PUBLIC
LIBRARY

52 W. LORAIN STREET
OBERLIN, OH 44074

Books by Charlotte Vale Allen

Time/Steps	1986
Matters of the Heart	1985
Pieces of Dreams	1984
Intimate Friends	1983
The Marmalade Man (Destinies)	1981
Daddy's Girl	1980
Promises	1979
Love Life	1976

TIME / STEPS

Charlotte Vale Allen

TIME / STEPS

Atheneum   New York   1986

Oberlin Public Library

The central characters in this novel are all creations, products of the author's imagination. Any similarities they might bear to people, living or dead, is entirely coincidental. Where reference is made to actual people who did live once upon a time, it is by design, and their words and actions, as reported, are historically accurate.

Library of Congress Cataloging-in-Publication Data

Allen, Charlotte Vale, ⸺
    Time/steps.

    I. Title
PS3551.L392T56   1986   813'.54   85-48138
ISBN 0-689-11773-6

Copyright © 1986 by Charlotte Vale Allen
All rights reserved
Composition by Westchester Book Composition, Inc.,
Yorktown Heights, New York
Manufactured by Fairfield Graphics, Fairfield, Pennsylvania
Designed by Harry Ford
First Edition

PL 31996

*For **Bette Davis,** with love—*

because there are more ways than one to give a life

Acknowledgments

I am enormously indebted to my friend Archie MacDonald, not only for making his extensive library of film history and biography available to me, but also for the many hours he spent assisting me with the research for this book. As well, I owe a large thank you to Linda McKnight, Valerie Thompson, Archie, and Prudence for all the hours they spent with me, at various times, watching and discussing movies of the 'thirties and 'forties; and to Kim, who learned in spite of herself to love Fred Astaire and Ginger Rogers, for valiantly watching even though it meant missing her favorite music videos.

Thank you to my wonderful friend Prudence Emery, publicist extraordinaire, for her willingness to discuss at great length the arcane logistics of the view from behind the scenes. And thank you, too, to my dear chum Rita Tushingham for many hours and much laughter in the course of numerous profound and insightful conversations on the view from inside.

And, finally, hugs and kisses to *you*, Claire Smith, for all the wonderful suggestions along the way, and the encouragement, and for your belief in this book.

This was a project of love that was endorsed and supported by many caring and interested people, all of whom have my gratitude and affection.

Part One

1917-1936

"Yes, there was definitely a black influence. In those early days, tap-dancing wasn't the accepted dance form it's become. And there wasn't one of us who, somewhere along the line, hadn't been influenced by the black dancers. Myself, I knew when I was a very small child and saw Bill Robinson dance that that was what I had to do. To this day, I remember every last detail of that night and the tremendous thrill I felt seeing the man dance. It's as if my life began right there.... Most of the dancers had a specialty, and Bill's was stairs. Mine was the tapping turns. But we all learned from each other, and there were a lot of people along the way who influenced me— Sandman, and Chuck and Chuckles. Sandman, you know, his special was sprinkling sand around and doing a wonderful soft shoe.... Oh, we challenged constantly. We'd get together and spontaneously start to dance; we'd do all our best steps, and that was our way of saying, 'Okay! There! Now, let's see what you can do!'... I remember once having a conversation with my old friend Becky—Rebecca Armstrong, that is—and she said that when she went to bed at night she'd lie there for ages, writing in her head. Then, the next morning, when she got up, she'd go to the typewriter and everything she'd written in her head the night before would come right out onto the paper. That's the way it was with my dancing. And every day there'd be something new to try.... It was years and years before I stopped thinking of myself as a dancer who acted...."

Beatrice Crane Interview
The Village Voice, October 1971

One

S HE was five years old when her mother and grandmother took her, one evening, down to the Elgin Theatre to a vaudeville show. Bea spent the first half of the show watching the audience, glancing at the stage every so often without interest. She liked the music well enough, but most of the acts didn't interest her. Then, halfway through the second part of the show, something happened. The orchestra struck up a very peppy introduction, the curtains parted, and a dapper dark man began to dance in front of the footlights. His feet tapped out amazing rhythms as he moved around the stage, dancing up and down a short flight of stairs that led to another level about four feet above the stage. Bea sat forward, clutching the top of the back of the seat ahead, and finally stood up in order not to miss anything. Clinging to the seat in front, she was unaware that her own feet had begun to move, trying to duplicate what she was seeing. The amused couple seated to her left smiled at the little girl dancing along with the man on stage.

When it was over, and the dark man was gone behind the curtains, Bea asked her mother, "Who was that man?"

"Bill Robinson. Come on! Let's get out before the crowd."

Bill Robinson. Right then, Bea decided she was going to dance just like Mr. Robinson.

Lillian laughed when Bea later told her, "I want to dance like the dark man."

And Agatha, Bea's gramma, said, "Nice girls don't go on the stage."

By the time she was seven, Bea knew that, according to the naming book at the library, "Beatrice" meant "she who makes others happy."

She was very pleased her mother had thought to give her the name, although she doubted Lillian had any idea what it meant.

By the time she was eight, Bea knew that her mother had been born in Hartford, Connecticut. At seventeen, Lil had found herself pregnant by the son of a wealthy West Hartford family. Upon learning of Lil's situation, the mother of the family offered Lil a lifetime income if she'd agree to take herself and her belly far away. Lil didn't mind. She signed a lot of legal papers, accepted the first installment, and, with her mother who'd been widowed four years before, relocated a few hundred miles to the north and west in Toronto, which was as far as the two of them were willing to go.

Bea learned the story in bits and pieces, partly from her gramma and the rest through her almost uncanny ability to remain still and silent for so long that people invariably forgot she was around and conversed freely in her presence, never dreaming their words might imprint themselves indelibly on their silent audience of one. Along with her capacity for stillness, Bea had an exceptional memory. Lil never had to write down her shopping lists for Bea; she merely said what she wanted, and Bea came back with everything she'd been told to get.

Since neither Lil nor Agatha especially liked children, Bea was, from the start, always well down on their list of priorities. They agreed that Bea was a very peculiar child. She didn't seem to need the company or friendship of other children and was content to spend hours, even entire days, amusing herself with only the radio or the Gramophone for company. She sang, she danced, she performed lengthy melodramas in which she acted out all the roles. And she could always be induced to absent herself from home for hours merely for the price of admission to the moving-picture show. Lil or Agatha rarely had trouble finding the five cents needed to buy themselves some free time. There was, they agreed, something downright strange about a little girl who'd spend hours on end singing and making a racket dancing around on the living-room floor.

By age nine, Bea knew what she wanted for her future and had roughed-in many of the details of the spectacular life she would one day have. All she needed now was to convince her mother or her grandmother to finance her dancing lessons. Both women insisted they didn't have money to waste on such nonsense, and hadn't they already told her enough times that nice girls didn't aspire to a life on the stage? Nevertheless, Bea persisted, certain she could wear them down. They displayed far more resistance than she'd anticipated. She was utterly frustrated, first, by her failure to convince them, and second, by her own enormous sense of urgency. She repeated her requests at regular intervals, convinced they'd finally break down and give her the money for the lessons just the way they always gave her the money for the moving-picture shows. She couldn't budge them.

By the time she was twelve, and ready to make one last, desperate pitch to prove to them the greatness of her need, something called "The Market" crashed, and the monthly payments from Hartford abruptly ceased, without notification of any sort. One month the money just didn't arrive. Lillian wrote at once to the lawyers in Hartford—getting Bea to check her spelling and make sure it was all right—demanding an explanation. Their reply came in the form of a three-word telegram: "FAMILY GONE BROKE."

"What do they mean 'gone broke'?" Lillian wailed. "How could they be broke, with all their money?"

"Must be some kind of trick," Agatha mused skeptically. "Their sort just doesn't *go* broke. Better get on the telephone, Lil, and see if you can't get some straight answers."

The two women marched purposefully down the street to the drugstore, to the enclosed telephone to one side of the front door. Bea hovered near the druggist, watching him shape little pills and then pour them into a brown bottle, while at the front of the store her mother shouted into the mouthpiece of the telephone as if, because Hartford was far away, it was necessary for her to raise her voice in order to be heard.

"They could probably hear her in Hartford without the telephone," Bea said softly to herself, chagrined and somewhat embarrassed by her mother's habits. She watched the druggist's nimble fingers shift powders and liquids, creating concoctions that went into various phials and tubes. The man glanced over at her and smiled.

Bea wandered up to the front of the store and stood by the magazine rack, waiting for Lil to finish on the telephone. Her grandmother stood just outside the booth, both arms folded across the handbag pressed flat to her breasts.

Her mother and grandmother looked a lot alike. They were both fair-haired and blue-eyed; angular women, their hipbones jutted prominently, and their arms and legs seemed too long and too thin; their breasts were large for their narrow bodies, and there was something about them that made men stare. Lil was very pretty, but her mouth had a kind of looseness, a prominence in the lower lip that contributed to the impression she gave of being malleable. Agatha exuded an aura of wiry strength. When it came to arguments, though, it was Agatha who always gave in, while Lil hung on with a ferocious tenacity that could be positively alarming. Agatha liked to threaten, but rarely made good her threats. Bea usually approached her gramma for the things she wanted. There was a better-than-even chance Agatha would forget why she'd been saying no and all at once give in. Where money was concerned, Lil never forgot a thing and couldn't be persuaded to part with a penny if she'd made up her mind.

Bea didn't look one bit like them. Although nobody ever actually came right out and said so, it was accepted that she took after her father. And according to Agatha and Lil, this was a downright crying shame, because poor Bea got stuck with too much dark brown hair—a good brushing session usually resulted in Lil getting angry and Bea starting to cry, until Bea was finally old enough to take over caring for her own hair—hazel eyes that were sometimes blue, sometimes green, and most often the color of cigarette smoke; and a nose Agatha was forever saying she hoped Bea would grow into. She had a strong jaw; a high, smooth forehead; and a wide, well-shaped mouth. Altogether, despite her diminutive stature, she had a very mature look.

"That child was born old!" Agatha said often, with slightly narrowed eyes.

Bea considered this a compliment. She'd long-since decided she didn't care that she wasn't a curly headed, big-eyed cutie like her mother. She was going to be famous one day, and probably rich, too. And when you were famous, it didn't matter if your jaw was kind of square, and your chin had a little dent in it, and your eyes, according to Lil, "kind of give me the creeps."

Lillian emerged from the telephone booth pale and distraught. "What're we gonna do?" she asked her mother. "They're not gonna send any more money."

Agatha sucked in her breath, then let it out slowly. "Well," she said, "I guess somebody around here's gonna have to go to work."

"*Not me!*" Lillian looked horrified at the prospect. "What do *I* know how to do?"

Agatha gave her what Bea thought was a not very nice smile, one that made Lil look even more horrified.

"If it comes to the worst, my girl," Agatha said, holding open the door, her words going directly into her daughter's ear as Lil went out past her in a daze.

As usual, they'd forgotten her, and Bea followed along after them like a small, dark shadow, listening to their worried exchange.

"We'll stop and get the papers, start looking at the want ads," Agatha stated.

The idea of want ads intrigued Bea. It was something she'd never heard of before, and she wondered if you could make up a list of all the things you wanted and then put it into the newspaper so people could read it and then go get you those things. If that was the way it worked, maybe she'd write out her own want ad and get it put into the newspaper. Maybe then somebody would finally give her her dancing lessons.

"Oh, and I suppose *you'll* be getting a job, too?" Lil snapped at her mother.

"How much've you saved, Lil?" Agatha asked calmly. "Years of money and how much of it did you put aside for a rainy day?"

"You know perfectly well how much I have!" Lil flared indignantly. "It went to pay for everything."

"Well, then." Agatha sniffed triumphantly. "People here will be going out to work, I do believe."

After her mother and gramma had gone indoors with the newspapers, Bea sat down on the top step of the porch, elbows on her knees, to view the passing traffic on the street. Through the open window behind her came Lillian's and Agatha's voices as they read aloud from the newspapers, then discussed the ads which, as it turned out, were nowhere near what Bea had thought. Annoyed at her own foolishness, she sat, her toes and heels tapping out a gentle rhythm on the wooden steps. If she just could have metal plates on her shoes, when she set her feet down there'd be a wonderful, clean click instead of the muffled, unsatisfying sound of leather soles meeting worn, splintery wood from which the paint was peeling. Swinging her knees back and forth beneath her elbows, she imagined a great, shiny expanse of something like marble where every step you took would click back at you with that swell sound.

Suddenly, she had an idea she thought might just work. She jumped up and ran into the house. At the kitchen door, she made herself go quiet, then moved inside and began opening and closing cupboards and drawers. Finding what she wanted, she shoved her hands into the pockets of her coat—she refused to wear clothes without pockets, an eccentricity that maddened Lil and prompted Agatha to accuse her of troublemaking—and stood for a moment watching Lil lick the tip of her pencil prior to circling something in the newspaper. Two empty teacups sat to one side on the table, and in the middle was an ashtray with lit cigarettes perched on two of the three metal lips.

Back on the porch, she undid her shoes one at a time and slipped them off. She placed a bottle cap on the toe of each shoe, put several rubber bands over the entire front of the shoe to hold the caps in place, then put the shoes back on. They felt tight and kind of lumpy, but she thought they really might work. Down on the front path she tapped her left foot experimentally, gratified by the slightly tinny but nevertheless metallic sound of the bottle cap meeting the cement. Heel toe, heel toe. She wished it wasn't so cold and that she didn't have to wear her heavy coat. She hated not being able to move freely. Heel toe, heel toe. It would've been better if she could've figured out some way to attach caps to the heels as well, but this wasn't bad. Pleased, she tapped her way down the length of the walk, doing quick little hops, a fast turn, and landed on her toes, her arms outflung.

"What're you doing?" a small voice asked.

Bea looked over to see Becky and Franny Armstrong. They were identical twins. Bea had always been able to tell them apart when nobody else could, because they walked and moved in totally different ways. She never could understand why she was the only one who could go right up to both of them and pick Becky out to talk to.

"Tap-dancing," she answered.

"Those aren't taps," Becky the pragmatist said, pointing.

"I didn't say they were," Bea defended herself.

"What're they, bottle tops?" Franny asked, about to laugh.

"They're magic buttons, if you must know. Buddy Rogers, the great movie star, gave them to me," Bea replied, then wondered for a moment if this might not just be true. Maybe this was how magic worked. You said something that you very badly wanted to be real, and saying it made it happen.

"Magic buttons," Becky repeated, her freckled brow furrowing slightly. "What makes them magic exactly?" Becky was the nicer of the twins, although she was forever asking all kinds of questions about absolutely everything.

"They're magic, all right. And if I tell you what they can do, they won't be magic anymore. They'll lose their power. I promised Mr. Rogers when he gave them to me that I'd never tell a living soul what they can do."

"Honest?" Becky asked, halfway to believing.

Captured by the potency of possibility, Bea tapped her right toe several times with pleasure, as she did, wishing with all her might for the money to pay for her lessons. Unfortunately, the friction was too much for the rubber bands which frayed and flew apart, causing the bottle top to drop from her shoe with a little *tink*. It lay, its metal interior revealed, on the path, and Bea regarded it ruefully, saddened by life's failure once more to provide magic.

"Magic button, my Aunt Hatty!" Franny scoffed. "That's just an old bottle top, and I knew it the whole time. Come on, Beck! Didn't I tell you, she's just silly!"

Offended as well as disappointed, Bea faced them, with deadly seriousness saying, "You'll be sorry you said that, Franny Armstrong. It *is* magic, and now you'll be cursed"—she paused dramatically for

10

impact—*"for the rest of your life."* The somber quality of her tone and the dire prediction undid Becky who burst into tears and began tugging frantically at her twin sister's arm.

"You take that back!" Franny demanded, shaking away Becky's hand.

"Oh, no. I'm afraid I can't." Bea lowered her already husky voice even more. "It has nothing to do with me. You're cursed now, because you didn't believe. I am very, very sorry for you." Enjoying her role as guardian of the magic button, she bent, retrieved the bottle top, and, holding it secure in her fist, walked—one shoe silent, the other squealing against the cement—back up the front walk to the porch. Behind her, Becky was crying, attempting to move her deeply offended sister back across the street to safety.

"I'm putting my own curse on you!" Franny raged. "I'm cursing you right this very moment."

"Oh?" Bea stopped at the top of the steps. "What's the curse?"

"Franny, you stop this!" Becky pleaded, positive terrible things would happen to all of them.

"One of these days you'll break every bone in your body!" Franny hollered. Since their mother regularly threatened to break every bone in her or Becky's body, this seemed to Franny the preeminent curse, and, satisfied, she turned, marched past her bleak-eyed twin, and crossed the street.

"She doesn't mean it," Becky told Bea wretchedly.

"Oh, yes I do!" Franny shouted from the middle of the road. "Oh boy, I sure do!"

"Better watch out for that car coming!" Bea pointed up the street, and without looking, Franny galloped to the far side, then turning, saw there was nothing coming and screamed at Becky to come home that very instant.

After pausing to remove the rubber bands and bottle top from her other shoe, Bea went inside to the living room. She shut the door behind her, folded back the rug, and began trying to drop her heels and toes on the hardwood floor in rapid succession, thereby producing a steady tattoo of sound, the way Mr. Robinson had. If only she could have met him. He could've showed her how to do all of it. She knew there were special steps she could learn that would enable her to create all kinds of different sounds—she could hear them inside her head—but she just couldn't figure them out on her own. She'd already made up lots and lots of steps, but she needed a teacher to show her more. And she needed taps for her shoes.

She had nothing to lose, so she asked again for dancing lessons, and this time Lil went wild. "Are you *nuts?*" she cried. "We don't

11

Oberlin Public Library

have *money* for *dancing* lessons! When, when, *when* are you going to quit nagging about those damn dancing lessons?"

"It's very important."

"Well, that's just too bad. You'll be lucky if we don't all starve to death."

"Why would that make me lucky?" Bea wanted to know.

Waving the hand that held her cigarette so that ashes scattered all over, Lil said, "Go to bed or something, and stop bothering me! I've got things to think about."

"It's only six o'clock. We haven't even had supper yet."

"Ooohhh!" Lil sighed. "Be a good kid, and go play for a while. Your gramma and I are trying to talk."

"Why'd you have me anyway if you never want me around?" Bea asked, wondering if this time she might get the real true answer instead of the usual runaround. Just once she'd have liked to hear her mother say the truth right out loud.

"Who knows?" Lil shrugged.

The usual runaround. Bea would've loved it if Lil had answered, "I had you for the money," or "I wanted a kid," or "Who said we never want you around?" But it was pretty silly to hope for that, Bea reasoned, from a woman who liked to tell strangers she was a widow when she didn't even have a wedding ring to wear.

"When's supper?"

"Soon," Agatha answered from the stove.

"How soon?"

"Half an hour."

"Okay. I'm going out for a walk."

"Don't you go too far!" Agatha called after her. "When I say half an hour I mean half an hour."

Bea strolled up the street, looking around, every few yards trying an experimental dance step. She *really* needed taps for her shoes. And somehow, some way, she had to get dancing lessons, and soon. If it took very much longer, she'd be too old to learn all the steps. Those lessons were just the most important thing in her life. She could already sing, and she knew she was good because a lot of the time she liked to sing out loud when she was going for a walk, and three times people had stopped to give her money, patting her on the top of the head and smiling at her.

Recalling the way people had stopped to compliment her, she thought maybe she'd just have to find a way to get the money for the lessons by herself.

12

Two

TO everyone's surprise, Lil loved being a waitress. She'd been ready to hate it, but the pink and white gingham uniform was flattering to her figure; the customers, particularly the men, were friendly and generous, not only with their tips, but with compliments and invitations; she could eat whatever she fancied on the menu free of charge; and for the first time in her life she had money she'd actually earned. Even with the tips, it didn't amount to a third of what she'd received from the family in Hartford, but bringing home the money gave her a new sense of self-respect. She went off humming in the morning, a freshly laundered lacy handkerchief tucked into the pocket of her uniform, and returned each afternoon good-naturedly complaining she was dog-tired, but not too tired to narrate the day's goings-on at the restaurant.

Agatha didn't fare quite so well. Her job, behind the counter in a bakery, left her with aching hips and legs and sore feet. Nightly she sat at the kitchen table with her red, swollen feet soaking in a pan of water. She, too, had stories to tell—about the bitchiness of the women customers, about the baker's foul moods and equally foul language, about the weevils she'd seen crawling in the sacks of flour out back and the mice the size of kittens that lived in the storeroom.

Along with Lil's job came a number of men to take her out in the evenings. She'd dated only sporadically in the past, but with the advent of her new career, suddenly she had more offers than she could handle. The only problem in the household was the chronic shortage of money.

"We'll just have to move," Agatha announced one evening. "We get a cheaper place, we'll have a little more to spend on ourselves." Suddenly angry, she said, "If I'd known giving up everything to come here with you would turn out this way, I'd never've done it."

13

Everything, Bea knew from overhearing the often-told stories, had consisted of a two-bedroom, clapboard cottage with a mortgage. Her late husband's insurance money had gone to make the down payment. They all knew Agatha's compromises for her daughter's sake were imaginary. She'd been as tickled as Lil at the West Hartford family's offer to pay, and the four hundred dollars she'd cleared from the sale of the cottage had gone on new clothes and luggage, so that the two of them could start fresh, looking respectable.

"I don't want to move," Bea said from the end of the table, where she'd been silently listening. "I like it here."

"You mind your beeswax!" Agatha fired at her, then continued on with Lil. "We get a smaller place, it won't need so much looking after. We might even find something closer to work and save on the streetcar fares."

"Gee, Ma," Lil said doubtfully. "I don't know." She looked around wistfully. "We've been here since the start. I'm used to it."

"What about my school?" Bea wanted to know. "I don't want to change schools. I like my school."

"Gee, that's right." Lil stared down the length of the table at Bea, thinking it was funny how that nose had looked just fine on Jackie Ellroy, Junior, but sure looked big on the face of a kid. "Bea'll have to change schools. It's gonna be a whole load of trouble, moving."

"You want a new dress now and then, or you want to be broke so Bea can stay at her school?"

Lil sighed again, and Bea knew it was over. They'd move, all right. It made her feel rotten. She got up and wandered down the hall to stand looking out through the glass of the front door. She'd have gone out for a walk if it hadn't meant dragging on galoshes, coat, scarf, hat, and mittens. With all that stuff on she could hardly move. She hated winter. Aside from being "cold as hell," as Agatha said every single day, every winter, the snow and slush and ice wrecked the sidewalks. You couldn't even hear yourself take a step. Someday, she promised herself, she'd live where it was summer all year long and you could always hear your footsteps on the sidewalk.

While the movers were loading the furniture into the truck, Becky came over to say good-bye.

"Where're you moving to?" she asked, standing on a clear patch of still snowed-over lawn, her eyes on the moving men.

"Not far," Bea hedged. Becky just couldn't help passing information along to Franny, and there was no way Bea wanted Franny to know she was coming down in the world when, all along, her plan was to be going up.

"I'll bet you're excited, huh?" Becky said.

"Oh, sure." Bea leaped into the opening provided. "Moving's always exciting."

"How do you know? When did you ever move before?"

"Well, you know what I mean."

"I guess so," Becky answered uncertainly. "I'd feel very sad if I had to leave our house. Sometimes, when I think about things—like moving, or somebody dying—I hate the thought of it so much, I just start crying. My father always says I think too much about things. He says I'm *over*imaginative."

"You probably are," Bea said, consideringly.

Franny began to call from across the street. Becky ignored her, asking Bea, "What school'll you be going to now?"

"I don't know yet," Bea lied.

Becky moved slightly closer and, with a flush overtaking her freckled features, said, "I've always liked your dancing a whole lot. I think someday you'll be really famous."

Bea soberly accepted this unexpected praise, saying, "When I am, I promise I'll still remember you, Becky. Okay?"

"*Becky!*" Franny bellowed at the top of her lungs.

"Okay." Becky glanced over her shoulder to where her sister was waiting. "I better go." She turned back to Bea and made a face. Then she shrugged and, with a smile, said, "Sometimes I could kick her. But she's my sister. You know?"

"I know."

"Will you come back and see me?"

"Oh, sure."

"Well, I guess I better go." Becky stood a moment longer, then turned and picked a careful path over the lawn to the sidewalk, pausing to wave at Bea before crossing the street.

The new apartment was on Dundas Street over a hardware store. It only had two bedrooms, instead of the three the old house had had. And the only place that got any sun was the bathroom. The neighborhood was entirely different. They were now on a main street with a streetcar line, so it was very noisy. In Bea's opinion, the apartment was just plain awful. She had to sleep now on the sofa in the living room. Still, the room did have a decent wood floor, and the radio and Gramophone were in here so she could stage her shows, and dance, and work out new steps when she felt like it. She just couldn't do it as often as before because most evenings Lil wanted

15

to use the room to entertain her gentlemen-callers. This meant that Agatha and Bea had to stay either in the kitchen or in one of the bedrooms. After a few weeks of falling asleep over her schoolbooks at the kitchen table, Bea began bedding down in her mother's room. Lil dealt with this by getting the man of the evening to shift Bea to the sofa before he left, or before he and Lil settled into her room for the night.

Lillian's sleep-over callers occasionally pressed money into her hands before departing, and she accepted their "gifts" with half-hearted protestations. Whenever Bea overheard her mother saying, "Oh, you shouldn't" or "You really mustn't," she knew Lil had just received another cash donation. Bea wondered why Lil couldn't hand over some of the gift money to her for lessons, but didn't dare ask. She also wondered if her mother's accepting money didn't make Lil a lot like those ladies Bea saw often outside the beer parlors. Obviously, Agatha was thinking along the same lines.

"Keep on the way you are," Agatha warned Lil, "and you're either going to wind up in jail, my girl, or pregnant again."

"It didn't work out all that badly the first time," Lil replied archly.

"That was then. Now is now. These men you're socializing with hardly have the price of a decent meal, let alone the money to pay you off if you're dumb enough to let yourself get caught."

"I won't get myself caught," Lil said haughtily. "I'm not stupid, you know."

You're not all that smart, either, Bea thought, but said nothing.

Agatha harrumphed and allowed the matter to drop.

Upon consideration, Bea thought she wouldn't have minded one bit having a baby brother or sister. It'd probably be all right if you could have someone from the day they were brand-new so you could show them how to grow up right and be an okay kind of person instead of a jerk, like Franny Armstrong, for example.

They hadn't been in the new apartment a month before Agatha and Lil were arguing again about money. Bea was fed up with hearing it. Noiselessly, she left the table and let herself out of the apartment.

It was May, but not that warm; at least the streets were dry, though, and she could hear her footsteps as she walked along Dundas, heading west. Trying a new route, she turned north on Palmerston Avenue. At College Street, she debated circling home but decided to keep on going. Her mother and gramma would still be arguing, and their fights over money made Bea feel blue, because she wasn't one bit closer to getting her lessons.

16

North of College, the street became Palmerston Boulevard and was totally different. The roadway was wider, the houses were huge and set well back from the sidewalk, and the streetlamps had round white globes on top of them. She walked along, admiring the houses, and came to a stop upon hearing piano music and the unmistakable sound of dancing feet. Turning, she saw heads bobbing in the ground-floor window of a house across the road.

She went right up the walk to the front porch and craned sideways to get a better view of what was going on inside. She saw a woman sitting at a piano, a tall, dark-haired lady demonstrating steps, and a gang of about ten kids sloppily trying to copy what the teacher was showing them.

Bea moved closer to the window, thinking they were just hopeless, these kids. The steps were so simple. Anybody could do them. Automatically, she started to follow, and easily danced along with the teacher. It was swell. Until suddenly the kids inside were pointing and yammering, and the tall, dark-haired lady had stopped teaching and was turning to see what they were talking about.

Bea saw a pretty, very surprised face, realized she was probably in big trouble, and took off. She bolted down the porch steps, cut across the lawn, hit the sidewalk on the fly, and was halfway back to College Street by the time the front door opened and the dark-haired lady was calling out after her.

She was glad as anything she hadn't got caught and tickled pink at having picked up a few new steps. At home, she went right to the living room, folded aside the rug, and started practicing the hops and shuffles and turns she'd seen. She did the steps over and over, changing their order and adding moves of her own, until Agatha appeared in the doorway, saying, "You don't stop that doggone clackety-clack racket this minute, I swear I'll break both your ankles. Turn off that machine and get yourself washed before supper. Then you go straight to bed."

"Which bed?"

"Your own, for a change. And make sure you remember to brush those teeth before you go to bed. They're starting to look downright green."

"Okey-dokey."

"You're sure chirpy," Agatha observed.

"I learned a whole bunch of new steps today."

"That and a nickel'll get you a cup of coffee."

It'll get me a whole lot more than that, Bea thought, skipping down the hall to the bathroom. It's gonna get me up on a stage someday.

Most of the time Bea tried not to think about how she felt, because when she considered the way her mother and gramma seemed to prefer life when she wasn't around it made her angry and sad and kind of scared. Knowing they didn't care all that much about her made her afraid they might just one day go off and leave her. She'd get home from school some afternoon, and the place'd be empty. They'd be gone. It wasn't that they didn't like her, just that they didn't care. And if they didn't care about her, then she wasn't going to care about them, either. She'd been working at not caring about them for a long time now and was pretty well convinced she'd managed to get born into the wrong family, which was why Agatha and Lil never bothered to pay much attention to her. Oh, sure, they looked out for her, made sure she ate her supper and brushed her teeth and everything, but that was as far as it was ever going to go.

The one thing she knew for absolute sure was that she was smarter than most other kids, except maybe for Becky Armstrong, and definitely smarter than her mother and gramma. Sometimes it was truly embarrassing to have to listen to the things those two talked about. Every time she had to go out with one or both of them, she was always waiting for the moment when something dumb would come falling out of one of their mouths, and then she'd have to pretend she was only visiting them or back up out of the way so people wouldn't think she was dumb, too, just because she was with them. And that kind of evened things up, she thought, because maybe they didn't care much about her, but she was smarter than both of them put together. And one day, when she was grown up and married and had kids of her own, she'd pay all kinds of attention to her kids and say how glad she was to have them; she'd get them singing and dancing lessons and clothes with pockets, if they wanted them. She'd never make them worry that maybe they'd one day come home to find she'd cleared out. Gramma and Lil didn't care about her, so she wasn't going to care about them either!

Once school closed for the summer, she offered to deliver prescriptions for the local drugstore, but the owner told her he couldn't afford to pay her, and anyway most folks came in to pick up their own medicine. She offered to deliver groceries at the market. The Italian owner was kind with his turndown, giving her a nice smile and an orange. After being refused work at half a dozen more stores where she applied to sweep up, stock shelves, or do any odd jobs that might need doing, she trudged along Dundas determined to find a way to make some money.

Part One / 1917–1936

The following Saturday morning, she stationed herself at the southwest corner of Yonge and Queen streets where her visibility was high and where a surging tide of people moved back and forth across the intersection between Eaton's and Simpson's department stores. Clutching an empty tin can with both hands, she began to sing all her best songs. She sang, "Sometimes I'm Happy," "My Blue Heaven," "Let a Smile Be Your Umbrella," "Makin' Whoopee," "You're the Cream in My Coffee" and was halfway through "Button Up Your Overcoat" when a police officer appeared before her, hands on his hips.

"You'll have to move along, little miss," he advised her. "Panhandling's against the law, you know."

"I didn't know about that." She emptied the coins from the tin can and put them into her pocket, then moved to go.

"Your folks know you're doing this?" he asked, walking along at her side.

"No," she answered truthfully.

"Having a rough time of it, are they?" His tone was sympathetic.

"Uh-huh."

"Well, I won't run you in this time," he said, "but don't let me see you down here again."

"No, sir, I won't."

"Hold on a minute there," he said, taking her arm.

She stopped and looked up at him.

"What's your name, little miss?"

"Beatrice Crane, sir."

"You're quite the singer, Beatrice; got a fine big voice for such a wee girl. But you want to be careful now, hear? Singing on street corners isn't a good idea. You don't want to do this again, do you?"

"No, sir," she lied. She'd had a whale of a time and would've loved to stand on that corner all day long, singing.

"You run along home now," he said with a sudden smile and pressed a coin into her hand. "Good luck to you, Beatrice."

"Thank you, sir." She returned his smile, said good-bye, and walked quickly away.

Some blocks farther along, she stopped to see that not only had the officer given her twenty-five cents, but her forty minutes' singing had earned her sixty-seven cents. She had almost a dollar. Now all she had to do was find out how much the dancing lessons cost.

The kids wouldn't tell her. They recognized her as being the one who'd danced on the porch a week earlier and refused to have anything to do with her.

"Just tell me how much the lessons cost!" she yelled after them.

19

"They don't cost nothin' if you stay outside on the porch!" one of the bolder girls yelled back.

"Oh, rats!" Bea muttered, turning to look toward the house where the dark-haired lady gave the dancing lessons. She wanted to go up and knock on the door, but was afraid the teacher would treat her the same way the kids had. Still, she had no choice. She went up the walk, then stopped to stare at the front door. "What're you so scared of?" she asked herself in a whisper. She was scared the teacher would say no. Well, it was the worst that could happen.

The woman recognized her, too. She stood with one hand on the doorknob, her eyebrows raised, and was smiling a bit. "Well, who've we got here?" she asked. She seemed like a person who enjoyed laughter, who smiled frequently.

"Beatrice Crane. I want to know how much you charge for your dancing lessons."

"You want to come for lessons, huh?" The woman's smile grew wider.

"I sure do," Bea said eagerly.

"It's a dollar a week."

"I've already got almost a dollar. I can get the other eight cents easily. I know where I can find some pop bottles. Unless somebody else already found them."

"The course is for ten weeks," she said almost apologetically.

"You mean it's *ten dollars altogether?*"

"That's right."

Bea was so disappointed she thought she might be sick. How could she possibly raise another nine dollars? If the policeman hadn't chased her away, she might've collected a bit more with her singing. But to make nine more dollars, she'd have to stand outside singing for days on end, maybe even weeks.

"I don't suppose you'd let me work for the lessons. I mean, I could run errands or clean up for you, sweep the front walk."

"You want them that badly?" The woman now appeared as disappointed as Bea.

"Oh, I do. I really, truly do."

"Why?" the woman asked, feeling herself drawn to this girl.

"I *need* them," Bea said fervently. "I already know how to sing, but I don't know enough dance steps."

The woman pushed open the door saying, "Come on in, Beatrice Crane. Let's have a little talk."

Bea followed her inside to the front room where the woman sat down on the piano bench, saying, "What steps do you already know?"

"I don't know what they're called."

"Would you like to show me what you can do?"

"Sure. D'you have any music? You know, Gramophone records or anything?"

"Anything in particular?"

"Have you got 'Yes Sir, That's My Baby'? That's my best number so far. I've been working on that one the longest."

"I think I can find it." The woman got up to look for the record, and Bea followed her every move, hoping and praying she was going to be as nice as she looked and seemed so far. Everything about her suggested she was someone who liked to have fun.

Lucy put on the music, and Bea started her dance. She felt kind of foolish at the beginning, but then she got tied up in the routine and the music and forgot herself, doing all her best steps.

As Lucy watched the girl dance, she had the oddest feeling. It was a sense that this touching little girl, with the big, soulful eyes, was going to change Lucy's life. Despite the crudeness of her self-taught routine, the girl had a natural stage presence and such determined energy that Lucy wanted to start instructing her then and there. Lucy had always had an impulsive streak that had prompted her to say and do things that often had unexpected results. As a child she'd found herself in trouble on a number of occasions for the comments and observations she'd made, without thinking, at the dinner table or right in the middle of a class at school. She'd managed to bring her impulsiveness under control by the time she reached twenty, but every now and then something would strike her and she'd go with the idea, unconcerned about the consequences. There was rarely a day in her life when her practical instincts didn't do battle with her desire to break free in some new, unanticipated direction. And she suspected that this girl was very like her.

"How old are you?" she asked, when Bea finished.

"I'm thirteen."

"I thought you were about nine. You taught yourself that routine?"

"I know it's not too hot. But if I knew more steps, I could do way better. I just know it."

"Tell you what. Be here Wednesday at four. Use your dollar to have the shoemaker put heel and toe plates on your Mary-Janes. And don't you dare be late."

"You mean you'll give me the lessons?"

"Yup. I'm Lucy Vernon, by the way. You can call me Lucy."

"Everybody calls me Bea. Gosh! You really mean it?"

"Uh-huh."

"Oh, thank you! You'll never be sorry, I promise."

Lucy watched the girl go running off down the street and smiled

21

to herself, reviewing the frantic little performance she'd just seen. There was definitely something there. All it needed was some discipline and some training. Another impulse, but what the hell!

"We've got another kid in the class," she told her sister, Julie. "She's gonna be very special."

There was no point to telling Julie that she wasn't going to be charging the new girl for her lessons. They argued enough as it was without adding more fuel to the fire of their perpetual, lifelong disagreement. Julie was entirely inward, self-absorbed; Lucy had always been completely outgoing and keenly interested in others. Lucy had her impulses, her hunches, and her determination to find pleasure in life. She'd been the first girl in their crowd to bob her hair, the first to wear make-up, and the first—although no one knew it—to surrender her virginity. Julie had her mysterious anger, her secrecy, and her contempt for her older sister who, to her mind, never took matters seriously enough. Each thought the other entirely misguided in her viewpoints and attitudes, so it was best not to say more—about anything, ever—than was necessary.

Lucy had no qualms about giving in to her impulse regarding Bea. In fact, the arrival of Bea in her life seemed to give her a new focus. She was eager, and very curious, to know more about the girl. Maybe, she thought, she ought to have her head examined, getting so immediately caught up in the challenge of shaping a raw talent. But, nuts! She smiled to herself, pleased. It'd be fun.

Three

B EA shivered with pleasure at first hearing the sound she'd tried so hard for so long to create: a perfect, clean-edged click. Head tilted to one side, she listened intently as she put first her toe, then her heel down. It was simply wonderful.

So enamored was she of the sound created by her newly armored

Mary-Janes that she wore them everywhere purely for the pleasure of hearing herself travel over the sidewalk. What she hadn't considered, however, was the hazardous aspect of the metal plates. Skipping along the street one afternoon, her feet shot out from under her, and she found herself sprawled on the sidewalk, pain shooting up her spine. The fact that a gang of kids saw her and pointed, laughing loudly, didn't bother her particularly. The thought of twisting an ankle or breaking a bone did. She stored the shoes thereafter behind the sofa and made a small ceremony of it each time she put them on to rehearse.

On the appointed Wednesday, she presented herself in the front room of the house on Palmerston Boulevard, staring down the gazes of the other ten kids, and an hour later came away with a series of new steps which she practiced throughout the week, adding variations, embellishing here and there.

By the end of the second class, Lucy held her back as the others were leaving, to say, "I think you'd better come on Saturday mornings from now on. You're a little too much for the beginners' class."

"Aren't I doing it right?" Bea asked worriedly.

Lucy put an arm around the girl's shoulders, already very fond of her. "You do better than all right, Bea. That's why I'm moving you into the advanced class. You're a very quick study."

"I am?"

"I've never known anyone to pick things up so fast. You see something just once and you're off and running."

Within three weeks, she'd outdistanced everyone in the advanced class and, again, Lucy held her back to say, "I think I'm going to have to work with you alone. You just don't fit into the classes."

As before, Bea looked concerned.

"Come sit here with me for a minute." Lucy led her by the hand to the piano bench. "What does your family think about your dancing, Bea? Tell me something about you."

"Oh, I don't think they think about it at all. I just do it. I've been putting on shows and making up dances since I was really small, since I saw Mr. Robinson in the vaudeville show. They're pretty well used to it by now. My gramma calls it 'making a racket.'"

Lucy had to wonder what sort of people could be blasé about a kid so obviously talented and committed. Bea had a kind of homeless air to her and, giving it thought, Lucy decided maybe it was this quality that touched her so. "What really matters," she told Bea, "is that I've never met an honest-to-Pete natural before. But that's what you are. You're a born dancer, Bea. And I'm going to teach you everything I know. You'll probably run though what I know in no time flat, but from now on, the two of us will work together. Okay?"

"Sure," Bea agreed readily.

For two or three hours every Saturday during the next ten months, Lucy gave Bea instruction. In very short order, Bea mastered single wings, double wings, and pendulum wings; time steps, double time steps, triple time steps, and double-triple time steps; bucks, double bucks, and triple bucks; struts, scootbacks, pullbacks, cross turns, jig hops, paddle turns, chorus kicks, cross springs, and soft-shoe turns. She learned the waltz clog, jig steps, stomps, and the riverboat shuffle.

She learned so easily and so well that Lucy extended their session an additional hour to school Bea in basic ballet. Arabesques, attitudes, and pirouettes. Lucy showed her how to shimmy and to cakewalk, how to prance and do high kicks. They exercised together, doing lunges and barrel turns, splits and slides. Lucy taught her how to spot—holding a visual fix—in order to do multiple pirouettes and otherwise dizzying combinations of turns.

"Don't ever forget," Lucy told her often, "that you don't just dance with your feet. Every part of your body's involved, right down to your fingertips. Keep your chin up always, your spine straight, your bottom tucked in. Keep those arms curved and graceful; nothing's uglier than stick-straight arms on a dancer. Unless you're doing a comedy number. And use your hands to indicate, to complement the steps. A good dancer can do anything. So practice your stretches, and do your warm-ups and exercises every day, without fail. Don't ever try to go into a routine with a 'cold' body! You'll pull a tendon, get a charley horse, or hurt yourself somehow. Dancing's hard work. You've got to get your body ready for the job. If you respect your body and take good care of it, it'll do what you want it to. And look after your feet. Dancers have the worst feet in the world."

The more Bea learned, the more she longed to burst into a frenzy of motion, putting to use every step and turn. But Lucy held her back. "You're not ready yet, Bea. Don't be in such a hurry. You've got years of dancing ahead of you. I know how you feel, how impatient you are, how everything inside wants to come bursting out. I *know* how that feels. I'm just the same way. I promise you, when the time's right, we'll choreograph a number for you that'll knock people's eyes out."

Bea listened, recognizing that Lucy really did know how she felt. No one had ever understood, until now, the anxious feeling Bea so often had that she had to get going, get moving, get started and keep going. But Lucy did, and Lucy was solid somehow, not someone who might pack up and just be gone when you got home from school one day. Yet, despite Lucy's advice, Bea couldn't keep away from the temptation of creating routines. On her own, she worked up complicated bits and put them to music, elated beyond measure each time she mastered something especially difficult. She spent hours every day teaching herself to tap while executing a series of pirouettes. Initially, it seemed impossible, but she was determined to make it work. And after weeks of telling her feet to keep tapping on the turns, it finally happened, and she was turning and tapping simultaneously. Having accomplished this, she worked on reversing steps. And when she was able to do any step both forward and backward, she went on to attempt elevated splits. Each time she was successful with some new move, she progressed to another variation. Lucy applauded, encouraged, and challenged her to do more, until it got so that Bea was spending five and six hours every day after school on her dancing, then getting up at five in the morning to do her homework before school. Her Mary-Janes fell apart. The straps disintegrated; the uppers shredded. The shoemaker shook his head, and said, "No can fix," but he did agree to remove the taps so she could use them on another pair of shoes.

To finance the new pair, she took a tin can down to the corner of Yonge and Queen and, her eyes peeled for any sign of the police, she sang and did soft-shoe dancing every day for a week. Luck was with her. Nobody from school came around to find out where she'd been, she had no run-ins with the police, and she managed to collect enough money for the shoes.

Eventually, Lillian noticed the change. Instead of the aimless, random sounds Bea had previously produced, there was now a compelling rhythm that accompanied the music. Standing unnoticed in the living-room doorway one evening, Lil watched her daughter do a series of whirlwind turns. The girl was dancing in her step-ins and undershirt, socks, and shoes Lil had never seen before, with her hair in pigtails pinned up on top of her head. Lil thought she looked cute as the dickens, spinning away.

"You're quite a dancer," she said admiringly.

"You think so?" Bea smiled automatically at this rare bit of parental praise.

"Where'd you learn to do all that, those spins and stuff?"

"Well," Bea began, "there's this lady, Lucy..."

Lil was looking at her watch, saying, "Oh, jeez! I gotta scram!" She turned and was on her way to the kitchen where Agatha sat, her feet soaking, reading the afternoon paper. "The kid's getting to be some swell dancer," Lil told her.

"Mmm-hmmn," Agatha droned.

"No kidding," Lil went on, collecting her hat and bag. "It's hard to believe she's never even had a lesson. I'll bet anything she could win prizes, she's that good."

"Hmmn." Agatha refolded the newspaper, experimentally lifted one foot from the water, looked at it, then set it back in the pan.

"Well, I'm going." Lil carefully pulled on her new cloche hat with the feather.

"Have fun," Agatha said routinely, without looking up.

"Always do."

In the living room, Bea put another record on the Gramophone. Agatha sighed, removed her feet from the water, dried them, then went to get the supper started. That goddamned tap-tap-tapping was driving her crazy.

As money grew tighter, more and more people lost their jobs, and one by one Lucy lost her students. Within a month she was left with only seven kids; she was down from thirty dollars a week to seven. And if that wasn't enough, Julie announced she was fed up with playing piano for the classes.

"I met a fellow," she told Lucy defiantly. "I'm going to New York with him. He says he can get me a job playing in a club there."

They argued bitterly, and within a week Julie was gone. Lucy tried to see a sunny side to the situation but couldn't. She was scared. Seven dollars a week just wouldn't keep everything going. After studying her options, she knew she would have to take some drastic steps.

"I'm going to have to close down," she confided to Bea.

"Why?" Bea was panicked.

"Mainly because dancing lessons are a luxury most folks can't afford for their kids these days. I've lost most of my students. And Julie's gone off to New York with some cake-eater who sold her a bill of goods. All I've got is this house and, at the rate I'm going, I won't be able to pay next winter's coal bill."

"Are you going to move away, Lucy?"

"I'm thinking about it," Lucy admitted. When she saw how upset Bea was, she tried to soften the news by adding, "Nothing's set yet, Bea."

"But where would you go?"

All at once, the bright side of the situation came clear. She could go off and start fresh somewhere else. "I could probably pick up some chorus work in New York. And then, there's California." She named the state lovingly. "Just imagine being warm all year round! And there's always a chance of getting in the movies."

Hearing Lucy speak dreamily of California and the movies, seeing what pleasure she derived from viewing the unknown potential of the future, Bea had, for the first time, an intimation of Lucy's youth. Because Lucy was tall and grown up, Bea had assumed she had to be pretty old.

"How old're you anyway, Luce?"

"Twenty-five. How old did you think I was?"

"I don't know. Just grown up."

Lucy laughed. "You thought I was *old!*" she accused. "Cripes, I don't *look* old, do I?"

"I don't know. Everybody over eighteen looks old to me. I mean, my mom's only thirty-two."

"You're joking!" Lucy had pictured Bea's mother as considerably older than that, although now that she thought about it she had no idea why.

"Nope. She went and got pregnant when she was seventeen, and the mother of the fella paid her to go away. So she and my gramma came here to have me. But I'm American because at the last minute Gramma decided maybe it wasn't so smart to have a Canadian baby. You know, in case they ever wanted to go back home or anything. So when it was time, my gramma took my mom over to Buffalo, and that's where I was born."

"Gee! So, what're they like? Is she nice, your mom? Are they good to you, Bea?" Suddenly, it mattered very much to Lucy that people should be good to Bea. And that confused her because she hadn't realized how deeply attached she'd become to the girl.

"They're okay. They're not mean or anything. When the 'Market' fell, the family in Hartford stopped sending the money, so Lil and Gramma had to go out to work. Lil's a waitress. She actually loves it, if you can imagine that. And Gramma works in a bakery. She's really fed up with Lil because ever since she started waiting table she's been going out with a lot of men. Sometimes they stay the night, and some of them give her money. Gramma says she's going to get herself arrested, or caught again, and then she'll really be in trouble because nobody's going to pay her for having a baby the way they did last time." Bea was having a good time. No adult had ever before offered to have a conversation with her. Not only that, but Lucy was

27

actually listening, smiling and nodding. "She's very pretty, Lil," she continued. "But I don't look anything like her, so I guess I must look like Jackie Ellroy, Junior."

"He's your dad?"

"Uh-huh. I wonder about him sometimes, you know. I mean, he's probably married and has some kids. And if that's so, then I've got brothers and sisters. It's kind of funny to think about that."

"I guess it must be," Lucy agreed.

"Will you be sad to leave here?" Bea asked.

"In a way." Lucy looked around the room. "But I like to try to look on the bright side of things, and it'll be a relief not to have to worry about keeping this place up."

"You're funny," Bea said with a smile. "Looking on the bright side and worrying all the same."

"That's me all over." Lucy returned the smile. "What do you want, Bea?"

"I want to be the best dancer there ever was."

"You do, huh?" Lucy's smile held.

"I *love* dancing. I love singing, too. But lots of people can sing. Dancing's different. You can *see* if a person's any good or not. Sometimes, when I'm dancing, it feels as if *I'm* the music. The notes are right inside of me, and there's nothing I couldn't do. Even the most impossible moves in the whole world, that nobody ever did before, I could do them because I'm part of the music. And sometimes, even when there isn't any music, I can start snapping my fingers and making a rhythm, and it's like music but without any notes. I start to dance, and I know that if I wanted to I could dance and dance until I just disappeared and there wasn't any me anymore. D'you know what I mean?"

"I don't know if I do."

"Gee," Bea laughed. "I don't know if I do, either. It's just this feeling I get, this terrifically sensational feeling."

"I'll tell you one thing," Lucy said. "If I'd ever once felt the way you described when I was dancing, I'd probably have been the greatest thing ever to get up on stage. I think maybe that's the way you've got to feel if you're really going to make it big. I've always known I was good; but up on a stage, I don't shine. You've got to have that extra something that stands out, that everyone can see. And that's what you've got."

"You think so, honestly?"

"Yeah, I do."

* * *

Part One / 1917–1936

It took Lucy four months to sell the house and furnishings. During that time, she gave up the last of her paying students and debated the pros and cons of New York versus California. Finally, she decided to try New York for six months, and if that didn't work out, she'd head west. With that settled, she started thinking about Bea, imagining the two of them going off to New York together. It was another impulsive, pretty whacky idea, taking on the responsibility for a fourteen-year-old kid, but in a lot of ways Bea was more grown up than most of the adults Lucy knew. And she'd become very attached to Bea. In a sense it was as if Bea were an extension of her own self, and she was convinced Bea would succeed in doing all the things Lucy herself might never do. She hated the idea of leaving Bea behind, especially when, from what Bea had told her, her mother and grandmother didn't care if the kid was there or not. Was she just begging for trouble? she wondered. Or was it that she believed she could offer Bea something she wasn't getting from anyone else? One thing for sure, she had a big soft spot for the girl. She was also giving this particular impulse one heck of a lot of thought.

"I sure wish I could take you with me," she told Bea several weeks before she was due to leave.

"You mean that?" Bea asked.

"Sure, I mean it."

"I've been hoping and praying you'd say that, because I'll bet anything my mom would let me go with you. They'd probably be *glad* to have me go. Especially if I told Lil I'd get work and send money home. The idea of the money would thrill her to bits."

"Now, wait a minute." Lucy tried to slow her down. "There's a whole lot more to it than whether or not your mother would let you go. There's also the question of money. I've got some, but not enough to pay for both of us. And then there's a bunch of legal questions to consider. You're a minor. I'd have to become your guardian, or something. People can't just go off with other people's children, you know. Are you sure your mother wouldn't say boo about your going off with me?"

"Lucy, I *have* to go with you," Bea said passionately. "You've been better to me than anybody ever. I really *want* to go with you. And, honestly, all I have to do is promise to send Lil some money and she'll even pack my bags. Please let me go with you."

Lucy was ready to give in right then, but she was determined to be practical. "That still," she said, "leaves us with a money problem. I don't have enough for both of us, Bea."

"Well," Bea said, "I do have an idea."

"What?"

"You *really* mean it?"

"How many times do I have to *tell* you?" Lucy flared.

"Don't get mad, Luce," Bea said quietly. "I just have to be sure. It's easy to fool kids, you know."

Softening, Lucy said, "I don't happen to be that kind of person."

"I know that. Okay, here's my plan: First, you'll come over and meet Lil and Gramma. I only just told them about you lately because when you said things were getting bad, I was hoping and hoping you'd want to take me with you. So, the way I figure it, if you show up looking and sounding okay, they'll go along. Then, after that, all we have to do is get some kind of paper signed saying you're my legal guardian."

"Okay so far. Then what?"

"Then, I enter that city-wide talent contest they've been advertising in the *Telegram*. First prize is five hundred dollars."

"Holy Hannah, Bea! Everybody and his brother's going to be entering that contest."

"Maybe so. But I'm going to win it. I've been working on my routine for ages now, and I'm going down to audition next Tuesday."

"When did you do all this?" Lucy asked.

"Oh, I planned to enter, from the very first day. I sent in my application right away. Once I have the prize money, we won't have to worry about your paying my way."

"You were that sure about me, huh?" Lucy grinned and gave her a hug.

Bea hugged her back, saying, "I only hoped. And I would've entered the contest anyway, so I could go to New York and we could still be friends."

Lucy took a long look at the girl. It was funny, but Bea really was a better, closer friend than any of the other, older, girls she'd known far longer. She knew, looking at Bea, that if she asked her there and then to do something—anything—Bea would do it without hesitation. There weren't many people she could count on that way. "What if you don't win?" she asked after a moment.

"Second prize is two hundred and fifty, and third prize is a hundred. I'll win some of that money one way or another. But don't worry. I'm going to win it all."

Lucy shook her head. "You sure got a lotta moxie for a little kid."

"I'm only short, not little. And you keep telling me how good I am. And I really love you, Luce. You're the best friend I've ever had, next to Becky Armstrong. So, what d'you think of my idea?"

"I think we better make arrangements for me to meet your mother. And after that, I think you'd better show me this prize-winning routine you've worked up. And do me a favor, will you?"

"Sure. What?"

"Next time you start making plans that include me, let me know. Okay? And one other thing. You're a pretty swell friend yourself. And I love you too."

Lil thought the idea was just peachy. Agatha was suspicious. "What's a grown woman want with a kid like you?" she asked Bea.

"What d'you mean what does she want? She's taking me with her to New York so I can be a dancer. She doesn't *want* anything. She's my friend."

Agatha laughed mirthlessly. "Oh, that's rich. That's really rich!"

"Don't be mean, Ma," Lil said. "Bea's a good little dancer. She'll make scads of money and look after her mom and gramma. Won't you, Bea?"

"That's right."

"Why, I bet she'll be a big hit on Broadway."

"Who's going to pay for all this?" Agatha wanted to know.

"I'll pay my own way," Bea answered.

"How?" Lil and Agatha asked as one.

"I'm going to win the money. In a talent contest."

"Oh, this is *really* rich!" Agatha gave a repeat performance of her mirthless laughter.

"You can laugh all you want," Bea said calmly, "but I'm going to win. What I want to know is, are you going to let me go to New York with Lucy?"

"Gee." Lil looked over at her mother. "It's something to think about."

"We'll have to make her my guardian," Bea hurried ahead, "in case there are problems. You know, to prove she's really in charge of me."

"I don't know," Lil said, still looking at her mother.

"You'll meet her first, of course. She's coming over on Wednesday to see you. Then, when you've met her and seen what a swell person she is, we'll get the paper signed. I asked Becky's dad, and he has a lawyer friend who said he'll do the paper as a favor to Becky's dad. Wasn't that nice of him?"

"Wednesday's no good," Lil said. "I've got a date."

"I figured you would, so I told Lucy to come at six. It won't take long. You two will have a cup of tea, and you'll talk. Then you'll go out on your date."

"This is the craziest thing I ever heard of," Agatha protested. "For

31

God's sake, Lil! You're going to let the kid go off with some woman you've never even met?"

"She's going to meet her," Bea corrected, "on Wednesday."

"And Bea's a good girl," Lil said. "She'll send money home. Sure," she told Bea, "you tell your friend to come on over Wednesday."

"Well, if this doesn't beat all!" Agatha exclaimed.

"Listen, Luce, I *know* her. All anybody has to do is talk money to Lil and they've got her complete attention. I could just see her thinking, adding up how much she'd save if she didn't have to feed me and buy my clothes. I've already got the paper from Mr. Armstrong's friend, so all you and Lil have to do is sign it. Are you changing your mind, Luce? Are you thinking maybe you'd be better off on your own, without a kid tagging along?"

"Listen yourself!" Lucy told her. "I'd be kind of a jerk if I didn't stop to think about what it means, volunteering to take you on. Sure I've been thinking about it. I'll probably be thinking about it for a heck of a long time, but I'm taking you with me. Never mind my worrying. I worry about all kinds of things. *You* worry about this contest. Now, show me the number."

Bea did it for her, then Lucy sat back saying, "Don't change a thing!" She shook her head slowly back and forth. "I can't believe you worked that up by yourself. We'll leave it for now. If you pass the audition, I'll take another look, see if there's anything that needs changing. And don't worry about me worrying about you. Okay?"

"I just want us both to be sure."

"I'm as sure as I'm going to get. I'm just someone who's always thinking of all the things that can go wrong. You'll get used to it."

"I'm already used to it." Bea gave her a wide smile.

There were hundreds of people waiting to audition. Most hadn't bothered to send in applications and were turned away. Those who'd applied properly were given numbers and told to wait backstage until their numbers were called.

"Write your number down on your music, if you've brought some, and hand it in to the assistant stage manager over there. If you don't need music, say so. If you need accompaniment, but don't have music, tell us before you're ready to go on."

Bea was briefly alarmed because it hadn't occurred to her she'd need sheet music. The A.S.M. assured her the piano player could do a creditable job of any song she wanted. "Just tell him your key."

"I don't know it."

"Don't sweat it, kid. Just go on over there, sing your opening notes, and he'll find the key for you."

"Gee, thanks."

From the wings she watched jugglers and singers, duos and trios, acrobats and dancers, all kinds of acts. There wasn't one of them, she thought, anywhere near as good as she was. One guy was a terrific singer, and a few other acts weren't too bad. Overall, though, she knew she was going to walk away with first prize. While she waited, she did her warm-up routine, wishing she had a costume. Once she won, the first thing she'd do would be to get a smart outfit to wear for the auditions she'd go to in New York.

When her number was called, her heart gave a tremendous leap, as if it was trying to jump right out of her chest. Swallowing hard, she walked out onto the stage and said to the piano player, "I'm doing 'Crazy Rhythm.' I don't know the key, but I start here." She sang the first two bars.

"Gotcha," he told her, at once noodling around in her key.

"I'm gonna sing it through once, then I'm going to dance it right from the top. Okay?"

"Okay."

"For the dancing part, I want it in double time. Okay?"

"Sure thing."

He played a four-bar intro; she wrapped her sweaty hands around the microphone stand and started. It sounded too naked, so she added the missing counterpoint with her feet. That was better. She got through the first chorus, waited out the next four bars, then went into her dance. She'd never before had this kind of space to move around in. It was terrific. She could really expand, cover a lot of territory. She let the music and the rhythm take her and danced with everything she had. The climax of the number was eight all-out, tapping pirouettes, topped by a flying split, and a final pirouette that came in right on the money, on the beat. She ended with her heels together, her arms outflung, and her chin high, smiling like crazy, because she'd never had a better time or more fun. And the applause that came at her from the wings and from beyond the footlights really was the bee's knees. She was halfway to winning that first-prize money. And she was going to dance on the very same stage that Bill Robinson had been on.

Four

THE meeting went well. Lillian relaxed at first sight of Lucy because Lucy wasn't as pretty as Lillian was. Looks meant everything to Lillian, and while Lucy wasn't unattractive, she was definitely no beauty. If she'd been prettier, Lillian might have worried about letting Bea go with her, because a pretty woman could always be tempted to go off with men. But it was easy to see that Lucy wasn't the type who'd drive men wild.

"What d'you want with her anyway?" Agatha demanded of Lucy.

"She's very talented," Lucy responded. "You'll see for yourself when she dances in the contest next week. You *are* going to be there, aren't you?"

"We sure are," Lillian put in. "I wouldn't miss it for anything. I love a good show."

"None of this sounds right," Agatha fretted.

"Lucy's gonna look out for me," Bea told them. "It'll be just fine."

"I've really gotta scram," Lillian announced, hastily applying fresh lip rouge. "I hate to keep a fella waiting. You understand." She smiled charitably at Lucy, certain Lucy didn't know a thing about fellas. "It's been real nice meetin' you. And I know you'll take good care of my little girl."

Agatha wanted to ask her how she could be so sure of that, but there was no chance. Bea would have liked to ask her mother when she had turned into Lil's "little girl." Lillian rubbed a little extra rouge onto her cheeks, checked herself in her pocket mirror, and was on her way.

"Well, I'll be," Agatha murmured as the door closed behind Lil. "You want a cup of tea?" she asked Lucy.

And that was that. Lucy had a cup of tea. Agatha talked about the

34

weather and the tough times. Then they said good-bye, and Lucy went home. It was all settled.

The next day Bea went to Lucy's house to work on her costume. Lucy had found a black leotard left behind by one of her students and was painstakingly sewing sequins and spangles on the shoulders and down each side. She'd already bought Bea a pair of pink tights and some pink ribbon for her hair.

"I'll come with you," Lucy offered, "keep you company and do your make-up and hair."

"What if they won't let you in?"

"They'll let me in. We'll just say I'm your mother. Have you given any thought at all to the possibility you might not win?"

"I'll win," Bea insisted.

"But if you don't, sweetheart, I'll have to go without you. And now that things are settled, I'm really looking forward to us going together."

"Don't worry so much." Bea placed her hand reassuringly on Lucy's arm. "Even if I only come in third, I'll still have a hundred dollars. That's plenty."

"Are you nervous?"

"I don't think so. There's going to be an orchestra, you know. A whole orchestra. I can't wait!"

There were twenty-two finalists in the contest. Bea was slotted second-to-last after the intermission.

"That's a good position," Lucy told her. "After seeing all those others perform, the audience'll be getting pooped out. I just pity the act that has to follow you."

"How come?"

"Think about it. Would *you* want to go on after you if you were a juggler or a singer? Boy! I sure wouldn't. Just one thing, Bea. You know that flying split at the end? I've been thinking about that. Do it side-to-side instead of turned."

"You mean face-on to the audience?"

"That's right. It'll knock 'em dead, I guarantee you. And that way, when you land, you won't have to do that extra half-turn to get into your final position."

Bea thought about it. "You're right. It'll be easier that way," she said.

"And don't forget to smile."

"I can't help smiling."

35

Backstage the theater was crowded with performers and their friends and families. The noise level was high.

"It'll settle down when the hangers-on clear off out front to watch the show," Lucy told Bea.

All the females were in one large dressing room, the males in another. Lucy directed Bea to a free area at the far end of the long, narrow, overheated room and began to set make-up out on the tea towel she'd brought along.

"Just relax," Lucy said. "You've got a long wait ahead of you."

"What's all this stuff?" Bea asked.

"Make-up. You can't go out there with a naked face. The lights'll bleach the features right off your face. We've got to make sure the people can see you, especially your eyes. But we won't do your make-up until the intermission. If we do it now, it'll be all runny by the time you're to go on."

"What'll we do while we're waiting?" Bea looked around at the others in the room, her attention caught by a stunningly beautiful blonde girl with huge blue eyes. A woman, presumably her mother, was fussing over her, fluffing her ringlets, then beading the girl's eyelashes. The blonde's dress was an amazing pink organdy concoction of layers and layers of ruffles that would have been far more appropriate on a much younger girl.

Following Bea's gaze, Lucy emitted a low whistle. "Isn't *she* the cat's pajamas?" she said admiringly. "What does she do?"

"She sings," Bea answered, her eyes still on the girl.

"Any good?"

"She's got this teeny tiny little voice, but she's not bad. Sort of like a singing mouse."

Lucy laughed appreciatively.

"No kidding. I figure she's at least seventeen or eighteen."

"Oh, easily," Lucy concurred.

"But look at her. That dress is for an eight-year old. And I don't know how she got into the finals. There were other acts way better than her."

"She sure is beautiful, though, isn't she?"

"Yup. What is that they're doing to her eyes?"

"Beading her eyelashes to make them look longer and darker."

"You're not going to do that to me, are you?" Bea asked warily.

"Nope. We won't bother."

"Good. What *are* you going to do?"

"Just a little this, a little that. Stay here, okay? I'm going to have a look around, see what's happening."

Part One / 1917–1936

The master of ceremonies was a slick-looking, silver-haired type, with a pencil-thin mustache and a mellow speaking voice. He introduced the judges: a fellow who wrote a daily column for the *Telegram*, a guy with his own radio show, an immensely large-breasted woman who was an opera singer, and an actor from Hollywood who'd played supporting roles in half a dozen movies and was in town promoting his most recent one. The judges occupied the center four seats of the first row in the orchestra stalls, and each stood in turn as they were introduced. The jam-packed audience applauded politely, eager for the show to begin.

Back in the dressing room, Lucy and Bea were alone. The others had crowded into the wings to watch the performances. Music trickled in around the edges of the dressing-room door, and Bea's foot tapped automatically to the beat.

"Why can't I go watch?" she asked, puzzled by Lucy's insistence that she remain in here.

"It's a bad idea," Lucy told her. "If you go out and watch, you might be influenced by the other acts. The best thing is to stay here and concentrate on yourself and what you're going to do."

"But what if I was in a real show?"

"That'd be different," Lucy said knowledgeably. "This is a *contest*, Bea. Anything goes. When money's on the line, people can be really ruthless. This one time, I actually saw a girl put glue in the rosin box to mess up another girl's audition. No trick's too dirty or too mean when money's involved. In this business, you want to keep your eyes open all the time, and your mouth shut."

"Boy!" Bea was mightily impressed.

"The only thing you've got to worry about, so far as I can see, is the blonde cutie."

"Why?"

"I don't know. Just a hunch I've got. Something funny's going on with that kid and her mother. They were awful chummy with the M.C. before the show started. I've got a sneaking suspicion there's a fix in tonight."

"What does that mean?" Bea asked, fearful her prize money was going to go to the wrong person.

"It's probably nothing. It struck me as kind of peculiar, all that friendly business. We'll see. You stay put here. I'm going to go have another look, see how things are progressing."

"Don't take too long, okay? This is really boring."

Things were really humming along, and the audience was having a good time. Every act had family members or friends out front who cheered loudly for them. But so far, Lucy thought, there hadn't been anything near a standout performance. Bea was probably right. She most likely would walk away with first prize. Unless...

"There!" Lucy smiled as she came through the door. "That wasn't long, was it? Only two more acts before the intermission. We can start getting you ready now."

They'd stacked all the best performers in the second half of the show. The opener was a young man with a fine Irish tenor who had half the audience dewy-eyed with his rendition of "Londonderry Air." He was followed by a family of acrobats who cartwheeled across the stage, leaped upon each other's shoulders, contorted themselves into impossible positions, and climbed into a human pyramid for their finale. After the acrobats came a mother and daughter who did a turn-of-the-century soft-shoe–and–patter number that was pleasant but not exceptional.

Lucy left Bea warming up in the dressing room and hurried to stage left to watch the blonde do her number. She sang "Blue Skies" in a watery, albeit pure, soprano. Her mother, Lucy noticed, stood in the wings stage-right with her hands clasped prayer-like and an expression of dedicated determination creasing her features as she mouthed the lyrics along with her daughter. At the bridge, forgetting herself utterly, she even mimicked her daughter's limp hand gestures. It was quite a show, made all the more interesting by the appearance in the shadows behind Mama of the M.C. As the girl finished her last eight bars, the M.C. patted Mama's arm significantly before gliding onstage to direct the rather doubtful applause. "Damn!" Lucy whispered, racing back to the dressing room. There really was a fix in, and Lucy could think of no way to scotch it.

Becky Armstrong had her entire family with her to see the show. By chance, the previous Saturday, she and Franny had been heading along Dundas to the movies when she'd spotted Bea's mother and had gone running over to say hello and to ask about Bea. She'd learned from Lillian about the contest and that same evening had launched her campaign.

"We've *got* to *go!*" she had begged her mother at dinner. "Bea's in the contest. She's one of the finalists."

"So what?" Franny had interjected.

"Now, just a moment, Frances," their mother had said. "Let Rebecca have her say. Remind me again, dear. Who's Bea?"

"You know!" Becky had moaned. "She was in our class at school. She's the one I told you about who's such a terrific dancer."

"Terrific, my Aunt Hatty!"

"Hush, Frances. I'm trying to hear what Becky's saying."

Becky had dragged out every argument she could think of and had had threats at the ready, should they prove necessary. She had been fully prepared to tell them she'd lie down on the streetcar tracks and let herself get run over if they didn't take her to the show. But her father had finally announced he'd already bought the tickets and had winked surreptitiously at Becky. Becky had been greatly relieved. She'd have hated to dirty one of her dresses, lying in the street.

So far, Franny had groaned and complained about everything from their seats to the performers, with the exception of the acrobats, whom she'd liked. Everyone else was having a splendid time, and Becky was beside herself with excitement at the prospect of seeing Bea perform.

"She's so wonderful," she told her father repeatedly. "Just you wait and see. I'll bet she even wins first prize. She's the best dancer you ever saw."

"Oh, sure," Franny put in. "So long as she doesn't break the rubber bands holding on her bottle tops."

Agatha thought the show was damned good value for the money, and Lillian loved every moment of it. She even entertained a certain romantic wistfulness about her own failure to go into show business. She certainly could have sung as well as the blonde, she thought, and she was every bit as pretty.

"When's Bea going to be on, I'd like to know?" Agatha murmured, halfway through the second part of the show.

"Soon, soon," Lillian assured her. "Isn't she something?" she said of the blonde beauty. "Just like a little doll."

"Who're they kidding?" Agatha hissed. "That little doll's twenty if she's a minute. And she can't sing worth spit. *You* sing better than that, for goodness' sake."

Gratified, Lillian sank back into her seat.

"When's Bea gonna be on?" Agatha asked again.

The blonde was followed by two sisters on roller skates who were doing a whiz-bang job until their feet somehow got tangled and there ensued a spectacular collision, culminating in an audible thud that actually shook the first few rows of seats. In a show of sympathy while privately elated by the spill, the audience cheered as the girls picked themselves up and gamely got through to the end of their routine, before limping off the stage.

A young couple came on after the skaters and performed a madly inventive apache dance with the husband quite convincingly beating the bejesus out of his wife to a pulsating tango. They received a good round of applause and skipped happily off the stage, congratulating each other as they went.

Next was a ventriloquist whose dummy was a rowdy little overalled fellow who sang while his master drank a glass of water and sassed back rudely each time the youthful fellow asked him a question. It was very funny, and the audience ate it up, clapping loudly at the end.

Then there was a woman of thirty or so who came out and sang "My Heart Stood Still" in a high, thrilling voice, accompanied by a minimum of hand gestures. Every note was perfectly placed and beautifully delivered. The audience loved her, and she had to come back for a second bow.

Bea and Lucy were waiting in the wings when the next act went on.

"This guy's a corker," Lucy whispered appreciatively, as the middle-aged, heavyset man sang, told jokes and funny stories, and closed with a nicely done soft-shoe. "Bet he was in vaudeville," Lucy said, clapping at the close of his number. "You can always tell. They have such a way with an audience. They know how to work a crowd."

The M.C. was back onstage, waiting for the applause to die down before introducing Bea.

"Are you all warmed up?" Lucy asked her. Bea nodded. "Don't forget to smile." Bea nodded again. "And don't forget about the side-to-side split." Bea nodded a third time, her eyes on the man onstage.

The M.C. was saying, "Here she is, folks, little Beatrice Crane. Let's give her a nice, big welcome."

Again there was that fantastic lurching of her heart as Bea made her way onstage accompanied by the sound of applause. She smiled, got to the microphone, counted down the opening, and, feet tapping the counter-rhythm, went into her song.

In the wings, Lucy wiped her damp hands down the sides of her skirt. Her heart was thumping like crazy, and she chewed on her lower lip, her eyes filling with proud tears. The kid was a natural, no doubt about it. She had a good, solid show voice, clear and strong, with a pleasing edge to it. She was a born belter, and the crowd was

40

with her from the first note. They knew they were seeing someone very special here.

When Bea pushed off into her dance in double time, she was like a small rocket spinning around the stage. The sequins and spangles on her leotard threw light off in a dazzling blur as she did combinations no one had ever seen before. Every single person in the audience was mesmerized, mouth agape, as Bea took off into her tapping pirouettes. And when she launched herself into her final midair, front-facing split, landing with her arms outflung, the whole place exploded into cheers and whistles, foot-stomping, and wild applause in a standing ovation. All the people in the wings were clapping too, except, Lucy noted, the mother of the blonde honey. To hell with her, Lucy told herself, turning her attention back to the stage where a laughing Bea was taking her bows. The audience didn't want to let her go. She was running back for her seventh bow when the M.C. waved the audience to silence and began his introduction for the final act.

"Sweetheart, you were a sensation!" Lucy crowed, scooping the barely winded Bea into her arms. "I'm so proud of you!"

"Great show, kid!" the older vaudevillian beamed at Bea. Most of the performers had gathered around to congratulate her, but Bea moved to approach the young man waiting to go on.

"You're gonna win one of the prizes," she told him. "You're the best singer I ever heard. Go out there and kill 'em."

He wiped imaginary sweat off his brow and gave her a smile. "I just hope I never have to follow your act again," he said. "You're a real pistol, kid."

"So're you. Good luck!"

"Thanks."

Lucy loved the girl for her instinctive showmanship, and loved her more for her generosity and grace. Her arm draped around Bea's shoulders, they listened to the young man do his song. Bea was right about him. He had a marvelous voice, and more, he was one hell of an actor. His rendition of "Brother, Can You Spare a Dime?" earned him the second standing ovation of the evening.

Then, the performances had come to an end and the M.C. was explaining that the judges would now confer before announcing the prize-winners. The four judges climbed up to the stage and moved to one side with the M.C. People in the audience chattered expectantly, energetically making bets on who'd take second and third prize. There was no doubt in anyone's mind that Bea was going to take the top honors of the evening.

Becky was so excited she couldn't sit still. Even Franny had to admit

Bea had been nothing less than a revelation. Lillian had a death-drop on Agatha's hand and tears of pride in her eyes. She'd already informed everyone within hearing distance that Bea was her little girl and had received hearty congratulations.

The M.C. separated himself from the judges and approached the microphone. An anticipatory hush fell over the entire theater.

"Ladies and gentlemen," he began, "I'm sure you'll agree with me that we've seen twenty-two very talented acts this evening." He looked stage-left, then stage-right, directing the audience in an enthusiastic round of applause. Then, holding up his hands for silence, he continued. "And now, for our winners." Again, the hushed silence. "In third place, for his heart-rending performance of 'Brother Can You Spare a Dime?,' let's hear it for young Andy O'Connor."

Bea whirled around, grinning, to exclaim to Lucy, "See! Didn't I tell you? I knew he'd win." She clapped happily as Andy skipped on stage to accept his prize envelope along with the accolade from the crowd.

Into another silence, the M.C. said, "In second place, we have the amazing young singer/dancer, little Beatrice Crane."

The silence held. People in the audience turned to look at each other.

"I knew there was a fix," Lucy whispered, as Bea walked on stage. No one in the audience moved; there was no applause.

Bea accepted the envelope the M.C. gave her, then took a step to one side, positioning herself next to Andy. The silence confused her. It obviously confused the M.C. as well, who hurried on to his final declaration.

"In first place," he said, his voice cracking, "for her lovely 'Blue Skies,' the beautiful Linda Everson."

As Linda ran on stage, an outraged and tearful Becky Armstrong broke the long-lasting silence by jumping to her feet, crying loudly, "THAT'S NOT FAIR! THAT'S JUST NOT FAIR!"

At once, a man sitting down near the front got to his feet, shouting, *"Something damned funny's going on here!"*

That did it. Suddenly, everyone was shouting. People were waving their fists at the M.C. and the four judges, demanding to know what was happening. The M.C. tried to speak, smiling and holding up his hands in an effort to quiet the crowd, but the people were enraged. Popcorn bags and crumpled papers began to pelt the stage. One man was so infuriated he ripped the arm off his seat and hurled it toward the stage, narrowly missing the M.C.'s knees. Everyone was shouting louder and louder; feet stamped on the floor; more and more projectiles flew through the air. Just at the point where pandemonium was due to break out, the judges hurried center-stage to pull aside the now very frightened M.C.

"Ladies and gentlemen," the *Telegram* columnist bellowed into the microphone. "Obviously, there's been a mistake."

"You're damned right there's been a mistake!" a very fat woman shrieked.

"Now, now!" The columnist held out his hands in a gesture of peace, and the standing crowd gradually quieted in order to hear what he'd say. "Our master of ceremonies has made a slight error and read the cards in the wrong order." He cast an angry look over his shoulder at the gentleman in question. "Didn't you, Bud?"

Bud nodded sheepishly and offered the house a weak smile. These people would rip him limb from limb if they got the chance.

"Miss Everson is our third-place winner, ladies and gentlemen," the writer went on. "And our first-place winner is, of course, the inimitable Beatrice Crane. Come on over here, Bea," he beckoned, "and get your prize."

The audience wouldn't buy it. Sure, they wanted the kid to get what was rightfully hers, but this whole contest was rigged, and they didn't care for that one bit.

"This whole show's a phony!" cried a burly man in the front row as Bea took the envelope from the columnist's hand. *"A phony from start to finish, and we're not going to put up with it!"*

Bea looked over to see Lucy frantically signaling to her. She looked back at the man in the front row as she made her way toward Lucy in the wings.

Everybody was shouting again and throwing things at the stage as Lucy grabbed Bea by the hand, and the two of them ran just before the audience surged up past the footlights onto the stage.

"We're getting out of here!" Lucy panted, pushing Bea's clothes and shoes and the make-up collection into her bag. *"C'mon!"* With a firm grip on Bea's hand, she directed the girl along the corridor toward the loading-bay door at the extreme rear of the theater. They pushed through the terrified group of performers who were all looking for somewhere safe to hide. Arriving at the door, they burst into the alley running behind the theater, rounded the corner, and scrambled for a streetcar that was just coming along Queen. Once safely on the car, they caught their breath, and Lucy helped Bea put her dress on over her leotard.

"Oh, my God!" Lucy exclaimed a minute or two later, remembering. "The prize money! Have you got it?"

"I sure do," Bea told her, and reached down the front of her leotard to pull out, not one, but two envelopes of prize money.

Lucy clapped a hand over her mouth, then burst out laughing.

"They gave me first *and* second prize," Bea said. "So I took them. Boy! Wasn't that something?"

"I knew in my bones there was going to be trouble. That's why I checked for another way out of the theater. I never thought they'd tear the place apart, though. I can't wait to read about this in the papers tomorrow. This ought to make headlines."

"You think it'll be in the papers?"

"Count on it! They'll never try anything like that again."

"I didn't really win, did I?" Bea said softly, absorbing this.

"You sure did, sweetheart. That's what all the fuss was about. Why d'you think those people went so crazy? Because you won. I'd just love to know what the payoff was gonna be."

"What payoff?"

"Well, how d'you figure it?" Lucy said reasonably. "Beautiful Linda and her mama were going to have to reward somebody somehow for that nice first prize."

"Oh!" Beatrice finished buttoning her dress, then jammed her hands into the pockets. "You mean...?"

"I surely do."

"I'd *never* do something like that just to win a prize."

"Never say you'd never, Bea."

Five

I T was exactly like a scene from a movie, Lil thought. At the last moment, as Bea was about to go out the door, Lil had to run to embrace her. She amazed them all with her sudden tears and overflowing emotion.

"You be sure to write to me," she told Bea. "Let me know where you are. And don't you forget us, will you?" Turning her tear-dampened face to Lucy, she said, "You'll look out for her, won't you?"

44

"I sure will," Lucy promised. "And we'll let you know the address as soon as we're settled."

Agatha, who'd remained at the kitchen table, smoking cigarettes one after another, finally got up—inspired not only by Lillian's demonstration of affection, but also by Bea's having donated the two hundred and fifty dollars of second-prize money to the household—to give Bea an awkward hug. In a hushed voice, audible only to Bea, she said, "You know us. We're not so hot when it comes to showing how we feel, and maybe we haven't done all that well by you, but things don't work out, you can always come home."

"Thanks, Gramma," Bea said, quite moved.

"And write to us, you hear?"

"I will," Bea gave her word. Why had they waited until now, when she was leaving, to give any sign of caring for her? Or was it that they were glad she was going and so were able to act as if they cared? It was a question that preoccupied her throughout the first several hours of the train trip to New York.

"Some women just don't take naturally to children," Lucy tried to explain. "Being a mother's not all it's cracked up to be. A lot of women don't ever take to it. Personally, I'm in no big hurry to have kids. You can't have impulses *and* kids."

Bea turned to look out the window at the passing scenery, feeling kind of shaky in the pit of her stomach. In the lavatory at the end of the compartment, her hand on the wall to keep her balance in the lurching motion of the train, she gazed at the bloodstain on her underpants and swallowed hard, trying to tie her knowledge of what this signified to her sense of herself. She certainly knew what was happening to her because once every month for as long as she could remember Lil had moaned and groaned, making a fuss and complaining about the weight she'd gained and the rotten cramps and how her breasts were all sore and swollen. She'd invariably gone on to warn Bea about "the miseries of being a woman." Bea had been waiting so long for it to happen that she'd started to wonder if there wasn't something wrong with her. At least now she knew there wasn't anything wrong, but she sure wasn't prepared. As a temporary measure, she folded a huge wad of toilet paper, placed it between her legs, pulled up her step-ins, and walked back to inform Lucy.

"Gosh!" Lucy said. "I just assumed . . . Never mind, sweetheart. I've got everything you need. We'll get you fixed up in no time flat."

"I guess I didn't really believe it was ever going to happen. You know? One part of me thought maybe there was something wrong with me. And the other part was kind of glad not to have to go through it. Lil always told me it'd happen, but I didn't want to believe her because she's so goldarned *dumb* and makes such a fuss over everything."

"Don't be so hard on her, Bea. She is what she is. You can't blame her for not being what you'd like her to be."

"I guess not. I feel as if I blame her for something, though."

"Come on. Let's get you fixed up."

The two of them returned to the lavatory where Lucy handled everything so matter-of-factly that it never occurred to Bea to be embarrassed. "Lucky I had these things along, eh? How d'you feel?"

"Okay, I guess."

"A little blue?"

"A little."

"Want an aspirin?"

"No, thanks. I'll be okay." She laughed suddenly. "Boy! These things are huge. It feels like I've got a pillow between my legs. What d'you do when you've got to dance and it's your time of the month?"

"I used to make a kind of plug, with cotton batting; roll it into a small tube and put on a little Vaseline to make it easier to insert. Thank heavens, there's a company that just started putting tampons out, so you won't have to go through all that bother."

"You put something *inside?*"

"Oh, sure. It's easy. When we get to New York, I'll show you how they work."

As they were heading back to their seats, Bea suddenly put her arm around Lucy's waist and leaned in close to her. "Thanks a lot, Luce. Lil would've made me feel just awful, but you didn't. I feel all right now."

While Bea napped, Lucy studied her, not in the least sorry she'd decided to bring Bea along with her. She seemed able to take things in her stride, easily, and with a very mature attitude. And, in a way, her attitude matched her features. At certain angles, Bea was fascinating to look at. The combination of her long, dark hair, pale skin, and smoky eyes was very appealing.

Bea opened her eyes, saw Lucy looking at her, and smiled. "Do I look funny?"

"No. I was just thinking."

"What about?" Bea sat up, glanced out the window, then looked back at Lucy.

"This and that, nothing in particular."

"Are you going to try to find your sister when we get there?"

"I've got an address. I'll get in touch to let her know I'm around."

"Are you sad you had to sell your house?"

"Not really. I inherited the house when Dad died, because I was the oldest. He'd only bought it in '28, when things were going really well for him. Eighteen months later, everything turned sour, and he had to take out a mortgage, and then a second one. The strange thing about this Depression, you know, Bea, is how many people there are around who've still got heaps of money. If you're out, walking on the street, it looks as if everybody's in a breadline, or panhandling, or selling apples. But that's not the way it is at all. Anyway, I didn't get much for the house. The people figured I had to be hard up, so they came in with a low offer and stuck to it, convinced nobody else was going to come along and offer me any more. So I had to take it. After the mortgage money and lawyer's fees were deducted, I didn't wind up with much."

"What happened to your dad, Luce?"

"He killed himself." She looked down at her hands, then out the window.

"Gee, that's terrible," Bea said.

"Yeah," Lucy sighed. "He put a gun in his mouth and pulled the trigger; did it at his office. I guess he did that so there'd be no chance Julie or I would be the ones to find him. It was pretty bad as it was. And then we found out all the money was gone, except for Julie's trust fund from our mother, which wasn't very much either, because Dad had invaded it. She had to quit music school a year early. She always dreamed of being a classical pianist."

"And what about you?"

"Oh, me. Well, I was older, and I thought I could look out for both of us. First I tried to get into the ballet companies. Then, when that didn't work, we put our heads together and hit on the idea of the dancing lessons. We started with ballet, but nobody was interested. Tap was all the rage, so I invested in a dozen lessons for myself, then went home and set up shop."

"Wasn't it hard, switching over?"

"It was just very different. Everything's outward, almost airborne in ballet. It's all in the extensions and how turned out you are; it's in your arms and shoulders and neck. Tap's a grounded kind of dancing. Your center of gravity's lower, and instead of trying for elevation, you're working downwards. But if you've got a good background in ballet, as well as tap, you'll always be a better dancer than the one who's only ever done tap. God! I just thought. What're we gonna do about school for you?"

47

"I have all the school I need. Grade Ten was boring anyway. Nope. I'm going to go straight out and start auditioning. And you know what else?"

"What?"

"I'm going to say I'm eighteen. The way I see it, I may be short, but everyone's forever telling me I've got a grown-up face, so I figure they'll believe I'm eighteen. Once they see me dance, nobody's going to care anyway how old I am."

"Where do you *get* it from?" Lucy wondered aloud. "I'm still worried about where we're going to live, and how, and you've got everything mapped out already. Slow down a little, Bea, and let the rest of us try to keep up with you."

"I can't," Bea said earnestly. "If you slow down, all the other people who want the same things you do will run right over you. And I've got this feeling I can't explain. I've just got to get going."

For a moment, Lucy was somewhat frightened by the intense light of Bea's eyes. They seemed lit from within by a cold flame and glowed with it, so that all you saw of her face were those huge, opaque eyes. Then Bea smiled and said, "Don't worry so much, Luce. I'll look out for you," and Lucy had to laugh.

Upon their arrival in Manhattan, Bea set out at once to acquaint herself with the city, quickly determining that the avenues ran north and south, and the streets followed east to west. To Lucy, it seemed Bea was fearless, with no qualms about the strangeness of the place, but rather an overwhelming curiosity and a need to put everything into a perspective uniquely her own. Within two days, she'd found the best inexpensive restaurants in a six-block radius of their rundown hotel on East Thirty-fifth Street. She'd located a good hand laundry, a shoemaker, several movie houses, and a newsstand that carried the trade papers.

Returning to their hotel room with the papers, she sat down at once with a pencil and began circling ads. There weren't that many for singers and dancers, but Bea was all set to go. Lucy tried to dissuade her.

"This isn't Toronto, you know. For every job there'll be hundreds of people, a lot of stiff competition. You need photos and some kind of résumé. You can just walk in off the street and hope to compete."

"I didn't come here to sit around in a hotel room. I came here to be a dancer."

"To get the chance, you've got to go by the rules," Lucy insisted.

"Maybe I won't have to. Oh, I'll get some pictures and whatever else I need. I just don't think it's good to fret too much about rules, Luce. If you do something the way everybody else does it, maybe you wind up never going anywhere because the rules are there to keep you in, not to let you out."

Lucy shut up and just stared.

"I know you want to help," Bea went on. "But I think there are other ways to do what you want. I'm good, and I know it. And I'll get people to let me show them what I can do. Sooner or later, somebody will see me and put me in a show."

"You put me to shame," Lucy said quietly. "Compared to you, I've got no guts."

"Maybe you're someone who doesn't need guts. You're a terrific dancer and a very nice person. I don't think you even want to be on stage, not really. And you know what else I think?"

"What?"

"I think everything'll work out fine, and you shouldn't worry as much as you do. We're together now. We've got enough money to get started, and we'll look out for each other. I've got to go now, Luce. There's an audition this afternoon, and I want to see what's what."

"Listen," Lucy said. "You be careful."

"I will be. *Don't worry!*"

Bea found her way over to West Forty-fifth Street, and from two blocks away she could see the crowd out front, waiting for the doors to open for the two o'clock audition. Undaunted, she circled the periphery of the crowd, noting there wasn't anyone who looked close to her age except for a boy about sixteen leaning against the building, a little apart from the tightly packed mob pressing against the doors. She studied the boy from about twenty feet away, liking the look of him, with his sandy brown hair, the freckles across his nose, and his round brown eyes. He had a pair of dancing shoes hung by their laces around his neck and looked perfectly relaxed and comfortable watching the people around him. Bea approached him, with a smile, saying, "Hi."

"Hi, yourself," he said, giving her the once-over. "What's up?"

She looked over at the others, then back at him. "I came to see what's what. You here to audition?"

"I am, if they let me."

"Me, too."

His eyebrows lifted, and he smiled. "You, too?"

"Uh-huh."

"What d'you do?" he asked, curious about this kid with the very sure demeanor.

"Sing and dance."

"You do, huh?"

"Yup. You dance, right?"

"That's right. You don't think you're maybe a little young for this?"

"I'm eighteen. How old're you?"

"*I'm* eighteen. You're about ten, eleven, I'd say."

She pursed her lips and gazed at him appraisingly. "You're not eighteen," she said, "and I'm not either. I figure you're fifteen, sixteen tops. And I'm fourteen."

He laughed. "You're pretty sharp. What's your name?"

"Beatrice Crane. Bea. What's yours?"

"Robert Ellis Bradley. Bobby." He held his hand out to her. "Glad to meetcha, Bea. You're a corker."

She shook his hand, saying, "Same here. Oh, look! They're opening the doors."

"Hold your horses," he told her. "The guys inside'll go through most of that gang in about fifteen minutes flat. Might as well wait and take our time. Half these people can't sing, and the other half can't dance. They'll weed out the would-be's inside half an hour, and then the real auditions'll start. You any good?"

"I sure am. Are you?"

"I'm the best," he said simply. "I've got a hunch you're not too bad, either. You sure you're fourteen?"

"Of course. And I wouldn't say I was the best," she said smoothly, "but I'm as good or better than you are. And I know there isn't anyone over there who's as good as either one of us."

"How d'you figure that?"

"I can tell just by looking at you."

"Sure are sure of yourself, aren't you?"

"Yup."

"Ever done anything?" he asked her.

"Just won first prize in a talent contest."

"Oh, yeah? Where was that? Somewhere important like Secaucus or Hoboken?"

"It happened to be in Toronto," she informed him.

"Isn't that in Canada somewhere?"

"That's right. And I'm sure it's a much bigger city than Sehobo or wherever."

"I'm sure it is," he agreed. "So you won first prize, huh?"

"I did. Out of twenty-two acts."

50

"Well," he said, "maybe they'll let you up on the stage, and we'll see what you can do."

"Say, d'you really think we should be waiting out here? I mean, we're about the only ones left."

"We'll give it a little longer. You watch. They'll start coming back out any minute now, in twos and threes."

"You've done this before, eh?"

"A lot."

"You wouldn't steer me off on a wild-goose chase, would you?"

He looked upset that she'd think him capable of that. "Say, sister! I wouldn't do anything that lousy."

"I hope not."

"So, you're from Canada, huh?"

"Yup. Except I was born in Buffalo, so I'm American. We've been here three days now."

"You and who else?"

"Me and my friend, Lucy."

"She 'eighteen' too?"

"Don't be silly! Lucy's a grown-up. She's twenty-six, for heaven's sake."

"Oh!"

"What about you? Where are you from?"

"Brooklyn."

"You live with your family?"

"Yeah. I'm thinking about moving out, though. It's crowded lately, what with everybody losing jobs and coming back home. Soon's I land a job, I'll find someplace on my own." He pushed away from the wall and went to peer into the theater. "A couple more minutes," he said, then stepped aside to allow those leaving to get by. "Didn't I tell you?" he said of the steady stream of people filing out of the theater. "Okay," he told her after five more minutes, taking hold of her hand. "Let's go. Ever done this before?"

"Once," she admitted. "For the talent show."

"Nervous?"

"Nope."

"Me, neither. I hardly ever get nervous." He unlooped the dancing shoes from around his neck, letting go of her hand. "Just stick with me, and do what I do."

Bobby approached a trio of two men and a woman who appeared to be in charge. Without looking up at him, one of the men asked, "Name? Singer or dancer? Agent? Last show?" and several other questions.

51

Bobby gave his name, then, "I sing and dance. No agent at the moment. My last show was with Gus Edwards in Atlantic City. I forgot my pictures but I can bring them next time, if you want me for a callback."

Still without looking up, the man said, "Okay, Bob. Over stage-left with the dancers. We'll be getting down to it in about ten minutes. Next!"

Bea stepped up. The man rattled off the same questions he'd asked Bobby, his eyes steadfastly on his clipboard.

She debated using some of Bobby's answers as her own, then decided to go with the truth. "My name's Beatrice Crane. I'm eighteen. I sing and dance. I don't have an agent yet, or any pictures, because I just got here. But I won first prize in a talent contest in Toronto— that's in Canada—and if you'll let me show you what I can do, I know you'll like me."

For the first time, the man looked up. There was a lengthy silence as he stared at her, then he nudged the man beside him as he asked Bea, "How old you say you were?"

"Eighteen. I'm short, so I look younger."

"You sing and dance and you just won first prize in a talent show where?"

"Toronto."

"Jesus!" He burst out laughing. "What're you, kid, nine, ten? And you won some talent show? That's a beaut!"

The man beside him didn't seem to share his amusement. "Shut up, Al," he said, looking at Bea's eyes. "We don't have a spot in this show for a kid," he told Bea. "I'll be fair and tell you that off the top. But there are always shows, and I'm always interested in new talent. You want to go up there and show me your stuff?"

Bea liked this man with the good smile, and the dark hair parted in the middle. She liked the laugh-lines around his eyes, and his honesty. "Yes, sir, I do," she answered. "I don't have any music, though."

"Don't worry about it." He turned to shout up to the stage. "Hey, Manny! Play for this kid, here." Turning back to Bea, he put a hand on her shoulder and gave her a slight push toward the stage. "Go on up there and tell Manny what you want him to play."

"C'mon, George," Al protested. "We're wasting time here. We got sixty, seventy people to audition."

"We got sixty-one," George amended. "You know something, Al? You're never going to be more than a stage manager. And you know why that is? Because you've got no intuition, no sense of adventure, no goddamned curiosity, and no eye whatsoever for talent. Now sit down, shut up, and let me see what we've got here. I like spunk, and this kid's loaded with it. You're lucky she didn't sock you in the jaw."

Bobby Bradley, standing with the other dancers, couldn't believe it. They were going to let the kid do her stuff. "Boy!" he said aloud, to no one in particular. "This is really something."

"Mr. White likes her," one of the girls whispered behind her hand. "I was watching. He was talking to her."

"This is amazing," Bobby said, watching Bea walk over to talk to the piano player. She sure was a cute kid.

Bea told Manny how she wanted to do "Crazy Rhythm," then leaned against the piano while she got her tap shoes on. As she straightened, she realized she'd have to sing in this big theater without a microphone. Well, she'd just sing louder than usual. She walked down almost to the apron, waited for Manny to lead her in, then belted out the lyrics.

Everyone on stage backed up to give her more room when she started to dance. Bobby whistled under his breath, astonished at the way she covered her ground. He noted her combinations, wondering who'd taught her. He'd never seen anything like it before. This kid wasn't fooling. She was better than anyone he'd ever seen. And he could tell everybody else thought so, too. Gee, but she was cute, he thought, watching her go. There was something about her that just made him smile. And her dancing!

When she finished, everyone applauded, and George summoned her to talk to him.

She ran back to the piano to get her street shoes and to thank the piano player.

"Say, kid," Manny said. "It was a pleasure. Where'd you ever learn to dance that way?"

"My friend, Lucy."

"Your friend could probably make herself a fortune if she could teach these hoofers to dance like you just did."

"I'll tell her you said so."

"Come on over here and sit down a minute," George invited, his hand again on her shoulder, directing her. "What'd you say your name was?"

"Beatrice Crane."

"And *how* old are you?"

"Eighteen."

"I wouldn't've believed that fifteen minutes ago. But seeing you dance, well"—he chuckled to himself. "Beatrice Crane, where did you come from?"

"Toronto."

"Beatrice Crane from Toronto. Can you take direction?"

"Yes, sir. I only have to see a routine once."

"I wish I had something for you in the show, Beatrice, but I don't. Never mind. There are always other shows, and there's bound to be a spot in one of them for a girl with your talent. Make sure Al has your name and where we can get hold of you. I want to talk to some people about you. Here's my card. Stay in touch, keep me posted on what you're doing. It was a pleasure." He extended his hand to her.

"Thank you very much, sir." She took his card, shook his hand, then got up and went to give Al her name and the address of the hotel.

As she was about to leave, Bobby Bradley came running up the aisle. "Hey! Wait a minute! Where can I find you? Maybe we could get together, you could teach me some of those swell combinations."

"Sure. I'd like that." She told him the hotel and her room number. "Good luck with the audition. And don't forget to come see me."

"You bet!" he called, racing back to the stage.

Back at the hotel, she hurried to tell Lucy about her audition. "He was really nice, Luce. He wanted to know who taught me, and so did the piano player, Manny. Manny said you could make a fortune teaching. And George told me to stay in touch, because he wanted to talk to some people about me." She gave Lucy the card.

Lucy looked at it, then, in disbelief, at Bea. "A few days in town, and you got to audition for *George White* of the *Scandals?* I can't believe it. You're starting to scare me, you know that? D'you have any *idea* who you danced for today?"

"George. He was very nice. I also met a boy. He's going to come over sometime and dance with me. He lies about his age, too."

Lucy rolled her eyes, then looked again at the card. "I'll be damned," she said, shaking her head. "George White. I'll never again doubt a word you say. I'm beginning to believe you can do *anything.* Who's the boy?"

"I liked him a lot. He pretends he's tough, but he really isn't at all. His name's Bobby." She gazed at Lucy, thinking how pretty she was with her curly brown hair and round dark eyes. Even when she was worrying over something or having a big "impulse," she always looked happy. It was one of the things that constantly drew her to Lucy. That and Lucy's willingness to have fun, to find something good in a situation, her inclination toward laughter were, to Bea's mind, as special as Lucy liked to say Bea's talent was. "You're so pretty, Luce," she said happily.

"Thank you," Lucy responded. "You're not too bad yourself," she said and smiled so that dimples appeared in her cheeks.

"Oh, I'm just me." Bea shrugged off the compliment.

"'Just you' is fine, sweetheart. Bobby, huh?"

Bea gave her a wide smile.

Six

THEY agreed on a small, furnished apartment in a brownstone on Twenty-eighth Street near Lexington, consisting of living room, bedroom, and kitchen. The furniture was all but indestructible; massive pieces of oak with horsehair stuffing that had survived countless previous tenants and seemed destined to last well into the twenty-first century.

Their landlady was a lively, oversized widow whose husband had had a long, successful career in vaudeville and about whom she spoke constantly. Mrs. Jolly was overtly fond of performers, and all her available rooms were rented to "show folk." The walls of her sitting room were completely covered by photographs and posters, primarily of her late husband, but also of departed friends and a few former tenants who'd gone on to better things.

Bea and Mrs. Jolly took an instant liking to one another, and when Bea wasn't chasing around town trying to push her way into auditions or agents' offices, she spent hours with Mrs. Jolly in her sitting room, going through the heavy scrapbooks that chronicled Mr. Jolly's career, listening avidly to the woman's ornately detailed reminiscences.

Bea decided that she, too, would one day have scrapbooks filled with programs and clippings; she, too, would have stories to tell, but not of someone else's life. She'd be able to talk about the stages of her own life. She'd have framed posters on the walls and glossy photographs of herself with famous friends. All these things would be in a special room in her home, not in the cramped sitting room of an apartment house. Not that she was judging Mrs. Jolly who was really very kind and couldn't help the way things had turned out for her, but rather that once she got to where she intended to be, she'd never lose it, no matter what happened.

"You can't count on things always stayin' the same, dearie," Mrs. Jolly cautioned her. "Y'always want to remember to be flexible; you gotta know when to bend, when to change. You remember that and you'll be right as rain. Get a fixed idea in your brain, and you might find yourself with nowhere to go. I think," she pronounced seriously, "you're gonna go a good, long way. I can always spot 'em. You'll be here and gone before anyone knows it."

"What does that mean?" Bea asked uncertainly.

"It means no dust'll have a chance to settle on you, dearie."

When she thought about her future and the way things were going to be, everything inside her went hard with certainty. All the images she'd ever carried inside her head were like negatives simply awaiting the printing process, and time would see to it that every picture emerged sharp and clear. Her opportunity would present itself, and then she'd be on her way. In the meantime, she'd used some of her money for a photographic sitting, the result of which was a package of eight-by-ten glossies showing her in her new dancing costume which was an abbreviated version of a man's cutaway in white satin, with white accessories, including a top hat and cane. She'd left dozens of them all over town, and people were getting to know her. When she went to auditions now, she exchanged greetings with faces that had grown familiar. She enjoyed the unspoken kinship, and the bantering and speculation that took place at the open auditions.

When Bobby Bradley appeared at their door one evening some weeks after they'd moved into Mrs. Jolly's place, Bea was so delighted she gave him a big hug before pulling him inside.

"I got the address from the hotel," he explained, somewhat taken aback by the effusiveness of her greeting. "I thought I'd drop by and find out how you're doing."

"Come on," she said happily, taking his hand to lead him into the kitchen. "Meet Lucy."

"This is the swell dancing teacher, huh?" Bobby smiled as he offered Lucy his hand. "Maybe when I get some money ahead, you'll give me a few lessons," Bobby said, unslinging his dancing shoes from around his neck.

"Maybe," Lucy said. "Let's not stay in here." She led the way to the living room where Bobby dropped down on the unyielding sofa.

"Say!" he exclaimed. "What's this thing stuffed with anyway? Bricks?"

"Did you get the job?" Bea wanted to know, sitting down beside him.

"Nah! It was pretty close, all right, but this other guy beat me out. He was a real sheik, you know. The way I figure it, half the trick is showing up looking like a million. Look like you need the job and they lose interest, won't even sit still to see what you can do. How're you making out?"

Bea shrugged. "I've gone to loads of auditions, but I'm always too young, or too short, or something. I'm not worried, though. One of these times I'll be the right age and the right height and then I'll be up there."

"You really believe that?" he asked doubtfully.

"Sure, I do. You've got to believe that. If you go along always thinking other people are better, or prettier, or whatever, then they will be better because you're letting them be better by thinking you're not as good."

"Whew!" Bobby wiped imaginary perspiration from his forehead. "You want to say that again in English?"

"How are things in Brooklyn?" she changed the subject.

"Not so hot. It was getting pretty grim, so I lit out a couple of weeks ago."

"You've got your own place?"

"Well, not exactly. I've just been . . . around."

"Around where?" Lucy asked.

"Oh, around."

"You don't have a place to stay, do you?" Bea said.

"I've got a line on a couple of things. And I'm going to an audition this afternoon. They're looking for a juvenile. It's a good part, too."

Lucy was touched by the boy and liked the look of him. But what intrigued her was Bea's reaction to him. If it hadn't been such a patently absurd notion, Lucy would've sworn Bea was in love with this boy. The way Bea looked at him, the obvious pleasure she derived from his presence there, were facets of her Lucy hadn't seen before.

"He could stay here with us," Bea said. "He could, couldn't he, Luce?" Turning to Bobby, she elaborated. "You could sleep here on the sofa until you get working and find a place of your own."

Lucy now looked doubtful, so Bea pushed it a little. "It'd be okay, wouldn't it, Luce?"

"I guess so. But we ought to clear it with Mrs. Jolly first."

"Oh, she won't mind," Bea declared. "I'll go down right this minute and ask her." She jumped up and went to the door. "You'll see," she told them both. "It'll be perfectly all right with her."

After she'd gone, Bobby looked down at his hands. "I, uhm, didn't come over with the idea of freeloading. That kid moves kind of too fast when she gets an idea."

"She does," Lucy agreed. "But I trust her instincts. You look as if a decent meal wouldn't do you any harm," she said gently, taking in his worn-thin clothing and underfed frame.

"I'm just naturally wiry," he said, finally raising his eyes to hers. "I never do eat much."

"How old're you?" she asked. "And *are* you any good?"

"Almost sixteen," he answered. "And I'm terrific. I used to say I was the best, until I saw Bea do her stuff. You taught her all that, huh?"

"I taught her some of it," she corrected. "The rest she did on her own. Bea's very special."

"I'll say," he agreed, then laughed. "Maybe she should be teaching us."

"Could be. Anyway, you're welcome to stay."

"You mean it? That'd be keen. It'd only be for a little while, until I get going. I could help out, clean up and stuff; take out the garbage. I won't get in your way."

"One of us is bound to land some work soon. It'll probably be Bea. I don't know what it is, but when she's around things just seem to happen."

Bea came bouncing through the door saying, "It's all fixed. I told Mrs. Jolly you were my cousin, and she said that was fine. So you're staying!" She seated herself once more beside Bobby. "It'll be fun," she told him. "Can you cook?"

"Boys don't have to know how to cook," he said, somewhat affronted.

"I was just asking. Well, never mind." She gave his arm a little squeeze. "We could work out some routines together, if you like."

"That'd be the berries!" he responded eagerly. "Got any music?"

Contrary to her prediction, it was Lucy who got work first. At Bea's urging, she went along to an open call for singer/dancers and, after auditioning half a dozen times in ever smaller groups, wound up hired for the chorus of a show called *Of Thee I Sing*.

"It's got the best songs," she told Bobby and Bea, "written by the Gershwin brothers. Course I haven't got a script yet and I haven't heard all the music, but from what I've heard so far, it's going to be

58

a big hit and I don't mean maybe. I just can't believe it!" she crowed, flushed with excitement. "I kept waiting for them to say, 'Thank you. You can go now,' but it didn't happen. *I'm in a show!*"

"That's just wonderful!" Bea threw her arms around her, and the two of them laughed jubilantly.

"I've got an agent to do the contract, *and* I'm going to join the actors' union. I don't believe it! Listen! We're going to celebrate, the three of us. I'll get cleaned up, and we'll go out for a big, fancy dinner." She hurried off to the bedroom, and Bea threw herself into the armchair, happily beating out a rhythm with her hands on her knees.

Bobby covered the envy he felt, but it was hard work. Lucy and Bea had been good to him; he owed them plenty. And while he was glad one of them had managed to get a job, he wished he could have been the one to come bursting through the front door with the good news. Maybe he was kidding himself, thinking he was good when he was nothing special. It wasn't easy to keep on believing in his talent when he kept losing out on one audition after another to lounge lizards who didn't have his timing or his voice but who had the wardrobe and the connections. All he needed was one chance to show his stuff and he'd never look back. But if he was wasting his time, he wanted to know it and to get out before it was too late.

Bea could see that Bobby was discouraged, and was fascinated both by his upset and by the way he tried to conceal it. He was making an effort to appear nonchalantly accepting, but small creases kept appearing and disappearing on his forehead and around his eyes and mouth, as if he were on the verge of tears.

"You'll get your break, Bobby," Bea said quietly. "You'll see."

"Yeah. And maybe I'm just kidding myself," he said dispiritedly, for the moment abandoning his pose. "Boy, I'd sure hate that."

"But you've done work before. You'll get more."

"Sure. And in the meantime, here I am sponging off two girls. How d'you think that makes me feel?"

"You'll pay us back when you start working," she said reasonably.

"Darn tootin' I will!" he said hotly.

"You will, so that makes everything all right."

Bobby stared over at her for a long moment. "How come you're so sure of things?"

"You have to be," she said simply. "I've told you before: If you don't believe, you'll never get the things you want."

"Don't you ever wonder if maybe you're not fooling yourself, playing kind of a game to make yourself believe things are one way when they're really a whole other way?"

"Nope! I know the way things are, and I know how they're gonna turn out, too. You're really good, Bobby, and you'll get your break. You just can't let yourself get discouraged."

"How d'*you* convince yourself of that, with all this time passing and nothing happening?"

"I say to myself, 'Bea, you've got to use this time to learn more and be better so you'll be ready when your time comes.'"

"Jeez!" Bobby sighed. "I don't know if I could ever be like you."

"You're not supposed to be like me. You're supposed to be like Bobby Bradley. There's only one of you, right? And nobody else is like you. So people are going to want the one and only Bobby Bradley in their shows, just the same way they're going to want me because there's only ever going to be one Beatrice Crane."

"That's a good thing, I'd say," he laughed.

She punched him on the arm. "You watch out, Bradley! Someday, when I'm a big star, I'll remember all this and I might not want to be friends with you then."

"Sure you will," he quipped. "Because *I'll* be so rich and famous you'll *have* to be friends with me."

"We'll always be friends," she said softly.

He smiled over at her, prepared to toss off another quick line, but was caught instead by the cute look of her and by the light in her eyes, and said, "You can count on that, sister."

With a bona fide offer in hand, it was no problem at all for Lucy to walk into one of the largest talent agencies in the city and ask for representation. Granted, she was turned over to one of the junior partners, but still she'd gained *entrée* to the theatrical world of New York. Her new agent, Jerry Greenswag, noted the details then told her to relax while he got on the phone with Sam Harris's office and haggled over the terms. When the call was completed, he folded his arms across the desk, grinned at her, and said, "You heard it. Seventy-five a week, eighty-five for the out-of-town tryouts. Welcome to the Maxwell Agency. Go home and organize your rehearsal duds. I'll call you when the contract's ready for signing. Congratulations."

She hesitated, wondering if she should tell him about Bea and Bobby, but decided it might be wiser to wait until everything was signed. After all, he was an agent, and agents were supposedly always on the lookout for new talent.

So, she went home and made her announcement to the kids and saw the genuinely pleased reaction Bea had to the news, and the envy or whatever it was that briefly choked Bobby before he managed to pull himself together and say how swell it was. She felt guilty and didn't know why.

As she changed her clothes, she wondered why her mood had swung so low. She'd managed to beat out dozens of other girls at a fair-and-square audition. She'd had to dance different combinations over and over until, at last, Mr. Kaufman, the director, and George Hale, the choreographer, had approved her. The Gershwins had sat through the entire process, from time to time turning to discuss this or that with Morrie Ryskind, the writer, or Charles Previn, the musical director.

Through it all, Lucy had felt almost ill with a combination of yearning and a miserable sense of inadequacy. Why would they choose her when there were other, more beautiful girls? She might be a better dancer and singer, but she wasn't beautiful. To her astonishment, they'd chosen her. She'd been hired, and rehearsals would begin in ten days' time. The tentative opening date was December 26. She was going to be in a Broadway show. She was thrilled.

Yet, hurrying home, she'd looked at the people selling apples on street corners and at the lines in front of soup kitchens, and it had all seemed wrong suddenly. With so many people out of work, who was going to pay good money to see a musical? None of it made sense. And so Bobby's reaction seemed more real than anything else. He was hungry, he was talented, and he couldn't get a job. She'd seen him dance, seen him working out numbers with Bea—the two of them in their stocking feet with the furniture pushed out of the way—and knew he was truly gifted. So were lots of the folks out on the street trying to sell apples. She told herself she ought to be happy, but she was scared.

"Once you start rehearsals," Bea said in response to Lucy's admission of fear, "you won't have time to think about anything."

"I hope you're right," Lucy said, fiddling with the salt and pepper shakers. "I've never had a feeling like this before, of being so absolutely, positively scared."

Bobby remained silent, listening, all the way through the meal. Just at the point when Lucy was framing something encouraging to say to him, Bea patted him on the shoulder, and said, "Bobby's turn is next."

"You really think so?" he said, brightening.

"I know so. And then you'll be the one getting the agent and signing the contract and coming down with a case of the heebie-jeebies."

Lucy looked at Bea and had to wonder why Bea wasn't jealous. Bobby's reaction was basic, and it was honest, too. Bea certainly

61

wasn't the goody-two-shoes type, and yet she appeared not to harbor the least bit of envy or resentment. "Aren't you just the tiniest bit jealous?" she asked Bea teasingly.

"Maybe a tiny bit," Bea allowed. "But not really." She looked off into the distance, saying, "All I want is to be up on a stage, singing and dancing. And if I squint my eyes a little, I can see myself there. I can even feel it. I know how it'll be when it happens, and I know it *will* happen, so that means I don't have to be jealous." She returned her eyes to Lucy. "I felt jealous once, when I first met Becky and Franny, because they were twins and I was jealous of that. I thought it would be the best thing ever to be twins. But being jealous felt terrible. So I decided I'd never feel that way ever again. It's better to feel good for the people you really care about. And I really care about you. So I feel good." She paused a moment and then smiled brilliantly. "See?"

Just over two weeks later, Bobby exploded into the apartment, shouting, *"I got a show! I did it! I got a show!"*

He danced around the living room, singing out the details of his audition for the Shuberts' production of *A Little Racketeer*.

"I'll tell you one thing," he said, finally winding down. "This Queenie Smith has nothin' on you, Bea. She's playing a part you could do blindfolded, with your hands tied behind your back."

"Oh?" Bea asked politely.

"From what I could make out, she's supposed to play a tomboy who wants to become a gangster. You could dance her right off the stage."

"Never mind," Bea dismissed it. "This is probably a good time to introduce you to Lucy's agent. What d'you think, Luce?"

"I'll run downstairs to telephone and ask him," Lucy agreed.

After meeting Bobby and going over the details of his contract, Jerry Greenswag smiled and winked at Lucy and said, "You got any other hot clients under your hat, Lucy? You might as well bring 'em all in now. The receptionist says there's a cute little girl in the waiting room who's quite the dancer."

After an impromptu audition that left him speechless, Jerry emitted a long, low whistle and said, "You three go on home. I've got some phone calls to make, Jesus H. Christ! Hey, wait a minute! You don't have a damned telephone. Bea, I want you here at two tomorrow afternoon. Bring your dancing shoes. We're gonna do some business."

Part One / 1917–1936

* * *

Jerry presented Bea over the telephone to Florenz Ziegfeld who, impressed by the agent's near-hysterical enthusiasm, urged Jerry to get in touch with Edgar MacGregor and Edward Clark Lilley who were set to direct the forthcoming Ziegfeld production *Hot-Cha!* in which there were several slots still open for strong female dancers.

MacGregor and Lilley agreed to see Bea at the Ziegfeld Theater at two-thirty the following afternoon. "We'll have Bobby Connolly there to put her through her paces," Lilley promised. "You better not be wasting our time with this hoofer, Jer."

"When did I ever not deliver?" Jerry countered. "When you see this kid dance, you'll beg to have her in your show. You'll never in your lifetime see another kid like this one."

"They're gonna go nuts over you," Jerry told Bea. "They're playing it close to the vest, but I happen to know there's a part in this show tailor-made for you. It's not big, but it'll put you on the map. One swell solo that could be a show-stopper. Say," he said, "don't you own anything that doesn't make you look twelve years old?" He closed his eyes, then opened them slowly and looked up at the ceiling. "I know," he addressed the ceiling. "You're twelve years old."

"I'm eighteen."

"The face is fifteen. The body's twelve, tops. Twelve doesn't work; eighteen works. You're eighteen. Come on." He got up from behind the desk, took her by the arm, and hustled her out of the office. "We'll go buy you a dress for an eighteen-year-old. You'll pay me out of your first paycheck."

"You're the doctor," she said, unruffled, hurrying along beside him. She liked this man even though he gave the impression of having spent most of his life worried sick about one thing or another. He was short, about five-six, and skinny, and his sandy-colored hair was worn thin on top as if his habit of constantly running his hands over his head had actually eroded the hair.

"We're gonna make you the hottest thing on Broadway," he promised, studying her from all angles in a simple but well-made blue jersey dress with a flared skirt and, naturally, pockets. "Just remember it was Jerry Greenswag who did it for you."

"What's he like, Florenz Ziegfeld? Have you ever met him?"

"A couple of times. He's the Big Cheese of all time, although the word is he's in pretty bad health right at the moment. You wanna

63

talk about class, kiddo. The man invented it. He's got not one, not two, but three telephones on his desk. *Gold.* He's got his own private railroad car. This is the guy who forked out a hundred and seventy-five bucks a night, every night, for a new costume for Marilyn Miller. Every single night, so she'd be fresh. Can you beat that? He never writes a letter. He's got the telephones, and he sends telegrams."

"Three gold telephones," Bea repeated, impressed. "Have you ever met his wife, Billie Burke?"

"To say hello at openings, you know. Now, listen. You sure you're not nervous?"

"I never get nervous. Except maybe for a second or two, right before I go on."

"You've got your music, right?"

"Don't worry, Mr. Greenswag. I've got everything."

"Jerry. Call me Jerry," he said shakily, ushering her into the theater. "Everybody else you call mister."

Seven

THE trio made a ceremony out of going to Capezio on West Fifty-second Street to buy shoes. The purchase of new dancing shoes represented the legitimate and irrevocable step forward into the world of professionals. They examined the ballet pumps and tap shoes and aesthete sandals with utmost seriousness and spent quite some time admiring and testing the new wing taps designed with special hollowing on the sole sides to give an amazingly clear, resonant ring.

Lucy settled on black kid ballet pumps and a pair of duo-type tap shoes with the new wing taps. Bobby, after due deliberation, bought black kid oxfords, also with the new taps. And Bea, surrendering to impulse, purchased the sensible duo-type tap shoes as well as a pair of low-heeled silver kid ones. "I know it's crazy," she told the others, "but I love these shoes," and held them to her chest as if to demonstrate graphically her love for them.

The sales clerk wrote up receipts and accepted their money with a gravity suited to the occasion.

"I think he knew how important it was to us," Bea ventured as they left the place.

"*I* think he probably works on commission," Bobby put in.

"Well, anyway, he was really nice," Bea insisted, carrying her packages with both arms. "That was one of the best times I've ever had. I don't think I'll ever forget it. Gee! Maybe I should've asked him his name."

"Why?" Lucy asked, bemused.

"So I'd always be able to remember it."

"Why would you want to remember some shoe clerk's name?" Bobby wondered.

"Just because," Bea said inadequately, unable to explain her sense of the significance of the occasion. She'd probably be buying dance shoes every few months for the rest of her life, but it wouldn't ever again be the way it had been this time when everything was new and exciting, and she was soon to be in her first Broadway show. Sometimes she had the feeling that the things that were taking place in her life now were things she'd always want to remember, and so she tried hard to study all the details—the names and faces, the places, what people wore, what was said, how things looked—in order to be able to recall them later on, when she might need them. It was a funny feeling, as if nobody else but she knew that everything only happened once, and so it was extremely important to watch and to make mental notes. When she looked toward her future, she knew she wouldn't be the same, way off then. And her being different wouldn't have to do with being older and physically changed. It had to do with the idea she had that she didn't see things the way other people did, and it would be her ability to absorb and remember details that would make her different. She'd always had the feeling that she wasn't like other people, that she didn't really fit in. Occasionally she'd experience a brief but terrible loneliness, knowing that no matter what she did, or how well she did it, she'd be forever set apart and isolated. Most of the time she was able to tell herself it didn't matter, and she could redirect her attention and energy into her dancing and her dreams. But every so often she'd look at Lucy, or at Bobby, or even at some sad Apple Annie on a street corner and be all but overwhelmed by how separate she was from other people. To help herself get past the moment she'd overpay for an apple just to see

the person smile, or she'd buy some small gift for her two friends—
a bow tie for Bobby or a pretty scarf for Lucy. The act of giving, the
gesture of helping out, made her feel connected, even if only for a
moment or two. Bobby couldn't seem to understand or accept these
gestures when she made them, and she didn't know how to explain
to him how good it made her feel simply to be able to give something—even if it was only a fresh cup of coffee or the first look at
the newest *Variety*. She wished with all her heart he could know how
happy it made her just to be able to look across the room and see
him. Perhaps, she reasoned, Bobby felt outside, too, and that was
why he had such a hard time accepting that people might like him
and want to give him things. Someday, though, he'd come to see that
it was all right to trust people, especially her.

Since Lucy's rehearsals began first, and Bobby's weren't due to
start until two weeks before Lucy's show opened, Bea and Bobby
spent their free days, while Lucy was away, working up routines
together and taking walks around town. It was Bobby who introduced
Bea to Gray's Drug Store on the south-east corner of Broadway and
Forty-third Street.

"This is a swell place to know about," he explained. "An hour before
curtain time, all the box offices send over their unsold tickets and
you can get them for half price."

"Really? That's keen! We could go to see tons of shows. We can
afford it now. Let's do it, Bobby! I haven't seen one single show yet,
and I've been dying to. We'll surprise Lucy," she decided. "She's been
wanting to see some of the shows, too."

And so, every few nights the trio met up at the drugstore, bought
half-price tickets, grabbed something to eat at the Automat or an
inexpensive restaurant, and then went to the theater. In the weeks
before Christmas, and the opening of Lucy's show, they saw *The Band
Wagon* with Fred and Adele Astaire; the Earl Carroll *Vanities* with
Lillian Roth and William Demarest; George White's *Scandals* with Rudy
Vallee, Ethel Merman, and Ray Bolger; *Everybody's Welcome* with Frances
Williams and Harriette Lake and the Jimmy and Tommy Dorsey Orchestra; *The Cat and the Fiddle* with Eddie Foy, Jr., and Bettina Hall
and Lawrence Grossmith; and *The Laugh Parade* with Ed Wynn.

Bea could have gone to the theater twice a day every day. She loved
it. Her special favorites were the Astaires, especially Fred. His dancing
made her want to run up onto the stage and join him. He had a
wonderful, misleading looseness and agility that made everything he
did look effortless and spontaneous, and every part of his body was

perfectly in synch, right down to the most seemingly casual hand gestures. She dragged Bobby back to see the show five more times and would have kept on dragging him back, but Bobby begged off, insisting, "I see any more of Astaire, I won't be able to remember how Bobby Bradley dances."

"But everybody's different," she argued. "How could seeing him change you?"

"You'll just have to take my word for it," he said doggedly. "I know what I'm saying. He's very stylized, very individual. So am I, and I want to keep it that way."

"Well, I guess I know what you mean," Bea allowed, mentally comparing the two. Bobby did have a very different approach, one that was more athletic and less flowing than Astaire's. She still couldn't see, though, how watching another dancer's work could be a bad thing. She gave up the argument and went to see the show three more times on her own, until she knew the choreography of every number in it.

On the opening night of *Of Thee I Sing* Bea was so nervous she could hardly dress herself. Bobby was ready half an hour ahead of time and sat on the arm of the sofa in the new suit Lucy and Bea had given him for Christmas, one leg swinging back and forth, as he wondered aloud why Bea was so worked up.

"I don't know!" Bea wailed, fumbling with the buttons of the blue dress Jerry had bought her. "I just am."

Her nervousness didn't let up, not through the dinner before the show with Jerry in the Rose Room at the Algonquin, right up until the house lights dimmed at the Music Box and the conductor raised his baton. She laced her fingers together in her lap and kept swallowing until the curtain went up after the overture and she spotted Lucy stage-left, carrying a campaign poster reading "Wintergreen for President." Only then did Bea's breathing steady; her arms and shoulders relaxed, and she was able to enjoy the show.

Afterwards, while they were moving with the crowd of people headed backstage, Bea decided she'd been afraid because she'd been unable to attend any of the rehearsals, and a tiny part of her had latched on to the awful idea that none of it was real, that Lucy had made it all up. It was real, however, and the show was terrific, especially William Gaxton and Victor Moore as Wintergreen and Throttlebottom. The songs were swell, too. She couldn't stop humming "Love Is Sweeping the Country" as she eyed the first-night celebrities in their swanky clothes.

Her fear gone, she was able to savor every aspect of the evening—the famous faces, the noisy excitement that was confirmation of a hit show, chatter about what were bound to be rave reviews. Everyone was smiling; toothy grins meant success, as did the electricity in the air backstage. It was tangible, this sense of success. It was in the ebullient laughter and in the congratulatory embraces; in the opening-night flowers whose scents mingled with the expensive French perfumes on the pearly shoulders of beautiful women and in the hair pomade of top-hatted men. Bea recognized Ray Bolger, and Fay Wray, and the handsome young English fellow Archibald Leach who'd been in *Nikki*. She saw Jack Haley and Lillian Roth talking with the Gershwins, and Helen Morgan smiling at Morrie Ryskind. Turning, Bea studied Bobby, curious to see his response to all of this. Unlike everyone else, he wasn't smiling but seemed solely determined to penetrate through the crowd to Lucy's dressing room.

"What's the matter, Bobby?" she asked, following close behind him as he pushed a path through the crush of people. "Is something wrong?"

He failed to answer, and she'd have pursued it but by then they'd arrived at the dressing room and she raced inside to throw her arms around Lucy, hugging her hard.

"It was just terrific, Luce, and so were you!"

"You think so?" Lucy laughed, elated. "It was terrific, wasn't it? Everyone says we're going to have a long run. I sure hope so." She kissed Bea on the forehead, saying, "Thank you for the flowers. That was wonderful of you, Bea."

"You're welcome. Was it fun? Are you having the best time ever?"

"I'll tell you all about it later. Say everybody!" Lucy addressed the other women sharing the dressing room. "I want you to meet Bea, and this is Bobby." Proudly, she presented the kids with her arms around their shoulders. Bobby gritted his teeth and groaned inwardly, while Bea smiled happily as the women, in keeping with the festive atmosphere, made a fuss of the two of them and, in turn, introduced their boyfriends and members of their families. Then Lucy shooed Bea and Bobby outside to wait. "I won't be five minutes," she told them.

Bobby leaned against the wall in the corridor, his arms folded across his chest, and gazed at the people milling about backstage. At his side, Bea looked at his profile and the freckles across the bridge of his nose. On his upper lip was the shadowy indication of a pale mustache.

"You'll be starting to shave soon," she said.

"What?" He looked at her, frowning.

"You've got a little mustache," she said, touching his upper lip with her fingertip.

"Well, what d'you expect?" he said rather angrily, brushing aside her hand. "I'm a man, after all. Men shave, you know."

"I know," she said quietly. "What're you mad at, Bobby?"

He saw that she was hurt and at once felt bad. "Not at you," he said, softening.

"What, then?"

"I don't know." He looked at her for a long moment in silence, then said, "You've grown. You know that?"

"I know. More than an inch. Is that what you're mad at?"

He laughed. "Don't be a dope! You're my best friend. Why would I be mad at you?"

"People have all kinds of reasons for the way they feel."

"Well, stop worrying. Okay? I feel just fine about you."

"Do you?"

"Sure, I do. I liked you from the first time I saw you. I thought you were cute as a bug in a rug."

"You don't say!" She was very pleased. "Same here."

They smiled at each other and, on impulse, Bea gave him a kiss on the cheek. "It's gonna be a swell party. You'll see!"

Perhaps, she thought, it was the wrong thing to say. His smile dissolved, and he turned away to resume gazing at the crowd.

They got home at six in the morning and sat at the kitchen table drinking coffee and going over the highlights of the show and of the party.

Bea's head felt full, too heavy with impressions—of marvelous clothes and elegant celebrities, of an amazing array of food, of snippets of overheard conversations, and, atop all of it, of a kind of golden glow. Throughout the evening, she'd had a sense of rightness and well-being she'd never before known, as if she'd located a place in the world that was utterly suited to her, among people she knew and understood. There'd been a unity and warmth among the cast members that she thought must be unique to the theater. She couldn't wait for rehearsals to start on *Hot-Cha!* so she'd be part of a team, the way Lucy was and the way Bobby likely was in his show.

He was again reading the reviews—in the *Times*, the *Herald Tribune*, the *World*, the *News*, and the *Mirror*. They'd go out and get the rest of the papers later, but had waited up to buy the early editions to see what the critics had to say about the show. As she looked at him, she experienced an odd, clutching sensation in her chest, and thought of the softness of his cheek when she'd kissed him. He was so sweet. Even his long, red-brown eyelashes were sweet. She wanted to hold his hand and tell him everything would be all right, because he was wearing his angry look again.

"Didn't you have a good time, Bobby?" she asked, staring at him over the top of her cup.

He lifted his head and, unsmiling, answered, "I had a swell time."

"You're sure nothing's wrong?" Lucy asked. "You look kind of down in the mouth."

"Nah!" He dredged up a smile. "I'm just beat. And I was trying to figure out how long it'll take me to pay the two of you back for everything—letting me stay here and buying me new clothes."

"The clothes were Christmas presents from both of us," Bea said quickly. "And we know you'll pay us back. You don't have to worry about it."

"I don't like being a sponger," he said strongly. "Soon's I get my first week's pay, I'll start giving back some of what I owe you two. And once the show's opened, I'll find a place and get out of your hair."

"You're not in our hair," Bea told him.

"I'm going to turn in." He pushed away from the table. "I've got rehearsals tomorrow." He paused to say, "Thanks a lot for tonight, Lucy. It was ..." He couldn't find an appropriate word to describe how he'd felt being a nobody surrounded by such a crowd of swells. One of these days the whole world was going to know who he was and then things would be different. He wouldn't just be a kid from Brooklyn in a cheap suit, getting elbowed out of the way at a ritzy party. He'd be the one they all crowded around, the one with the spiffy clothes and the important name. And he'd be free and clear, in the money, tipping headwaiters and cabbies with five-dollar bills. He'd take Lucy and Bea out to the Stork Club and 21 and pay the way with a pocketful of twenties. "I had a great time," he said unconvincingly, placing his coffee cup in the sink before heading for the living-room sofa.

While she and Lucy were preparing for bed, Bea considered aloud what could possibly be bothering Bobby.

"It's male pride," Lucy told her. "He wants to be able to pay his own way, and because he can't, he doesn't feel like a real man."

"But he's only sixteen years old."

"Honey, age doesn't have a thing to do with it. I think they're born with that pride, and a girl spends her whole life tiptoeing around it."

"But why? And what about female pride? How come they don't go tiptoeing around us?"

Lucy stopped in the midst of rolling off her stockings. "I guess maybe we're not supposed to have any," she said, thinking it through. "At least not so it shows."

"That's hardly fair."

"Not a lot *is* fair, Bea." She finished taking off her stockings, then moved around the room nude, putting her clothes away.

Bea watched her, admiring Lucy's very white skin, long muscular legs, and full, round breasts. "You've got a really nice figure, Luce," she said appraisingly. To her surprise, Lucy blushed and grabbed for her robe.

"I've got good legs," Lucy said, belting the robe tightly. "The rest of me's about average."

"Do you wish you had lots of beaus?"

Lucy laughed. "I think about it now and then. But I don't really have the time, and men take up a lot of a girl's time."

"Wouldn't you like to get married one day and have babies?"

"Maybe. I carried a torch for a fella back in Toronto for a while."

"What happened?"

"He married somebody else."

"He wasn't very smart."

"He was probably very smart. I'd make a lousy wife. I hate housework, ironing, cooking, all that. And anyway, I like working. You get married, you have to give it up."

"I want to be married someday, and have a nice house and babies sleeping upstairs. I'd like to live near the water, and have a dog and a cat. And a garden, with lots of flowers, all colors under the sun."

"What about becoming rich and famous?" Lucy asked. "Would you give all that up?"

"I don't see why I'd have to. I'll sing and dance *and* have a family."

"You'll probably do it, too." Lucy yawned. "If I don't get to sleep, I'm gonna fall on my face. Be back in a tick," she said, and went off to the bathroom.

While she was gone, Bea undressed then examined her reflection in the wardrobe mirror. She was starting to grow every which way, and the sight of her own body made her feel peculiar. In all her thoughts of growing up she hadn't considered the possible ways in which her body would alter. It was odd now to cross her arms and find that her new breasts got in the way. Already a couple of her dresses were sort of tight across the hips and backside. She pulled on her nightgown silently praying she wouldn't get great big breasts like her mother's. Maybe, she thought, the women in Jackie Ellroy, Junior's family had sensible little bosoms that a dancer could live with.

The two of them settled finally in bed, Bea reached to turn off the light, saying, "I'm really happy for you, Luce. I was so excited and proud, seeing you up on stage and having you introduce us to the other ladies in your dressing room."

"Sometimes you feel like my own kid, if you want to know the truth," Lucy murmured, half asleep.

"I wish you were going to be able to come to my opening night."

"I'll work something out. Go to sleep now."

In a minute or two, Lucy was asleep. Bea folded her arms under her head and gazed into the darkness trying to make everything fit— Bobby's "male pride," Lucy's sudden embarrassment at Bea's compliment, and her own strange feeling at the sight of her naked body. She drifted off before being able to reason her way through to any satisfactory conclusion.

March 12, 1932

Dear Mama and Gramma,

Hope you both are fine. Things are just swell here. Lucy's still working in her show and has to soak her feet a lot now, just like you, Gramma. Bobby's show posted the closing notice and he's kind of blue because he was hoping it would run for a really long time so he could save up some money.

I sure wish you could've been there for the opening of my show. It was really exciting and lots of famous people came back to the dressing room to say I was good, and Mr. Ziegfeld sent everybody flowers, and we had a big first-night party. Lucy got another girl to stand in for her so she could come to see the show, but Bobby had to work, so he couldn't come. He sent me some beautiful flowers, though. When I did my big solo number the whole audience stood up and clapped like anything and I had to go back for six curtain calls and people whistled and shouted. It was terrific.

We all went to the bank and opened savings accounts, and Jerry gives me an allowance every week, then puts the rest in the bank for me so I'll have money for my future. He's kind of mad right now at Bobby because Bobby spent most of his money buying new clothes and renting a room and now his show is closing and he doesn't have hardly anything put by. But Jerry says he might be able to get Bobby booked into a show that's opening in Atlantic City.

I'm sending you fifty dollars with this letter, and I'll send you some more soon. I've grown two whole inches. Write soon, okay?

Lots of love,
Bea

March 27, 1932

Dear Bea,

Thank you dear for the mony. It come in very handy especialy since your granmother had to quit her job at the bakery as it was just too hard on her feet standing all day. Were both fine and glad the winters about over. Its been a rough winter here with snow day after day right to the tops of the streetcars. Things are a little slack at the restaurant but good enough to keep me in a job. Were moving to a smaller place over on Manning where it'll be quiet for a change without the streetcars day and night. My friend Don whos a big reader says he saw your name in some magazine I forget the name of it but he said it was all about you being a dancing whiz and the talk of New York, I just cant get over it my little girl being on Broadway. Maybe next youll be out in Hollywood making movies. You keep on saving your money Bea thats the smart thing to do. You always were real smart. You must be getting very tall with all those inches you keep telling about. Be a good girl and take care of yourself. Gramma sends her best.

Love,
Lil

Eight times a week Bea stepped out on stage to do her solo number, and loved poured back to her across the footlights. Everything, from the first rehearsal, to each night's performance, made her happy. She loved the theater, the dressing rooms, the stage-door man who called her "Miss Beatrice," the other cast members, the conductor, the fellows in the orchestra, the little light bulbs rimming her make-up mirror, the smell of sweat and cosmetics and perfume in the wings, all of it. With the heat of the spotlights full on her, and the rows of unseen faces turned expectantly toward her, she felt absolute happiness. She performed with all her heart and every last bit of her energy, and she was rewarded with cheering approval. She and these others, including the audience, were a part of something intimate and thrilling. And for a couple of hours they gave and took, back and forth: performance onstage, acceptance offstage. This was what she'd hungered for, what fed and sustained her now.

Her only disappointment, and that was too strong a term for the pinched little realization, had been in at last meeting Buddy Rogers who was one of the stars of the show. He'd been her hero, but he was just a man, after all, and not the larger-than-life idol she'd made of him after seeing *Wings* and half a dozen other films. People, she'd come to realize very quickly, even if they were famous, could be charming and nice or mean with self-importance, but they were only people after all. Working every night with stars had showed her that the sole difference between ordinary folks and famous ones was in the fame itself. In private, everybody did the same kinds of things: had colds, got into arguments, used bathrooms, slept at night, and got up in the morning. Of course talent played a part in that difference, but she'd personally seen loads of talented people at one audition after another, trying constantly to get to be the next famous people. It was, she thought, like a great big circle, going around and around, with people trying to climb to the top while others were right behind them, at their heels.

The only time she could get any real idea of the audience was during the curtain calls. With the lights up full there was always a spillover when she came out to take her call. She'd look out into the first few rows of the orchestra and smile at someone who was smiling right at her. She carried the smiles away with her as she and Lucy met up to return home together.

The apartment wasn't the same now, without Bobby. Bea missed him, missed being able to look at him when he didn't know she was doing it; she missed picking up the clothes he left draped over the furniture. With him gone, she often had the feeling that a part of herself had been taken away. Occasionally, they managed to get together on a Sunday afternoon to sit around the living room with their shoes off and look through the weekend papers and talk backstage gossip about who was going out with whom and the rumors about this person or that. Bobby adored gossip. Lucy didn't care much for carrying tales, and Bea listened in silence.

Even though she was now a part of this world Bobby so loved to talk about, when she was away from the theater she simply felt like herself and not like someone who quite often signed programs outside the stage door after the show, who'd sung twice on the radio, and who'd been all the way to Washington when the show was doing tryouts out of town. It didn't seem important to her that Bert Lahr was being paid $2,250 a week, or that Bobby thought that that was more than anybody was worth. She thought her salary of a hundred and fifty dollars a week an absolute fortune and couldn't imagine wanting or needing more than that. She was able to send money to her mother and grandmother and to buy new clothes as she outgrew the old ones, and sometimes she treated when she and Lucy went out for a meal. Bobby thought everything came down to money.

"It proves what you're worth," he insisted.

"That doesn't make sense," Bea disagreed. "It shows what you're worth if people want to keep on hiring you."

"Boy, you've got it wrong, and I don't mean maybe. Oh, sure it means something. But it means more when they're willing to pay you the big money and put your name up on the marquee. And to get the money and the light bulbs for your name, you've got to play the game the way the big boys want, and you've got to know the rules."

"What big boys? What rules?"

"Aw, I'm not going to get into all that now. Anyway, it probably wouldn't mean anything to you. *You* seem to get to make up your own rules as you go along."

"What d'you mean by that, Bobby?" Lucy asked, setting aside her newspaper.

"I'm only saying what you've said yourself about her."

"What?" Bea asked, looking from Lucy to Bobby. "What d'you say about me, Luce?"

"She says you make things happen," Bobby said defiantly.

"That's not quite what I've said," Lucy said angrily. "You're making it sound as if I'm implying something, and I've never said anything except that things *do* happen with Bea. But it's because she's special and because people are attracted to her. Why're you twisting my words? Why're you trying to start something, Bobby?"

"I'm not 'starting' anything," he backed down a bit. He stole a glance at Bea and knew he should've kept his mouth shut.

"What is it you think I do, Bobby?" Bea spoke very quietly.

"Nothing. I shouldn't've said anything."

"You don't think I should be in the show? Or you think I didn't get to be in the show honestly?"

"He's jealous, Bea," Lucy interjected. "Even friends get jealous now and then."

"No, they don't. Not if they're real friends. Real friends are happy for you. They don't try to make it sound as if you did something dirty . . ." She broke off and shook her head. "All I ever wanted, all

I still want is to be able to go out on stage every night and sing and dance. It makes me happy, but I don't think you want anybody to be happy."

"Wait a minute!" he cried, angry with himself and the turn the conversation had taken. "Course I want you to be happy. And I didn't mean anything dirty or anything."

"You don't trust anybody," Bea said miserably, "not even the people who trust you. What happened to make you this way? Don't you see what you've done? You've made it so we can't be friends anymore because now I know that you're not happy for me, the way I've been happy for you all along." With that, she broke into tears and ran off to the bedroom.

Stunned, Bobby watched her go, then began trying to explain himself to Lucy.

"Don't waste it on me," she said sadly. "I understand what you were trying to say, Bobby, but you're wrong. Bea's right, you know. Sooner or later, all of us have to trust someone. Bea's smart enough to know what really matters. And it's the people who're there for you when you come home at night. Keep on the way you are and there'll never be anyone there for you. I think you'd better go now."

"But I didn't mean..." He gave up, pushed his feet into his shoes and went to the door where he stood looking at the closed bedroom door. "I'm sorry. It all went haywire."

"Maybe you should sit yourself down and think it all through again."

"Yeah," he agreed. "Maybe I should."

After he'd gone, Lucy knocked on the bedroom door, then opened it to see Bea sitting on the side of the bed staring out the window. Lucy sat down and put her arm around the girl.

"He didn't know what he was saying, Bea. He's out of a job and he's scared."

"It's not my fault his show closed and he spent all his money."

"Of course, it isn't. But boys, men, they get themselves all tangled up and can't find a way out, so they have to blame someone else for their problems."

Bea rested her head on Lucy's shoulder. "It feels awful. Why'd he have to say those things?"

"He's angry and he's scared, so he took it out on you."

"What if he doesn't come back?"

"He'll be back," Lucy promised.

"I'm always happy when he's around, Luce. I'm happy just looking at his face or watching him read the papers."

"He'll be back," Lucy said again. "I've got a hunch the two of you are going to spend the rest of your lives fighting and making up."

Eight

"JERRY, couldn't you please find something for him? He's so good. You know he is. All he needs is another chance."

She didn't look or sound like a kid today, Jerry thought. In fact, the scene played as if she were a middle-aged matron pleading with the prison warden for a stay of execution for her child. Bea sat across the desk from him, her ankles primly crossed, her hands clasped in her lap, and an expression on her face that, in the deepening afternoon light, added years to her. Was he the warden? he wondered, pulling himself out of the third or fourth reel of what could've been a D. W. Griffith melodrama. The only thing missing was a river and some ice floes.

"Why're you going to bat for him, Bea? Okay, he's one hell of a dancer, but he's got this big problem. He wants to go from here"— he held his hand flat above his desk—"to there"—his hand soared into the air—"without taking the necessary steps in between. *Racketeer* had forty-eight performances. He gave his all every single show. No problems there. But he goes out like a drunken sailor and puts every cent he earns on his back."

"Is that really so terrible?"

"No, it's not so terrible," he conceded. "His attitude now, that's pretty terrible."

"It's been months, Jerry. You could make a few telephone calls."

She leaned forward, her hands still folded in the lap of her pale gray wool dress that was almost the color of old snow. "Would you do it for me?"

His brain shifted back into the fourth reel. He could almost see the celluloid looping around mental spools. Was he actually sitting here watching and listening to a fifteen-year-old kid—nineteen to the rest of the world—begging him to help another kid? She was the best

77

performer ever to walk into his office. No one else even came close. Except maybe for Bradley. He ran his hands over his head, then slouched back in his seat, studying her eyes. Why hadn't he ever taken notice of her eyes? Here he'd always thought they were blue, but they were gray. And they dominated her pale face, framed by dark lashes and her almost black hair which was pinned up today, off her neck. She'd changed a lot in seven or eight months. Of course kids her age shot up right in front of your eyes. You could practically see it happening. His own kids were a constant mystery and joy to him.

Bea watched him closely; she could feel him deciding and silently willed him to give in, for her sake, and help Bobby. Right now wasn't the moment to say anything more. She wanted to throw herself on the floor at his feet and beg; she'd promise him anything if he'd just put Bobby back to work. She forced herself to be still, thinking how wrong Lucy had been. He'd stayed away for weeks until Bea had gone to his rooming house uptown to look for him. The landlady had told her his room had been rented to somebody else three weeks earlier.

"But where did he go?" Bea had asked.

"Dunno. He didn't leave no forwarding."

She'd had to come to the office to get his new address from Jerry's secretary. And then she'd gone across town to Tenth Avenue, to find Bobby washing dishes in a greasy spoon in return for a bed in the storeroom.

"Please come back with me, Bobby," she'd asked him, standing in the doorway of the storeroom, looking at the cobwebs wafting in the corners and the paint that had bubbled and was peeling from the mildewed walls. All his beautiful clothes were carefully pressed, on hangers suspended from nails in the wall.

"What're you doing here?" he'd wanted to know, angry at being found and yet happy to see her.

"Sometimes," she'd said slowly, "I don't think anybody really knows anything. Lucy said you'd come back. I thought you would, too, so I've waited home every day for you, until it was time to go to the theater. And every night, when the show's over, I hurry back, positive we'll get to the top of the stairs and there you'll be, waiting, with your dance shoes around your neck. Why didn't you come back?"

"How could I, after all that dumb stuff I said?"

"It didn't matter."

"Sure, it did. I shouldn't have said any of that. It wasn't what I meant to say. Making you cry." He was angry with himself just thinking about being responsible for her tears.

78

"You were so angry. I thought maybe I really did do or say something..." She broke off, her eyes moving over the canned goods stacked on warped shelves, coming to rest on his several pairs of well-cared-for dancing shoes aligned on the floor.

"I wasn't ever mad at you." He gazed at the floor between his feet. "It was me. Don't you get it? I was mad at myself."

"But why?"

"I don't want to talk about it. And you shouldn't have come here." He looked up again at her. "One show, in and out, and end of career. I was pretty lucky to get this job, you know. No money, but it's inside, out of the rain, and all the leftovers I can put away. I was going good there for a while, but I guess it's over now."

"This is stupid," she said impatiently. "You're feeling sorry for yourself, and I suppose you'd like me to feel sorry for you, too."

"Hey! I didn't ask you to come looking for me."

"No. But that's because you're stupid. Just because you made some mistakes doesn't mean you have to go out next time and make the same mistakes again. So you didn't save your money, and you bought all those clothes. Now you've learned your lesson, and you'll never do it again. Why don't you get your clothes and your shoes and come home! I'll bet you haven't even been trying to get another show. Jerry told me he hasn't seen you in weeks. You're not even *trying!*"

"You're not my mother!"

"Boy! You're just proving how stupid you are, Bobby! Get your stupid stuff!"

"I *can't* come back there with you!" He stood up, jamming his hands into his pockets.

"And why not?"

"Because I'll start getting mad all over again."

"*Why,* for heaven's sake?"

"Because I'll start noticing things the way I did before, and then I'll get these whacky ideas, and then I'll be mad again."

"What things? What ideas?"

"*Jesus H. Christ, Bea!*" he sputtered. "*You!* In your pajamas, or running out of the bathroom in your underwear and me happening to look over and see you, or you're backstage in just your wrapper and how can I help but look at you!"

It took her several seconds to absorb what he was saying, and then she exclaimed, "*Bobby!*" in a shocked whisper and covered her mouth with her hand.

They stood staring at each other. Bobby could feel perspiration trickling down his spine as the heat of his shame threatened to melt him down to bare bones. He couldn't have looked away if he'd wanted to, so intrigued and frightened was he by the possibility of what she might say.

She thought of her mother, and the men who'd come to spend the night, and of Gramma warning Lil she'd get caught. She thought of how, after Bobby had left, it had felt as if something in her chest had broken under the burden of her hurt and disappointment and loneliness.

"What should we do?" she asked finally, floundering in unfamiliar territory.

"What d'you mean what should we do? I'm seventeen. You're fifteen. I guess fellas my age think about stuff like that. I mean my brothers sure did. But you're just a kid, for crying out loud."

"I can make babies," she said defiantly, then flushed deeply realizing she'd just confided something terribly intimate.

"*Oh, brother!*" he groaned.

"Well, I'm not a little kid."

"I can *see* that!"

"But I'm definitely too young for *that*."

"We're *both* too young for that. Damn!"

"What should I do?" she asked him.

"I can't tell you that, Bea. I don't even know what *I* should do. You think I like saying rotten things I know will hurt your feelings, just because I'm mad at myself, because I can't stop looking at your chest and your legs? It's no good. I'll stay here. You go on home."

She didn't answer at once but looked at his furrowed features and was suddenly angry herself that this was happening to them. "I guess," she said, "we need to be older. Will you at least go see Jerry?"

"He's miffed at me."

"No, he isn't. Promise me you'll go see him! Please?"

"Okay. I'll go see him."

"Good." She wet her lips and took a last look around. "Come on Sunday," she invited. "Lucy and me, we miss you."

"We'll see."

"Bobby?"

"Yeah?"

"I really wish we were older, or that I knew more."

"See you in church, kiddo."

"**W**hat is it with you and this kid?" Jerry asked, breaking the silence.

"We're friends."

"You sure stick up for your friends."

Part One / 1917–1936

"It's important."

"I'll see what I can do. No promises, but I'll make a couple of calls."
She gave him a sudden wide smile that erased the illusion of age.
A kid again, she jumped up from the chair, leaned over the desk to
kiss his cheek, then waved good-bye, and all but skipped out of his
office.

Exhaling tiredly, he sat a moment, then reached for the telephone.

June 14, 1932

Dear Mama and Gramma,

Hope the two of you are fine. I've been really busy, working
in *Hot-Cha!* still and doing a few more radio shows. Lucy's show
is still running, too. And Bobby's going into *Face the Music* to
replace one of the dancers who's going off to Hollywood to have
a screen test. Jerry says he's had calls from a couple of talent
scouts to see if I'd be interested in going to Hollywood because
they're doing tons of musicals out there now, but he won't let
me go unless they're willing to give me a contract. He says going
for a screen test is a mug's game and a waste of time unless you
want a nice paid vacation. I don't even know if I'd want to go,
but it would be fun to see how movies get made. Anyway, I'm
sending you fifty dollars with this letter and I promise I'll try to
write more often.

Love to both of you,
Bea

June 26, 1932

Dear Bea,

You sure are good the way you send us the money. As I always
say it comes in handy. Now that the nice weathers here your
Grammas a lot happier and shes got herself a new job behind
the noshuns counter at Kresges. She likes it there likes the hours
and getting the discount they give to the people work in the
store. The new place is okay not as big as the one on Dundas
but not so noisy. You be sure to let me know if your going to
Hollywood to be in movies Ive always had a yen to see what its
like out there and Id sure love to come visit if you go. Take care
of yourself and dont forget to keep in touch.

Love from me and your Gramma,
Lil

"**J**erry says the screen test is just a formality. They want me for this one picture, and after I do it, *if* I do it, then I can come back *if* I want to. He says George White's planning a new show for next year and has asked about me. It's called 'Melody' or something like that. And Mrs. Ziegfeld's going to produce another *Follies* with the Shuberts, and they'd maybe like me to do that."

"What's the matter, Bea?"

"Oh, Luce, I don't know. I think maybe I would like to go to California and do the movie. The thing is, if I do, I won't have Jerry there. Or you."

"Don't you worry about me. D'you really think I'd let you go out there by yourself?"

"You'd go with me?"

"Of course I would."

"But what about your show?"

"I've been thinking, too," Lucy said. "I guess you were right when you said I didn't really want to be up on a stage. I'm sure not cut out for a long run. Doing the same thing every night and two matinees a week is starting to get me down. If you decide to go out west, I'll tag along as your bodyguard, or chaperone, or something. I've always wanted to see California, you know. I'd love to go with you."

"If I went for a few months, then I'd be able to come back and . . . things would be different."

"This is really about Bobby, isn't it?" Lucy guessed. "What's that louse done to upset you?"

"He's not a louse, Lucy," she defended him, even though now that he was working he still hadn't come around to see her. And she couldn't go back to him a second time. "Jerry thinks it would be good for me to make the picture. He says it'll jack up my asking price and make them offer me even better parts here when I get back. I need to think some more about it." She stopped, and looked at her hands. "Why does everything have to change?" she asked plaintively.

"Sometimes things have to get worse before they get better. This Depression isn't going to last forever. Prohibition's bound to end soon. Maybe they'll find the Lindbergh baby; maybe Roosevelt will get elected; and maybe you'll forget about Bobby Bradley and start having some fun again. You're too young to be making yourself so miserable over a boy."

"Maybe, maybe. What do *you* think I should do?"

"I can't decide that for you, Bea. I wouldn't. If it was the wrong

82

decision, neither one of us would ever forgive me. You've got to make up your own mind."

After the show that night, Bea sat at her dressing table wishing she could stop thinking about Bobby. If she could, she knew life would be so much easier. But she couldn't stop. In her free time, she kept remembering the fun they'd had together, the routines they'd worked up; she'd go back over things he'd said and done, and the way he looked when he laughed. She'd think about the first day when she'd seen him leaning against the wall outside the theater, with his shoes slung around his neck, and feel miserable, missing him.

There was a knock at the door, and Mr. Sam, the stage-door man, poked his head in to say, "There's a gent asking to see you, Miss Beatrice."

At once thinking Bobby had relented, she smiled. "Did he give his name?"

"He sent this." He handed her an engraved calling card. The raised letters spelled out "John Ellroy." Underneath was a company name and an address in Hartford.

For a moment she was so stunned she couldn't speak. Then she looked at Mr. Sam and said, "Give me a few minutes, then send him back, please."

"Okay, Miss Beatrice." Sam pulled the door shut behind him.

She pulled on her wrapper and waited, her throat dry with apprehension. When the knock came at the door, she jumped up, her heart pounding. She opened the door and took several steps back.

Hat in hand, dressed in what had once been an expensive, tailor-made suit, but was now slightly shabby, stood a tall, dark-haired, gray-eyed man who looked as nervous as she felt.

"I know this is an intrusion," he began, "but I think you know who I am."

"Jackie Ellroy, Junior?"

"One and the same. May I come in?"

"Oh, sure." She waved toward a chair and gratefully sat down at the dressing table. "Boy!" she said with a wobbly smile. "This is some surprise."

"I hope you don't mind," he said, positioning his hat on his knees.

"Gee, no. I don't mind."

"You're probably wondering why I've appeared suddenly, out of the blue." He smiled rather shyly at her, and she knew he couldn't be anyone but her father. She looked just like him, right down to the cleft in his chin. "I had a letter from Lil," he explained. "Hadn't heard from her in a lot of years, so you can imagine how surprised I was to get her letter."

"She wrote to you? What about?"

"She wanted to know when her payments were going to start up again." He made a face and glanced around the dressing room. "I was taken a little off guard, as you can imagine. The family's barely hanging on. Business hasn't been good enough to do more than pay the bills, but we're grateful we're able to do that. Of course, with the election coming up, everyone's hoping for a change. But right now, we're getting by from day to day. I didn't know about you, Beatrice. I had no idea you even existed."

"You didn't?"

"I'm afraid not. I always wondered why Lillian was there one day and gone the next. Now I know my mother made certain arrangements." At the mention of his mother, his expression tightened angrily. "To tell you the God's honest truth, I was astonished by Lil's letter, by her asking for money after all these years, and by the news about you. You see, I have a family. A wife and two children."

"I see." Bea swallowed, sensing where he was headed.

"Jackie, my son, is nine, and my daughter, Emily, is just seven."

Bea nodded, waiting. I have a brother and sister, she thought. And I'm never going to see them or meet them. She was beginning to feel sadness, like a chill, creeping over her skin, and pulled the wrapper closer around her.

"I'm not in a position to send your mother anything," he continued.

"I send her money every month," she said, as upset with her mother as he was. "I can't imagine why she'd do a thing like that."

"I destroyed the letter at once. If Alice, my wife, ever saw it . . . Well, I'd be in quite a fix. I don't know how I could begin to explain to her that I had a child I'd never even known about. But I thought the very least I could do was come here and see you. So I took the train in after work, to see the show. I knew the moment I saw you that Lil hadn't made any of it up. I could, I can . . . see myself in you. This is very difficult." He looked into her eyes. "I don't know you; we don't know each other. But I want you to know I felt very proud, seeing you. If I'd known, things might've been very different. Who's to say what might have happened? I was very young. We both were. But I would've done right by Lil. I certainly wouldn't have sent away a young girl . . . in that condition. I thought about confronting my mother, but it seemed pretty pointless to go into it at this late date." He looked again at his hat, repositioning it on his knees. "I wish I had known," he repeated, meeting her eyes.

"It's all right," she told him. "I understand."

"You do, don't you?" he said, surprised. "I had a speech prepared, but I don't have to make it, do I?"

"No. I know what you want to say. I'll write to my mother and tell her to leave you alone. And I'll stay out of your life."

"This is dreadful!" he declared heatedly. "You have to know I'd have been willing to honor my obligations, but I was never given that option. I simply didn't know about any of it. And now it's too late. There are other people to consider."

"I know, and I really do understand."

"You're a very intelligent young woman," he said appraisingly. "Talented and bright. You'll do well, I can tell." He got to his feet, saying, "I've got a train to catch, back to Hartford. I'm glad I came, that I had this opportunity to meet you. You're a lovely girl, Beatrice."

"Thank you," she said thickly, standing now, too. "Thank you for coming to see me."

He got the door open, his eyes still on her. "I wish I could say that if there was ever anything you needed you could come to me, but I can't even do that much. It makes me feel like a bastard, because nobody consulted me, nobody gave me a choice in the matter. I do wish you well. I hope you have a good life. And I hope you'll forgive me."

"Thank you again for coming." She held on to the back of her chair for support. "And don't worry. I'm not one bit like Lil. I'd never turn up out of the blue asking for money. And anyway, I'll be going to California soon, so I'll be out of the way."

"Oh, damn!" he said softly, then hurried away.

She stood staring at the empty doorway for quite some time. Finally, she straightened her spine and walked over to close the door.

Nine

"ACCORDING to the *Motion Picture Herald*, the top ten stars are Marie Dressler, Janet Gaynor, Joan Crawford, Charles Farrell, Greta Garbo, Norma Shearer, Wallace Beery, Clark Gable, Will Rogers, and Joe E. Brown. What do you make of that?" Bea asked, looking up at Lucy.

"Next year you could be on that list."

"Oh, sure!" Bea scoffed.

"Anything's possible."

Bea put aside the *Herald* and looked out the window. They were on the Twentieth Century Limited, heading west.

"We've got quite a long stopover in Chicago," Lucy said. "Several hours to get our baggage transferred to the Dearborn Street Station to pick up the Santa Fe Chief. Jerry's got every last detail written down here." She leafed through the several typed pages Jerry's secretary had prepared. "The studio's supposed to have somebody waiting in Chicago to help us get across town to change trains."

"Good," Bea said distractedly, watching the night sky. So far, she had merely taken in the details of the trip without knowing what her reactions were. She felt numbed, had felt that way since the night her father had come backstage. She hadn't told anyone about the visit. She wasn't sure she could describe how it had felt gaining and losing a father in the space of a five-minute visit, or what it meant to know she had a half-brother and half-sister living in Hartford. Primarily, she was furious with Lil, not only for having gone begging to Jackie Ellroy, Junior, but also for having told him about her. Lil's having written that letter had moved Bea into a state of active disgust. How could Lil have been so stupid, so greedy? It was bad enough she'd started hinting around in her letters about coming to California if Bea decided to go, but to ask Jackie Ellroy for money when she was receiving more than enough from Bea was going too far. She really didn't care now if she never again saw her mother. She'd keep on sending money regularly, but that was as far as it was going to go. Every time she thought about that idiotic letter, and about the painful meeting with her father, she felt sick with humiliation.

Lucy suspected something had happened, but Bea hadn't volunteered a word of explanation. She'd announced, "We're going to California. I'll go see Jerry in the morning," and as of that night she'd stopped referring altogether to Bobby.

"I don't want to hear his name," she'd told Lucy. "I don't want to know about him. If he doesn't want to see me, I don't want to see him. We're not friends anymore and that's all there is to it."

Whatever had gone on, it had changed Bea. There was little left of the girl she'd been. She'd acquired an aura of hard-won maturity, and it showed in her eyes and the set of her mouth.

"You hardly laugh these days," Lucy observed, folding the memo back into her purse. "I wish you'd tell me what's bothering you. I might be able to help."

"I just want to get away," Bea answered without turning from the window. "Once we get there, I'm sure I'll feel a whole lot better. Maybe we'll like it so much we'll never go back to New York."

"But, Bea, I thought the plan was to go back as soon as you've finished the picture."

Bea turned from the window saying, "You're right, you know. It's been ages since anything struck me funny, since anything was fun. I want to feel happy again. Way back when we were first planning to go to New York, I was always happy. There was something to look forward to every minute. I keep telling myself I ought to be happy now. After all, I do have something to look forward to, don't I? Jerry said I've got the part, that the screen test is just to let them see how I look on film."

"It scares you a little, huh?"

"It scares me a lot. It's not like doing an audition where I know exactly what's going to happen. I don't even know what a screen test *is*, what I'm supposed to do."

"There'll be people to tell you that."

"Sure. But I don't like not knowing how it works. I mean, I've always loved the movies, but I've never stopped to try to figure out how they actually get made. Have you?"

"You had no reason to," Lucy said sensibly.

"All these fan magazines and newspapers"—Bea indicated the stack on the table of their drawing room—"don't tell you one thing about anything *real*. It's about the stars and what they eat and drink, and where they eat and drink, and who they eat and drink with, and what they wear while they're eating and drinking, and the kind of pets they have. Who *cares* about that junk?"

"Obviously, a lot of people. Aren't you excited, though? I am, and I'm not even the one who's going to be making the movie. Imagine seeing yourself up on the screen!"

"I'm ugly, Luce. People will hate me."

"You are *not* ugly. And maybe people'll think you're the best thing ever."

"I wish I was older," Bea said wistfully. "Things'd be so much easier."

"Don't count on it. From where I sit, it doesn't seem as if age makes one bit of difference. In just over three years, I'll be thirty. In some circles, that's way over the hill. All the girls I went to school with have been married for years. For all I know, so's my sister Julie."

"Gosh! What d'you suppose ever happened to her?"

"It's like she disappeared off the face of the earth. The whole time in New York I kept thinking I'd run into her somewhere, see her on a bus or in the street."

"D'you miss her, Luce?"

"To be honest, I don't. We never got along. I'm closer to you than I ever was to Julie. She had no sense of fun. She never thought anything was funny. And she thought I was a lost cause."

"Why?"

"Oh, because I liked a good laugh, because I liked the boys, because even though taking chances was always scary I went ahead anyway."

"But those are all the reasons why I like you," Bea said.

"Which is why"—Lucy grinned—"I'm here on this train with you, headed for California, and not back on Palmerston Boulevard in that drafty old barn. I guess some folks might say I was taking advantage of the situation, riding along on your coat-tails. And maybe they wouldn't be that far wrong."

"They would be wrong," Bea said with energy. "You're the only one in the world I can really talk to, the only one who really cares about me." She sighed and rested her chin on her arm that was extended along the back of the seat. "I'm scared, Lucy. I'm scared I'm giving up the one thing that really makes me happy. Every time the curtain went up, and I could feel the audience out there, it was this wonderful thing where they were waiting to see what I could do, and I was going to show them and make them glad they'd come. It was something to look forward to every day, and I loved it. It's only been a matter of weeks since the show closed and it feels like somebody died. I miss Mr. Sam, and my dressing room, and the way it smelled backstage, and my friends in the company. I miss how it felt waiting in the wings for my cue, and that moment when I went on, and the lights were up full and hot, and all I could hear was the music, and then the applause."

"It's not forever, and you could be back there in a few months. You've got standing offers."

"I don't think I'll be going back." She sat up and looked at Lucy, for a moment taken again by Lucy's prettiness, her warm brown eyes and delicate nose, her pointed chin, her soft-looking mouth. For some reason, the sight of Lucy compounded her sadness. "I've got this awful feeling I'll never go back, Luce. And when I think about that, I want to get off this train in Chicago and get on the next one back to New York. But I won't, because I said I'd do this, and I will."

"You're running away from Bobby. Isn't that it?"

Bea shrugged. "He said he was mad at himself because of the way he kept looking at me, at my chest and my legs. He said it didn't have anything to do with me, except that it did, because he made me feel awful, Lucy, as if it was my fault that I had to grow up instead of staying a kid for the rest of my life. I didn't know what to do, but I knew I couldn't do *that*. I did think about it for a minute or two, but I just knew I couldn't. I don't *feel* that way. I still feel peculiar when I see the hair under my arms, and when I go to cross my arms and realize I've got breasts. I mean, maybe my body's old enough, but I'm not. Oh, I knew what he was talking about, all right. Considering all the fellas who came parading through to spend the night with my idiot mother, and Gramma forever warning her she was going to get herself 'caught' again, I'd've been pretty stupid if I didn't know.

"He came to see me, you know. Jackie Ellroy, Junior. He came backstage and gave me this whole line of applesauce about how any man would be proud to be my father, except he'd never even known he had a kid—aside from the two he's already got—until good old Lil wrote asking for money. So he came to see the show, to see me and to make sure I wasn't another Lil come along to mess up his life. I'd really like to know why I had to get a mother with a brain like a walnut. And I don't know why I'm talking about Jackie Ellroy, Junior, the way I am, because I *liked* him. He was nice, and I know he meant every word he said. But I wanted him to be my father, Lucy. The whole thing was a big dream. I've never had a father, and now I never will have one."

"Bea, why didn't you tell me about this?"

"What for? What could *you* have done about any of it? Here I am sending that fool of a woman my hard-earned money, and she goes and writes asking *him* for more. She's got a change-purse where her damned brain's supposed to be. I was so *ashamed*. All the years I thought of how it'd be meeting my father, the things we'd say to each other." She shook her head miserably. "That stupid tart! Why did she have to go and do that?"

Lucy got up and went over to sit beside her, taking care to maintain a little distance between them. "I'm really sorry, Bea. I wish you'd told me. Don't you know I care what happens to you? Don't ever do this again, not to yourself, or to me. It's no good to save up your feelings this way. You do that and one day you just can't hold them in anymore and the next thing you know, you blow up. It can't feel good."

"It feels lousy." Bea smoothed the skirt of her dress with a two-handed yank, then let her fists rest on the seat either side of her. "Why are people so stupid? First Bobby, then my mother."

"Who knows? At least now I can make some sense out of everything."

"Oh, good! Maybe you'll explain it to me."

"Don't take it out on me," Lucy warned.

"Sorry. I'm sorry."

"You're right about one thing. You're not ready for what Bobby had in mind. But if he had the guts to say that to you, he's just gone way up in my estimation."

"Why?"

"Because he did the right thing by you, Bea. He was in a situation he didn't understand and couldn't handle, so he got out of your way. That had to be hard for him. He's not someone who's used to thinking too deeply about things. Most men aren't, in my opinion. I guess he thought hard and long about this one. I suppose I should've spotted it, but I never dreamed things had become so . . . well, serious, between you two."

"But *I* didn't know it, either."

"No," Lucy said sympathetically, sliding her arm around Bea's shoulders.

"Have you done it, Luce?" Bea asked her.

Lucy's face flamed. She smiled, embarrassed, then said, "Uh-huh."

"I thought you probably had. Did you like it?"

Lucy rolled her eyes. "God!" she laughed. "This is embarrassing. Yes, I liked it."

"What's there to like about it?"

"Oh, sweetheart, there's a lot to like about it. It has to do with being close, with feeling good, with touching someone you like an awful lot and wanting them to touch you."

"I couldn't see myself taking my clothes off in front of Bobby. I tried to picture it, but it made me want to laugh. And it's not supposed to be funny, is it?"

"Sometimes it's pretty funny. I mean, if you stop and think about what you're doing, it's ridiculous. The thing is, you *don't* stop and think about it. You're there, doing it. This is the single most embarrassing conversation I've ever had in my life."

"Why?" Bea asked her.

"I don't know. It's just something people don't talk about."

"Well, I can see why not," Bea said with such indignation that Lucy had to laugh.

"I promise you you'll grow out of that."

"Lucy, I miss him. I thought at the very least he'd come to say good-bye."

"Did he know you were leaving?"

"Jerry told him."

"Maybe it's better this way."

"Who for?" Bea wanted to know.

"Both of you. The two of you are too young to be involved."

"But we weren't 'involved.' We were friends. I miss him, and I worry about him. I can't help it. If you weren't around, I'd miss you and worry about you."

"You'll see each other again. And maybe next time, you'll be older and able to handle it better."

"We *have* to see each other again," Bea said determinedly. "I'd just hate it if we didn't. We had such good times. All the things we talked about, the routines we worked up. We danced so perfectly together, Luce, as if we were parts of the same body. I always knew his next move, and he knew mine. I felt so happy being with him."

"I'd say he felt pretty good being with you, too."

"You think so?"

"I think so."

All in a rush, Bea said, "I thought someday we'd get married. I really did. I thought we'd get married, and have a home of our own, and three or four babies. I could *see* it, Luce. Then, when he said those things, it made me feel as if I'd been playing dress-up, as if everything I'd dreamed about was a great big lie, and my getting taller and looking older was the worst lie of all because inside I was still just a kid and I didn't want to know about the way it made him

91

feel looking at my chest and my legs. I felt ashamed, because it wasn't my fault that he had to keep looking and thinking the things he thought."

"I know," Lucy consoled her. "But you'll stop feeling that way soon enough."

"Not soon enough to suit me! It's terrible. It's like walking around behind a big photograph of somebody else, and it's wearing out my arms holding the dumb thing up." She laughed at the image.

Relieved to see Bea coming back to herself, Lucy changed the subject, asking, "Come on now, admit it. Aren't you just dying to meet some of your favorite movie stars?"

"I don't know. I always thought I'd like to meet Joan Crawford until I read that dumb stuff she said in *Photoplay* last year. 'Spend! I, Joan Crawford, I believe in the dollar. Everything I earn, I spend.' That's one of the craziest things I've ever read. I suppose she thought that was going to make people standing in breadlines feel really swell. There she is out spending her money and that's supposed to be encouraging. I don't know, Luce. Every time I read one of those movie magazines, and there's a story about someone I like, I've stopped liking the person by the time I've finished the article. Oh, God!" Her expression froze. "You don't think they'll do that to me, do you?"

"They might."

"I don't think I'm going to like Hollywood."

"I think you're gonna love it. And they're gonna love you."

"I'm scared all over again. I'm letting myself in for what feels like more than I can handle."

"Let me tell you something," Lucy said seriously, taking hold of her hand. "I don't honestly think there's a single thing that you couldn't handle. And I mean that. Don't forget I'm with you, and as long as I am, nobody's going to hurt you, not if I have anything to say about it. I love you, Bea, and I'll look after you. Sometimes I'm not sure who's in charge, you or me. At moments, I'm convinced you're the smarter, more grown-up one of the two of us. And at other times, I realize I'm the one who's been alive for almost twenty-seven years and has the experience under her belt. I know a thing or two, and I'm willing to put my money on you, girl. I believe in you, and you'd better know that."

Bea hugged her hard, whispering, "I wanted my father, and I wanted Bobby. I couldn't have my father and didn't know how to have Bobby. I hate being young, Lucy. It's so hard."

"Life is hard, sweetheart, right from start to finish. Don't expect it's going to get easier just because you get older." She started to laugh and eased Bea away, again taking hold of her hand. "I think I'll embroider it on a pillow," she laughed. "Life is hard, and then you die."

"God!" Bea blinked at her for a moment, then started to laugh.

Ten

WHILE the make-up man fussed over her, Pete, the publicist, ran down the schedule.

"After the test, we'll get you cleaned up, then you meet Mr. Meyers, the executive producer. After that, lunch. Then, this afternoon, you'll have a session with the publicity department, and at four you've got a photo session. Shooting starts three weeks from Monday, so we've got a lot of ground to cover. I've got some calls to make, but I'll be back to take you to the sound stage." He closed his notebook, gave her a pat on the shoulder, and went off.

Bea's eyes met Lucy's in the mirror. Lucy shrugged and smiled, astonished by the enormous amount of make-up being applied to Bea's face. It looked heavily overdone, but maybe the studio lights would wash out the shading on her cheeks and nose and chin and cut down the lurid effect of the thick false eyelashes, the darkened eyebrows, and the vivid red lip rouge.

When the make-up man stepped back to study his work he seemed very pleased.

Bea was horrified and looked inquiringly at Lucy.

Trying to be tactful, Lucy ventured to say, "You don't think it's a little strong?"

"Strong?" The man turned to look at her, then back at Bea. "Strong? I don't think so." He shooed Bea out of the chair, saying, "Next door, to hairdressing," and busied himself returning to order his brushes and powder puffs and pots of make-up.

The hairdresser, looking anything but happy, unpinned Bea's hair, let it fall, took several steps back to stand staring at the hair, then at her face, then back at her hair. At last, he said, "You really should have this cut. It's far too long."

Bea's temper was giving way. "You don't mean to tell me nobody out here has long hair!"

"Not this long," he answered self-assuredly. "You can't wear it down, and the way you had it's very unflattering to your profile. There isn't time now, but you really should come back before you start shooting and let me cut it for you. Up to here, at least." He held his hand at her earlobes. "For now, let's just put it back up." With several twists, the insertion of a number of pins, several of which felt embedded in her scalp, and another twist or two, he'd created a fuller, softer-looking version of the bun she'd been wearing to begin with.

As he was finishing, Pete returned. "They're ready for you," he said from the doorway, waiting for Bea to collect her purse.

He led the way, and Lucy hung back to walk with Bea.

"I look like Minnie Mouse," Bea whispered. "I can't go in front of anybody, let alone a camera, looking this way."

"What're you gonna do?" Lucy asked, glancing at the publicist's back.

"Excuse me," Bea said, stopping Pete. "Is there a ladies' room where we're going?"

"On the way. I'll show you."

While Lucy and Pete waited outside, Bea dashed into the lavatory to see what could be done about the garish make-up. The hair was all right, but the eyelashes were ridiculous. Gingerly, she peeled them off and dropped them onto a tissue. Working quickly, she got out her mascara, wet the brush, and darkened her lashes. Then, with a fresh tissue, she rubbed off some of the thick, gluey-tasting lip rouge.

"That's better," she addressed her mirror image, having returned her mouth to its normal dimensions with her own lip color. Folding the tissue with the false lashes into her purse, she hurried out, to go along to the immense sound stage.

Several technicians were moving about on the set. A number of men were hammering away at flats; two others were shifting huge lights, and one was carrying an armload of props. A knot of four men stood together, talking in undertones. Pete took Bea by the arm to introduce her.

"Here she is!" he announced, causing the four men to turn. Only one of them smiled, a tall, lanky fellow in shirt-sleeves and a bow tie. The other three just stared, their eyes narrowing, as Pete continued with the introductions. "This is Gregory Robinson, who'll be directing. Henry Donovan is A.D. for the picture. Ike Allborn's the cameraman, and Fred's the sound engineer." In the background hovered the hairdresser and the make-up man.

"Where's her make-up?" Robinson asked angrily.

"I'm wearing it," Bea answered. "They put so much goop on my face I could hardly hold my head up."

The assistant director, Henry Donovan, laughed delightedly and extended his hand to her. "I'm Hank," he said. "I saw you in *Hot-Cha!* You were just great. It's a real pleasure."

"Thank you," she said, responding to his welcoming warmth, and the gentle pressure of his hand enclosing hers. "This is my friend, Lucy Vernon."

"The *hair*, the *make-up!*" Robinson complained, looking accusingly over his shoulder at the two culprits who were now conferring in whispers.

"It's all right, Greg," Hank said. "Let's get on with it. It'll be fine. Lucy, why don't you have a seat there while I explain to Beatrice what we're going to be doing." He indicated several canvas chairs behind the camera, and Lucy, after a moment's indecision, went to sit down. The only one of these people, aside from Pete, she'd have spent more than five minutes with was Donovan. The rest of them were like fearful robots.

"All you'll have to do," Hank explained, leading Bea onto the cleared set, "is relax and talk to us, follow whatever direction Greg gives you. Once we have the film, we'll be able to decide on your hair and make-up, think about how we'll want to light you. You'll be doing this again for the wardrobe, so we can see how the costumes photograph. I know you can't imagine it now, but you will get used to all this."

"You don't want me to sing or dance?"

He smiled again. "We already know what you can do. And you'll get your fair share of singing and dancing once we start principal photography. Okay, here's how it'll go. In a couple of seconds, we'll hit the lights and do a quick sound check for the voice level. The clapperboard will identify the test, and we'll roll. Greg will talk to you, maybe ask you some questions, get you to turn this way or that, and that'll be it. The whole point of this is to see how you handle yourself on camera. Some people start out cool as can be and the minute the camera starts rolling, they freeze. I know that's not going to be a problem for you, though. Nervous?"

"No. Yes. D'you think they'll get in trouble because I took off most of the make-up?"

"I really don't think so," he said kindly. "Have they put you someplace nice?"

"The Hollywood-Roosevelt."

"That's good. Are you comfortable there?"

"It's very nice," she said politely.

"Once shooting starts, you might want to think about renting a place. It'll be a lot less expensive for you. Now, be sure to let me know if there's anything I can do to help."

"What exactly is it that you do?" she asked him.

He laughed. "The A.D.'s kind of a general dog's body. You could say I'm kind of the set foreman. I make sure the director's got everything he needs—actors, extras, special equipment, whatever. I'm the first one here in the morning and the last one to leave at night. I do the paperwork, look after any little problems the crew might have, try to keep the actors happy, and make sure the whole thing rolls along without too many problems."

"It sounds like an awful lot of work."

"It is, but I like it. Now don't forget. Anything you need, let me know."

"Thank you very much, Mr. Donovan."

"Hank. Just relax, and look right into the camera unless Greg says otherwise. Okay?"

"Okay."

"Good. Don't worry. You'll do just fine."

He left her and went back to the chairs behind the camera where Lucy and the director were now seated. He bent to exchange a few words with the director, then straightened and shouted, "LIGHTS!"

There was the sound of a switch being thrown and suddenly Bea was flooded with hot white light. The director moved to stand to one side of the camera, tilting his head this way and that, then he said something to Hank who, in turn, shouted, "GIVE ME SOME KIND OF KEY LIGHTING ON HER LEFT!"

The light shifted, and the heat intensified on the left side of her face.

"OKAY! THAT'S GREAT. READY FOR A VOICE LEVEL?"

A disembodied voice shouted back, "READY!"

"Just count to ten, Bea," somebody instructed, and she began counting, feeling like a complete dodo and starting to perspire under the tremendous heat of the lights.

"VOICE LEVEL'S FINE!"

"OKAY! MARK IT!"

Out of nowhere, a young man appeared, held what Bea guessed was the clapperboard up in front of the camera, said, "Bernice Crane, Test," then ducked out of the way. The camera, looking like nothing so much as the front of a train, seemed to close in on her, and she suddenly found the entire situation too funny for words. Smiling, she folded her arms comfortably across her chest, letting her weight shift to one hip.

"Tell us about yourself," Robinson said from the shadows.

"Well," she said, still smiling. "I'm Beatrice, not Bernice, Crane, and I sing and dance. I was born in Buffalo, New York, but grew up in Toronto. That's in Canada. More?"

"Go on," Robinson said.

"I'm twenty, almost twenty-one. I'm five feet four inches tall and weigh one hundred and two pounds."

"Turn to your left, will you?"

She turned.

"Okay. Now to your right."

She turned again.

"Okay, front to the camera."

Unable to help herself, she started to laugh and tried to swallow it.

"When you're finished," Robinson said somewhat sarcastically, "perhaps you'd be good enough to say a few words about why you're here and what you'll be doing."

Managing to put a lid on her amusement, she said, "As far as I know, I'm here to play somebody's kid sister called 'Peaches' in the musical *Upside Down*. I haven't seen a script, but my agent has and he thinks it's a swell part. So here I am."

"Okay, just hold it there, will you?"

She stood perfectly still and gazed into the hard eye of the camera for what seemed like several hours until a voice she recognized as Hank's yelled, "CUT! PRINT THAT!"

The lights shut down, and the air was almost instantly cooler in the sudden darkness. Picking her way off the set over thick cables, she approached the group that was once again in conference. Lucy got up and came over, asking, "How d'you feel?"

"I thought it was pretty silly, if you want to know the truth."

"Seemed pretty silly to me, too."

As Pete was about to lead them out, Hank came hurrying over. "Pete's explained everything to you, has he?" he asked.

"Some."

"There'll be a script waiting for you by the time you get back to the hotel. I apologize for that. Somebody botched things up."

"That's all right."

"Say, how about if I take the two of you out to dinner?" he suggested with another of his seemingly habitual smiles.

"That'd be swell," Bea said at once.

"Okay. I'll pick you two up at seven and show you a little of the local nightlife. We'll go somewhere casual, so you don't have to worry about getting dressed up. By the time you finish here, you're not going to want to have to do anything more strenuous than picking up a knife and fork. I'll see you at seven," he said, and went back to his conference.

After the make-up man creamed Bea's face, Pete walked her and Lucy across the lot to meet Ludovic Meyers.

"I want to warn you," he said before they entered the building that housed the executive offices. "Ludie can be a gruff son of a gun, or he can be nice as pie. Whatever way he happens to be, don't take it to heart. Underneath it all, he's one very sharp guy, and he knows exactly what he's doing, and what everybody else is doing, too. People are pretty excited about you making this picture, so you've got nothing to worry about."

The secretary showed Bea into a vast, luxuriously appointed inner office where behind a clear expanse of highly polished mahogany desk sat a small, round man with owlish eyes behind wire-rimmed glasses.

"C'mon in and siddown," he told Bea, beckoning her over with a manicured hand.

She walked across the thick carpet, acutely aware of being studied from head to toe. Upon arriving at the desk, she held her hand out to him. The move seemed to surprise him. His eyes widened, then he smiled, took her hand, and give it a hearty shake.

"I heard you had gumption," he said approvingly. "Sit, sit. Good. Relax. I like people with gumption. You got dancer's legs, too. Nothing like 'em. Beautiful legs. So, tell me. How'd the test go?"

"It went," she answered, making herself comfortable in the leather armchair. "I'm afraid I found it funny and laughed a lot. I don't think the director cared very much for that. I don't think he cared very much for *me*. But Mr. Donovan, Hank, was very nice."

"It *is* funny," he said, enjoying her candor. "Everything okay? No problems?"

"No, sir. So far, everything is just fine."

"That Jerry Greenswag, he held me up for ransom to get you. You know that? I don't give one-picture contracts. You know what it says in your contract? You know we've got an option after *Upside Down?*"

"Yes, sir. I know that."

He tilted his chair back and turned slightly, still staring at her. "Polite," he said. "I like nice manners. So, twenty, huh?"

"Almost twenty-one. That's right."

He laughed. "You wanna be a movie star, kid?"

"I don't know," she replied truthfully.

98

"Go on!" he laughed some more. "*Everybody* wants to be a movie star!"

"Everybody, huh? I'm not everybody." She smiled at him. "But I'll think about it."

"You as good as they say?"

"Probably. Of course, I've never made a movie, so we'll have to wait and see if I'm not better back on Broadway."

He let his chair come forward and crossed his arms on the desk. His eyes hadn't once moved off her. "Tell me," he said. "What d'you want?"

"You mean now, or eventually?"

"Eventually."

"What I've been doing, singing and dancing."

"But not necessarily a movie star."

"Maybe I won't be any good."

"Every single person who comes in here wants to be a movie star, thinks they're God's gift. You, you don't know necessarily. It's a nice change. Now, you listen here to me. You listening?"

"Yes, sir."

"You deliver for me, and I'll look out for you. You understand what I'm saying?"

"I think so."

"Make it so you *know* so. You give this picture everything you got, and we'll put you right on top. *I'll* put you there myself. You're a smart girl. You got a chance here there's dozens would cut your throat to get. You stay clean, you do your job, and we'll take care of everything else."

"All right."

"Okay, good. So, go have your lunch, and don't give my publicity boys any bullshit. Those boys are going to be what stands between you and the outside. Make friends here, kid. It's the best advice anybody's gonna give you."

"Thank you very much." She stood up and again shook his hand.

As before, he looked surprised and pleased. "You got a lotta class for a kid," he said admiringly. "Just make sure you mind your p's and q's."

"I liked him," she told Lucy over lunch in the commissary, while Pete was off again, making more phone calls. "He was round and kind of cute and stared at me the whole time. Pete wasn't kidding. He's very smart. It's as if he can see right through you, read what you're thinking. I think he liked me."

"Well, that's good." Lucy looked around. The place was crowded with people, many in costumes, many with well-known faces. Lucy's eyes went round and she blushed as she leaned across the table whispering, "That's John Barrymore! And over there, Jeanette MacDonald! I think I'm going to faint."

Pete returned and slid into his seat saying, "I was talking to Hero, the choreographer. He'd like to meet with you after you finish with the publicity boys. You dance, too, am I right, Lucy?"

"Right."

"She sure does," Bea chimed in.

"He heard you were available and would like to meet you, too. He says he's got a spot open for dance captain, if you're interested. The girl he was gonna use went and got pregnant."

Lucy lit up. "I sure am interested."

"How's your lunch?" he asked, looking at their plates. "Mind if I smoke?"

"Go right ahead," Bea told him. "I like the smell of tobacco. The lunch is fine. I'm still trying to get it into my head that we're actually here."

"You'll have the whole weekend to take it easy and look around," Pete said. "And remember, don't take any of what goes on around here personally. Unless, of course, somebody hits you in the kisser with a fish or something. That, you take personally."

Bea laughed.

"You got any objections to doing part of the photo session at the beach?" he asked.

"In a bathing suit, you mean?"

"Yeah. You got any?"

"No. I don't even know how to swim."

"We'll go over to wardrobe after we see Hero and pick up a few things, a couple of swimsuits, maybe a dress or two for the indoor session. The boys'll want to start feeding stuff to the press right away, get the public worked up about you so that by the time the film's ready for preview they'll already know your name. The next few weeks, you'll be going out on the town most nights, to get your name in the columns. The boys and I'll make the arrangements, probably have you seen with some of the other contract players. And we'll get a whole campaign going with the fan mags, dribble a few choice tidbits to Parsons."

"I'm not sure I have the right kind of clothes for that," Bea said anxiously.

"Don't worry about it. Ludie'll put through an advance on your salary to cover some new duds. We'd better get a move on now, if

100

you're finished." He crushed out his cigarette and stood up. "Always be on time, and you'll never have a problem. Around here, you'd better believe time is money. You never keep a crew standing waiting. When you get a six a.m. call, you show up at six. They want you in publicity at two, you get there on the dot. We've got ten minutes, but it's not far."

Behind half a dozen desks half a dozen men sat, most of them with their feet propped on open drawers, and threw questions at her like firecrackers: Got any hobbies? Got a boyfriend, a mother, a father, sisters, brothers? Born where? Grew up where? School? Is that your real name? How about changing it to something catchier, say Brenda, or maybe Roberta? No soap on the name, huh? Okay. Height? Weight? Measurements? Skip the measurements. Age? Who's your good-looking friend? How come you need a guardian? How come they're in Canada and you're out here with a guardian? Hey, guardian, how about dinner and dancing one night? Make sure I've got your number. Okay. Favorite male stars? Gable's good. Farrell's good. Cooper? Cooper, that's great! Maybe we can do something with Cooper. Both have the same kind of eyes. You go to church? Okay, skip that. Ever done anything we oughta know about could come up lookin' ugly later on? You're absolutely sure? You got any nasty little secrets, tell us now, before we get out there and start peddling you. Okay, swell. No offense intended, just asking. Have to, you know. Anything else, boys? Okay. We'll work on the Canadian-import angle for now. We'll get together for more stuff next week. Hey, guardian! Bring those dimples back here and give us your number.

Hero was calm and soft-spoken, a soothing break after the raucous publicity boys. An elegant, graceful man, he wore a white silk shirt, exquisitely tailored slacks, and handmade calfskin dancing shoes. He wore his hair brushed straight back so that his blue eyes were his dominant feature. He held himself very tall, his shoulders a wide line that broke with rippling suppleness as he shook hands with both of them and offered them a warmly open smile. "Come sit down," he invited, indicating a grouping of chairs in the otherwise empty rehearsal sound stage. "I have a rehearsal record. I thought we'd listen through, then discuss a few ideas. You've got two major numbers," he told Bea, over the start of the music. "One with the juvenile lead, the other with him and the full chorus, a big production number. We'll shoot the first number all in one take so there're no jumpy little

101

Oberlin Public Library

offsteps when the film's down to the fine cut. Now here," he said, drifting over into the center of the floor, "is the beginning of that first piece." As he told them how he envisioned the number, he began to dance. Bea and Lucy watched, entranced, as his body shaped itself to the music. "We'll have plenty of rehearsal time," he said, "with Clark Boland who's the musical director. Okay. Right here is where it breaks." He walked toward Bea as the music shifted into double time. His eyes fastened to Bea's, he dropped onto his haunches directly in front of her, grasped both her hands, and said, "If you have any ideas, please feel free to contribute. I want your impressions."

Bea had never encountered anyone remotely like this man, yet she liked and trusted him immediately and completely. With his eyes, and his hands holding hers, he transmitted many things—that he also liked and trusted her, that he recognized her need to dance, and their mutual compulsion to transform their feelings into motion. Their eyes and hands linked, Bea listened through both numbers, then asked if they could go back to the top of the first one. He nodded, rose to his feet in one fluid motion, and went to place the needle back at the start of the recording. Setting aside her bag, as if in a trance, she got up to meet him on the floor where she duplicated the steps he'd demonstrated until they got to the break into double time. Hero glided away to watch what she did with the music. And watching her work against the time, rather than trying to conquer it, filled him with excitement. She surpassed his expectations. "That's good," he said, as she suddenly broke time, then broke it again, then slipped into the meter. He couldn't help smiling with pleasure at witnessing the natural choreography that flowed out of her. "I like it very much." At the end, he went to lift the arm of the Gramophone saying, "If you agree, we can work this up together."

"I'd love that. The music's wonderful. Who's going to be the juvenile lead?"

"It's not cast yet. We're having trouble finding the right face. We need a kid who can sing, who can really dance, but he's got to look good. Fresh, but kind of tough, too."

"I know someone who could do it. A friend of mine in New York. He'd be perfect. He's a bit older than me and he's a terrific dancer."

"In New York, huh? That's a shame. We've got to use someone here. Time's running out. But maybe we'll get your friend in on the next one." He put an arm around her waist and pushed her off into a spin to which she responded automatically, allowing herself to be reeled back into his chest with a happy little laugh. Releasing Bea, he held his hand out to Lucy, saying, "Let's see how you'll do as

102

captain." And Lucy, as mesmerized as Bea by this magnetic, charming man, stepped forward, extending her hand.

"I knew the minute I saw her you were right. She's exceptional, Hank."

"I told you."

"I know you told me. But, admit it, you're not exactly qualified to rate dancers."

"It doesn't take a genius to see that that girl's one in a million."

"For a while there, I was beginning to wonder, you know."

"About what?"

"You know. Since when did you ever make a fuss like that over some girl?"

"Well, I'm glad you agree. I've got to get off the line. Robinson's chewing up the flats."

"Are we on for dinner?"

"I promised to take Bea and what's-her-name to dinner. I'll see you at the screening. You'll be there, won't you, Hero?"

"Wouldn't miss it. Thanks for finding her, Hank. Nice work."

"Thanks for agreeing. Christ! What a relief!"

Feeling paper pale, Bea posed sitting on the sand, standing at the water's edge, and, finally, did some jumps and attitudes to make it seem as if she were actually doing something sensible. After the beach, they piled into Pete's car, to relocate indoors at the studio where her make-up was altered for the lights and, in a series of unbecoming and hastily pinned evening frocks, she was posed this way and that on a chaise longue and told to smile fetchingly.

"This is the stupidest thing ever!" she complained to Lucy, between shots. "Look what they've done to my eyebrows! And they've painted over my upper lip again, so I'm back to playing Minnie Mouse!"

Ludie Meyers went through the contact sheets with a magnifying glass, his expression growing darker and darker until he tossed the sheets into the wastebasket, pounded his fist on the desk, and yelled, "She's a *kid*, goddammit! Get that *crap* off her *face*, put her into some *normal* clothes, and *reshoot*! Do I have to do *everything* myself around here? Tell those *morons* in make-up I want she should look like what she is: *a fresh, young kid!* Enough with the eyelashes and the big lips and the artsy-fartsy dramatic backlighting. Goddamn baggage smashers! All they know is how to make one face—Constance Bennett's—and they put it on everybody! Out! Find a photographer knows what he's doing. Let him take pictures when she's dancing, singing, something. *Not this!* You come back with more crap like this I'll throw all of you the hell off the lot!"

Bea could have wept. "We've got to do it all *again?*"

"Ludie had a fit," Pete explained apologetically. "It'll be better this time. No more Constance Bennett make-up. Ludie said even pigtails would be better."

"Well, thank heaven for something."

Back at the hotel, Bea dropped on the bed, pushed off her shoes and gave a long, exaggerated moan.

"I couldn't agree more," Lucy said, sprawled in the armchair.

Bea adjusted the pillows and sat back. "The whole day was ridiculous and unbelievable, but you know what?"

"What?"

"For forty minutes, I was absolutely, I mean absolutely, happy. I'm going to adore working with Hero. Did you see the way he *moves?* He's like liquid; he *pours* from place to place." She sat up and wrapped her arms around her knees and smiled over at Lucy. "I think it's all going to be worth it just to be able to work with that man. Don't you think?"

"Agree, hands down."

"And you know who else I really liked?"

"Who?"

"That tall lanky fellow with the copacetic smile who's taking us to dinner."

"Hank."

"He's really nice."

"Um, Bea, I don't think you want to get interested in someone so much older than you."

Bea laughed. "He was *nice,* Lucy. Everybody else we met today, except him and Hero, they were all . . . working. You know? But the two of them acted as if they cared about other people, and about what they do. Pete wasn't bad. The rest of those guys made my hair stand on end."

Eleven

"I HAVE a confession to make to you," Hank said halfway through dinner at the Brown Derby. "If this entire experience out here turns out to be less than your heart's delight, you'll have me to blame."

"Why?" Bea asked.

"Because after seeing you in *Hot-Cha!* I wired Ludie Meyers to say I'd found the perfect ingenue for *Upside Down*. I kept sending telegrams and calling his office, making such a fuss, that he finally sent one of the local scouts to catch the show. Fortunately, he agreed with me. The two of us got Ludie so worked up that by the time he started negotiations with your agent, he was convinced he'd discovered you himself. Not that I mind," he added. "I'm just happy we managed to get you."

"Well, I guess *I* should be buying *you* dinner," Bea told him, smiling. Her initial impression of him was solidifying more with every minute she spent in his company. Not only did she like his easy, sincere manner, she also liked his clothes. This evening he was wearing an argyle vest over a white shirt. He had on another bow-tie, this one dark red, almost burgundy, that picked up the predominant color in the patterned sweater. Gray flannel slacks and a navy blazer completed the outfit, and she thought he looked more like a college professor than someone who worked in moving pictures.

"Next time," he returned her smile. "This time, it's my pleasure entirely. So, now, tell me. What d'you make of it all so far?"

"It's strange, and I can't get used to how hot it is. Things seem to happen awfully fast here."

"Not always. Sometimes projects can drag on for years. Did you get the script all right?"

"Yes, I did. Thank you."

105

"Good." He turned to Lucy. "I hope you don't mind my taking the liberty of recommending you to Hero. I saw your show, too, and Hero usually trusts my judgment. We've been friends quite a while."

"No, I appreciate it," Lucy thanked him. Then, lowering her voice, she asked, "Is that really Janet Gaynor over there?"

He turned to look. "It really is."

"God!" Lucy sighed. "This is like a dream."

"Believe it or not, after a while, you get used to it."

"How long have you been here?" Bea asked him.

"Just over eight years. I worked with von Stroheim on *Greed* up in Frisco. By the time we'd wrapped, I was hooked but good, so I came along down here and worked my way up from prop man to A.D. I want to direct, and so far Ludie won't let me, but one of these days he'll give in. He's sick of my memos, my begging letters, my suggestions, my scripts, and all the rest of it. The way I figure it, I'll just keep on until he gives in."

"You're from San Francisco?" Lucy wanted to know.

He nodded. "Born and raised."

"What was it like, working with von Stroheim?" Lucy asked. "You don't mind all these questions, do you?"

"I love it. It gives me a chance to show off what I know." He smiled again. "Working with that man was an education in itself. First of all, he did the adaptation from Frank Norris's novel *McTeague* himself, and he was obsessed with translating the book literally. He insisted on absolutely authentic detail. So he rented this old, empty place on Gower Street, furnished the rooms exactly the way Norris had described them, and shot inside with just some lamps and whatever daylight we got. Drove the cameraman crazy, but the film looked surprisingly good. Believe it or not, he was so determined everything be right he made the cast *live* in the place. He shot miles of film, forty-two reels. Of course, the studio went nuts and told him he had to cut it down to ten. He refused, so they brought in another director, Rex Ingram, who managed to get it down to eighteen reels. Anyway, it finally got cut to ten, and it was a disaster. The cutting destroyed what most of us thought was a masterpiece. But he kept a lot of us working for a good, long time, and I met some swell people—Chester Conklin and ZaSu Pitts, Jean Hersholt. And I learned most of what I know from watching him, seeing how he operated. He's a tough guy, but I think he's a genius, and it's tragic that the whole business just about ruined him here. Okay. Enough of that. I have to warn you, it's dangerous to get me started. I can go on for days. And I don't want to talk about me. I want to know about Beatrice Crane."

106

"There's nothing to tell," Bea demurred. "And I think the publicity boys ran me dry this afternoon. Do they do that to everyone? I had the feeling it was kind of like an assembly line."

"The publicity people can be your best friends and staunchest supporters," he explained, "or they can make your life a misery. My advice is to string along. They can make you a household name without your ever appearing on the screen. The fanzines are very important. You wait! A couple of days after the first stories about you appear, you'll start getting fan mail. They'll tell you what they think you should wear, how you should do your hair, what they like and don't like about you, about your clothes. Plenty of people here take the fans very seriously. Crawford, you know, took her name from a fanzine poll."

"No kidding!" Lucy said. "I didn't know that."

"Believe me," he said earnestly. "The fans are going to be the most important people in your life. As long as they want to see you on the screen, you'll have a career. Don't ever make the mistake of underestimating them or taking them for granted!"

"I certainly won't," Bea said, certain now that she could learn everything she'd ever need to know from this man.

"The really big power in town," he went on, "is Lolly Parsons. She happens to like you and says something about you in her column in the morning *Examiner,* by noon everybody'll be talking about you. Same thing if you get on her wrong side. And *nobody,* from the top on down, wants to do that. The publicity boys all feed her stories, and a lot of producers even consult her about casting. She's got eyes and ears everywhere, including her husband, Dockie Martin, who's the studio physician over at Twentieth Century-Fox. Sooner or later, the boys'll drag you over to her house, or to her table in some restaurant where she's having dinner, to have you say howdy-do and put your best foot forward. No matter what you might think of her, be nice. She can do you an awful lot of good. Basically, she's a pretty decent woman. And don't let her fool you with that vague act she likes to put on sometimes. She never forgets a thing."

"Do you have to go through stuff like that, too?" Bea wondered.

"They're not interested in the guys behind the scenes. Unless we happen to get ourselves involved with somebody who's in front of the camera. Lucky for me, I've never been interested in being out front. My place is back of the camera. I'm happy there. There's a lot you can do with pictures, you know, and there's only a handful of people who've really done good, first-quality work."

"Is Gregory Robinson one of them?" Bea asked.

107

He shook his head. "He's competent, but definitely not inspired. He's smart enough to get the best people on his team, right from the cameraman to the grips and gaffer."

"What's a grip?" Lucy interjected.

"A grip is kind of an all-purpose handyman, sort of the movie's counterpart to a stagehand in the theater. They're usually hefty guys with some muscle."

"This is like being back in school," Bea laughed. "You honestly don't mind us asking you all these questions?"

"I told you: I love it."

"I think you look like a professor," Bea told him.

"I'll let you in on a secret. I nurture that impression. I can't stand the guys who go around in jodhpurs and riding boots, the guys who get into costume to work behind the scenes. That's such crap. As if what they wear has anything to do with making pictures. I don't mind looking scholarly. I was one anyway, once upon a time."

"Well, if you're absolutely sure you don't mind," Bea said. "Then, tell me, who d'you think are the good directors?"

"Let's see. There's Capra and Cukor; Wyler is first-rate; Lubitsch is pretty good. Von Sternberg's a little crazy, but he's not bad. I already mentioned von Stroheim. King Vidor has moments, but the moments don't save a lot of his pictures. He tends to get carried away with tricky camera angles. There's Goulding, although I personally think he's a better writer than director, but maybe he'll catch up with himself; Archie Mayo's up and coming. I think he's going to do some very good stuff."

"And there's you," Bea teased, "Professor Donovan."

He laughed happily. "Some day. I've got my fingers crossed. You want to know all of it, don't you?"

"Sure. I figure if I know how it works, I'll have a fighting chance of doing a halfway decent job."

"Smart girl," he approved. "Feel free to ask me anything, any time." He was having a wonderful time, delighted his initial impressions of her had been so accurate. He liked everything about her, and especially her unusual looks. Properly lighted, she just might turn out to be one of those people the camera loved. He was anxious to see the screen test and glanced at his watch to check the time.

She saw him steal a look at his watch and wondered if he found her boring.

"Don't worry about my doing that," he said, picking up on her having seen him check his watch. "I have to be back at the studio by ten to see your test. Where were we?"

108

"You were encouraging me to enroll in the Donovan school of picture-making."

"Right! I was. You're so young," he said, studying her eyes. "I don't very often get a chance to talk to someone your age."

"I'm not *that* young."

"Heck! I could probably be your father."

"I don't think you're old enough," she countered. "But if it makes you feel better, I'll call you 'Pop.'"

"I can't stand it," Lucy whispered. "That's John Barrymore again."

"He's probably following you," Hank told her, then, turning to Bea said, "Obviously he's following her."

"Oh, obviously."

"Don't I wish," Lucy said longingly.

"Anyway," Hank said, "one of these days I'll get to direct pictures, and maybe Ludie will stop giving every script to some other guy just because I asked to do it. I begged and pleaded to do *Upside Down*," he explained. "So if you see me off somewhere, banging my head against the wall and having hysterics, you'll know why. How about a tour on Sunday? I'll give the two of you a viewing of local sights of interest."

"Lucy?" Bea nudged her to get her attention. "Sunday, a drive with Pop here?"

"Fine, fine." Lucy continued to look around the restaurant.

"Fine, fine," Bea repeated to Hank.

"I know of a small house for rent. You might want to take a look at it, while we're out. It's easier to adjust here if you're not stuck in a hotel. So, I'll pick you up at twelve. We'll have lunch somewhere, then go for a drive."

"Great! And maybe," Bea laughed, "you'll get to eat some of the lunch."

"I talk too much," he admitted, looking down at his barely touched dinner.

"No, you don't," she disagreed. "I'll expect to hear lots more Sunday."

In the small screening room sat Ludie Meyers, Gregory Robinson, Hero, Ike Allborn, and Hank. They sat apart from each other, something Hank had never been able to understand. Always, when viewing dailies, or a test, they ended up talking to each other over the backs of their seats or across the room.

Ludie instructed the projectionist to run the film, and the five men sat back to watch. When the brief clip ended, Ludie explained angrily, "She looks terrible! This isn't the same girl I saw today! What *happened?*"

"She has wonderful eyes," Ike Allborn, the cameraman, said quietly, as if to himself.

"A good smile," Hero contributed, dismayed nevertheless by the test.

"What are we *doing?*" Ludie wailed. "We spend all this money to sign her, bring her here, and we get *this?* I feel sick. *Who* did I *see* today?"

Greg remained silent.

"I'll be *bankrupt!*" Ludie moaned. "Who *did* this to me?"

"She's a marvelous dancer," Hero defended her. "She's got excellent ideas for the dance numbers."

"Listen, Mr. Meyers," Ike put in. "With the right lighting and decent make-up, she'll be better than all right. We're just going to have to light her carefully, make sure we point up her eyes. The way I see it, I'll shoot all her scenes slightly up-from-under, focus on her eyes. She'll look terrific."

"*This* you can make terrific?" Ludie looked over at Ike in disbelief. "*This?*" His hand pointed wildly at the screen.

"She's got everything going for her," Hank chimed in, wondering why Greg was keeping out of the discussion. "Listen to her voice. She's got a lovely speaking voice, plus she sings up a storm, plus you've never seen a dancer like her. Who can tell anything from a five-minute piece of film with no lighting, lousy make-up, and nothing for her to do? Maybe we should have another look at the test and think about her good points. I'm convinced that audiences'll love her."

Wearily, Ludie said, "I'll look again. Maybe there'll be a miracle."

The projectionist rewound the film, and this time Hank kept up a running narrative. "Hear that voice?" he said. "It's got a nice, husky depth to it. And look at that smile, those eyes! God, will you look at those eyes! We do something with her hair, the make-up, and she'll walk away with the picture, I'm telling you. Look at her!" he insisted. "She looks *real*. And not only does she sing and dance, she can act, too."

"And how do you know that?" Greg spoke for the first time, addressing himself to Hank.

"I know it. She can."

"I think you're dreaming," Greg drawled, lighting a cigarette. "So what if she can sing and dance, who's gonna believe anybody could fall in love with that face?"

110

"Everybody!" Hank was getting angry. It was clear Greg was less then enthusiastic about working with Bea. "I'm telling you, Mr. Meyers," his voice rose fractionally, "you're looking at someone who's going to generate more money for this studio than you ever dreamed of. People stood up and cheered for this girl on Broadway. What she can do to an audience has to be seen to be believed. It's time we went out with a different face, a different look. You're always complaining that everyone comes out of make-up looking like Bennett. Well, here's our chance to change the trend, set a new one. Let the girl keep her eyebrows and her hair. Let's work with what she does have: great eyes, a lovely smile, and more talent than most of the women in Hollywood combined."

"What do we think about this?" Ludie asked the room, impressed by Hank's impassioned declaration of faith in the kid.

"I'm with Hank," Ike said. "She's got something. I like her."

"Me, too," said Hero.

"She'll be box-office poison," Greg said flatly, turning the cigarette between his fingers. "All the make-up and clever lighting in the world isn't going to turn a skinny kid with a big nose into a star. I vote no."

Ludie sat back to think. Hank held his breath as, after a minute, Ludie began giving voice to his thoughts. "What're our choices?" he asked rhetorically. "We could bring in Powell, but she's too old for the part. We don't have time to go on a talent hunt for another kid, not when we haven't settled yet on the juvenile. Hero, you like her. I trust you when it comes to that. Ike, you know what's what. You say you can make her look good, I gotta believe you. And Hank, you, I think, you're maybe in love. Years now with the memos, the notes, not once did I ever see you excited like this. What worries me is Greg; you don't like her you won't work so good with her, we wind up with a crummy picture, and I'm out of business. I don't know."

Greg put out his cigarette and turned in his seat to look at Ludie. "What're you saying exactly?" he asked.

"What I'm saying is you don't like this kid. These guys," Ludie jerked his thumb at Ike, Hank, and Hero, "wanna put their money on her. Me, I liked her myself, I gotta say. So a choice gets made. And what I think, I think we go with the kid. We go with the kid, it means we move Hank in to direct, swing you over to *Time Enough*, which you wanna do anyway." He paused and looked at each of the men in turn. Greg's features were frozen with surprise. He'd fully expected Ludie to get rid of the girl and allow Greg to select an ingenue of his own choosing. He knew just the girl and had been planning all along to bring her in as a replacement. Hank had to work hard not to reveal his sudden jubilation. Ike merely nodded. And Hero

111

smiled. "Yeah!" Ludie went on, his mind set now. "Greg moves out to *Time Enough*, and Hank you step in." He clapped his hands together and stood up. "Yeah!" he said again. "This, I think, is good. But you," he pointed to Hank, "you better deliver me a movie star and a hit picture, or you'll be doing props on oaters for the rest of your life. Same goes for you!" he threw at Hero and Ike. "Me, I should have my head read. A month from now, I'll probably be on the street. *Feh!*" He left the screening room and the four dazed men.

"You guys finished in there?" the projectionist asked over the intercom.

"We're finished," Hero told him, then looked at the others. "I guess that's that," he said, keeping his voice uninflected.

"Suits me fine!" Greg declared. "It's your ass, Donovan. If you want my opinion, you've pitched for that kid and probably put an end to your career. Which is no great loss. See you guys around."

The minute the door closed, Ike muttered, "Asshole," and gave the other two a rare smile. "My money's on you and the kid," he told Hank. "See you tomorrow."

After Ike left, Hero and Hank stared at each other for a moment, then burst out laughing and pounded each other on the back. "He *gave* it to you!" Hero crowed. "The last thing I thought he'd do, and he did it."

"I've been waiting so long for this chance," Hank said almost tearfully. "Bea's going to do it for all of us. I knew the minute I saw her she was going to be important to me. Do you *realize* what this means? We make a go of this one, we'll be able to do more. We'll have our own damned *unit*, with you and me, Ike and Clark. We could make *terrific* pictures!"

"Don't get ahead of yourself," Hero cautioned. "Let's get this one made first."

"Hell! Let's go celebrate! I feel as if my career's finally beginning."

Twelve

"THIS is Grauman's Egyptian Theater," Hank told them. "As you can see, it's meant to resemble an Egyptian temple." He walked ahead of them, stopped, and turned. "I will now do the official tour-guide spiel." He cleared his throat, then began. "The deep forecourt," he intoned, "is enclosed on each side by high walls. Kindly notice the spotlights placed on the top of the walls. They are there to illuminate the illustrious during premieres and the like. Also, please note the pillars supporting the portico. All very tasteful and in keeping with the general motif. Inside, which unfortunately we haven't time for today, there are ornate murals and more artifacts of the era. The theater was named and designed to coincide with the discovery of King Tutankhamen's tomb, and the auditorium has carved columns and sphinxes flanking the stage. I happen, off the record, to be nutty about this place, but I'll allow you to make your own decisions. If you're ready, we'll move along."

"This is fun," Lucy said happily, as they headed in the car to the Chinese Theater.

"How do you *know* so much?" Bea asked.

"I love this town," he said simply. "And I've also got one of those memories. I remember absolutely everything. I could tell you about things that happened thirty years ago, right down to what everyone wore and what they ate."

"Come on!" Lucy scoffed. *"Thirty* years? How old are you anyhow?"

"Okay, Twenty years. I'm thirty-five, almost."

"You talk like you're sixty-seven."

"Sorry. I'll try to talk younger."

Lucy gave him an open-handed whack on the shoulder, then said, "Well, go on!"

113

"Do you realize I've been saving up all this information for years? I'm deadly serious. This is my first chance to show the town to total newcomers. Indulge me. Here we are!" he announced. "Everybody out!

"Okay, this theater was intended to be a museum as well as a movie house. Obviously, it's built in the shape of a pagoda. Inside, there are imported bells, more pagodas, Fu dogs, and all kinds of rare artifacts. Below our feet, if you'll be good enough to direct your eyes down, you'll see that a fair number of celebrities have put their hand- and foot-prints in the cement. This silly business started because Sid Grauman walked across the forecourt one day and was confronted by his chief cement mason, Jean Klossner, who raised hell with him for walking in the freshly laid cement. Well, Sid looked at what he'd done, and the proverbial light bulb went on in his head. He went at once to call Douglas Fairbanks, Mary Pickford, and Norma Talmadge to come over and put *their* footprints in the new curbstone. Too bad for Sid, the cement was nearly dry and the impressions were too faint. Not to be put off a good idea, three weeks before completion of the construction, Sid had Pickford and Fairbanks come back and, this time, in a formal ceremony, they placed their hand- and foot-prints in the center of the forecourt here. A few days after that, Talmadge came back, too. She, tricky devil, added the date of the official opening, May 18, 1927, which was several days *after* she actually made the impressions.

"The interior has a magnificently carved ceiling, more murals, lovely plush carpeting, and more ornate columns. As I said, I prefer the Egyptian. Our next stop will be the wonderful Pantages Theater which is, by far, the grandest of them all. It has a vaulted lobby which is the biggest in Los Angeles, flanked by twin stairways. Over the whole thing is a very modern, very original ceiling done in shades of gold and henna. It also has the largest stage in town, seventy feet wide by one hundred and eighty feet long."

After they'd finished the theaters, he drove along Hollywood Boulevard, telling them about the Santa Claus Lane Parade. "The parade's held here every year, and since it started back in '24, it's been getting bigger and bigger. Last year, they lined the street with metal Christmas trees that were each sixteen feet high, weighed seven hundred and fifty pounds, and contained a hundred and sixty lights. They've got *big* plans for this year, and if you're both very good girls, I'll bring you to see it. There's going to be bands, and movie stars, equestrian teams, and a Santa Claus float. Oh yes, and during the Christmas season, Hollywood Boulevard is known as Santa Claus Lane."

114

"Seven-hundred-and-fifty-pound *metal* Christmas trees?" Bea made a face. "Are you making this up?"

"Scout's honor. You wait, you'll see. They've got real ones, too, but nothing like you're used to in New York, We're going for a little ride now, so I can show you the 'Hollywoodland' sign and do my best party piece."

"I thought that was there to let everybody know this is Hollywood," Lucy said.

"Quite wrong, I'm afraid. Movie people have nothing on the land promoters here. I hope you're prepared to be stunned by the depths and breadth of my knowledge. That sign, my good ladies, was built in 1924 at a cost of twenty-one thousand dollars. It was erected by Harry Chandler, who was one of the builders of the Hollywoodland sub-division, to attract attention to the home sites they were hawking on five hundred acres of property here. The letters are each fifty feet high, and they sit on the side of Mount Cahuenga. Out here, *that's* considered a mountain. Oh, well.

"Each letter is thirty feet wide and composed of three-foot by nine-foot sheet-metal panels painted white and attached to a framework of pipes, wires, scaffolding, and telephone poles, all dragged up that hillside by caterpillar tractors and a lot of sweating laborers. The sign has four thousand twenty-watt light bulbs, placed eight inches apart around the perimeter of every letter. The burned-out bulbs are re-placed by Mr. Albert Kothe. In September last year, Lillian Millicent Entwhistle climbed up to the top of the letter H and jumped to her death."

"My God!" Lucy said. "That's terrible."

"Yeah," Hank said softly. "I wasn't making light of it. It was tragic. Anyway, there you are. Quite something, isn't it?"

"How do you know the name of the man who changes the light bulbs?" Bea challenged him.

"Simple. I asked him," Hank answered. "We'll go back through town now, and I'll tell you practical and impractical bits of informa-tion. We have to go that way to get to the house I want to show you. Okay?"

"Sure," Lucy and Bea chorused.

"I should've told you to bring notebooks," he quipped.

"Don't worry," Bea said. "I've got a pretty good memory myself, although it doesn't go back thirty years."

"All right. We'll have a little quiz first thing Monday morning. Here goes: If you want to get your hair done and ogle the celebs while you're at it, Weaver-Jackson's is extremely popular. Same thing goes

115

for household furnishings: shop at Barker Brothers. Jewels, my dears, only from Stromberg's. When you reach the point where you don't care what anything costs, order your groceries from Young's, either the Hollywood store or their Beverly Hills branch. Clothes you get at I. Magnin's or Bess Schlank. Your imported cigarettes you get from Max Lickter. And your flowers, naturally, from the House of Flowers. Coming down a notch or two, you can buy your footwear either at Wetherby-Kayser or at Innes. If you need the police, call the Hollywood Division. Now, restaurants. The absolute, A-number-one most superb food on earth is at Musso-Franks Grill. You go there when you've been out on location in the desert for six weeks, and all you've thought about day and night is delectable tidbits served by staff who want you to be *happy*. The Brown Derby you've already seen. So much for telephones at your tables and having yourself paged. For your informal meals there's the Pig'N Whistle, and Henry's Delicatessen, and the in place for lunch is the MGM commissary, but I'm afraid they won't let you girls in. Unless, of course, you make friends with some of the contract players over there. Where was I? Nightlife. There's the Cocoanut Grove at the Ambassador Hotel on Wilshire, the Hollywood Roof Ballroom on Vine, or the Armstrong-Carlton on Hollywood. If you're suddenly taken ill, get over to Hollywood Hospital. And if you have to drive along this street, watch out for the goddamned trolley cars!" He hit the brakes, stopping inches from the back of a trolley, and apologized. "I'd better stop showing off and start paying attention to what I'm doing here, or we'll *all* wind up in Hollywood Hospital. Oh, Jeez. I forgot to tell you about Bullock's Wilshire, which is a swell department store. And the newspapers. You do want to know which papers to buy, don't you?"

"Of course, we do," Bea said with a laugh.

"Humor me," he said, delighted by her laughter. "I'm almost finished. There's the *Daily Graphic*, the *Examiner*, the *Citizen News*; there's the *Hollywood Reporter* created by Billy Wilkerson who's an amazing guy; there's *Variety*, and *Daily Variety*, and, of course, six or seven dozen fanzines. And that, patient ladies, is it for today. Now I'll take you to see the house. Oh, and by the way, Greg Robinson's been given the old heave-ho, and I'll be directing *Upside Down*."

"*Hank!*" Bea cried. "That's fantastic! When did this happen? Why didn't you *say* anything?"

"Ludie decided Friday night. And I was saving it, sort of like dessert. You think you'll like working with me?"

"I think I'll *love* it! I was worried sick about Mr. Robinson. I could tell he didn't like me."

"Well, stop worrying. *I* like you fine."

116

Part One / 1917–1936

They rented the little house in North Hollywood and then, pooling their money, bought a Chrysler roadster that Lucy fell in love with on sight. It was black and yellow, with a convertible top and a sleek running board, at the front of which, on the driver's side, was mounted the spare tire.

"You need a car to get around," Hank said, approving the purchase, "and this is a honey."

The money they had to lay out for deposits on both the house and the car, as well as for Bea's new evening clothes, seriously reduced the balances in both their savings accounts. It bothered Bea, but she didn't want to take an advance on her salary. She had the feeling it would be too much like starting out in debt to the studio. Still, studying the new balance in her account, she promised herself she'd start adding back to her savings as soon as her money began coming in from the studio.

They moved into the house one week after they arrived in town, and Bea hung away her clothes, then stood staring at her several new gowns.

"They're so pretty," Lucy said from the doorway. "From the sound of it you're going to be out every night. I think I'm jealous."

"Don't be. I told them today I won't go without my chaperone."

"Your what?"

"Lucy, they think I'm twenty-one. I keep getting mixed up and saying I'm twenty, then saying no, I'm twenty-one. But they think I've been going out on dates for *years*. I had to make up this whole story about how I never had time or the opportunity in New York because I worked every night but Sunday. You've got to go with me. And they loved the chaperone idea."

"But I don't have the right clothes..." Lucy began.

"We'll have to get you some. Please do this for me, Luce. At least you know what to expect on a date and, with you along, nobody's going to do anything funny."

"I guess you're right. I wasn't thinking."

"I had *no idea* this was going to be so *crazy*. We just got started working out one of the routines this morning, me and Hero and Clark, when two of the boys came rushing in to say I had to be over on the other side of the lot to do another stills session. That meant I had to go to make-up first. This time they didn't throw five pounds of goop on my face, but they still took forever, and I came out looking like someone I've never seen before. Then, after that, I had to get cleaned up and get back to the rehearsal stage only to have Hank tell me

they'd like me to test tomorrow with a fella they want for the juvenile
lead."

"Who is it, d'you know?"

"Dickie something. I never heard of him. The thing is, we rehearsed
for a total of maybe an hour. Lucy, if this is the way they work here,
I think I'd rather be back in New York."

"Just think of it. Slush in the gutters, freezing winds. You're right.
We'd both be better off in New York." Lucy walked over and tugged
at Bea's hand. "I've got an idea. Let's go to the movies. It's your last
free night before you start going out on the town. What d'you say?"

"I'd *love* it."

The only thing that was familiar, and into which she fell gladly,
was working with Hero and Clark Boland in the rehearsal sound
stage. The three of them plotted every step, discarding ideas that
wouldn't work, accumulating ones that did. Clark patiently went over
and over eight-bar blocks, sitting swiveled to one side in order to
keep his eye on the evolving routine.

The first of the numbers, a song called "Heavenly," was fairly bal-
letic, to be done in soft shoes, and included solo segments from both
partners, as well as a climactic paired segment with lifts and a synchronized run up a staircase.

"On the big production numbers," Hero told her during one of the
breaks, "we'll shoot in pieces, from different angles. Hank and I are
working on the set-ups now. But for this number, we'll concentrate
on one take."

"That means we only have to do it once?" she asked, flexing her
arms and legs so her muscles wouldn't cramp.

Both Clark and Hero laughed. "It means we only have to do it once,
maybe eight or ten or fifteen times, depending on whether we get
lucky and don't have to cut halfway through. It ain't easy," Hero said
good-naturedly. "But you'll be happy with the end product. Once
you've seen the first dailies, you'll have a better idea what I'm talking
about."

"That's the film you've shot that day?"

"Right. We take a look every evening at what we've shot, make
sure we're getting what we want, in the way we want it. Then, next
morning, we do some more. By the end of the shooting, we've covered
every conceivable angle, with medium shots, close-ups, reaction shots,
the whole works. Then we cut out the stuff we don't want, keep the
stuff we do, edit it all together, and you've almost got a picture. A
few other things like orchestrations and dubbing, maybe some loop-

ing, come into it, but that's later on, after we've got all the principal photography and a rough cut. You should be talking to Hank. He's the guy who knows it all from A to Z."

"He knows *everything* from A to Z," Bea agreed. "When do we do the test with the new juvenile?"

"Couple of hours. He's all set, though. You two'll do the test, then I'll bring him up on the choreography while you're doing your wardrobe and make-up tests. By the time everything's organized, you'll both know the routines and can start rehearsing together."

"D'you ever sleep?" she asked with a smile.

"Hardly ever. Wait till we've got the whole chorus *and* the principals in here. Then you'll find out I'm not really a choreographer but a drill instructor. That's what Busby was, you know."

"No, I didn't know." She sat back, recognizing the signs. Like Hank, Hero also knew a great deal and had, several times, rattled off stories about people and their histories that fascinated her. "Come on," she coaxed. "Tell me about it."

"Busby went to a military academy as a kid and, during the war, while he was in the army, he conducted parade drills. The regulation routines bored the pants off him, so he started working out trick drills where he had twelve hundred guys all marching in different patterns at the same time. After the war, he tried acting, at the same time scrambling for work producing or directing. Cantor saw him choreographing *Fine and Dandy* and got Goldwyn to bring him out here. The rest is becoming history even as we speak. Okay! Let's try the next eight, before we lose you to Hank and the boys."

Hank looked at Bea and lost his temper. Taking her by the arm, he walked her back to make-up.

"I told you," he addressed the make-up artist, "not to do this to her!" He pulled Bea forward and pointed at her face. *"This* is precisely what I asked you *not* to do! You're off the picture! Ivy," he beckoned to a woman at the far end of the room, "take all this muck off Bea's face and redo her. She's *young.* She has wonderful eyes and a good mouth. That's what I want to see when she comes back for the test."

"Sure thing, Hank." Ivy smiled and directed Bea over to her chair.

After creaming clean Bea's face, Ivy studied her from every angle for close to five minutes. At last, she let out her breath, smiled, and said, "We'll just tweeze a little under your eyebrows to raise them a bit, make your eyes look even bigger. Your eyelashes are nice and long, so we won't bother with false ones. Some shading across the bridge of your nose and the tip to bring it down a little, and we'll fill out your lower lip a bit. What worries me," she said, coming around to the front of the chair to look at Bea directly, "is the weight of your hair. With it pulled back, it's too severe. There's just too much of it, and you need some softness to take attention away from the prominence of your nose. How about if we get Phil next door to cut it just to your shoulders?"

"How would I wear it?"

"We'll get him to give you a nice, long bob, fluff it up a bit, part it on the side. Here, let me give you an idea what I'm talking about." She pulled the pins from Bea's hair, then draped it so that a natural parting occurred on the left side. "How would you feel about that?"

"But what if they want my hair the way it is?"

"I think Hank'll be happy, and so will you. It'll be sophisticated, but not too old a look. The only other thing I'll do is put a tiny little red dot at the inside corner of each eye. That way your eyes'll photograph darker. Well, what d'you think?"

"You're the doctor."

Ivy laughed. "Okay. Let's take you next door and get Phil to do your hair."

When Ivy brought Bea back to the set, Hank broke into a wide grin. "That's more like it! Nice work, Ivy. Okay, Bea. We'll let Ike have a look at you now, see what he wants to work out with the lighting."

Ike, too, was complimentary. "It's a swell job," he said, tilting her face this way and that. "Okay, Hank, here's what I think. The dark hair and her light skin are going to be a small problem. Dark hair absorbs light," he explained to Bea. "I think we'll aim a good strong light at her chin. That'll give us a shadow and show the definition of the cleft and the line of her jaw. Our best bet is to shoot her a hair off full face, and use a baby spot at maybe a 35- or 45-degree angle above the eyes. That'll blend in the forehead and the hair and really show off her eyes and mouth. Any close-ups, I'll come in slightly up-from-under."

"Sounds right," Hank nodded.

"I'll get the gaffer to set it up." Ike moved off.

"What's a gaffer?" Bea asked.

"Chief electrician," Hank told her. "Ike'll tell him what he wants, and the gaffer'll get the crew to shift the big Kliegl lights, the inkies, and Seniors, and baby spots until everything's set." He pointed up to the lamp rails where lights were suspended. "Once everything's tested and approved, those'll be your lights until we've finished shooting."

"Everybody has special lighting?"

"The principals do. For the production numbers, we'll use general

120

floodlighting." He led Bea over to a row of canvas director's chairs. "How it works is this: Ike and Hero and I get together and break down the script, scene by scene, deciding overall on how we want to shoot it. We've set the photographic key for the various sequences, and now we're working on the individual settings. If, for example, we're shooting a big, jolly number, we want a high key of light. If it's a mood scene—like the one with you and Dickie when he misunderstands and thinks Peaches doesn't want to go to the party with him and she winds up home alone after he storms off—we go for a lower, deeper, contrasting key. Follow that?"

"I think so. How many cameras are there going to be?"

"Oh, just one. The more cameras you use, the harder it is to light everything the way you want, because with more than one camera you've got that many more angles of light to consider. Ike's bringing in two additional cameras for the finale, for that very reason: so we can cover all the angles, and get a lot of variation to cut into the final print."

"It's so complicated," she said. "I guess I thought the actors just came out in front of the camera, did their piece, and that was it."

"It is pretty complicated," he concurred. "But it'll all make sense to you once you see how it actually works." He patted her on the arm, saying, "Relax for a few minutes, then we'll do the test."

In every free minute, Bea studied the script, learning not only her lines but most of everybody else's. Every evening she was on the arm of some young man at a party, or at the premiere of a new picture, and she kept reminding herself to smile for the inevitable cameras while relying on Lucy to put a word in at the appropriate time so they'd get home at a reasonable hour. Every morning they got up, drove to the studio, and separated to go to opposite ends of the rehearsal stage. After only a week of this routine, Bea felt worn out, but the publicity boys were insistent.

"We've got to keep you out there, get you seen a lot," Pete told her. "We'll slack off once shooting begins," he promised. "By that time, the first of the articles will be out, and the fanzines will carry us until you finish shooting."

Three times she was presented to feature writers from the magazines who came to interview her. They asked often silly questions, and she tried to give reasonably truthful and sensible answers. After each interview, time had to be taken for her to pose for the magazines' photographers because the studio didn't yet have enough hand-out stills from their in-house sessions.

121

On the first day of shooting, a car came for her at four in the morning. At five, she was in make-up; by six she was on the set, her script tucked under her arm. Hank rehearsed her and Dickie on the set, telling them the general moves he wanted them to make. Then the lights were turned on, the clapperboard marked the take, there was utter silence, and the camera started rolling.

Bea thought the scene was going well. Dickie was reacting when she spoke her lines, and he didn't appear nervous. When Hank called "CUT!" she looked around in surprise.

"Dickie," Hank said, coming on to the set. "When you do that last bit, try not to mug. It's too big. I know you're used to stage work, but for the camera you need to bring it down. And Bea, you're projecting too much. Don't worry about being heard. The sound engineer will pick everything up. Just speak normally. Okay? Let's take it again."

They did the scene seventeen times. By the time Hank was satisfied, Bea felt like a performing monkey. The lines no longer made sense. Her make-up felt caked into her pores. The dress-shields they'd sewn into her costume were saturated, and she'd lost all idea of what they were trying to do. She retreated to the sidelines to read her script again from the beginning, trying to retrieve her sense of the characters.

"We're ready for the close-ups now," the A.D. informed her. "We'll do Dickie's first. You'll be right over here. When you get the cue, just feed him the lines."

Ike wasn't happy with Dickie's key light, so there was a fifteen-minute break while the gaffer and his crew climbed up on ladders to shift several of the spots. Then they moved them again, and again. While this was going on, Bea watched Dickie, thinking he was rather unfriendly. But maybe he was just concentrating. He certainly was good-looking, in a kind of non-Latin Valentino-ish way.

Dickie's close-ups took six takes. Then it was her turn.

Sweating under the lights, she couldn't reel in her attention. Dickie was simply reading, and there was nothing for her to react to. She was afraid to stop, but Hank cut the take and came over to ask, in an undertone, "Something's wrong. What is it?"

Grateful that he'd noticed, she told him. "When we did it together, for the two-shot, I could react to his delivery. But he's not reading the same way now, so it's hard for me to get the right reaction."

"I'll talk to him." He walked away and spoke for several minutes to Dickie, then announced, "We'll do it again."

This time, Dickie put some inflection into his reading, and she was able to respond. Still, she kept expecting Hank to cut the scene, but it didn't happen. They got all the way through it; Hank said, "PRINT THAT!"; the lights shut down; and Hank came smiling over to say, "Perfect! We'll break for lunch and start again on the next set-up in an hour. Are you okay?"

She was watching Dickie leave the set, wondering about him. He didn't seem to like her. Right through her close-up, even though he'd delivered his lines with some punch, his expression had been almost angry.

"I guess so," she answered Hank. "I only wish I was more sure of what we're doing. It's hard to stay in the mood when we do a scene over so many times."

"Come along tonight and see the rushes. Then you'll have a better grasp of what's happening."

Alone in her portable, she picked at the salad sent over from the commissary and continued reading the script. This was the first day, with another twenty to follow. So far, making a picture seemed to involve a lot of sitting around and waiting, followed by doing one scene repeatedly until it was meaningless.

"Hey!" Lucy said, stepping inside. "Has it been that awful? You look very down in the mouth."

"We did the scene seventeen times. And then, we only did my close-ups twice."

"You should see the mob over on the rehearsal stage," Lucy smiled. "A hundred left-footed hoofers driving poor Hero nuts. It sure is a heck of a way to earn a living."

"Hank said I could see the dailies tonight. Or rushes, or whatever they call them."

"Can I come? I'd love to see what *you've* been doing. It couldn't be worse than what's going on over there. I've got to get back. I just wanted to know how you were doing. You'd better eat that." Lucy pointed at the tray of food. "The last thing you want is to pass out under the lights from not eating. I'll be back when we wrap up."

"Okay, Luce. Thanks for coming over."

"That's what a guardian's for. Keep your chin up, sweetheart." She gave Bea a kiss on the top of her head and went to the door. "I'm crazy about your hair that way. If nothing else, at least you got a good haircut out of the deal."

Bea laughed. "Oh! That makes it all worthwhile."

Lucy ran off, and Bea turned to look at herself in the mirror, touching her hand to the side of her hair. "All this for a haircut," she said to the mirror, then found her place in the script, picked up her fork, and started to eat.

123

Thirteen

November 12, 1933

Dear Mother,

I hope you and Gramma are well. I've been so busy I hardly have a minute to myself. We're halfway through the picture, and it's quite a job, getting up at four in the morning and not finishing sometimes until six or seven at night. By the time Lucy and I get home we're so tired it's all we can do to go over some lines and have a bite to eat before we fall into bed. Hollywood is supposed to be glamorous, but I sure haven't seen any of it, except for that couple of weeks when I had to go out every single night to get seen.

No, I'm not still angry about your writing to Jackie Ellroy. I think we should forget about it. Okay? I'm enclosing another money order for one hundred dollars, but you have to understand I'm not rich and I can't keep sending you more and more money every time you ask for it.

Jerry's coming out here to set up a west-coast office for the agency and when he gets here I'll talk to him about making arrangements to send you money automatically every month. If you know the money's coming, you should be able to work out some kind of budget or something. Okay?

There's going to be a story about me in the December *Modern Screen*, so be sure to get a copy. And don't worry about writing to me in care of the studio. I get my letters right away. Take care of yourself and Gramma, too.

Love
Bea

Part One / 1917–1936

November 21, 1933

Dear Bea,

Thanx a lot for the extra money. I hate to ask you you know but things are still hard here especially since your grammas home permanent now with her bad legs and busness is really fallen off at the restaurant. They already had to let one of the girls go so Im working two sections all alone its very hard on me. Thatll be good having something regular every month itll help out a lot and I sure apreciate it. Your gramma says send us a picture so we know what you look like these days its been such a long time since we saw you. Maybe one of these times well come out for a visit and meet some of those famous movie stars your living among nowadays. It must be a real thrill to work with Glenda Farrell and Jack Oakie maybe you could get theyr autographs. Were waiting to read the article that ought to be really something my little girl in the pictures. Whens the movie going to be in the theaters? Let us know so well be sure to go see it. My friend Harry loves the movies and hes dying to take us to see yours. You be a good girl and be sure to do what they tell you.

Love from me and Gramma,
Lil

Hank had been right, up to a point, in suggesting that seeing the dailies would enhance her understanding of the work they were doing each day. But she learned more from listening to him discuss the set-ups with Ike and Hero and from watching from the sidelines. It was an incredibly slow process, yet as she watched Farrell and Oakie do their scenes, taking note of how they knew not to get beyond their lights, how they always hit their marks, and how they delivered back and forth to each other, it all began to make sense.

Seeing herself on the screen was hateful and demoralizing. She was unrecognizable to her own eyes, but everyone said they were very pleased with her, so she had to accept that this was the truth. Slouched low in her seat in the screening room, she tried to connect the smiling, large-eyed girl on the screen to the person she knew herself to be. The connection was a slim one. She had to keep reminding herself that not only was she playing a part, but she was also cleverly disguised to do it. This was make-believe being played for real, with the view in mind to making a lot of money for the studio. The movie, she thought, probably would do well at the box office. The songs were catchy, and the orchestrations Clark Boland had done were

125

first-rate. Hero's choreography was inventive and far more than the parade-ground drill he laughingly called it. And her two numbers with Dickie were very good, if she said so herself. As she watched them on the screen, she forgot about the twenty-eight times they'd had to do "Heavenly" before Hank and Hero were satisfied, because all the takes had been worth it. It flowed from start to finish and was a complete little story in itself. What struck her funny, though, was how, at certain angles, it looked as if she were dancing with Bobby. Maybe that was only because she'd pretended it was Bobby; she'd thought about him through every one of the twenty-eight takes; she'd thought of him in every scene she'd done with Dickie.

Even so, she couldn't enjoy the sight of herself on the screen. Things she did that Hank and Hero approved made her shrink inside. She looked thin and sounded terrible, her voice gravelly and her accent peculiar. But in spite of all this, there was something fascinating about seeing herself, utterly transformed and far larger than life. She wanted to watch, yet she didn't; there were aspects of her film character she quite liked, and others that made her want to run somewhere and hide. Overriding her personal reactions was her mounting enchantment with the process and with the results it produced. And in order to prevent her personal feelings from getting in the way, she stopped going to see the dailies.

It was a good decision. Her work before the camera at once became easier. She lost the self-consciousness those fragments of film she'd seen had induced in her, so she was able to forget about herself and get on with being Peaches.

When the filming ended, there was a party on the sound stage for the cast and crew. Gifts were exchanged; all previous constraints were gone; everyone let go, and the party was a laughing, noisy success. People danced, and overate, and drank too much. It was just like a closing-night party on Broadway.

She sat on the sidelines with a plate of food balanced on her knees, watching Lucy dance with half a dozen different fellows, one after another. And as she watched, she realized that Lucy loved it here and would be in no hurry to go back to New York.

"Why aren't you joining in the fun?" Hank asked, pulling a chair over beside hers.

"I'd rather watch. I just now realized how much Lucy likes it here."

They both turned to look over to where Lucy was dancing with one of the men from the chorus. She was laughing, her head thrown back, and appeared to be having the time of her life.

"That bothers you?" Hank asked, striking a match on the underside of his shoe and then lighting a cigarette.

126

"It doesn't bother me. I'm just . . . surprised."

"Why? Because you thought she'd feel the way you do?"

She shifted around to look full at him. "Why d'you say that?"

"I think half of you would love to hop the next train back to New York, and the other half would like to start a new picture first thing in the morning."

She smiled at the rightness of his observation. "You always seem to know what I'm thinking, Henry. Why is that?"

"Who knows? Maybe I'm good at guessing games."

"You think I should stay, don't you?"

Choosing his words with care, he said, "I think you could have an important career here. Oh, I know you don't get the same charge out of it you do working in front of a live audience. Here, everything gets broken down into small pieces, and a lot of the time it's close to impossible to make sense of the pieces. But when you see the final cut it's bound to hit you that there are things you can do here you could never do anywhere else."

"Such as?"

"Well, for one thing, this is permanent. You'll never be any older than you are on the celluloid. It's proof for all time of who you are and what you can do. Fifty or a hundred years from now people will look at *Upside Down* and meet Beatrice Crane for the first time. That's a kind of immortality, Bea. For another thing, being purely selfish, I'd like you to stay so we can make more pictures together. And third, once Ludie sees the rough cut—never mind the final cut—he's going to pick up your option. Maybe he'll want to tie you to a long-term contract."

"But what if I don't want to do that?"

"It's his option, not yours. He'll get on to your agent, and the two of them will come up with a new deal."

"That makes me sound like nothing more than words on paper, like a piece of furniture or something."

"It's the way the studios operate. Sure, you're tied down in some areas and told what to do and how to do it. But on the plus side, you've got an entire organization behind you, to protect you if you need it and to reward you with plenty of money. And, admit it, Bea. You've got the bug. You like all this. Not very long ago you had no idea how movies got made. Now you not only know how they're made, you're actually in one."

"I hate seeing myself on the screen."

"You'll get over that. By the time you've got a couple more pictures under your belt you'll be able to look at yourself and see objectively what's good or bad about what you've created. You've got so much going for you—exceptionally good concentration and a memory that's almost as good as mine." He gave her a smile. "You've taught yourself in just a few weeks how to find your mood and sustain it, for days, if you have to. But what's more important is that when you're on the screen nobody looks at anyone else. And d'you know what that is?"

"What?"

"It's star quality. And you've got it. Not only do you have it, but you're talented, too. It's a killer combination. There's no end of beautiful faces—men and women who look so good on the screen it hurts. But there's not more than a handful who compel the eye *and* who back it up with honest-to-god talent. If you don't stay, you'll spend the rest of your life wondering what it might've been like if you'd stuck with it."

"Every time you say things like that, I feel as if you're talking about somebody else. You always talk to me as if you believe there's not a single thing you could say that I wouldn't understand." She stopped for a moment to look again at Lucy who was dancing now with Ike Allborn.

"You're one of the least stupid people I've ever encountered."

"If I tell you something, will you promise not to tell anyone?"

He put his hand on her arm. "Don't you know yet you could tell me *anything* and I'd go to my grave with it?" He gave her another smile, adding playfully, "You tell me your secret, and I'll tell you mine."

"I'm not twenty," she whispered against his ear. "I'm only sixteen." She sat back, looking at him, waiting for his reaction.

"I kind of guessed that, I'm afraid."

"You did?"

"I don't think most folks will even question it, but I had to read the program notes twice when I saw you on Broadway, to make sure I hadn't read them wrong."

"Gosh!" She glanced around to make sure they weren't being overheard.

"Don't worry, Bea," he reassured her. "As far as everyone else is concerned, you're twenty, and no questions asked. You look it on film, and you look it in the publicity stills. I know how hard it is at sixteen to decide on things that'll affect the rest of your life, but you've got a damned good head on your shoulders. And you trust me, don't you?"

"Absolutely! I've liked you right from the start."

"Well, the same goes for me. You're very special to me, Beatrice Crane. I care an awful lot about you, and I want the best for you, in

128

every way. You have my promise that I'll never steer you wrong. If
you do decide to stay, I'll look out for you. And for Lucy, too. Nothing
would make me happier. Would you like me to teach you how to
swim?" he asked with sudden brightness.

"Sure I would." She blinked, confused by the abrupt turn of direction.

"When we've finished the editing and I have some free time, we'll
go to the beach, and I'll teach you. Okay?"

"Well, sure."

"I've taught quite a few people," he said, his eyes moving away
from her. "I was big on sports at school. Football, ice hockey, swimming. I even gave some thought to playing professional baseball at
one time. But a rumor got started, so I went back home to Frisco. I'd
been living in the east for a while, after I graduated from college in
'21. I went to Yale," he explained. "I didn't know what I wanted to
do back then, so I took a degree in fine arts." He shook himself
impatiently. "I'm digressing." He turned back to her. "There was
someone I cared for very much," he told her in an undertone. "We
had all kinds of plans. Everything blew up in our faces."

"Why? What happened?" she asked, her tone matching his.

"He confided in his brother. His brother told the rest of the family,
and that was that."

He gazed at her, waiting.

As his words connected in her brain, she looked into his eyes and
saw a pain there that seemed, all at once, to become her own. She
felt hurt for him, and immediately protective of him, and took hold
of his hand. "What happened after that?" she asked.

"I bummed around for a couple of years, doing this and that. Then
I landed the job on *Greed* and finally knew what I wanted to do. So,
when it finished, I came along down here."

"Did you ever see him again?"

"Nope."

"Would you want to?"

"Not any more. For a while there, he was all I could think about.
But I got over it. And then I met someone else. We have to be very
careful, you know; but we get along well; we're interested in the same
things. It's been a couple of years now."

"That's good. I'm glad." Her grip on his hand tightened.

"You're the only girl I've ever really cared about, Bea. There isn't
anything I wouldn't do for you, but I thought it only fair to let you
know how things are with me."

"I'd never tell anyone," she promised fervently.

"I know you wouldn't."

"I'll tell you another secret: I'm illegitimate. So now we both know about each other."

He leaned forward and kissed her on the cheek. "I *know* you," he said quietly. "From the minute you walked out on that stage in New York, I knew who you were and the way you'd be. And maybe that's why, sometimes, I seem to know what you're thinking. You make sense to me in ways most other people don't."

"You do to me, too." She took a deep breath. "I feel so much better, don't you?"

"Yeah, I do. You're not put off, are you?"

"No!" she said strongly. "Why would I be? What's important is that people care about each other. It isn't really important who those other people are. Is it?"

"I don't think so, but then I'm not the one who makes up the rules."

"Well those people who make up the rules can just go to blazes! You're my friend, and you always will be."

"You're a peach."

"I'm a tired peach. D'you think maybe you could drive me home? It looks like Lucy's set to dance all night, and I'd really like to get some sleep."

"Sure thing," he said readily. "Let me do a couple of quick things, then I'll be back to take you home."

He got up and walked into the crowd. Bea's eyes followed him, and she watched with interest and approval when he stopped to talk briefly with Hero. Hero smiled and nodded, then Hank moved, signaling to Lucy, calling to her that he was taking Bea home. Lucy grinned and waved, then looked around for Bea, saw her, and called out, "I'll see you later."

Bea smiled and waved back, then stood up as Hank returned.

After waiting to make sure Bea got safely inside the house, Hank drove toward home, thinking of how she'd reacted to what he'd told her. Maybe she'd responded as she had because she was only sixteen and didn't fully comprehend the implications of his story, or maybe she was the rare, innately sensitive girl he believed her to be. Whichever was true, she'd given him something that no one else in his lifetime had: a viewing, from an entirely new perspective, of himself as someone of value simply by dint of his ability to care. She hadn't recoiled from him, hadn't displayed the slightest hint of disgust. She'd

130

accepted him at face value, and still claimed to like him. It was a gift of such enormous proportions and it moved him so utterly, that he had to pull the car over to the side of the road where he sat for close to an hour, examining from every angle the completeness and perfection of his love for her.

Certainly there were other people he loved—Hero, for one, and his late mother, for another—but he'd never felt for anyone what he did for Bea. Just imagining any harm coming to her made everything inside him seize up, caused his hands to tremble and his jaw to clench. He loved her. Even if she decided to return to New York, and he never set eyes on her again, he'd love her. Oh, he could readily envision how certain people might react were he to confess his feelings for her! He could hear the laughter, the snide comments about a thirty-four-year-old homosexual falling in love with a sixteen-year-old actress. None of it mattered. He couldn't concern himself with the reactions of others to what felt as if it might be the single best thing he'd ever do in his lifetime. To be allowed to love Bea, in his fashion, gave his life new scope, new dimensions. And nothing would be permitted to interfere with his devotion to her.

At last, he wiped his face with his handkerchief, started up the car, and drove home.

Bea awakened to the sound of the front door opening. She heard Lucy whispering, and two pairs of feet tiptoeing through the living room. There was a sudden, quickly stifled burst of Lucy's laughter, followed by silence. The door to her room opened, then closed. Another silence and then, through the too-thin wall separating their bedrooms, Bea recognized sounds she'd heard before and knew all too well.

She pulled on her robe and went out to the kitchen. In the moonlight, she read the time on the wall clock. Three-forty. She looked around the shadowy room, then cautiously opened the back door and stepped out. The grass was wet under her bare feet; the air smelled of dormant flowers and tasted faintly of salt. Her hands in the pockets of her robe, her back to the house, she walked slowly across the lawn to the grouping of furniture at the bottom of the property.

The cushions on the chaise were damp to the touch, but the air was soft, the night mild. She stretched out and lay staring up at the improbable moon, with its odd markings and its deeper-than-usual yellow. Glancing over at the house, she saw the lights were off in

Lucy's room. The only sound was of a light breeze as it combed through the leaves of the half-dozen trees surrounding the house, and a kind of low whistling in the grass. She looked again at the moon and wondered where Bobby might be at that moment. Probably out on the town. Or perhaps asleep. She smiled to herself, picturing him asleep, with his arms and legs awkwardly outflung, his face pushed into the pillow, and his sandy hair poking in jagged points from his burrowing into the pillow. Occasionally she'd got up in the night to go to the bathroom and had stopped in the living room to look at him, asleep on the sofa. When he slept, he looked like a discarded toy. Thinking of him now, she experienced a sudden, wrenching pain and drew her knees up to her chest, then wound her arms tightly around them.

She might have been the only person on earth, out in the darkness on a damp chaise, gazing at the moon with only the all-but-silent rising and falling of the leaves and the faintly whistling grass. She wished she were older, or not alone, and tried not to think about what she knew Lucy was doing over there in the dark, with someone she'd brought home from the party. But for a few minutes she could think of nothing else, seeing Lucy naked with some faceless man, doing what Lil had done those nights when she'd brought fellows home with her.

Even though Lucy had admitted to previous experiences, still Bea somehow had never connected the present-tense Lucy she knew with a grown woman who actually did that sort of thing. It was what Bobby had wanted to do, and she had no better idea now why anyone would want to do that than she'd had before. It seemed ridiculous. Yet obviously everybody thought it important. Maybe there was something wrong with her; maybe, she thought, she should've been eager to make love with someone, Bobby, someone. But she wasn't eager. The idea of it actually made her feel squeamish.

When she awakened with a start some time later, it was to the sound of a car accelerating away from the house. The light was on in Lucy's room and, as Bea watched, the kitchen lit up and Lucy was there, filling the coffee pot at the sink. Watching Lucy was like being in the screening room; it was a movie. Lucy got the coffee started, then left the kitchen. The bathroom window glowed yellow, then, after a few minutes, went dark, and Lucy reappeared in the kitchen. She got down some cups, went to the icebox for cream, put things on a tray. Not much of a movie, Bea decided, yawning, as she looked up at the moon to see clouds, like thin smoke, drifting across its face.

"I wondered where you were," Lucy said, setting the tray with the

132

coffee down on the table near the chaise. "Did I wake you up before?"

"No," Bea lied. "I couldn't sleep, so I came out here."

"I brought you some coffee." She sat down beside Bea on the chaise. "Everything all right?"

"I'm okay."

"Poor Bea. We did wake you up, didn't we?"

"Honestly, you didn't. Who were you with?"

"Ike. I got a little pixilated. Heck! Everybody did. It was a swell party. Are you upset?"

"Oh, no. Why would I be?"

Lucy's hand curved against Bea's cheek. "You're such a sweet kid," she said softly. "I wouldn't want you to get any wrong impressions. I mean, it's not the kind of thing I usually do."

"I know that, Luce."

"Every once in a while, nature gets in the way. I'd hate you to think I was some kind of floozy."

"You could never be that. My *mother* was a floozy. You're not that dumb. If you had a good time, I'm glad. You like him, Ike?"

"Uh-huh."

Bea sat up and picked up one of the cups to hand it to Lucy, then took the other for herself. "This tastes wonderful. D'you ever notice how things almost always taste better out of doors?"

"Can't say I've ever given it much thought."

"Lucy?" Bea kept her eyes on her cup.

"What, sweetheart?"

"How does it make you feel?"

"Excited, I guess. And a little crazy."

"But good?"

"But good, uh-huh."

"Hank thinks I should stay on."

"So do I. You know that. But it's up to you to decide."

"I guess I'll get used to it here. You don't suppose Jerry will be bringing Bobby with him, do you?"

"I don't know. You could ask him."

Bea thought about that. "No, I couldn't."

"No," Lucy agreed, "I guess you couldn't."

"I'm lonely for him, Luce. I'm lonely altogether."

"It'll go away."

"Will it?" Bea's voice was so hushed it was almost lost to the night.

"You bet it will."

There was silence as they drank the coffee and breathed slowly in the gradually lifting darkness.

"Hank said he'd teach me how to swim," Bea said at last.

"Better watch out. The 'boys' get wind of it, there'll be two hundred photographers there to catch it on film."

They both laughed, then Bea said, "At least Jerry will have the latest news on what Bobby's been doing."

"What're we gonna do about you?" Lucy said, again touching Bea's cheek. "You just can't get over that boy, can you?"

"I've been trying, really hard. But I keep thinking about him."

"Maybe he's thinking about you, too."

Bea shook her head.

"Well," Lucy sighed, "we can't sit here all night guessing about it. Drink up, and let's get to bed. I'm bushed. And we don't want you coming down with a chill from sitting out here on these wet pillows."

"D'you really think he might be thinking about me?" Bea asked her.

"He could be. If it's meant to be, sweetheart, it'll be. Come on now."

Fourteen

"CRIPES! Listen to this hokum, Luce! It's enough to make you sick." She folded open the magazine, found her place, and read aloud. "'. . . it was Beatrice herself, her dark hair falling gracefully to her shoulders, her full mouth shaped into a welcoming smile.' Okay, wait a sec. It gets better. 'There was something wonderfully fresh and young and vibrant about her—at nine in the morning, no less! She was wearing an adorable short-sleeved dress of navy blue silk with white polka dots.' *Adorable*," Bea groaned. "'What is your real objective? I asked the young charmer. What have you always wanted to do? I just want to sing and dance, do the best I can do, she answered with admirable frankness.' *Young charmer*." Bea rolled her eyes. "Here's the best bit. 'People should be grateful for nice, wholesome girls like Beatrice Crane. She's not one of those types who thinks the world owes them a living. She's prepared to work, and work hard. We predict a very bright future, indeed, for the open-hearted, candid, young performer.' This is the worst crap I've ever read!"

"Oh, I don't know," Luce said, looking through her copy of *Modern Screen*. "Turn to page a hundred and seven. Now *that's* the worst thing *I've* ever read. 'She's an ex-Airedale,'" Lucy read dramatically. "'Hollywood saw that she was beautiful, but movie people work under pitiless lights, play in glaring sunshine. They called her an *Airedale* because her arms and legs betrayed superfluous hair. You'll never guess her name—for she is now one of the most perfectly groomed women in the world—thanks to X-Bazin Cream. With X-Bazin, *any* woman can be exquisitely free of hair on legs, arms and under-arms.' I think the best is the picture." Lucy decided, laughing over the photograph she showed Bea of a woman in a black bathing suit and white high-heeled shoes supposedly sitting on a beach beside an Airedale. Her arm was raised as if she were waving to someone, and there were large black X's, one under her arm, another on her leg, and one approximately where the dog's under-arm would be.

"No, no!" Bea cried. "The best one's on page ninety-one. 'He went and told his mother,'" she read. "It's killing. In the first cartoon, the lovely neighbor lady offers the little boy a rose, and he says he'll give it to his mummy 'cause she's feeling sort of blue. Then, in the next frame, the nosy little brat's eavesdropping on the lovely neighbor lady while she tells her friend that the little brat's mummy is careless about B.O. So, little brat goes home to ask Mummy, 'What's B.O.? Mrs. Allen next door says you dot dot dot.' And Mummy thinks, 'B.O. Can that be why folks are so distant with me? I'll get some Lifebuoy at once.' A week later, there's the little brat raving about Lifebuoy and Mummy's raving about how extra clean it makes you feel. And then in the last cartoon, in great big letters, it says, 'B.O. GONE dot dot dot She's, 'one of them' now!' and they're inviting her and the little brat to go to the movies. Maybe we should rush right out and buy a whole bunch of that soap, Luce, so the neighbors will invite us to go to the movies with them."

"We'd better make a shopping list," Lucy giggled. "Lifebuoy goes at the top, then the X-Bazin Cream. We really must get some Madame Berthe Ab-Scent Deodorant Stick, and some Dr. Ellis' Quick-Dry Wave Set because 'Beautiful Women know this secret,' and some De Wans Special Facial Hair Remover. And let us not forget our Ipana Tooth Paste, so we can avoid 'The dangers of Pink Tooth Brush'—a fate worse than death. What the *hell* is 'Pink Tooth Brush'? Oh, and we'd better have a few bottles of Inecto Rapid Notox so we can be the girls we used to be; *and* we'll conquer our 'nervousness' with Konjola, America's Wonder Medicine!" Lucy tossed the magazine aside and blotted her eyes with her handkerchief.

"People believe all this stuff," Bea said wonderingly, still turning pages. "I can't imagine why."

"People believe what they want to. If a company says 'Use our products and you'll wind up a movie star,' who's to say it might not happen? Would *you* want to be thought of as an *Airedale?*" She started laughing again. "*Who* thought *that one* up?"

"I think I'd prefer to be an Irish Setter, if anything. Or maybe an Afghan hound. An *Airedale?*"

The two of them lay on the floor, howling and barking. When their laughter subsided, Bea flopped over on her back, folded her arms under her head, and stared at the ceiling, asking, "D'you honestly think a story like that and a dumb photograph are going to mean anything?"

"It's not a dumb photograph. I think you look cute as a button. I'll admit the story's kind of gushy, but it couldn't hurt you any. An awful lot of people read that magazine, Bea."

"Why d'you think they've got all that stuff in there for women? All kinds of junk to take every last hair off your body, gunk to keep the only hair you're allowed to have, which is on your head, stiff as a board; medicine for nerves, stuff for your teeth. And the only things they've got for men are things like cigarettes, and Noxzema if he gets sunburned, or Griffin Allwite to keep his shoes clean. It's as if women are smelly and hairy nervous wrecks or something."

"Oh, they probably figure it's mostly women who read those magazines, so the ads are for them."

"But why ads for things that mostly have to do with making sure we don't smell? I mean, honestly. Some of the grips sure could've used Lifebuoy and Ab-Scent. How come they don't picture men using all that stuff?"

"I guess the point is that girls're supposed to look and smell good so the fellas will like us. I don't mind. I mean, you want to look and smell good, don't you?"

"Sure, I do. It's just kind of funny. You really think it's an okay story?"

"I really do."

Bea couldn't get over Jerry's pallor. He wasn't sick or anything; he just didn't have the golden suntan everybody else around seemed to have. He certainly hadn't changed, though, and ran his hands over

136

his hair after greeting her with a hug and a kiss on the cheek.

"Sit down, sit down," he urged her, returning behind his desk. "I don't know about this place." He looked out the office window, narrowing his eyes at the sun glare. "A week we've been here, already I miss the noise and the rotten weather back east. Brenda and the kids love it. We got a place with a pool. They've been in the water since the minute we got here. They'll never want to go back to New York, and I'll be stuck out here with the goddamn palm trees and lizards. You look terrific, kid. How's it going?"

"All right, I guess. It's boring, waiting around now. I haven't done a thing for weeks but work out with Lucy and go to movies."

"You won't be bored for long. Meyers is already making positive noises about picking up your option. He's got another property ready, and just wants to see how the preview's gonna go."

"What kind of property?"

"Shakespeare," he said. "A musical. What did you think? They'd cast you maybe as Lady Macbeth?" She laughed, and he went on. "I get together with Meyers next week after the sneak preview. Then we'll see what's what. You like makin' movies?"

"Uh-huh, I do."

"Word is you're gonna walk away with the picture. What d'you think of that?"

"I don't know. In one way, it makes me feel kind of embarrassed. I mean, I'm not the star. Miss Farrell is, and Mr. Oakie. If I were either of them, I'd be pretty upset to think people were going around saying somebody was walking away with my picture."

"What d'you care?"

"Maybe that's the way things happen out here, but that doesn't mean I have to like it. I hate the idea that somebody else might get hurt because of me."

"You want everyone should be happy," he said, with a smile. "I'll tell you, that ain't possible, Bea. Somebody else is always going to be getting hurt by the new kid in town. If the somebody doesn't have what it takes to stay on top, they'll get bumped out of the way. It's not your lookout. It's Farrell's, or Oakie's; it's Garbo's worry, or Shearer's."

"And someday, it might be my turn," she said shrewdly. "And I hate it."

"But you want to get back to work, right?"

"Yes, I do. I can't stand sitting around, doing nothing."

"So, okay. You want to work, you've got a choice. You can be one of the best, or you can hang around here for a few years playing second banana until they get tired of your face and find a new kid who's got a bigger appetite than you do and wants billing above the title. It's up to you. You don't want to push, we don't push. Personally, I think you're a little nuts and a whole lot naïve, but it's not my life. I don't think you're going to have much of a choice once Ludie claps his eyes on the final cut. Whether you want to or not, you'll be going back to work, and they'll be running around like sons of bitches to keep building you. Course, you can always lay down on the job, play temperamental, show up late on the set, pull a bunch of stunts, and you'll be out of business in no time."

"I'd never do any of that!" she said indignantly.

"No," he smiled. "Course not. So, it's just a matter of a short time before everything's signed, sealed, and delivered. And then the big machine's rolling, and Ludie Meyers is putting everything he's got behind you to make you the biggest thing since chewing gum. All we've got to iron out it how long, how much, and the fine print. They love playing games, these people. Star you in one picture, give you five lines in the next. We wanna make sure it's the starring part every time. When it comes time to talk, we all sit down together, thrash it out."

"How's Bobby?" she asked, unable to contain her curiosity any longer. "Have you seen him? Is he working?"

"He's rehearsing for the *Follies*. They still wanted you, but I had to tell them no soap. Ludie's got dibs on you. Kid's in the chorus, but he's happy with that. He's pulled himself together, got rid of that chip he was carrying around on his shoulder; he's putting his money in the bank and behaving himself."

"Oh, that's good."

"He's had a couple of nibbles from RKO. They'd like to put him under contract, but he wants to get more experience. The Shuberts have their eye on him for a new show they want to open around July or August. He keeps his nose clean, he might land himself a nice part in what looks to be a helluva show. Arlen's doing the music, and Ira and Yip Harburg are doing the lyrics. He's okay, Bea. He's doing fine, sends his regards."

"He does?"

"Well, sure," Jerry replied, made sad by the way this small lie visibly gave her a lift.

"If you're talking to him, be sure to say I said hello."

"Sure," he agreed, for a few moments clearly able to see Bobby as the chink in Bea's armor. The kid was nutty over that hoofer, anybody could see it. Maybe it wasn't so smart to feed her lies, encourage her.

"Jerry, could you do something for me?"

Thinking they were still on the topic of Bobby, he answered warily. "Name it, and we'll see."

"I'd like to have a place where I could rehearse, work things out. I thought maybe you could ask Mr. Meyers if there's some free space at the studio. I was thinking that if I know I can go there every day and work for a few hours, I won't feel as bored as I do hanging around the house."

"I can ask. Anything else?"

"One thing more. I'd like to set it up so my mother automatically gets money every month. Maybe the bank could take care of it."

"How much were you thinking of sending her?"

"A hundred and fifty a month?"

He gave out a low whistle. "You sure you want to fork over that much?"

"Well, I'm getting four hundred a week now, and I'll be getting that for another month until the contract ends. I thought, since you and everyone else are so convinced Mr. Meyers will take up my option, they'll pay me at least the same, so I should be able to afford it."

"They want you," he said sharply, "they'll be paying a helluva lot more than four bills. I plan to get them up to six, seven hundred, at least."

"So, that should be all right, then. The bank could send her a hundred and fifty, and she'll quit writing, asking me for more all the time."

"What're you gonna do when word gets out about the kind of money you're pulling in, and she comes back at you for two-fifty, and then three-fifty?"

"How would she find that out?"

"Are you joking?" His eyebrows shot up. "Have a look at this!" He pushed around among the papers on his desk and came up with a copy of *Screen Book.* Finding the page he wanted, he said, "Here! Cast your peepers over that!" He held the magazine out to her.

In a box centered on the second page of the article, under the title "How Today's Stars Rank Differently in Salary and Box-Office Value," was a chart showing Will Rogers receiving fifteen thousand a week, the top salary, and ranking second in popularity. At the bottom of the list, at sixty-five hundred a week and ranking eighth in popularity, was Ronald Colman. Garbo was getting thirteen thousand, and Constance Bennett eight. The salaries were not in direct proportion to their popularity rank.

Intrigued, Bea scanned the article, noting the statement that before a major feature started about forty-seven percent of the budget was written off for salaries. Further on, her eye was caught by Buddy Rogers' name, and she read, astonished, that at the time he'd made

Wings, he'd been paid seventy-five dollars a week as the industry's most popular male star. And, later on, when he was declining, he drew twenty-five hundred a week.

She closed the magazine and returned it to Jerry's desk. "I can't imagine being paid fifteen thousand dollars a week. What would anyone do with that much money?"

"Plenty. And ten percent of it," he reminded her, "goes to a very happy agent. Four hundred's peanuts, Bea. You're gonna get way more. I'm just worried about this mother of yours deciding it's okay to freeload off you for the rest of her life. From what you've told me about her, I can't believe it's what you'd want."

"But how could I stop her? She is my mother, after all."

"But you can't stand the woman," he argued. "And according to you, she's never done a thing for you."

"She didn't give me away, either, or let me die."

"Fine! It's up to you. You want her around your neck, it's your funeral."

"What could I do?"

"There are ways and ways, if it should come to that. For now, we'll make the arrangements with the bank and keep our fingers crossed she doesn't come back too soon asking for more."

Bea insisted the others go on ahead into the movie theater. "I'll come in in a few minutes," she told them. "I want to wait for the lights to go down."

"I'll wait with you," Lucy offered.

"Okay, so you two will wait," Jerry said, and went in with Hank and half a dozen other men from the studio.

"Walk with me?" Bea asked.

"Sure, honey." Lucy fell into step at her side. "Nervous, huh?"

"Terrified. What if those people hate the movie and see me trying to creep out? They'll stone me, or something."

"What if they're crazy about you?"

"They won't be," Bea said glumly.

"Shows what you know. And if you're worried, you can sit way down in your seat and stay there until everybody's gone. The boys're gonna be busy as all get out reading the preview cards. To tell the truth, I'm kind of nervous myself." She squeezed Bea's arm. "Sometimes, I just can't believe we're actually here. And now we're going to see your movie. It's just amazing."

"I feel as if maybe I'm going to hurl. My stomach's jumping around like nobody's business. If this picture does go over, I swear I'll never come to another preview as long as I live. This is awful."

Lucy looked at her watch. "We ought to head back. The picture'll be starting." Lucy swung Bea around, and they retraced their route to the theater. "This is kind of like an opening night," Lucy observed.

"It's worse. What if it's terrible, if *I'm* terrible?"

"Then we'll pack up and go back to New York. Here we are." Lucy held open the door.

Sitting at the very back in the loges, her jaws clenched and her nails digging into her palms, Bea watched the picture. She was impressed by the clean cuts from one scene to the next, by the musical lead-ins, by the way the audience laughed in all the right places and, at the end, applauded enthusiastically. She didn't even mind the sight of herself, although, really, it was like watching a stranger. She paid close attention to Dickie, wishing she could understand what it was about him that had kept her on edge through the entire twenty-one days of shooting. It had something to do with his eyes and the way he held his mouth. She told herself she was reading too much into nothing.

"Tomorrow," Jerry whispered momentously in the lobby after the audience had gone, "we have a chat with Mr. Meyers, talk a little turkey."

"You want to stick around and read the cards?" Hank asked her.

"I'd rather go home. But you could come over later, if you want, and tell us about it. I'll make coffee."

"Okay, will do." He gave her a happy smile. "It's a hit, Bea. Count on that. The cards'll confirm it."

Pete and another publicity man, Hank, Jerry, and Ike, each stood with a handful of cards, reading, their excited voices overlapping.

"'That girl's the best dancer I've ever seen.'"

"'The young kids who danced are just the best.'"

"'How old is Beatrice Crane and is she going to be in another movie soon?'"

"'Farrell and Oakie are okay, but the two kids are the real stars.'"

"'I think I'm in love with Dickie DeVore. He's swell.'"

"'I want to take Beatrice Crane home and introduce her to my mother and father. She's the kind of girl they've been after me to marry.'"

"'It's nice to see someone in a picture who looks like a real person, not a glamour queen. When's Crane's next movie? I'll line up for it.'"

"'Dickie DeVore can park his shoes next to mine any time.'"

"'Where were Farrell and Oakie? Must've missed them, I was so busy watching Crane and DeVore.'"

"'Beatrice Crane looks exactly like my cousin Gert, but Gert can't sing or dance and Crane sure can.'"

"'More Crane, less Farrell and Oakie.'"

"'Beatrice Crane's just the sweetest thing I've ever seen. And can she dance!'"

"'When she sang "Heavenly" she just broke my heart. What a lovely kid! When's her next one?'"

"They're all raves for Bea and Dickie," Pete exclaimed. "There's not one pan in the bunch."

"Listen to this," Ike said. "'I don't usually bother filling out these cards, but this time I just have to. I'm a big movie fan, and I'd put my money on Beatrice Crane any day of the week. In fact, if they were issuing stock in that girl, I'd go right out and buy some.'"

"I can top that," Jerry put in. "'Not only can she sing and dance, but there's something about her that had me all choked up even when she was happy. It was like watching Chaplin. You can bet I'll be back for her next one.' This one," he announced, "I'm hanging onto to show Ludie."

"Overall," Hank said, having reviewed all the cards, "every single person rated it either good or excellent. *Hot damn!*" he yelled. "We did it!"

"**W**ell," Ludie smiled expansively, "it looks like our girl here's a smash."

"She's not your girl yet," Jerry smiled too. "There's the matter of this option."

"Already we've got another property," Ludie told Bea. "A pip. We'll put you together again with Dickie."

"A thousand a week, one picture deal," Jerry said.

Ludie lost his smile and much of his color. "Five years, working up to a thousand."

"Three years. The first at seven-fifty, the second at a thousand, and the third at twelve-fifty."

"Five years," Ludie countered, "starting at six, ending up at eleven."

"Three years, starting at a thousand, ending up at fifteen hundred."

"*Are you crazy?*" Meyers all but screamed. "Five years, the last at twelve hundred."

"*Three,* starting at twelve-fifty, third year at seventeen-fifty."

Bea followed this exchange in astounded silence, as Ludie grew

142

redder in the face and Jerry became quieter, until they suddenly broke off, and Ludie leaned back in his chair, steepling his stubby, manicured fingers in front of his face and peering at Jerry through them.

At last, Ludie lowered his hands to the desk, leaned forward, and spoke with quiet finality. "Three years," he said. "Seven-fifty, a thousand, twelve-fifty. And she tours for this picture."

"Tours?" Bea interrupted.

"You go across country and appear in movie theaters to promote the picture," Jerry told her.

"Do I go alone? What do I do? For how long?"

"Three weeks," Ludie said. "We send Dickie out with you. You'll do one of the numbers from the show. Ten, twelve major markets."

"We'll get to perform live?"

"Yeah."

"Jerry, I want to do it."

Jerry looked at her for a long moment, then said, "Okay. You've got yourself a deal." He grinned, rubbing his hair. "You're in luck, Ludie. The kid wants to tour."

"Lucky, hah!" Ludie made a face. "Highway robbery."

"I'll have to have Lucy with me," Bea added.

"Okay, okay," Ludie agreed.

"We'll be in touch." Jerry stood up to shake hands with Meyers, then waited while Bea also shook hands with the man.

As they walked toward Jerry's car, he said, "Rehearsal space is being set up for you. And they're getting you your own trailer. You're about to become important around here. Make sure you keep your nose clean."

"What does that mean?"

"Just what I said. Stay out of trouble."

"Why didn't you tell me you were going to ask for so much money?"

"What difference would it've made?"

"I don't know. It's scary. It's such a lot."

"You're worth it, kid. And besides, don't think for one minute they're not going to make you work damned hard for it. But I'm holding him to no more than three pictures a year."

"And what'll I do the rest of the time?"

"Whatever. Practice, get a tan, take up tennis. They'll keep you on the go, the publicity boys."

"Where will the tour go?"

"All the major burgs. New York'll be the big one. They'll probably have you two kids appearing all over the place, making sure they get their money's worth. You like the sound of that, huh?"

"I do. It'll mean live audiences again, and getting to do an entire number from start to finish without having to stop twenty times to adjust one of the spots or to have six guys come rushing onto the set with rags and cans of Energine to clean the Bakelite floors. D'you have any idea what it's like to dance on those floors? They're like ice, they're so slick. Most of the time, I'm worried half to death about taking a spill."

"It sure looks great, though."

"That's what everything is here," she said, gesturing at the sound stages. "It's all about how things *look*."

"You're right on the money on that score. Remember that, and you won't have any problems."

"Seven hundred and fifty dollars a *week?*"

"Every week for a solid year. The next year, it's a thousand a week, and the year after that it's twelve-fifty. Take my advice and sock it away like you've been doing."

"Even when I'm not working?"

"Week in, week out. With four weeks guaranteed vacation time." He gave her a hug. "Three years from now, when we sit down again and negotiate some more, we'll maybe double or triple that."

"I can't wait to tell Lucy. She'll have a fit. Thank you, Jerry."

"Thank *you. I* can't wait to tell the east-coast boys. Let 'em know we'll be paying the rent, and then some. You're going to be one of our big clients." He opened the car door, then turned back to her. "By the way, it's all set, the money for your mother. The bank'll look after it on a standing order."

"Oh," she said distractedly. "Good." She watched Jerry drive off, thinking she might be able to track Bobby down while she was in New York. She could imagine how surprised he'd be to see her. And just thinking about it, her heart gave a little leap.

Fifteen

THE premiere was not dissimilar to others Bea had attended before on her dates arranged by the studio. But because she was involved in this one, more was required. There was the matter of an appropriate dress. She and Lucy shopped for three weeks before finding something they both agreed was perfect—an ankle-length gown of pale pink peau de soie, with a narrow ribbon sash; short, slit, ribbon-trimmed sleeves; and a scalloped neckline dotted with seed pearls. They then had to buy white shoes to be dyed to match the dress.

"You look like an angel," Lucy declared, inspecting her prior to the arrival of the limousine. Bea's hair was upswept into a loose knot, which accentuated the length of her neck. A little mascara and some gray shadow in the crease of her lids made her eyes the focus of her face. The pale pink was a most flattering color to her pale complexion. "You've got the sweetest little face," Lucy laughed, kissing her on the forehead. "I love your stubborn jaw and that dimple in your chin."

"I'm jealous of your bosom," Bea admitted, her eyes on Lucy's cleavage, framed elegantly by her simple, long black dress.

"Oh, cripes!" Lucy looked down at herself. "I wouldn't be, if I were you. One of these days, they'll be resting somewhere down around my knees, and then you'll be glad you've got nice, small ones that don't have anywhere to go."

Bea laughed, then swallowed. "I'm so nervous."

"Don't be. You won't be on your own."

"Dickie and I are going to get fed up with each other pretty fast, they way they keep pushing us together."

"I'm sure he understands.'

"He's so much prettier than me. Every single time they send me out, it's with some guy who'd make a better-looking girl than I do."

It was Lucy's turn to laugh. "Looks aren't everything."

"Go on! In this town, they sure are."

"That may be, but on the screen you're every bit as good-looking as Dickie, and don't you ever forget it."

"I don't *live* on the screen, Luce."

"You'll be up on a stage in less than a week. Then you'll be pining to get back here and start another picture. Face it, sweetheart. This is where you want to be." Lucy turned to look out the front window. "Grab your bag, and let's go. The car's here."

There were giant Kliegl lights set up in front of Grauman's Egyptian Theater, and the spotlights on top of the forecourt walls were aimed down at the crowd. Hank had fought hard and long to have the premiere held here, and Bea smiled to herself, glad he'd succeeded. She imagined he was pleased as punch at having his first picture premiere in his favorite theater.

Crowds of people filled the sidewalks in front and lined the walkway set up through the forecourt, many of them clutching autograph books which they thrust at the celebrities as they made their way through.

As she walked toward the theater door with Dickie on one side and Lucy on the other, Bea had the sudden, strange feeling of being one of the crowd of watchers and saw herself through their eyes. She wasn't any different than the girls on the sidelines, and yet she was. She had abilities they didn't have, but aside from that and the money her abilities provided, she was exactly like them. For the length of time it took to walk from the limousine through the forecourt, she felt split in two, part of her on the sidelines, and the other part playing out some role she didn't quite understand. Overall, she felt mortified and turned to look at Dickie to see his reactions. He was beaming, waving to the crowd, enjoying himself.

"You really like all this, don't you?" she asked him, marveling yet again at his exceptional good looks. He was so handsome, his features so perfectly chiseled, that looking at him was like studying a piece of sculpture or a centuries-old painting.

"I sure do," he answered readily, glancing down at her, with his smile revealing white, even teeth. "This is what it's all about. And it's going to get better and better. Next time around, they'll be begging *me* for my autograph. After tonight, they'll know who I am."

"You really want that?" she asked.

He gave her an incredulous look. "Don't you? What're you *doing* here, otherwise?"

"I just wondered," she answered, made uncomfortable by the ferocity of his determination. There was a quality about him, about his hunger for fame and his willingness to do absolutely anything to get it, that not only mystified her, but frightened her, too. She'd never met anyone like Dickie, although she'd heard plenty of stories since she'd come out west about others just like him, and worse. They were people so set on fame and fortune through careers in the movies that they'd try anything, say anything, do any kind of stunt, perform like circus animals for the publicity boys, just to get it.

She'd really been very lucky, she thought, turning in her seat to look at the rest of the audience. Yes, she'd had to go out on dozens of dates arranged by the studios, and she'd had to have her photograph taken, almost daily, it seemed. But it had all been done *for* her, in a way. She hadn't had to do or be anything other than what she was. She'd even been somewhat reluctant to stay on here, but she could see now Hank had been right in saying she'd never have forgiven herself if she left. Still, if her career here ended tomorrow, she'd be all right; she'd go back to Broadway. She couldn't conceive of what Dickie might do if his dreams failed to materialize. He seemed to have left himself no options. Everything he had was riding on his making it big in the movies.

The premiere gave every indication the picture would be a great success. The audience clapped and cheered and gave Hank, Hero, and Ludie a big round of applause, after the stars and Bea and Dickie had received one. At the party following the show, photographers worked the crowd, taking shots of anyone in any way involved with the movie. Bea was maneuvered into groups with Hank, Hero, and Ike, as well as with Farrell, Oakie, and Dickie. Even Lucy found herself fitted into the foreground of a number of shots.

At last, Bea was left alone with Hank, who gave her a glass of champagne so they might drink a toast to the success of the picture. "Excited?" he asked, admiring how well she looked, touched and pleased every time simply by the fact of her existence.

"I am, but mainly about having a chance to get back onstage, even if it is only promotion for the picture."

"Most other people would be dreading it, the one-night stands, the climbing on and off trains, the sleeping in hotels and waking up in the morning not sure which city you're in."

"It sounds as if you've done it a few times yourself."

"I've heard enough about it from folks who have."

147

"I don't care. I'm going to love being in front of a live audience again." Her eyes drifted over the crowd and came to rest on Dickie who was gesturing animatedly while talking to a trio of eager-eyed young women.

Following her gaze, Hank said, "He's eating it all up like birthday cake."

"He really is, isn't he?" She shrugged and turned back to Hank, linking her arm through his. "So, Pop, when do I get my swimming lessons?"

"Soon as you finish the tour. And while you're away, Hero and I will be breaking down the musical numbers for the new picture. They're already doing rewrites on the script."

"What's it like?" she asked. "And when do I get to read it?"

"A lot of catchy one-liners, not a bad boy-meets-girl-loses-girl-wins-girl-back plot. Some reasonable dialogue and six great songs, including one that's bound to be a very big hit.'

"What's it like?"

"A number called 'Without You,' that's sung by the male lead. It has some of the best lyrics I've ever heard. There's one line, in the last chorus, that goes something like, 'Now I'll never again have to be alone, without you.' Gave me chills, I swear."

"Featuring me and Dickie?"

"Starring you," he corrected. "Dickie's not set yet. His agent's pushing hard for a lot more money, and Ludie's holding off, waiting to see what the gross is gonna look like and what the general audience reaction's gonna be to young Mister DeVore. So far, the response has been pretty favorable, but altogether, you're coming out on top."

"Dickie won't like that," she said astutely. "Every so often, I get the feeling he doesn't think I should even be around, that *he's* the one everybody's really crazy about."

"Well, he's very much mistaken!" Hank said strongly. "Don't you take any guff from him on the tour, Bea."

"Oh, I'm sure he wouldn't try to give me any."

"Still, remember you don't have to put up with any nonsense. You have any problems, anything at all, call me and I'll make sure it's taken care of."

"I'll call you anyway, just to say hello." She smiled up at him.

His arm slipped around her waist, and he gave her a hug. "You do that. I'm going to miss you, miss all the tap-tapping echoing inside the rehearsal stage. I love watching you do your stuff." He felt a powerful surge of affection for her, and, involuntarily, his arm tightened around her narrow waist. Sometimes the size of her took his breath away. She was such a tiny girl; he could easily have spanned her waist with his hands. Looking at her, noticing the length of her eyelashes, he thought, I'm going to make you someone the world will never forget. He'd do it because it was the only viable way in which he could ever demonstrate his love for her. He wished, not for the first time, he was capable of loving her as she deserved, but it simply wasn't in him. His mind loved her, and his heart, but he could never be for her what some other man might. Hadn't he tried a couple of times, only to suffer the abject humiliation of failure? No, the course of his life, and his preferences, had been set a long time ago; it wasn't possible to change his instincts, no matter how much he might wish to.

"Please be careful," he told her, "and take care of yourself."

"I will," she assured him, secure inside the circle of his arm.

Things went well on the tour until they reached Chicago. Despite the fact that the traveling and performing were every bit as grueling as Hank had warned her they'd be, the response of the audiences buoyed her, inspiring her to put every ounce of energy she could summon up into "Heavenly" which she and Dickie did after each showing of the movie along the route. But in Chicago, halfway through the number, Dickie failed to follow through on one of the lifts, and if she hadn't quickly redistributed her weight to brace herself, she'd have fallen. Since the remainder of the number went as always, she decided his action had been unintentional and put it out of her mind.

Until Cleveland. There, not only did he fluff the lift, he also added several extra steps into the routine so that when they reconnected center-stage, they were no longer in synch. It made the dance look sloppy, and there wasn't anything she could do to fix it.

"What's he up to?" Lucy asked backstage, helping Bea out of her costume. "I caught that little extra bit he threw in."

"I don't know," Bea admitted. "It's as if he's trying to make me look bad."

"He's only making himself look clumsy." Lucy folded the dress into a bag to be cleaned. Bea had three identical dresses to perform in, so that she'd never have to work in a soiled, sweaty garment. In those cities where they stopped for more than one night, the dresses were sent out to be dry-cleaned. "What're you gonna do?"

"There's nothing I *can* do. I guess I'll try to talk to him."

Dickie stared at her, his brows pulling together, the corners of his mouth curving downward. "What d'you mean?" he wanted to know.

149

"Three times now that lift has gone wrong. I was wondering if there was some problem."

"The only problem I can see is maybe you're getting a little hefty. You're no feather, you know."

Refusing to take umbrage, keeping her voice low, she said. "I weigh exactly what I did when we filmed that number and did take after take. You didn't seem to have any problem with my weight, *or* the lift, then. If there *is* something wrong, I wish you'd tell me about it so we can set it right."

Wearing a mask of innocent incomprehension, he said, "I really don't know what you're talking about," and walked away.

His subtle tricks proliferated and, in direct proportion, so did her anger. She simply couldn't understand why he was risking, not only making both of them look like clumsy clods, but also his career, with these ridiculous and dangerous pranks. By the time they were preparing backstage for the opening at Radio City Music Hall she was, for the first time ever, filled with dread at the prospect of going out live. Dickie was bound to do something, and since it was no longer possible to predict where in the number he might do it, she was tense and testy as Lucy helped her into her costume.

"*I* can't help what's going on!" Lucy said, stung. "It's up to *you* to do something about him. Just don't take it out on me."

"I'm sorry, but I know he'll pull some stupid prank," Bea worried aloud. "And tonight's so important. All the newspaper people are going to be out there ... He pretends nothing's wrong, or says I'm too heavy so he can't do the lifts. For Pete's sake, I weigh even less now than I did when we were making the stupid movie! He's making me hate him, Lucy. He's spoiling everything."

"Let's sit down here for a moment." Lucy pulled her by the hand over to the couch in a corner of the dressing room. "You're not a kid anymore, Bea. The studio's got their money riding on you, and your career's on the line. There's a lot I'll do for you, but I absolutely will not fight your battles for you. Stop and think about everything, and make up your mind how you want to handle the situation."

"I don't want to get anyone in trouble," Bea said miserably.

"So, you'll let him make you look like a mug."

"No, but ..."

"You don't have to put up with it."

"It's just that I hate to make a fuss."

"You'd rather look bad?'

"No! Of course not."

"Bea, listen to me! Sooner or later, it happens to everybody. We all get to a point where we've got to take charge of our own lives. You're at that point right now. Either you're going to let people push you around, walk all over you, or you're going to assert yourself, stand up for yourself. Nobody else can do that for you."

"Let's see how it goes tonight. Maybe it'll be all right."

Lucy could see how nervous she was and didn't want to push the issue further. Taking hold of Bea's hands, shocked by how cold they were, she said, *"Maybe* it'll be all right. But if it isn't . . ."

"If it isn't, I'll have to do something." Firming her grip on Lucy's hands, she said, "Why does there have to be something to spoil it, Luce? That's what I don't understand." She looked around at the floral arrangements placed about the room. "Any word from Bobby?" she asked.

Lucy shook her head.

"He doesn't have much money," Bea said, then wet her lips. "I'm going to go see him. I know where he's rehearsing. I spoke to Mark in the New York office, and he found out for me."

"Okay." Lucy smiled. "No harm in that."

"I'd give *anything* if I could be going out tonight to dance with Bobby. He'd *never* do stuff like that. *Why* is Dickie *doing* this? Why?"

"Who knows? He's awfully good-looking, but he's not too bright, when you come right down to it."

The A.S.M. knocked on the door and called "five minutes." Bea's hold on Lucy's hands tightened even more as her heart seemed to lurch against her ribs. "I'm so scared," she whispered. "If I only knew where and when he was going to do whatever it is he's planning, at least I'd be prepared. But this way, I feel as if I'm going out there naked, and everybody's going to laugh at me."

"Don't cry," Lucy said softly.

"I *can't* cry!" Bea laughed bitterly, wrenching free her hands and jumping to her feet. "All this black crap on my eyes will run." She went to lean close to the make-up mirror, automatically picking up the powder puff and dabbing at her nose and cheeks. "I could kill him," she hissed, meeting Lucy's eyes in the mirror. "I could honestly kill him. Keep your fingers crossed, Luce." She threw down the puff and raced out of the dressing room.

From the wings, Lucy watched, her arms tight against her sides, weighted with apprehension as the orchestra played the introduction and the curtains pulled back to reveal Bea and Dickie in position stage-left. Applause, and then the two started the dance.

It went beautifully, without a hitch, until the top of the second chorus. Lucy could tell from the way Dickie pulled Bea into the lift that he was going to throw her so that she landed wrong. Her fists clenched, she watched him take a half-turn—seeing it as if in slow

151

motion—and Bea's head lift fractionally with awareness of what was happening. Instead of handing her down out of the lift, he all but threw her from him.

"Correct it, correct it!" Lucy whispered frantically, suddenly sweating as Bea came down awkwardly, her arms automatically seeking to balance her. Dickie was smiling, as he filled in each beat as choreographed, as if absolutely unaware of what was happening.

Bea had two choices. She could either go into the off-kilter landing, skip a beat or two, and try to pick up the routine, or she could take the landing and make something of it, abandoning the routine altogether. In the split-second left to her, she decided to improvise, took the crude landing and turned it into an attitude she held for the beat, then broke loose and did the next twelve bars in double time, adding in eight whirlwind pirouettes circling Dickie and four bars of broken-time tapping while he, thrown totally, simply stood and watched her go, hearing the audience erupt into shouts and wild applause. Then she picked up at the start of the final eight and dragged him with her through to the end of the number, with the original choreography.

After the many calls, as they were leaving the stage, he whispered furiously, "What the hell did you think you were doing there?"

She waited until they were safely in the wings before allowing her anger to flood to the surface. "I could've *broken a leg*, the way you *threw* me! Tonight's the *last time* I dance with *you!* I don't know *why* you've been doing what you have, but you're *never* going to get a chance to do it again!" She was so angry, it was all she could do not to strike him.

"Oh, yeah? We'll see about that!"

"You're darn tootin' we will! *You stupid son of a bitch! You need your goddamned head examined!*"

Lucy hurried over, put her arm around Bea's shoulders, and directed her away, murmuring, "Thank God you corrected. I was so afraid you were going to fall."

"I'm *never* working with him again!" Bea fumed. "He's completely insane!"

"Poor you, you're shaking."

As she stripped out of her costume back in the dressing room, Bea said, "I saw his face, just for a second, before he threw me. He did it on purpose." She stepped out of the dress, pulled off her tights, pulled the slip off over her head, and reached for the robe Lucy was holding out to her. "He looked so..." She shuddered, belting the robe around her. "If I'd broken every bone in my body, nothing would've made him happier. Oh, he'd have made a big fuss, pretending to be concerned, but he'd have been thrilled. *What kind of person does things like that?* I'm going to call Hank, and Jerry, and maybe Mr. Meyers. I can't and won't work with him again. I couldn't."

"But, sweetheart, you've got the rest of this tour to get through."

"I know that. But I've got an idea."

The dance captain was putting the chorus through its paces. Bea stepped inside the rehearsal hall and stood to one side of the door, overcome by the gladdening familiarity of the scene—the tinny incompleteness of a piano thumping out music, the chaotic mix of rehearsal clothes, the flex and stretch of well-trained bodies, and the air stinking of cigarettes, perfume, and sweat. She leaned against the wall, her bag tucked under her arm, and watched until the captain called a halt.

"Okay, take five," she said, "and then we'll add in the next eight."

The dancers relaxed their spines. Several stretched out on the floor. Bobby stood for a moment talking with one of the girls, smiled, then turned away, heading for his bag which was on one of the chairs against the near wall.

Bea tracked his progress across the room, noting the changes in him, elated by the very sight of him. He was taller and broader; he no longer looked like a boy. In the nine or ten months since she'd last seen him, he'd made an important transition. He'd moved into manhood, and it showed in the way he moved, in his carriage, even in the set of his jaw. She couldn't stop staring at him, so taken was she by the change in his appearance.

She moved to his side, touched his arm, and waited for him to turn. When he did, his eyes, for a moment, were blank. Then recognition clicked in, and he let out a whoop of laughter as he threw his arms around her, lifting her clear off the floor and swinging her around.

"What're you *doing* here?" he asked, holding her away to look at her. He couldn't get over how grown-up she looked in a close-fitting dark red suit and a cloche that completely concealed her hair, framing her face. "How'd you know where to find me? You look sensational!"

"So do you," she managed, unexpectedly choked by emotion. "Jerry told me you were doing the show, so I had Mark in the New York office find out where you were rehearsing. I'd really like to talk to you."

"Me, too," he said eagerly, his hands still on her shoulders. "Gosh, it's wonderful to see you. Can you wait? Or do you want to meet me somewhere after I finish up here? We've only got another hour."

"If it's all right with you, I'll wait."

"I saw your picture, you know."

"You did?"

"I begged and pleaded and finally got one of the studio reps to let me in at a preview. It's terrific, Bea. *You're* terrific! It was all I could do not to start shouting, 'I know her! She's a good friend of mine.' I was so damned proud of you."

"Let's go, everybody!" the dance captain called, clapping her hands together.

"You sit down here and wait for me." Bobby directed her into one of the chairs. "Don't make a move. Okay?"

"Okay." She smiled at him, feeling she might begin to cry.

"I can't get over how you look," he told her. "You'll wait, you promise?"

"I'll be right here."

He went back into formation in the center of the room, and she undid the buttons of her suit jacket, settling in to enjoy an honest-to-god rehearsal. It was, for an hour, like returning to a favorite room, one she'd almost forgotten existed. Everything in her longed to get up and join in, but she contented herself by tapping out the rhythm with her foot, watching, impressed by the great improvement in Bobby's dancing. He was still athletic, and by far the most limber of the male dancers, but he'd lost his previous tendency toward abruptness in his transition steps. His moves now were clean and smooth. There wasn't another dancer in the room with his presence or anything like his ability.

At the end of the hour, he dashed over and said, "I'll be five minutes and then we can go somewhere. Okay?"

"Okay."

He grabbed his bag and ran off to shower and change his clothes, so excited at seeing her again that he hardly knew what he was doing.

Settled in a booth in a nearby coffee shop, she got right to the point. "I've done something you might not like, Bobby."

"What could you possibly do that I wouldn't like?" he quipped.

"I'm serious. I've taken kind of a liberty and I'm hoping you won't mind." She paused, studying him as he lit a cigarette. He'd acquired new confidence, and it showed in his every move and gesture.

"Go on," he said, dropping the spent match in an ashtray.

"I was on the telephone for hours last night and most of this morning. First I called Hank. He's my director and a very good friend. I mean, he directed the picture I just did, and he's set to do the next one. Then I called Jerry, and he called Mark in the New York office. And after that, he spoke to Hank, and then to Ludie."

"*Ludie Meyers?*"

154

"That's right."

"What for?"

"I know it was wrong of me to go ahead without asking you, but time's really important, and I thought maybe it'd be better to get their okay first before talking to you. So, here it is." She took a deep breath, then told him about what had been happening with Dickie.

"What a crumb!" he sympathized.

"I've never done anything like this in my life. I mean, I never thought I could, or that I'd have to. But I couldn't keep on working with him. So, everybody's willing, that is, if you are, to have you step in. I could teach you the routine in one day easily. Then, you'd do the rest of the tour and travel back to Los Angeles with Lucy and me. They want to test you for the new picture. Hank says he'll take my word for it that you can do the part. And Ludie wants to see a piece of film of you, but it's only a formality. I *know* they'll go for you, and Jerry thinks so, too. So, what d'you think? Would you like to do it?"

"Holy Cow! Are you saying they'll give this Dickie jerk the heave-ho and let me step in, *just like that?*"

"On my say-so."

"And they'll foot the bill for my fare to Los Angeles, and test me, and all the rest of it?"

"Yes."

"Well, I guess I'd have to be crazy not to want to do it."

"Oh, Bobby, I know they'll want you, and that you'll be wonderful onstage and in the picture."

"But what about the Ziegfeld show?"

"That's not a problem. Mark says they can easily get you out of your contract."

"When would I have to go on?"

"Tomorrow night?"

"Tomorrow night? Brother! You sure I can learn the number in only one day?"

"Knowing you," she laughed, "you could learn it in about half an hour. I've got a rehearsal record, and we can work in one of the rooms backstage at the Music Hall. Everything's arranged."

"And what about this Dickie guy? What's he gonna say about it?"

"I *don't care* what he's gonna say!" she replied hotly. "He almost threw me off the stage last night. And anyway," her anger began to cool, "RKO's already interested in taking over his contract. They've got a picture they'd like him for. He won't go hungry."

"Why would you do all this for me, Bea?" he asked. "I didn't exactly treat you too well last time we saw each other."

"You couldn't help it. And neither could I. We were both a lot younger then."

He laughed at that. "Neither one of us is all that much older now."

"No," she conceded. "But we both sure *look* older."

"I can't argue that. I'm wild about your new haircut. And the clothes. You look like a million bucks!"

"So do you," she said quietly. "I've missed you an awful lot."

"Me too, you," he said. "I kept kicking myself for being so rotten to you that time."

"It doesn't matter now."

"I'm not sure if I can believe all this," he said.

"Oh, you should," she told him. "It's going to happen."

"You've been nothing but good to me since the day we met," he said seriously. "You, and Lucy too. Say, where's Luce?"

"She's here, at the hotel. I wanted to see you first, on my own." She looked down at her untouched coffee, then back at him. "Sometimes I thought I'd never see you again, and I hated the idea of that."

"I thought the same thing," he admitted. "I'll tell you one thing: I won't let you down, Bea. I'll be the best damned dancing partner anybody ever had."

"I know that." She smiled at him. "I've always known that."

Sixteen

LUDIE had approved Bobby's test and signed him to a seven-year contract. Bobby had rented a small cottage not far from Lucy and Bea, and rehearsals for the musical numbers of *Big City* were underway. Everything was going just as Bea had hoped it would, and, as well, she'd started receiving fan mail.

In the first week after *Upside Down* opened nationwide, the studio called and asked her to come collect her mail. Imagining there was yet another begging letter from her mother, she got Lucy to drive her over and was bowled over to find a sack containing two hundred and eleven letters and postcards, the majority of them from girls between the ages of thirteen and twenty-one. A week after that, there were three hundred and nineteen pieces of mail, and the third week brought four hundred and forty-two letters.

Initially, Bea thought she'd sit down and respond to each individual letter and card. It quickly became clear she wasn't going to be able to do it.

"Why don't I take care of the fan mail?" Lucy suggested. "If I find anything special, I'll pass it along to you and you can write a personal note. But trying to answer all these"—she waved her hand at the accumulation of letters and cards—"would take you the rest of your life. You'd be an old lady by the time you got finished. You'd have no time to do anything else."

"I couldn't ask you to do that," Bea argued. "It'll take up all *your* time. And when'll *you* get any work done?"

"To be honest," Lucy told her, "I'd really enjoy doing this. Maybe it's curiosity, or nosiness, or something, but I really like reading the letters and answering them, sending out your photos. If it makes you feel better, you can call me your personal assistant and pay me a salary. I'm not proud. Make me an employee."

"That wouldn't be right," Bea protested.

"Sure it would. I *want* to do it. You don't have the time. And while we're at it, maybe you should give some thought to getting someplace permanent to live. It seems kind of foolish wasting money on rent when it could be going toward a place you'd own. I've always believed paying rent was about the same as lighting cigarettes with dollar bills." Seeing Bea wavering, Lucy hurried on. "I can do the looking while you're at rehearsals. The point is to let me do the things you don't have time for. I want to do it, Bea, so why don't you just say okay, swell, and let me get on with it. I'll take care of the fan mail, find a decent house, and hire a housekeeper."

"Are you sure?"

"Positive."

"Well, if you're really sure, it'd be great."

"Good." Lucy smiled, noting not for the first time the transformation that had occurred in Bea with the return of Bobby to her life. "Look at you," she teased. "You're so distracted. It wouldn't surprise me a bit to have you come marching in one afternoon to announce you and Bobby, the wonder boy, are running off to get married."

"Lucy!" Bea flushed.

"There's nothing wrong with being in love. It happens to the best of us."

"It's not like that at all."

"It sure *is* like that. You've always been crazy about that boy."

"Of course I've always liked him."

"Of course," Lucy agreed, then wisely let the matter drop. "I'd better get to work. I've got to run over to the studio to pick up a fresh batch of photos and envelopes. You will have to sign the photos, you know."

"I know," Bea answered. "You think I should actually *buy* a house?"

"Why not? You've got plenty of money coming in to pay for it."

"I keep thinking all this'll end any minute, and I'll be back in New York, going to auditions or dancing on street corners with a tin can in my hand."

"It'll never happen."

"Something like that can always happen. I read the papers; I've seen those stories about how so-and-so used to be a big silent-film star, and spent every cent he ever got on big parties, fancy cars, ritzy clothes, and diamonds for his girlfriends, and was discovered the other day waiting tables in some dive."

"You don't do foolish things with your money," Lucy said. "You're a sensible girl, altogether."

Bea frowned. "Not altogether," she disagreed.

Lucy looked at her watch. "You'd better get a move on, or you'll be late. And we don't want to keep Bobby waiting, do we?"

"You're rotten," Bea laughed, flushing again.

Bobby was riding high, and he owed everything to Bea—his contract, his weekly salary, a place of his own, swell new clothes. She'd even prepared him for every single thing that would happen—the publicity, the photo sessions, the screen test, the arranged dates to get him seen around town, all of it. Nevertheless, he'd had no idea what it would be like when they sat down with Hank to look over the shooting script.

Bobby stared at the breakdown spread out on the table, mystified by what looked like some kind of architectural drawing.

"Don't worry," Bea reassured him. "Hank'll explain everything."

"I don't want everyone to think I'm some kind of idiot."

"She's right," Hank said with a smile. "Don't worry about it."

Hank's analysis laid out everything from the main titles to the timing of each segment, its location, which cast members would be involved, whether the scenes were indoors or outdoors, the opticals— fades, wipes, dissolves—the estimated running time to the second, a brief analysis of each scene, and whether or not there'd be music;

plus notes on singing, dancing, or novelty bits. There were also blanks to be filled in for the timing on the rough cut, as well as for the final cut.

"What's the difference between rough and final?" Bobby asked her.

"Rough is before the last editing and scoring. Final is what people see when they pay the price of admission."

He shook his head, awed by the complex, detailed breakdown, with its careful notations: Scene 45—Action: 2–8/9 minutes; Dialogue: 3 minutes; Total time: 5-8/9 minutes.

"What if it goes over or under?" Bobby wanted to know.

"It's only an estimate," Hank said. "This is for me and the crew to worry about."

"How did you learn so much?" Bobby asked Bea.

"I asked."

He couldn't ask. It made him feel too stupid. But he did pay extra close attention to everything that went on, making mental notes in order to remember each face he encountered on the set. He couldn't get over how many people it took to put a piece of film together. As they were preparing to start shooting, he counted thirty-six technicians on the sound stage and, out of curiosity, made a list in a small notebook he'd taken to carrying around with him. It included Hank, the gaffer, Ike, and two assistant cameramen; the key grip, the best boy or assistant gaffer; a dialogue assistant and an assistant director; a technical adviser, several set painters, a script clerk, the unit production manager, a sound-boom man, stand-ins for himself and Bea, two make-up people, a hairdresser, two people from wardrobe, Clark Boland, Hero, and Pete, the publicity man.

"Are you nervous?" Bea asked him before their first scene together. "Don't be. Just concentrate on what we're doing. If there's a cut during a take, remember where you were, what you were doing, and how you felt doing it. It's really important to concentrate so that when it comes to the cutting, it'll match. When we get to your close-ups, I'll be right here to feed you the lines. The only thing we've got to worry about is the number of takes we'll have to do on the dance numbers and the damned floor which they'll keep as slick as ice. You'll be fine, Bobby. I know you will."

"I sure hope so." He took hold of her hand, marveling at how small it was. Her bones seemed too minute, as if they couldn't possibly be strong enough to support her. His eyes traveled upward over her as he continued to examine her hand, feeling jolted as he did every time he had contact with some part of her or happened simply to look at her. Without fail, he had to wonder how she could be so complete in his thoughts, so all of a piece; and how, in reality, she could appear

159

to him a complete puzzle. The look and sound and feel of her in his arms when they danced was bewildering and magnetic.

He had, in their time apart, had his first relationship with a woman. An older woman. At the outset, he'd been overawed at the symmetry of man fitting to woman and the paroxysmic pleasure of it. With time and continued exposure, however, he'd grown dissatisfied because he'd started thinking again of Bea, understanding more fully what it was he'd felt that had caused him to run away from her. Understanding it in no way diminished her ongoing impact on him. They danced together, for hours every day. They shared a rhythm, whether together or apart, and he was being drawn closer and closer to her. Yet she seemed not to share his feelings, and he had to keep telling himself to resist impulses like the one just now that had prompted him to take hold of her hand, because he didn't want to do or say or even think anything that would result in their being separated again. What he hadn't known a year or so ago, but knew now, was that he was crazy about her. It was grown-up stuff, these feelings he had for her. And neither one of them was really grown-up, despite what it said in their contracts. Sure, he had the edge on her in the age department, and he'd had those few months with Lydia, but none of that had prepared him to cope day after day with Bea. He told himself she thought of him as a friend; he told himself not to do anything that might mess it up; he told himself to do the work and keep the rest of it to himself.

"You've gone off somewhere," she said, breaking his long silence. "Is anything the matter?"

"What if we're a flop and people really want to see you dancing with old Dickie?"

"Bobby," she said with quiet, but absolute, conviction, "we could *never* be a flop!"

She was right. The *New York Times* said of *Big City*, ". . . their dancing is peerless, and what they give in emotion to each song is impressive in its depths."

The Los Angeles *Examiner* said, ". . . they dance their way into your heart. These two are the perfect screen match."

Variety said, ". . . to hear Bobby Bradley sing 'Without You' is to have your heart-strings tugged. To see him and Crane dance is an experience without parallel."

The New Yorker said, ". . . something rare and wonderful has come to the motion-picture screen: a young couple of outstanding musical talent who simply dazzle. Director Henry Donovan continues to deliver, in this his second feature, a production packed with good things to look at and to hear, with no unnecessary frills or jagged edges."

After *Big City,* they did *Early Birds,* and then *Fancy Dress,* followed by *Clear Sailing,* and *Starlight.* Each picture drew excellent reviews and ever bigger audiences, so that after their second year and their sixth picture, Bea and Bobby ranked together as number six on the list of box-office top ten. Bobby had an apartment at the Château Marmont, a closet full of hand-tailored clothes, a new Chrysler sports coupe, and thirty-six pairs of dancing shoes. Bea had a ten-room house in Beverly Hills, a wonderful housekeeper named Molly, a driver's license and a new roadster, her own collection of dancing shoes, two thick scrapbooks Lucy faithfully kept up to date, and a mounting malaise.

Their production unit at the studio had its own offices and full-time staff, including Pete who now worked exclusively on their publicity. The nucleus of the unit consisted of Ludie as executive producer, Hank, Hero, Ike, Clark Boland, Bobby, and Bea and was referred to by everyone as the Crane-Bradley unit. The two of them had permanent dress models in wardrobe, as well as files full of publicity stills. They were sent out to do publicity between pictures, sometimes together, most often with other partners. Bobby dated. Bea refused to go out unless Lucy was along to chaperone. Bobby kept expecting Bea to announce her interest in some other fellow, but it didn't happen. And he began to feel guilty when he went out for an evening with some starlet from one of the studios and found himself having a good time. He hated feeling guilty, hated feeling like a louse for being able to enjoy himself with someone other than Bea. But most of the time she balked at doing publicity, claiming she preferred to stay at home in the evenings. She said she'd rather read, or listen to music, or have dinner with Hank and Hero, or go to visit Bill Robinson than dress up and go out for the evening.

She'd asked to be introduced to Bill when she'd heard he was working with Shirley Temple on *The Littlest Rebel,* and Pete had paved the way, arranging the introduction. He'd then taken Bea over to Fox himself and, during a break in the shooting, he'd presented Bea to the little girl, and to Bojangles.

Bea had been enchanted by the child, and speechless at meeting the man who'd been indirectly responsible for her career. "I saw you at the Elgin Theatre in Toronto in 1922," she told him, "when I was five years old. And when I saw you dance, I knew that was what I wanted to do."

"I've seen you," he said with a smile, "and you'd have been there dancing even if you'd never set eyes on me."

They'd become friends, and whenever possible, Bea would drive over to talk to the man or to sit listening to his tales about his vaudeville days. When he agreed to do the choreography for *Dimples,* another upcoming Temple feature, Bea heard out his ideas, impressed anew by his great knowledge. Often, when she'd drop by for a visit, other dancers would be there, and they'd regularly, spontaneously, start in to dance. She felt, more and more, as if the hours she spent with Bill were somehow keeping her sane.

When rehearsals started for *Happy Go Lucky,* she and Bobby spent hours alone together in the rehearsal sound stage, working up the routines along the guidelines Hero had suggested. Bobby felt himself sliding out of control. He'd study the way the muscles in her thighs moved beneath the taut surface of her flesh or the slim width of her torso as she fitted into the circle of his arm; he'd look at her extraordinary eyes and forget himself, caught by the light depthlessness there that was like the ocean at daybreak.

For her part, she felt often as if she were sinking below the surface of something as silvered and heavy as mercury. The intense happiness she'd felt at the onset of their sanctioned partnership had, during the subsequent two and a half years, altered subtly day by day until she couldn't stand to hear the tales of yet another party Bobby had attended with yet another beautiful newcomer to the studio. She didn't want to know who'd been at the party, or what sort of food had been served, or what kind of deals had been made over cocktails before dinner. When politics obliged her to put on a ludicrously expensive gown she'd be able to wear only for that one occasion and accompany some improbably handsome young man to, say, the Academy Awards ceremony at the Biltmore Hotel, she felt put upon and was quietly livid at being unable, at the very least, to attend with Bobby. But the studio was determined that their link should be advertised only through their pictures together and not socially. She was compelled to suffer through an evening with some vapid but beautiful young man while she watched Bobby escort yet another gorgeous blonde starlet who, no doubt, was also vapid. Mercifully, there was always Lucy along to keep things going, to make pleasant conversation. And most often, Ike made it a foursome. Lucy and Ike were spending much of their free time together, and Bea was waiting for Lucy to make an announcement.

Being around Bea, Lucy thought, had become a little like walking around carrying a time bomb in a suitcase. Bea was pleasant enough and seemed to enjoy the new house, but she was always ticking away just beneath the surface. Often, without warning, she'd abandon

162

whatever it was she'd been doing, jump up, grab her keys, and rush out of the house. She'd drive off and return hours later subdued and ready for sleep. When Lucy casually asked where she went, Bea responded, "I just drive. Sometimes I go to look at the ocean or to visit with Bill. Sometimes I drop in on Hank or Hero, and we talk."

When Lucy ventured to ask, "Are you all right?" Bea answered every time, "I am perfectly all right, couldn't be better, thank you."

It was a lie, of course, and they both knew it. Finally, Lucy forced a confrontation. After waiting up until four in the morning for Bea to return from one of her flights from the house, she ushered her into the living room, sat her down on the sofa, and declared, "Something's going to have to be done, Bea."

"About what?"

"About you. At first, it was all right as long as you were working. Oh, you'd come home at the end of the day and let off steam, but that was to be expected. But now," she said, "it's all the time, and you're wound up like a spring. If you don't ease off, I'm afraid to think what'll happen."

To Lucy's great surprise, Bea sat for a long moment with her elbows on her knees, then she jumped up, wound both hands into her hair, threw her head back, her eyes closed, and she emitted a sharp, choking shriek. She remained standing, pulling at her hair, her eyes ground shut, every muscle in her body tensed. "I can't stand it!" she groaned, opening her eyes to look at Lucy. *"I can't stand it!"*

"What?" Lucy asked, alarmed.

"The way I feel." She let go of her hair, and her hands dropped to her sides, her fingers immediately curling tightly into her palms. "I think maybe I'm going crazy, Luce."

"Why? What's happened?"

"If I have to go to one more party, one more 'function,' and sit there with some idiotically pretty young man while I watch Bobby dancing attendance on one more of those grinning little would-be movie stars, I swear I'll kill someone. I know I'm getting a reputation for being difficult, that Louella's taken to hinting that I'm not the sweet thing I was when I got here; I know I'm not *fun*, but I can't help it. I don't *want* to be difficult, but I have to say *something* when they hand me dialogue no self-respecting eight-year-old would believe. And I can't just say thank you when the designer comes in with a dress that doesn't move and expects me to dance in it. And not even Hank can make me believe there are reasons why our pictures are making the studio a fortune but still nobody takes them seriously. I'm beginning to think I've sung and danced my way into a corner I'll never get out of. I'm tired of playing variations on the same character over and over until I can do the lines in my sleep. I'm tired of all of it." She stopped abruptly and did something utterly out of character. She broke into silently convulsive weeping that prompted Lucy to take her in her arms and hold her until Bea had regained some measure of her control.

"Come sit down," Lucy said gently, directing her back to the sofa where Bea sagged against her, her chest heaving with the effort to contain her anguish. "This doesn't have a thing to do with any of what you've been ranting about," Lucy said incisively. "Every bit of this has to do with Bobby and nothing else. I'm right, aren't I?"

"I *hate* crying!" Bea said furiously, grinding her fists into her eyes.

"You're not answering my question."

"I *can't* answer. I don't know. I only know I've never felt so wretched, not ever. I feel like dying, except that I don't want to die. I have everything; I've even got a friend like Bill Robinson. When I had nothing, I used to be so happy. Remember? Remember when I wanted you to give me dancing lessons, and you said you would? And I always knew how things would be, how they'd work out. I knew we'd all get work in New York, and we did. And I knew Bobby would be a big hit here . . . So many things I knew once, and now I don't know anything. Years of my life are passing, whole years. It seems as if I go to bed at night, and when I wake up in the morning, it's another year, and I don't have the things that used to make me happy. When I have to go to the studio, I get up dreading it because I'll go there, and we'll work together, hour after hour, and as long as we're actually working I feel in charge of myself, as if I know that this is the way things are supposed to be, and it's all all right. But then we finish, and he changes his shoes and leaves, and I stand there waiting for something that never happens. That's when I think about dying." She turned slowly to face Lucy and in a voice even deeper than normal said, "He doesn't love me, Lucy. I don't think I can bear it one more day. Nothing else seems to matter. It's all I think about."

"Oh, sweetheart," Lucy sympathized, "you can't know that. Not for sure, you can't."

"You love Ike," Bea said reasonably, "and he shows you that he loves you, doesn't he?"

"Well, yes, I guess," Lucy agreed, taken aback. "But that's different."

"Why is it different? Why?"

"Because . . . Because we're older. Because Ike's been married, and because at a certain point way back I made a decision about what was . . . acceptable, I suppose, about what I was and wasn't willing to do."

164

"You're talking about sex, about making love."

"Yes, I am."

With a terrible expression of yearning, Bea said, "For years now I keep coming at you, asking questions that turn you red from head to toe, and I still only know what I think I know, Lucy. Sometimes, I look at myself in the mirror and hate me, hate what I see because the only thing I know how to do is dance. I'm nineteen years old, and that's not so young. So why am I still just a kid?"

"Because you are. Some people grow up faster than others, that's all."

"*How* can I still be a kid when I've made all these movies, and support that fool of a mother of mine, and can drive a car, and do all the things I do? I'm *tired* of being a kid. I'm sick to death of it. It's time I got to be a grown-up. My press kits say that I am. My press kits make me sound like the most sophisticated thing to walk down a street in the last hundred years. They do up my hair, they do up my face, they put me into evening gowns that have no backs and not much front and then they backlight me so you can see through the damned things. You *know* what I'm saying," she insisted.

"I know."

"So what am I supposed to *do* about it?"

"I don't know."

"*You see!*" Bea cried, and wound her hands again into her hair. "What'm I supposed to *do?*"

"I don't know," Lucy repeated. "But ripping your hair out at the roots isn't the answer. Maybe you should have a talk with Bobby," she suggested.

Bea laughed, allowing her hands to fall into her lap. "I don't want to *talk* with Bobby," she said, then covered her face with her hands, feeling the heat pulsing in her cheeks. "We'd better get to bed now," she said, jumping up. "I'm sorry you were worried. I'll let you know next time where I think I'm going to be." She almost ran toward the hall.

"Bea!" Lucy called after her, causing her to stop. "It isn't wrong, you know, to be human and to want certain things."

"Are you telling me it's all right?" Bea halted in the doorway, and turned to look back. "Are you giving me permission to give myself away, Lucy?"

"Maybe I am."

"I don't know whether or not that helps, but thank you." She said good night, and went off up the stairs to her room.

"God!" Lucy whispered.

They worked until nine on the evening before they were to begin shooting. Bobby sat on the floor taking off his shoes, and Bea leaned against the practice bar, watching him.

"Does it feel to you as if we're doing the same thing over and over?" she asked him.

He looked up at her as he shoved his shoes into his bag. "No," he answered, slightly confused. "Is that the way it feels to you?"

"Sometimes. Do you read the fan magazines and the trades, Bobby?"

"Sometimes. Why?"

"They say all kinds of things about us. Have you noticed? Parsons is forever hinting we fight like cats and dogs on the set. And the fanzines say that off the set we're the new Gilbert and Garbo. Which is pretty funny, I think. I just wondered what you thought about it."

He finished tying the laces on his street shoes and got up. He thought she looked odd, very tense, the muscles in her upper arms flexing as they bore her weight against the bar. Her hair was scraped back from her face in a tight knot, but strands had come free and adhered wetly to her temples and to the back of her neck. Without make-up, her skin was very white; she looked vulnerable, almost naked.

"I guess," he said, leaving his bag on the floor and coming over to stand beside her at the bar, "I don't think much about it one way or another." He glanced sidelong at her, studying the way her left leg was bent for support and the way perspiration caused her blouse to cling. Certain she had to have guessed at his reaction to her, he averted his eyes. "Do *you* think about it?" He tried to keep his tone casual.

"I think about all kinds of things, about how it feels to go out shopping and I'm just another customer until I write a check and hand it over the counter. Then the girl reads my name and she looks at me, and I can see the reaction on her face. First, she's excited because she's seen me in pictures. Then, she's confused and disappointed because I'm not one bit glamorous. In fact, if she didn't have the check in her hand with my name right there, she'd never believe I could possibly be Beatrice Crane. I'm just too ordinary. I've even got a big nose. She'll go home tonight and tell everyone she met Beatrice Crane today and there wasn't anything so hot about her.

"I think about the letters people write, about how much they claim to love me. I've had marriage proposals," she laughed. "And girls have written to criticize the way I walk or the false eyelashes they had me wear in *Early Birds*. There are people who'd like to meet me, and people who've threatened to kill me. At first, it scared me. But then, when I thought about it, I realized it'd be just like the salesgirls when I go shopping. If I go out looking like myself and not like a movie star, not many people give me a second glance. But it makes me feel peculiar because I have two lives, the one I live on the screen and the one I try to live off the screen. To the people out there, I'm one thing. But inside here, in my life, I'm someone else."

"But all of it's you," he said. "After all, you *are* the person on the screen."

"I *play* the person on the screen, Bobby. I play that person as hard as I can, as well as I can, with everything I've got in me. And, sure, that girl's part of me. But I don't go on living her life after the final dissolve. It ends. I change my clothes, take off the make-up, and go home. But sometimes, sometimes, I have to wonder... about it. Who's the real Beatrice Crane? Maybe the real person *is* the one on celluloid. Maybe she's the very best of me, and I'm nothing more than some kind of transparent bag that gets stuffed full of different characters who say and do the things Beatrice Crane can't do. So," she sighed, "I have to wonder why it's so important to everyone to speculate about us the way they do."

"It's just publicity, Bea. If it's not us, then it's Lombard and Gable, or some other hot item. That's what sells magazines, what gets people to go see the pictures."

She wanted to prolong the conversation but felt so suddenly awkward that she couldn't. She could feel heat radiating from his body and smell the lemony cologne he'd taken to using recently. All she could think about, for a moment, was the number of times they'd kissed for the cameras, with thirty or forty crew members in attendance, and how, during those kisses, she'd had to hold herself together inside, as if Beatrice Crane had become a small package that could be hidden anywhere. It wasn't quite so simple, though, and after the take was done, she'd found herself left with an agitated sense of incompletion and an emptiness she'd had to struggle to hide. She'd be certain that her eyes were staring wildly and that everyone on the sound stage could see right through her, direcly into the knot of confounded emotions she had to contain behind her skin.

"Are you happy, Bobby?" she asked, her treacherous voice going thick. Why, she wondered, couldn't she be content with what she had? Why did she have to be someone who was thinking all the time and couldn't seem to turn off her brain? At some moments she'd have given anything to have no brain at all.

"I guess so," he answered uncertainly. "What about you?"

It was going wrong, she thought frantically. She'd given misleading cues, and he'd asked the trigger question. Nobody wrote a script for life; there was no one to call "cut" on the take. She opened her mouth thinking to give some glib, dishonest answer but, to her utter dismay, she found she couldn't speak. She made an indecipherable sound that was going to be, she knew, only a brief prelude to tears. She shoved away from the bar, bent on escape, but he caught hold of her arm and she had to stop and look at him, frightened of the situation's potential. Why couldn't she be complete within herself? Why did she have to want more? How important was a life, anyway?

"I'm not all that happy," he said, searching her eyes, "if you want to know the truth. What are we doing, Bea?"

She shook her head, mute. If she tried to say one word now, she'd start to cry, the way she had with Lucy. And she'd never forgive herself if that happened.

He waited for her to answer, his eyes holding hers. He could hear his heartbeat in his ears. When she failed to answer, his attention slowly shifted and he became aware of his hand on her arm. The sound stage seemed all at once like a cave in the dead of winter, silent but for the sound of their breathing: his steady, hers uneven. "I don't think I can do it anymore," he said almost inaudibly. "It feels like a bad marriage or something." He gave her a grim smile. "Something that went bad without ever having been good."

"What?" she managed.

"Playing hands-off with you, Bea. I go home from here every night tired to my bones, and the minute I lie down, I'm wide awake thinking about you, thinking about the things I want to say to you but can't, about touching you but never being able to. I go in my car and collect some dame who's just another name at some address the studio boys've given me; they've told me to take her to the Cocoanut Grove or some other damned place to be seen, and no matter what I do, I can't make her you. They're most always willing, you know. At first, I could hardly believe my luck. But, thanks to you, I've got a name that means something now, and the way these dames figure it, going to bed with me might do their careers some good. So they're willing. It doesn't do *me* any good, though. And later on, when it's over, I have to wonder why the hell I did it. I mean, aside from the possibility that one fine day one of those girls might get wise and decide to hit me with a paternity suit, I don't give a damn about them, didn't even really *want* them. But they were there, they offered, so I took what was offered because I'm not smart enough, or something, to say no. And I keep thinking maybe I'll find someone if I keep on looking out there, because it gets harder every day playing the game in here. Hands off, Bradley! You can't have what you really want because . . . because . . . I don't even *know* why. It's just the way it is. And now, all of a sudden, you want to know if I'm happy. Hell, no! I'm not happy, Bea. But I can't stop thinking maybe I could be, if I could just get you to stop and hold still for a couple of minutes."

"Me? Hold still?" she said stupidly.

"Yeah," he answered.

"Do you care for me at all?" she asked, agonized.

"Weren't you *listening?*" his voice rose. "You're *all* I *think* about, for chrissake!"

He glared at her, and she searched his eyes, desperation and need making her legs suddenly rubbery. "I love you," she whispered. "Nothing has ever hurt the way loving you does."

"Why does it have to hurt?" His brows drew together. "Why are we putting each other through this?"

"Because there are rules," she said sorrowfully. "All kinds of them. Some I made up for myself, and a lot of others this place has made for me. I don't think I can care anymore about the rules."

They were at the brink, he thought. And for a long moment, he was awed and more than a little frightened by a vision of the re-sponsiblity both of them faced if they went one step further with this. He looked at her eyes, then at her mouth, then again at his hand on her arm. The decision made itself. All he had to do was tighten his grip on her arm and pull. She moved. So simple. The air between them thinned, evaporated. He took a step and they were breast to breast, and all that remained between them was damp clothing.

In the last few seconds before their mouths met, she had a dreadful insight into what this meeting would signify. You'll break my heart, she thought. I'll give myself to you, and with the best intentions in the world, you'll hurt me somehow. She saw this, acknowledged it, and then allowed it to drift away. There were no technicians to see, no silent witnesses behind the lights and camera. There were just the two of them, and she was about to leave something behind, but she couldn't care. She could only close her eyes and feel, at liberty finally to measure the breadth of his shoulders with her hands, the length of his arms. She could only respond, her entire being suspended in anticipation of new knowledge.

Without a word, they ran to her trailer and, once inside with the door locked, they tugged at each other's clothing, frantic to dispense with the final barriers. And when they stood together, skin to skin, she breathed shallowly, tremulously, thinking there couldn't possibly be any feeling finer than this. To have the warm, solid length of his body molded to hers was the ultimate perfection. In shedding her clothes, she'd discarded her childhood, her anxiety, and her igno-rance. She could never retrieve that girl, but it didn't matter. Having him kiss and caress her, having his hands and mouth touch against what seemed to be raw nerve-endings and having him explore her body triggered a kind of madness that inspired her to envelop him in whatever fashion she was able, so that she might perpetuate the madness. She'd have been willing, at the apex of her pleasure, to die. What she'd wanted and needed for a very long time came in the form of this man who could, with his touch, blind and deafen her to everything but this. Just this. A brief, stabbing pain that turned her gelid. And then engulfing heat that brought in its wake astonishment. She was shattered by the way in which he lost himself to her, crying out her name before subsiding. She cradled his head to her breasts, gently ferocious in her love for him, and mute again, rendered voiceless by the enormity of their ability to merge.

She had to touch and know every part of him, had to see how he looked when his hands fitted themselves to her body. And when he slowly slid away down the length of her body, she watched him, initially amused, thinking he couldn't possibly be serious, couldn't possibly do or want to do what it appeared he intended. But he was serious, did have intentions. His aggressively determined actions were like a bullet to her brain, destroying those last segments of her self that had sat apart, taking note of and commenting on what was happening. She closed her eyes, so that she never saw herself go. She gave access, and he claimed her. She was scalded, convulsed, and ultimately, reborn.

Suddenly, she couldn't understand what had kept them apart for so long, why they'd gone to such lengths to avoid one another when, the entire time, each had wanted the other to come near. "We were such idiots," she laughed, gathering him into her arms. "I should've known better," she chided herself, and him. "Should've known better than to buy your tough-guy act when I've known from the start what a softie you really are."

"I'm no softie," he argued.

"Oh, you are," she disagreed. "You try so hard to cover it up, but I know better."

"You *think* you do."

"Let's not talk."

She was happier than she'd ever imagined it possible to be, and everything made sense. Her energy was limitless. She could work all day, then sneak away with Bobby and make love half the night, then be up again at four in the morning ready to work some more. Six days a week, the two of them sweated under the lights, and on

Sundays they drove in Bobby's car as far as they could get from the studio. On some deserted stretch of beach, they'd sit together on a blanket and talk until words were no longer sufficient and they had to find a place—an out-of-the-way tourist cabin, or the back of the car, or the house of some discreet friend—where they could be naked together.

"Now I have everything," she told him, in a state of ongoing astonishment at the pleasure they could give each other. "I just wish we didn't have to sneak around this way."

"It won't be forever," he said, wishing he knew how to tell her what she meant to him. He never seemed able to frame his feelings for her in words, and he sometimes doubted that his actions revealed what he wanted her to know—that he loved her so utterly, that he felt her to be so much a part of him that when they were apart, even for a few hours, he couldn't see, or hear, or even think properly. When they made love, he felt as if he wanted to become permanently attached to her. He even dreamed one night that he began taking bites out of her, going on and on until he'd swallowed her entirely. The dream alarmed him, and he thought about telling her but decided it would be too easy to misinterpret the dream's significance.

"Imagine!" she whispered to him, one afternoon on the set. "I used to make faces at the idea of making love."

"You were just a little slow on the uptake, sister," he whispered back.

"Bobby." She reached for his hand and held it tightly. "I'm so happy."

"Me, too," he said, then freed himself. "We shouldn't be taking chances."

"I wish I knew why we can't come out in the open."

"Jesus, Bea! You're the one who's been telling me about the rules since day one. Don't tell me you've forgotten them all of a sudden?"

"No. You're right. I'll meet you at eight." She peeked out around the edge of the flat, turned back to smile at him, then hurried away to use up the hours before they could be together again.

Her body, and his, fascinated her. She was shameless and refused to feel guilty. They made love until she was too swollen and sore to continue. Then she lay in his arms and weaved dreams of their future, breathing in the smell and feel of him, thinking repeatedly of that afternoon when she'd seen him for the first time outside the theater, with his dancing shoes around his neck. "I love your freckles," she told him, "and the way you sleep, with your face buried in the pillow. I love your elbow," she declared, and laughed.

"You're nuts, sister," he told her, delighted.

171

"You're not supposed to say that. You're supposed to tell me all the things you love about me."

"I can't recite to order."

"Come on. Tell me."

"Your legs. I love your legs."

"That's it? That's all?"

"Bea," he moaned, "I can't do it."

"There must be something else about me you're mad for."

As she watched, he flushed darkly. "Yeah, there is," he admitted, and held her down to show her. She had to know, he thought. She had to be able to feel it, because no matter how hard he tried the right words just wouldn't come to him. He despaired, at moments, of ever being able to display all she aroused in him. "I'm crazy for you," he told her over and over. "Crazy for you."

Seventeen

HANK sat alone in the screening room after the others had gone and had the projectionist run the day's takes again. Then he let the man in the booth go home. In the dark, Hank lit a cigarette and gazed at the blank screen, able to see again what had been so manifestly clear in the dailies since principal photography had begun. The chemistry that had existed previously between Bobby and Bea had flared, with this picture, into an explosive dynamism. It wasn't bad, it wouldn't hurt the picture any, but in some barely tangible fashion, Hank was hurt. He tried to remind himself of certain, harsh realities, but the truth in no way ameliorated the nagging presentiment he had of trouble. He wanted to be happy for Bea, and in one sense he was. She was in love, and she shone with it. She'd never looked so beautiful. She glowed, she simmered, she seemed to vibrate.

And to be fair, it had done wonders for Bobby, too. Their scenes together, especially the dance numbers, were nothing short of miraculous. They flowed like something elemental, their timing so attuned, their meetings so inevitable that people were going to line up for days to see them. They were just so goddamned young, he thought, and so naïve that they couldn't manage to conceal their emotions entirely, although they made a damned good effort at it.

Ludie knew. He'd called Hank into the office that afternoon to say, "You keep an eye on those two. Don't let this get out of hand. Maybe somebody should put a word in, they should be separated. Who knows?"

"Ludie," Hank had said quietly, "it's bad enough they're hounded everywhere they go. They can't stop someplace for a cup of coffee without people popping out of the woodwork to take their picture or ask for autographs. D'you really think we should start telling them what to do and how to do it, when they're on their own time?"

"I got plenty tied up in that girl. In Bradley, too. We got another story in the works."

"Your investment's already paid off a hundred-fold. Bea's nobody's fool. I don't think you've got a thing to worry about."

"I want everybody keepin' an eye on those two, they shouldn't go running off in the middle of the shoot. They want to get married, they do it right. We make something of it."

"Everything will be fine," Hank had told him. "They're not small children, Ludie. And they do have a right to their private lives."

"Yeah. We'll see."

Bea was a sensible girl, and Bobby was no dunce, either. But there was a difference between the two of them that Hank could see effortlessly. Bobby didn't have the independence, the same sense of self Bea did. He was talented, a good kid, a solid performer. But he was one of the hungry ones, and hunger could prove a stronger appetite than any other. Sure, he'd acquired a degree of maturity in the past couple of years, and he'd paid attention to what Jerry, among others, had told him. He'd been taking care of his money, accepting sound advice; he'd grown. And Hank was genuinely fond of him. Still, the two of them were kids, nineteen and twenty-one. They seemed somehow moist, as if they hadn't quite finished ripening.

He was going to have to talk to Bea. He couldn't see any way around it. They had a week of shooting left, and then a couple of months free before they started work on *Moonlight*, the sequel to *Starlight*. And maybe when *Moonlight* was out of they way, he'd take some steps toward making a go of one of the projects he'd been nursing for so long. He wanted to try his hand at a non-musical production; he wanted to film something that would have a different kind of impact. He had two scripts ready and, if necessary, he'd go to another studio with the projects. What he dreamed of was putting Bea in a solid, dramatic role. He suspected she'd like the challenge, and he had no doubt whatsoever she'd be able to do it. What he couldn't decide was how her involvement with Bobby might affect her professional decisions. There was also the matter of convincing Ludie to allow her to do it. Ludie had a number of limitations, not the least of which was his inability to let something go until he'd milked the last possible penny from it. Still, Ludie was going to have to renegotiate with Jerry soon, because after *Moonlight* Bea's contract would be up.

With a sigh, he put out his cigarette, but made no move to leave. Instead, he lit a fresh one, recrossed his legs, and stared again at the dark screen. Admit it, he told himself. You're jealous. No, not jealous. That was too strong. Envious, perhaps. Something. Who the hell knew what it was? And what right did he have even to think about her? Not only was he eighteen years older, he was also physically incapable of making good any commitment he might have wished to make to her. So what did he think he could offer her? And where did that leave Hero? There were existing commitments on everyone's part. Bea was in love with Bobby, and the two of them fled from the studio at the end of each day like giddy school-children playing a fabulous, secret game. He didn't want to see either of them get hurt. He had no right to try to evaluate their affair. Except that he couldn't help himself. He was a lot of years older. Years represented experience, and God only knew he had enough experiences under his belt. Experience built wisdom, if you allowed it. He'd allowed it, he had it, and now he was powerless to do anything but sit on the sidelines and watch, hoping to God it all worked up to a happy ending.

Stubbing out the cigarette, he reached for the telephone. Lucy answered and said Bea hadn't come in yet.

"Tell her I called, Lucy," he said wearily. "I need to talk to her."

"Is there a problem?"

"Ludie's afraid there might be."

There was a pause, and then she said, "It's getting around, isn't it?"

"I'm afraid so."

"Damn!"

"Hell, Lucy! You know what a goddamned goldfish bowl this town is. I don't want to be making this call any more than Bea's going to want to get it."

"I know that, Hank. What should I tell her?"

174

"Tell her to come home tomorrow night. I'll be along as soon as I can get away."

"She's so happy. Why won't they leave her alone?"

"Lucy, there's a reality here you're ignoring. And so is Bea. When she signed that contract, she did a whole lot more than put her name on the dotted line. She turned her life over to the studio and, more specifically, to Ludie Meyers. So far, she's been lucky, or maybe just smart. Right now, she's not being so smart. They made her, but they can break her, and she's about to find out that she doesn't own as much of a percentage of herself as she thought."

"You sound so angry," Lucy said nervously.

"I *am* angry. D'you think I like being turned into a messenger boy for Ludie? D'you think I like being told to play watchdog? I love Bea, and if she's happy, that makes me happy. But every last one of us has a career on the line. So I've been delegated to 'talk' to her. It makes me *sick.*"

"I'll talk to her for you," she said. "I know what you're going to say anyway."

"It stinks!" he railed. "Nobody should have the right to call the shots in somebody else's life."

"No," she agreed. "They shouldn't. But they do. So I'll talk to her. It'll be all right, Hank. Don't be upset."

He took a breath and sat back in his seat. "Let me ask you something."

"Sure. What?"

"What d'you get out of this? What do you, personally, get from it?"

"Me?" She had to think for a moment. "I don't know how to answer that. I guess what I get is the right to be with her, to try to look out for her, to help if I can."

"And that's what you're going to do for the rest of your life?"

"I don't know about the rest of my life. But for now, for a while, yes. Somebody has to, Hank. Aside from everything else, I love her, too. She's the only kid I'm ever likely to have, and she's more mine than that dizzy blonde's in Canada. I'll talk to her," she promised. "What exactly is it Meyers wants?"

"To put it crudely, and I'm quoting: He doesn't want them fucking in the public eye."

"Jesus!" she exclaimed. "Have they been seen?"

"Not so far. But he's heard talk."

"It's not fair!" she protested.

"When you find something that *is,* please share it with me. I'm going home now. I'm sorry, Lucy. But maybe it'll all just quietly go away and neither one of us will have to do very much of anything."

175

Lucy waited up, and when Bea came in at midnight, Lucy repeated her conversation with Hank.

"You're going to have to be very, very careful," Lucy wound down. "Or, you're going to have to let Ludie throw you the wedding of the century."

"We've talked about getting married," Bea said, reeling, "but not now. I mean, I don't know. It wasn't going to be right away, but . . . I don't know. This is so awful. I had no idea people knew." She looked around the room, then over at the windows. "It's as if they've got spies in the shadows, watching everything you do with binoculars." She shivered, then wet her lips. "Lucy, for a few months I've been completely happy. I suppose I thought somehow no one could see us. We stay away from each other on the set, and we've stayed away from this house, and from Bobby's place. We've stayed away from every place where anyone might conceivably see us. We've had to sneak around . . . We've never been able to spend one entire night together, or even be . . . I think I'm pregnant. I want a baby, and I want Bobby; I want us to live together and be a family."

"*Why* didn't he *protect* you?" Lucy asked angrily. "What kind of idiot *is* he?"

"Don't blame him, Lucy. It's really not his fault. When I first thought I might be pregnant, I was so excited. I was planning to go to a doctor next week, after we wrapped the picture. And then, then I thought I'd tell Bobby, and we'd go somewhere, get married. We can still do that."

"And what about your career?"

"What about it? Just because I get married and have a baby doesn't mean my career has to end."

"I think that's *just* what it might mean."

"I thought you'd be so happy for me," Bea said disappointedly, looking for a long moment at her friend. Even upset and angry, Lucy was soft-looking, lovely, with her short curly dark hair, creamy skin, and brown eyes. The sight of Lucy, Lucy's presence in her life, was always reassuring, even when they disagreed, as now. "I thought," Bea went on, "that I'd marry Bobby, and you'd finally be able to get together with Ike. I know it's what you've been wanting."

"What I want hasn't anything to do with this. They're not going to let you do it, Bea. It isn't that I'm not happy for you, because under other circumstances I would be. With all my heart. It's just that I know Meyers will never sit back and let you go off into the sunset with Bobby while he's got a new picture set for you, while you're still top

176

ten at the box office. And then there's Jerry. What d'you think he's going to say when you tell him you can't sign a new contract because you're going to have to take time off to have a baby? And, let's not forget Bobby. I assume you haven't told him yet. Bea, if they put his back to the wall and say he's out of work, he's on suspension if the two of you go through with this, what d'you imagine he'll do?"

"He won't let me down."

"Okay." Lucy pulled back. "Okay. If it's what you both want, then that'll be fine. You can fight this together. I only hope to God this turns out the way you want it to."

"You don't think it will, though, do you?"

"I know it doesn't sound that way right this minute, but I love you. You're like my kid and my sister; you're my friend, and sometimes you're like my mother, the way you look after me. But I think you're riding for a big fall, and it scares the hell out of me. It scares Hank, too. We *all* love you. What you're doing, what you're talking about doing, just isn't smart. You keep thinking you can have your career and some kind of fairy-tale life, too, but you can't. That's not the way things work around here. There's a *price* you've got to pay for getting to the top and staying there, and sooner or later, they'll come around collecting. If Bobby goes along with you, if Meyers and Jerry and everyone else goes along, no one will be happier for you than me. But I'll tell you this: I don't think for one minute any of it's going to happen. I think the time's come when you're going to have to pay, and pay big. I hate it, but that's what I think."

"You're wrong," Bea insisted. "You'll see. You're wrong."

"I'd give every last thing I've got to be wrong," Lucy said sadly. "But I know I'm not."

Two days after they wrapped the picture, Bea drove herself off to keep an appointment she'd made with a physician in the San Fernando Valley. She underwent the first internal examination of her life and tried not to reveal her shock at the procedure. When it was over and the doctor said he was fairly certain but would wait for the test results and confirm by telephone later in the day, she went out to the car filled with dread, no longer certain of anything. It was as if the rude shock she'd just had was merely a foretaste of worse things to come. Why had no one ever told her there were aspects to being female that would necessitate experiences as offensive as the one she'd just undergone? And why, suddenly, did she doubt that Bobby would support her?

She returned home to wait for the doctor's call, pacing the length of her bedroom for hours, until the telephone rang and she snatched it up to hear the words that were the formal acknowledgment of what she'd known was the truth for close to two weeks. She was going to have a baby in just over seven months.

When she was thirty-nine, her baby would be twenty years old. The prospect no longer elated her; the dread had expanded until it was like miles of netting that enshrouded her and from which there seemed no possible freedom. Her mouth dry, her heart drumming, she picked up the telephone and dialed Bobby's number.

"I have to see you."

"What's up?" he asked. "You sound funny."

"Meet me at our spot at the beach in an hour. It's very important."

He was already there, sitting cross-legged on the sand, pitching pebbles into the water, when she arrived. As she walked from her car, her eyes on him, she felt as if all the love she had for him might suffocate her. She only had to look at his mouth, or his hands, to experience a need for him that was instant and so total that her interior went liquid in anticipation; she only had to think of him and her entire being yearned for him. Don't let me down, she prayed, moving toward him. Please, don't let me down.

Folding her skirt under her, taking care to keep a healthy distance between them, she sat on the sand and, gazing out at the sun-glazed surf, told him, then waited.

"I guess," he said after a few seconds, "you and I are going to get married, sister."

She turned to look at him, feeling the tightness in her chest easing a little as she studied the sweetness of his smile, the freckles on the bridge of his nose, his amber-brown eyes. "Is that what you really want, Bobby?"

"I love you," he said, the smile holding. "I guess I'm always going to. I can't see myself with anybody else."

"Would you fight for me, Bobby?" she asked him. "If it came right down to it, would you?"

"I'd *kill* for you. Are you kidding?"

"It's not the same thing," she said gently, feeling all at once many years older than him, infinitely older. "The real issue is this: You and I both have contracts with the studio. Yours has another four and a half years to run. Mine is up for renewal after we finish the next picture. They *own* us, Bobby. They can tell us when to dance, and for how long. So, what I need to know is if you're willing too fight for me, if you're willing to face Ludovic Meyers and say, you don't care what he does, you intend to go through with this, even if it means your contract's in jeopardy."

178

"I'm willing," he said without hesitation.

"Okay," she said, still only partially eased. "Okay." She looked out at the water for a time, then said, "Maybe I shouldn't say this, but I'm going to anyway. It feels as if it might be dangerous to say what I'm thinking. It really does. My hands are shaking, and inside I feel queasy, because it's so important and I have to make you understand. I believe you, Bobby. I believe you really do love me. I'll *always* believe that, and not just because I want to, but because I know it's the truth. The thing is, you see, I love *you*. I love you so much that having to spend two and half years looking across a room, or a theater, or whatever, and see you with somebody else was like swallowing ground glass. If I'd had a choice in the matter, if feelings were something I could control, like pulling back on an attitude or holding for an extra beat, maybe I would. Maybe not. I don't know. I do know there isn't any part of me that doesn't love you. I always will, no matter what happens. I think maybe I'll get to be very old, *very* old, and everything I feel for you will still be there. There are other people I love, and probably people I'm going to meet in the future that I'll love, too. But no one will ever mean to me what you do, and I want you to know that, to understand it."

"I do," he said, somewhat cowed by the intensity of her declaration. "I do know it. And I feel the same way about you."

She had to look at him, to see how he appeared saying this. She shifted on the sand, her fingers sinking into the sliding warmth, and smiled. You'll break my heart, she thought again. You will, and somehow I'm going to have to go on living. "Let's go somewhere," she said hoarsely. "For a little while. Mr. Meyers wants to see both of us first thing tomorrow."

They met up outside the executive offices at nine the next morning. Jerry was there, and so was Hank. In silence, they filed inside and waited until the secretary told them they could go in. Ludie sat behind his massive desk watching as Bea and Bobby took the two chairs directly in front of the desk, and Jerry and Hank seated themselves to one side.

"So," Ludie said, looking first at Bobby, and then at Bea. "The little lovebirds, we've got here. This is very nice."

Bobby couldn't restrain himself. "Mr. Meyers," he said. "Bea and I are going to get married."

Ludie smiled and, watching him, Bea was for the first time aware that beneath the superficial benevolence he'd always displayed for her was a quality of ruthlessness as well as a kind of horrific cowardice.

Ludie was someone who, when threatened, would cover his fear with aggression. Bobby was out-matched, and she knew it.

"You plan," he said, "to do this when?"

Bobby looked at Bea then back again at Meyers. "Right away."

"And you," Ludie directed his gaze to Bea, "will put an expensive project on hold for six or seven months while you have this baby. Am I right?" Seeing her surprise, he went on. "You go see some doctor, you give him a cockamamie name, and you think he doesn't go to the movies on a Saturday night, or his nurse doesn't? You think his nurse doesn't figure she'll pick herself up a few bucks with a hot tip? It *cost* me to buy that hot tip!"

She looked over at Jerry who gave an almost imperceptible shake of his head. Hank had knitted his fingers together in his lap and was staring down at them. Bobby gaped at Ludie, his face ashen.

"I'm sorry," she apologized. "I thought no one would recognize me. People never seem to."

"You thought wrong. For a smart girl, you've been doing a lot of wrong thinking lately. So somebody else is going to have to do the thinking for you for a while. And this is what's going to happen: You're gonna get this taken care of, and the two of you're gonna get to work on the new picture. You"—he pointed a thick finger at Bobby—"are gonna keep your nose clean, your pants buttoned, and get your-self seen around town with some new girls. And you"—he turned the finger on Bea—"are gonna get a new contract and a nice fat hike in salary. And I'm not gonna hear one more word about the two of you, or babies, or any of it. You wanna talk about getting married, we'll see what's what after the picture's in the can. And that's how it's gonna be."

Bea turned to Bobby, silently urging him to fight for her. You can fight him, she told him with her eyes. We don't have to give in. Look at me! she willed, but he wouldn't meet her gaze.

"You understand me, the two of you?" Ludie asked.

Bobby swallowed hard and answered, "Yes, sir."

Bea couldn't speak. She simply nodded, then got up and walked out. Hank came hurrying after, grabbed her hand, and pulled her into the nearest empty sound stage. She sagged against the wall, her eyes deadened, and he held both her hands saying, "Don't blame Bobby for this, Bea. I know you wanted him to tell Ludie to go to hell, but he couldn't do that and you knew all along he couldn't. But you hoped he would, didn't you? You wanted him to be just a little more than he is. I'm sorry. Christ, I'm sorrier than I can say. But there'll be other chances. This isn't the end of the world."

"Have you got a cigarette?" she asked.

"Sure." He fumbled his pack of Camels out of his jacket pocket, gave her one, and got it lit for her. "You don't smoke, for chrissake."

"I just started," she said coolly. "I think I'm going to need some bad habits." She gave him a wry smile and folded her arms across her chest. "It's okay, Pop. I'll be a good girl and do what I'm told."

"This is..." He stopped, groping for words that would appropriately describe what he thought of the situation.

"I spent most of last night sitting looking out the window, thinking about the things that could possibly happen this morning," she said, taking a puff on the cigarette. "There were only two possibilities, really. The first one didn't happen. So, obviously, I'll get on with the second." She picked a piece of tobacco off her tongue. "We'll *all* just get on with it."

He'd expected her to cry, but he could see now she wouldn't. She'd found an icy degree of control and was exercising it, drawing it into her lungs with the cigarette smoke and exhaling it steadily.

She looked past him into the murky depths of the sound stage with its vaulted ceiling and said, "Don't you wonder sometimes about what it is we do here, Hank? Making musicals while people are starving."

"You could do more."

"I suppose I could. Perhaps I will. Who knows?" She dropped the cigarette, then stepped on it. "I have a feeling there's going to be more to it," she said somewhat mysteriously.

"No. This is over," he said.

"*This* is over. But there's going to be more. I feel as if I'm standing way up there"—she pointed to the ceiling—"looking down. And from my P.O.V.," she smiled up at him, "I can see what no one else can. You're a very dear man."

"God, don't!" he said. "I'm just another notch on Ludie's gun."

"In the midst of all this, I've got a date tonight to go to the latest party with some *wonderful* young man from RKO. The publicity boys never sleep. I'll go out tonight in a two-hundred-dollar dress I'll wear precisely once. And in the morning, the kindly studio doctor will perform a small surgical act that will enable me to fulfill my obligations to the studio."

"Cancel out on tonight," he told her.

"Oh, never! This is the game, and these are the rules, and I will be ready this evening at seven. I'm all right, Hank. Really, I am. Bobby will be all right, and so will you. Life goes on. And we'd better get back out there where they can see us. Otherwise, they might think something's going on with the two of us."

"Don't let what's happened turn you bitter," he begged her.

"I'm not bitter, Hank," she said, surprised. "I think I knew all along

181

what would happen. And I'm not sorry. I'm really not sorry." It was true, she thought, searching the corners of her mind for any possibility that she was merely layering words over top of her true feelings.

He stared at her, aware that she'd changed. Irrevocably, she'd moved beyond herself into another, new, aspect of Beatrice Crane. The underlying person was the same, but her dimensions had altered. She'd taken the first major steps into adulthood, and he despaired of, but also admired, the woman who was emerging.

The studio doctor and the two nurses assisting were deferentially impersonal and handled her with a practiced efficiency that implied boredom. She didn't realize how frightened she was until her legs were lifted into the stirrups and pushed into position behind padded posts that prevented any possibility of her closing her thighs. At this, fear filled her chest, making it exceedingly difficult for her to breathe. Worse still, the doctor wore spectacles and, with the bright lights of the small operating room, she was able to see herself reflected in the lenses. One of the nurses placed a steadying hand on Bea's shoulder. She redirected her eyes to the ceiling and gazed steadfastly upward as the doctor scraped away what Bobby had placed inside her. Her stomach muscles fluttered; her clenched hands were wet. She thought she knew the precise moment when the baby was separated from her, when its cells were detached, and she experienced a sensation of emptiness and loss that was so overwhelming and painful she didn't think she could survive it.

She rested for a short time, and then Hank helped her out to his car and drove her home. Throughout the trip he kept glancing over at her wordlessly, his face creased with anxiety. She'd have liked to reassure him but her attention was turned inward to the stripped and brutalized interior of her body. Lucy met them at the door wearing a similarly anxious expression.

"I'm fine," Bea told them both. "I'm going up to bed."

She paused at the foot of the stairs to say, "Thank you, Henry, for everything," then went slowly, cautiously up the stairs. Her thigh muscles ached; blood seemed to course from her body with every heartbeat. After quietly closing the door to her room, she lay down, pulled the blankets over her head, and wept until the last of her strength was gone.

Hank drove directly to Brentwood. Hero came to the door, took one look at Hank, and said, "You'd better come in and sit down. I'll fix you a drink."

182

The drink helped. After he'd downed half of it, Hank looked across at Hero who was sitting, staring at him.

"How do we resolve this?" Hero asked quietly.

"I can't resolve what I don't even understand," Hank answered.

Hero sat back and crossed his legs, placing his hands on the arms of the chair. As usual, his white silk shirt was immaculate, as were his navy slacks, his doeskin loafers, and his meticulously trimmed hair. "It isn't that I don't understand what you see in her," he said, "because I do. My real concern is you. And me, of course."

"All I know is that, whatever happens, nothing is going to change between you and me. You know what you mean to me."

"I think so," Hero replied. "But you're getting more involved every day in this girl's life. I'd hate to see you get hurt. I don't have to tell you what *you* mean to *me*. I gave up the directorship of the ballet to live in this insane place just so we could be together. I was happy to do it," he added quickly, "and I'd be happy to do it again. And, all things considered, I can't complain. Meyers pays well. I do like this house. I simply don't want to see it all go up in smoke."

"She understands," Hank said helplessly.

"I'm glad one of us does," Hero quipped, and then laughed softly. "Did it go badly?"

Hank shook his head. "She didn't say a word. But it was terrible. Her face..." He had to stop, choking up.

Hero got up and came over to sit beside him on the sofa. "I'm sorry. What can I do to help?"

"I love both of you," Hank lamented. "The last thing on earth I thought could happen."

"Just promise me I won't find myself in an adversarial position," Hero said calmly.

"That could never happen," Hank promised. "I'm my own adversary in this situation. You," he said, turning to look into the sane blue depths of his friend's eyes, "are the anchor that keeps me from flying off into space."

"An anchor, huh?" Hero gave him a smile. "Well, I've been called worse. Want me to freshen that?"

Hank looked down at the glass in his hand. "Not just yet. I'm starting to feel better. Christ! It was terrible. She thanked me for going with her. As if I could have let her go through something like that alone."

"I know," Hero consoled him, his hand on Hank's arm.

"All the time she was in there, I kept thinking, 'What if she dies, what if she dies.' I want both of you in my life. But it feels as if that's not fair to either one of you."

183

"I'm not going anywhere," Hero told him. "But you may not be able to work this one out in the editing room."

"Are you jealous?" Hank asked anxiously.

"I'm too old to be jealous. And I'm in no position to select your friends."

"But you've got the right to feel . . . however you feel."

"I feel concerned about you. It's pretty simple: if you're happy, so am I. And it's not as if she's some worthless piece of fluff. The girl's going somewhere. Let's just wait and see."

Hank took some more of his drink, then put the glass down to light a cigarette.

"You need a haircut," Hero observed, watching Hank run his hand over his hair. "And I'll bet you haven't eaten. I'll have Dee fix you something." He got up and stood for a moment. "I'm not jealous. I'm very fond of her myself. I've actually missed her the past couple of months. I liked it when she used to drop in for a visit, or she'd pick me up to go with her to visit Bill. Relax, and stop worrying. I'm not," he repeated, "going anywhere."

Eighteen

BOBBY kept calling. Bea refused to accept his calls, until Lucy said, "You've got to talk to him. This is wrong. It's not fair to either of you."

"All right," Bea relented unexpectedly. "I'll talk to him next time he calls."

It was only a matter of hours before he telephoned again, and Bea said, "Come here, to the house. I'll be waiting for you."

He agreed, sounding greatly relieved. She put down the receiver and went through to the rear of the house, out to the garden where she spent the time between the call and his arrival admiring the flowers and bushes, thinking yet again of the power of the studio. They could, it seemed, arrange anything. An abortion got put down in the files as a D and C. Two people's lives could be set at a distance, and it undoubtedly went down on some interoffice memo under the heading "New Publicity Campaign." In one sense, having the studio in control of her life was like being the adopted child of wealthy and domineering parents who knew best and who would dictate the terms for every step she was to take. Inherent in that parental control was a substantial degree of protection, and the implicit promise of ever greater financial rewards. On the negative side, her right to make personal choices had been lost. Between her and the public stood a phalanx of studio officials—everything from personal physicians to private police. Her life was now such that she had to rely on that studio intervention for protection from a public that swore, in letters, that they adored her but who would, given leave, invade what small degree of private life remained to her.

"Why wouldn't you talk to me?" Bobby asked mournfully as he came up to her. "I've been going out of my mind with this whole business." He'd have liked to embrace her but her posture cautioned him against making any physical approach to her.

"I couldn't," she said flatly, blinking into the sunlight against which he was standing. He seemed to be a featureless presence placed between her and the sun. "Let's sit down," she suggested, and walked across the grass toward a grouping of white wrought-iron furniture positioned in the center of the garden. She sat down and waited for him to follow suit. Able now to see his face, she reached into her pocket for a pack of cigarettes, removed one, and lit it while he watched with an expression bordering on astonishment.

"Since when do you smoke?" he asked, as twin streams of smoke emerged from her nostrils.

"It's been almost a month," she said casually, resting her hand with the cigarette on the broad, lacy-patterned arm of the chair. "It made me very dizzy at first, but I quite like it now. How are you?"

"Never mind about me," he said, puzzled by her attitude and demeanor. It was as if she'd aged ten years in about a month, and the aging showed in the tone of her voice and in the way she used her body. Even her dress, a simple cotton affair with short sleeves, a full skirt, and a belted waistline, seemed older. "You're the one," he said. "I've been going nuts worrying about you."

"There's nothing to worry about. It's all over and done with. In fact, the good studio doctor told me last week I could resume my sexual life in another two weeks. For some reason, I found that funny. I laughed, and he looked at me like I was crazy."

"That *is* crazy," he said. "Why would you laugh about something like that?"

185

"I've been reading," she rolled on. "In fact, it's almost all I've been doing lately. Reading, and starting back into my workouts, getting into shape again. I don't know why, but I had the idea I'd walk out of the doctor's office and the next day put on my rehearsal clothes and go to work." She paused to puff on the cigarette. "That's not quite the way it was."

He shifted uncomfortably in his chair, praying she wouldn't go into graphic details of what she'd been through.

"So, tell me what you've been doing," she invited.

"I've *told* you," he said hotly. "I've been worrying myself half crazy about you." He looked at her, floundering, trying to think what he could say that would retrieve their former closeness. It felt as if something immense and impenetrable filled the few feet of space between them, and he had no idea how to get past it to reach her. Frustrated, frightened, and ashamed, he took refuge as always in gruffness. "We're not talking!" he declared accusingly. "Why won't you talk to me, really talk?"

"But we are," she said, studying now the lit end of her Camel, watching for a moment the way the paper shriveled, turned gray, and drifted down from the burning tube.

"No," he disagreed. "I'm *trying* to talk to you, and you're playing at something. I know you blame me for what happened. I blame myself. Why don't you say what you really think?"

"I don't blame you," she said, growing more quiet as his voice gained in volume. "How can I?" she asked reasonably. "I knew what I was doing. I took chances. It didn't work out."

"You're writing me off," he insisted, feeling overwrought. "Don't write me off this way! I love you."

"I love you," she replied, watching the color spread over his face. "That hasn't changed. I told you: I'll always love you."

"Then why do I feel as if there's six feet of solid steel between us? Why do I get the feeling you only asked me to come over here so you could tell me to go away and stay away?"

"You feel guilty," she said, leaning forward to extinguish the cigarette in a small glass ashtray on the table around which their chairs were arranged. "Don't."

"Is it over between us?" he asked. "Is that what you're trying to tell me?"

"I've been thinking about that," she said, crossing her legs and turning more toward him. "I've been thinking about it a lot. I don't want to give you up. Even Ludie doesn't want me to give you up. He just wishes the two of us would stop sleeping together, so there won't be any chance of my getting pregnant again. The studio would prefer it if we got married, but they'd like to be able to decide when and if, if we got married, we'd begin having babies. I always thought," she said with some sadness, "that I'd be the one to decide about when and how I got married and had a family. I see now that everyone's been trying for ages to tell me that I gave up certain things when I signed on with Ludie. It's interesting, you know. I've been playing a little game for the last few years since I came out here. It was this game where I told them and myself that I didn't *really* want to be a star, that I'd make some movies and then go back to Broadway where I was truly happy. Maybe I did it to protect myself somehow, because, after all, if I didn't care one way or another, if it didn't matter to me, then I wouldn't get caught up in it, and no one would be able to control me. I'll tell you something, Bobby. I've wanted all this since I was a little kid. I wanted to be a movie star; I wanted to be rich and famous; I wanted fan mail, and a swell big house in Beverly Hills, and a car, and evening gowns, and everything else that goes with it. I also," she went on, "wanted to have it both ways. I wanted you, and I wanted you to fight for me. But there's nothing I've wanted so much that, in the end, I wasn't willing to give in and do what *they* wanted. So, you see, you really shouldn't feel guilty. Because if I'd wanted to keep the baby, I would have. The truth is, I want this more. It's not over with us, unless you want it to be. It's all I can do to sit here and not reach out to touch you. But it's critical that we both know where we stand. I *never*," she said vehemently, "want to go through that again. Not ever. I don't think I'll ever be able to put it entirely out of my mind." Her brow creased, and her eyes turned momentarily inward, as if she were seeing and experiencing the abortion again.

"So what are you saying?" he wanted to know, confused.

She sighed and turned even more toward him, folding both her arms on the arm of the chair. "I don't know exactly. I suppose I'm saying that in two more weeks, if we still feel the same way about each other, we'll try to pick up where we left off. I love making love with you, Bobby," she admitted. "I don't think I care to give it up."

"I want you," he said, certain terms were being set down that he was failing to pick up on. "If it's marriage you want, then I want it, too. There's no one else I'd ever marry."

She smiled, and again he saw that newly aged quality to her. "Neither one of us is really old enough, or ready, to get married."

"I sure as hell *feel* old enough. And you're certainly acting like you are. I can't get over the change in you."

Her shoulders lifted and fell. "I know things now I didn't know a month or so ago."

187

"And those things you know have changed you."

"I can't help that. After lying in bed bleeding for days on end, you tend to view things a little differently."

He made an agonized face and held up his hand, saying, "Don't!"

"Oh," she said, "I think you should have some idea of what it's like, Bobby. You really should. They strap your legs apart, and then they reach up inside you and scrape. It's monstrous. Your thighs tremble, your stomach quivers. It's a nightmare of pain, and there's nowhere for you to go. When it's over, you bleed and bleed, and you're sure you'll die of it. But you don't. Amazingly, you don't die."

To her consternation, his face screwed up, he bent his head into his hands and began to weep noisily, as if this emotional act was physically excruciating. She watched him cry, saw the way his back curved into it, and felt an aching pity for him. She reached to put her hand on his shoulder, thinking to comfort him even though she fully accepted that she'd wanted to see evidence of the suffering he claimed to feel.

"And you say you don't blame me!" he shot at her through his tears, revealing his face to her. "If you didn't blame me, you wouldn't force me to hear all that."

"I'm only trying to explain to you why I'm not going to allow it to happen again. We'll just be very careful in future."

"I don't get it," he complained, like a small boy rubbing his fists into his eyes. "I don't know how you can say you're willing to pick up with me and go on, after . . . after what's happened."

"I can't help it, Bobby. I love you."

"Jesus!" He let his head fall back, and his eyes raked the cloudless sky. "Jesus H. Christ!" After a moment, his emotions somewhat subdued, he lowered his eyes to hers. She was pale as always, her eyes almost transparent in the afternoon light; her face, with its strong straight nose and determined jawline, was, for a few seconds, unrecognizable to him. Her head tilted slightly, and he stared at her, at the way the sun highlighted the prominent, somehow stern, bridge of her nose. "Okay," he sighed. "So where do we go from here?"

"Next week, we'll start working out together again; we'll meet with Hank and Hero and Clark and go over the breakdowns of the musical numbers for the new script. And the week after that, after my final checkup, we'll go somewhere and be alone together. We'll keep on making movies as long as they want us to; the movies'll keep on making Ludie and the studio heaps of money; and on and on it'll all go. Don't worry," she said again. "At least, the whole thing gave me a chance to think matters through, to decide what it is I really want."

"And now you know that?" he asked, afraid to have her tell him what she'd decided was important to her, because the chances were it wasn't him.

"Yes, I do," she said firmly, sparing him the details of her decision. "I do."

While Hero diagramed the moves on a large, standing blackboard, explaining as he went along how he viewed the overall number, Bea and Bobby listened, occasionally interjecting comments about what they thought would or wouldn't work. They'd long since acclimated themselves to the protocol of their work as a unit. All four of them contributed ideas to the musical theme of each picture, laboring to come up with new and different ideas. It was vital there never be any duplication, anything too closely resembling what they'd done in previous pictures. In between their efforts to map out the choreographic aspects of the script, Bea went along for costume consultations and fittings, as did Bobby, although the costume demands were far simpler for him. Bea's clothes had to be more than merely glamorous; they had to be fully functional—with pockets, of course—so that they moved with her, accentuating each line of every step she took. Initially, and to her surprise, after *Upside Down*, her "look" had influenced fashion. Suddenly, every girl wanted pockets in her dresses, and a shoulder-length, side-parted hairdo. There were Beatrice Crane look-alikes popping up all over the map. It made her feel odd, even bemused. That anyone should wish to emulate her looks, should want to be as much like her as they could, seemed silly. It was flattering, but more disconcerting than anything else. With time, she'd become used to being copied, but that in no way diminished her obligation, and the studio's, to keep her worthy of being copied. So, for each film, there came an extension of her "look" in the form of cute day dresses and smart evening clothes whose secondary function was to ensure envy in the hearts of the women who were her biggest fans. The sketches were approved, the fittings got done, the costumes were tested and approved. And in a small secret place inside her, she enjoyed both the attention paid to her as an important personage in the studio hierarchy and the public adulation that continued to generate hundreds of fan letters weekly, along with a constant interest by the press and the fan magazines that regularly featured articles about her. She willingly publicized each film, as did Bobby, but had to remind herself not to become annoyed at being asked the same questions over and over. She'd evolved a format for her responses and rarely deviated from it. She and Bobby were great chums and had been for ages; yes, she had a housekeeper, because the stresses

189

of her position were such that she was unable to maintain so large a house on her own; her hobbies were reading, listening to music, and swimming, which her wonderful director, Henry Donovan, had taught her; she disliked parties and preferred entertaining small groups at home; her circle of friends was a limited, close one, that included primarily members of the Crane-Bradley Production Unit and, of course, her beloved guardian and friend, Lucille Vernon. Variations were forever played on the basic themes, and the reporters embellished wherever possible, except for Louella who was forever digging, on the alert, it seemed, for the slightest hint of anything out of the ordinary taking place in Bea's life. It amused Bea to visit with the woman and let slip some piece of information that made Louella's eyes bulge slightly as she thought to herself she'd finally got a scoop. Louella was all right, Bea thought, and basically not malicious. So she played this harmless game with the woman, always amused when Louella discovered her "scoop" was already common knowledge.

Where the press was concerned, Bea was hard work, but newsworthy. So, despite knowing they'd get the same story every time, they pursued her through Pete and the rest of the publicity boys with patient, long-term persistence. There was always a contingent from the press waiting to interview and photograph her when she showed up for some function the studio insisted she attend, or even at a restaurant if she and Hank, or she and Lucy, decided to go out for dinner. There were always sessions with the studio photographers for new publicity stills and moments during shooting when she'd have to hold a pose for the still photographer who roamed the set, often taking shots that would wind up on lobby cards and posters to advertise the picture. It was all part of the job; she tried to be gracious about what she felt were the more foolish aspects of it.

As the days of preparation for *Moonlight* added up and the first day of shooting drew closer, she found herself feeling strangely reluctant. She couldn't have said why, but she wasn't looking forward with her usual heightened sense of anticipation to this picture. Things were going well between her and Bobby, although when they were together now, periodically the abortion and its frightful aftermath melancholy interfered with her ability to find pleasure in being with him. Or perhaps it was the new, premeditated aspect to their love-making that disturbed her. Where before they'd come together with all but explosive spontaneity, meeting to throw off their clothes in a silent frenzy of mutual longing, now there were steps that formed a necessary prelude to their unions. One or the other of them was compelled to prepare physically against the possibility of conceiving, and in making

190

those preparations a degree of her ardor got lost. They still took tremendous satisfaction in the ongoing exploration of each other's bodies, but the alteration in her commitment, no matter how subtle, did exist. She had been informed in absolute terms of her responsibility to the studio, and that responsibility had infiltrated her private life to such an extent that she couldn't make love with a man she wanted with every particle of her being without being aware that every time they took off their clothes and lay down together, the studio shared the bed with them. The adoptive parents had managed to penetrate her more successfully, more completely than this man she loved. She simply couldn't ignore the risks they ran every time she opened her body and welcomed Bobby into it. Love-making had become a form both of salvation and of crucifixion. It allowed her to lose much of the tension generated by a day's work, but the moment her flesh began to cool her awareness blossomed, and she felt pangs of guilt. She had to wonder if she'd spend the rest of life unable to give herself over to anything or anyone without having to fear the possibility of repercussions.

Since they'd made no plans to marry, the studio had no compunction about sending them out to be seen with other partners. Often, politely but firmly, she refused, her justified defense being her need to conserve energy for the production in progress. Bobby, however, couldn't quite bring himself to defy the system again. He felt he'd caused a serious breach once and didn't dare risk another. His involvement with Bea was as much as he could handle. Flack from the studio, from Ludie, was something he couldn't have taken.

"Go ahead," Bea told him repeatedly. "I understand, and I honestly don't mind. You know I hate all those do's, and I'm happier to stay home at night and go over my lines."

"Maybe we should get married," he said just as often, in a permanent quandary about their unresolved, unofficial status.

"Not yet," she told him every time.

He'd go off for his public evenings, and she'd either go home or drive into town to spend an hour or two with Bill, or with Hank and Hero. The time she spent with Bill was like a holiday. Often as not, they'd end up trying out steps, challenging each other until they finished with laughter. They rarely talked of anything but dancing and music. With Bill, as with Hank, silences were never uncomfortable. There existed an understanding that made talking all but unnecessary, and so there was a luxuriousness to the time she spent in each man's company. She could simply be, without any pressure to perform to anything other than her own inspiration. Bill commented

191

only once about the possible dangers of her friendship with him.

"You might be getting yourself into a whole mess of trouble," he told her.

"I'll tell you something," she'd responded in a deadly tone. "They can tell me who to date, who to love, what to do with my body; they can run me like a goddamned train. But the first time *anyone* questions my right to be friends with you, it'll be the *last time ever* they get to interfere in my life. No one will ever decide for me who my friends are!"

She and Hank worked on the script, playing with the dialogue, trying to give life to some of the more hackneyed situations. Or they sat together in thoughtful silence, eating a meal prepared by his housekeeper or fetched in by the housekeeper's husband from some restaurant or another. There seemed to have been an inevitable evolution in their lives that didn't merit questioning. The success of the pictures they'd done had changed their lifestyles, bringing much-needed hired help into their lives, along with increased incomes. Both she and Hank now had secretaries with offices at the studio; both of them had moved into larger quarters to accommodate, not only their personally expanded lifestyles, but their public images. A movie star and big-time director were obliged to live in ways commensurate with the public's expectations.

"It's all a load of crap," Hank said good-naturedly, "but I'm not complaining. One of these days, Ludie's going to let me do something more, something different. I'm willing to wait."

"I'm sure you'll get what you want," she told him. "D'you know where they're sending me next week?" she asked, reaching for her bag and keys. "The White Mayfair Ball. Lombard's worked herself half to death for it, and I couldn't refuse. All white this year, Pop. I've got a final fitting tomorrow evening for my *white* dress. Everyone's got to wear white, and *everyone's* going to be there, including Ludie and Mrs. Ludie. They've got me fixed up with some clown from RKO." She made a face. "Lucy can hardly wait. I'm hoping I come down with pneumonia, even if it is for charity."

"Bite your tongue," he chided, walking with her to the door. "You'll have a hell of a time."

"Of course, I will. I'll stand around all evening while my escort gets himself seen at the Do of the Year. In a couple of weeks the magazines'll have big spreads on the whole bash, and by then there'll have been four other big bashes. It makes me feel like a performing seal. The dress is pretty, though."

"Go home." He kissed her on the forehead, then swung open the door. "Sometimes I think the highlight of your life is complaining about these things."

"It's the best part of it," she conceded with a laugh. "What would life be if I couldn't bitch about having to go to a party people would kill to be at?"

"Drive carefully," he said, seeing her into her car.

"Always." She fitted the key into ignition, then reversed into the road, tooting the horn at him before driving away.

"**I** wish I was going with you," Bobby said, the night before the ball.

They were at his apartment at the Château Marmont. He was sitting on the end of the bed watching Bea put on her clothes. He had the radio turned on low, and music drifted almost, but not quite, out of reach.

"I'd love to have a movie of you doing that," he said, as she buttoned her dress. "From start to finish. I'd run it backwards and forwards, make myself crazy."

"You have overactive hormones or something."

"Don't be a jerk," he said. "You've got the best legs I've ever seen." He pushed off the edge of the bed and knee-walked over to wind one arm around her hips, pressing his face into her belly, his free hand slipping up under her dress to caress the bare flesh of her thigh between the top of her stocking and her step-ins. Her muscle contracted under his hand, and he kissed her belly through the dress.

"I've got to go, Bobby." She stepped backwards, then went around him to the doorway. "Were you planning to see me to the car in that condition?" She pointed at him from just inside the living room.

"Maybe I will," he retorted, standing now, hands on lean bare hips.

"All right, then, but hurry up."

He laughed, said, "Hold your horses!" and rushed to pull on a shirt and trousers. Jamming his feet into loafers, he grabbed up a pair of silver-backed brushes—last year's Christmas gift from Bea—and applied them to his hair before escorting her out of the building.

He leaned in through the car window to give her a kiss, murmured, "I'd give anything to be going with you," then kissed her again.

"It's a duty visit," she told him. "I'll put in an appearance, stay two hours at most, and be home in bed by eleven. And think about this, if it's any consolation: You know perfectly well that the fella they're sending over from RKO is going to be better-looking than any girl either one of us knows. He'll certainly be better-looking than me."

193

"He won't have your thighs, though."

"Thank you. I feel so much better knowing that."

"I love you, sister."

"Me, too. I'll see you tomorrow."

As she drove home, staying at exactly the speed limit, she thought of how much she would've preferred to go to the ball with Bobby. Instead of fulfilling an obligation, she'd have been out for an evening of fun. Maybe it was time to change matters. If she and Bobby were officially engaged, they'd have every right in the world to go out together in public. Bobby was more than willing. And being engaged didn't have to mean they planned to get married right away. Engagements had been known to last for years. They'd talk about it, she decided. She was fed up with going out with strangers, fed up with beautiful men whose interest in her was as non-existent as hers in them. It was definitely time she and Bobby stepped out together.

Nineteen

LUCY was heartbroken. On the morning of the ball, she awakened with her head stuffed, her nose and eyes streaming, and her throat raw.

"I can't possibly go in this condition," she half cried. "And I've got that gorgeous dress."

"Maybe if you stay in bed all day, dose yourself with aspirins and hot tea, you'll feel well enough by this evening to go." Bea tried to sound encouraging, but one look at Lucy's red-rimmed eyes was enough to convince her Lucy wouldn't be fit to go. "And if you're not well enough, maybe I'll stay home and keep you company."

"Don't you dare even *think* about that!" Lucy protested. "We can't waste *two* gorgeous dresses."

"Go back to bed, and we'll see how you feel later. I'll get Molly to keep you supplied with hot tea and lemon."

Sniffling, wiping her nose with a tissue, Lucy trudged off back to bed. Bea went down to the kitchen to have a word with Molly, the housekeeper. Molly was an easygoing, almost black-skinned woman in her early thirties who kept the house spotless, cooked not elaborately but well, and had a wonderfully wry sense of humor.

"Lucy's sick," Bea told her, going over to the stove to pour a cup of coffee.

"You gonna eat before you go?" Molly asked.

"I can't. I'll have something at the studio. Will you make her some tea with lemon and honey?"

"Sure thing."

"And keep me posted. Call me at lunchtime."

"Okay."

"That dress is going to need pressing," Bea remembered. "You'll be very careful, won't you?"

"I'll take care of that dress like it's a child of mine," Molly promised. "Anything else?"

"If Lucy's still feeling punk by this afternoon, maybe you'll want to give Dr. Shannon a call. I just hope it's not 'flu."

"I'll take care of Miss Lucy like she's a child of mine," Molly said, leaning against the counter with her arms folded comfortably in front of her, her eyes on Bea as she gulped the coffee.

"I've got to run." Bea plonked down the half-empty cup, grabbed her handbag, keys, and rehearsal bag, and raced off.

At midday, Molly telephoned to say, "I called the doctor, 'cuz I think maybe it's 'flu after all. She's got a high fever. I took her temperature, and she didn't like that one bit, I can tell you. But I took it anyway, and she was at a hundred and three, so I thought I'd better call him. He's comin' over this afternoon."

Bea thanked her, hung up, and went back to her lunch. They had three or four days of filming left at most, but those days would be spent on the big finale. It was going to be a spectacular number, with more than a hundred dancing extras, and a running time of almost ten and a half minutes. The singing was planned to go for two minutes, and the dancing for just over eight; a very big number. After that, she'd have to come back to dub her taps and do any final close-ups Hank might decide he wanted.

What she wanted, she thought, was a vacation. She'd never had a holiday, and after eight pictures, it was time for one. The strain of three productions back to back, with consultations on the script and choreography in between, was beginning to take its toll. She felt tired

195

and when, that afternoon, Hank had them go back over one small scene again and again, she thought she might start screaming. He kept calling, "CUT!" until at last she demanded, "Why are we doing this over and over?"

"Because it's not right," he answered implacably.

"What's not right about it?"

"It's just not right."

"If you could please tell me what's not right about it, maybe I could fix it. It doesn't make sense to keep shooting this one bit over and over. Are we both hitting our marks?"

"Yes."

"Are we both in our lights?"

"Yes."

"Is the dialogue right?"

"Yes."

"So then why are we doing it again and again?"

"It's not right. Let's do it one last time."

The exchange struck her as so absurd that there seemed no point in pursuing it further. She sighed, turned, held still to have her face powdered and her hair smoothed down, then went back to her mark, convinced they were all, every last one of them, including her, completely crazy. Why else would they be doing this?

He called "cut and print" on the next take and, relieved, Bea moved off the set. "What was that about, Henry?" she asked him out of range of anyone's hearing. "Could you please explain it to me?"

"Bobby kept masking you. It wasn't intentional. It was just the angle, and I wanted to keep the set-up as it was."

"Well, why didn't you *say* so? It would've saved us all a lot of agony."

"I had to see how it'd play, Bea. It's not as simple from my side of things as it sometimes might seem to you from yours. And you should know by now that I have reasons for the things I do."

"I can handle anything, if people just explain it to me. What I can't handle is doing something that doesn't appear to make any sense."

"Come see the rushes. Then it'll make sense to you."

"You know I loathe it. I won't do it. I get so depressed it interferes with my next day's work. It's one thing for me to do this, but it's something else entirely to have to sit in the screening room, suffering at the sight of myself. Maybe in twenty years I'll feel more at ease sitting through one of our pictures, but right now, it makes me cringe. Are we finished? I want to get out of here, go home, and get some rest before the goddamned ball tonight."

"You're angry," he observed.

"I feel furious," she conceded.

"With me?"

"With the whole insane business. Sometimes I wonder what the hell I'm doing here." She paused to take a breath and, softening, said, "I'm not really angry with you, Pop. I just wish I didn't have to go to this stupid affair tonight."

"As long as we're still friends," he said, draping his arm across her shoulders as they headed for her trailer.

"Ah, Hank, we'll always be friends," she relented. "I needed to blow off steam, that's all."

They stopped outside her trailer. She turned and gave him a chaste peck on the lips. "Wish me luck," she joked. "I'm going out tonight with some brilliantined beauty from the land of RKO."

"I wish you luck, and I'll see you back here in the morning."

"Yes, you will," she sighed, then, with both hands, straightened his bow tie. "We can't have you less than perfect." She smiled up at him. "Three or four more days, then we're finished, and I'm taking a vacation. I don't care what hot new property Ludie's got in the works. Even slaves get Sundays off from chopping cotton."

"Lordy, Miss Beatrice," he chirped, "I'm sure I don't know. Have a good time tonight," he said in his normal voice, and moved to go.

"Hank?"

He turned back.

"D'you suppose they'd let Bobby and me go off somewhere together for a holiday?"

"One can but try."

"Would you hint around for me and test the waters?"

"I'll do my best."

In his street clothes, Bobby stopped by to sit watching her cream off her make-up. "I still wish I was going with you," he said, his eyes on hers in the mirror rimmed with small light bulbs.

"Look!" She swiveled around to confront him. "Let's drop it, okay? Lucy's home sick with the 'flu. We've spent hours doing one dopey scene until all I can hear inside my head are those eight lines. I'm tired. I'd like a vacation. I'd like a vacation with you. Hank's going to find out if we can swing it. I'd rather be doing almost anything I can name than going to this ball tonight. Unfortunately, I'm committed to going. There's a white orchid corsage from my escort sitting at home in the icebox, and Molly's having a nervous breakdown

197

ironing my dress. My feet hurt, my back aches, and I'm in a lousy mood. Please, be a darling, and leave me alone. Don't nag me anymore about this goddamned ball!"

Chastened, he got up. "I'm sorry," he said stiffly.

"Come give me a kiss, and then get out of here." She smiled at him as she removed the last of the make-up. "Let's not make things any more complicated than they already are."

He bent to kiss her, then straightened saying, "Sometimes I get the feeling you're about twenty years older than me. It makes me feel kind of dumb."

"That's because you *are* kind of dumb. But I love you. Now, good-bye."

"Good-bye," he said, and went off.

After the door closed, she turned back to the make-up mirror, even more tired than she'd been a few minutes before.

Upon arriving home, bent on an hour's nap before starting preparations for her evening out, she went up to look in on Lucy. Her features blotched with fever, Lucy was asleep. Closing the door quietly, Bea returned downstairs to the kitchen where Molly was staring balefully at the white silk dress suspended on its hanger from the top of the pantry door.

"Don't you never make me do nothing like this ever again!" Molly warned. "I need a big drink after fussing with *that* half the day." Without pausing for breath or changing her inflection, she went on. "You had some calls, and there's a letter the studio sent over from your mama."

"Who called?"

"I put the letter in your room. Mr. Bobby called, said not to go out before you call him back. Mr. Hank said about the same thing. And the publicity fella from RKO called to say your date'll be here seven-thirty sharp. Name of Richard something. Man said it so fast I couldn't hardly get it."

"What did Dr. Shannon say about Lucy?"

"He says it's just a bad cold. He give her some medicine and told her to keep to her bed a few days. You want anything? Bet you didn't eat a scrap all day."

"No, thank you." Bea lifted the dress down gingerly from the door and stood holding it, one arm extended to keep the hem off the floor. "I don't want to talk to anyone. I'm going to lie down for an hour."

"You're in a fine mood," Molly observed.

"I'm in probably the worst mood of my life."

"You *better* lie down," Molly said, "else you'll scare everybody off with that face you're wearin'."

"If Hank or Bobby phones again, say I'm in the bath or something."

"I'll do that."

Bea looked at the older woman for a moment, then asked, "D'you have a family somewhere, Molly?"

"I've got my mother and a brother back in Mississippi."

"Are you close? D'you miss them?"

"We're close, and I miss them at times. But bein' here, doin' work for you, pays for them."

"I'm sorry," Bea said inexplicably.

"Why're you sorry? You give me this job when nobody else would. Leastwise, Miss Lucy did. And I like it here, like the two of you."

"Do you? I like you, Molly. I think you're the only sane person I know right now."

"Go on up 'n take your nap," Molly told her. "I'll come in an hour, bring you somethin' to put in your stomach before you go out."

"Thank you," Bea said, and went off with the dress.

The letter was months old. Attached to the envelope was a note from the publicity department apologizing for its having been mislaid by one of the new employees. Bea tore open the envelope impatiently and sat down at the foot of the bed to read.

March 17, 1936

Dear Bea,

I guess your real busy these days with your career which is why I haven't heard from you but the money comes every month thank you. Ive got some sad news your gramma died. She wasnt feeling so hot and complaning about her feet and legs and chest pains like always but when I come home from work one day she was just gone. The doctor who come said it was her heart and she went quickly there wasnt a thing I couldve done if I was here. Its not the same without her I never thought Id miss her so much as I do and I thought youd want to know. The funeral and everything cost me almost four hundred dollars but it was worth it my friend Harold said it was a real nice service. Me and Harold been talking about getting married maybe in a couple of months and maybe wed come out there to see you. I havent decided yet cant make up my mind. Here I am almost 38 and I never been married makes you stop and think. Anyway I thought Id bring you up to date on what alls been happening. Theres always big lineups for your pictures Ive seen them all thats a

199

very cute fella you dance with. I hope your taking good care of yourself not staying out to all hours at those parties theyre always having I read about.

> *Love,*
> *Lil*

Bea got up, walked around the bed, picked up the telephone, and dialed Jerry's office number. He'd still be there. He usually stayed until at least seven or eight, in case any calls came in from New York.

When he picked up his line, she said, "Would you arrange with the bank to send my mother five hundred dollars? My grandmother died in March, and Lil wants the money back she laid out for the funeral."

"I'm making a note of it right now. How's everything? You sound down."

"Jerry, doesn't my contract say I have the right to four weeks' vacation time every year?"

"It does."

"I've never had one week of it, and I want to take some time after we wrap *Moonlight*."

"I'll talk to Ludie, see what I can arrange."

"Thank you. I'd appreciate it."

"Anything else?" he asked tolerantly.

"No, not at the moment. Am I sounding unreasonable?" she asked.

"I wouldn't say so. It's been my experience that, among my numerous unreasonable clients, you rank somewhere down around the bottom."

"That's good to know. Are you going to be there tonight?"

"There's some kind of bug going around. The kids are sick, Brenda doesn't want to leave them, so we canceled."

"That's too bad. I'm really sorry. Give them my love. I'll talk to you in the next few days."

"Take it easy, sweetheart. I'll get on to the bank, and to Uncle Ludie, first thing tomorrow."

She laughed, said, "Thank you," and put the receiver down. After pulling the plug from the wall, she stretched out on the bed.

Lucy came in clutching a handful of tissues while Bea was putting the final touches to her make-up.

"You look so pretty," she wheezed, folding into the armchair near

200

the dressing table. "I'm so mad I'm not going. I'll probably never get another chance to wear that dress."

"Sure you will," Bea outlined her mouth with a lipstick brush. "I had a letter from Lil. It got lost over at the studio for months. My gramma died."

"Gee, that's too bad."

"I know I should feel sad, but I don't feel much of anything, so I feel guilty instead." She put down the brush and picked up a tube of rose-colored lipstick, pausing to look over at Lucy. "Lil says she might be getting married and wants to come visit. The very thought of it makes my hair stand on end. She's getting two-fifty a month from me now, and every other letter from her hints it's not enough. Every so often I have the feeling she's like something attached to one of the veins in my arm. She's never interested in knowing how I really am, or what my life's like. She just wants highlights of the juicy parts."

"You don't have to see her if you don't want to." Lucy pushed the handful of tissues against her nose and sneezed before going on in more nasal tones. "All she's got is the studio address. It's not like she's going to show up on the doorstep."

"She's greedy and dumb, and if you want to know the truth, I've always been a little mortified at being related to her. I know it's awful of me, but I can't help it. It's not as if she was ever anything like a real mother."

"I know that, hon. I don't think you've got any cause to feel guilty. You've been very damned generous with that woman."

Bea turned back to the mirror and sat for a moment contemplating her reflection. Then she pulled over a box of pins, reached for the hairbrush, and adeptly pinned her hair into a loop at the back of her neck.

The telephone could be heard ringing downstairs, and Lucy looked over at the bedside table, noting the disconnected extension. There was silence from below, then the sound of Molly's feet on the stairs.

"You still not talkin' to anybody?" she asked from the doorway.

"Still," Bea answered around a mouthful of hairpins.

"It's Mr. Bobby."

"Tell him I'm locked in the bathroom, and I'll see him in the morning."

"Okay." Molly shrugged and left.

"The two of you have a fight?" Lucy asked.

"No. I'm just not in the mood to talk to him. Sometimes," she said, taking the last of the pins from her mouth and returning them to their tortoise-shell box, "when we're together, I'll look at him, and I'll think

201

about the way he knuckled under in Ludie's office that day; I'll think about how he wouldn't, or couldn't, fight for me, and I feel as if I'll never be able to forgive him. Then, a minute to two later, he'll say or do something that's so sweet, so dear, I feel as if I'll strangle, caring so much for him."

"That's the way it goes," Lucy said. "I'm beginning to believe it's impossible to be in love all the time. There's always something that you hold back. I guess the secret is to find the one you hold back the least from."

Bea got up, shrugged off her wrapper, and went to lift the dress down from its hanger.

Lucy sneezed again, coughed, blotted her nose with the bunched-up tissues, and said, "That sure is a gorgeous gown."

Bea held it away from her, looking at it. Weightless white silk, it had a sweetheart neckline; the bodice was hand-embroidered in glistening cream silk threads in a design of interwoven leaves and flowers. Bea stepped into it carefully, then moved across the room so Lucy could do up the zip.

"You look like a dream." Lucy smiled, bleary-eyed, as Bea examined her image in the full-length mirror on the back of the walk-in–closet door.

The gown fit very closely from shoulders to waist, then fell from dozens of tiny tucks in a wide sweep of fabric to the floor. Additional embroidery circled the hem, and when she turned, the silk strands reflected the light.

"It looks like a wedding dress," Bea said dismissively, picking up a pair of white, elbow-length gloves and the white silk evening bag that completed the ensemble. "If I didn't like Carole, if I didn't know she's worked like a dog on this ball, I can promise you I wouldn't be going. But I gave my word."

"I want to hear every detail," Lucy said with all the eagerness she could muster. "Wake me up when you get home. I don't care what time it is."

"It doesn't feel right, going without you."

"If you're nervous, you can call me after you get there and tell me how it's going."

"I'll call you at ten-thirty. If you don't hear from me," she laughed, "send out the militia."

The doorbell rang, and Bea swore. "He's early, damn it! And the corsage is still in the icebox."

"Molly will have it for you, you'll see."

Giving herself a final check in the mirror, Bea wondered aloud, "How d'you suppose we ever managed without her?"

Sure enough, Molly was waiting at the foot of the stairs, ready to pin the orchid to the left shoulder of Bea's dress, as she did, whispering, "I put him in the livin' room to wait. He's another pretty-lookin' fella. Seems nice enough."

Bea stopped cold in the living room doorway at the sight of her date.

"Hello, Bea." Dickie smiled, and got up from the sofa, as he did, emitting an admiring whistle. "Say, that's a sensational gown!"

"Thank you." She gave him a stiff smile, then said, "I'm running a bit late. Give me another minute, would you?"

"Sure. Take all the time you need."

She flew back up to Lucy's room. "It's Dickie," she whispered frantically. "*He's* my date from RKO. How could Pete *do* something like this? Listen, he's waiting, and I've got to go. If you don't hear from me by ten-thirty, send somebody over there to get me. Call Pete at home, or at the studio, if you have to. I *really mean* it! I *don't understand* how this could happen."

"It'll probably be all right," Lucy said doubtfully.

"Don't take any bets on that. I'll call you later." Lifting her skirt with both hands, she tore off.

Dickie held open the passenger door to his sleek new roadster and waited, smiling pleasantly, until she'd managed to get herself seated inside.

"Just everybody's going to be there," he said excitedly, as he reversed the car. "Lombard's really outdone herself this time. I've heard they've even got footmen rigged out in white." When Bea remained silent, taking her time to light a cigarette, he continued on with his eager narrative, speculating on who might be there, and about the pre-dawn breakfast party that would take place at Carole's house after the ball. "They've got Cab Calloway and his orchestra, and Eduardo Durantes' Latin Band."

Feeling called upon to make some comment, she gave him another stiff smile and said, "It sounds wonderful."

"I'll bet it was some surprise, me turning up."

"It certainly was."

"*Photoplay* had a contest to come up with a new name for me," he told her. "So I'm Richard Vere, these days. Everybody likes it. The folks over at RKO thought 'Dickie' was a little too far over on the boyish side. And I *am* twenty-four."

"I see." She took another puff on her cigarette.

"It's been kind of tough, these last couple of years, starting from scratch at a new studio."

"But you're doing very well," she said, somewhat taken aback. "I

203

understand RKO's been working hard to build up your name. I've seen all kinds of print about you."

He shrugged. "Yeah, well, it's coming along."

Why, she wondered, did this conversation sound like grade-B dialogue? It was probably nothing more than her enormous surprise at finding he was her escort for the evening. Yet *she* hadn't changed her name, so why had he agreed to be her date? She sat quietly, smoking her cigarette, enjoying the soft breeze that flowed through the open car windows.

It did seem as if "everybody" was there. Within half an hour after their arrival, Bea had caught sight of and exchanged greetings with Claudette Colbert, Spencer Tracy, Marion Davies, and Basil Rathbone and his wife. She'd also seen Jeanette MacDonald wafting past in a pale mauve, almost pink, gown and thought it was kind of rotten of MacDonald not to play by the rules for the occasion.

Dickie excused himself to go to the bar for drinks, and Bea stood looking at the assembled crowd, admiring all the stunning white gowns, exchanging greetings with smiles and waves to Ludie and his wife as they passed by on their way to the table. Just as Dickie was returning to her side, drinks in each hand, a whisper started up and heads began to turn. Norma Shearer had arrived. In a bright crimson gown. Unable to help herself, Bea covered her mouth with a gloved hand, as her dismay emerged in the form of laughter. It was too awful, she thought, seeing Carole frozen with outrage near the door. Everyone but Shearer and MacDonald had followed instructions to the letter, and the crimson gown was like fire moving through the crowd. People muttered angrily on all sides, including Dickie who, his eyes tracking the woman's progress, whispered, "Who does that bitch think she is?"

"Poor Carole," Bea said in an undertone, more to herself than for Dickie's benefit. "Perhaps," she said, in normal tones, "we should join Mr. Meyers at the table."

"Oh!" he said. "Sure." His eyes lingered on the woman in red, and his expression mildly alarmed Bea. He looked almost as if he would willingly have murdered Shearer. Granted, people were visibly upset with her, but Dickie's reaction seemed incredibly overblown.

She made an effort to have a good time but was completely chagrined, while dancing with Dickie, at his attempt to turn a fox trot into a full-fledged routine. People were watching, eyebrows raised, and Bea could do no more than keep a smile plastered to her face while steadfastly resisting his moves to turn her and his silent physical urging to show off. As they were returning to the table, she glanced surreptitiously at his watch. It was only nine-thirty. The evening was going to last an eternity.

As they got to the table, she was relieved when Mrs. Meyers suggested Ludie dance with Bea. "Go on," Mrs. Meyers told him, then addressed Bea. "Believe it or not, Ludie's a wonderful dancer."

"I didn't know that," Bea said, pleased. "Now, I'll have to insist we have a dance, Mr. Meyers."

For an overweight, middle-aged man, Ludie was indeed a fine dancer, light on his feet, and able to lead without undue pressure. His fingers placed on her spine signaled in advance his moves. It was a surprisingly professional gesture.

"You're a nice kid, you know that," Ludie said as they circled the floor. "I want you to know I'm sorry about that mess a while back."

"I understand," she accepted his apology.

"You havin' a good time?" he wanted to know.

"Very nice, thank you. You dance very well."

"You," he grinned, "you're a feather. It's a pleasure."

She laughed, and he expertly reversed her into a turn. Maybe the evening wouldn't be so terrible after all, she thought, looking over toward the table to discover Dickie's eyes on her. At once, she averted her gaze, but she couldn't help being disturbed by the almost glowering intensity of his expression. She'd give it another half-hour, she decided, then ask Dickie to take her home. If he was unwilling, she'd get a taxi and be home well in advance of the time she'd promised to telephone Lucy.

Twenty

THE telephone kept ringing and, finally, Lucy picked up the extension beside her bed. It was Bobby.

"D'you *know* who Bea's out with?" he demanded without preamble.

"Bobby," she said tiredly, "I know."

"The guy's nuts, Lucy! I've got half a mind to go down there and get her."

"You can't *do* a thing like that!" Lucy argued.

"Why not? I was invited. I just didn't want to go and have to watch Bea with some other guy."

"Bobby, please calm down. I'm sure she'll be fine. She's due to call me in about half an hour."

"Call me right after you talk to her," he pleaded. "I've got to know she's okay."

"Why wouldn't she be?"

"Luce, I've heard some things, and they haven't been good. I won't rest until I know she's home safe. So call me as soon as you've talked to her."

"What exactly have you heard?" Lucy wanted to know, feeling the first stirrings of unease.

"You don't want to know. Just call me."

Not five minutes later, the telephone rang again. This time it was Hank.

"I happened to run into Pete a few hours ago, and he told me Bea was going tonight with Dickie."

"What's *wrong* with everybody?" Lucy asked. "Bobby's been calling nonstop, and now you."

"Why aren't you with her, Lucy?"

"I'm sick in bed, that's why."

"I hauled Pete over the coals for this stunt," he said feverishly. "It's the dumbest damned thing ever, pairing Bea up this way with a guy she had dumped off the lot."

"What's the story about him, Hank?"

"There are some nasty rumors, very nasty."

"About *what*, for God's sake?"

"About Dickie and women, about the kinds of things he's been getting up to lately."

"But they're surrounded by dozens of people..."

"He still has to bring her home. I'm arranging to have Pete go down with a limo to get her."

"You're *scaring* me, Hank!" she accused.

"Maybe I'm being an alarmist, but I don't like the idea of her being out with that guy. I'll get back to you."

Just before ten, Dickie drained his glass, plonked it down on the table, reached for Bea's hand, and said, "I can tell you're not enjoying yourself. Why don't I run you home?"

Relieved and grateful, she gave him a smile. "I have a headache, to tell you the truth. If you wouldn't mind, I really would like to go. You can drop me, then come right back."

"Sure," he agreed, then waited while she said her good-byes.

The car was brought around, Dickie tipped the white-suited car jockey, then went to slide behind the wheel as the jockey held the door open for Bea.

"I'm just wild about your dancing," the boy confessed to Bea with a smile as he smartly closed the car door. "Goodnight now, Miss Crane."

Bea thanked the young man, then opened her bag for a cigarette. She paid no attention to the route they were taking but relaxed with her head back against the seat, savoring the cigarette and glad to be on her way home. It wasn't until they'd been driving for about ten minutes that she straightened to look out the window and failed to recognize any familiar landmarks.

"Where are we going, Dickie?" she asked him.

"I want to show you something before I drop you. Ever seen the view from up in the Hills?"

"Not recently."

"It's fabulous at night. You'll see."

What difference could a few more minutes make? she told herself, and sat back again.

The road was slow-going, winding up into the Hills, with hints, in the clearings, of what did indeed promise to be a spectacular view. When at last he pulled the car to a stop, she looked down at the panorama spread below and sighed with pleasure. "You're right," she began, when something collided stunningly with the left side of her head.

Automatically, her hand rose to her head as she turned to look at him questioningly, trying to imagine what might somehow have come loose in the car and struck her. Before she could think or speak, his hand flew out, and he hit her again. Immediately, she threw herself against the door, groping for the handle. She couldn't find it, her hands sliding in the darkness over the leather-covered interior of the door. Just as her fingers seemed to have a grip on the handle and began to pull it down to open the door, Dickie's fingers fastened like a vise around her upper arm.

"We're gonna be here for a while," he said softly, his fingers digging into her flesh.

"What is this?" she asked, barely able to see him now that he'd turned off the car lights. "What d'you want, Dickie?" Her face was throbbing from his blows, and her breathing had turned shallow.

"*Richard*," he corrected her. "Thanks to you, I can't even use the name I've had all my life."

"You told me it was the studio's idea. What's your name got to do with me?"

Almost lazily, his left arm drifted through the air and connected with her face in another open-handed blow that snapped her head back with its force.

"I had *everything* going for me, and *you* scotched it. You're over there with Ludie Meyers making pictures with Bradley when it was supposed to be *me*. You're the one that soured everything!"

"Your agent wanted too much money," she reasoned with him. The man was insane, she thought, trying to stay calm and think her way out of this. He threw open the door on his side and began dragging her out of the car. She resisted, fixed on the arbitrary idea that safety resided in the car's interior.

"*Get out here!*" he commanded, using both hands to pull at her. "You've got to see the *view!*"

If she did what he wished, maybe he'd stop this, and she'd be able to go home. She quit struggling and allowed herself to be yanked out of the car. His grip on her arm so fierce her hand was going numb, he propelled her forward in the darkness until they were at the edge of a steep incline.

"*Look at it!*" he ordered.

Obediently, she looked. If she could break free of his hold on her arm, she'd be able to find somewhere to hide and, eventually, make her way back down that road and get home.

All at once, he released her. Immediately she looked around, seeking an escape route.

"Take off your clothes!" he said, his voice now maddeningly soft.

"What?" Her voice emerged as a whisper.

"You think half the world doesn't know about you and Bradley? I'd hate to have to rip such a pretty dress. It must have set you back four or five hundred, at least."

Suddenly, she was enraged. And now that he no longer had hold of her, her courage flooded back. "Never mind worrying about ripping the dress," she barked at him. "You'll have to kill me to get me to take off my clothes."

"All right," he said, sounding as if he were smiling.

She took a step to the side, mindful of the sheer drop behind her, but he seemed somehow immense as he blocked her path. The only place she could go was backwards, over the edge.

"You'll never get away with this, Dickie," she attempted again to reason with him. "Everyone knows I left with you. Dozens of people saw us together. You harm me, and your career will be finished forever. You're not thinking."

"You won't tell anyone about this," he said with demented confidence, so close she could smell the scotch on his breath.

"I won't, if you stop this right now and let me go. I'll walk home. That ought to be punishment enough, making me walk all the way back down that road in high-heeled shoes, in the pitch dark."

"I have no intention of forcing you to walk home. I brought you; I'll take you home. When we're finished."

"**P**ete got there with the limo, and they'd already gone. Is she home yet?" Hank asked.

"Not yet. They're probably on their way."

"No. They should've been there by now. According to Pete they left the ball forty minutes ago. I'm going to call the studio police."

"Don't you think we should give her a little more time?" Lucy asked.

"If anything happens, *if* anything does, we've got to cover Bea, protect her. I'll call the studio, then come over to the house. I'll be there in half an hour." He put down the phone, and Lucy replaced the receiver as Molly knocked and opened the door.

"What's goin' on?" she asked. "What's happenin' with all these phone calls? Somethin' wrong with Miss Bea?"

"I don't know." Lucy looked over at the telephone. "Hank's on his way over. I'd better get dressed, I suppose. Maybe you should make coffee, or something."

"Somethin' happened to Miss Bea?"

"*I don't know!*" Lucy cried. "Please go make some coffee! God! I'll never forgive myself," she whispered. "I knew I should've gone with her. The one time I couldn't go..." Remembering Molly, she looked up and said, "I'm sorry. I didn't mean to snap at you. Please go on. I'll be down in a minute."

Resolutely, Molly turned and left the room.

It wasn't yet ten-thirty, Lucy saw by her alarm clock. Hank was jumping to conclusions, making a fuss because he'd always had a crush on Bea and often liked to act as if she were something he'd created single-handedly.

He's *never* acted any such way! she rebuked herself harshly. He's never done anything that wasn't in Bea's best interest; he's always been there for her. He was the one who went with her that day, waited while she had the abortion, then brought her home. He adores her, and you know it.

As she dressed, she kept looking over at the telephone, willing it to ring. And downstairs, while she waited for Hank to get there, she strained toward the instrument, hoping for its shrill summons.

Bea couldn't believe this was happening to her. The pain was real enough, all right; but some segment of her brain kept insisting she'd awaken to discover this was only a terrifying nightmare. Her exquisite dress was nothing more than a series of white shreds against the black of her surroundings. One long piece had fallen into the brush and lifted and fell with the breeze. The petals of the orchid had been ground into the dirt. She kept her eyes on the wafting bit of silk just over there, while Dickie pounded the last of the resistance out of her. She had no fight left. She could only keep her eyes fixed on that slip of lightness as his weight bore down on her, taking her past the rocks and dirt beneath her, into the heart of the earth. It seemed as if this would never end. His voice would go on and on forever, whispering vile threats into her ear as he thrust himself with more and more force inside her, as if he wanted to rip her apart as he had the gown.

It did end, finally, and he paused for a moment, shuddering, his breathing gone haywire. Then he abruptly pulled out of her, causing her, involuntarily, to gasp. Rising up on his knees, he straddled her and began shrieking incoherently, as his fists drove into her belly and breasts, into her arms and shoulders. When he redirected his fists to her face, she sought instinctively to protect herself, but he shifted, bringing his knees down on her arms. Then he went back to striking her, and there was an instant of engulfing pain before she fainted.

Hank paced back and forth in the living room, halting every few minutes in front of the telephone where he waited expectantly. Nothing happened.

"You've *got* to tell me what he did," Lucy insisted. "Bobby refused to be explicit. *Please*, Hank! The two of you are scaring the *hell* out of me!"

He stopped, came over to the sofa and sat down beside her, his hand coming to rest on her wrist. "The word," he said fearfully, "is that he went out on an arranged date a week or so ago with some girl."

"And?" she prompted.

"And for no reason she could think of, she claims he beat her black and blue."

"My God!"

"She's being paid to keep quiet about it."

"The poor girl."

"The thing of it is," he continued somberly, "she says he kept calling her 'Bea,' and that he told her repeatedly he'd kill her. She kept telling him her name wasn't 'Bea,' and it suddenly seemed to register, and he stopped. He pulled himself together, apologized profusely, gave her several hundred dollars, and took her home. Pete didn't know about any of this or about the name change." He swiveled around once more to look at the telephone, then back to Lucy who, wide-eyed with apprehension, was holding several tissues to her nose. "*Nobody* knew about it until the girl got in touch with the powers-that-be this morning. Somebody had heard about Bea going with him to the ball tonight and called me in the afternoon, but I couldn't get back to him until late in the day. And Bea wouldn't take any calls. If he hurts her, I *swear* I'll *kill* him." He held his fists on his knees. "Why the hell doesn't somebody *call*?" he said. "They've got most of the studio cops out there, looking for them. Maybe we should bring the police in, too. I hate to do that, though. The publicity." He shook his head, got up, and resumed his pacing. "Pete's beside himself," he said. "He just didn't connect Richard Vere with Dickie DeVore."

She regained consciousness as Dickie was shoving her across the front seat of the car but kept her eyes closed, afraid to do anything that might provoke him further. Her whole body pulsed with pain,

211

and she held her breath as he started up the car, put on the headlights, then slammed closed his door.

Please, she prayed, let him be taking me home.

The speed and motion of the car felt all wrong, as if, instead of descending, they were climbing higher. There was nothing else she could do, so she pretended she was coming around and slowly pulled herself upright on the seat to see where they were going. Dickie was driving very fast, muttering under his breath. Everything seemed to be speeding past the car at a tremendous rate as it lurched around curves, the tires spitting rocks and dirt against the undercarriage.

Tyring to cover herself with what remained of her slip, she had the idea all at once that Dickie intended to go as high up into the Hills as he could and then throw her from some cliff.

"Please take me home," she pleaded, aware the instant she spoke that her lips were split and bleeding. Touching trembling fingers to her face, she felt blood oozing down her nose and over her chin.

"SHUT UP!" he shouted, looking away from the road and halfway raising his arm so that she shrank away from him.

There couldn't be much road left, she thought. She had to do something, had to get him to stop. She didn't want to die. Completely gripped by panicked conviction, she threw herself across the seat in an attempt to wrestle the steering wheel from his hands. They were headed, so far as she could see, into space. There was nowhere left to go.

"DICKIE, STOP THE CAR!" she screamed. "STOP THE CAR!"

Beyond the windshield, there was only air.

Dickie turned and with his right arm flung her away from him. The force of the gesture propelled her all the way across the seat and against the passenger door that, unlatched from her earlier efforts to open it, swung free. She sailed out of the car and was turning in darkness, then landing with a pain so tremendous she knew, in her last instants of awareness, she couldn't possibly live. She rolled over and over, dark earth indistinguishable from dark sky, and knew that the car was gone. All motion stopped. She lay unmoving. There was only silence, and the utter darkness, and the pain.

The ringing of the telephone awakened Lucy who'd fallen asleep on the sofa and she jerked upright, her head pounding with the suddenness of the motion. Hank leaped from the armchair where he'd been sitting most of the night, chainsmoking while he'd waited for the call he now dreaded receiving.

He walked across the room, lifted the receiver, and held it to his ear as Lucy watched him numbly. He listened for what seemed a very long time. At last, with all the color drained from his face, he hung up."

"They found her just over an hour ago," he said thickly. "She's going into surgery at Cedars of Lebanon."

"*Surgery?*" Lucy's stomach lurched.

"They say she's in very bad shape."

"Oh, no!" Lucy bent forward over her knees.

"Dickie's dead. The car went over a cliff and burned up with him in it."

"Was she in the car?" Lucy lifted her head.

"Apparently she was thrown clear, but she landed on some rocks. They thought at first she might be dead, too."

Molly appeared behind him in the doorway asking, "Miss Bea all right?"

"They don't know, Molly. We'd better get over there."

Sick and dizzy, Lucy got to her feet and looked around for her handbag.

"You're in no fit condition to go anywhere," Hank told her.

"Don't you *dare* tell me what I'm fit to do! Molly, phone Bobby and tell him to meet us at the hospital. Cedars. You know his number?"

"Yes'm. I know it."

"I'll keep you posted," Lucy promised, and hurried out with Hank to his car.

As he drove at top speed toward the hospital, he said, "They had to call in the police, because of Dickie. God, let her be all right!"

"Tell me what they told you," she implored him.

"I talked to the chief of the studio cops. He was only repeating what he was told. And he was told by one of the two guys who found her."

"*I don't care! Tell me!*"

"They didn't want to wait for an ambulance. They were afraid she'd be dead by the time it got there. So they put her in the back of their patrol car and took her right to the hospital, then called the city police from there. The guy that phoned in said she looked like she'd been beaten half to death, and that the fall she took had done a lot of serious damage. I can't say any more, Lucy. Please don't ask me. I'll break down if I have to say one more word."

Pete was already there. He'd installed himself at a pay phone with several dollars' worth of nickels and broke off from speaking into the mouthpiece to say, "She's still in surgery. No word. I'm working out

213

the story with the RKO boys." He turned back to the mouthpiece and resumed talking in a low, urgent voice.

"We'd better find somewhere to wait," Hank said, and directed Lucy into a nearby waiting room.

Not ten minutes later, Bobby arrived, looking terror-stricken. "How is she?" he asked the two of them. "Is she okay? What happened?"

"I don't know," Lucy told him. "We're just waiting. Hank's going to look for someone who'll tell us what's going on. Pete's out there on the phone..."

"I know. I saw him."

"Nobody's saying anything."

"Jesus, Jesus!" Bobby ran to the doorway, looked up and down the corridor, ran a few yards toward the nurses' station, then returned to the waiting room. He couldn't remain still. Again he went to the doorway, looked up and down, and was startled by the sight of half a dozen reporters pushing in through the emergency entrance. "Shit!" he whispered. "How'd they find out so fast? The press," he told Lucy, turning a white face to her.

"Tell Pete!"

Bobby flung himself out of the room and raced down the corridor, signaling wildly. Pete shouted into the phone, "The press! Get on this fast!" pushed the receiver back into its rest, squared his shoulders, and went to cut off the reporters.

By eight-thirty in the morning, Jerry, Hank, Lucy, Bobby, two studio cops, a team of publicists from RKO, and a detective from homicide were all crowded into the small room. When finally the doctor appeared, Lucy got up on unsteady legs and went with him some distance up the corridor.

"I'm sorry," he began.

"Oh, God!" she cried. "She's not *dead?*"

He placed a calming hand on her shoulder. "She's not dead. But she's in critical condition. Her back's broken, so are both her hips. I can only think, in her fall, she landed squarely on her spine and buttocks. Her left leg's broken in five places."

Lucy began to sob helplessly.

"There's something else I think you should know," he said.

"What?"

"She was raped and badly beaten. Several bones in her face are broken."

Lucy wept harder, so dizzy now she felt faint. She had to ask, "Will she be all right?"

"We'll know in the next forty-eight hours. It was a lot of work, setting so many bones. It's a tremendous shock to her system, especially combined with all the other trauma she sustained. I'll be completely honest with you. If she does make it, it's touch and go whether she'll be able to walk. It's hard to determine at this point the extent of the damage, whether or not there's any spinal-cord injury. I don't think so, but I can't be entirely sure. Are you going to faint? Here, sit down." Gently, he eased her into a chair and urged her to put her head down.

Her voice muffled, she said, "Please don't tell her! Don't tell anyone! But for God's sake, don't tell Bea! She wouldn't want to live if she knew she couldn't walk, let alone dance."

"I won't say a word to anyone," he promised. "Stay as you are. I'll have one of the nurses bring you something."

He left her, and Lucy remained with her head on her knees, the back of her neck prickly and cold, her mouth flooded with bitter fluid. Her brain reeled drunkenly back and forth over what she'd been told. The only coherent thought she could form was that she should have gone with Bea, regardless of how she'd been feeling. She should've gone with her.

Pete was having a rough time with the press. They were refusing to leave until they had something they could print. They already knew Dickie had died in the crash. Now they wanted to know what the two of them had been doing up there in the Hills and the details of Bea's injuries.

Unable to satisfy them, Pete at last resorted to part of the truth. "Look," he said exhaustedly. "The girl might not live. If she does, she's going to be in bad shape. *Please*, just say she was injured, that the extent of her injuries isn't yet known, and leave it vague. You wouldn't want her to find out her condition by reading one of your papers, would you? Would any one of you want to be responsible for that? As soon as I've got anything solid, you've got my word I'll call you back for a conference."

Grumbling, the reporters and photographers backed off. Pete mopped his forehead with an already damp handkerchief and headed once more for the pay phones. He'd neglected to call home and let his wife know his whereabouts.

Only Lucy was allowed in to see her. With a nurse offering her arm as support, Lucy went along to the room, stepped inside, and

215

gasped at the sight of Bea. She hadn't yet regained consciousness, the doctor had told Lucy, but her vital signs had stabilized.

Bea's face was swollen beyond recognition. Both eyes had been blackened, her nose and several bones in her cheeks were broken. Blood was crusted in her ears and in her hairline and down the sides of her neck. Her body was encased in plaster from mid-chest to her thighs, and one leg was in a heavy cast and suspended by some kind of traction device. Intravenous needles were taped to both her arms. Her fingernails were broken and clotted with dirt, as were her feet.

"Why hasn't anyone cleaned her up?" Lucy whirled around. "Why have you left her like that?"

"Don't worry," the nurse said, holding up a placating hand. "She'll be cleaned up shortly. Please don't stay for more than a minute or two."

"God!" Lucy exhaled tremulously, and stepped closer to the bed, shaking her head in mournful disbelief at the sight of Bea's battered face. Biting her lower lip, she placed her hand with utmost care on the top of Bea's head. Then, sickened and afraid, she got herself out of the room and along to the ladies' room where she bent over the sink and splashed her face and neck with cold water until the worst of the sickness had passed.

Lucy refused to leave. To accommodate her, the head nurse brought in a comfortable chair and allowed her to remain in the room with Bea so she could be there when Bea came around. That didn't happen until very late that night. Lucy looked over, and Bea's eyes were open. At once, Lucy jumped up and went to lean over, smiling down at her, softly saying, "Hi."

Bea's impossibly thickened lips parted slightly, and she tried to moisten them with the tip of her tongue. Lucy dipped her finger into the water jug on the table and very lightly ran her wet finger over Bea's lips.

"I thought I died," Bea got out. "I'm so scared!"

"You're going to be fine now," Lucy lied. "There's no need to be scared. It's all over. Close your eyes and rest." She remained standing, watching, until Bea's eyes fluttered closed.

Hank and Bobby were still in the waiting room. They, too, had refused to leave. They'd dozed on the narrow sofa and the uncomfortable chairs while keeping their vigil. Pete had gone off many hours

216

earlier and had been checking in by telephone at regular intervals. Jerry had left at noon to go to the office, after eliciting their promise they'd keep him informed. Hank had been calling Hero on the hour.

Both men looked up as Pete burst into the room. "How is she? Have you heard anything more?"

"She's gonna make it," Hank said, studying his hands. "We won't know the rest of it for a while yet."

"Okay. I'll be back first thing in the morning."

Bobby, on the sofa, drew his knees up to his chest, wrapped his arms around his calves, lowered his head to his knees, and sobbed. Hank looked away.

After three days and nights at the hospital, Lucy simply had to go home — to bathe, to sleep for a few hours, to change into fresh clothes.

Hank had finally, midway through the second day, gone off to see Hero.

Bobby had hung on until the morning of the third day when he'd confessed to needing sleep; he'd left after assuring Lucy he'd back by evening.

As soon as Lucy walked through the front door, Molly said, "You better call Mr. Greenswag. He said the minute you come through the door you got to call him."

Weary beyond measure, Lucy went to the telephone.

"There's some half-assed dame who's called a press conference, says she's Bea's mother, and she's being kept from her daughter."

"Christ! As if everybody hasn't been through enough."

"Is she the McCoy or what? Talk to me! I've got my hands full trying to deal with this nutsy woman."

"Did she tell you her name?"

"Lillian Crane. She's got some hairy thug with her."

"It's her," Lucy said in a dulled voice.

"I've gotta know what to do here, Lucy. Give me some help!"

"Let me think for a minute. I'm so tired. It's hard to get my thoughts straight."

"SHE'S THREATENING TO GIVE PARSONS AN EXCLUSIVE!" he shouted. "HELP ME HERE!"

"She can't be allowed to see Bea. It'd be the worst possible thing. Bea's only barely able to talk. She's so scared that when the doctor came in to see her, she took one look at him and started screaming. She doesn't know yet about her condition, Jerry. Stall Lil off for a couple of hours! Put Pete on it! Tell him Bea can't stand her mother, that she's the last person on earth she'd want to see. He'll know what to do. I'll get cleaned up and go back to the hospital, find out how Bea wants to handle it."

While Lucy was gone, one of the nurses accepted a call. Upon hearing who was on the other end of the line, she became obsequiously obedient and held the receiver to Bea's ear.

"I'm so sorry, dear," Louella said. "Such sad news. I'm sure it must be a terrible blow to you, having your career end this way."

"What?" Bea asked.

"Your wonderful dancing. Such a pity."

Before she could go on, Bea started screaming, her eyes bulging, the cords in her neck like rope. The nurse was so shattered, she dropped the receiver, abandoned the screaming Bea, and ran for help.

By the time Lucy returned, Bea had been sedated, and the nurse had been removed from the floor after having been dressed down in no uncertain terms by the attending physician.

"Why didn't anyone tell me?" Bea rounded on Lucy as she came in, twisting her head around in order to see her.

"Tell you what, sweetheart?"

"THAT I'M CRIPPLED!" Bea shrieked.

"You are *not* crippled! Who's been telling you rubbish like that?"

"TELL ME THE TRUTH!"

"It *is* the truth," Lucy persisted. "There's no nerve damage. You're not crippled. You're just..." She had to stop, then start again. "You'll be able to walk..."

"I just won't be able to dance. Is that it?"

"Bea, I'd give anything if it could've been me. *Anything.* We were waiting. We wanted to break it to you slowly."

"Did you think it would hurt less later on?"

"I don't know. Maybe."

"God! How long am I going to have to lie here, flat on my back like this?"

"I don't know that, either. Please don't get yourself so worked up."

"What's the rest of it?" she asked, closing her eyes.

"Your mother's in town, threatening to hold a press conference if she doesn't get to see you. Jerry's half crazy. He doesn't know what to do."

"Keep her *away* from me!" Bea said, her voice rising again. "Give her money. Pay her off. It's all she wants. I don't want her near me. Just pay her!"

218

"Oh, sweetheart," Lucy said miserably, "I don't know how to tell you how I feel about all of this."

With difficulty, Bea turned her head once more to look at her. "It's okay, Luce. I know you care."

Undone, Lucy began to cry again. It felt as if it was all she'd done for days on end.

"Go on home, Luce. You're worn out, and whatever they gave me is putting me to sleep. Don't worry. We'll figure out some way to muddle through."

Lucy bent to kiss her forehead, whispering, "I love you with all my heart. Nobody means more to me than you do."

"It hurts, Luce," she whispered.

"Oh, God!" Lucy was choking. "I'll get them to give you something."

"They already did. Please go home. And tell Jerry I don't care what it costs. Get rid of her. If I have to see her, I don't know what I'll do."

After Lucy had gone, drained, Bea shut her eyes, willing herself away from the pain. And gradually, the medication overcame her. She slept again.

Twenty-One

SHE did her best to put a good face on things. She couldn't help but see that, in some way, it was expected of her. The people who came to visit her at the hospital approached tentatively, nervously, expecting her to behave in a hysterical fashion. It amazed her to find herself in the position of having to console her friends, rather than the reverse. While there was, without question, a therapeutic aspect to her ongoing endeavor to ease others and reassure them of her basic stability, it nonetheless generated in her a slow-banking anger at their refusal to allow her to display her fear and anger and uncertainty. She exhausted herself playing out the role of courageous survivor for her friends, especially since every time she closed her eyes she was back in the Hollywood Hills and Dickie was once more punishing her for imaginary crimes against him.

All she felt, constantly, was fear. It came over her at the most unanticipated moments. When it did, her body turned alternatingly hot and cold, and she had to struggle to conceal the terror from whoever happened to be visiting. When she slept, the incident gained even more in depth and intensity. The blows fell upon her, her body was invaded, she was thrown from the car out into space, over and over, until sleep was anything but a refuge, and she found it, too, fearsome.

The only person who seemed to have some measure of understanding of her agony was Hank. He alone appeared not to expect to be entertained when he came to sit with her in her hospital room. He came, he held her hand, and, for long hours at a stretch, he allowed the air to expand around them while his empathy drew some of the ache from her body. He didn't need her to talk or to express false optimism for her future. He expected nothing at all. He held her hand, stroking it, studying it, transmitting through these gestures a caring for her so fundamental to his own nature, and so lacking in ulterior motives, that she could no more have refused it than she could have told any of the others to stay away.

By dint of her injuries, she was a captive audience to whatever her friends wished to say, or to display, and it was difficult for her to maintain control over her periodic outrage at their failure to see the selfishness of their tacit demands. There were moments when she felt as if she hated these well-intentioned people for their failure, and their refusal to allow her to vent her rage and sorrow at her misfortune. All that saved her from flying out of control was her daily growing dependence on Hank's mainly silent ministrations. He sensed her pain, and he was prepared to help her bear it.

As the weeks of her confinement passed, she became aware of a number of things. The most significant was her building attachment to Hank, to this man eighteen years her senior who freely admitted that he loved her but who could never be more than a deeply committed friend. The second, and almost equally significant, was her inescapable aversion to the very act Hank was incapable of performing. Each time Bobby came and made an attempt to kiss or touch her, she shriveled; terror swelled her veins so that the blood rushed through her system too quickly, leaving her giddy with misgivings and suspicion. She had no desire to be touched or kissed by Bobby, and she couldn't understand why he didn't recognize that. She thought if he'd been able to show, in any way at all, some small sense of her losses, she might have been able to get past the fear and display some portion of her ongoing love for him. Inside her, in what felt like a shallow bowl, her caring for him sat like evaporating liquid. She reminded herself daily, hourly, of how young he was and how ill-equipped to have any comprehension of the kind of torment that had been inflicted on her. But these reminders weren't enough to ease her dissatisfaction with him. Never once did he come to visit without attempting too show his love for her in physical terms. Not once, no matter how hard she tried to transmit it to him, did he see how horribly uncomfortable he made her. She suffered through his mercifully brief kisses, tried not to let her revulsion show when he claimed possession of her hand, or her arm, and caressed her. She wished, finally, he'd go away for a time and leave her to get on with the arduous task of coming to terms with her life as it was now.

After his first few visits, Jerry seemed to guess that she'd prefer to be alone, so he reported to her by telephone regularly and made it clear that if she had any need of him he'd come at once. He'd paid off Lil, against his better judgment, furious at having to dole out more than half Bea's savings to this woman. Nine thousand dollars, a restraining order, and the signing of documents waiving her rights, had sent a happy Lil and her seedy new husband off into their future. Jerry had no doubt they'd go through the money in no time flat and try coming back for more and so had arranged the added precaution of the restraining order. He'd tried, and failed, to make the woman see that she was robbing her own child, not only of her hard-earned capital, but also of her security at a crucial time in her life. Lil had been oblivious. It was the husband who drove the bargain, who pocketed the cashier's check, and who, with a contented grin, directed the dizzy blonde out of Jerry's office.

When Jerry tried, both in person and by telephone, to explain to Bea the precarious position she'd placed herself in by giving so much away, she refused to listen. Jerry was scared for her. Sure, Ludie was being a sport about paying her salary while she was incapacitated. But nobody seemed able to say when, or if, Bea would be fit to resume her career. And it was abundantly clear that her dancing days were over. Ludie wasn't going to go on paying her indefinitely. So what was she going to do? She had a few thousand in the bank, the house, and the car, and Hank. And it was Hank Jerry was banking on, because Hank had stated emphatically that he could, if Bea proved willing, take her career in an entirely new direction and would demonstrate that her talent went far beyond singing and dancing.

"Very strong words, those," Jerry had said, halfway convinced simply by Hank's forcefulness and sincerity.

"I have some ideas," Hank told him. "Just leave her be for now. It'll be months before she's even able to sit up. There's no rush."

"I'll take your word for it," Jerry said, and, like Bea, placed his faith in the tall, earnest man.

Hank's ideas had been shaping in his mind for a long time, and he knew he was taking a calculated risk, but he had no alternative but to suggest them, at last, to Bea.

The conversation took place toward the end of her third month in the hospital. Although her face had healed, and she looked once again like her old self, she was still trapped, flat on her back, by the cast that covered her from above her ribcage to the tops of her thighs. Her leg had healed well but was withered from being encased so long in plaster. And no physical therapy would be possible until her hips and back had mended.

"I'd like to take care of you," he told her, having completed the daily ritual of lighting a cigarette and giving it to her, then positioning the ashtray on the right side of the bed so she could tip off the ashes. "You might decide what I'm going to say constitutes some of the dumbest things you've ever heard," he smiled, holding her left hand, "but here goes." He paused, took a breath, then said what was on his mind. "You know how I feel about you, Bea. But in case I haven't made myself clear before now, I'll tell you again. I love you. I'd like to look after you, in any way I can. When you're up and about, I've got a project I think you could, and should, do, and I've already started my campaign to get Ludie to let us do it." Again, he smiled. "He's coming around to my way of thinking, but, like all the rest of us, he's waiting to see how you're going to come through this. He doesn't know you the way I do, doesn't know you're going to come through everything just fine. I'll get back to this in a minute. I want to get the important things said first, so you can tell me I'm crazy, and then we'll come back to the other stuff.

"I know how close you and Lucy are. And I also know you're aware of how things stand with Lucy and Ike. They've put things on hold, but they'd like to get married. *I'd* like to marry *you*. I'm sure that's not what you ever had in mind, but before you say no, let me say a few more things. Okay?"

"Yes, okay."

"If you and I were to get married, there'd be obvious advantages, as well as disadvantages. You already know the disadvantages, but

Part One / 1917–1936

I'd want you to understand right from the start that I know there'd come a time when you were bound to want to be with someone—Bobby, or someone else. It would be inevitable. It really would. No, please. Hear me out. Right now, you feel as if you never want to see another man as long as you live. But you're still very young, Bea, and someday you'll get past that feeling. When the time comes, I wouldn't stand in your way, because part of everything I'm saying has to do with Hero. So I'd never stand in the way of what you wanted. Do you follow?"

"I think so."

"As long as we're both discreet, there's no reason why we can't work the whole thing out. We can live together, and make pictures together, and maybe, at some future date, we can even adopt some kids and have a family. I *want* to take care of you. I know there are a lot of people who'd find the arrangement pretty questionable, but we could swing it. Okay. Now back to my starting point.

"I don't want to spend the rest of my professional life making musicals for Ludie. They're hot right now, but the public's going to get tired of them eventually. What they'll never get tired of is good, solid stories, well produced, well directed, and well acted. I'm willing to put my money on you; I'm willing to bet everything I've got that you can make the shift over to straight acting without missing a beat."

"Hank, I'm not a dramatic actress."

"You sure are. You just don't know it. Let me tell you something, Bea. One of the reasons the public's so crazy about you is precisely because you're one of the most dramatic goddamned actresses I can name. And you know what? You get more so every day."

"That makes me sound phony, as if I'm putting it on or something."

"That's not what I'm talking about, and you know it. Life's doing it for you, Bea. Reality's doing it. Right from day one, every time I look at the rushes, I get this shock at seeing what you put into lines that, if they came out of anybody else's mouth, they'd be garbage. You take risks like no one I've ever seen. ZaSu put a lot of that on the screen in *Greed*. But von Stroheim pulled it out of her pores. Nobody has to persuade you. You dig around inside yourself until you find some kind of central core, a heart, to the character, and then you deliver it. The boy you like in the script rebuffs you. The camera comes in for the close-up while the orchestra plays an intro, you open your mouth and start to sing, brave little soul, about your broken heart, and even the toughest mug up in the back row of some theater in Peru, Indiana, knows what he's seeing isn't just some actressy dame faking it for the camera. He's seeing *you*, the heart and soul of

223

you, bent to fit some idiot girl called 'Millie' who comes out with immortal lines like, 'Gee, Buzzy, I guess if you really can't make it tonight, I understand.'" He pitched his voice high and delivered the line with widened eyes and a trembling lower lip. She laughed, and he said, "See! A real howler. Who'd buy it? *You* deliver the line, and everybody's got tears in their eyes because, looking at you, they know it's from the heart. Nobody can fake that, Bea. All these movies later, you've got technique. You always hit your mark; you're always in your light; you're where you're supposed to be. But more than that, you've found a way to use your eyes, to tilt your head, to look into the camera, to use your voice, your hands, your body, every last part of you to make the audience believe stuff they wouldn't buy from anyone else on earth."

"I'm not that good," she scoffed.

"You're better than that even," he insisted. "*I'm* telling you, and I should know."

"It's only because you like me."

"I *love* you. And what I'm saying doesn't have a thing to do with my feelings for you. It's plain fact. There are plenty of movie stars who can hang on with pure technique. There are some with talent you can practically reach out and touch, it's so real. There are some you wouldn't buy on a bet, who have to stick to the glamorous roles, the safe parts. *You* could take chances from now until forever and the audiences would only love you more. And if you'll trust me, I'll prove it to you. If you'll trust me, instead of going to the Awards ceremonies to be seen, you'll be going to collect one."

"Henry, I'm *not* that good," she argued, forced to smile at his visions.

"I won't push it any more for now. As for the other, just think about it. Take your time. I'll look out for you, whatever you decide. If you're curious, I'll bring along a script next time I come and read you the part I wrote for you."

"You wrote a part for me?"

"I sure did. About two years ago. You can even check the date on it, if you don't believe me."

"I believe you. What's going to happen to *Moonlight?*"

"Nothing. It's going to be scrapped. We can't salvage it without the finale."

"And what d'you think they'll do about Bobby?"

"They're already scouting a new girl for him to partner."

"I see," she said. "That's fast."

"Yeah," he agreed. "It's fast. It's also the reality of life here, Bea.

224

Sentiment has its place, but only for a while. People care sure enough, but ultimately we've got to keep going. All of us."

"If we did do it," she said, thinking aloud, "where would we live? Could we keep Molly? And my house?"

"Wherever you want, whatever you want; whatever it takes to make you happy."

"Why would you do all that for me, Henry?"

"Because I want to. Because I love you. It's not a whole lot, I grant you, but it's everything I've got to give."

"Don't *talk* about yourself that way!" she said, hurt. "I *will* think about it. I'll think hard and long. Henry Donovan," she said, choked, "you're such a dear man. I couldn't have made it through this without you."

"I'll run along now," he said, releasing her hand. "You want another smoke before I go?"

"I think I need one."

He lit a cigarette, passed it to her, then said, "We'll talk again."

"Thank you, for everything."

After he'd gone, she lay back, thinking and smoking the cigarette. The only thing that had moved her as deeply as the conversation they'd just had were all the flowers, months before, that had come in from the dancers. As the arrangements had arrived, and Lucy had read aloud to her the cards from Eleanor, and Ruby, from Bill, and Fred, and a number of others, she'd felt less alone, less isolated by her losses. There were people who knew what had been taken from her life, and they'd sought to console her. She was still unable to imagine her life without dancing, without the perpetual rhythm that had been as constant an underscoring to her life as her own heartbeat. She could no longer dance, and the studio was arranging a new partner for Bobby.

The newspaper headline "Actress Injured in Crash" and the wire-service story had generated a tremendous public response. There'd been so many floral offerings she'd had to ask the nursing staff to leave her the cards and deliver the flowers, after she'd seen them, to the children's wards. There'd been hundreds of cards and letters, even stuffed toys and baskets of fruit; there'd been amazing gifts from all sorts of people—a silk bed jacket from a debutante in New York who'd broken her back in a spill from a horse and conveyed her sympathies, an entire carton of books from a New York publisher whose wife was a great fan of Bea's, a butter-soft cashmere blanket from the wife of an orthopedic surgeon in Seattle; chocolates, and perfume, and even a radio. There'd also been one very special letter,

225

culled by Lucy from the sacks of mail sent over weekly from the studio; a letter that had made her feel both very old and a little girl again. She kept it under her pillow and reread it periodically, trying to frame her reponse. She finished the cigarette, then reached under the pillow for the letter.

September 8, 1936

Dear Bea,

You probably won't even remember me, that is assuming this letter ever reaches you, but I read about your dreadful accident in the newspaper, and I had to write to tell you how heartbroken I am about what's happened. I keep remembering how wonderful you were at that talent contest, the way you danced, flashing like a little gem with the lights reflecting off you. I smile every time I think of it. I think I'll always remember you, the way you were that night, and how excited and proud I was to think that I knew you.

I'm just starting my second year at the University of Toronto. I'm studying English, with the idea in mind that someday I'll be a writer. Franny got married six months ago and is expecting a baby. Everyone's pushing me to find someone and settle down, but every time I look at Franny's burgeoning belly, all I can think is that I'd prefer to wait, thank you.

I hope somehow you get this letter. I'd like you to know that I think of you very often and that I believe with all my heart that nothing could ever keep you down. If there's ever anything at all I could do for you—I guess that's a pretty far-fetched idea, given your status—I want you to know I'd be happy to do it. I still miss you, and all my thoughts are with you.

Your old friend,
Becky Armstrong

It made her cry, as did thinking about Hank's proposal, as did her deeply rooted fear that she'd never again be able to live anything remotely resembling a normal life.

When Lucy came later that same day, Bea looked at her for so long and so hard that Lucy became fidgety and finally had to ask, "Is something the matter, Bea?"

"No. I was only trying to see you as if you were someone I was just meeting."

Laughing with relief, Lucy said, "What's it in aid of?"

"I think you should go ahead and marry Ike."

"Now, wait just a minute..."

"No, I mean it. I might be cooped up here for years. You can't waste your life answering my fan mail and looking after my house, and my bills, and my messes. A secretary could do that. Jean from the studio could do it. In fact, I'll probably ask her. Go ahead, Luce. Do it."

"And what about you? Who's going to look after you?"

"Hank's offered to. He'd like to marry me."

Lucy's eyes went wide with surprise. "*Hank*? But what about Bobby? You're not seriously considering that, are you?"

"I'm *very* seriously considering it."

"But, Bea, you love Bobby. You've loved him since you were fourteen years old. And he's wild about you. Why would you marry Hank, of all people?"

"I haven't said yet I'm going to. I said I'm thinking about it."

"But where does that leave Bobby?"

"I don't know where it leaves him, or me, for that matter. That's why I'm talking to you. Things have got to start happening. The whole world can't hang suspended while my bones mend. It's not fair to anyone. And first off, the person it's most unfair to is you. Please, go ahead and marry Ike."

"You're going to do it, aren't you?" Lucy's eyes narrowed, as if the truth was something so small she had to squint to see it.

"I don't know," Bea repeated. "But I want your word you won't delay any longer for my sake with Ike."

"You're not in charge of my decisions, you know!" Lucy declared, her confusion taking the form of anger. "I'll get married when *I* think the time is right."

"I know you're not really angry." Bea smiled at her winningly. "I know you're not."

"No," Lucy backed down. "I guess I'm not. It just throws me the way you've always played big sister to me when I'm the one who's older, who's supposed to know better. It's always 'Don't worry, Luce' or 'Just you wait and see, Luce,' and nine times out of ten you're right. Sometimes I wonder if you're not too smart for your own good."

"If I was really smart, I'd've sent Dickie packing when he showed up at the house that night. But I'd given my word that I'd go, so I went. I'm beginning to think giving my word might be kind of dangerous."

"You wouldn't know how to do it any other way."

"I probably wouldn't. Which is why maybe I need someone like

227

Hank to take care of me. No matter how I look at it, I can't see that Bobby would know how."

"No, he probably wouldn't. Not now, anyway."

"So, you see?" Bea said. "It's not such a strange notion. And the way I feel right now, I don't ever want to *think* about being touched by a man."

"You're not going to feel that way forever."

"I can't worry about how I'll feel in five years, Lucy. It's how I feel *now*. Bobby wants to marry me. I can guarantee you he'll ask me again when he comes tonight. *He doesn't understand*. He'd want to make love, and maybe the first few times he'd be sympathetic. But after a while, he'd get mad when I didn't want to, or couldn't, and he'd be bound to take it out on me. With Hank that problem would never exist. It just wouldn't."

"It's a mistake," Lucy said doggedly. "He's too old; he's not interested in women. The whole thing's wrong. And how do you know he wouldn't be using you as a blind, to protect himself?"

"You know Hank would never do a thing like that."

Exasperated, Lucy gave up and changed the subject. "What're we gonna do about Molly?"

"Why?"

"She's wondering if you're still going to need her when you get out of here."

"Tell her I'll definitely need her. Tell her that, okay? And tell her not to worry, I'll keep paying her salary. She needs the money, Luce, for her family."

"Why do I have the feeling I'm being browbeaten here?" Lucy asked rhetorically. "Probably because I am. What else? I've got the distinct impression there's more."

"Just one small thing." Bea got out Becky's letter. "I want to answer this letter."

"Fine." Lucy held out her hand. "I'll take care of it."

"No. If you could get a pen and some paper, I'd like to dictate an answer for you to write. Okay?"

"I guess so. What am I missing?"

"You know something, Luce? Aside from you, I don't have any female friends. That's scary, but it's the truth. One of the things that happens when you have a name and a face people recognize is that you become suspicious of other people. You can't open up and be friendly, because you're not ordinary anymore. You've become something else, and there are tons of people who'd like to get close to you, not for yourself, but because you're somebody, and maybe they'll get some of the glory for themselves if they can get next to you. I can't help wondering how many friends I may have lost along the way because it's no longer safe to trust what seem to be the good intentions of others. It's just plain luck I got Becky's letter. It could've been lost for months, like that last letter from good old Lil."

"You can't have it both ways," Lucy said sensibly. "Maybe friends are part of what you give up."

"I don't want to believe that. This letter made such a difference, Lucy. Becky's still my friend, and I want to keep that."

"You're scared," Lucy saw. "It's understandable."

"I'm scared because you're right: I can't have it both ways. I can't make movies and have chums the way ordinary people do. But that's what I want. There are some awfully nice people around this town, and they've made a point of inviting me to their homes, to their parties, and sometimes I've gone along and had a swell time. But I look at their lives, at their families, their cars and houses and swimming pools, and I wonder if any of it's real or if it's only another set on another sound stage. I can't tell real from not real anymore, except for a handful of people, including you and Hank. And I'm only able to tell about all of you because you've been there from the beginning. So that's why, I guess, I'm going to marry Hank as soon as I can stand up without help. Because he's real, and I know he is, and if I know he's real, then I must be, too."

"God," Lucy said. "I hope it makes you happy. You're going to break Bobby's heart."

"He broke mine when he wouldn't fight for me, or for the baby."

"Who ever thought it'd turn out this way? I sure didn't."

"I can never go back to being ordinary, Lucy. For years, there'd always be somebody who recognized me. So if I can't go back, then I'll do what Hank wants and try to switch over to straight acting. If I fail at it, then I'll stay home and look after Hank's house, or mine, or whatever. But I'm not going to fail, because he believes in me, and he doesn't frighten me, and I know I can live with him. So be happy for me, Lucy. And go ahead and marry Ike."

Initially, Bobby took the news as a joke. Then, when he saw she wasn't kidding, he tried to talk her out of it.

"The man's a fruit, for chrissake!" he raged. "You're out of your mind! You *know* you love me! Why the hell are you *doing* this?"

"Don't *ever* speak of him that way, Bobby! Without him, you'd still be in the chorus back on Broadway. He's the one who agreed to hire you sight unseen, and then got Ludie to sign you; he's the one who's brought you along every inch of the way. It's been Hank who's advised you to save your money, to make good investments. Someday you'll be a very wealthy man and you'll owe every last bit of it to Hank. Don't you ever say *one word* against him!"

"*You're* the one who did it all, not him! Why're you giving *him* all the credit?"

"Because I could only recommend you, Bobby. He's the one who made good on it."

"Okay, okay. But you love me. I know you do. Why're you splitting us up? Is it because of the baby? Is that it? Because I didn't fight Ludie? You *do* blame me for that. I *knew* you did!"

"That's only a very very small part of it. The big part is the way you keep avoiding what happened to me. Maybe it's because it upsets you to think about it, so you push it out of your mind. Why is it I have to get graphic with you every goddamned time before something gets through to you? He *raped* me, Bobby! He raped *every part* of me! He ripped me apart; he made me *bleed*. He did things that were unspeakable! Just the *thought* of making love makes me sick. I can't bear to touch you, Bobby. I can't bear to have you keep coming here, touching me. Now, do you get it? I don't want *anyone* to *touch* me!"

It finished him. He sat staring at her for one minute, then another, as images detonated in his brain. He tried to speak, couldn't and stared at her some more. He looked at the tears on her face, and words galloped through his brain, but none of them seemed to form into a grouping that would persuade her to change her mind or feelings. He couldn't find any way to wipe out what had been done to her.

Seeing him struggling, she took pity on him and offered him an out. "You're right about one thing," she said quietly, wiping her face with the back of her hand. "I do love you. I told you I always would, and that still holds. But I couldn't live with you. I'd make both of us miserable. You deserve better than that."

"I thought we'd get married," he said, near to tears. "I had all these plans..."

"You'll find someone else."

"No! See, that's where you're wrong. If I can't marry you, I won't marry *anyone*." He couldn't say more. He'd used every last one of his arguments, and still he'd failed. Lowering his eyes, he got up and left.

She watched him go with the sense that she'd just severed herself from the one person capable both of making her dreams come true, and of destroying them. She *did* love him; she *would* love him always. But he had it in his power, because she loved him, to hurt her more deeply, more long-lastingly than anyone else ever could. "I'm sorry," she whispered to the air where he'd been. "I'm really sorry."

Part Two

1938-1946

"I started out as a prop man, back in San Francisco. It's really a very good point to begin. The prop man's a kind of general factotum for the director, handling everything from the set dressing to getting coffee for the director, and playing unofficial host to visitors to the set. It was damned good training, and a lot of fellows have gone forward into other areas after putting in their time on props. John Wayne, you know, started out in the prop department. So did Henry Hathaway, and Henry's a fine director, very fine. *Lives of a Bengal Lancer* is a particular favorite of mine. . . . My own favorite? That's a tough one, but I'd have to say *Jeannie*. There are a lot of reasons why. First, because I'd been wanting for a long time to do a non-musical, to break out of that and into straight features. And second, because I knew Bea had a very special quality that would make it more than just another 'women's weepie.' There were holes in the script—I wrote that picture—that she instinctively filled. She's always been a very intuitive actress, and no one else could've done what she did with that part. I also think it had a lot to do with how much we all cared about the project—me, because I was putting myself on the line for something I believed in; and Bea, because she'd never before done anything remotely like it. Neither had Ike, and it was the beginning of a new era for him, as well. Everything came together just beautifully. Other pictures I've done, I'll look at them and see shots that could've been more carefully framed or editing that could've been tighter here and there. But *Jeannie* still holds up; it has it all."

Henry Donovan Interview
American Cinematographer, October 1947

Twenty-Two

"I T'S just that I want you to know things aren't going to change," Bea said, trying to gauge Hero's reactions to what she was saying. It was hard. Outwardly, he seemed as unruffled as ever. Physically, facially, he'd so far revealed only an interest in hearing what she had to say. "I've known since the beginning," she went on, "how important the two of you are to each other. If I thought I was going to interfere with that, well, I'd stop everything now." What was he thinking? she wondered, this man with his impeccable clothes, his aura of tranquility.

Hero saw what difficulty she was having expressing herself, but for the moment couldn't help her. He thought perhaps he should be angry, or afraid, or resentful, yet none of these emotions was present. When he looked at her, all he could think of was what had been taken away from her and what a tragic loss that was, not only for her, but for everyone. His sadness interfered with the other, perhaps self-preserving, emotions he might have entertained.

"Do you hate me?" she asked at last, looking full at him.

The question shook him. He moved, finally, bringing his eyes to hers, and he answered softly, "Why would I hate you? What could you possibly do that would make me hate you?"

"I don't know," she answered. "I keep thinking I'm going to interfere . . . I'll destroy something that's very important to the two of you. I need to know that you accept me . . . just as I accept you."

"What a strange little girl you are," he said, lighting a match for her cigarette. "All the things you care about, the things that worry you." He shook his head, then blew out the match. "If you were anyone else, probably I would resent you, maybe even hate you. But

235

you are who you are, and I believe you, Bea. And aside from that, Hank adores you. I've always loathed unpleasantness of any kind. This doesn't strike me as a situation that warrants it."

"It doesn't?" She looked surprised.

"Did you really think I'd come here and make a scene?" he asked her. "Did you think," he asked, eyebrows lifted, "I'd play the other woman?"

She laughed, then apologized.

"Don't apologize," he said. "It's an entirely reasonable hypothesis."

"I know." She took a puff on her cigarette, then said, "The day we met, you held my hands as we listened to the music, and you felt like someone I'd known forever. I don't want that to change. I want you to come over, and Hank to go see you just the way it's always been. The only difference will be that Hank's moving house. That's all. That's really all."

"What about Bobby?" he asked, crossing his legs, then smoothing the crease in his trousers. "How many people are getting married here, Bea?"

She puffed again on the cigarette, then put it out before replying, taking the time to frame her answer. "I love Bobby," she said, almost in a whisper. "Part of why I do is because I know how much he loves me. I don't know if that makes very much sense, but it's how I feel. He's stupid sometimes, and he likes to play tough guy to cover up the way he really is. He does that because he's afraid that if he shows people what a softie he is they'll take advantage of him. Maybe that happened a lot when he was a kid, so he started covering up. I don't know. He doesn't talk much about his childhood or his family. He's inside of me, Hero." She turned to look at him, a beseeching light in her eyes. "He's part of me, the way my hands are, or my eyesight. And I know that it's the same way for him. We're always hurting each other, because only people who really love each other can feel the pain. With other people, it's just a kind of game. You pretend you're angry, or upset, because you heard somewhere or read that you're supposed to feel that way. But with Bobby it's real. And I think that's the way it is with you and Hank. And it's why you have to know that I do understand."

"You haven't answered the question," he said gently.

"I can't. I don't know the answer. I love Hank very much."

"But it's different."

"It's different," she allowed, "but it's just as real, in another way. Will it be all right?"

"Oh," Hero smiled and patted her arm, "I think so."

236

Bea wanted to slip out of town and get married without any fuss. Hank tended to agree. But Ludie got word of their intentions and phoned up to say, "You can't do that. You want to get married, fine. But give the press a break. You run off, you elope, you'll offend the press and you don't want that. It's too big a story."

Hank repeated all this to Bea. "We're going to have to give a press conference," he wound down. "We just can't get out of it."

"Could we give it *after?* Could we go get married quietly somewhere, come back, and then give the press conference?"

"I don't see why not."

"Then, let's, please, do it that way."

Hank made the arrangements, and on the morning of February 2, 1938, with Lucy and Hero along as witnesses, they drove to Somerton, Arizona, got their license, and were married at the home of an Episcopalian minister. The four of them then piled back into the car and made the long drive back to Los Angeles.

Early the next morning, a group of studio police came to stand guard outside the Beverly Hills house, while Molly set up a breakfast buffet in the living room. By nine-thirty, the first of the reporters arrived. Within an hour, the living room was packed with press and photographers, and the official conference began. Hank and Bea posed for pictures, fielded questions, then invited everyone to help themselves from the buffet. The food vanished off the plates; gallons of coffee, and champagne, and orange juice were consumed. At last, Hank explained, "Bea's a little tired, folks. You understand," and got the place cleared out in fifteen minutes.

Bea *was* tired. It was painful for her to remain standing for any length of time. After fifteen or twenty minutes, her hips began to ache, sending tremors radiating down both legs. Every morning when she awakened, she threw back the bedclothes and attempted to swing her legs over the side of the bed only to discover anew she could no longer move with anything even resembling the mobility she'd taken for granted fourteen months before. But at least she could walk, she reminded herself as she sat on the side of the bed before rising. And one day, she'd be able to dance again. It was a vow she'd made during the months of physical therapy when she'd learned how to balance her weight when upright, as the muscle tone had returned to her left leg.

She sat in one of the armchairs in the living room and smoked a cigarette while Hank escorted the last of the reporters to the door, and Molly began clearing the buffet. He closed the door and came back running a finger inside his tight shirt collar and, smiling, dropped into the chair opposite.

Once she'd agreed to his proposal, they'd thrashed out the details of how they'd live. Hank had insisted, not only on selling his place, but on using the sale money to pay off the mortgage on her house. "That way, we're starting off equal," he'd told her. They'd shopped together for a number of new pieces of furniture, fitting them in among the items she'd already had and those he'd brought along. Both of them were entirely satisfied with the arrangements.

"Well, that's over," he said now, "thank God."

"Now we can read about overselves for weeks to come."

"You won't have too much time to sit around reading," he said. "I've got a meeting with Ludie this afternoon, to set up a shooting date. You'll be back in the saddle again," he laughed. "Wardrobe fittings, the whole works."

"I hope you know what you're doing," she said doubtfully.

"Of course, I do." He folded one long leg over the other. "Having second thoughts?"

"Third, fourth, and fifth. Maybe the public won't buy me in this part."

"They'll buy you if *you* buy you. We've had this discussion several dozen times, Bea, and we both know you're the only one who could do *Jeannie* justice."

"I do love the script," she admitted. It was the truth. She saw the role as being perfectly suited to her, as being a part only someone who knew her as well as Hank did could've written. The story line was a little shaky, but the relationship between a young shopgirl and her illegitimate daughter had a lot of impact. "It's just a pity," she said, not for the first time, "that the Hays Office would insist Jeannie has to be punished. If it was up to me, I'd let the girl live happily ever after."

"You can't have a child out of wedlock and live happily ever after. You were naughty, and you have to acknowledge it, otherwise you're in defiance of the Production Code. And I quote, 'Impure love must not be presented as attractive and beautiful.' And Jeannie getting herself pregnant by a man she isn't married to falls into that category. We show the affair as better than attractive; it's a love match, and the guy gets killed in a freak accident; she winds up left alone, pregnant, scared. So she leaves town, sets herself up as a widow, starts her little dress shop, has the kid, and is actually happy. Wrong. There's got to be a conflict. So we supply one. To save the day, she marries a jerk, struggles to make the marriage go—all for the sake of her daughter. The jerk makes off with her money, so that puts Jeannie back in the right; she'll get a divorce eventually, and everybody winds up cheering for her. It's great stuff."

"I just wish it was a little less . . . I don't know . . . melodramatic, I guess."

"It won't be, not the way I intend to do it. I'm going to change clothes and drive over to the studio." He stood up, removing his bow tie. "You look worn out. How d'you feel?"

"I don't know." She looked at the platinum and diamond wedding and engagement rings on her left hand, then smiled up at him. "It's going to take some getting used to."

"Not sorry, are you?"

"Not one bit. It'll be so good to get back to work. Molly'll be glad, too. She's sick to death of having me around. You don't think there'll be any problems, do you?"

"I can't think of any. I'll call you as soon as I come out of the meeting."

"**G**reg Robinson's set to produce," Ludie announced.

"Greg?" Hank couldn't hide his shock. "But he's a director." And not a very good one, he silently added.

"He's moved over to producing. He's read the script; he likes it. He's waiting outside to talk. You got any problems?"

"I won't know whether or not I do until I've heard what Robinson has to say." He wished he could ask Ludie straight out why it was that every so often he liked to throw Greg in his face, as if Greg was an ongoing barometer Ludie used to measure Hank's mettle.

"So, we'll get him in here." Ludie got on the intercom and told his secretary to send Greg in.

Hank held his breath. This wasn't good.

"**W**hat's wrong?" Bea wanted to know. "I can tell there's something. I can hear it in your voice. I can see it all over you."

"Ludie's putting Greg Robinson in as producer."

"As *producer?*"

"Maybe it won't be so bad. He's happy with the script, and he agrees with my choice of Robert Taylor for Jeannie's lover."

"What's the bad news, Henry?"

"He wants you to test for Jeannie."

She didn't speak for a moment, battling her instinct to take offense. She was in no position to be offended, or even to refuse. "All right," she said. "I'll test. You were dreading telling me, weren't you? I know you. You thought I'd have a fit."

"You have every right to," he said angrily. "It's a hell of an insult, asking you to test."

"It doesn't matter. Honestly. Set it up and I'll do it."

"It's nothing more than a formality, Bea. You've got the part. I'm the damned director, and the casting's up to me."

"I want to make the picture. I *need* to do it. If I have to sit around this house much longer, reading, and playing gin rummy with Molly, and listening to the radio, I'll lose my mind. I dream I'm dancing," she said, looking toward the windows and the garden beyond, where the heat held everything immobilized. "Almost every night, I close my eyes and Bobby and I are doing 'Starlight' or 'Without You' or a routine from one of the other pictures. I want to stop thinking about it, dreaming about it. The only way I can do that is by getting to work again." She turned back to him. "Do you dream, Hank?"

"Yeah," he said dispiritedly. "I was dreaming when I thought Ludie would let me make this picture the way I want to. I can't figure out why he's sticking me with Robinson. It's as if Ludie sets up tests that make sense only to him. Nobody knows the rules, except him. And you don't find out who won and who lost until you're at the point where you hardly give a damn anymore, because you're so fed up with having to take the imbecilic test at all."

"Does Robinson know how to produce?"

"It doesn't take a great genius to keep track of the pennies, to make sure we bring it in on time and don't run over the budget. But he could make life very unpleasant for everyone if he decides to throw his weight around. The producer's credit goes above the director's, remember. It's the only reason I can think of why Greg would be interested. That, and the fact that he's had a few flops of epic proportions in the past couple of years. Who knows? Maybe it's Ludie's way of trying to ease him out. Let him flop again as a producer, and then Ludie can legitimately give him his walking papers. But why do it to *my* picture? That's what I'd like to know."

"Go ahead and make the arrangements for the test," she told him. "I promise you I don't mind."

It was a lie. She minded so much that, for nights on end before the test, her sleep became a battleground where she raged against Ludie Meyers for subjecting her to such humiliation. Arguments splattered like raw eggs against the backdrops of her dreams, flung back and forth by herself, by Ludie, by Hank, by Gregory Robinson. She was fighting, it seemed, not just for her right to work but for her very life, and she woke up each morning with her jaws aching from having spent the night hours grinding her teeth together in furious frustration. She'd go through with it, for her own sake as well as Hank's; she'd put a good face on it. But she would only be able to view Ludie, from this point on, as a benevolent tyrant.

Everyone at the studio greeted her with effusive warmth. Ivy was there to do her make-up and gave Bea a hug, saying, "We've missed you around here. You look wonderful."

"It's good to be back," Bea said, sliding into the make-up chair.

Pete appeared as Ivy was powdering Bea's face and came to stand behind the chair, grinning at her in the mirror.

"So how does it feel?" he asked. "All set to go to work?"

"I'm as ready as I'm ever going to be. Are you assigned to the picture?"

"I'm assigned to you. There'll be a whole raft of stories about your return to work, how you're tackling a tough dramatic role. You know the drill. From soup to nuts, including x-rays, for which you've got a sitting scheduled next week with Hurrell. How d'you feel about working with Taylor? Nah," he laughed. "Don't answer that. Just getting you primed. Mind if I come watch the test?"

"I don't mind," she said, maneuvering herself out of the chair. "How's your wife, and the kids?"

"Aces," he answered, walking with her toward the sound stage. "We're having another."

"Congratulations! That's great!"

"We keep on the way we're going, we'll have our own baseball team soon."

He slipped away as Hank came over to have a word with her.

"Taylor's being a real sport about this," Hank said in an undertone. "How d'you feel?"

"Nervous as hell."

"Don't think about it. Just do the scene. We'll screen it tonight and then we can stop horsing around and get to work."

Taylor was so handsome, all Bea could think of was how badly she was bound to come over next to him. They rehearsed the lines while the lights were set, and for the first time she was fearful of going before the camera. Everything was riding on this picture. What if, for some reason, they decided she was wrong, or not pretty enough? She was working herself up to a case of nervous paralysis when Lucy arrived. At the sight of her, Bea's confidence returned. Lucy waved, went to have a word with Ike who was shooting the test, then sat down beside Hank as he called for quiet.

241

A two-minute scene, and by the time it was finished, Bea was wet with perspiration. Her fingertips were buzzing, her throat was parched, her spine felt exposed, and she was convinced she was going to be violently sick. Hank conferred with Ike, and then told Bea they wanted to do it again.

"I'm sorry," she apologized to Taylor.

"Perfectly all right," he said, and offered his face to Ivy to be powdered down, while the hairdresser came to tuck stray strands of Bea's hair back into place.

They did it again, and then it was over. The lights shut down, and Hank discreetly assisted her off the set, saying, "Lucy came to take you to lunch. Go out and forget about this. I'm going to be home late tonight."

"I'll wait up."

They stared at each other for a moment, then Hank gave her hand a squeeze, kissed her on the mouth, and said, "Put it out of your mind, dear heart."

Over lunch at the Colonial Drive-In, Lucy asked, "Are you okay? You're awfully quiet. And you're not eating."

"How did it look to you, Luce?"

"Good. It looked good."

"Are you just saying that to make me feel better?"

"Why would I do that? You're set for the part, and Taylor's terrific."

"I look like something from the zoo next to that man. And with Greg Robinson producing...I don't know. Hank's very worried, I can tell."

"Don't anticipate," Lucy cautioned.

"I can't *help* it. My career's riding on this picture. I honestly thought I was going to hurl on the set. I've never been so scared in my life. And it's bound to show in the test. God! Have you heard anything about Bobby?"

"Only that he went on a three-day toot after you and Hank got married."

"He's all right, though, isn't he?"

"So far as I know. They're fixing him up with yet another partner. The last picture wasn't so hot, didn't do too well at the box office. But Ludie's still high on him."

"Poor Bobby."

"My foot!" Lucy snapped. "Don't waste your sympathy on him. He's gonna make out just fine. The women still line up at the box office for days to see him. Worry about yourself, if you're gonna stew about anyone. Not," she added, "that I think you've got a thing to worry about."

"You're so wrong. I've got plenty to worry about."

"Everything's okay with you and Hank, isn't it?"

"Hank is perfect. He's kind, and generous, and unbelievably thoughtful. And he doesn't snore."

"The two of you are sleeping together?" Surprise lit Lucy's eyes.

"We share a bed. What did you think we did?"

"I don't know. I guess I assumed you had separate rooms."

"I have nightmares," Bea lowered her voice. "He stays with me." She doubted she could have made it through a night without him there to comfort her, to hold her until her fear subsided and she was able to sleep again.

"Oh!" Lucy sat back, thinking.

"I feel safe with him," Bea elaborated.

"I guess that makes sense."

"It makes very good sense. He's there when I need someone to hold on to." Bea studied Lucy, almost able to read her thoughts. "You're wondering how I can do it, aren't you? Well, I'll tell you something. It's good to know that he's not going to try to comfort me in the one way that would upset me the most. He's warm, and he's there. We lie in the dark together, sometimes for hours, and talk. And when I hurt, he massages my back and legs."

"But doesn't it bother you? I mean . . ."

"It doesn't bother either one of us, Luce. When you're comfortable with someone, you stop fretting, you stop feeling self-conscious. You just enjoy each other's company."

"Maybe that's the ideal," Lucy thought aloud.

"Aren't things going well for you and Ike?"

"Six months of marriage is hardly time enough to decide."

"What does that mean?"

"It means we're both pretty set in our ways, and that it's hard learning how to live with somebody else's habits. But we're working on it."

"Aren't you happy, Luce?" Bea's concern was immediate.

"I'm not unhappy. I guess it's just not the way either one of us thought it'd be. I miss seeing you every day. And maybe I'm spoiled, but I'm used to having my own money. Every time I have to remind Ike I need housekeeping money or a new pair of shoes, I feel guilty and embarrassed. Don't you feel that way with Hank?"

"No. But then I haven't had to ask Hank for anything."

"You're lucky."

"I think so."

It was Lucy's turn to stare appraisingly. "It's really good for you, isn't it?"

"I love him very much, Lucy. And I know he loves me. It's not the same as what I still feel for Bobby. But in an awful lot of ways, it's better."

"What about Hero?"

"Hero will always be welcome in our home. I don't have the right to tell Hank who he should and shouldn't care for. The two of them have a lot of history, just like you and I do. Hank would never dream of interfering in my friendship with you. So why should I tell him who he can see? If you need money, Luce . . ."

"I'm okay," Lucy cut her off. "I've still got some savings. Don't even *think* about offering me money. I owe you enough as it is. And you need what you've got. Every time I think about that woman fleecing you that way . . ."

"She doesn't matter. You know I'll help you. I honestly don't mind."

"You don't. But *I* do. It was one thing when I was actually doing a job for you. But now that I'm not . . . It's too much liking scroung-ing. I know you mean well, and I appreciate it, but I've got to live with myself."

"I'm still getting a fair amount of fan mail. Nowhere near as much as before. But if you want to, you can take it back over. Once Pete starts feeding out press releases, and the interviews begin for *Jeannie,* I'm going to need help."

"We'll see," Lucy said.

"You sound just like a mother," Bea laughed.

"I might as well act like one, then. Will you please *eat?* You're way too thin. If you're going to be working from six in the morning till all hours, you're going to need to build up your strength."

The lights went on in the screening room. Greg lit a large cigar, puffed at it to make sure it was going, then said, "Okay. Here's how I see it. She needs all kinds of work. That nose is terrible. Maybe in musicals she could get away with it, but in a picture like this, with all kinds of tight close-ups and side by side with Taylor, she looks lousy. She needs her nose done, and her teeth fixed, maybe some molars pulled to give her cheekbones a better look. Then there's that scene she's supposed to do in a slip. She's flat as a goddamned board. Something should be done about her tits."

Ludie rested his chin on his hands, listening.

This was a test, all right, Hank thought. Ludie was going to put his marriage to Bea through the wringer to see what kind of stuff both of them were made of. Seething, Hank looked over at Ike.

"I don't know about that," Ike offered. "Like I've always said, she's got great eyes and a good mouth. Her jawline's strong, her chin's balanced. We could light her..."

"You can't get away from the fact that she's got a big, goddamned nose. And I don't care where you put her key light, and how much highlighter you use to try to make it look smaller, when she turns profile to the camera, it's goddamned ridiculous!"

"She looks real," Hank said evenly, keeping his temper down. "She looks right for the part. The role doesn't call for glamour. And it's always possible, you know, that the public wouldn't like her with a new nose, and big breasts, and all the rest of it. Ludie! For God's sake, what're we talking about here? Bea's got a proven track record. Women love her. She comes across. She's perfect for the part. I *wrote* it for her."

"Maybe," Ludie said, "Greg has a point."

"What? What point does Greg maybe have?"

"About the nose, for one thing. And she doesn't have much in the way of sex appeal."

"You're crazy!" Hank exploded at Greg. "This is *my* picture, *my* project."

"And your wife," Greg put in coolly.

"Bea's being my wife has nothing to do with it! She's one hell of an actress, and that's the only thing that counts here. The *only* thing!"

"She needs her nose fixed, her teeth fixed, her hairline fixed. She needs *fixing!*"

"And what if I say to hell with *you?*" Hank challenged. "What if I say I'll find independent financing and produce and direct the picture myself? What then?" he demanded of Ludie.

"You still need distribution. You want to go independent, that's fine by me. But you want this studio to distribute your picture, you're going to have to do something about the way she looks."

"Let me get this straight," Hank said, so angry he could feel his pulse beating in his hands. "If I put up my own money, say, you're still going to hold me up on the distribution unless Bea gets work done on her face? After all she's been through, you'd force her to go through more, just because this, this... because *he* says so?"

"It's not such a big deal," Ludie said. "Maybe you should talk with Bea, find out if she's willing."

"I wouldn't *ask* her!" Hank insisted.

"Maybe you should," Ludie told him, meeting his eyes. "You're telling me you can make her into something different. Maybe you can. Who knows? I'm saying we'll find out at the box office, and by then it's maybe too late, and one of us is out a few hundred thousand. You want to do your own financing, it's okay by me. I've got other places to put the money. We'll do a deal on the distribution. But *only* if I see a face I could wake up to in the morning."

So here it was: Ludie was going to see how far both he and Bea were willing to go for a chance to begin again in a new direction. Ludie was going to push them both into corners to see if they'd knuckle under or if they'd come out fighting. "You didn't mind waking up to the sight of the receipts her pictures brought in for the last four years!"

"Don't get so mad," Ludie said mildly, confirming Hank's suspicions.

"This is *my* picture!" Hank cried. "First you bring in this clown who can't even direct to save his life, and then you listen to him when he tells you to change every single thing about the girl the public's crazy for. Why would you *believe* him?"

"Who the hell're you calling a clown?" Robinson yelled. "And what've *you* done lately? You're still trying to peddle that bum Bradley to the public, and he's not worth spit without Crane. She's not worth a plug nickel without him. But never mind that. You've got visions of sugar plums and you think you'll take that dame and shove her down eighty, ninety million throats as someone a guy would *die* for? You're out of your goddamned head!"

Hank choose to ignore him and directed himself to Ludie. "What if I offer a co-production deal? What if I agree to go half and half with you on the financing? What then?"

"I don't know," he said doubtfully.

Having found the wedge he knew he could drive into Ludie, Hank charged ahead. "I can't *work* with that man!" Hank argued. "Why don't *you* produce, or co-produce the picture with me, Ludie? Think of the credit you'll get for producing the picture that puts Bea back in the spotlight in a very big way!"

"Hmmn, maybe. It's possible."

"You'll wind up a laughing-stock," Greg predicted.

He'd gone too far. Ludie sat forward in his seat and pointed a stubby finger at Greg. "You, you shmuck, you beg me for a chance to produce, and now you talk laughing-stock to me? You got some balls, for a guy half in, half out the door."

"Now, hold on a minute..." Greg backed down rapidly, groping for safe territory.

"To hell with your minute! Get off my lot! Get your crap and get off my lot!"

"But we had a deal..."

"So now we don't have a deal. For years I'm carrying you, and you make break-even money. Enough is enough."

There was a silence as Greg looked at Ludie, mutely appealing to him for an oportunity to redeem himself. When the silence held, Greg dropped his cigar in the ashtray, stood up, and said, "You'll have to settle with me. I've got a contract."

"Go home and read it," Ludie said tiredly. "I got clauses. You got dreck. You can't push me."

After Greg had gone, Hank lit a cigarette and asked, "Where does that leave us, Ludie? The last time we went around and around with Robinson, I wound up directing Bea's first picture. You've had no reason to regret giving me that chance. Can we get together on this?"

Ludie sat back again and laced his fingers together over his belly. "You could be throwing your money away on this deal. You know that?"

"I know it, but it's a gamble I'm willing to take."

Ludie made a face of concession. "You're willing, I'm willing. I like the idea of producing her comeback picture. But I still think she needs some fixing."

"What are we talking about here?" Hank wanted to know.

"We'll compromise. She gets the nose done, gets a little something in the way of a bosom, we'll forget about the teeth, the hair, and the rest of it."

"You know I can't agree to any of that without Bea's say-so."

"So you'll talk. She's a sensible girl. She'll see what's right."

"And you're telling me that's the only way you'll go ahead with the project?"

"You want me to produce, put my name right there on the credits, I want a product with a face I can smile at. You'll talk with her, and you'll let me know."

Hank sighed. He'd passed his part of the test. Now it was going to be Bea's turn. Ludie was going to have contracts signed in blood.

Bea sat in bed, with three pillows supporting her spine, and listened in silence until Hank was done.

"How much of your own money would you have to put in?" she asked.

"I've got the picture budgeted at four hundred and fifty thousand. If I go back over it again, I can probably bring it down to four hundred. But that'd mean twenty-one days shooting and not one minute over. It'd mean we'd have to cut corners everywhere, and work like sons of bitches to bring it in on time."

"And your share would be two hundred thousand dollars? Have you got that kind of money?"

"It'd be every last cent I've got in the world."

"It's such a lot to risk."

"It's not a *risk*. I believe in the picture, and in you. I *know* we'll make it back."

"So that's your share of the risk. And mine is to have more surgery. Henry, I have to think."

"I'll go down and make some coffee." He rose halfway off the bed, then sat down again and took hold of her hand. "Look at me," he said, with his hand on her chin, turning her head. "Nobody really has the right to ask you to do something like this. If you decide you can't, or won't, do this, I'll be one hundred percent with you. We'll shop the script, find another studio who won't ask for impossible commitments from us. You have to believe I love you exactly the way you are. He's asking one hell of a lot, and I don't approve, Bea. But *I* don't have the right to make your decisions. I also don't have the right to hold any of what went on back from you. At the very least, you deserve to know what the stakes are. Now, I'll go make the coffee."

He left, and she remained where she was for several minutes before making her way into the bathroom. The door locked, she got out of her nightgown and stood naked in front of the mirror, slowly turning this way, then that. Facing forward again, she reached for the magnifying mirror and held it close to her face. After a time, she put down the mirror and started the tub filling. While the water gushed into the tub, she stared down at it, wondering if she had sufficient courage left to deal with more surgery, more doctors, another stay in the hospital. The very thought of a hospital made bile rise into her throat. She closed her eyes and saw Dickie; he forced her down on her hands and knees, and then . . . Her eyes flew open and she held her hands over her breasts, pushing away the horror. Yet she couldn't rid herself of it entirely, because everything that was happening now was Dickie's doing. If she consented to the surgery, how much more would be asked of her after that? Was this the way it was going to be for the rest of her life, with endless demands to be satisfied only in payments of her flesh?

She bent to turn off the faucets, then unlocked and opened the door before struggling to get herself into the tub. Settled, finally, with the heat gnawing away at the pain like some invisible animal that fed only on ravaged nerve endings, she told herself she'd known from the start that she and Hank would have to pay dearly for the privilege of stepping outside the boundaries of what Ludie found it acceptable for them to do. Oh, he might have given Hank the go-ahead on the picture if Hank hadn't insisted on her playing the starring part. But

Hank had not only married her, he'd defied Ludie. And no one defied Ludie without suffering the penalties only he could impose.

"You talk about people's rights," she told Hank when he came in and placed her coffee on the side of the tub. "You talk about *my* rights, but you don't say a word about yours, Henry. And I don't have the right to hold you back, to stop you doing something that means as much to you as this picture does."

"That's not true," he disagreed.

"It sure is! Christ! This is a *marriage*, Henry! I can't expect you to go on and on making concessions for me while I sit back and accept them as my due. I don't want to do it. The idea of it frankly terrifies me, but I don't have a choice. Not really. I just want one thing. I'll have the surgery, but I will not stay in a hospital, not for one night. As long as I can come home here after it's done, I'll do it. I'll recuperate here, but I won't spend one extra hour in a hospital."

"This doesn't seem right," he told her. "Maybe we should tell Ludie to got to hell."

"We can't afford to do that. People around here have fancy operations every day of the week. If they can do it, so can I. As long as I can come straight home."

"I want to be sure, Bea. I feel rotten about it."

"*I* feel rotten that Ludie made you crawl. So that makes us even. I've made up my mind, and I won't go back on my word."

Three days later, she went in for the surgery. It had been arranged that both procedures would be done at the same time, by two different doctors, one who specialized in the face, one who had a decent reputation for the more arcane forms of cosmetic surgery like breast enlargements, hip reductions, and tightening sagging bellies.

Coming out of the anaesthetic, Bea vomited blood into an enamel basin, the stitches under her breasts protesting the violence of her retching as blood gushed from her mouth. Falling back finally, nauseated and exhausted and still under the lingering influence of the anaesthetic, she whispered, "It hurts terribly," and managed to raise one impossibly heavy hand toward her face. Her hand was rudely plucked away by a nurse who placed an icepack over her eyes and nose, then gave her an injection to deaden the pain. Bea slept again and awakened an hour later, desperate to get out of there.

Upon seeing her, Hank became completely distraught.

"They didn't say a word about any of this," he cried, her blackened eyes and swollen face reminding him of the night of the Mayfair Ball.

"I'm not supposed to raise my arms for six weeks," she told him.

"And if I look as bad as I think I do, judging from your reaction, it's hard to believe I'm going to look better after going through all this."

"You couldn't look worse," he told her, and then laughed. "I'm sorry."

"Don't be. I'm laughing inside. It just hurts too much to do it on the outside."

He carried her upstairs and tenderly put her down on the bed. "I feel like goddamned Rasputin," he said, arranging the bedclothes over her, then propping the pillows to keep her head elevated.

"I think you're worse than that," Molly stated heatedly, pushing Hank aside. "Making the poor girl go through more operations. Just look at you! What a mess!"

"It looks worse than it is, and don't blame Hank."

"You allowed to eat anything?" Molly wanted to know.

"Of course, she is," Hank answered.

"Don't it hurt?"

"It did when I first came arround, but they gave me a shot. Now I'm just sleepy."

"What-all'd they do anyway?"

"They broke my nose in four places," Bea answered, "then they fiddled around inside, filing down the bone, removing cartilage. I highly recommend it."

"The both of you're crazy!" Molly declared. "I'll go fix you some soup." She bustled off, muttering under her breath.

"She thinks picture people are crazy," Bea said. "Will you get me the hand mirror from the dressing table?"

"We *are* crazy, and I will not. You don't want to see yourself. There'll be time enough for that next week when they take off the bandages. I *must* be crazy," he said, "letting you go through this."

"I volunteered. I want to make that picture."

"By God, you will! We'll show Ludie what we can do, all right!"

Twenty-Three

S HE studied her face from all angles, fascinated by the difference made by the reshaping of her nose. The surgeon had thinned down the bone, reduced the width from brow to tip, removed cartilage, and shortened it. As a result, her eyes looked even larger, and her mouth seemed more generous. Altogether the face in the mirror was very pretty, even elegant. It simply didn't look like hers. Neither did her body. It would still be weeks before she could move her arms freely without having to fear doing some damage to the slow-healing incisions hidden beneath the weight of her new breasts. Those, she thought, were too funny; mercifully they weren't overly large, but just sufficiently enhanced to require a new model to be constructed by the wardrobe department and the abandonment of at least half her personal wardrobe. Overall, the changes she'd undergone frightened her. No matter how often she told herself there were reasons for these alterations, she couldn't quite convince herself they were valid.

She'd undergone surgery in order not only to continue her career, but to have what Hank was determined would be a bigger and better one. Here she was doing things she'd never have believed herself capable of doing. And it felt as if she hadn't any real choice in the matter, because she could no longer dance. With that ability gone, she couldn't keep the hope of someday returning to Broadway as an ace in her sleeve. She'd never be able to go back—to Broadway, or to being the original Beatrice Crane. How much more, she wondered, would get changed along the way? Was she going to end up completely unrecognizable at the other end of the line? And when she got to the other end, who'd be there? She'd already surrendered one child as hostage to her career, and being married to Hank meant it was unlikely she'd ever have another. So what did she have? A small, neat nose centered perfectly on her face; cleavage to fill out the bodice

251

of the slip she'd wear in the film; and a full set of misgivings.

"Are you pleased?" Hank asked her.

"The doctor said it'll be at least six months before the swelling's entirely gone from my nose."

"It looks even better than I thought it would," he said carefully, unable to read accurately her reactions.

"Yes, it does," she agreed. "I'll be ready to do the make-up tests next week."

"You're upset, aren't you?"

"Not upset, a little scared. Henry, if I keep changing everything about me that's recognizable, who am I going to wind up being? And what are people going to think when they see this face? Maybe they won't know who I am."

"They'll know, all right. And most people won't even notice. They'll think you're doing something different with your hair or your make-up. Some will notice and comment, but it won't matter."

"I wish it didn't matter to *me*. I can't even brush my hair. I have to get Molly to do it. It feels as if they stuffed me full of liquid rubber that's slowly turning hard. I miss sleeping on my stomach. I don't know if all this is worth it."

"It will be, I'm certain."

"Well," she said flippantly, "if I do flop, maybe I'll go back to being flat-chested. It'll be some consolation."

"You won't flop. And I'd like to remind you my reputation's on the line, too."

"I know that. That's a big part of why I'm so scared, why I'm whining, and complaining, and behaving like such a dolt."

"We've got every component, Bea, and the key one is you."

"Every time you say that, it makes it worse."

"It shouldn't. I believe in you. When the picture hits, the two of us stand to make a lot of money, not to mention finally gaining some recognition."

"God! I just hope I don't let you down."

"You could never let me down." He came across the room and stroked her hair. "You're still you, Bea," he sought to console her. "You've only changed the outside. And that's not the part that's important to me."

She leaned against him and closed her eyes, soothed by his stroking hand.

In the weeks prior to the start of shooting, she and Hank approved the costume sketches. She went for fittings, did the make-up and wardrobe tests, and, in every free moment, studied her lines. Hank conferred with the art director, oversaw the construction of the sets, and completed casting on the supporting and minor roles. Everything was going to be shot either on the sound stage or the back lot in order to keep the budget in line. Bea came along when Hank interviewed mothers offering their infants for use in the early part of the film and agreed with his choice of a month-old baby girl with an exceptionally placid nature. She was also there when they auditioned five-year-olds, one of whom would play her daughter in the latter part of the film. Bea loved the children, some of whom were so spunky and independent they reminded her of herself as a youngster. And she fell in love with the girl Hank ultimately hired. Elizabeth Hansen had Bea's dark hair and pale skin, and a face of amazing mobility. Everything she felt showed. Elizabeth's mother, however, was something else again. The woman was demanding, pushy, and so overly protective that her behavior with her daughter bordered on abuse.

"We're going to have to keep her out of the way while we're filming," Hank mused aloud to Bea. "If she's around, I've got a hunch Elizabeth'll clam up and we won't be able to get a thing out of her. I *hate* working with kids!"

"But you *like* children!"

"I'm crazy about them. It's the goddamned stage mothers I can't stomach."

"How are you going to keep her off the set?"

"I'll think of something. Maybe the front office can find some kind of temporary work for her, sorting fan letters or something. I don't want her anywhere around here. She's the sort who'll worry her kid into such a state of nerves, the kid won't be able to open her mouth."

"She's such a sweet little girl."

"You'd love to have a gang of kids to look after, wouldn't you?" He looked up at last from his shooting script and the breakdown chart he was painstakingly creating.

"I've always wanted children."

"Okay. One of these days, we'll get you some."

She went to sit on his lap and rested her head on his shoulder, her eyes on the work spread out over the desk top. "Let's get through this first," she told him, lifting his hand to examine the ink staining his fingers. "A couple more weeks, and I'll be able to lift my arms. I probably won't remember how. I feel like a duck with broken wings."

"Go back over there and do some more work on your lines. When I finish this scene, I'll run them with you, if you like."

"We've got those love scenes," she said tentatively.

"Nervous about them?"

She nodded. "I seize up inside every time I get to that part of the script."

"We'll take it nice and easy. You'll keep telling yourself it's not for real, and if that's not good enough, I'll keep telling you, too."

In general, he disliked shooting out of sequence, but because the weather was gray and heavy with impending rain, he decided to set up on the back lot and get some of the exteriors done.

"We might as well take advantage of what nature's giving us," he told Bea. "And it'll put us a couple of days ahead of schedule right off the bat. We'll shoot you and Elizabeth walking through the rain outside those storefronts. The crew's working tonight to get the fronts ready. I know you thought we'd be starting Monday, but you won't mind working tomorrow and Sunday, will you?"

"Not at all. Have you set it up with Elizabeth's mother?"

"It's set. My only real concern is Mama, hanging on the sidelines, fussing."

"Why don't we call Lucy?" she suggested, inspired. "We could get her to come over and babysit Elizabeth's mother."

"How?"

"Lucy'll be able to distract her. She's good at it. She did it for me, for years, any time I got a case of the jitters. As a matter of fact, she might be grateful for being put on the payroll. There's a lot she could do, besides running interference with Mrs. Hansen. And if the money's a problem, just deduct it off the top of my fee. Lucy would never have to know."

"Ike might not like it."

"Why do you say that? Why should he mind?"

"I don't know. He just might. You want to call her?"

"I think you should. I don't want her to feel she's getting a handout from me. If you call, it'll be on the up-and-up. It'll keep Ike from minding, too. She really could use the money, Hank."

"Doesn't he give her any?"

"It's hard for her to ask. She's used to paying her own way, and I think he's a little mean about money."

"Has she said that?"

"She wouldn't. It's just the way I read it."

"He averages twenty thousand a picture, and he's on four or five pictures a year. That really surprises me, that he'd be mean about his cash."

"Maybe he isn't. It could just be something they haven't worked

254

out yet. But I know she'd be glad of a job. Aside from everything else, she's bored silly, sitting home all day."

"Okay. I'll call her."

Lucy was elated. "Don't worry about a thing," she told Hank. "I'll keep the woman out of your hair. I'll be more than happy to do it."

Encouraged by her response, he said, "When that part of it's done, we've got a few other things we'll be able to use you for. If that's acceptable to you."

"It's more than acceptable. Give Bea my love, and I'll see you on the back lot in the morning."

After the call, he turned to look at Bea who was smiling expectantly. "Well, you were right on that score. She was thrilled to death."

Setting aside her usual trepidations, Bea came back to the studio after the weekend's shooting to see the dailies. She sat next to Hank in the screening room, her teeth clenched, waiting for the projectionist to run the film.

"Christ, you look beautiful!" Hank murmured, taking hold of her hand. "And Elizabeth looks enough like you to be yours. I knew in my bones it'd be a perfect match."

Bea didn't respond. She was too taken with the quality of the film he'd shot. Unlike the musicals, with their brilliant lighting and glossy look of newness, these pieces of film were grainier, more natural. The quality of the light was extraordinary, endowing everything, from a puddle, to the close-ups of her and Elizabeth, with an almost opalescent beauty. And he'd chosen to do footage of details she doubted anyone else would have thought of—of Elizabeth's small hand enfolded in hers, of rain spatters on the backs of their legs. She knew, all at once, that this picture was going to be better than good. This was not only her opportunity to give all she had to a role, it was also Hank's chance to show everything he'd learned about movie-making.

"It's going to be a marvelous picture," she whispered to him, tremendously excited. "This footage is incredible!"

"Count on it!" he whispered back, his hand tightening around hers. "I'm gonna make you a star, kid," he imitated Ludie. "You'll be the hottest thing goin'." They both laughed; they both knew he was serious.

She felt no need to see any more of the dailies and turned her attention to the script and their work on the sound stage. She'd managed to get through the first of the love scenes and knew every-thing would be all right. Taylor was playing well, giving her a lot to work with, and their scenes together had a lovely lightness on top, with a mounting emotional content underneath. The second love scene was going well, the lines and actions building smoothly. When Hank called, "CUT IT!" Bea was startled, and watched him approach, trying to imagine why on earth he'd stopped a scene that had been going so well.

"Something's wrong," he said to her in an undertone. "We'll break for half an hour," he told the crew, then directed Bea behind the flats, out of anyone's earshot.

"What is it?" she asked, bothered by his expression.

"Look!" He pointed at her slip, then shook his head. "You can't see it. There's something wrong," he said again, and began removing his cardigan. He wrapped it around her, saying, "Let's go to your trailer. We'll talk there."

Once inside the trailer, he stood her in front of the make-up mirror, withdrew his cardigan, and said again, "Look!"

"My God!" She stepped closer to the mirror, fingering the spreading yellowish discolorations on the slip. "Something really *is* wrong," she agreed, fearfully lowering the top of the slip to examine the incisions beneath her breasts.

"This isn't right," he said worriedly. "I don't care for this at all."

"I think they're infected," she said, dabbing at the raw-looking incisions with some tissues, then looking at the tissues. "I'm going to have to see Dr. Shannon. What'll we do about the slip?"

"I'll get wardrobe to bring over another. Maybe we should shut down until you've seen the doctor."

"*We can't do that!* We can't afford to lose half a day, Hank, and you know it. Get wardrobe to bring some gauze, too. I'll cover these up with the gauze, and hope it doesn't leak through again before we finish. Lucy can phone and make an appointment for me to see Shannon later."

"Are you sure? Losing a little time doesn't matter that much. You're too important. And why Shannon?"

"Henry, the scene's going too well. If we stop, we might not be able to get it back. Send for wardrobe, and get Lucy to make the call. I wouldn't go back to that other guy if I was dying. At least I trust Shannon."

"If anything happens to you . . ."

"Nothing's going to happen. Go on!"

"I just *knew* I shouldn't let you get that done."

"It's done! It's too late for second thoughts. Please!"

Reluctantly, he went. A few minutes later, the wardrobe woman came with a roll of gauze bandage and a fresh slip.

"Jeez!" she exclaimed, watching Bea place a folded wad of the gauze beneath each breast. "That's a mess."

"I know it is. You'd better see if you can get that slip cleaned up in a hurry, in case I need it."

By the time the shooting finished at six-thirty, her breasts felt so engorged and tender she was certain the slightest pressure would cause them to split wide open. Leaving off her undergarments, she buttoned on one of Hank's cotton shirts, pulled on a baggy pair of old rehearsal trousers, and went with Lucy to her car.

"Are you okay?" Lucy kept asking, glancing over every few seconds as she drove.

"No," Bea answered. "It hurts like hell." Reaching up under the shirt, she could feel liquid seeping down over her ribs. "It's as if whatever was put inside is leaking out."

"Shit!" Lucy's foot eased down more on the accelerator.

"Well, at least the scene's in the can. I don't have to worry about showing the world my new cleavage anymore. At this rate, another ten minutes and they'll just explode off my chest."

Lucy laughed, then was angry again. "I don't know how you can crack wise at a time like this."

"You tell me: What else am I going to do?"

Dr. Shannon hustled Bea into an examining room, frowning and tut-tutting at the sight of the inflamed, oozing incisions.

"Whoever did this ought to be taken out and shot!" he said angrily. "Don't tell me his name! I don't want to know it. These incisions have to be opened, cleaned and drained, then restitched."

"Then I guess you'd better do it."

"Listen to me, Beatrice." He came to the head of the table and leaned directly over her. "Whatever he's put in your breasts is being rejected by your natural tissues. Do you understand that?"

"No. What does it mean?"

"It means that if we don't take it out, your whole system's going to be poisoned. Why the hell did you *do* this?"

"Look, Dr. Shannon," she said tiredly. "I had to do it. Now it's gone sour, and we've got to fix it. I'm in the middle of shooting. I've got to be back at the studio at six in the morning. Please, do what you can."

"You'll be out of commission for a good week, maybe two. You've got a very serious infection here."

"I *can't* be out of commission, and we're wasting time talking while you could be fixing it."

"I could do it with a local anaesthetic," he said with misgivings, "but it won't be fun. You're going to feel some of it."

"Just do it!"

Seeing she was determined, he shrugged and said, "Okay. Just relax. It'll take me a few minutes to get scrubbed."

She refused to make a sound. She fixed her gaze on the overhead light and lay motionless while the nurse bathed the area with alcohol, and then Shannon injected the local. She felt an odd sensation as he reopened the incisions with a scalpel but tried not to listen as, from behind his mask, he gave instructions to the nurse. He swore several times as he worked. Neither Bea nor the nurse paid any attention. As he finally closed the incisions, she felt each insertion of the needle and chewed on her lower lip, keeping her eyes on the light above. The procedure seemed to take forever, and she wondered if Lucy wasn't frantic out there in the waiting room, not knowing what was going on in here.

"It's done," Shannon said at last. "I'll give you a couple of pre-scriptions, one for painkillers and one to try to knock out the infection. You're going to hurt like hell for a few days. I can write you a letter for the studio, if you want to reconsider. You're insured. The insurance will cover the delay in shooting."

"I don't want to reconsider, but thank you."

"You'll have to keep the incisions clean, and don't do anything strenuous for a couple of weeks. Don't lift anything heavy, and above all, keep those dressings clean. I'll give you some ointment. I don't think you have any idea what you're doing, and it makes me madder than hell to have you come in here in that condition so I can patch up some idiot's handiwork. The same fella do the work on your nose?"

"No."

"Well, thank the good Lord for something. It didn't seem reasonable to think a man could do such fine work on one part of you and such butchery on another. Take it nice and easy now, Bea." He pressed his hand on her shoulder. "Lie down every chance you get. And if there's a problem, call me. I make house calls, you know. Far as I'm concerned, you got more guts than brains. You know that?"

"Thank you for everything."

"Rest for a few more minutes, then you can go home. And don't forget to get the prescriptions filled! I promise you, you're going to need those painkillers."

Part Two / 1938–1946

* * *

"**I**'m sorry it took so long," Bea apologized as Lucy drove her home. "I was imagining all kinds of things."

"I'll bet you were. I've got a couple of prescriptions to get filled."

"Give them to me. I'll take care of it. Should I dare ask what he did?"

"He opened the incisions, took out whatever was put inside, cleaned it out, then sewed everything back up again."

"Christ! Didn't it hurt?"

Bea gulped, said, "Yup," then allowed herself to cry.

"Is all this worth it?" Lucy asked in a low, serious tone.

"It better be." Bea blotted her eyes on the sleeve of Hank's shirt.

Hank hurried home as soon as he'd seen the day's takes.

"How is she?" he asked Molly.

"She's sleepin'. Miss Lucy dropped her home a couple hours ago, then went off to fetch the medicine for her and come back with it. I woke her up 'bout an hour ago to give her the medicine an' she went right back to sleep. She's gotta take it every four hours. She needs lookin' after, and that's for sure."

"Maybe you should come with her to the studio for the next few days to do just that."

"It's what I was thinkin'. I'll be ready in the mornin'."

He tiptoed into the bedroom, fearful of disturbing her sleep.

"You don't have to creep around," she said in the dark. "I'm awake. Please put the light on. It wasn't dark yet when I got back."

He went to put on the bathroom light, which was kept going every night, because it made her feel less afraid. On those occasions, at the beginning of their marriage, when he'd forgotten and she'd awakened in the night, she'd cried out in terror at being unable to see where she was.

Returning, he sat on the side of the bed, found her hand and held it, asking, "How are you, dear heart?"

"It hurts, but not the same as before. I think this is from the anaesthetic wearing off. Shannon was furious, but he's a good doctor. I'll be right as rain in a few days. Are you coming to bed?"

"In a few minutes." He touched her forehead. "You're hot."

"It's a muggy night."

"Five minutes. I want to take a shower."

By the time he slipped into bed, she'd fallen back to sleep. He lay at her side listening to the sound of her breathing, thinking of how she'd lowered her slip and stared at herself in the trailer's mirror. He'd been sickened and frightened by what he'd seen. Now, worn out, but unable to sleep, he vowed he'd allow no further harm to come to her, in any way, shape, or form. Enough is enough, he thought, folding his arms under his head. You could only ask so much of someone, and she'd been asked too much already.

"You're not her guardian anymore," Ike said hotly. "You're not responsible for her."

"I'll *always* be responsible for her," Lucy shot back. "I'd like to know why you're getting so hot under the collar."

"You need money, all you've got to do is ask me. I don't like you fetching and carrying like some kind of servant."

"This is ridiculous!" Lucy said disbelievingly, looking at the man she'd married. Six feet tall, heavy-boned, with blond hair and Nordic blue eyes, a pencil-thin, all-but-invisible mustache. She recognized him all right, but she couldn't have said she knew him. "Are we fighting because you're jealous of my friendship with Bea?"

"I don't like seeing my wife being told to run here, then run there."

"Ike," she said, "it was what I did when we met, and you didn't mind it then."

"Well, I mind it now. It makes me look bad."

"It does nothing of the sort. Everybody knows I'm Bea's guardian, or was. Everybody knows we're very close. And aside from that, I'm being *paid* to fetch and carry, as you put it, on this production. I've even got a title, for God's sake—assistant to the director. It's the first time in months I've felt I was more than some kind of living decoration around here."

"What's wrong with this place?"

"Nothing. It's a perfectly nice little house."

"Oh, I see. It's too small for you."

"You're being a real jerk. It's fine for me. Maybe we should've stayed as we were. We never used to fight."

"Maybe we should've," he agreed bitterly. "You can't cook, you hate housework, I'm forever having to remind you to pick up my shirts from the laundry. And we hardly ever sleep together anymore."

"I never *said* I could cook; I never *said* I liked housework. And I've never had to worry about getting anyone's shirts from the laundry. I never once told you any differently. And if we don't sleep together much lately, it's because half the time you're at the studio till all hours, and the other half of the time you're either too busy, too tired, or more interested in picking a fight."

"So what d'you want to do?" he asked defiantly.

"I don't know. What d'*you* want to do?"

"How the hell should I know? The only thing I do know is that this arrangement's no good."

"Then maybe we should try going back to the way we were."

"And how do we do that?" he wanted to know.

"I guess I can go live with Bea or find a place of my own. And you and I will see each other when we can, the way we used to. I don't know what else to suggest."

All at once, he caved in, his arguments and his energy draining away. "This isn't what I wanted," he said unhappily.

"Me, neither. We haven't even been married a year."

"Maybe we should give it some more time."

"You know what I think, Ike? I think if two people can stay married in this town, it's because they've got something going for them that's outside any studio, outside ambition, outside of everything. I'm not sure we've got something like that. So maybe we should split up and start dating again, see if that doesn't put some of the fun back into it for us."

"I wasn't trying to blame Bea, you know. She's a great girl, and I know how you feel about her. I guess I wish you felt the same way about me."

"I do care about you," she said. "But Bea's a whole other matter. You and I could never have that same kind of friendship. For one thing, you're a man. Men and women can't seem to care about each other the same way two women can. Women don't pretend with each other, the way we do with men. Then, once we get married, we stop pretending, and nothing's any good anymore. I wish I knew why that was, but it's a fact."

"Yeah," he agreed. "I kind of know what you mean." Suddenly shy, he glanced away, then with a somewhat chagrined smile said, "I wouldn't mind, you know. If you're in the mood."

She laughed and went closer to him. "It takes all the pressure off, doesn't it, knowing we can both stop working so goddamned hard to make a go of it?"

"You know I'm crazy for you," he told her, his arms going around her.

"I know that. It'll be better this way."

Lucy got to the studio at just after six the next morning. Bea was already in the make-up chair.

"I need to talk to you. How are you feeling?"

"Not bad. Ivy, could you give me and Lucy five minutes?"

"Sure thing," Ivy agreed readily. "You both want some coffee?"

"That'd be swell," Lucy said. "Thanks."

"What's happened?" Bea swiveled in the chair as Lucy came to stand looking at Ivy's exotic array of cosmetics.

"Ike and I are having a few problems. I was wondering if my old room's available."

"Have you split up?"

"We're going to try dating again. I wouldn't want to get in the way, but if you could see your way clear, I'd really like to come back."

"Of course, you can," Bea told her. "Do you think you two will be able to work it out?"

Lucy shrugged. "We're going to try. I guess I'm really not the marrying kind after all."

"That's what you've been telling me for as long as I can remember."

Lucy smiled. "It looks like I was right. It's kind of humiliating to be thirty-two years old and come running back to you, as if you were my mother."

"Don't feel that way, Luce. I'm sorry things haven't worked out."

"I guess there's no harm done. I miss answering the fan mail anyway."

"If Hank's right, you'll have permanent writer's cramp once this picture's released."

"Fine by me. D'you take your medicine this morning?"

"Yes, ma'am, I did."

"Good." Lucy picked up a liner brush, examined it, then put it down.

"I know how you feel," Bea said quietly. "But if you think it's for the best, then it is."

"Probably."

"We're going to have quite a crowd in the trailer," Bea said, striving to lighten the mood. "Hank insisted Molly come along to make sure I don't strain myself powdering my nose or drinking my coffee."

"I've been missing you," Lucy said. "And Molly, too. You don't think Hank'll mind, do you?"

"Hank won't mind," she said firmly.

"God, you're lucky! That man adores you."

"It works both ways. Don't forget that."

"No. I won't."

Twenty-Four

"**D**ON'T waste your time trying to threaten me, John. I've gone far past the point where I can be frightened—by anyone. You don't seem to realize that when you put a person's back to the wall, that person has two choices. She can give up altogether, or she can come back fighting, because there's nothing left to lose. I've got nothing to left to lose now. Bonnie's safe. You can never get to her. And me, well, I've stopped being so afraid—of you, of what people might think. Can you understand that? You're going to have to find someone else to work on, some other fool of a woman who starts out thinking you're the goods and ends up realizing she should've taken a closer look at the package. Go on. You're all washed up here, so go."

"You haven't seen the last of me, sister!"

"I have, and you know it. Can't you get it through your head? I'm not afraid anymore."

There was a three-beat pause, and then Hank cut the scene.

"That was perfect!" he congratulated Bea and Carson. "Let's get the close-ups, and then we can wrap."

There was a break while the crew rearranged the lighting for her close-ups. Bea was sweating, tired, and could feel a tightness at her temples that would evolve into a headache. She'd never worked harder than she had in the previous three weeks. Molly came over with a glass of ice water, Ivy close on her heels with the ever present powder and puff.

"Take this here pill," Molly ordered, and stood guard after Bea had swallowed it to make sure she wasn't going to be needed further.

"Where's Lucy?" Bea asked Molly as Ivy took the shine off her nose and chin.

"She went to take them two home. That woman was refusin' all the way to let the child stay for the party. And poor Elizabeth had her heart set."

"What a bitch!" Bea muttered.

"Some people don't deserve their kids, and that's a fact!"

Ivy stepped back, examined her handiwork, then went off, leaving in her wake a drift of pale face powder.

"You oughtn't to be stayin' for no party yourself," Molly said. "You're about ready to keel over."

"I've *earned* this party. I wouldn't miss it for the world."

"It's for sure nobody's gonna stop you, so I might's well save my breath."

"A very good idea." Bea smiled at her, drank the last of the water and returned the glass. "Thanks, Molly. That helped."

The close-ups finally were finished. Hank announced, "THAT'S A WRAP, FOLKS!" and the cast and crew cheered. The sound stage doors were thrown open, and the caterers began setting up for the party.

Lucy had returned and was in the trailer, playing gin rummy with Molly.

"I take it you couldn't talk her into letting Elizabeth stay."

"That hag yelled at the kid all the way home because Elizabeth wanted to stay, and when she found out she couldn't, she started crying and couldn't stop. The more Mama yelled, the harder Elizabeth cried. I never wanted anything so much in my life as I wanted to belt that broad in the chops."

"I'm going over there to get Elizabeth and bring her back to the party," Bea stated, getting out of the sweat-soaked dress she'd worn for the final scenes. "I *dare* that woman to say one word to me. Just one word!"

"I can't wait to see this!" Lucy said eagerly.

"No. Hank's taking me." She sat at the dressing table and began creaming off her make-up. "She won't dare refuse the two of us." She was so angry her hands were trembling as she snatched up a towel and wiped her face. "My mother may have been stupid, but at least she wasn't cruel. I've had to watch that bitch mistreat Elizabeth for three solid weeks. I won't let her get away with this. Elizabeth deserves some fun."

She was so outraged that Molly and Lucy could do no more than watch as she finished at the dressing table, jumped up, and grabbed a dress from its hanger. She was so thin the bones in her chest looked like a narrow little ladder inserted beneath her skin; her upper arms were no longer as rounded and muscular as they'd been. Since the accident and the therapy, she had a hipshot way of walking that people who didn't know about her injuries considered a gross affectation. Those who did know watched her get about with quiet respect and a certain fear that she might, at any moment, lose both her strength and her coordination and simply topple over.

Without bothering to look at herself in the mirror, she dragged a brush through her hair, picked up her bag, said, "I'll be back inside an hour," and left the trailer, slamming the door so hard it bounced open again.

Both women watched her stalk awkwardly across the set to where Hank was waiting.

"Boy, ain't she mad, though!" Molly said admiringly. "I ain't never seen her get so mad."

"Me, neither," Lucy said. "I'm sure glad I'm not Elizabeth's mother."

It wasn't much of a contest. Mrs. Hansen made a short-lived attempt to state her reasons why Elizabeth couldn't attend the party, citing the child's present overly excited state and generally frail health.

"All the more reason why she should be allowed to have a little fun," Bea cut her off.

The woman looked at Bea, prepared to argue, then reconsidered.

"Why don't you get Elizabeth now?" Hank said quietly. "We'll see she's home well before her bedtime."

Mrs. Hansen frowned. It was clear she was considering the possible repercussions of her continued refusal. Word would get around, and Elizabeth's career might be cut short. She gave up and, without saying anything further, left Hank and Bea on the doorstep as she went to get Elizabeth who could be heard sobbing in the distance.

"Why is she like this?" Bea wondered aloud in a whisper.

"It's vicarious," Hank replied. "If she were Elizabeth, she'd play 'star' to the hilt. She'd be unavailable, reclusive when it suited her, rude, showy, and totally temperamental. She'd keep people waiting on the set; she'd hold up production for hours on a whim. However, since it's a five-year-old we're discussing, she can't do any of it."

The woman returned, pulling Elizabeth along by her arm. "She's not dressed for a party," she stormed, pushing the child forward.

"She's dressed perfectly," Bea said, with a smile for Elizabeth. "Come on, sweetheart." She held out her hand. Elizabeth wavered, looking doubtfully up at her mother. Then she reached to take Bea's hand.

"Who's gonna look after her?" Mrs. Hansen called. "Maybe I should come, too . . ."

"She'll be well looked after." Hank paused on the walk to answer. "Not a thing to worry about."

Bea sat with Elizabeth on her lap while Hank drove them back to

the studio. Seeing how upset she was, Bea settled her more comfortably, then, with a smile, said, "There's going to be ice cream and
cake and lots of good things to eat. And there'll be some other children, too."

"Who?" Elizabeth asked, turning her small serious face toward Bea.

"Well, let's see. My agent's two children, and Pete's kids. He's got
five, if you can imagine that. And some of the crew's families. You'll
have a great time."

"I'm not supposed to get dirty."

"If you do, we'll clean you up before you go home. How's that?"

"I don't know," Elizabeth fretted.

"Don't you worry." Bea tightened her arms around her. "Little girls
are supposed to get dirty and have fun. Everything will be fine. You'll
see."

Elizabeth allowed herself to be held, and Bea rested her cheek
against the girl's dark, silky hair, wishing she could keep her, that
she'd never have to send her home. Why was it the wrong people
were the ones who got the children?

Arriving back at the sound stage where the party was in full swing,
Elizabeth once again became apprehensive and hung back tearfully.

"Come to my trailer," Bea invited. "I've got something for you."

Hank went ahead to join the others, turning back to watch Bea
walk off with the child. They seemed, he thought, to be contained
in a bubble of silence and meaning that involved only the two of
them, and he was reluctant to intrude.

Elizabeth looked around warily as Bea went to the dressing table
to get the gift.

"My mother says I'll be very famous one day, and I'll have to be
careful, then."

"She does, does she?" Bea sat down and beckoned the child to
come sit with her. "What will you have to be careful of?"

"Oh, lots of things." Elizabeth sat herself down beside Bea, sighing.
"Lots and lots of things. I can't remember them all."

"Do you think you'd like to be famous?" Bea asked her.

"Uh-uh." Elizabeth shook her head. "I'd like to be a nurse. Nurses
are almost as important as doctors."

"So they are. This is for you." Bea placed the package into the girl's
hands.

Elizabeth looked at the gift, then at Bea, her face clearing so that
she appeared to be a little girl instead of the prematurely aged creature
she seemed so often.

"Open it!" Bea urged.

"Honestly?"

"Sure. Go on."

Elizabeth got the wrappings off, opened the box, then gazed trans-fixed at its contents. "It's a *baby!*" she breathed.

"It's a baby doll, for you."

Elizabeth lifted the doll from the box and clutched it to her with a rapturous expression, then held it away to look at it.

"I think there's something else in the box," Bea said.

"There is?"

Holding the doll to her chest with one hand, she used her free one to push past the tissue. "Is it for me, or for the baby?" she asked.

"It's for you. Would you like me to put it on you?"

Elizabeth nodded and obligingly bent her head so Bea could fasten the gold chain with the dainty heart around her neck. Then she ran her fingers over the chain until she found the heart and looked down at it.

"It looks very pretty. Do you like it?"

In answer, Elizabeth hooked her free arm around Bea's neck and hugged her fiercely. Bea held her for a long moment, then eased her away to say, "I like you very much, Elizabeth."

"I like you, too. You're nice."

"If there's ever anything I can do for you, or anything you need, I want you to come to me. Okay?"

"Okay."

"Do you understand?"

"Yes, I do," Elizabeth replied soberly.

"Good. Now! How about some cake and ice cream?"

"Okay! Can I bring the baby?"

"Of course. She's yours."

"What's her name?"

"She doesn't have one yet. You'll have to name her."

Elizabeth thought for a few secods, then said, "I think I'll call her Leonard."

Bea laughed. "A fine name," she said, and took Elizabeth's hand.

Periodically, throughout the party, Hank stopped to study Bea with the child. Much of what Elizabeth aroused in her had showed in their scenes together. Each frame seemed endowed with a special light that emanated from Bea and spread to embrace the girl. Upon seeing this, he'd worked to enhance it further by shooting their scenes with the utmost delicacy and care. It shouldn't have surprised him that she'd be willing to do battle for the girl, but he'd gone along viewing Bea herself as barely beyond childhood. It had been a mistake. In the past eighteen months, she'd been thrust into a confrontation with her own resources and had chosen to find a new strength rather than give in to defeat. He'd seen this, yet he'd failed to see she was no longer a child, but a woman, with all her instincts intact. She wanted children, and she'd never really be content until she could have them.

Since his love for her was, in part, predicated on his belief in his ability to take care of her, and, in part, on his fascination with her talent, he'd neglected to keep his perspective of her accurate. He promised himself he'd never again allow this to happen. It was his responsibility, as her husband and friend, to be as aware of her off-camera as he was on.

When, as they were taking Elizabeth home, he glanced over to see the girl asleep in Bea's arms and saw Bea's expression of sad longing, he could have wept. He'd have given anything, just then, to be able to provide her with what she most wanted and needed.

"She'll harm that child," Bea said, after they'd returned Elizabeth to her mother. "It's dreadful. I can't tell you how tempted I was all evening to run away with that little girl."

"You should have children," he observed.

"I should," she agreed. "Except I can't stand the thought of what you have to do to get them. And you"—she smiled at him—"have no interest, thank heaven. One of these days, we'll adopt a bunch."

"You may change your mind about all kinds of things, Bea."

"Possibly. For now, I want to get caught up on sleep, and maybe get started putting this body back into condition. I need exercise, and I have to find a way to walk that doesn't make me look like a mechanical doll with broken hinges."

"But it's attractive, the way you walk."

"It's absurd," she laughed, her anger forgotten. "Someday though I'm going to get up on a stage again and dance. I swear to God, I will. And the first step is to start exercising."

"Maybe that's not such a good idea," he began.

"Hank, I've got to. I'm a dancer. *Was* a dancer. Everything I see and hear becomes a dance in my mind. I can't even sing anymore because that was part of the dancing. Every time I open my mouth to sing, I start to feel the rhythm, and I want it to be there, in my feet and my legs, but it's gone. It's as if the bottom half of me has turned to wood." She thumped her fists on her thighs for emphasis. "Maybe I'll never be able to do it, but I've got to try. You can understand that, can't you? I can't just give up and forget about it."

"Sure I understand."

She slid across the seat closer to him, saying. "You always do. It's what I love best about you."

"I want you to come see the rough cut when it's ready."

"If you think I should, I will."

It was a revelation to her. She was so intrigued by what he'd effected overall in the picture that there wasn't room for her to be as self-conscious and overly critical as she usually was of herself on screen. The surgery was in no small way a contributing factor, because she looked so unlike herself that it was like witnessing some other woman's performance. And that other woman gave Bea goose bumps. Of course it was a combination of factors—the lighting, the sets, the way in which Hank had created tight groupings and had dispensed, for the most part, with odd angles and overhead shots. There was a breathless kind of intimacy to every scene that he'd accomplished through the use of carefully composed medium shots and a minimum of extreme close-ups; he'd done it by turning the actors halfway to the camera or moving them partially out of the frame; he'd done it by focusing on a reacting face while the actor delivering the lines was out of sight or had his or her back to the camera; he'd done it by closing in on someone's hands or profile and cutting these pieces into a given sequence so that points of view were shared simultaneously by the character reacting at the moment and the person to whom he or she was reacting.

As she'd seen at the outset, the quality of the light was exceptional, as if the light itself was another character. And as frustrated and confused as she'd often been during the shooting by Hank's repeated cuts and takes, she could see now what he'd been aiming for in getting her to keep her eyes averted in one scene, to pitch her voice very low in another. Everything gelled. There was nothing rough about what they were seeing.

"The score will be the italics," Hank told her, "and the punctuation. I'm keeping it minimal, just here and there. I don't want the picture overwhelmed, or put off balance, by the score."

She had to take a long look at this man she'd married, to see if there wasn't something about him she'd previously failed to notice. He seemed the same. Yet perhaps he'd grown so familiar that she was no longer able to see the external signs that would've given her the clues to his talent and vision.

"Why're you looking at me that way?" he wanted to know, a bemused smile on his lips.

"That's an amazing picture you've made, Henry Donovan. You see things no one else seems to. I even didn't mind myself, and that's quite a feat."

269

"Well, I'm satisfied," he said, "because I knew all along you could do it. And there's a hell of a lot more you'll do before you're finished."

"You're the one who did it. I only took direction."

"Don't minimize it, Bea. All the elements of who and what you are transcend the character. Yes, you're playing a part. But it's merely an extension of the basic you. It's your tremendous energy, and your determination, and your style that make Jeannie what she is."

"I just do what I'm told," she argued. "The entire thing is yours."

"Maybe it's because you're so young that you'd like to think I'm some kind of optical Svengali. You're going to have to take my word for this: What you saw up there is a collaboration. It's not any one person's show. I'm damned proud of this picture, and I'm equally proud of you. Just remember one thing: Don't ever take on a part your instinct tells you is wrong. Stick with your instinct, and you'll be okay."

"You make it sound as if I'm going to go off tomorrow and never work with you again."

"You'll work with other directors, dear heart. It stands to reason. For one thing, not every picture I'm going to do will have a part for you in it. And for another, there'll be parts you want to play that Ludie won't own. Then you'll have to fight for the chance to do those pictures."

"You're scaring me, talking as if we're going to get separated for some reason."

"That's not it at all. Bea, you're going to *want* to go after the good parts, and you'll be prepared to fight for them, because it's the only way you know how to do things; you'll do it the hard way, just as you always have. And you know what else?"

"What?"

"The reason I know all this is because, in my own way, I'm just like you." He smiled, and held her hand against his cheek. "If I'd been born a woman, I'd have been you."

Twenty-Five

A FTER digging out her old rehearsal clothes, Bea shut herself into one of the guest bedrooms, put a record on the portable phonograph, and positioned herself on the floor to start some stretching exercises. Less than five minutes later, she was winded, her hamstrings protesting every attempt to bring her chin to her knees as she held on to each foot in turn. Her hips didn't want to cooperate; her arms trembled from the strain; her abdominal muscles ached.

The record ended and the needle slid back and forth in the center of the disc. She brought her legs together and leaned back on her hands until her breathing slowed. Then she got up, turned the record over, sat down, and began the next set of stretches, with one foot tucked into her groin, attempting to bring her upper body down flat over the extended leg.

Three minutes of this, and she was in pain. Maybe it wasn't possible. Maybe she'd never again have any real degree of control over her body. The notion outraged her. It had been almost nineteen months since she'd been thrown from the car. Why did she think a few minutes of exercise would undo all those months of atrophy?

She stood up, went to the machine, selected another record, then positioned herself in the middle of the room. Go slowly, she told herself. A little every day. Build up to it. She lowered herself into a cautious plié, keeping her spine straight, her chin lifted. The tendons in her thighs felt as if they'd snap. She rose slowly, began another plié, and had to stop. She was off-center, and she was terribly afraid of falling. Sometimes, in her dreams of dancing, she fell, and her bones shattered like glass. The pain of the fall radiated outward from her broken hips, traveling up into her arms and down to her feet. There'd be a dreadful dream-overlapping where instead of finding herself on the floor of a stage, she'd be hurtling through darkness, colliding with jagged rock outcroppings. She hated being so afraid, especially of a body that had always been completely under her control. She wanted that control back, and she'd have it, if it was the last thing she ever did.

Lucy knocked and opened the door, took in the scene, and said, "You'll kill yourself."

"Of course I won't!"

"You will, you know. You'll destroy whatever flexibility you've managed to gain. You can't jump in and do exercises meant for a trained body in perfect shape."

"So what should I do?"

"You'll have to go right back to the beginning and start from scratch. I wouldn't mind working with you, if you like." Lucy watched Bea trying to decide if she'd be willing to have anyone see her struggle like an infant with her impossible body. "I know you're not too hot on having anybody watch you, but I could help. As a matter of fact, I need to get back into condition myself. I'm starting to get kind of flabby. If you promise not to look at my flab, I'll promise not to notice any trouble you have with the exercises."

"It's all still there in my head," Bea said angrily. "I should be able to do it."

"You'll have to go back and start over."

Bea sighed. "I know you're right. Okay. Yes, thank you."

"You'd better go soak in a hot tub before you stiffen up."

Bea turned off the music, then paused with her hand on the machine to ask, "Do you honestly think I can do it?"

"Well, *you* do, and that's what counts, isn't it?"

"*Do you think I can?*" Bea persisted.

"Yeah, I do." Lucy smiled at her. "Go on now, and put plenty of Epsom salts in the tub."

"I will do it, you know."

"I know."

"*I will!*" Bea went off along the hall in her odd, canted walk.

"**L**udie's waiting to see how *Jeannie* does after it opens. He's promised to let us do *Wait for Morning* if he's happy with the receipts," Hank told her.

"When would we start?" she asked eagerly.

"Two months, maybe three. He likes the script. He just wants to see how the audiences react to the picture."

"He doesn't think people are going to like me?"

"He's hedging his bets. *He* likes you. He couldn't get over your performance. Now he's going around telling everybody it was *his* idea to produce your comeback picture. We're going to be okay. While you're in New York, promoting your heart out, I'll keep a fire under him here."

"I wish I were going to the premiere with you."

"So do I, believe me. But the east-coast promotion will help put the picture over. You've still got a big public out there who'll stand in line to see you."

"You'll phone and tell me about it?"

"No," he teased. "I thought I'd let you read about it in back issues of *Variety* when you get home."

She draped her arms around his neck and pressed her forehead to his. "Listen, Pop," she said, her voice gruff, "you'd better call me the minute the damned thing's over or I'll get the boys to rough you up."

"Bea," he chided, "you know I will."

She remained with her forehead against his. "Are you happy, Hank?"

"Very. Are you?"

She lifted her head, and he looked at her eyes, perennially drawn by the constantly changing moods they expressed. At this moment, her eyes were luminous, darker than usual.

"Yes, I am." She smiled at him, then rested her head against his shoulder as she looked at the room. "I love this house. And it feels complete, now that Lucy's home again. Does it make me selfish to be glad she's back?"

"I don't think so."

"When I was kid," she went on, "I used to think I'd love to live someplace where it never snowed and I could always hear my footsteps. Lately, I've started thinking about snow, about sitting inside a warm room and looking out a window, watching it fall. You lose track of the seasons here. You go to bed one night and it's summer, and when you wake up the next morning, it's Christmas."

"And where would you go, if you had your choice?"

"Somewhere with snow, so that when you wake up and it's Christmas, you don't have to worry about how you're going to decorate the palm trees this year."

He laughed and gave her a squeeze. "We could always make plans to spend a Christmas back east, if it's what you want."

"I have no idea what I want," she admitted. "I'd better go make sure Molly doesn't pack all the wrong things." She pushed away and stood up, then turned back.

"What?"

"Nothing. Just jitters, I guess. It's the first time we'll be apart since we got married. It doesn't feel right, going away without you."

"It's only for a month. And you can always call it off, if you're really uncomfortable about going."

"You know I'd never do that. Nope! It's back I go into the circus, smiling for the camera and giving interviews."

"It sells tickets."

"I know that. Yes, I do."

"By the time you get back, we'll be up to our necks in preproduction for *Wait for Morning*."

"Not a doubt in your mind, huh? You're going to make back all your money, and I'll be launched. You don't see me as the new Anna Stench?"

"It wasn't her fault," he laughed. "And you're rotten."

She waggled her fingers at him, then went to supervise Molly's packing.

Some of the questions were tough. She had to take her time responding to how it felt now, being unable to dance. There were numerous questions about the accident and Dickie's death, and she told lies, expressing sadness at his loss when, in truth, simply having to speak his name made her feel ill. If he hadn't died, she'd have killed him. Publicly, she was obliged to say, "It was a tragic accident," and wait for the next question, praying it would be along other lines. She hated having to lie so blatantly.

Regarding *Jeannie*, she credited Hank with being a superb director. "He's brilliant," she stated unequivocally. "And I thought that long before I ever married him." The comment was met with fond and approving laughter. Everyone seemed to approve of their marriage, and the fan magazines were forever referring to them as Hollywood's "ideal couple."

On went the questions. No, they weren't planning on having children in the immediate future. They were both far too busy with their careers. Yes, another picture was in the works, a second script Hank had written and was set to direct. Yes, she very much enjoyed the challenge of dramatic acting, and yes, it was entirely different from doing musicals. Of course she missed working with Bobby, but he was immensely talented and bound to do well with other partners. No, she had no comment on the fact that he'd had different partners in each of his last three films, except to say it was difficult to find someone whose style coincided with one's own. Yes, they were still good friends; she hoped they always would be.

No, *Jeannie* was not a "women's" movie. It was a movie for people, period. Hank had intentionally steered clear of all the trappings, the traditional settings that categorized a picture strictly for women. Robert Taylor had been loaned out from MGM for the picture, yes. And he'd been most professional and hard working. A serious man, and a very nice one, too.

After the press had gone, she sat with her feet propped on the coffee table, drinking a cup of coffee and thinking about Bobby. She hadn't seen or heard from him since the evening she'd told him she intended to marry Hank. There were frequent stories about him in the fanzines and items in the gossip columns, always having to do with whom he'd been seen with lately. He was still good copy but, according to the trades, his pictures weren't grossing what they should. The general opinion was that the public didn't want to see him dance with anyone but Bea. The chemistry just wasn't there with his other partners. The consensus was that his dancing was as impressively innovative as ever, but his recent pictures lacked the spark that had existed with Bea. She read the comments and felt hurt for him. It wasn't fair that he be judged by her absence, rather than on his own merits. He *was* impressive. Bobby was incapable of turning in anything less than his best.

"That was some session," Lucy commented, watching Bea from across the room. "You handled yourself beautifully."

"They ask the damnedest questions sometimes, as if I'm not a person and don't have the right to my own life and my own thoughts. Why do people think they have the right to ask me when I'm planning to have a baby? I mean, they might as well come out and ask me how often we do it, or whether we do it at all. No one ever asks men questions like that. And all that stuff about Bobby. They were so snide, the way they talked about him, as if they think he's on his way out and they'd like me to endorse that fact. God! People are only interesting if they're on the verge either of making it big or of falling off the mountain. Bobby doesn't need me for his career. They make it sound like we got divorced or something."

The telephone rang, and Lucy automatically picked it up. Bea rarely answered the telephone. Too often fans managed to get hold of the number—of the house or of a hotel she was staying in—and called up asking to speak to her. Lucy, Hank, or Molly almost always screened the calls.

Lucy covered the mouthpiece with her hand and said, "It's the agency. They've had a call from some woman who says she knows you and would like to see you. What's her name?" Lucy said into the mouthpiece, listened, then covered it again. "Becky Armstrong?"

Bea sat up and reached for the receiver. "When did she call? Is she in town?"

"Hi, Bea. It's Mark Rosenberg. How are you?"

"I'm fine. What about Becky?"

"She called, oh, an hour ago, said she understood you were in town and could we put her in touch with you. Naturally, I held her off until I could check with you."

"Did she leave a number?"

"I told her to call me back."

"Tell her I want to see her. If she's in town, send her over. And call me back as soon as you've spoken to her."

"Will do. Everything okay? Hotel good?"

"Everything's fine."

"They're taking care of you?"

"Mark, it's all perfect. Ludie's boys have been rushing around, organizing us like there's going to be no tomorrow. Pete's with us, too. The suite's lovely. Thank you for the flowers. Tell Becky to call me right away. Okay?"

"Okay."

She put down the receiver and turned eagerly to Lucy. "God! I hope she's actually in town. I'd love to see her."

"She's the girl from Toronto, right? The one you've been writing to?"

"Last time she wrote, she said she was still at the university but she was pretty bored with it."

"Maybe she's left school and moved here."

"Who knows? I just wish she'd hurry up and call." She sat with her elbows on her knees, periodically looking over at the telephone. Then she smiled and said, "I'm being a horse's ass. It might be hours before I hear from her." She returned her feet to the table, picked up her cup, and drank some of the now lukewarm coffee. "What time is it?"

"Almost five."

"A couple more hours and Hank'll be dressing to go to the theater. I hope he remembers to wear the new cufflinks and studs I got for him."

"I imagine Ike's trying to find clean underwear." Lucy laughed and shook her head, watching Bea set aside her coffee and light a cigarette.

"D'you think it's going to work out for the two of you?" Bea asked.

"Doubtful. I'm enjoying being on my own again. And I think he probably is, too."

"That's too bad, Luce."

"We gave it a try and it didn't work. At least I've got it out of my system now. I won't be in any big hurry to go getting married again."

The telephone rang, and Bea froze as Lucy reached to answer it.

"Who's calling? No, I'm sorry. She's not available at the moment. I'm afraid I can't tell you that. No. Oh. Well, I suggest you get in touch with the publicity department, talk to them. That's right." She hung up and groaned. *"How* the *hell* do they *find* you?"

"A fan?"

"Thinly disguised as a reporter. As if every member of the press didn't know about today's conference."

"Male?"

"Female. 'I'm with the *Times*,' she said. I'll say one thing for them, they've sure got nerve."

"What time is it?"

"A few minutes later than it was when you asked a few minutes ago. You're really worked up about seeing Becky, aren't you?"

"We've got about two hours before we have to go to this do tonight. I've never felt less like going out in my life. I think they created public appearances just to kill off actors, or whoever else has to do them. The idea of getting all dressed up to go to some banquet and smile a lot..." She was interrupted by the telephone.

"This is really something," Lucy said, letting the phone ring a second time before lifting the receiver. "Yes? Oh, hi. No, we'll be ready on time. No, it went great. When's the car supposed to be here? Right, that's what I thought. No, everything's fine. I don't know about that. I'll have to ask her. Hold on a sec." She covered the mouthpiece with her hand. "Pete says you're getting some kind of award. You know anything about it?"

"What award? Tonight?"

"What's it for, and when's it happening?" Lucy asked, then relayed the information to Bea. "It's the key to the goddamned city," she laughed, "and they're giving it to you tonight."

"But I thought this was a banquet for some charity or something."

"You're sure about that, Pete?" Lucy asked. "He's sure," she told Bea. "La Guardia himself's going to make the presentation. Apparently, he's a big fan of yours."

"Why didn't anybody tell me?"

"How come we weren't told?" Lucy said into the mouthpiece. "Oh! Somebody messed up. Wonderful! What? Jeez! Okay, I'll tell her." She hung up and said, "You have to give an acceptance speech. Pete says five minutes."

"Oh, holy Hannah! What the hell am I supposed to say?"

"'Thank you' would be good," Lucy said lightly. "You can always wing it, tell them how much you love New York and what a great honor it is, and like that."

Bea lit a fresh cigarette, then lifted the lid on the coffee pot. "Could you order some more coffee, Luce?"

"Sure. Anything else you want?"

"Just the coffee, thanks." She listened to Lucy call room service, becoming more nerved-up by the moment. "This is hopeless!" she announced after five more minutes had passed. "I'm going to soak for a while. If Becky calls, keep her on the line. I want to talk to her."

She threw off her clothes, closed herself into the bathroom, and eased herself into the scented bathwater. At once the heat began to unlock the stiffness in her lower spine as well as the sudden tension created by finding out she'd have to make a speech. A few more hours and the premiere would be over. Hank would be calling to let her know whether it was a hit or a miss.

The telephone rang, and she sat very still, listening. When, after a minute or so, Lucy failed to call out to her, she stopped listening and concentrated instead on slowly raising her legs, one at a time, as high as she could. Her flexibility was only slightly improved after weeks of exercise. And the cold and damp here in the East seemed to have a very adverse effect, causing her hips to hurt which, in turn, made her walk even more hipshot than usual.

Having lifted each leg twenty times, she rested, looking down the length of her body. She still hadn't gained back the weight she'd lost after the accident. Her ribs showed, and her hipbones looked sharp enough to puncture her skin. She thought again of Bobby and experienced a pang of longing so absolute she could do nothing more for several long moments than marvel at her body's treachery and her disloyalty to Hank. She told herself it was nothing, just an absent-minded kind of spasm, a purely physical thing that hadn't anything to do with the actual facts of her life. Yet she did miss him. She'd never thought he'd go away and stay away, making no attempt to maintain their friendship. Maybe it wasn't possible to go back to being friends after having been lovers. Lovers. The very word affected her body. What *was* this? Why was it happening?

Stop it! she told herself. That part of her life was over; there was no point to speculating about Bobby. She pulled the plug and climbed out of the tub to wrap herself in one of the hotel's thick Turkish towels as the water flooded noisily down the drain.

In the bedroom, belting her robe, she stared at the open closet, looking at the gown she'd planned to wear that evening, wondering if it was dressy enough, or too dressy. She opened the door to the living room and started into the room, thinking to ask Lucy's opinion, and came to a stop at the sight of Lucy on the sofa talking to a very pretty auburn-haired woman. Both Lucy and the woman went silent and turned to look at Bea who was unable to stop staring at this surprise visitor. She had lovely brown eyes and smiled so expectantly that Bea felt completely at a loss as the woman got to her feet.

"You don't recognize me," she said, taking stock of the slight figure in the doorway. She'd forgotten how petite Bea was. They were almost the same height, but Bea was a good fifteen or twenty pounds lighter. And she was so charged, she seemed to cause the air around her to shiver with barely contained energy. To meet her smoky, questioning eyes was like risking everything you had ever believed to be true about yourself, because if you'd been suffering from illusions of any sort, Bea would disabuse you of them simply by her gaze. "I knew you wouldn't. You look just the same, but that's probably because I've never missed one of your movies."

"My God! Becky!" Bea opened her arms to embrace her, then had to stand with her hands on Becky's shoulders, exclaiming, "You grew up beautiful!"

Becky laughed, and shook her head. "No, I just grew up."

"There's fresh coffee," Lucy said, slipping away to her adjoining room. "I'll take the calls in here," she said, before closing the door.

"Would you like some coffee? What are you doing here? Come sit down and tell me everything! This is wonderful!"

"You're just the same," Becky said appraisingly. "You still have more energy than any ten people put together. I'd love some coffee. I'm not holding you back, am I? I know you've got an engagement tonight."

"No, no. Tell me! I want to hear all about you. Are you living here now?"

"Actually, when I read you were going to be here, I decided to come down and try to see you."

"I'm so glad you did."

"I hope you won't think it's presumptuous, but I've brought something along for you. I'm sure people must be after you all the time, hounding you about this and that, so if I'm out of line you have to promise you'll say so."

"What is it?"

"It's a script, a movie script. I wrote it for you. I think it's pretty good, but I don't know too much about writing movies, so it might be perfectly dreadful."

"You wrote it for *me*?"

"When you said in one of your letters that you were going to try

279

straight acting, I started thinking about it, and the next thing I knew, I'd written a hundred and fifty-eight pages, complete with dissolves, close-ups, and fade-outs."

"Have you got it with you? I'll read it right away. Where are you staying? Do you have to hurry back to Toronto?"

"If you've got some free time, and we can get together, I'll stay for a few days. There's nothing going on I'm worried about missing. I'm so bored at school, it's a treat not to have to be there. Is this horribly pushy of me?" she asked, looking around the lavish suite, noticing the huge basket of fruit on a side table and several elaborate floral arrangements. "Please tell me if I'm in the way."

"This is the best surprise possible. Honestly!" Bea assured her. "I'll read the script tonight, as soon as I get back. And we can talk about it over breakfast. How would that be?"

"That'd be terrific. God! It's so good to see you! I can't believe I'm really here, that you're really here."

"Becky, you're just gorgeous. You look more like a movie actress than I do."

"Oh, no," Becky disagreed. "You've got the presence. You just *fill* an empty room. I'm too—*brown.*"

Bea stared at her. "I haven't the faintest idea what you're saying," she laughed.

"Neither do I," Becky admitted. "I had the hardest time trying to find you. You're tougher to get to than the president or the prime minister. All those people I had to go through. First the Canadian office. They put me on to the New York office. Then *they* put me on to the Maxwell Agency. And those people thought I was just another one of your fans. D'you mind if I ask you something?"

"Ask me anything."

"Is it awful not being able to answer your own phone and having to have people around to keep other people away? Or do you love it?"

Bea finished pouring two fresh cups of coffee, then sat back and crossed her legs, pulling the robe closed over her knees. "I don't know about how awful it is," she said thoughtfully, "but it's necessary. I guess maybe it is a little awful. In some ways, though, it's what I need. I'm sorry you had such a hard time. It won't happen again."

"It was worth it." Becky smiled happily. "Knowing which hotel you were in and being able to tell them downstairs I was expected was kind of a thrill. It made me feel special, even privileged, because I know you."

"Your being special could never have anything to do with knowing me. You mustn't ever think that way—about anyone. I'm just another person, Becky, who happens to be an actress, staying in a big suite in a ritzy hotel while the studio foots the bill."

"Surely not for all of it. There's a big part of this you, personally, have to maintain, isn't there?"

"I suppose so. Yes, all right, there is."

"You're a star, after all," Becky said, absorbing the details of Bea's reality—her thinness and energy combining to give the impression that she was composed of countless tautly drawn wires; her dark hair pinned haphazardly atop her head so that the length of her neck seemed extraordinary; and her eyes which, at close range, were even more penetrating, more questioning.

"I'm not nearly old enough to be a star," Bea said decisively. "Just thinking about it makes me feel foolish. I mean, women like Shearer and Crawford and Swanson work night and day at that. I prefer to concentrate on what I'm trying to do."

"Which is?"

"Becoming a decent actress. Do you always ask so many questions?"

"I'm afraid so."

"It's unnerving. I have to keep reminding myself I'm not being interviewed. Never mind. Come keep me company while I dress. Bring your coffee. You can fill me in on what you've been doing."

Twenty-Six

"**O**F course you can't gauge reactions accurately with a premiere audience, but I thought it was damned good. There was a great round of applause at the end; we got first-class coverage by the press. So I'd say we're off and running. And how are you? How was the banquet?"

"Oh, it was all right," she said impatiently. "The exciting news is that Becky's here. You remember; I've talked about her."

"Your friend from years back."

"Hank, she's brought me a script she's written. I have a hunch it's going to be good. If I like it and I want to buy it, how much should I offer her?"

"Hold on, Bea. Before you go offering anything, I'd like to read it."

"Don't you trust my judgment?"

"Sure, I do. But whether or not it's produceable is something else again."

"But if I want it, what'm I supposed to do?"

"If she's willing, why not bring her back here to talk? Let me read it, then we can think about negotiating."

"Bring her back with me?"

"Why not?"

"I don't know. All right, I'll talk to both of you after I've read it. I love the title. It's called *Strange Paradise.*"

"That is good. By the way, Ludie sent over a script for you."

"What d'you mean, he sent a script?"

"A picture he wants you to do."

"What about *Wait for Morning?*"

"It's being shifted to the back burner. He wants you to do this other picture first."

"But why?"

"I don't have a whole lot of say in what he decides for you, Bea."

"What if it's terrible?"

"Wait and see," he counseled. "At least he's excited about you again. That's something. And," he reminded her, "it is *his* contract."

"God! All right, I'll wait and see. I'm going to go read Becky's script now."

"Why don't you get some sleep?" he suggested. "You sound frazzled."

"I'm not tired. I'll read it and call you back."

"I hope you're not running yourself ragged, Bea, or letting the publicity boys do it for you."

"I'm *not* tired," she insisted.

"Okay. I'll get out of this monkey suit, have a drink, and wait for you to call."

"I love you, Henry," she said urgently. "I wish you were here."

She really was running near empty. He could tell it from her voice, from the things she was saying, from her near-manic level of energy. It worried him, but there was little he could do long distance to calm her down. "Go read the script," he told her, "and I'll wait up to hear from you."

She put down the phone feeling suddenly shaky. One minute she

was telling Hank she loved him, and in the next, all she could think
about was Bobby. Like portraits in a gallery, images of Bobby were
on display in every area of her brain. The result was an almost in-
tolerable agitation. She got into her nightgown, then stood holding
Becky's script, looking at the bed. Why had everything suddenly taken
on new significance? Why was the bed all at once more than a bed?
In disgust, she carried the script into the living room and settled
herself in a corner of the sofa, lit a cigarette, and began to read.

When she got to the last page, she sighed, lit a fresh cigarette and
reached for the telephone, then waited while the operator put through
the call to California.

"Well?" Hank asked good-naturedly. "What's it like?"

"It's amazingly good. The dialogue is very original, very true-to-
life. It's about this terribly shy woman who decides to write a book,
and the book becomes a great success, and the publishers want her
to make personal appearances to promote it, all that sort of thing.
But she's so nervous and shy that she convinces her best friend to
pretend to be her and make the appearances. Well, the friend goes
off thinking it's great fun and a big laugh, but then she gets caught
up in it and starts enjoying all the attention she's getting. She plays
it to the hilt, dating men who think she's the actual writer, making
commitments to the publisher, and so on, without bothering to tell
the other woman. Meanwhile, the real writer is sitting at home in
this small town, and aside from the money she's making off the book,
her life is just as dreary as it was before. When she tries to get in
touch with her friend, the friend keeps giving her the bum's rush.
So, finally, the writer decides it's time to reveal the hoax and let
everybody know she's actually the one who wrote the book. The
friend doesn't care for that one bit, and there's a wonderful scene in
the hotel room where they meet, and the writer realizes what a monster she's created. Anyway, they hit on a compromise and the writer
agrees to play secretary to her friend so she can stick around and at
least enjoy a little of the reflected glory.

"Well, soon enough, people start finding the secretary a lot more
interesting than the friend, because the friend's so superficial it's hard
to believe she could ever have written a letter home, let alone a best-
selling novel. And as the friend starts realizing the game's going to
come to an end, she pushes the writer to get to work and do another
book, so she can keep the whole show going. At last, the writer's
had enough. She sees that if she doesn't put a stop to this, she could
easily spend the rest of her life playing second banana while her friend
takes the credit and gets all the glory. So in this terrific climax, the

writer gets her courage together and has it out with her friend. She throws the woman out on her ear and gets ready to take control of her life."

"Is there a love interest?"

"Oh, sure. There's this guy who's her editor. He's the one who found the book in the first place and fought to get it published. And all along he's been doubtful and confused about the friend because she doesn't seem to have any frame of reference for what she's written. In the end, the two of them, the editor and the real writer, are planning her next book, and she's still a little shy, but she's talking about something she knows, with someone who really admires her, and the audience knows they're going to wind up together. Hank, it's so good. I *want* this script!"

"When are you seeing Becky again?"

"In a few hours, for breakfast."

"Why not tell her how enthusiastic you are and see if she might be interested in coming back here with you?"

"What if she doesn't *want* to? I really do want this!"

"One step at a time. If she can't, or won't, we can still negotiate. It doesn't mean she's going to take her property somewhere else."

"God! I wish I could phone her right now and talk about it."

"Bea, get some sleep," he advised. "You've still got another two weeks of personal appearances to get through. You're trying to take on too much."

"I won't sleep. I'm too excited."

"I'm starting to get worried about you," he admitted. "You sound like someone who's burning up with a fever."

"I'm perfectly all right," she insisted. "I'm just not sleepy."

"Okay," he backed off. "But don't wake the poor girl up in the middle of the night. Call me tomorrow and bring me up to date. Okay?"

"Of course okay. Goodnight." She hung up, then sat looking around the room. It was three-forty in the morning. She was wide awake and hungry. She got up and went over to examine the basket of fruit, selected a banana, and returned to the sofa. She hated having to wait—for morning, for other people to get up, for an appropriate time.

"To hell with it," she said aloud, and picked up the telephone.

Becky answered at once, sounding wide awake.

"Did I wake you? It's Bea."

"I thought you might call," Becky told her. "I kept imagining you sitting there, reading the script, and I was too nervous to sleep."

"Well, I read it, and I love it. Can you come over? I want to talk."
"I'll get a taxi and be there as soon as I can."

Becky was so fascinated by Bea, by everything about her, that she felt certain she must be giving a totally misleading impression of herself. But she couldn't help watching Bea, studying her, noticing she had definite eccentricities and mannerisms so uniquely her own that on anyone else they'd have been ludicrous. She also appeared to be even more electrically charged than she'd been half a dozen hours earlier. She lit cigarettes one after another and smoked them furiously, talking with a low, rapid delivery that had an edge almost of hysteria to it. She couldn't seem to sit still. She'd perch on the edge of the sofa or one of the chairs—lowering herself in an awkward, painful-looking fashion—and then be up again a minute or two later to go halfway across the room, then stop, positioning herself absent-mindedly as she seemed to snatch ideas out of the air. All the while she smoked furiously, scattering ashes everywhere, pausing to extinguish one cigarette and dump the contents of the ashtray into the wastepaper basket before lighting another. Becky had never known anyone who seemed so positively driven, and she was so lost to her fascination that Bea's enthusiastic comments about the script scarcely seemed important. Here was a young woman who, not very long ago, had been a peculiar little girl living across the street. This Beatrice Crane had been a big-eyed kid with bottle-tops on her shoes, and an odd kind of separateness, an aura of differentness that had so effectively removed her from the realm of little-girlhood that she'd been able to frighten and charm the child that Becky had been. Of course, Becky had always been more than halfway willing to believe in magic and supernatural powers, and Bea had, in her own way, represented both. In some ways, it seemed perfectly logical that Bea should have evolved into the woman she now was. There wasn't anything pretentious, or contrived, about her behavior. She simply seemed to be under the influence of unimaginable pressures.

"You're a writer!" Bea said abruptly, stopping six or seven feet away from where Becky was sitting in one of the armchairs. Her eyes widening, she looked hard at Becky, saying, "I've always believed writers could be dangerous people."

"How?" Becky asked, intrigued, her attention completely caught. "In what way?"

"Because you're always watching, because you see things the rest of us don't. And you're a very good writer, Rebecca. A *very* good writer." Bea backed up, turned to see where she was going, then sat on the edge of the sofa, her eyes still fused to Becky's. "When you were here before, a few hours back, you wanted to know if I liked having people around; you wanted to know how it made me feel; you wanted to refer to me as a movie star; you ate up everything in here, including me, with your eyes, and questions popped out of your mouth like gumballs from a penny machine. Let me tell you something. I *need* to have those people around—Lucy and Hank, Molly, Pete, the publicity boys, the studio people, the agency boys. I need them because I'm not what I used to be. Your dozens of questions made me think about myself, my life, made me see a lot has changed.

"At the beginning, I was all agog because people were interested in me. I was just starting in pictures, and I was grateful for the attention because that meant print space, it meant being mentioned in the columns, it meant I was on my way. I'm still on my way, but it's on a different level. And somewhere along the line, without stopping to think much about it, I started accepting that my position had changed. I just accepted it. I wasn't the same as I'd been. I was a moving-picture actress. People knew who I was, and for reasons I don't begin to claim to understand, they wanted to get near me, touch me, talk to me, even marry me, for God's sake. So, somewhere back there, it stood to reason there had to be people between me and the public. It made good sense. Why should I question it? Success didn't make me crazy or give me a swelled head.

"I remember going to the Biltmore in '35 for the Awards dinner. It was the most amazing crush: a thousand people in the dining room, six thousand jammed into the lobby and the foyer. And counting the votes took forever, right up till eight o'clock. Everybody was so nervous. Anyway, *It Happened One Night* swept the awards, and Gable won. He was stunned and kept repeating over and over, 'I'm still going to wear the same size hat! I'm still going to wear the same size hat!' I loved him for that, because it meant he knew what he'd paid to get there, he'd done it, but he wasn't going to let any of it change the man he'd finally become. Do you understand what I'm saying?"

"Sure, I do."

"Okay!" Bea was up again, pacing back and forth for a minute or two before, once more, posting herself in front of Becky. "Okay, if you understand that, then understand this: I'm Beatrice Crane, and it's too late in the day to change who she is and what that name means. The studio and Ludie are slaving away to make me into a household staple like butter and eggs. They've been building my career since the day I got off the Santa Fe Chief in Los Angeles. And

286

it's *what I've wanted.* Now, I've come to a point where certain things just *are,* as a matter of course. I don't have to ask the price if there's something I want to buy. I accept that attention will be paid to me. I accept that I need people between me and the public. I have the clothes, the money, the lifestyle, and I accept all of that, too. Now, I've invited you, and you've agreed, to come back with me, and I'm not sure you really know what it means."

"I think I do," Becky began.

"No, wait!" Bea held up her hand. "You said you felt special because you knew my hotel, because you were expected, you were someone I knew. Get that out of your head! Knowing me and some small change will buy you a cup of coffee, but not a lot else. I think you've got a few ideas of your own about not being ordinary, and I also think you're going to wind up someone important in your own right. But until that happens, I'm giving you a position in here." She spread her arms to indicate she meant not only the room, but her life. "I can't trust many people. I don't dare anymore."

"I understand that . . ."

"If you're going to be my friend, *be my friend.* Accept me, just as I've got to accept everything that's part of *being* me, without having to buy bigger hats. That means that whatever you see or hear inside my home, inside my life, is private, Becky. I'm willing to cope with the fact that you're a living, breathing, walking question; that everything you see is information that gets filed away somewhere in your head. I'm willing to share myself with you, but please don't ever make me sorry for trusting you. Sometimes I feel very naked, like a window without a curtain. You're tremendously talented, and I want to do your script. I know how to play the game, I know how to give the interviews, and I know how to make movies, but I don't know how to live without people I trust and care about. I need friends as much as I need the career, as much as I need to work at something I love. Just, *please,* don't ever use what you see or hear on the inside of my life."

"I never would," Becky promised.

"And one last thing. Don't take any guff from anyone, me included. Okay?"

"Okay."

"I've got to lie down for an hour or two. You can stretch out on the sofa, if you like. We'll have breakfast at nine. My first appointment's at ten."

"I could go back to my hotel."

"Whatever suits you." Bea stood a moment longer, some of the heat gone now from her eyes. "I really have to lie down," she said, as much to herself as to Becky, as if surprised by how suddenly bone-tired she felt.

After she'd gone, Becky let out her breath and sagged back into the chair. She was beginning to have a very clear picture of how Bea had achieved the degree of success she had. She was strong, even ferocious; she was alert to the merest hint of dishonesty; and she was so vulnerable it was positively scary. Becky felt exhausted, and humbled, and slightly ashamed at having been so impressed by the trappings of Bea's success and at having been caught out at it; she was also more than a little afraid. Maybe the smart thing to do would be to let Bea hang on to the script and take herself home to Toronto.

But she wouldn't do that, she thought, pushing off her shoes. She couldn't possibly do that. She was already too involved.

"**B**ut I'm all wrong for this part, Mr. Meyers. Hank and I have two scripts that I *am* right for. Why use me in something that won't work for any of us? I can think of half a dozen other actresses right off the top of my head who'd be perfect for this picture."

Ludie was immovable. "You start shooting the end of the month," he told her.

She wanted to weep. "Look," she gave it one last try. "I understand you've bought this property. It's not at all a bad script. It's just that I'm not the right female for the lead. You need someone blonde and beautiful, someone with . . . Oh, God, I don't know. A lighter touch than mine. You saw *Jeannie*. You know that's the kind of part I can do. I don't know how to *do* comedy."

"So the next one you'll do *Wait for Morning*. Right now, you do this one."

"All right," she sighed, conceding defeat. "But we do *Wait for Morning* next, okay?"

"Sure okay. I already told Hank, as soon as he's finished with what he's doing, and as soon as you're finished with this, you do this 'Morning' thing. And after that, we'll see what's what with 'Strange' whatever. You should eat more," he said unhappily. "Everywhere I see bones."

"Clothes look good on bones," she said mirthlessly, then said goodbye.

Hank was waiting outside with the car. One look at her face told him Ludie had got his way.

"I could scream," she said from between her teeth as she climbed into the car. "It makes absolutely *no sense* to put me in this part."

"It does to him. He figures your name above the title will bring in more box office than somebody else's."

"Please don't be reasonable about this." She turned, glaring. "We're going to be held up for months because of this piece of lightweight rubbish." She brought the script down hard on her knees. "All the people they've got under contract, and he has to have me to play darling Alice—with a blonde wig, no less. Here we go and do a film that gets rave reviews and is making pots of money, and all he can see is a way to capitalize on my so-called *name* by wasting *my* time and *his* money on a picture that won't draw flies."

"It's only a couple of months," Hank said, waving to the guard as they drove out through the studio gates.

"And what about *you?*" she rounded on him. "Don't tell me you're ecstatic about doing a western!"

"Well." He shrugged. "Maybe it'll do both of us some good to work with new people, learn some new things, freshen our perspectives."

"Jesus! I don't *need* my perspectives freshened. And I want to talk to Jerry about my goddamned contract. It's one thing to have the studio behind me. It's another thing altogether when Ludie starts making arbitrary decisions and throwing me into the stew like a carrot or something."

"Think of it this way: It'll give Becky time to do the rewrites, not to mention getting herself settled and the legalities taken care of with her visa."

"Okay, okay," she backed down. "Everyone's made his point. I'll roll over and play dead like a good dog."

"This might cheer you up." He pulled an envelope from his inside jacket pocket. "From the *New York Times.*"

She pulled the cutting from the envelope, lit a cigarette, scanned the review, then went back to read it more slowly. "...this new Beatrice Crane is a revelation, giving a performance that is powerful and controlled. Her voice, which seemed only appropriate for the reedy ingenues she depicted in her previous films, becomes, with *Jeannie,* a force in itself. Husky and resonant, it has a singer's pitch and tone that lend an interesting contrast to her obvious youthfulness. Her other great attribute, which director Henry Donovan has used to perfection, is her eyes. Those eyes can convey worlds of emotion and meaning, and in several scenes, most notably those with young Elizabeth Hansen who plays Crane's daughter, the combination of her impressive stillness and her pale, sorrowing eyes, have an impact that is all but overpowering. One can only hope that in future films we have more opportunity to see Crane used so simply, and so well."

289

"So?" Hank glanced over as she returned the clipping to its envelope.

"It just makes it even harder for me to understand why Ludie's insisting I play in this piece of crap."

"You'll have to work very hard and try to make something out of it."

She turned to look again at him. "I'm supposed to find this a *challenge?*"

"I don't see any other way you *can* look at it. Bea, I want to say something, and I want you to try not to get angry. Since the accident, but especially in the last few months, you've been like something smoldering. You're very, very angry, and every so often you misdirect your anger. I think I know why you feel the way you do, and I'm not for a moment suggesting you don't have damned good cause. But having a lot of unfocused anger, with no outlet, can be a very bad thing. You've got to try to work it out of your system, find some way to turn how you feel to your own advantage. Because being angry with everyone and everything is doing something to you I'm not sure I care for. Poor Becky's a nervous wreck around you. I don't know what you said to the girl, but most of the time it's as if she's afraid to open her mouth. You're starting to get irascible, and the next thing you know it'll spill over and affect your work. You'll bark at a technician or a grip because something isn't the way you want it, and before you know it, you'll have yourself a reputation for being difficult on the set, hard to handle. You really don't want that to happen. *I* don't want to see it happen. And there's something else I want to say, too. *Please* don't blow your stack, but I told you quite some time ago that things might change, that you'd be surprised to find they probably would. I think a lot of your anger is because you're starting to get back to yourself, you're starting to find out you still care for Bobby, and maybe you've begun thinking about what you gave up. I don't want you to live like a nun for my sake, Bea. I'd hate it. It'd make *me* feel guilty and angry." He stopped and waited for her to respond, but she remained silent, gazing at him. When the silence began to grow cumbersome, he chanced another look at her, saying, "I don't want to see you get hurt, dear heart."

"I know that." Her tone was sadly reflective. "I'm starting to feel as if there's too much going on, too many people in every room. And what if I'm wrong, bringing Becky here, making her feel as awful as you say I do?"

"It was *her* decision, not yours."

"But I feel responsible."

"Well, you're not!" he said flatly. "Don't make the mistake of assuming responsibility for *everything* that goes on. Just be responsible for your own actions. The rest of us can fend for ourselves."

He stopped in the driveway, put the car in neutral, pulled the handbrake, and switched off the ignition. "Look, I know you want to get on with our other projects, you want to work with Becky on her script; you want to feel as if the things you're doing have some kind of sensible direction. Now Ludie's insisting you make a picture you don't want to do, and you feel like going out and murdering somebody because all the anger's bubbling to the boil." She gave him a small smile and, encouraged, he reached out to place his hand on her cheek. "I've been there more times than I care to remember. But try to think of it this way: At most it's a couple of months out of your life. It'll keep Ludie happy. And Ludie happy will keep on building you. You're making a trade. You might not like it, but it won't kill you."

She breathed out slowly, then inhaled until her lungs felt as if they'd burst, and let the air gradually escape until her seemingly ever present anger had been shifted to one side. "You always know the right thing to say to me. I know I've been ranting and raving at everyone. I know I have, and I'm sorry. It's so damned hard sometimes to keep myself all in one piece. I work myself half to death because there's something I want. And then, I get it, and I don't know what the hell to do with it. I don't know if you're entirely right about Bobby, but you're partway right. It doesn't matter, though, because he's cut me out of his life, and maybe that's for the best."

"You'll figure everything out. Give yourself some time. You don't have to get it all done in one day, or one month, or one year. You've got your whole life still ahead of you. Now, come on." He leaned past her to push open the passenger door. "You've got lines to learn for Uncle Ludie's new picture."

She made a face, then got out of the car.

Twenty-Seven

HANK lay awake, his arms folded under his head, listening to the night sounds that seemed augmented both by the lateness of the hour and by his inability to get to sleep. He felt anxious, unsettled, and didn't know why. Turning on his side, he held his breath, trying to see Bea in the sliver of light escaping from the all-but-closed bathroom door. He couldn't tell if she was asleep. Always, she lay so still, her breathing was so subtle, he sometimes experienced a bursting terror at the thought that she might be dead. It was his worst and most private fear, that he'd open his eyes one morning to see her lifeless body beside his in the bed. He'd never dreamed he'd be capable of such an enormous emotional investment in anyone. But Bea was everything to him. She was doting mother on those infrequent occasions when he felt unwell; she was friend, and confidante, and sister. She was also his wife. At moments, the knowledge that they were married, that the word "wife" carried with it all sorts of connotations, made him feel quite drunken with caring and with a profound sense of possession and commitment. Certainly, he felt affection for other people, but even in his most intimate moments with Hero there was lacking that thrill of recognition in unconditional belonging.

Now, to his astonishment and confusion, his feelings for her had turned themselves to reveal an additional facet. He knew precisely when it had happened, and just thinking of that moment, months after the fact, caused him to undergo once again the strange, perturbing reaction he'd had then.

"Are you asleep?" he asked in a whisper.

"No," she answered at once, her head turning toward him. "What's the matter, Poppy? Can't you sleep? Don't you feel well?"

"Bea," he began uncertainly, and had to stop.

"What is it?" she asked, her hand moving through the near-darkness to settle on his arm. "Are you feeling punk?"

"No, no. I'm okay." He paused again, then said, "I want to tell you something, and I'm not sure how, or where, to begin."

She pushed against the bedclothes and came closer, her hand stroking his arm. "Is something wrong, Henry?"

He closed his eyes, touched by the simple signals of their communication. When things were going routinely well, he was Hank. When she was in a particular teasing mood, he was Pop. If she was concerned about his physical well-being, he was Poppy. When matters were serious, he was Henry. Regardless of the credit she gave him for interpreting her moods and silences, she was equally adept at picking up on even the subtlest of his cues.

"Tell me," she urged, close enough so he could feel the heat from her body, could smell the lingering fragrance of her perfume.

"It's strange," he said. "You remember that day I had to cut the scene because your incisions had gone bad?"

"I remember."

"And do you remember we went to your trailer, and you looked at yourself in the mirror, then you lowered the top of your slip so you could see what was wrong?"

Her hand stopped moving on his arm. He waited. She didn't speak.

"It was the first time," he explained, "I've ever felt that way. About a woman, I mean. I was completely thrown, didn't know what to think or how to react."

"Henry," she said very softly, "are you trying to say you want to make love to me?"

"I know how you feel about that," he said quickly.

"*Henry*," she interrupted with gentle force, "just answer me. Do you?"

"I don't know. It feels as if I do, but I'm not sure."

She lay very still, thinking. Until this moment her sexual fears had seemed intact, impenetrable, despite her unsettling thoughts of Bobby during her stay in New York. Now everything was changed, and her fears had suddenly been displaced. She sat up and pulled off her nightgown, then lay back down, her hand once more stroking his arm. His uncertainty transmitted itself to her through his skin, and she was strengthened by the discovery that not only was this something she could do for both of them, but that it was a very small return for all he'd given her. Her hand slid down the length of his arm, found his hand and placed it on her hip. "We can try," she whispered.

"Are you sure? I don't want to force anything on you."

293

In answer, she held his face in her hands and kissed him. "We'll try, and if it's no good, we'll just hold each other until we sleep. Don't worry, Henry. I'll help you."

Nervous but determined, he got out of his pajamas, then sat for a moment on the side of the bed. "Should we have the lights on?" he asked.

"On or off, whichever you prefer."

"I don't know."

"Then we'll have them off. We can always turn them on later. Come here, Henry." She held out her arms to him, and he found his way into her embrace, stunned by her softness. She'd always appeared to him so small and underfed that he'd expected to come into contact with tiny jutting bones and hard, angular surfaces. But she was all soft pliability, a warmth into which he seemed to sink and to which, to his amazement, his body was eagerly responding.

"You feel good," she said, winding her arms around him.

"So do you."

"Is it peculiar?"

"Just different."

"I love you, you know, Henry."

"I know."

"Kiss me again."

All their prior embraces and kisses had familiarized him, he'd thought, with the look and scent and feel of her. But he'd been wrong. He'd known nothing about her before now. She was female, and she'd given herself before, countless times, and she possessed a knowledge he'd simply never considered. The sweetness of her mouth and the sudden shifting of her body beneath his galvanized him, as did the realization that she was entirely his to claim, that the parting of her thighs was an act of private invitation he'd never envisioned. Her entire being was accessible to him; all he had to do was take hold. Her breast fit neatly into his hand, his mouth found its home in the warm curve of her neck. He caressed her and she sighed, her thighs tightening reflexively.

From moment to moment he couldn't believe any of this was happening. One segment of his brain stood in awe of the simple fact of his making love to his wife. Another segment was rapidly recording each new sensation as well as his reaction to it. His body had never before been touched so lightly, so provocatively. Still another segment of his brain was bewildered by the absence of sinew and the utter strangeness of this compliant female body. Yet overall he was being inexorably drawn by curiosity and caring into this unique union, and

294

nothing could have turned him away from seeing it through to completion.

He refused to concern himself with thoughts about the origins of her knowledge. It didn't matter. He could only be grateful, because without her prior experience this couldn't have happened; she wouldn't have known that he required leading. She knew, and with what he viewed as enormous generosity, she unselfconsciously directed him, holding herself open to accept him.

She couldn't possibly contain him, he thought, briefly alarmed. She was too small, her body too tightly compact. But again he was mistaken. It was extraordinary, but not only could she contain him— making good the union with a slow upward thrust—her soft gasp was, he soon ascertained, one of pleasure.

"It's all right?" he asked anxiously, inundated with sensation.

In answer, she fastened her mouth to his as her hips began a metered, mesmeric roll that made him think he might be dreaming, so effectively was he caught in the tidal motion.

"Turn with me," she whispered. "Hold on, and turn with me."

Maintaining the connection, even more deeply captured by the illusion of being towed along in a deep, watery flow, he found himself coasting—a raft, beneath a naked swimmer—as the length of her body undulated upon him. Her rhythm was so persuasive he could only follow her lead, surrendering himself to whatever direction she might choose to take. So caught up was he in the sleekness of her heated flesh and the eagerness of her mouth, that all capability of thought abandoned him until her rhythm peaked and her small body shuddered on his, bringing back his awe and further heightening his need to get to the end of the mystery. Holding her secure, knowing her affinity, he found his own, familiar rhythm and followed it to its completion, then lay with her clasped to his exhausted flesh, waiting for his heart to slow.

"I didn't know this was going to happen," he said, after a time. "Are you all right?"

She leaned away to turn on the light, and they both blinked tiredly until their eyes adjusted. Leaning her chin on her folded arms, the length of her body centered atop his, she looked down at him and smiled. "It was lovely, Henry."

"Really?" He found that difficult to accept.

"I thought I'd lost everything, but you've just shown me that I haven't. I can still do this with someone I care about. I thought I never would again." She raised herself to push the hair out of her eyes, then asked, "Was it the way you thought it might be?"

"I don't know," he answered truthfully. "But I love you even more than I did before for allowing me to see you this way, to know how you are."

"But you're not sure you'd want to do it again."

"I don't think I know anymore what I want."

"It doesn't matter. Honestly. This wasn't a part of what we agreed on."

"I've never lied to you, Bea. Maybe this was inevitable, and I'll find out it's something I want to have happen again."

"I really do understand."

"I've told you from the beginning that I knew a time would come when you'd want to get all the way back into life. This doesn't change any of that, Bea, for either one of us."

"Why is it people are forever giving me permission to do one thing or another? I know what you said then, and I know what you're trying to say now, and it's all right. I'm not stupid, but maybe you are, just a little. Okay, so maybe there'll be someone, and I'll want to be with him. And you'll always be involved with Hero. But none of that has a thing to do with *us*, with you and me. I've always known that. I'll admit I didn't think I could ever again stand to have someone touch me. But you're not just someone, Henry. I'm *married* to you, and I love you. There's no one who could ever come between us; no one, not ever."

"Bea, think about what you're saying. Think about Bobby for a minute. I know what the two of you had."

She sighed and lifted her head again to look at him. "Yes, I loved him. Yes, I still do. But it's not the same as what you and I have. It couldn't ever be, because he wouldn't fight for me."

"Bea, he didn't know how."

"That doesn't matter."

"Yes, it does. I know you. I can see you wondering day after day why he doesn't call, why he's made such a complete break from you. And if he called right now, you'd get up and go to him. Don't deny what you feel for him," he said kindly. "It *is* different, and I don't resent the part of you that's held in reserve for him. If you want to know the whole truth, a little while ago I felt grateful you'd had him because he gave you something you were able to share with me. And," he added importantly, "you've never resented Hero."

"No, but..."

"Well, I don't resent Bobby. What you and I have together is rare and very special, and I won't let anything—not my curiosity or your guilt—interfere with it." He held the hair back from her face with both his hands. "You're wonderful, Bea. You're so wonderful it's hard

296

for me to believe sometimes that you're in my life, that I can lie here at night and listen to the sound of your breathing and think to myself, 'This is some kind of miracle. There's someone in the world I can love with all my heart who doesn't judge me, who doesn't feel superior because she knows her preferences and I thought I did until tonight.' You've been important to me from the beginning, and you will be until the last day of my life. What amazes me is that you're still so young, that you've got years and years of living yet to come, and with any luck at all, I'll be around to share that."

"Don't say any more. You'll make me cry."

"Okay. But thank you for tonight."

"I *told* you not to go on!" she protested and, dropping her head, began to cry.

"I do so love you," he crooned, stroking her hair. "I could never love anyone more."

In a sudden gust of motion, she embraced him fiercely, kissed him hard on the mouth, then pushed herself away and ran into the bathroom. He remained where he was, touching his fingers to his lips.

She stood in the shower, struggling to bring her emotions under control. She felt devastated. Her thighs and pelvic region ached, not only from the unaccustomed sexual activity, but also from her staggering flight away from the things Hank had said to her. Why did he have to be so decent, so tolerant, so sympathetic and understanding? Why did he so consistently display for her the bounty of his affections, when she too often felt unworthy of them? And how could he know and still condone her caring for Bobby? It was, in many ways, horrendous to be so well loved, so well understood. Life would have been infinitely simpler, clearer, if Hank had been a little less than he was. But he was what he was, and that's why she'd accepted his offer of marriage in the first place. Now, by attempting to expand his love and comprehension, he'd erased her fear and, as a result, created an even deeper love for him within her. Because he was so important to her, and because she'd known implicitly how momentous an occasion this had been for him, she'd been able to put her many reservations to one side in order to honor the feelings they had for one another. Yet, despite all of it, he had the wisdom to sense what she'd been making such an effort to conceal from herself: that she was still preoccupied with Bobby, still loved him.

"Why," she confronted Hank upon emerging from the bathroom, "aren't you more selfish? Why are you so willing even to think about sharing me with anyone else?"

"Beatrice, no one has the right to sole and exclusive control over anyone else's life. And let me ask you something. Why are *you* so willing to share *me* with someone else?"

"That's different."

"It is *not*. It is precisely the same thing. Why is it all right for you to be magnanimous where other people are concerned, but positively stringent about yourself? Don't you realize that this is reciprocal, that I'm only trying to return a part of what you give me?"

"You're far more giving than I am," she disagreed.

"You," he pronounced, "are the most giving human being I've ever known. I can't for the life of me see why you apply one set of standards to yourself and an entirely different set to everyone else." He gave her an encouraging smile, the one that made him appear most professorial. "You think that because you're capable of caring for two men, for totally different reasons, it makes you unworthy of the love of either one of them." Seeing that this was indeed the crux of the matter, he went on. "Where does it say we're only allowed to care for one person at a time? Where is that written? And have you ever considered how exceptional you are to be *able* to give such a lot of yourself without ever claiming to feel cheated in any way or left wanting? I know for a fact you never have. You give and give and give, and then feel guilty because your emotional funds are temporarily running a little low. Somewhere along the line you've got to accept that it's your right to take as well as give. My greatest happiness is in having you take whatever it is I try to give you, whether it's advice, one of my long-winded bits of history, an argument, or love. Don't drive yourself crazy because you find it so hard to accept what's being offered. It's being given out of love, and it's only your due."

"Maybe," she said at last, "I'm never going to feel I have the right to so much."

"It was a mistake, wasn't it," he said, "what we did?"

"Oh, Henry," she cried, folding herself over on his chest, "no, no. I'm so . . . *proud* that you'd trust me that way. I'm sorry. If I'd thought I'd make you doubt yourself, I'd never have said a word. You do honor me. That's what's so hard for me. Just when I think there couldn't possibly be more, that no one could *do* more or *be* more for me, you go ahead and do more, become more."

"That's the way I feel about *you*, dear heart."

"God! Why does love have to hurt so much? Why does it have to feel as if it'll split you wide open?"

"I think," he answered carefully, "because it's the ultimate state of nakedness. And it's terrifying to allow other people to see you that way."

298

Hero was silent for quite some time, his features creased in a frown, his hands braced rigidly on his knees. A minute or two passed, then he cleared his throat; his face and arms relaxed. "What else are you trying to tell me?" he asked, his emotions once more in check.

"What else?" Hank stared at him. "There's nothing else. I just felt I had to discuss this with you."

"Why?"

"Because it pertains to you, to us."

"Does it? Does it change anything?" Hero kept his tone conversational.

"Not between the two of us. But maybe in my own mind. I don't know."

"Come sit down," Hero said. "I think we have a few things to straighten out."

Uncertainly, Hank went to sit down. "I shouldn't have said anything," he began.

"Yes and no," Hero cut him off. "Yes, because it's important to you. But I want you to see all the aspects of this. I've been around long enough to know that you and I can't ever have another conversation like this. I respect your feelings for Bea, and if what happened strengthens those feelings, fine. It puts me in a very uncomfortable position when you confide something like this. So, for all our sakes, whatever goes on in future, please don't tell me any more of it. It's not fair to Bea to discuss her with me. And I know you don't discuss me with her. Let's keep it that way. If any one of us knows too much about the other . . . Well, I think you get my point."

"Bea's right," Hank said, looking at his hands. "It does hurt; it does feel as if it'll split you wide open." He took a long, deep breath. "I had to tell you."

"Yes, you did." Hero nodded. "I don't see that you had a choice."

"But I wasn't thinking. I won't subject you to any more of it."

"You didn't subject *me*," Hero corrected him. "You did it to yourself, and to Bea. All right, yes, maybe a little to me. But I've been waiting for this to happen, to tell the truth. It seemed inevitable. I just wasn't quite . . . prepared. You had to tell me. I've listened. Now I'm warning you of the possible side effects. So we all know where we stand."

"Things are too goddamned complicated."

"No, they're not, Hank. But they will be, if you let them."

"I won't allow that. You have my word."

From the first day, everything about *A Drop in the Bucket* seemed destined to go wrong. Charlie DuMont, the director, was a diffident, moody man who gave the impression that what they were embarking upon was a project of such immense scope and value that it would undoubtedly earn everyone involved Academy Awards. The crew, with telling cynicism, went about their work wearing expressions of bemusement. The sets were unspecial, functional but without charm; the art director seemed bored. The costumes were numerous and pretty but lacked line and any definitive style. The cast stayed away from each other for the most part, arriving in time to do their scenes and departing the instant they were no longer needed. John Barrymore, who was sharing title billing with Bea, required prompt cards, which were held off-camera by the prop man. This caused a lot of sniggering on the sidelines which, in turn, made Bea feel sad and defensive on Barrymore's behalf, but she couldn't find any way to communicate either her sympathy to him or her anger with the crew for their unkindness and meanness of spirit. Despite his need for the cards, Barrymore, with his many years of experience, outshone everyone else.

Bea felt like a fool in her blonde pageboy wig and had trouble walking in the very high-heeled shoes that went with every last one of her costumes, even down to a pair of satin mules to be worn with a frivolous peignoir. She was so constantly fearful of taking a spill that she could barely free herself to put any punch into the delivery of her lines. She worked instinctively, almost without help from DuMont, telling the cameraman, "I need a little more room." He pulled back, switched lenses, at the same time telling one of the gaffers to spread the overhead a little. The sound man wanted to know, "When're you gonna move? What's the word cue?" She had to stop, figure that out, deciding she'd make her move a beat after the end of the line, before John's next one. DuMont stood by and watched all this happen, without offering either comment or argument.

During the rehearsals between takes, no one seemed able to come to a decision as to a given scene's focus. Charlie paced back and forth, chainsmoking, encouraging the cast to make their own decisions. After three days of this rather bizarre lack of direction, Bea was starting to panic, missing Hank's clear-cut direction.

Barrymore, who was plainly not in the best of health, took the time to sit with her while they were waiting for a set-up on the fourth day and observed in an undertone, "This picture will be about as funny as a road accident unless we get together. Charlie DuMont has no feel for comedy."

"*None* of it feels right," she agreed, studying the famous profile and finding something terribly touching about the man.

"When I first started in film," he told her, "I found I overacted

300

many of the scenes. I had a feeling that if I worked hard enough I could make the electrician and the cameraman laugh, and they'd take the place of a theater audience. The result was woeful and unreal. Charlie lacks the lightness this sort of piece needs. He certainly doesn't know how to use you to advantage. May I offer a word of advice?"

"Please do. I'd be grateful for any help at all."

"Play it seriously. The key to comedy is the characters' belief in what's happening to them. If one goes for the broad stroke, it simply comes across as grotesque. People will be leaving the theater in droves. So, in spite of Charlie's ponderous hand, play it delicately but for real. I've watched the way you work, seen how you concentrate, and you're very good. I think you may find it helps your focus if you keep the idea firmly in mind that your character doesn't find any of this the least bit amusing."

"Thank you. I'll try to remember that. It makes good sense."

He smiled at her and, for as long as it held, he looked younger and healthier. "You have splendid eyes, splendid eyes. A lifetime ago, I'd have insisted on inviting you to a discreet rendezvous."

She returned his smile, and then, very abruptly, he got up and moved off to one side where he remained, looking at his shoes, until they were ready to shoot the scene.

He gave her sound advice. The insight enabled her to get a grip on the character so she could get through the filming feeling considerably less detached and disoriented. Charlie DuMont either didn't notice or care that she'd changed her approach to the part. The scenes with Barrymore went particularly well, she thought. He gave a great deal, allowing her much room for reaction. She found him very generous and altogether professional.

They got through it on schedule, even under budget, and she and Hank attended the wrap party for purely political reasons. She presented small gifts to the crew and the supporting cast, gave Charlie DuMont a pair of gold cufflinks, then went over to Barrymore to present him with the only gift she'd found suitable.

Barrymore opened the envelope, looked at its contents, and emitted peal after peal of delighted laughter.

"I couldn't have asked for anything better!" he declared. Then to Hank, he said, "You will forgive me, I hope, for this slight liberty," and gave Bea a kiss.

"What did you give him?" Hank asked on the way home.

"An antique dance card. I dated it 1839 and filled his name in for every dance. I knew he'd like it."

To everyone's surprise, *A Drop in the Bucket* did very well at the box office, despite mixed reviews and Bosley Crowther's observation in the *New York Times* that "... it was disappointing, but not entirely, to find Beatrice Crane the centerpiece of this limp-wristed farce. It's becoming clear that she's incapable of turning in a bad performance, regardless of the material she sometimes has to work with. There are moments with Barrymore that are worth the price of admission, but she deserves better fare."

In the course of a lengthy and vociferous meeting with Ludie, Jerry battled to get her, not only a hefty increase in salary, but script approval as well.

"There may be more *Buckets*," Jerry told her on the telephone afterwards. "He wouldn't go all the way, but he's promised 'consultation.' You might as well know he's already talking about some piece of dreck he's sending over for you to read, but I think you might be able to stamp your little foot and say no."

"Well, thank heaven."

"Don't thank heaven, sweetheart," Jerry chuckled. "Thank me."

Twenty-Eight

"MR. Bradley's certainly busy as a little beaver these days, 'being seen' with half the women in Hollywood," Lucy said, turning the pages of *Photoplay*. She was sitting at the kitchen table with Molly. In the background played "Lux Radio Theater," to which Molly listened devotedly. Her other favorites were "Allen's Alley," "Suspense," and "Fibber McGee and Molly." The radio provided a constant accompaniment to everything that went on either in the kitchen or in Molly's room. She'd been more excited about Bea's doing the radio adaptation of *Jeannie* on "Lux Radio Theater" than almost anything else Bea had done, and Molly had sat with her ear nearly touching the Atwater-Kent's speaker, scarcely daring to breathe until the show ended.

"In the last month," Lucy went on, "he was 'seen' at the Cocoanut Grove with Joan Crawford who's on the loose again after the 'tragic break-up' of her marriage to Franchot Tone. He also attended the premiere of Crawford's latest, *The Women*, with 'beautiful young redhead Susan Hayward, who's currently featured in *$1000 a Touchdown.'* Sounds like one swell movie." Lucy made a face. "He was also spotted dining 'head-to-head' with Elizabeth Ruth Grable, better known as 'Betty' who, 'it is rumored, is about an inch away from splitting up with hubbie Jackie Coogan.' Grable, in case we're interested, is work- ing on what will undoubtedly become a masterpiece called *The Day the Bookies Wept.*" Lucy took a breath, then continued. "In this same month, the high-stepping Mr.Bradley was seen having lunch at the Brown Derby with up-and-coming starlet Constance Keane, who's presently appearing in yet another classic for our times called *Sorority House.* He was *also* seen in the company of Norma Shearer, if you don't mind; and Ann Sheridan who 'recently split up with hubbie Edward Norris'; *and* screenwriter Zoe Akins; *and* Mae Busch who is about to go into production on something called *Women Without Names;* and last, but not least, newcomer from Broadway, Betty Field. Makes you wonder when he has time to sleep, never mind getting any work done."

"Sure sounds like one busy fella," Molly agreed, selecting a copy of *Screen Romances* from the stack of magazines on the table. After flipping quickly through the pages, she said, "You got the new *Modern Screen* there? Says here this month's true-life story's about Miss Bea. 'The girl who was born of poor parents in a humble home in Canada, who came to Hollywood a poor but talented creature, is gone. At least outwardly so. In her place is a beautiful and fascinating person- ality, a woman of the world, cultured, famous. The highlights and depths to her life story have left a suggestion of tragedy about her, a sort of wistfulness that is apparent even when she smiles. The private life of one of the screen's most glamorous personalities, the complete true life story of Beatrice Crane appears in the May issue of *Modern Screen.* Now on sale for ten cents.' I sure would be interested in reading about that," Molly said with sarcasm.

"You know it's all hokum," Lucy said, pushing through the peri- odicals. "It was here somewhere."

"Don't matter," Molly said. "I didn't specially want to read it any- how."

"It's the usual crap, with stills from *A Drop in the Bucket* and some supposedly candid shots of Hank and Bea on the golf course." She snorted, put down her magazine, and got up to fill the kettle. "The golf course, for Pete's sake! Next thing anybody knows, they'll have the two of them on horseback."

The doorbell went, and Molly got up, saying, "Who could that be this time of night?"

Lucy didn't bother to answer but put the kettle on the burner and opened the cupboard to get the teapot. Molly returned with Becky in tow.

"I was bored, so I thought I'd come over, see what everybody's doing," Becky told them.

"We're reading the lastest crop of fan mags and shooting the breeze," Lucy said. "Want some tea?"

"Sure, thanks."

Becky sat down and pushed aside some of the magazines, leaning her arms on the table. Molly went to turn down the volume on the radio.

"How's the writing going?" Lucy asked, setting out an extra cup.

"I'm almost finished."

"You *think* you're almost finished. Wait till they've got you in a portable on the set with a typewriter, doing rewrites while they're breathing down your neck."

"Where's Bea, and Hank?" Becky looked around.

"They're at the premiere of Bobby's new picture. Personally, I think she's crazy, but they went. There's a bash after, at the Trocadero."

"Why is she crazy to go?"

"Ancient history," Lucy said. "He's still carrying a big torch for her, and he keeps trying to put it out with every woman in town. He'll be there tonight with some blonde beauty, and it'll upset the hell out of Bea. She'll probably come home fit to be tied."

"So, then, why go?"

"Lots of reasons. First, to be seen. It's publicity. Second, to get it mentioned that they've just finished *Wait for Morning*. And third, because she wants people to see that even though neither of them acts as if they are, they're still friends."

"Oh!"

Lucy put tea into the teapot, then added the boiling water. "So, Becky, how d'you like it out here so far?"

"It's strange. I have a lot of trouble believing it's real. I mean, there's a coffee shop where I go sometimes for breakfast when I've been up all night working; it's just an ordinary coffee shop, nothing special. But every time I go in there, you'd swear everybody in the place is auditioning for something. Nobody looks normal. Everyone's posing. Maybe it's just me. Who knows? Anyway, the weather's nice, and I like being able to go to the beach whenever I feel like it."

"But you'd rather be up to your knees in snow." Lucy smiled as she poured the tea.

"Maybe. I keep seeing the strangest people. There's this one woman, she wears a long, long blonde wig, and all this make-up on her eyes, with little lines drawn underneath—you know, the way they draw the eyelashes on dolls? I keep seeing her, and she makes me feel so sad. I wonder about her, wonder if she used to be someone once upon a time. And there's this other woman, who wears the most amazing clothes, skin-tight, and the highest high-heels I've ever seen. She's pretty old, probably around fifty. And the strange thing about her is that the clothes actually look pretty good. I mean, she's got a decent figure, and she doesn't wear strange make-up or anything. It's just the way she walks. I swear she used to be a dancer; she's got that very straight spine, and she turns out when she walks. Then there are all the men with the Van Dyke beards, and the artist's smocks, and the riding boots. I mean, who *are* those people? I start making up stories for them, and the next thing I know, I've been sitting in the coffee shop for three hours and I've had so much coffee my bladder's about to explode." She laughed. "Anyway, I'll stick around for a while. I wouldn't want to miss seeing the picture get done." She lifted a magazine then let it drop. "You don't really read all these every month, do you?"

"I go through them, cut out anything about Hank or Bea. A few of the articles I read. We get them as soon as they come out, then Molly and I sit around for a couple of evenings, going through them, having a good laugh."

"Tell me about Bobby," Becky asked. "What's the story?"

"Uh-uh." Lucy shook her head. "Ask Bea, not me. Why're you so interested anyway?"

"Just curious. I saw all their pictures, so I suppose I'm wondering what went wrong."

"It's pretty simple," Lucy said, keeping a rein on her suspicions. "Bea can't dance anymore, so no more pictures with Bobby. And she married Hank." Becky asked one hell of a lot of questions, and although Lucy instinctively liked her, her relentless questioning sometimes struck a wrong note, a note that moved Lucy to wonder if there was more to Becky's curiosity than simple interest. Then she'd look at Becky's guileless brown eyes and decide, as Bea had, that curiosity was part of Becky's equipment as a writer. Nevertheless, every so often it was hard to buy that, primarily because Becky never let up. She asked about everything and anything and, from time to time, it became extremely irritating. Several times Bea had exploded, scaring Becky half to death, by shouting at her. Becky had apologized, falling all over herself trying to explain. And Bea had, in turn, said she was sorry, too, but would Becky please try to read the prevailing mood, at the very least, before letting fly with her endless questions.

"You think I talk too much," Becky said as Lucy brought over the tea and sat down. "I know I do," she went on, as if revealing a terrible personal flaw. "I honestly can't help it. I have to know why things are the way they are, how they got to be that way, why people do the things they do. It drives everyone crazy, I know. I tell myself not to do it, but the next thing I know I'm asking away, and everybody's pulling back from me. I know Bea hates it, and I get upset because it's just me and I don't mean anything by it."

"Maybe you should learn to watch," Lucy advised cannily. "Keep your eyes and ears open. That way you'll find out what you want to know, and you'll still have some friends left down the road."

"It's very strange, this town." Becky turned her teacup around and around. "If people aren't auditioning everywhere you go, they're watching everybody else to make sure they don't steal their ideas, or their thunder, or their husbands, or their part in some movie. This is the whole world, and nothing else exists. Most folks I've met don't even know there's a war going on in Europe, and the ones who do know don't care. I don't think I can live this way for very long, so cut off from reality."

"It takes special skills," Lucy told her.

"The way I see it, it's sort of like a great big game, and everybody wants to play."

"That's about right."

"What doesn't make sense is why someone as practical as Bea would want to stay here."

"She's got a career here, Becky."

"I know that. But she could still have her career and live somewhere else."

"Oh? Where would you suggest?"

"I don't know. New York, maybe."

"And if they called her and said be ready to start shooting next week?"

Becky nodded. "Point made. I guess I'm lucky, really. I can do what I do, and I don't need to be here to do it."

"But you want to stay," Lucy said, beginning to get a fix on the girl, "because you haven't got the whole thing figured out yet."

Becky looked over and smiled. "You sure have got my number."

"Just go easy on the questions," Lucy told her. "Especially around this house. You've got a very powerful friend in Bea."

"That's the thing that really amazes me about her," Becky said eagerly. "She *does* have power, but she doesn't even seem to know it. Or if she does, it's as if she doesn't care. And I don't get it. I thought the whole thing was about power, about getting it, and keeping it, and using it."

"You don't know Bea," Lucy said quietly. "Maybe she does have it, but she could care less about keeping it or using it. Except where she can see something good might come out of it. She used it for Bobby. And now she's using it again for you. That's why I'm telling you: Don't keep pushing away with all your questions. It could, if you're not careful, blow up in your face."

Bea's favorite designer, Howard Greer, had created her look for the evening. The dress was of black silk, with a square neckline scalloped to fall flat just over the tops of her breasts, with ribbon-thin shoulder straps. The bodice was shirred to the hips, where the fabric gave way to free folds that fell to the floor. Under Howard's supervision, her hair had been sculpted cleanly back from her face and, behind the ears, it was shaped over a large, curved rat so that it sat, smoothly full, from above her ears to the nape of her neck. She wore a heavy necklace, Egyptian in design, with four tiers of red, white, and green semi-precious gemstones; her earrings and bracelet matched the necklace, and her only other jewelry consisted of her wedding and engagement rings. Over her shoulders lay a chinchilla stole. Her nails had been lacquered a pure red to point up the color of the necklace. She wore little make-up, just mascara, a hint of rouge, and lipstick to match the nailpolish. The black dress and the bright red lipstick complemented her pale skin and dark hair, and Hank couldn't stop commenting on how beautiful she looked. She, too, was very pleased. Her only problem was the shoes—black silk with heels that were somewhat too high, so she had to move slowly, which emphasized her hipshot walk.

Tip-Top showed that Bobby had lost none of his energy or inventiveness in the dance numbers, but the plot was almost nonexistent, and his most recent dancing partner was, despite her exceptional good looks and lithe body, no match for him. There was polite applause as the lights came on, and then people started up the aisles.

Outside, screaming fans crowded the bleachers that had been set up for the occasion, and searchlights sliced the sky. Over a loudspeaker, a voice announced the arrival of the departing star's cars. Constance Bennett climbed into the wicker-box body of a Rolls Phaeton as a spotlight held her. Tom Mix, wearing a white ten-gallon hat, drove himself off in a white, open Packard. Marlene Dietrich's black Cadillac was brought up by her chauffeur, Briggs, who was known to carry two revolvers and who, in winter, wore a uniform with a mink collar. Finally, Hank's Packard Phaeton was brought up. He held open the door, Bea got in, he ran to climb behind the wheel, and then they were on their way to the Trocadero on Sunset.

Bea was laughing as they left the mob scene behind. "I think the fans are disappointed we don't have someone like Briggs to hold the crowds at bay with a pair of six-guns."

"They'll have to live with it," he said with a laugh. "I prefer to drive myself, thank you very much."

"Promise me we'll have something to eat, then get out of there and go home."

"If that's what you want. But I don't think you'll be able to sneak away all that easily. For one thing, Jerry'll be there with Brenda. So will Ludie. More photos of everyone having a swell time. You look positively glorious."

She finished lighting a cigarette. "Maybe we could get Howard to do all my pictures. He makes everyone look so good. He used to do Pickford, he told me, and Theda Bara, Swanson. What ever happened to Theda Bara, do you know?"

"Ah! A question for Professor Donovan," he laughed again. "Theda Bara," he said, as if the name had a good taste. "Fox created her out of nothing. All told, she lasted maybe four years from start to finish. She was entirely a figment of the publicity boys' imagination.

"Theodosia Goodman: a nice Jewish girl from Cincinnati, daughter of a tailor. Her one gimmick was her fascination with the occult. Fox's director, Frank Powell, met her in New York, and all that occult business appealed to him. So he cast her in *A Fool There Was*, as a vampire, no less, back in '15. The public loved 'the vamp,' and the next thing anybody knew there were wild rumors and stories about her—planted by Fox, of course. They sold her as 'the exotic horror,' and the public ate it up like candy. Fox kept her busy; thirty-five or forty pictures from '15 to '19, rafts of interviews and personal appearances, and four thousand a week. She had the good sense to retire, and for the last however many years, she's been *the* Hollywood hostess. She gives gourmet dinner parties, and she's bored out of her mind, otherwise."

"Who goes to these parties?"

"The older set. Not us, sister. We're nouveau, I'm sorry to say. But you never know. Stick around long enough, and we might get ourselves invited to chow down with Theda."

"Oh, God! We're here already." She stubbed out the cigarette and opened her bag to check her lipstick in the pocket mirror. For the eighty-four minutes while the film ran, she'd managed to relax, secure in the knowledge that for those minutes there was no possibility she'd encounter Bobby. The film had ended, and her tension restructured itself during the time it took them to leave the theater and get into the car. Ten or twelve minutes of reprieve while they drove from the

308

theater to the restaurant, and now her hands were so unsteady she could barely get the lipstick to her mouth.

Hank said, "If you'd honestly rather not do this, we can turn around and go home."

"*That* would be *criminal,*" she quipped, not without effort. "I'll never be able to wear this outfit again."

He put his hand on her arm. "You could always hold a fashion show for me. I'll take the wing chair in the living room, then you'll put on dress number one and make an entrance."

"Henry," she said tremulously, feeling the need to weep suddenly building inside her chest, "every so often, life goes out of control. Tonight is one of those occasions. The only way I can get through this is by getting through it. If I kiss you, I'll make a mess of both of us."

"Then you stay perfectly still, and I'll kiss you." Holding her shoulders, he kissed her on each cheek, then asked, "Ready?"

"Ready."

The car jockey who'd been patiently waiting curbside leaped into action the moment Hank moved to get out of the car. He opened the passenger door for Bea just as Hank got there to offer his hand to help her out. It was one of those gestures people assumed were mannerly. But in reality she needed his assistance to get out of the car without appearing all but crippled. Her arm secure through his, they entered the club, to be hit at once by the noise of the assembled crowd. The air was thick with cigarette and cigar smoke and the yeasty fumes of alcohol-tainted breath. For a few seconds, she wished she was a kid again, concerned only with the sounds her feet could create; she wished she could go back to a time when all this had seemed magical and hardly believable. How was it possible she'd become accustomed to the life she was leading? There'd been so many experiences that had brought her to this point; she'd managed to acquire a personal history, an inventory of past circumstances that affected everything she did, thought, and considered now. Everywhere she went, she carried with her some portion of that inventory. And no matter how badly she might have longed to enter into a given moment unencumbered by anything more than her own enthusiasm, it would never again be that way.

She didn't want to have to see Bobby with another woman and couldn't help remembering his anger years before when he'd talked about how he'd felt seeing her with other men.

Too many times in the last couple of years she'd had to make appearances at functions only to see Bobby with some woman draped over his arm. It might have been tolerable if she and Bobby had had any vestige left of their former closeness. Since they didn't, the sight of one woman after another clinging to him was, to Bea, like discovering she'd unwittingly presented herself in the midst of an immense gathering with one breast bared. She checked herself repeatedly to be certain her worst and most private fear hadn't been realized, yet she could never rid herself of that feeling of being denuded. On the occasions when they came face to face, they exchanged words and smiles, even on-the-cheek kisses, solely for the benefit of whoever might be nearby watching, and for the cameras that were always there to document their activities. It was agony for her, and she wondered each time what Bobby must think.

"Are you all right?" Hank was asking in an undertone.

"No," she answered, "but I'll survive. Where d'you suppose our table is?"

"I see Jerry over there, in the middle. Last chance," he offered. "We can still get out of here and go home."

She looked behind them to see they were holding up the others crowding in through the door. Automatically, Hank followed her gaze, saw, and moved with her to one side to allow the others to go by. She leaned against the wall, and he looked at her, all at once able to see how she was going to look in twenty or thirty years' time. Apprehension shadowed her eyes and tightened her mouth. Perhaps it was no more than an illusion created by the dim lighting in the foyer, but he could have sworn she was actually aging right in front of his eyes. It was alarming, especially since her hand had tightened on his arm as she looked away into the interior of the club. He lowered his eyes to see her shiny, red-polished nails embedded in his sleeve. For some reason, he was always surprised by her hands which he thought of as small but which were, in fact, quite large and long-fingered, broad in the palms. He'd once imagined dancers would have beautiful feet and had been shocked to discover that dancers' feet were more often than not misshapen and anything but beautiful. So many illusions. Everyone had them about all sorts of things. But he had none about what was happening just then.

Bobby was at the center of a good-sized crowd. On his arm was the mandatory beautiful woman. This one was a long-haired, sloe-eyed blonde Hank had seen before, called Keane. Bobby was smiling and nodding, but his eyes were on Bea. And Bea, like something skewered by a sword, was fixed helplessly beneath his gaze, breathing shallowly, her lips slightly parted. As Hank watched, Bobby said something to the blonde and detached himself to begin working his way through the crowd. Turning, Hank saw Bea come away from the wall, her grip on her arm easing gradually until there was no more contact between them.

"Hello, Hank." Bobby offered his hand, and Hank shook it. "Do you mind if I have a minute with Bea?"

Bea seemed to tear her eyes away from Bobby with great difficulty. "I won't be long," she told Hank. "I'll join you at the table."

"Certainly." Hank took one step away, and another, then turned and headed toward the table where Jerry and his wife, and the Meyers, were already seated.

"Let's get some fresh air," Bobby suggested, and taking her arm, he propelled Bea out of the club. Instead of starting along the street with her, as she'd expected, he directed her into the parking lot, walking with her until they were at the very rear of the lot, out of sight of anyone but the car jockeys who were far too busy to pay any attention to them.

She looked toward the front of the lot, watching the progress of one of the young men as he jumped from a silver Rolls and raced back toward the entrance. Bobby pulled a sterling cigarette case from his pocket and held it out to her. She took a cigarette, then waited for him to light it. The air was cool but heavy, as if a giant fan somewhere had iced the top of the air while, underneath, it remained thickly liquid. It would undoubtedly rain in the night.

"So," Bobby tried for an offhand note. "How's married life these days?"

"Surely you didn't bring me out to the parking lot to talk about my marriage?" she rasped, her voice deep with anger and too many cigarettes. "It's fine! We're very happy."

"Well, good. I'm glad to hear it."

"Christ! You're not glad in the least to hear it," she accused. "You'd love it if I were to stand here and confess that I'm miserable, that I wish I'd never done it."

"You're right. I would love that."

"Well, sorry. Hank and I are very happy. Why are you doing what you are?"

"What am I doing?"

She puffed on the cigarette, trying to think how to answer. "It would seem," she said, selecting her words with deadly precision, "that you've become a one-man consolation crew, soothing every woman in town who's either on the brink of a divorce or just got one. I suppose you were hoping I'd admit I was going to be the next in line, in need of your services."

311

"That's a hell of a thing to say! You know damned well most of these things are arranged. I go where I'm told, when I'm told, with whom I'm told."

"Spare me! You're past that stage, and so am I. Neither one of us *has* to do that sort of thing anymore. You do it because you want to."

"Well, there's where you're wrong. I do it to keep from going crazy. Of course, I could always stay home nights and drink myself to sleep, but I've never been much of a booze-hound and it's kind of half-assed to think about making myself sick just to live up to somebody's romantic notion."

"Notion of what?"

"Let's drop it. I didn't want to get into a fight."

"What *did* you want?"

"Who knows?" He took another drag on his cigarette, then dropped it to the ground and stepped on it with the toe of his handmade patent-leather evening pump. "Maybe I thought I'd get you alone for a minute or two, say a few words, and straighten some of this out."

"What were the magic words going to be?" She drew so hard on her cigarette that she burned her fingers. She winced and, disgusted, threw it away. It landed on the ground a few feet away in a small burst of sparks.

"I love you. I miss you. I'm going crazy without you. I hate dancing with anybody else. I've never been so lonely. I don't know what anything's about anymore. Nothing's changed. Everything's changed. I'm starting to lose my hair, bunches of it in my brushes. I stand there and look at the brushes and think, Jesus Christ, I'm getting old. I'm out here in Wonderland, playing with the ladies, supposed to be having the time of my life, and it's rotten, all of it."

"Oh!" She reached to pull the chinchilla more closely around her shoulders, feeling the chill.

"That's it?" he asked. "That's all? 'Oh'?"

"What d'you want me to say?"

"Say you love me, you miss me, you're going crazy without me, you wish you could be dancing with me, you're lonely."

"I *can't* say any of that."

"Okay, you can't say it." He shrugged and tossed his head, jammed his hands into his tuxedo pockets, and looked at her. "You can't say it, but do you think it?"

"Bobby, I really should get back inside..."

"Just tell me the truth, and we'll go back in."

"Yes," she admitted in a whisper. "I think it."

"You're cold," he said suddenly, his hands going to adjust her fur. He came closer, and she looked up at him fearfully.

"Don't!" she said softly. "I have to go back in there, and if you . . . if we do, I won't be able . . ."

"Okay." With an exaggerated motion he held his hands well away from her, backed up a step, and returned his hands to his pockets. Then, determined not to lose the moment, he said, "If I call you, will you meet me?"

She lowered her eyes briefly, then looked again toward the front of the lot where two of the jockeys were having a race back to the entrance. "I think we should leave well enough alone," she answered.

"*Well enough?*" He laughed bitterly. "You consider this 'well enough'?"

"I thought we'd be friends . . ."

"Hank won't hold you back."

"I *love* Hank."

"I really believe you do. But you love me, too."

"Why don't you marry one of those women?" she said despairingly.

"I'll tell you something," he said harshly, grabbing hold of her wrist. "I'm not marrying *anyone*. Got that? Not anyone, not ever. Unless it's you."

"*Jesus Christ, Bobby!*" she cried, wrenching her arm free. "*Leave me be!*" She started across the parking lot, forced to walk at less than desired speed because of the dangerous shoes.

"IF I CALL YOU," he shouted after her, "WILL YOU MEET ME?"

She stopped halfway across the lot, turned fully, and, trembling all over, cried "YES!" then blindly hurried, as best she was able, back to the club.

Twenty-Nine

BOBBY didn't call. Ludie did, however, to say, "I've got this picture I want you to do. The script's on its way over."

"We're in preproduction for *Strange Paradise*," she told him. "You know that, Mr. Meyers."

"So you'll put it on the shelf a couple months. This one you'll do first."

"Mr. Meyers..."

"You'll get the script, you'll read it, then we'll talk." He put down the telephone, and she was left with a dead instrument in her hand and an immediate anger. She called Jerry.

"I thought you told me there wasn't going to be any more of this. We're about to get going on Becky's script, and now Ludie's sending over another 'pictsha' he wants me to do. What's going *on*, Jerry?"

She knew at once from his tone that he'd been aware of Ludie's move. "Wait and read the script," he said placatingly.

"We all know Ludie's got a passion for the garbage everybody else turns down. I don't have to wait to read this one to know it'll be all wrong for me. And if it's not all wrong, it'll have the worst dialogue ever and no characterization."

"Before we can start fighting him, you've got to read it."

"*Okay!* I'll read it! And if it's as rotten as I know it's going to be, I'm saying no. *Why* does he keep doing this? He's approved *Strange Paradise*, for God's sake! Hank's set; the crew's set; everything's set. Now he wants us to put back the starting date, rearrange our lives, and make magic out of his latest overpriced turkey."

"Calm down, Bea. A copy's on its way over to me, too. Let's do our homework and then we'll talk."

"I'll tell you right now: If this is as bad as I think it's going to be, I'll go on suspension before I agree to do another picture that makes me look like I woke up one morning in somebody else's house."

Jerry laughed. "Call me after you read it."

Within half an hour, a studio messenger delivered the script. She carried it, and a cup of coffee, up to the bedroom, sat down, lit a cigarette, took a swallow of the coffee, then started to read. An hour and a half later, she was so livid she thought she might start screaming and never stop. She stormed downstairs to the dining room where Hank sat working on the shooting script for *Strange Paradise*. She threw Ludie's script down on the table, her rage overflowing.

"*He wants me to do that! It's even worse than* A Drop in the Bucket. *I won't do it!* I'd rather never work *again* than have to do these asinine scripts. I can't keep making a good picture that gets good reviews, does terrifically at the box office, then move along into a piece of *crap* so Ludie can capitalize on the good movie. A few more of these and people will stop going to *see* my pictures."

"Is it that bad?"

"It's worse! Jerry's waiting for me to call him. I think he thinks I should do it, just to keep Ludie happy. Hank, I *can't!* Why doesn't he get Glenda to do it? She's happy going from a starring role in one picture, to playing a bit part in the next; she says it gives her a chance to get some rest. She wants to rest, let *her* do this! I'm sick of being used by Ludie like some kind of human bandage he puts on sick scripts."

"Sit down a minute," Hank said. She did, and held her hands knotted together in her lap. "You're talking about going on suspension. If you do that, not only will you be suspended for the duration of the picture, but Ludie has the right to suspend you for half that amount of time again as a punishment. On top of that, the entire length of your suspension will be tacked on to the end of the contract. So not only will you be out several months' salary, but you'll have another three or four or five months' additional servitude to Ludie, to boot."

"I don't care!" she flared the instant he stopped speaking.

"You've *got* to care! If you take suspension for that"—he indicated the script—"it not only means you'll sit home twiddling your thumbs, it also means we might find ourselves without financing to do *Strange Paradise.*"

"*Why?*" she asked, shocked.

"Because Ludie won't take your refusal lightly. I mean, did you seriously think he'd just let you go on suspension and then, when the time was up, give you his blessings to get on with what you'd really wanted to do all along? Never. He'd *never* go for it."

"So what should I do?"

"See what Jerry has to say. You may have to swallow your pride and do the picture."

"I won't do it!"

"How bad is it, anyway?" he asked, leaning across the table to pick up the script.

"It's not that terrible," she relented. "I'm just wrong for the part."

"Answer me this: *Could* you do it? Is there anything you could make out of it?"

"Oh, sure," she replied, "if I turn into a contortionist, or maybe apply my character from the outside in, with make-up, like Muni. *God damn it!* I don't *want* to do it! I don't want to have to worry myself sick trying to figure out how to get an audience to buy me as another featherweight, with gelatin for brains."

"But you could do it," he prompted.

"I could," she conceded. "But I won't."

"Bea, you may have to."

She stared at him feeling as if the burden of her frustration might cause her to burst apart at the seams. She didn't want to believe what

315

he was telling her; yet, unarguably, he was right. "I'll call Jerry," she said, getting up. "But this isn't over yet."

Jerry's remarks were merely a variation on Hank's. He wound down with, "You could end up in a lot of hot water, Bea. Suspension's serious business. You don't want to do anything rash."

"I *do*, Jerry! I want to be rash as hell. I want to drive over to the studio, march into Ludie's office, and tell him in no uncertain terms what he can do with this piece of garbage. *Back Door*, for God's sake!" She drew in her breath, then let it out slowly before asking, "Tell me what you think he'll do if I say I'll go on suspension before I agree to do this picture."

"He's not that predictable. He could decide he admires you for taking a stand and let you off the hook. Or he could decide you're getting too big for your britches and take you down a peg or two. In the end, naturally, it's your decision, but I'd advise against confronting him." He hesitated, knowing he was risking her not inconsiderable anger, then said, "I know you hate the part, but I've got to say I think you could do something with it. You're good enough to make the part your own."

"My own *what*? I'm supposed to find that some kind of incentive, Jerry?"

"I'm only saying it's not a one-hundred-percent total loss, as parts go. I've seen better, and I've seen worse."

"You're saying I'm so goddamned good I can turn this pathetic gutless creature *into* something and, by some mystical process, that'll make it a good picture. Let's just, for the sake of argument, say I agree. What's to stop Ludie from doing this to me over and over again?"

"Now, that's something we can talk about. My suggestion is this: We'll set up a meeting. We'll go in and say you're prepared to do the part *but*. The 'but' is, number one, this is the last time he can shuffle you around this way, and we get it in writing; number two, we insist on your having script approval. The thing is, Bea, if you go into him prepared to make a concession, he'll be more inclined to give you what you want. But nobody faces Ludie point blank with flat-out refusals. It tends to make him a little vengeful, not to mention angry. So we use this script for leverage. Between this one and *Strange Paradise*, your contract time will get used up, and we're back to negotiating. I say we negotiate right now."

"You said last time that I'd be able to stamp my little foot and say no. I'm here stamping like crazy and saying no, and you're telling me to say yes. Why should I believe you? I keep winding up in the soup."

"Not this time," he promised. "Here's what I'm going to get for you: the right to make a picture a year for an outside studio; the right to choose your own cameraman; director approval; supporting-cast approval; the right to park your goddamn car on the studio grounds instead of using the lot; the right to pick your own make-up man, hairdresser, and crew. *And,* we'll get Ludie to knock out the morals clause in your contract. So you could have yourself one pip of a scandal, and he wouldn't have the right to fire you because of it."

"Jesus, Jerry! Does anybody actually have all that?"

"Lombard does, for one."

"And you think you can get him to give me the same?"

"I'm sure of it. He needs you, Bea. You're pulling in a lot of box office. You've been back in the top ten two years running. Don't you think he wants to keep you there?"

"If this backfires, Jerry," she warned, "I'll quit before I do another compromise deal. I'll leave the goddamned *country* first."

"It won't backfire. I'll call Ludie and set up an appointment."

"Damn!" she swore, returning to the living room.

Hank looked up from his notes. "Let *me* tell *you,*" he said with a smile. "You can make something out of the part. And if you agree to do this, this one last time, Jerry's going to get you everything, from triple your present salary to your own private plane."

"Close," she said wryly.

"You're in a good bargaining position."

"I'm glad you think so."

"Jerry won't let you down."

"He'd better not because if he doesn't get everything he promised, I'll get the hell *out* of this stupid business!"

"No, you won't," he said, pulling her down onto his knee. "And I happen to agree that you could do something with the part. I was looking through the script while you were on the phone. I'll admit it's on the skimpy side, but you could take this girl and turn her any way you like."

"It'll put us a minimum of three months off schedule for *Strange Paradise.*"

"I'll make you a deal," he said. "You'll do Ludie's potboiler, have a couple of weeks to do the wardrobe testing and the rest of it, then we'll get this baby shot. After that, you and I will take a nice, long holiday, go somewhere and relax. Tell me where you'd like to go, and I'll take you there."

"It's a deal. We leave Molly and Becky and Luce to fend for themselves, and you and I will go off to Vermont or wherever and have

317

snowball fights." She gave him a war-weary smile and slipped her
arm around his neck.

Becky watched for twenty minutes and then, unable not to comment, said, "I don't think I've ever actually seen someone abuse
herself before. Why are you doing that?"

"Since you haven't," Bea grunted, "as you say, actually *seen* anybody do this," she grunted again, shifting position, "allow me to
inform you that this is called," she huffed for air, "exercise, not abuse."
She completed the set of stretches, then lay on the floor, catching her
breath.

"But it *hurts* you," Becky argued. "How can doing something that's
so obviously painful be good for you?"

"This," Bea said momentously, turning her head sharply toward
Becky, "is *my body*. It is the *only* body I'm ever going to have. It used
to do any goddamned thing I wanted it to. Now, it barely takes orders.
I will be *damned* if I'm going to give in and let this body dictate how
I live my life! Can you understand that?" she demanded, pushing
herself to a sitting position.

Somewhat cowed, Becky said, "Only philosophically. On a purely
pragmatic level, I still think you're punishing yourself."

"Oh?" Bea cocked her head to one side. "And for what, do you
imagine, am I punishing myself?"

"I don't know. Maybe because you're having to work on this picture
and you hate it."

Bea stood up, walked across to the bar Hank had had one of the
studio carpenters install for her, gripped it with both hands and, with
her back to Becky, began doing shallow pliés. "You're absolutely
wrong," she said. "I don't 'hate' it. I *despise* it. The director's a perfectly
sweet clod. Charlie Bickford's a lovely man and a fine actor and plays
my father just beautifully. Mr. Robinson is a swell gangster, as usual.
A few years later, and little Elizabeth has gone from playing my
daughter to playing my kid sister. The cast is fine. The crew is fine.
Who the hell knows if there's anyone out there who'll believe for five
minutes that I'm the girl reporter of the century, so hot on the trail
of a scoop that I'll actually sleep with a gangster to get it. If this gets
past the censors without being gutted, it'll be a miracle. The whole
script is tissue paper, and I'm supposed to fling it around and blind
people to the fact that the so-called plot hinges on the fact that a nice
girl would go to bed with a not-nice man just to get a newspaper
story. *And* still be a nice girl at the end." The pliés completed, she
faced Becky again, her hands on either side of her, wrapped around

the bar. "I am, however," she went on, "being amply rewarded for participating in this soufflé, with scads of money and sundry other concessions that nearly gave Ludie a massive coronary."

Becky stared at her. She was soaking wet, red in the face, and so clearly furious that, for a moment, Becky cringed, certain she was again about to become the target for Bea's anger.

"Well?" Bea challenged.

"I guess," Becky fumbled, "I don't like seeing you put yourself through such . . . Well, it looks like torture."

"It *is* torture. Now let me ask you a question, Rebecca Armstrong. Is there *anything* at all you accept purely on faith?"

"Not very much," Becky answered truthfully.

"Then it must be a testament to my fondness for you that I don't sock you on the jaw regularly. You are the goddamnedest, most maddeningly curious human being who ever lived."

"I know." Becky smiled.

"I've got to soak now. Come keep me company."

Another aspect of Bea that simply amazed Becky was her complete lack of self-consciousness. She seemed to have no compunction whatever about stripping down to her skin in front of other people. Becky had been to the set a number of times lately and had watched an almost nude Bea get handled by the wardrobe people like some kind of mannequin. It was as if, to Bea, her body was merely another part of her overall equipment as an actress. And now, here she was doing it again, utterly unconcerned that Becky was there.

She started the water going in the tub, tossed in some Epsom salts, then threw off her clothes, shoved them into the hamper, and carefully climbed into the water. Once immersed, she closed her eyes and said, "You've got to understand, Becky, that if I just gave in, gave up, and said, Okay, this is the way it's going to be forever, I'd never be able to get around for any length of time without feeling the pain start up; I'd never be able to match the music in my head to the steps my brain still thinks I can execute. If I took that tack, I'd be giving up something so important that I'd be hard-pressed to give anyone, let alone myself, one good reason for my staying alive."

"But you're such a marvelous actress . . ."

"Spare me that. I do the best I can with what I've got. I still have to come home and live some kind of life. Acting is my career. I refuse to allow it to become a substitute for living."

"I'm confused."

"So'm I," Bea admitted disarmingly, opening her eyes. "There are things I have to do, and I don't have reasons for some of them. I'm *not* something you *wrote*, Becky. I'm a person, and the reasons I do

319

have aren't always logical. I might not make very good reading. I wish, God how I wish, you could get past your being so taken with my being an actress that you forget sometimes I'm human."

"You hurt all the time, don't you?"

"Everybody hurts all the time."

"Oh, come on, Bea. I hate it when you get all actressy and start waxing profound. Level with me. You never sit still for longer than five minutes. You're up, then you're down, then you're up again. At first, I thought it was part of your incredible energy. But I've finally figured out that you *can't* sit for longer than five minutes. Yet you never complain; you never say anything."

"Wouldn't that be attractive, me whining to anyone who'd listen?"

"But it's the truth, isn't it?"

"So what?"

"*So what?*" Becky repeated, disbelievingly. "It makes a difference, you know, Bea. It's very easy to misinterpret the impression you give."

"Fine. I'll be misinterpreted. It won't be the first time or the last."

"Okay," Becky backed down. "I can tell we're not going to get anywhere with this."

"You're not, no."

"I happened to hear something I think might interest you."

"I swear to God," Bea teased, "if I find out you've been taking notes, plotting how you'll turn me into a book one day, I'll come after you, wherever you are, and rip you limb from limb. What did you hear?"

Becky laughed and pointed at her. "You, with that scrawny little body, *you* are going to rip *me* from limb to limb?"

"Scrawny looks good on camera."

Becky rolled her eyes, then bent closer to Bea, asking, "Doesn't it embarrass you, having people see you nude?"

"Oh God!" Bea groaned. "What *is* the matter with you? This is hardly a body to inspire lust or envy, for chrissake! *What* did you hear?"

"Your old friend Bobby's been hit with a paternity suit."

Bea sat upright. "You're *not* serious!"

"I sure am."

"Where did you hear that?"

"Can't say, and you wouldn't like it if I did say, because that would only make you more suspicious of me than you already are, despite your protestations to the contrary. What I heard was that the lady in question showed up with a year-old baby and announced to Ludie that it was Bobby's kid, and she intended to sue for damages and support. Needless to say, Ludie had apoplexy, got in all the studio lawyers and Bobby, and smartly put a lid on the whole thing. According to my source, Bobby's never even met the girl, let alone given her a baby as a souvenir. Apparently, he went berserk and the studio brass had to hold him down to prevent him from physically going after the tootsie in question. Anyway, rather than face a court case and all the publicity, they're going to settle with her and make sure she's out of town by sundown."

"How long has this been going on?" Bea wanted to know.

"A month and a half, maybe. It's just about wrapped up now, but my source says Bobby's so furious with Ludie for not being willing to expose the whole fraud in court that he's gone on suspension rather than show up at the studio. Ludie's been firing off telegrams to him on the hour, but nobody knows where Bobby's gone, and he refuses to come back until the four months of his suspension are up."

Bea sat motionless for one minute, then another. Then she said, "Becky, please go home now. I'll see you tomorrow evening when I get back from the studio." She wrapped her arms around herself and drew her knees up to her chest.

"Are you angry with me for telling you?" Becky asked, confounded by the way Bea had become suddenly body-conscious at the introduction of Bobby into the conversation.

"Angry?" Bea's eyes clicked into focus on her. "I'm not angry. I'm terribly grateful. Please, leave me alone now."

Becky got up and walked over to the side of the tub. "I seem to have a talent for upsetting you," she said apologetically.

Bea shook her head. "You keep my brain alive. You're one of the few people who says what she thinks and doesn't pussyfoot around."

Becky bent to kiss her on the forehead, said, "I'll see you tomorrow," and left.

Bea pulled on her robe, then went directly to the telephone.

"Jerry, where is he?" she demanded.

"I don't know."

"You *do* know. And if you don't tell me, not only will I never forgive you, I'll get myself another agent. *Where is he?*"

"Bea, stay away from him now. Let the situation cool down."

"Don't you *ever* tell me what to do, Jerry! Don't ever even *think* of telling me what to do! Where *is* he?"

With a sigh, he told her. She gave him a curt, "Thank you," and hung up.

He was hiding out in a borrowed house in Laurel Canyon. She pulled into the driveway, marched up to the front door and rang the bell, then waited, drying her damp hands on a tissue. When he came to the door, she said, "You told me years ago you'd one day get hit with a paternity suit."

"Jesus! Did you come here to gloat? I suppose you broke Jerry's arm."

"Only his eardrum. No, I didn't come here to gloat. Are you going to let me in?"

"It wasn't my goddamned kid!" he said furiously, in his best tough-guy posture, swinging away from the door. She took note of his every move, so perennially aware of him she could almost feel his rage throbbing in her veins.

"So I'm given to understand." She closed the door and followed him into the sparsely furnished living room. There were French doors at the far end of the room that opened on to a deck. The view was a good one. He came to a stop halfway across the room and turned to look at her.

"Why are you here?" he asked, thinking she looked a hell of a lot more like herself without the fancy hairdo, the fur, and the evening clothes. She looked younger, too, in a long-sleeved shirt and baggy trousers.

He was so deeply enmeshed in his anger she was suddenly afraid she might no longer have the skill to bring his basic sweetness back to the surface. What if she'd left it too long, and all she loved in him was gone? "I don't know," she answered, her momentum lost. "I thought I did, but now I'm not sure." Where was he? Had he been lost in the distance between them?

"You want a drink?"

"No, but don't let me stop you."

"Don't try to make me sound like some kind of lush!" he snapped. "I'm not hiding up here drinking the time away."

"No? What are you doing, then?"

He waved his arm impatiently at the corner of the room, and she looked over to see a heap of shoes on the floor. On a small table sat a file. He'd been working on his taps.

"When I've finished with those," he said, "I've got letters to write. All kinds of things to do."

Searching his face for signs of accessibility, she thought of the previous afternoon when she and Becky and Lucy had gone to the beach. They'd walked along the hard-packed sand at the water's edge, talking, and Becky had said, "I feel homeless. I don't know where I belong. I used to think I'd stop feeling that way when I fell in love, but I felt even more homeless when I did. I guess I thought whoever I loved would bring my home with him, but that wasn't the way it was at all. And I was better off, happier on my own because I could get up at three in the morning, if I felt like it, and start writing. Which I do," she'd confessed with a little smile. "So, here I am better off, but I still want to feel as if there's somewhere I belong."

"I think that's an occupational hazard for writers," Lucy had contributed. "At least that's the impression I get from the two or three of them I've dated. You all," she'd laughed, showing her dimples, "like to ask questions nonstop, and you all feel like orphans."

Bea had listened, wondering how Becky could bear to live, feeling as she did. "Are you lonely?" she'd asked Becky. "Is that what you're saying?" There'd been a silence then, as if the introduction of loneliness into the dialogue was in the worst possible taste. People seemed to hate to talk about it.

Becky broke the silence finally, saying, "Some of the time. Maybe most of the time. Maybe, though, it's the way it has to be. I don't connect the way you do, or you, Luce. Everything I feel seems to be in my brain, not in my emotions. Oh, I care...about even the least little thing. But I care up here"—she tapped a finger against her temple—"not in here." She held her hand over her breast.

"That's not true," Bea had said. "You're very caring. What does it matter which part of you it comes from?"

"It matters," Becky had replied. "It's the difference between committed and casual. You're committed. I'm casual. And you know exactly what I mean."

Bea did know, she thought now. She'd been bound up in commitments to Bobby since their first meeting, and the reasons were like those unseen organs inside her that kept her alive.

"Why didn't you call me?" she asked him.

"I couldn't," he said flatly. "How could I? I was up to my ass in accusations and lawyers." He glared at her, then slowly began to smile. "Christ!" he said. "What does this remind you of?"

"I don't know. What?" He was beginning to emerge, poking beyond the edges of himself.

"Don't you remember, years ago, back in New York, when you came to find me in that dive where I was washing dishes?"

She now smiled. "Do you remember what you said to me then?"

"Not exactly. I know I wouldn't go back with you, though."

"You said you wouldn't come back because you'd start noticing things again, and you'd get whacky ideas that'd make you mad. Remember?"

"Yeah."

"Me in my pajamas or backstage in my wrapper."

"Yeah."

323

"Has that changed?"

"Nope."

"I'm not fourteen years old anymore, Bobby."

His smile dissolved. "That's for damned sure." His forehead creased with uncertainty.

"Neither are you."

"No."

"You were the one doing all the talking in the parking lot a while back," she reminded him.

"Yeah, I guess I was." He slid suddenly back inside himself, out of her view.

"I don't think I can keep this up very much longer." She hadn't thought she'd be, but she was afraid—of things she thought she wanted, of her inability to be satisfied with what she already had, of his capacity to hurt her, of almost everything.

He began to move and came to a stop a foot or so away from her. "What about your husband, Bea? I can't figure any of it anymore. There used to be a time when I thought I was *so* smart. I knew it all. I don't know shit. I had this plan that life was a place we were going to go to, where we'd live happily ever after. It didn't have one god-damned thing to do with anything real, like getting up at four in the morning and going to work in a hot sound stage all day, putting together pieces of film like some big moronic jigsaw puzzle. I don't *know* what I know. That's the truth. And what about you? What about your husband, Bea?"

"I didn't come here for this." Was it gone forever? Had she lost the ability to bring him out of himself?

"No? Then what the hell *did* you come here for? How, *how* did everything get so fouled up?"

"It just did." She took a step away from him. "I guess I thought...Nobody's really a part of anybody else, Bobby, not really. We feel what we feel, but we can't ever get as close as we'd like to. Hank and I aren't the same person. We're separate. We do different things. We all have to live inside our own heads, our own bodies. He understands."

"Does he? Lucky guy. I wish I did."

She took another step away, and he grabbed her arm. "Wait a minute!" he said angrily. "Wait! You go too fast. You always do. You're forever five steps ahead of everybody else and you don't want to give the rest of us time to catch up. I don't know *how* I feel. Don't you get it? Can't you try to see it from my side of things? I actually *like* your goddamned husband, Bea. Just that fact makes me feel like a son of a bitch. He's one of the most decent people I know."

324

"Yes, he is." She nodded stiffly, her head feeling top-heavy.

"But he'd understand this, wouldn't he?"

"He's understood all along."

"I wish to Christ I did. Do you?"

"No. I just know how I feel about both of you."

"And how is that?"

"I love you both, " she admitted, feeling completely helpless. Her eyes filled. Her mouth was too dry. Her chest was tight. She was near to defeat.

"Oh, Jesus Christ!" He put his arms around her. She seemed impossibly thin, insubstantial. "I wanted it to be the two of us," he told her, breathing in the scent of her hair. "We were going to be together, we'd make each other happy."

"You've always been able to make me happy."

"Yeah, but not for very long." Again, he was stepping outside himself.

"Things keep happening," she said inadequately.

He kissed her temple, then kept his lips pressed to her skin, feeling the pulse beating there. "Tell me about the way things are. At least help me understand what I'm up against. Are the two of you really married?"

"Sometimes."

He made a noise somewhere between a laugh and a sob. "I guess I hoped he couldn't."

"If it wasn't for Hank, I couldn't have come here today. I wouldn't even be able to touch you. Please don't make me feel disloyal to him by talking about him with you."

"Okay." Putting a little distance between them, but still keeping hold of her, he looked at her mouth, then into her eyes. "I want to take your clothes off."

She shivered, her eyes filling with a feral light. "Where is it? Where do you sleep?" He was himself again, utterly familiar and lovable.

"Over here." Taking her by the hand, he led her to the bedroom, brought her to a halt just inside the door, and asked, "Is this a mistake?"

"Would it make any difference?" She was worn down from the struggle.

"No."

"Then make love to me." She walked away from him to the side of the bed, where she sat down and began removing her clothes. After a moment, he followed, and knelt in front of her, plucking her hands from the buttons she seemed to be having such trouble with.

"I'm nervous." She tried to smile.

325

"Don't be." He got the buttons undone and eased the shirt off her shoulders. She was so involved in the moment, so taken by the efficient way his hands laid her bare, that she forgot she was no longer the same as she'd been the last time they were together.

His head snapped back suddenly, and his eyes were round with shock. "*Jesus Christ!*" he breathed, feeling weak. "What happened to you?"

At once, she covered her breasts with her hands, ashamed.

"No, don't do that!" He pried her hands away to trace with his fingers the ridges of scar tissue. "What *happened* to you?"

He looked as if he was going to disintegrate, and she felt sorry, all at once, for both of them, because whatever they might represent to the rest of the world, to each other they were the same bewildering people they'd always been. They could make each other laugh, and they could wound each other more skillfully, more knowingly, more lastingly, than anyone else ever would.

"The movies happened to me," she said simply.

"I'm sorry," he said, gazing up at her as if for absolution. "I'm so goddamned sorry."

"Never mind," she dismissed it, drawing him to her. "It doesn't matter."

Becky sat on the side of the pool, her legs idly swinging in the water. She thought perhaps she should have felt used, or put upon, or disturbed in some fashion by what was happening. But she didn't. If anything, her brain was inundated with impressions, ideas. She was actually happy, and smiled at that, certain it was a sure sign of perversity that she could feel worthwhile in a situation that, by rights, should have been depressing.

Here she was, at Bobby's house, sitting at Bobby's pool while, inside, Bea and Bobby were together behind the locked door of his bedroom. Becky was there as the live red herring, the false clue. She liked the role. It was one of those infrequent occasions when she acted on faith, without need for an explanation. She was in love with Bea's love affair and was therefore willing to help in any fashion conceivable to facilitate it. She loved the idea that the two of them were over there, in bed together, and that it could happen because her presence validated Bea's being in the house. She loved the thought that she was providing a valuable service, making it possible for the two of them to be together.

She'd come to the house on two prior occasions and had settled herself out at the pool with a novel, her notebooks and script, content at having finally been able to prove herself worthy of Bea's trust. It was incredible to think what the newspapers could make of this, were it to become known. Incredible and terrible. She glanced over at the house, thinking that if it came down to choices she could never choose a life like Bea's. She preferred her invisibility, her facelessness, as a writer. She wouldn't mind having an important name, but having an important face set dreadful limitations on your life. And she'd only had a true glimpse of the extent of those limitations in the past couple of months when, Lucy being unavailable, she'd volunteered to come here with Bea during those few hours Bea stole from her life in the way, Becky thought, a clever bank manager might invade some client's trust funds.

Bea was quiet on the drive home, smoking a cigarette and looking out the window.

"Are you all right?" Becky asked.

Bea shrugged, then turned halfway around on the seat. Unexpectedly, she put her hand on Becky's hair and gave her a smile. "Do you think I'm contemptible?"

"God, no!" Becky responded. "Why would I think that?"

Again Bea shrugged, her hand still on Becky's hair.

"I'm just glad you trust me," Becky said, and brought the car to a stop in the driveway.

"I love you." Bea held her with her eyes for several seconds, then leaned forward to kiss her cheek before getting out of the car.

Late that night, standing in the living room looking at her desk and typewriter, Becky reviewed that moment in the car and, without warning, began quietly crying. She had no idea why.

Thirty

THE Hollywood *Citizen News* said, "*Back Door* would be more appropriately titled *Where's the Door?* Despite Charles Bickford's earnest portrayal of a long-suffering father and a refreshing appearance by Elizabeth Hansen as the younger daughter, the weight of this thinly sliced loaf falls squarely on the shoulders of Beatrice Crane who not only staggers under the load but actually appears dumfounded at finding herself carrying it in the first place."

Look said, "Who's doing this to Beatrice Crane, and why? She is rapidly becoming one of our national treasures, and to see her miscast in such a turgid epic is all but heartbreaking."

Howard Barnes, writing for the New York *Herald Tribune,* said, ". . . regardless of the all-too-obvious flaws, the picture is redeemed by Beatrice Crane's performance as Mimi. She manages to breathe life into flaccid dialogue and be both convincingly ruthless and vulnerable. But star acting alone can't save this dreary piece."

Variety said, ". . . shame on everyone for wasting such a fine cast in such a blighted enterprise."

Bea said, "I hope this proves to Ludie once and for all that his judgment leaves a lot to be desired."

Hank said, "You've already won. Why are you still fighting?"

"Because I don't like feeling as if the critics think I'm so stupid I don't know a good script when I see one."

"Bea," he said quietly, "there's a definite subtext to this conversation. Could you please tell me what it is you're really so hot under the collar about?"

She stared at him, then let her tensed shoulders drop and went to sit with him.

"Talk to me," he coaxed. "All these months later, you can't possibly still be angry about *Back Door.* I know you better than that. What is it?"

She picked up the pack of Camels from the coffee table, shook one out, got it lit, then sat back, plucking a stray bit of tobacco from her tongue. She had no idea where to start. Not only did she feel that history was repeating itself in the vilest possible fashion, she also knew she could never keep anything from Hank. She shifted around, leaning with her back against the arm of the sofa to look at him. His shirt was perfectly white, the creases in the sleeves crisp; his V-necked sweater was a becoming shade of royal blue; and his red bow tie had been, as always, knotted to perfection. His hair was starting to go gray, and there were lines radiating outward from the corners of his eyes. He was eighteen years older than she. And one of these days, she thought with horror, he was going to die and she'd be alone. There'd still be Bobby, of course. But Bobby could never know her in the ways Hank did; Bobby could never empathize to the degree that Hank did. She could never feel free with Bobby, as she did with Hank, to elaborate on feelings and experiences without having to fear Hank would place his personal interpretations on what she said and felt. Somehow, Bobby invariably managed to bring things full circle back to himself, so that her thoughts became *their* thoughts, and her feelings became mutual territory. She was made so suddenly afraid by the prospect of losing Hank that it momentarily outweighed all her other fears.

"What would I *do* without you around?" she wondered aloud. "I can't imagine how I'd live without you."

"I'm not going anywhere." He regarded her with open curiosity. "Are you about to tell me something so terrible it'll drive me out into the night?" he asked with a tenderly mocking smile.

"That wasn't what I was thinking."

His eyes remained on her, and she felt too transparent. Turning, she crushed out the just-lit cigarette. "I'm pregnant," she blurted, then covered her face with her hands and sobbed. *"God! I hate telling you this!"*

"What would you like to do about it?" he asked, not totally surprised.

"I have no choice." She sniffed hard, wiped her eyes on her sleeve, and reached for another cigarette. "You know I don't. We start principal photography in a week."

"That has nothing to do with anything."

"All right! I just can't do it! I can't have another man's baby, bring it home, and pretend the two of us are mama and papa. I couldn't do it to you or to Bobby; I couldn't do it to the baby or to myself." She looked at the burning cigarette and put it out. Her chest was fluttering, her hands were shaking, and she felt she was about to slide off the edge of her sanity. "Don't," she warned, pointing a trembling finger at him, "don't you dare say anything decent! I swear to God, if you play Saint Henry right now, I'll go stark raving mad. I can't do it. *Henry!*" She swayed as if she might topple off the sofa. "I know you *say* you understand. It's what you always say. But we were so goddamned careful, for the most part. We were, and this has happened anyway. I just can't stand it. I want a baby! I want children."

"You could always divorce me and marry Bobby," he suggested.

"No! I couldn't do that!" Bobby and I can't live together; we never could. And I want to be married to you. I'm *happy* being married to you."

He'd never seen her so distraught, and thought if he failed to say or do the right thing she might harm herself in some way. "I'll go with you, see you through," he told her, his voice dropping in direct ratio to her climbing hysteria.

She gazed at him and, as he watched, the madness seem to drain away, leaving her ashen and ill-looking. "I will never," she whispered emphatically, "go through this again. Never! I feel as if I'm dying, Henry. Why do I feel this way when I'm supposed to be so lucky? Why doesn't somebody warn us when we dream that having the dreams come true probably won't make us happy? Why couldn't the two of you have been one person? It would've been so perfect. I'm sorry." She clutched at his hand. "I do love you. I do, very much. I hate myself for doing this to you. Please forgive me, Henry. You don't deserve this."

"I'll go with you," he said again.

When it was done, she began to cry and simply couldn't stop. She felt she might cry herself to death. Hank put her to bed, then pulled over a chair and sat holding her hand, so grieved himself that, for once, he was at a loss for appropriate words. The longer her tears went on, the more afraid he became. He was tormented by a vision of entering the bedroom to find it empty and, proceeding to the bathroom, he'd open the door to discover her lifeless body abandoned in a swamp of blood. So bereft of consoling ideas was he, that he surrendered to pure instinct and did the only thing he could think of: He lay down on the bed beside her, gathered her against him, and just held her until, thankfully, he saw that she'd fallen asleep.

While she slept, he thought about the great conflict between a life lived publicly and the difficulty that that public life created for the private person; he thought about whether there was truly any value to attaining celebrity if it deprived you of the right to do something

330

as simple as walking unimpeded along a city street; he thought about the stars he'd encountered over the years who'd been undone by the very success they'd coveted. They'd become so convinced of their own potency and allure that anyone's refusal to accede to their slightest whim became an affront of such monumental proportions that it had to be punished on the grandest possible scale; these were people who'd become so accustomed to being wined, dined and generally feted, admired, and adored that they lost all ability to deal in a remotely normal fashion with people; they came to believe the contents of their own press packages so utterly that they wound up bearing no resemblance whatever to the people they'd once been; they evolved into golden monsters nothing could satisfy, and they resorted to all sorts of devices, embellishments, chemicals, disguises, and distortions in order to find something, anything, that would please them— for however long or short a time. They sold their original identities, even their native intelligence, for the opportunity to have fame and money, only to discover that they lacked the skills or the knowledge of how to live with what they'd managed to get. Other people then had to bear the blame for the failures, whether personal or professional; just as they had to bear the responsibility for keeping these tawdry monsters permanently elevated, either in the public's eye, or in their own minds.

Whenever he thought along these lines, invariably he recalled Marion Davies and the way Hearst tried to run every area of her life. Hearst was so jealous and protective of Marion that he was suspicious of every man on the set when she made a picture. He so totally disapproved of her drinking that she took to hiding bottles of Moët et Chandon in the many powder rooms, often in the toilet tanks, of her various establishments. And in the end, she was better known for being Hearst's mistress than for her talent.

He'd seen and heard too many variations on the theme, and he despaired of it happening to Bea. He was willing to do anything in his power to preserve all about her that was real, and good, and valuable. And there was only one way he could see to do that.

When she awakened an hour later to find herself still cradled to his chest, she sensed at once that he'd come to an important decision of some kind. She could see it in the set of his features; she could feel it in the way his eyes tracked his hand as it traveled up and down the length of her arm.

"I've put you through such a lot," she said guiltily.

"That's what I'm here for." He laid his finger across her lips to ensure her silence. "If you're willing, and I know how badly you want children, I think it's what we have to do. It may not even work. We

331

both know we can't count on my being consistent in that department, but I'm prepared to try—once you're well again, of course. The only real difficulty, as I see it, is Bobby. But you're going to have to settle that part of it yourself. I can't tell you what to do. I wouldn't try, because neither one of us would be happy with me if I did. I know the last few months have been hard as hell for you. And I know how divided you feel. I have my own moments, you know, Bea, when I sometimes have the feeling maybe I'm not giving you or Hero the best of myself. So I do know the feeling. Just think about it. All right?" He lifted his finger from her lips and touched his mouth to hers, then returned to stroking her arm.

She lay unmoving for a very long time, so long he had to check to be sure she hadn't gone back to sleep. She hadn't. Her eyes wide open, her lips parted, she was staring at nothing.

She thought about the abortion a few hours' earlier, feeling the slow, steady seepage now of blood from her body and the interior throbbing behind her pelvic bones. Twice she'd had to give up what she most wanted, and the pain was more than merely physical. It was in her bones and her brain cells; it was in her eyes and on her tongue; even her hair felt desiccated. For a few minutes she hated being female and wished with everything in her she was neuter, incapable of desire or conception. Being a woman was, just then, the worst state of existence she could imagine. Womanhood equated with endless, lifelong pain. Men could never suffer in the way women did. They could never even begin to understand it. And yet, that wasn't true. Hank understood it; he always had, he still did. Even Bobby did, in his own way. She thought of how it might be to spend the remainder of her life free of sexual need, free of the all-too-regular craving she had to impale herself on pleasure. The very thought of it made her bereft.

"You really do love me, don't you, Henry?" She turned her eyes to him, at last, touching the fine hair behind his ear.

"I really do."

"More than anything else, I want a child."

Here was his answer. He touched his mouth again to hers, saying, "Try to sleep now. I'll go down and get Molly to make you some broth."

"Will you ask Lucy to come up, please? I need her."

He held her close for a few seconds more, then eased himself away.

"Why am I always the last one to know, the one who never gets any say in what goes on? Why is that, Bea?"

332

"It was a decision I alone had to make. It wasn't easy. None of this is *easy*, Bobby. Not one stinking bit of it. You and I, we keep making babies, and then they have to be taken away, when I'd give anything in the world to have two, living, children right now instead of the sickness I feel every time I think about them being taken out of me."

"It's your career," he said bitterly. "Everything boils down to your career."

"*My* career? *Please*, let's not drag in issues that have nothing to do with this."

"The careers have *everything* to do with this," he insisted.

"What's the point in blaming what can't be changed? Would you tell me that? Even if both of us were to walk away from here tomorrow and never come back, there'd be people for years to come who'd recognize us. 'Aren't you Bobby Bradley? Aren't you Beatrice Crane?' It's too late. We can't change what's already a fact of life. And I don't want to. I've been working most of my life to have what I have, be who I am. And what would we do, live off our investments? You'd be fine, I've no doubt. From the sound of it, you own a good part of downtown Los Angeles. I might last about two years on what I've saved. I love my work, and so do you. So why go on about what's essential to both of us?"

"This is what it always comes to, isn't it? We get to spend four or five months together, happy as clams. And then it blows up in our faces. If it isn't Ludie telling us what to do, it's Ludie one step removed doing it. What I can't seem to figure out—and maybe it's just because I'm not quite as smart or as fast as you are—is why I'm getting the heave-ho this time. Or does Ludie know about your latest medical experience, and you're just not telling me he's put the squeeze on again?"

"No one knows but you, me, Hank, and Lucy."

"And the trusty doctor, of course."

"Yes, the trusty doctor." She made a face and opened her bag for a cigarette.

He saw how unpleasant she was finding this, but he felt hamstrung because he wasn't being given any room in which to maneuver. "Well," he said, "it's probably for the best that I'm off suspension and can bury my sorrows in work."

"Go ahead, be sarcastic! I'm not going to fight with you. You have every right in the world to hate me."

"Maybe I would, if I knew the score." Why couldn't they touch? Why couldn't they push their way through all this weighted air between them and relocate their true feelings for one another? Here he was, sitting opposite a woman whose flesh he knew as intimately as

333

his own. There wasn't any part of her he hadn't touched and tasted. He knew where she was ticklish and where a caress would instantly turn her receptive. He knew so many things about her, so why wasn't that enough?

"It's not all that complicated." She drew hard on her cigarette, then faced him squarely. "I can't have your baby and allow Hank to raise it as his own."

"Why not? Would Hank object?"

"It would be a nightmare for everyone. You must be able to see that!"

"I see it. So I'm out on my ass, and never mind how I might feel."

"I *do* care about how you feel. I'll go to my *grave* caring about how you feel. But the truth is you and I could never live together under one roof, no matter how much we love each other."

"*I* think we could."

"*I* know we couldn't."

"And the fact that I love you doesn't make a goddamned bit of difference, right?"

"Bobby," she sighed, "I'm *married* to Hank."

"Marriages bust up every half-hour around here."

"I *want* to be married to Hank. He's good to me, he understands me, he helps me, he's taught me everything. I feel safe with him."

"And what am I? Jack the Ripper?"

She shook her head, took another puff on the cigarette, then put it out. "I have to go now. I've got wardrobe fittings in an hour."

"The career," he said, acid eating into his words.

"Yes, the career. The fittings, the luncheons, the banquets, the Awards ceremonies, the drop-in chats with Louella, the seventeen takes, the shoes with heels too high, the getting up before dawn and the going to bed at nine-thirty, the publicity, the fan mail, the photo sessions, every last goddamned bit of it: *the career*. It's what I damned well *do*. It's all I've got *left* to do. AT LEAST," she shouted, her voice out of control, "YOU CAN STILL DANCE! I can't stand anymore even to listen to music on the car radio because it hurts too much! Don't you *ever* think past what isn't right under your nose? Could you possibly imagine what it means to lose all the things that mean the most to you?" She got up and tucked her bag firmly under her arm. "I get *so sick* of you feeling sorry for yourself! Nobody's ever strapped you to a table and raked your insides! Nobody's ever tried to kill you, rape you, beat you senseless. Nobody's ever done one goddamned thing to you but love you. And you mess that up every time. *You* were the one who couldn't wait! *You* were the one who thought just once wouldn't get me pregnant! *You're* the one who says it's like taking a

334

bath with your goddamned socks on! Trust me, you said. Dear God!
If I kept on trusting you, Bobby, I'd wind up with no insides left at
all, no husband, no career, nothing. *I love you.* The sight of your
stupid face makes me happier than anything I can think of, but you
just don't think! I prayed all the way over here I'd be able to make you
understand, that we wouldn't have to fight, that I wouldn't have to
get explicit the way I always do before you finally see the light. I wish
to God loving you didn't make me feel most of the time as if I'd be
better off dead!"

"You're right," he said wretchedly. "I am stupid. But I never said
I was any kind of genius. You go on and on blaming me for all the
things I'm not and never give me a bit of credit for what I am. I love
you, too, for the record. And it's no picnic for me either, getting to
spend a few months with you every three or four years. But I'll take
it, if that's all I can get."

"What are you saying?" she asked, her anger evolving into alarm.

"Sooner or later, we'll get back together again. Maybe next time
you'll be back to trusting me. I'll be around."

She looked away from him, blinking rapidly. "I must go."

"Can I at least kiss you good-bye?"

She looked up at the ceiling, her throat working. Finally, she was
able to direct her eyes to him and nod. He gave her a sad little smile
and kissed her on the cheek. She hugged him hard, murmuring, "It
would be so much easier if neither one of us gave a damn," then
pushed him away and hurried out.

"Take care of yourself!" he called after her.

Molly stood at the foot of the stairs and bellowed, "It's for you,
Miss Bea."

"Who is it?"

"Mr. Bobby."

"Okay." Bea rushed from the spare bedroom along the hall to the
master suite to pick up the telephone.

"I wanted to let you know I've signed up."

She had to sit down. *"Signed up?* You're going overseas?"

"I don't know about that yet. I figured since we're in this war now,
I might as well do my duty, so I've joined the navy."

"Oh, Bobby, I don't know what to say. When do you go?"

"Soon. I wanted to let you know, that's all."

"Damn! Will you write to me?"

"Sure, if you want me to. I'll even make you the beneficiary on my
government life insurance."

"That's *not* funny!"

"I didn't mean it to be. Hey! I saw your new picture. You're going to win every award going. So will Hank and Becky and Ike. I'll bet you make a clean sweep. I was so damned proud of you. You were terrific, sister."

"Bobby, please don't get yourself killed."

"Don't worry. They'll probably have me dance my way through this thing."

"I mean it. Please come home in one piece. And write to me. Let me know where you are."

"I will." He paused, then said. "I'll be thinking about you. I love you, Bea."

"Oh, Jesus Christ! I love you, too. You know I do. I won't be able to draw a deep breath until you're home safe."

"You could check on my place every so often, make sure the gardener's doing his job. I'd hate to come home to a house full of dead plants."

"Of course I will."

"Name the first one 'Bobby,'" he said with a laugh. "Good-bye, Bea. Look after yourself."

"I *love* you. Don't die!"

Thirty-One

October 12, 1942

Dear Bea,

I'm sorry not to have written sooner but the truth is I didn't know what to say, and I guess I was afraid that if I sat down to write, everything would come spilling out and I'd wind up saying a lot of things I don't have the right to say to you. But I've been thinking about you night and day. I'll go a couple of hours and then it'll hit me that two or three whole hours have passed and I was busy entertaining the boys or rehearsing with the band, so

I didn't think about you. Then I feel guilty and start thinking about you again, and when I do it's all I can do not to lay down in my berth and just stay there. Maybe it's not what you want to hear, but it's the truth. I don't know what's tougher, being at home missing you when you're only a couple of miles away or being at sea missing you when you're thousands of miles away. Either way, it's rough. I'm getting through this in kind of a fog.

I read about you and Hank and Ike and Becky all getting Oscars for Becky's picture and got choked up picturing you going up there to get yours. I think it's a shame that because of the war you didn't get the real McCoys, but just plaques. Still an Oscar is an Oscar, and you deserved it, and I'm prouder than hell of you. Be sure to tell Hank and the others congratulations from me.

They ran *Big City* one night for the boys, and it was a big hit, especially since, for the most part, the pictures they've got on board are old westerns with lousy, jumpy cuts. They keep promising us new releases, but so far all we've got is the same old crap. Anyway, it was pretty hard for me to watch the two of us. We were so damned young. We look kind of like we got taken out of the oven too soon, before we'd finished cooking. But it was great to be able to sit there for 83 minutes and remember the way things were when we were making the picture, how dumb I was, and how much you already knew about all of it, and the way you explained everything to me. Seems like a hundred years ago now.

I'd love to hear from you. We pick up mail in the ports where we stop, so I'm putting an address you can write to at the bottom. I dream about you, Bea. I dream about making love to you. Maybe I made every mistake in the book, but none of it was intentional. I'm just never going to be as smart as you are. Write to me, will you?

All my love,
Bob

January 21, 1943

Dear Bobby,

When did you start calling yourself Bob? I think I'm going to need some time to get used to that, so I hope you won't mind if I keep on thinking of you as Bobby.

I was so happy and excited to get your letter. It took months to get here. I just hope this doesn't take as long to reach you. I read your letter over and over and I've actually been carrying it around with me, in my bag, so I can look at it now and then.

We finished *Bad Company* just before Christmas. It was a long shoot, with two weeks on location north of San Francisco. Then, after we wrapped, we had to do a lot of looping because so much of the sound was dirty, with noises nobody heard apparently when we were up there. So we had to redo almost half the location dialogue, but it's finally finished. The final mix is done, and Hank's busy with the post-editing. He's hoping it'll be over in another week so he can get it out for sneak previews. He's already picked the theater but he can't book the picture in until he's one-hundred-percent happy. Anyway, enough of that.

Becky's gone back East for a while. She went home to Canada first, and now she's staying in New York, working on a book. Lucy is seeing Ike again, and they're even talking about trying marriage a second time. As for me, I've got three months off, so I'm reading, and keeping up my exercises, and going to the movies with Luce, and working a couple of nights a week in the kitchen at the Canteen.

I miss you, too. To tell the honest truth, I was worried sick when I didn't hear from you for so long. Please don't ever do that again. If you only knew the kinds of things I imagined, you'd never make me suffer that way. As you say, it's one thing when you're just a few miles away and I know I can drive over to the studio and drop in at whatever stage you're working on. But not knowing where you are, with this war going on, is just awful.

I know what you mean about seeing our old pictures. I can't look at them. I tried once, thinking maybe it would cheer me up. Hank set up the projector, but seeing the two of us the way we were somehow only made me worry even more about you.

It's funny, Bobby. I still dream of dancing, but now when I do, we're both naked and it's terrible. I can't explain it. *Please* take good care of yourself, and write me often. I hate having you so far away.

> Love,
> Bea

April 4, 1943

Dear Bea,

I was sure one happy guy when I heard my name at the mail call. Aside from a couple of letters from Jerry, I haven't heard from a living soul. Your letter made my month, never mind my day. Be sure to tell me how the sneaks went for your picture and, if it's been released, how it's doing. Are you going to win another Oscar, do you think? You've turned into one hell of an actress, Bea. I've gone to see a couple of your pictures when I've had shore leave, and even though I'd seen them before I was just bowled over. I think *Jeannie*'s my all-time favorite. I mean *Strange Paradise* was swell, with terrific dialogue and all the rest of it. And I got a kick out of you with no make-up, glasses and a bun, without the usual payoff where the girl takes off the glasses, lets down her hair, and whammo, she's a beauty. You sure have guts to play all-out the way you do. But there's something about *Jeannie* that gets to me, especially those scenes with the kid. I give Hank a lot of credit. He has an amazing eye, and the pacing's always good.

I want to know everything you're doing. Just keep on writing, and so will I. If it's possible, I'm thinking about you even more now than before. It's hard sometimes when I have to tell myself that you're not just on your own there, waiting for me. There's Hank, too. And even though I know why you did it, and what a terrific guy he really is, I forget and start thinking about how it'll be to see you once this war's over and done with.

I've been reading a lot too, mostly old newspapers and some books that are just about falling to pieces from having been passed around so many times. I've been working up new routines too, now that jitterbug's so hot. We've come up with some pretty cute numbers with one of the boys in the company. The best part is how much the boys love the shows. It feels really worthwhile to make them laugh, to get out there and entertain them. It's kind of funny, though, to think about how this is real and making movies isn't. I get confused because I have the feeling I'd like to be back on stage again in front of a live audience, but then I want to be back there too, close to you.

Boy! Look at how many pages I've filled up. I guess I'd better break off for now. I love you, Bea, and I'd give anything to see you. I'll tell you that part where you wrote about dreaming about the two of us dancing naked did some pretty interesting things to me. Now you've got me doing it too. Write soon and fill me in on what you're doing.

All my love,
Bob

June 15, 1943

Dear Bobby,

I may never get used to thinking of you as Bob. Don't be mad, okay? As usual I was delighted to get your letter. I laughed like crazy at the mental picture of you and some skinny kid jitter-bugging. You forgot to tell me whether he's in uniform or dressed up like a girl. I need to know so I can have an accurate picture in my head. And speaking of pictures, will you send me a snap-shot of you in your uniform?

We're in the second week of a very patriotic picture called *Homecoming.* Ludie insisted we do it; the script's a little on the tearjerker side, and Hank and I have been working with the writer almost every night to tone it down a little. Parts of it are pretty good. As you can imagine, I'm playing the brave little wife who sends her young husband—an awfully good new guy, Bill Hol-den—off to the war and then waits for him to come home. Mean-while, I'm doing war work in a factory, and we did two weeks on location in San Diego. The women were terrific, although the noise in the place was tremendous. I don't know how they can stand it day after day. But I really admired them and felt sort of embarrassed to sign autographs when I felt they were a lot more important than I could ever be. Not because they were involved with the war effort so much, but because they were just such wonderful women. It's one of the few times I've been able to sit and talk with other women and find out that I thought a lot the way they did and felt the same way, too. They were so cheerful and good-natured, and I was so proud of them, Bobby. It's hard to explain, but people admire movie stars because of what they *think* we are, and I admired them because of what they *really* are. I hope that makes sense to you. As I said, it's hard to explain.

Anyway, it's good to be working again. It's pretty late now, and I've got to be up early. You know how it is. So I'll close now. Stay well, and be sure to write again soon.

All my love, as ever,
Bea

November 3, 1943

Dear Bobby,

Three letters in one week! I could hardly believe it. It was like winning the Irish Sweepstakes. Hank laughed at how excited I was. He said I reminded him of a kid coming home from summer camp after living on hard-boiled eggs for six weeks.

You're starting to sound tired, Bobby, and I hope you're not

340

wearing yourself out. You won't be any good to anyone if you come home a wreck. And I hope you're eating decently. I'd send you a food package if I thought for one moment it would reach you in a reasonable amount of time, but judging from how long it took for you to get the books I sent, I don't think I should risk it.

Ludie was after us to do another war picture, but the script was just a bad rehash of *Mrs. Miniver* so we turned it down, and I'm staying home again, reading and going to movies with Lucy and putting in evenings at the Canteen. I think I told you I sang a few times, but it's been too long. I smoke too much, and I'm too rusty, so now I just help make sandwiches and go out to talk to the servicemen. That part of it's hard, because when I see all those boys I get lonely for you.

Hank's working on a loan-out to Paramount and seems pretty pleased with the picture. It's amazing, but at the start of this year there were 110 musicals planned. And all the studios are getting heated up about doing color pictures. By the way, did you read about Hedy suing MGM for refusing to increase her weekly paycheck from $1,500 to $2,000? I would've just shut up about it, myself, at a time like this. Oh, well!

Of course I still miss you. And of course I love getting your letters. And of course I think about you. Sometimes it's downright embarrassing the things I think about you. Take good care of yourself, and don't work too hard, please.

All my love,
Bea

March 1, 1944

Dear Bea,

It's starting to feel as if I've been gone half my life. I'm dying to get home and sleep in my own bed again, get back to making pictures, get back to you. I had a good laugh over that clipping you sent about the 70 drive-in theaters opening up. Just think, we'd never have to be worried about getting mobbed. We'd just climb in the car and stay there, see the show, then start up the car again and go home. It'll probably go over big.

To tell you the truth, I've got this photo of you, one of the ones from way back when, when we were making *Happy Go Lucky* and had to do the stills session twice because something went wrong with the chemicals when they were developing the first batch. Remember? Anyhow, I've got it right over my berth, so you're the first thing I see in the morning and the last thing I see at night. It'd be so great if you could be there waiting with all the wives and sweethearts when this tub finally sails back into a U.S. port. I lie awake sometimes and try to figure out why you and I can't ever seem to make it work. I can't find the answer and I keep thinking if I could, maybe we'd be able to start all over again. I know it's just daydreaming, but being at sea for months on end, there's too much time for thinking. So if I'm way out of line, chalk it up to cabin fever. I know how you feel about Hank. And you know I'm fond of the guy myself.

Oh yes, I got your little joke about my "old chum" Constance Keane becoming quite the sensation. So she's Veronica Lake now, and everybody's walking around with her peek-a-boo hair. You know damned well I haven't laid eyes on the girl in years. It was pretty funny, though, I must admit. You sure have a strange sense of humor, sister.

Before I forget, would you please find out for me if Foulke & Morgan on South Olive Street have a new catalog? And would you check on the Hollywood Theatrical Shoe Co. on Hollywood Blvd. too? They're two of my regular places for rehearsal shoes and, of course, buying new ones is going to be one of the first things I do when I get home. The other thing will be to take you and Hank and Luce and everybody to Musso-Franks for a swell dinner, on me, natch. Hank won't mind, will he?

Keep writing. I miss you like crazy.

All my love,
Bob

PS: Why didn't you tell me *Homecoming* was picked one of the ten best by the *NY Times*, and that you got yourself another best-actress nomination? Didn't you think I'd want to know? Some friend you are. Love, B.

September 22, 1944

Dear Bobby,

Since your last half a dozen letters keep nagging for inside news, I thought I'd better give you the highlights right off the top. So here's some fascinating business news. The powers that be are holding the number of prints of each picture released at 285. (You're going to be sorry you asked!) A big group, some of them studio heads and top actors, have formed something called the Motion Picture Alliance for the Preservation of American

Ideals. Hank says they're a right-wing group who oppose "Red" activity in the industry. Not only do I not know what "Red" activity is, the whole thing sounds kind of scary to me.

Business is booming, as you probably know. They're breaking attendance records right, left, and center. And I didn't tell you about the nomination because I knew I wasn't going to win, and I didn't. Maybe someday someone will be able to explain to me why the picture made the top-ten list, because I thought it was a pretty dreary effort.

I wish you were home. At least if you were I wouldn't be going to the studio every day with my handbag stuffed with paper and pens and envelopes. (I spend most of my time between set-ups writing to you.) We're doing a picture now called *Dawn,* and I get to play a pretty bad sort for a change, a dame called Letty who's hard as nails, except with these amazing horses she breeds. I'm petrified of the horses, but they're using a double for all the riding shots. It has a neat kind of switch ending, and the cast's terrific, with Jack Carson, who's just dear, and the good-looking Mr. Taylor (again), and Hank's great old chum ZaSu. The atmosphere on the set is friendly, and we're zipping along right on schedule.

When am I ever going to see you again? We might be in rocking chairs by the time this ends. Everybody dreads telegrams now, and nobody wants to open them because they're usually bad news. It's really put a crimp in Ludie's style. You know how he's always loved to fire off telegrams. I try not to think about the war. It's not easy. What's happened to our lives, Bobby? Hank and I have tried and tried, but I can't seem to get pregnant now, and I keep thinking of how easily you and I seemed to make babies. It seems wrong, as if this is the pay-off for not keeping them when I could have.

I'm sorry to get depressing. I worry so much about you. *Please* stay alive and come home soon.

> *I love you,*
> *Bea*

April 7, 1945

Dear Bea,

I never thought when I asked for news that your letters forever after would arrive stuffed with clippings from just about every paper anyone ever heard of. And I thought you told me you'd stopped reading the papers. So who's cutting the clips, sister? Never mind. I love reading the stuff, and thanks for the fresh supply of books. The boys all appreciate them too.

Listen, Bea, I can't help feeling this won't go on very much longer. I don't know how I could've got through it without hearing from you, even though sometimes it's weeks on end between letters. Be sure to tell me how you really are when you write next. You always give me the news about everybody else, and I'm left guessing about you. I mean, it's nice that Becky's in such fine form and she's got a second book coming out. I'm tickled for her. And I'm pleased as all get out that Lucy and Ike are getting on so well. *But what about you?* From one letter to the next, you go up and down, and I get worried about *you*, in case you didn't know it.

Did you really mean it that you'd come to meet me, if and when? I'd be the happiest man alive if I knew I could look forward to coming down the gangplank and there you'd be, waiting. I'll do my absolute best to let you know the minute I know. I never thought it was possible to be as lonely for anybody as I've been for you. Still, I'm only one of hundreds of guys on this tub who'd do just about anything for the sight of their girls. Oh, sure I know you're not officially my girl. But that's the way I'm always going to think of you. I don't know if we can ever work that out. But it's practically all I think about these days, and I'll tell you one thing. Maybe I did think too much of myself, but I won't make that mistake again. My life stinks without you in it, so I'll just have to do something about changing the parts that don't work with the two of us.

I hope you're all right and that taking the time off only means you wanted a breather and nothing serious. I see this is getting to be another one of my long letters, so I'll cut it short now. I love you, Bea. I don't know what I'd do if anything ever happened to you. So take care of yourself for me. And for Hank, too. I guess if it had to be anybody, I'm glad he was the one. At least I never have to worry that he'd do you dirt.

All my love,
Bob

. August 2, 1945
DEAREST BEA STOP ARRIVING FRISCO AUGUST 20 A.M. STOP
WILL YOU BE THERE STOP LOVE YOU BOB STOP

Thirty-Two

S HE'D had Lucy book a suite. It was all very discreet, except for the complimentary basket of fruit and the flowers from the management, along with a bottle of champagne. She'd stopped by his house and brought along some of his clothes.

"I thought you might be anxious to get out of uniform," she explained. "The plants are thriving, by the way. The house looks great. Everything's ready for you."

All the way home he'd imagined making love to her, but now that they were actually together he found, to his surprise, that he wanted more to talk with her, to listen to the sound of her voice and see her reactions. So they sat and talked and drank the champagne, and he found her altered. Her previous high energy had been replaced by a mysterious serenity that was an intriguing new aspect of this revised edition of someone he no longer seemed to know quite as well as he had.

She could see him puzzling over the changes and, finally, too excited to keep the information from him any longer, she smiled at him, saying, "This is a new you, Bobby. The old you would have come right out asking what was different."

"I've come to the very important conclusion that nothing, absolutely nothing, is ever the way we think it's going to be."

"Why do you say that?" She immediately pulled back on her news.

"Because all I've thought about for months and years was being back with you. But we're not doing any of the things I thought we'd do. Not because of you," he qualified, "because of me. I pictured the two of us making a run for the nearest bedroom. But when I saw you

345

waiting there on the pier, I realized that if it was going to happen, it'd happen, but I wanted this more; just to sit and talk and fix up my mental picture of you. See?" He smiled widely. "That's what happens to a guy who lives for too long with a photograph that's years out of date."

"It's funny, isn't it, how we never really think people are going to change, but they always do. Do you suppose we're too old to make a run for the bedroom?"

"It's got nothing to do with age. It's just been a hell of a long time. I guess I'm not as confident as I used to be, or something. And anyway, it's been years."

"Yes, it has."

"We could always walk casually, but purposefully, to the bedroom."

"Yes, we could," she agreed.

"That much hasn't changed."

"That much will probably never change. I'm exercising incredible restraint."

"Oh yeah?" He gave her a big grin. "You mean that?"

"Absolutely. Ever since I was old enough to understand what it meant, and even before that, actually, I knew I wanted you. I've also always known that the only hope we have of preserving whatever we feel for each other is to stay apart."

"Soooo," he said slowly, "the more things change, the more they stay the same. I get to play in the outfield permanently. Well, I'll try to be a good sport about it. It beats hell out of being out of the game altogether."

She laughed, then went silent, looking at him. He allowed the silence to hover between them, waiting. At last, unsure of her timing, she said, "I drove up. I thought I'd deliver you right to your doorstep. If that's all right with you."

"What's going on, Bea? We're backing and filling here. I'm starting to get kind of nervous."

"There's no need to be nervous. I just wish we could figure out how to get started. This feels like a bad first date."

"Do you do it on the first date?" he asked, fitting his hands to her waist.

"In your case, I'll make an exception."

"Thank Christ!" he said, relieved, his hands moving up her ribcage and over her breasts. "This better not be another dream."

"No dream," she whispered. "Let's go in there." She took hold of his hands and tugged at him.

When they lay down together, he said, "So much for old photographs. Christ, I've missed you!"

346

This was different too, he thought, as urgency overtook both of them. It was as if she'd shed her skin at the door so that he was making love to her exposed nerve endings. She felt feverish, her flesh hot beneath his hands, melting at his touch, splitting open, over-ripe. He parted her thighs. Her eyes seemed to grow larger, to be glowing as she watched him. Then he lowered his head, and she reached to put her hands on his face, holding him to her.

What she and Hank did together was something she thought of as an exchange of love. They didn't *make* love, they simply nurtured what already existed between them. But with Bobby, it was a re-invention of love-making every time. He came to her so filled with eagerness and appetite, with such an immense passion for all the parts of her, that she could only hope to match his appetite with her own. No one else, not the several men she'd slept with in his absence, and not Hank, could create in her anything close to the hunger she had for Bobby.

It was such simple madness. They could join and, breathing each other's air, sharing a single rhythm, achieve perfect pleasure, all the while intoning, I love you, I love you. Simple.

It wasn't until some time after they'd made love twice more that she told him. She sat smoking a cigarette, her free arm wound around her drawn-up knees, and said, "I'm pregnant, Bobby."

He reached for his cigarettes on the table by the bed and got one lit.

"We kept trying until I felt terrible for putting poor Hank through it. So we stopped, and I threw myself into my work. D'you realize I've made more than thirty pictures? Some of them are so bad I'd rather be burned at the stake than have to see them."

"So you're having a baby." This was the way it always happened. They were separate now, their bodies cool. It was the time for revelations.

"I'm very happy, Bobby," she said almost pleadingly, as if it were within his means to destroy her happiness.

"I'm happy for you. When's it going to be?"

"Are you really?" she asked, her head cocked to one side.

"Sure I am. I know how long you've wanted a kid. Now you're going to have one. Why wouldn't I be happy for you?"

"Lots of reasons," she said quietly.

"Well, I'm happy if you are, and that's that. When's it going to be?" he asked again.

"Seven and a half months. I get to pick the day I want. I'm going to have a caesarian section."

"So what day have you picked?"

347

"April fifteenth?"

A spectacular smile overtook his features. "You picked *my* god-damned birthday! Why'd you do that?"

"I don't know," she said with a shrug. "I had the idea you might be kind of pleased."

"Jesus!" he said shakily. "And here I was working myself up, getting ready for another big heave-ho. I was so convinced you were figuring out how to tell me this was it for me, this was where I got the shove for good and always."

"I wouldn't do that to you."

"Tell me something. How does Hank feel about it?"

"He's thrilled he's going to be a father. And I think, although he'd never show it, he's relieved as hell. It's been an awful strain on him, and on Hero, too."

Was all this tolerance real? he wondered. Was it possible for Bea and Hank to show each other this degree of deference? Obviously, it was. And he couldn't help feeling envious of Hank for his firmly established position in her life.

She could tell there were things he wanted to say, and watched him set them to one side.

"Well," he said at length, "I guess I have to ask you what this means to you and me."

"It means we'll be able to see each other."

For how long this time? he wondered. There'd be something he'd be bound to say or do that would trigger an argument or send her hurrying home to Hank. The only times they could ever be completely unguarded with each other were when they were naked, locked in intense, silent communion. Then, the moment they separated, he'd put back up all the defenses he needed to protect himself.

"I've never known you to be this way," she said, twisting to put out her cigarette.

"What way?"

"You're thinking over every word before you say it; you're being very—cautious."

He looked at her slowly, at her long, beautiful legs and her small breasts, at her throat and the dimple in her chin; he studied the way her flesh was so tight to her bones he could clearly see each of her ribs. "I could pick you up like a baby," he said, "and rock you to sleep." And then, because it seemed such a reasonable thing to do, he lifted her into his lap and held her against his chest, tracing the veins in her arm with his fingers. "I've had a lot of time to think things through, Bea. A few minutes ago you were telling me about throwing yourself into your work. I guess it's what I'm going to be

348

doing from now on. See, I always had it in the back of my mind that you'd find some way to sort things out for yourself, and I would, too, and then we'd be together. But that's not going to happen now." He took hold of her hand and held her palm to his mouth. "You planning to quit work now?" he asked, keeping hold of her hand and kissing her shoulder.

"For a little while. I've worked all my life. I don't think I'd know how to stay home day after day, indefinitely."

"But you're going to give it a try." Wonderingly, he molded his hand to her breast, pleased at how well hand fit to breast.

"For a while."

"Uh-huh." With great care he brought his thumb and forefinger together on her nipple. She turned abruptly and kissed him, then shifted so she was sitting astride his lap. "And what's my official position going to be with Miss or Master Donovan?"

She put her arms around his neck, lacing her fingers together, and leaned away from him, arching her back. He bent his head to touch his tongue to her nipple. She arched more. "Uncle Bobby? Or godfather? Both? How do you see yourself?"

He lifted his head, his hands sliding under her. "Dangerous question. Balding dancer of no known status sees himself as—what? In need of a good hairpiece. In need of all kinds of things. If I'd known at the start I'd wind up in emotional hock to you for the rest of my life, I probably wouldn't even have said hello to you outside that theater. Jesus!" He kissed the side of her neck. "But I've always been a sucker for cute girls, especially cute, spunky girls. And you're spunky, sister. I remember that day like yesterday, better even."

"Me, too. Isn't it strange, growing older?" She bent her knees and shifted closer so that her breasts grazed his chest.

"It's the shits, toots. If there'd been choices, I wouldn't've picked it. I had to go talk to you, and now, here we are. Are you really happy, Bea?"

"Now that you're home in one piece, I am; now that I'm finally going to have a baby I get to keep."

"And Hank's not going to mind Uncle Bobby hanging around?"

"Hank knows I love you."

"What a guy! I guess I could never give you what he does."

"You give me other things. Like this, for instance."

"I am definitely going to give you this for instance. Uncle Bobby." He laughed and shook his head, sliding his hands the length of her thighs. "What're you going to call this baby?"

"It'll be a girl. I just know it. And I'll name her Melinda. Melinda Donovan. What d'you think?"

"Sounds good. No middle name?"

"*I* don't have one. Should she, do you think?"

"Nah." He eased one hand between her thighs.

"Oh, God, I'm glad you're home."

"Me, too."

She lifted, then came down slowly. So simple.

Through most of the filming of *Crossroads*, she was ill. Between set-ups she had to sit in her trailer with her head between her knees, battling the nausea that prevented her from eating and frequently wakened her at night. Lucy and Molly accompanied her to the studio each day. Molly was forever offering cups of broth, or glasses of milk, or the vitamins Dr. Shannon insisted she take. Everyone was solicitous, especially Hank, with the result that there was an abnormally high level of tension on the set.

"I'm supposed to be growing fat and happy," she complained to Lucy near the end of the shoot. "Instead, I'm turning into a cadaver, and everybody's treating me as if I've got the plague."

"We're all worried about you," Lucy corrected her.

"I wish you'd stop. How'm I supposed to do my job with all of you, from the grips to you and Molly, watching me out of the corners of your eyes, ready for me to keel over? I'm not dying. I'm just having a baby."

"Well, you *look* like you're dying!" Lucy snapped. "Maybe when and if you ever do start getting fat and happy, we'll all be able to relax and get on with whatever the hell we're supposed to be doing. Maybe if you'd eat something and take the goddamned vitamins..." She broke off, then tried again. "It's a good part, in a good picture. You're sick as a dog, and it's scaring everybody. We all care about you, Bea. Would you rather have us pretending everything's hunky-dory?"

"I *hate* being sick!"

"Now, there's a big surprise." Lucy smiled. "You hide it so well."

"Thank you," Bea replied, examining her ankles. "My legs are like sticks, and my damned ankles are swollen."

"Not so's anybody would notice."

"Maybe if I put ice on them."

"I'll get you some," Lucy said, prepared to go.

"There's no time now. Maybe after the next set-up. Do you realize it's been years and years since we heard anything from Lil?"

"I realize it." Lucy stood aside and watched her get to her feet, smoothing down her skirt.

350

"I would've thought she'd be back long before now, trying for more money."

"You ought to be glad she hasn't."

"Oh, I am. Believe me." At the door, she paused. "This'll be the first year I'll miss the Awards dinner. I'll be busy having the baby."

"You don't eat somethin' soon, you'll be busy bein' dead," Molly put in.

Bea laughed loudly, opened the door, and left the trailer.

"D'you have to blurt out everything that comes into your head?" Lucy demanded.

"It's okay for you but not me?" Molly defended herself. "That girl don't weigh eighty-five pounds. She don't eat enough to keep herself alive, let alone no baby. I don't want to sit around watchin' nobody die."

"Then go home, for God's sake!"

"Don't go getting all huffy with me. You know you're thinkin' the very same thing as me."

"Get some ice, will you? Please?"

"Yes, ma'am. I'll get some ice, ma'am. Want me to shuffle?"

It was Lucy's turn to laugh. "You're turning into a monster."

"We all's turnin' into monsters. It's what happens to folks in the movie business."

"Since when are *you* in the movie business?"

"Since when I come to work for that scrawny girl an' live in her house. It sure ain't no place for sensible people."

"Bea's sensible," Lucy said.

"Compared to some. Maybe she'll get a whole lot more sensible when she's got that baby to look after. Maybe she'll stop tryin' to split herself up 'tween two men in two different houses, and then maybe she'll have the strength to deliver up that baby. You better git on over there. She'll be wantin' you."

Lucy went to the door, then turned back. "You know this is only temporary, Molly. We depend on you. And I'm sorry about lashing out at you that way."

"Yeah, I know that. I still don't like watchin' nobody that sick."

"She can't eat. She vomits everything up."

"Then she oughta go back to Doc Shannon. I don't think neither one of you's got the brains of a squatty chicken."

Lucy looked out the door at the activity on the set, then again at Molly. "Maybe you're right," she said.

"Sure I'm right, an' you know it. Just cuz I'm Nigra don't mean I'm stupid."

"Just cause you're Negro doesn't mean all white people don't like you. I happen to come from the country that was at the end of the underground railway, you know."

"Yes ma'am, I know. I just don't happen to recall seein' you on the train."

Lucy burst out laughing. "The ice?"

"I haven't forgotten. Go on, git!" Molly flashed a smile at her.

Bea sat waiting for the crew to finish on the set so she could do her close-ups. She lit a cigarette, took a puff, and had to put it out. Just one inhalation of smoke had the bizarre effect of distancing her from what was happening not ten feet away. Like a suddenly tele-scoped shot, she felt as if she'd been moved to the far end of a tunnel and, from where she sat, her view of the goings-on around her had become miniaturized. Hank was conferring with Ike on how far to shift the camera. Someone was adjusting her key light, as her stand-in patiently stood on the mark.

Was it possible one puff of a cigarette could alter things so much? she wondered, looking at her hands and the veins standing promi-nently just beneath the surface of her skin. There was a buzzing in her fingertips, a tremor somewhere deep inside her. Over there, the make-up lady was standing ready to apply the mandatory powder puff to Bea's nose before she went in front of the camera. So much noise. She placed her hand over her stomach. Nothing, just the slight-est roundness. A baby inside. But where? Members of the crew were shouting to one another. The noise was terrible. Hank had turned and was looking at her. He looked peculiar, and came forward with exaggerated slowness. His voice echoed shatteringly in her ears.

"We're ready for you, dear heart." The words clanged, cymbals against her eardrums.

She got up, to discover she'd grown very tall. Her head was at least ten feet above the ground. Her legs seemed well beyond reach.

"Are you okay?" Hank's whisper was a roar.

"I'm fine. Let's get this done."

"Tomorrow we'll wrap," he promised.

She held one hand now against her ear, keeping herself immobile as the make-up lady scrutinized her face. The hairdresser came up from behind and fussed infuriatingly. Bea longed to push everyone away but held her ground until Hank took her by the arm to lead her to her mark. He let go of her arm and called to someone to mask something that was placed distractingly in Bea's eye line.

"Are you okay?" he asked again.

"I'm fine," she repeated. *Let's get this over and done with. Get it done!*

She had to stand for interminable minutes, waiting. Ike was set with the 75mm lens he favored for her close-ups. Because it had a narrow angle and a shallow depth of focus, he could close in sharply on her eyes, leaving the area around her ears and the front of her nose slightly softer. She would never, in reality, look as fine as Ike made her look on film. Ike was a genius with a camera, a wizard with magical lenses. *Just stop fussing!* she silently begged everyone, feeling the tremor moving closer to the surface of her skin. Again, surreptitiously, she laid her hand flat over her abdomen. Something? No.

The A.D. called, "QUIET!" then turned to Hank, to say, "Okay?"

Hank nodded, and the A.D. said, "TURN 'EM."

Ike got started, said, "RUNNING."

Bea felt herself beginning to shake. No one seemed to notice. She wet her lips. Her tongue felt swollen.

The sound mixer watched his dials, got to running speed of ninety feet per minute, and said, "SPEED."

The assistant cameraman held up the slate, said, "Scene eighty-nine, take one," and clapped the clapperboard so the cutter would, eventually, be able to synchronize the sound and the picture. The assistant scurried out of the way, and Hank called, "ACTION!"

All this had happened hundreds of times before. Routine, part of a day's work. She got her mouth open, and the well-rehearsed lines began to come, except that everything sounded wrong, gluey and indecipherable. Perhaps she was the only one able to hear the wrongness, so she kept going, with mounting distress finding her vision telescoping again. The camera was dollying away from her as if pulled by some powerful magnetic force. She maintained her eye line, trying to contain her fear as a great roaring thundered against her inner ears, and she turned, thinking to apologize to Hank, to the crew, for blowing the take, but she couldn't speak at all; her mouth was stuck open around something like congealing paste, and everything tilted terrifyingly so that she threw out her arms to steady herself, but it was too late. She was unable to protect herself from the sudden, somehow inevitable, meeting of her head and the floor.

"We just won't use close-ups for that final scene. It's not going to affect the picture. In fact, I think it'll probably be better. We've got all the shots we need, and you have my word it'll be fine. Will you trust me, please? You know I wouldn't lie."

"You *would* lie, Henry, if you thought you had a good enough reason."

"Possibly," he allowed. "But this time it happens to be the truth."

"When can you get me out of here?" she asked, looking with distaste around the room.

"A couple of weeks."

"You promise?"

"Word of honor. They want to build you up, make sure you're strong enough to get through the second half of this."

"So I spend the next four months in bed?"

"Pretty well. But we'll have a baby at the end of it."

She managed a small smile. "For some silly reason, I always thought I'd just go on about my business, take time out to give a push or two, have the baby, and that'd be that."

"Not in this version."

"Obviously. God, I'll go out of my mind with boredom."

"I doubt it. Becky's on her way from New York. And Bobby's been phoning every hour on the hour. You'll stay home and entertain in quiet elegance."

"Hah!"

"Bea, don't fight on this one. I've never been so scared. Why didn't you say something, tell me you felt ill?"

"I thought I'd get it done and go home."

"Nothing's worth your life. And passing out during a take's a hell of a way to make the columns. Parsons did a whole item. It was sick-makingly sweet. Now she's determined to have a bedside exclusive. See what you've brought on yourself?"

She rolled her eyes. "Take me home and I promise I'll behave perfectly until the baby's born. I'll eat everything. I can't stay here, Hank!"

"Two weeks!" he said angrily. "I want to be able to leave here knowing you're being looked after. So stop asking me, Bea! I won't put you at risk."

She'd never seen him angry in quite this way. The skin around his mouth had gone white, and there was a deep furrow between his eyes.

"Are there things you're not telling me?" she asked uncertainly.

"No. I'm *telling* you! Two weeks here, then bed at home until it's time to come back to deliver the baby. You're sick! You can't keep on the way you have been. If you do, there won't *be* a baby! And if you need convincing, I'll be happy to set up a projector in here and run that last little piece of film for you. What're you trying to prove, Bea? What? That you're the first and last of the all-time great stoics? That you'll work until you literally drop? What does that prove, huh? What? Does that prove something to you? You want to have archival film somewhere showing how you died? Is that what you're after?

354

Headlines reading, 'Actress Drops Dead on Set. Husband Stands By Like Patsy, Watching.' It's *my* baby, too. I'm involved in this, too. *Two weeks,*" he repeated. "You don't come home one minute before that. For God's sake, Bea, stop being stupid." He dropped his voice, and some of the color returned to his face. "No movie's worth your life or the life of a baby you want as much as you want this one. You're no good to me dead. And please stop thinking of this as punishment. It's only a hospital, and it's only two weeks. You *need* to be here."

"All right. I'm sorry."

"And stop that, too. Don't be sorry. I don't want to hear that you're sorry. I know what you've been doing; I know all about how you are when you give your word. You gave it, the picture's in the can, that's it. Period. Stop fighting. Get some rest, let them fatten you up, and then you'll come home. Okay?"

"Yes, okay. Don't be angry with me. It frightens me."

"Good. Just this once, you need to be frightened."

"You've succeeded. Please stop now."

He shook himself, rubbed his face with his hands, then let his hands drop, saying, "It's my turn to apologize. No more lectures."

"Becky's coming?"

"She got on the train yesterday. She working on another script, so the two of you will have plenty to talk about."

"Did she tell you what it's about?"

He closed his eyes, then laughed. "You're hopeless. I give up. You are hopeless. I've got to go." He gave her a kiss then pointed a finger at her. "You behave, or I swear I won't be responsible for what I do."

"Yes, sir." She saluted him.

He laughed again. "I'll be back later. If I find out you've so much as twitched, there'll be big trouble."

"I won't twitch."

"Be good," he begged. "I love you."

After he'd gone, she looked around at all the flowers, then slipped her hands under the bedclothes and over her belly. Only two weeks, not thirteen months. No casts, no traction, no broken bones, no bruises, no blood. A baby. *A baby.* She'd have to think hard about the baby, to quell the panic that reached out to take hold of her every time she thought about where she was. Just two weeks. Only two weeks. And when it was over, she'd never spend another night in a hospital, not ever. A baby, inside, behind the protecting flesh, curled into itself, dreaming in liquid, a baby.

Part Three

1947-1976

"Mother held court every afternoon, wherever we happened to be, in the bathroom. She sat in scalding water up to her neck, and people came and went, in and out, as if there was nothing in the least extraordinary about a naked woman entertaining guests in her bathroom. Every afternoon when I returned from school, it was expected that I would change out of my uniform and then present myself in the bathroom for my daily half-hour visit with Mother.

"I was friends the year I was ten with a girl named Janet. I visited with her at her parents' flat in Maida Vale at the weekends and, occasionally, for a night. After a time, Janet began to complain that I never invited her home and, eventually, I decided to do just that. I got permission for her to spend a night, and she returned home with me after school ended one Friday.

"As always, I changed out of my uniform, then asked Janet to wait while I went to have my visit with Mother. I was sitting, as usual, on the white enamel stool near the tub when Janet suddenly appeared in the doorway, her face positively alight as she took in the scene before introducing herself, over my protestations, to Mother.

"Within moments, Janet had posted herself on the side of the tub and was inundating Mother with all sorts of questions about her films, more animated than I'd ever seen her. Mother was polite and talked with her, every so often looking over at me if I'd committed an unpardonable breach of conduct, first, by bringing Janet into the house at all, and second, by encouraging the girl to intrude upon our time together.

"It simply wasn't possible for me to explain. Mother was so furious she wouldn't listen. I was furious with both of them, Mother for holding court in the bathroom as she did and Janet for taking advantage of our friendship in order to gain access to Mother.

"From that point on, I was exceedingly careful in the friendships I made. And I never again spoke to Janet."

Excerpt from Melinda Donovan, *Private Lies*
(New York: Crompton House, 1976)

Thirty-Three

BEA had hoped to take some time off after Melinda was born, but less than three months after the baby's birth she was at work on Becky's new script, *Endings*. When that wrapped, Ludie made a deal for her to be loaned-out to Twentieth-Century to do a costume epic that, despite its fine script and huge budget, turned out to be a complete failure at the box office. She was about to start work on a pet project of Ludie's which he was personally producing, when Ludie died at his desk of a massive coronary. Production at all the studios was stopped for an entire day, while hundreds attended his funeral.

Ludie's death seemed to mark the beginning of the end of an era. While Bea had had any number of run-ins with the man, what she kept remembering was how they'd danced together the night of the White Mayfair Ball and his gruff apology. Ludie had made her career; the studio machinery had kept his plans for her in operation; now Ludie was gone, and brash business types who exercised regularly at the Hollywood Athletic Club had stepped in to reorganize the studio. Hank was delegated to take over Ludie's picture and see it to completion, which he did, but not without a lot of interference from the temporary head of the studio.

"I don't like the way things are shaping up," he told Bea. "All of a sudden, too much is happening. There's an undercurrent, not just here, but at all the studios. People are going around whispering about Communists, as if gangs of them are waiting outside the studios for a chance to move in and take over."

"I dropped in for a chat with Ivy," Bea said, "and she was gone. Just gone. When I asked around, Ferd, in hairdressing, got all red in the face and started mumbling something about Ivy's having been a

Party member. No one would talk about her. It's as if she died of something highly contagious and you could contract it just by mentioning her name. What's going *on?*"

"I don't know," he said. "But I don't like it."

By the time Ludie's picture was ready to be shown at a sneak preview, Bea's contract had expired.

"Just sit tight," Jerry advised her. "You might be better off in the long run free-lancing for a while, until we see how the new management shakes down. Things are peculiar around town right now. All anybody wants to talk about is Communists. Let me see what's what and I'll get back to you."

Bobby moved over to MGM without missing a beat. His pictures were gaining again in popularity; he was back on the top-ten box-office list but still changing partners regularly.

"D'you get the feeling something's going on?" he asked Bea one afternoon. "I sure do." He looked over to where Melinda was crawling on the carpet and stared at the baby for several moments. "Nothing's the same," he said at last. Then brightening, he smiled at her. "Beatrice Crane—Mother. I can't get over it."

"Me, neither." She looked now at the baby and smiled. "She changes everything. Hank's fascinated by her. He'll go into the nursery in the middle of the night, pick her up, and carry her around in his arms for hours, just staring at her. He's a wonderful father; he's so much more patient than I am. D'you ever have the sense that we're in the last reel, only we don't know it?" She turned back to him. "I do. I've felt that way since Ludie died. The atmosphere around town is unbelievable. We were out to dinner the other night, and there was none of the usual table-hopping. People were just eating. All very subdued. Hank's on edge. The only time he seems to relax is when he's with the baby. He says he doesn't know how much longer he can work with everyone acting so suspicious of everyone else."

"You know how I feel?" Bobby asked, scooping up the baby and holding her on his knee. "I feel like we're about to do a Hollywood version of 1936 Berlin, only instead of going after Jews, they're out to get Commies. And all the Commies happen to be writers." Melinda sat looking at him for a few seconds, then her face screwed up, and she began to howl. At once, he handed the baby over to Bea. Melinda quieted and started tugging at Bea's necklace.

"The kid hates me," he said.

Bea laughed. "Of course she doesn't hate you. You're not used to babies, and she can tell."

"Nope," he disagreed. "I know hate when I see it."

"Fool! I think you're jealous."

"Damned right! I was there, remember. I watched you with one hand on your incision and the other on the baby while she had the time of her life nursing. *I* never got twenty minutes on each side."

"You never asked."

"An actor of my stature doesn't have to ask."

"You know what Monty Woolley said. 'Scratch an actor and you'll find an actress.'"

"Ssshhh! There's a third party here."

She laughed and leaned across the baby to kiss him.

On October 20, 1947, the House of Representatives Committee on Un-American Activities began hearings to investigate the Communist infiltration of the motion-picture industry. They started with a week of testimony by witnesses who were "friendly" to the committee's work, among them Jack Warner, George Murphy, and Ronald Reagan.

"They're naming names," Hank said. "They're turning in their friends as Communists. Subpoenas are going out right, left, and center, and everybody's looking squinty-eyed at everybody else. This is bad, very bad. What the hell does anybody here have to do with subversive plots to overthrow the government? All this crap about the writers putting Communist propaganda into scripts. Christ, Bea! I'm starting to think seriously about quitting the business or getting the hell out of here."

"You don't think it's going to blow over?"

"No, I don't!" he declared. "I think this is only the beginning. When they start appointing House committees to investigate a bunch of people who do nothing more sinister than make movies, I think we're in a hell of a lot of trouble. These *fools* are marching in there, thinking they're doing the good, all-American thing by giving up their friends to the goddamned committee. Where's the threat? That's what I want to know."

"You're saying Morrie and Coop were wrong to testify?"

"Who the hell knows? All *I* know is that people we've known for years are being railroaded just because ten or fifteen years ago they belonged for a while to the Party. I even thought about joining up at one time. The only reason I didn't was because I didn't have the time. I was busy, working. Now, they've slapped contempt charges against ten of my friends because they refused to cooperate, because they wouldn't do more than give their name, rank, and serial number. What the hell good's the Constitution if a bunch of state-appointed zealots can ignore the First Amendment and charge ten guys for contempt of Congress because they won't talk?"

"What should we do?" she asked. It was only the second time ever she'd seen him so upset and angry.

"I don't know about you," Becky put in, "but I'm not going to stick around to find out. They're out to prove that everyone who belongs to the Screen Writers' Guild is a card-carrying Party member. The most threatening group I've ever belonged to is the Girl Guides, for God's sake. I'm heading back to New York. I'll finish the new script there."

"You're leaving?" Bea asked her, shocked by the suddenness with which their lives were being upended.

"I'm scared," Becky admitted. "Maybe I'm just a naïve Canadian girl, but it seems to me this country's going nuts, looking for subversives under every rock. I belong to the Guild, Bea. I don't want to wind up facing contempt charges because I won't go in front of some committee and rat on my friends. The next thing anybody knows, they'll be burning people at the stake."

"This is a nightmare," Bea said, looking for help to Hank. "Should we be getting out, too?"

"I'm considering it," he admitted. "I think Becky's got the right idea. Things are going out of control fast."

"But what about the picture? How can we work on it if you're back in New York? Can we still do it?" Bea turned first to Becky, then to Hank.

"I'll get it done," Becky promised. "I just want to get out of here."

"You honestly think these investigations could affect you?" Bea asked her. "Am *I* the one who's naïve here? Isn't the point to prove we've got nothing to hide?"

"I don't care about proving points," Becky said. "I never dreamed that being a writer would wind up something I'd have to apologize for, and I'll be damned if I'll let people hang over my shoulder, looking through every word I write for secret messages. I'll get it done in New York, and the two of you can fight it out here while people pick the script apart. For all I know, maybe I *have* written something wildly subversive. I just can't stay here. I'm too scared."

For Hank, everything ended at the beginning of October 1950, when DeMille decided to oust Joe Mankiewicz as president of the Screen Directors' Guild. Under the Taft-Hartley Labor Act, all officers of all the unions and guilds in the country were required to sign a loyalty oath. As president of the Guild, Joe had signed it. It was DeMille's thinking that it should also be mandatory for every other member of the Guild to sign the oath as well.

The way Hank heard it, in the course of a frantic telephone call from Willy Wyler, Joe's position was what while he'd signed the oath required by the government, he wasn't prepared to sign one demanded of him by DeMille.

"He considers it an infringement of his rights as a citizen under the Constitution," Wyler told Hank. "Now, all of a sudden, items are appearing in the papers hinting Joe's a 'pinko,' and a 'Communist-inspired left-wing intellectual' who's busy slipping Communist propaganda into his films. We've got to round up people who'll support Joe. Where d'you stand? We've got to have a meeting."

"When and where?" Hank asked, feeling he'd been forced, finally, to take a stand.

After the call, he told Bea, "There's going to be a general meeting to discuss the recall of Joe as president of the Guild. DeMille and his gang don't want the meeting to happen; they've been planning to push through a recall vote before anybody can organize support for Joe."

"Henry, is there a chance you'll get blacklisted for taking sides in this?"

"You know what?" he said furiously. "I don't give a damn anymore. I know what's right and what's wrong. And this is bullshit, Bea. We let DeMille railroad Joe this way, and the next thing anybody knows, DeMille will be running the goddamned *world*. I've got to go. We're meeting up at the Guild office to get addresses of the members so we can send out a petition. We need twenty-five people to sign. No, sorry," he corrected himself. "There are already six of us."

The place was locked up.

"What the hell's going on?" Wyler demanded. "It's a business day. Somebody's supposed to be here."

"We've got to get the petition signed, notarized, and turned in to the executive secretary before DeMille gets his recall votes in and counted. If we can't get into the office to get the addresses, how do we get the damned thing out to the members?" Joe Losey asked the others.

After much discussion in the parking lot, Hank wearily suggested, "Let's see a lawyer,"

"Who?"

"Martin Gang," Losey said. "He's the best in town."

Gang said, "I'll take the case. But I want to point out to you that, according to the current bylaws of the Guild, unless a member's signed a loyalty oath, he's not in good standing. And on top of that, signatures on the petition will be invalid unless each signing member also swears he's not a member of the Communist Party and doesn't support any organization that believes in or teaches the overthrow of the government by force or by any illegal or unconstitutional methods."

"Wait a minute!" Hank said. "You've telling us we can't save Joe unless we sign the very thing he's against. There has to be another way. All of us have already signed goddamned oaths, and now you're telling us we've got to sign more? When does this end? Pretty soon we'll have to swear our loyalty just to go to the toilet!"

"Come on!" Wyler said. "Do we want to be coerced into spending the rest of our professional lives making 'safe' pictures, pictures devoid of any ideas whatsoever? The only thing we're going to get out of playing it safe is mediocrity, and I'm not willing to go that road. Let's show a little courage here."

"Okay, okay." Gang raised his hands for quiet. "This office will write up a legal petition. Then it's up to you to find twenty-five members to sign it. When you've got that done, you'll call a meeting, and you can fight this thing out with the full membership."

Hank returned home and went directly upstairs to look in on Melinda. He stood for quite some time watching his daughter sleep, wondering if he was doing the right thing. It didn't feel as if he had a choice.

"I'm involved now up to my eyeballs," he told Bea. "We've got lunatics shoving oaths under our noses every half-hour, asking us to put it in writing that we're loyal, God-fearing Americans. I *loved* this place," he said miserably. "I loved the history, and the madness, and everything to do with making pictures. And they're taking it away; they're destroying it with this stinking witch-hunt. It'll never be the same after this."

"Let's see what happens at the membership meeting," she said. "If you can keep Joe in as president, maybe it'll mean the tide's turning."

"Bea, I want you to think seriously about what it would mean to you to leave here. I'm giving it a lot of serious thought myself. *Very* serious thought. I've got friends in jail. People are afraid to talk to each other now. I can't live this way; I can't work this way."

"All right, Henry," she said softly, putting her arms around him. "I know what you're trying to say."

The meeting was held in the ballroom of the Beverly Hills Hotel, and the entire membership showed up. Joe made an hour-long opening speech on the loyalty oath, saying, "I'm unalterably opposed to an open ballot, a blacklist, and a mandatory oath. All three are un-American!"

DeMille then got up to defend his faction's position, but he was a poor public speaker and, looking around, Hank could see the audience getting bored and restless. Then, DeMille singled out the twenty-five directors who'd signed the petition, saying, "... most of them are affiliated with un-American or subversive organizations and theories, and many of them are foreign-born." At this, there was a communal gasp of disbelief from the audience. Then some of the members began to hiss and boo. Hank was so outraged he could feel the blood pounding in his temples.

Joe rapped his gavel, and there was silence. "Mr. DeMille has the floor," he said.

DeMille stood a moment longer, then sat down.

Fritz Lang stood up to say, "For the first time, the fact that I speak with an accent makes me a little afraid."

Delmar Daves rose and said, "My family's been in California for four generations. And I can't begin to express my contempt for your attack, Mr. DeMille, on the foreign-born directors who signed..." He had to stop, breaking into tears.

Speeches were made with endless charges and countercharges. For four hours directors attacked or defended DeMille or Mankiewicz. Finally, Hank stood up. "I ask that Mr. DeMille retract his charges against the twenty-five directors."

"I will not!" DeMille flatly refused.

George Stevens took the floor. "I'd like to offer my resignation from the board of directors."

The members refused to accept his resignation.

Stevens then launched into an articulate, devastating list of charges against the executive secretary and the anti-Mankiewicz members of the board. He finished by saying, "I'm asking Mr. DeMille to recall the recall movement."

DeMille demanded an act of contrition from Joe in exchange, which Joe refused.

Stevens said, "I have nothing more to say," and sat down.

With the exceptions of John Ford and the small group sitting around DeMille, the entire membership got to their feet to applaud Stevens' speech. Hank clapped, pausing to wipe his eyes. There were good people here, but it didn't mean they'd carry the day. As the applause died down, he looked over at Ford, who'd been silent through all of this. He sat in his baseball cap and tennis shoes, sucking thoughtfully on his pipe. From time to time, he'd put the pipe away, take out a dirty handkerchief, wipe his glasses with it, and then chew on it for a while. Now, as Hank watched, Ford raised his hand, stood up, and faced the stenographer.

"My name's John Ford," he said. "I make westerns." He paused for a moment to let this bit of information sink in. "I don't think there's anyone in this room who knows more about what the American public wants than Cecil B. DeMille—and he certainly knows how to give it to them. In that respect I admire him."

Hank had his hands clenched, fearful of where Ford was headed.

Ford looked over at DeMille and said, "But I don't like you, C.B. I don't like what you stand for, and I don't like what you've been saying here tonight. Joe has been vilified, and I think he needs an apology."

He stared at DeMille. So did everyone else. DeMille stared straight ahead, making no move.

Finally, Ford said, "Then I believe there is only one alternative, and I hereby so move: that Mr. DeMille and the entire board of directors resign and that we give Joe a vote of confidence—and then let's all go home and get some sleep. We've got some pictures to make tomorrow."

"I second that!" Hank jumped up, with his hand in the air.

Ford sat down and lit his pipe.

Hank slowly sat back down, thinking perhaps he'd just signed his death warrant. But if he had, he was in damned good company.

The membership voted in favor of Ford's motion. DeMille and the board resigned; Joe was given a unanimous vote of confidence, with only four abstentions.

Drained, Hank told Bea about the meeting. Near to tears again, he said, "I couldn't believe C.B. would say things like that about the men who signed the petition. We're talking about people like John Huston and Joe Losey, and Negulesco, for God's sake. DeMille's gone off the deep end. He's so goddamned busy helping search Hollywood for Communists he doesn't know which way is up anymore. I need a drink." He went to pour himself a hefty scotch with a splash of water, then came back to sit beside Bea on the sofa. "I was one of the men who signed that petition, Bea. I had a moral obligation to sign it. But I've had as much as I can stand of this insanity." He took a swallow of his drink, then held the glass between his knees as he gazed at the floor.

"I had a very interesting conversation with Jerry today," she said quietly.

"Oh?" He lifted his head to look at her.

"All the agency's clients are being asked to sign loyalty oaths, so

Jerry and the others in the office can honestly say they don't represent any subversives."

"Jesus!"

"According to Jerry, it's the studio that wants the signed oath. Since I'm under contract until this picture's finished, they want an absolute guarantee of my loyalty."

"What did you do?"

"I refused to sign. Jerry said if I didn't sign, the studio would stop production and scrap the picture. He pointed out to me that that would put an awful lot of people out of work."

"Jesus!" he repeated, shaking his head. "It's all gone too far."

"So," she said, "I signed the damned thing. Then I came home and listed the house with a real estate agent. After than, I sat down with Lucy and Molly and told them we'd be leaving. Lucy said she'll go with us, wherever we decide. Molly said she didn't want to be away from her family. She's broken-hearted, but I've left the offer open. After that, I put in a call to London and said I'd be free to do that picture they've been after me for. I also took the liberty of saying I thought you'd probably be agreeable to directing. We've got to leave, Henry. If we stay, you'll only become more and more unhappy. And if you're unhappy, I will be, too. I've made a date to see Bobby tomorrow, to tell him."

Hank took another swallow of his drink. "I have felt worse," he said, "but I can't think when. I thought we'd work out our careers here, then retire and maybe write our memoirs." He laughed ruefully. "I've been procrastinating," he admitted. "You did the right thing. So did I, tonight. Doing the right thing doesn't leave a particularly good taste in my mouth. I'm too goddamned old to be pulling up my roots!" he railed.

"Fifty-one isn't that old, " she said with a smile. "And at least we won't be expected to sign any pledges of loyalty to the British government."

"I'm going to look in on Mel," he said, getting to his feet. "I don't know how I'm going to break the news to Hero."

"You'll tell him, and he'll understand."

"I wish *I* did, Bea. I don't think I'll ever understand why all this had to happen. What did we ever do here that was so wrong or so terrible? We made a lot of pictures that gave a lot of people pleasure. There was no harm done. They'll never be able to get back what we had here. Never."

"You'll make more pictures that'll make lots more people happy, Henry. And you'll be allowed to make them in the way you want."

"I *loved* it here," he said.

"I know," she commiserated.

He straightened his shoulders and turned to look up the stairwell. Then, with a sigh, he turned back to give her a small smile. "I've always wanted to see Europe. I'll just go check Mel."

"**H**ank, I've got three more pictures to do for MGM. My name's on the dotted line. I can't even begin to think about making any kind of move until somewhere around next Christmas."

"But would you consider relocating?"

"Of course I'll consider it," Hero replied. "But I'll be honest about this. I've been here almost as long as you have, and I'm used to the place. I'm also fifty-six years old. I finally have the house just the way I want it. And it's been in the back of my mind for quite a while now that once these pictures with MGM are out of the way I'd retire. I can't imagine what it's going to be like without you."

"You could always keep the house, maybe spend part of the year here and part over there."

"I'm going to look at all the options," Hero promised.

"You will come at least to visit us?" Hank asked, near to tears.

"Probably sooner than you think." Hero got up and went to the bar to fix drinks. "There's going to be such a huge hole in my life," he said, his composure slipping. "Why the hell did this have to happen?"

"I can't stay in this town," Hank got out. "I've seen too much already."

"Has Bea told Bobby?" Hero asked, giving Hank a drink.

Hank nodded.

Hero flopped gracelessly onto the sofa, sighing loudly. "What a stinking mess! How did he take it?"

"About as you'd imagine."

"I thought that was probably why he's been the old Bobby the past few days, playing with a hard edge." Hero shook his head. "I'll be over as soon as I possibly can. I really don't know what I'll do without you."

Hank gave up and wept.

The week before they were due to leave, Bea received a letter postmarked Toronto. It had been addressed to her in care of the studio.

Part Three / 1947–1976

December 30, 1950

Dear Miss Crane,

I thought you'd want to know your mother passed away the twelfth of last month. It was pretty sudden, and she just went one night in her sleep. I thought you should know. I've got the two girls staying with my mother for now until I get things settled here. I had to take a loan to pay for the funeral and the plot. I guess that's everything.

Sincerely,
Harold Crewes

Bea carried the letter out to the garden. Poor Lil, she thought. Fifty-one, the same age as Hank. It was awfully young to die. She stood on the grass and looked back at the house, the breeze catching the letter, almost taking it from her hand. She smiled suddenly, recalling Lil saying in one of her letters that she was almost thirty-eight and never had been married. Well, at least you got that, Lil, she thought. Even though, according to Jerry, Harold was a hairy thug. Two girls staying with their grandmother. It reminded her of Agatha, with her feet soaking.

January 2, 1951

Dear Mr. Crewes,

Thank you for writing to tell me about the death of my mother. My family and I are leaving tomorrow for England, but I wanted to write before we left. The enclosed check should cover the funeral expenses, and I hope you'll use the balance for your daughters. Again, thank you for letting me know.

Sincerely,
Beatrice Crane

Thirty-Four

Dear Bobby,

We're finally ensconced, at least for a while, in a lovely house we've rented. We had to spend the first few weeks over here in a hotel. Then Hank was busy scouting locations for the picture and finalizing the shooting script, so Lucy and I made the move in between interviewing nannies for Mel. The girl we've hired is wonderful with Mel, and Mel adores her. Hank and I go on location next week.

Lucy loves it here and has been dating the associate producer. Brian's very easygoing and loves to dance. He's been showing her the sights and has generally been a great help to all of us.

I don't know why, but I assumed we'd land and then go about our business. But there was a crowd at Southampton waiting outside the customs shed. And when we arrived at the Savoy they had policemen there to keep order. Evidently it was "leaked" we were coming. We ended up giving a press conference, and there were quite a few questions about you. I'm sure you'll be pleased to know you're extremely popular over here.

I've been able to take Mel for walks, and the few times I've been recognized, the people have just smiled or stopped to say a word or two. It's very civilized, and the English so far have been warm and friendly without going too far.

Mel is growing almost in front of our eyes. I can hardly believe she'll be five in another couple of months. She's her own little person, and if she decides she doesn't want to do something, nothing will move her. As I said, Sarah's good with her, fortunately.

Aside from the dreary weather, we're all in love with London. I can't wait to start work again, and Hank's looking forward to it, too. It's certainly nothing like back home. All the production people we've met have been nicely business-like but nowhere near as aggressive as the types we're used to.

The only part of this I'm not enjoying is that you're not here. I miss you terribly. I miss sleeping with you. In fact, I miss just seeing you. I hope you're looking after yourself, and not filling the gaps with endless parties and blonde divorcées. Please write and let me know how you are, and keep me up to date on what you've been doing and the latest happenings there.

My love, as ever,
Bea

March 24, 1951

Dearest Bea,

God, but it was good to get your letter! Next time, please don't make me wait so long to hear from you. I'm glad to know you're all okay and that you like it over there. I've been playing around with the idea of coming over to visit, maybe this summer when I'm between pictures.

Talk about missing someone! I've had to drive by your house a couple of times, and it felt all wrong knowing you weren't there. Do you have any idea how long you're going to stay away? Not for good, I hope. I couldn't stand that. I'd probably have to do something drastic, like selling up here and coming after you.

More and more of our old crowd are bailing out, moving to Mexico or to London. A couple of weeks ago Joyce O'Hara, the acting president of the Motion Picture Association, made an official statement saying that movie people who didn't deny Communist ties would find it "difficult" to get work in the studios. Jesus!

The hearings started up again a few weeks ago, and they absolutely destroyed poor Larry Parks. He and Betty are going to pack up and get out of here, because he's dead as far as his career goes. Everybody's getting subpoenaed, and the studios are putting the screws on to make sure their employees "cooperate" with the committee. The joke, if you can call it that, going around is about the variations on the Fifth. They're saying Carl Foreman used the "diminished fifth" denying he was a Party member at the time he testified, but wouldn't answer any questions about whether he'd been a member in the past. And Bob Rossen did the "augmented fifth" saying he wasn't a member of the Party, wasn't sympathetic to it, and wouldn't say if he'd ever been a member. Every time one of these guys has to testify, he's out of a job the next day.

I feel like a lousy coward but I've been staying home nights for the most part. It's safer that way. And I'm not interested in blondes, anyway. I'm used to you, and you know it. I won't kid you and say I'm living like a priest here. The truth is it's not fair to the girls I do see to make love to them and think about you while we're doing it. This is like the damned war all over again, with the two of us thousands of miles apart, back to writing letters.

Good luck on the new picture. Give my best to Hank and Lucy, and a big hug to Mel. I love you, Bea. And happy birthday, by the way.

> *As ever,*
> *Bob*

The constant dampness undid much of the progress Bea had made with her faithfully maintained exercise regimen. For the first time in years, when she awakened in the morning it was to discover she'd lost a little more of her flexibility. Her working-out sessions with Lucy continued but she was laboring just to remain mobile. She returned to the house in Chelsea after each day's shooting at Elstree to go directly to the bathroom to soak in a tub of hot water. After they finished the picture, her hour in the tub became a daily routine. It was the only thing that eased the permanent ache in her hips and legs.

Initially, Melinda seemed puzzled by this new habit of her mother's. Sarah would bring her down from the nursery and leave her to visit for half an hour with Bea. Sometimes, Lucy would be there, too, or the housekeeper, Mrs. Pepper, would come in to ask some question or other. It seemed very odd to Melinda that her mother would talk to all these people who came and went while she was all naked in the bathtub. And Melinda invariably spent the half-hour asking questions, trying to make sense of the situation.

Bea tried to explain, saying, "I have to do this, Mel. If I didn't stop and take the time for this even when I'm not working, after a few days I wouldn't be able to get up the stairs. It helps me feel better, and then I can do all the things that have to get done."

"But *how* does it make you feel better?" Melinda wanted to know.

"It just helps me, sweetheart. You like having your bath every night, don't you?"

Melinda nodded. "But I play in my bath, and you just sit there. You don't have any toys or bubbles or anything."

Bea laughed. "You're right," she said. "I should have toys and bubbles, shouldn't I?"

"Why can't I come play in the bath with you?"

"Because the water's far too hot. You'd get burned."

"Why don't *you* get burned?"

"Because I'm used to it."

"Sarah says it's an aff-eck-tay-shun," Melinda enunciated carefully.

"Sarah said that?" Bea suddenly sat up very straight so that Melinda could see the funny white lines on her chest and the other one on her tummy. "When did she say that?" Bea asked, controlling her voice and her incipient anger.

"She said it lots of times," Melinda told her, fanning the air with the bottom of her dress. "She said all fill-um stars have aff-eck-tay-shuns."

"What else did Sarah say, Mel?"

"Oh, let's see." Still holding up the bottom of her dress, Melinda looked at the decorative tiles placed around the perimeter of the tub. "She said I'm a very lucky little girl to have her because she can tell me all the things that are right and wrong that you won't tell me because you're too busy and fill-um stars make terrible mothers and fathers. Is Daddy a fill-um star, too?"

"Your father *directs* pictures, and sometimes he writes them. He's not an actor, Mel. You know that."

"Uh-huh. But how can you be a fill-um star and be my mummy, too? Sarah says you can't be both, you have to be one or the other."

"That's *not* true, Melinda. I work in pictures. It's my job, just like Daddy's job is working in them, too. But even when we're not at home with you, we're still Mummy and Daddy."

"Yes, but sometimes people know who you are and want to talk to you and have you write your name for them, even when you're just Mummy and we're out for a walk."

"That's because of my work, darling. You know that. We've explained it to you dozens of times, and so has Aunt Lucy."

"Sarah says Auntie Lucy is a toady, and she's not my really aunt at all."

"Sweetheart, I'm going to get dressed now, so why don't you run along up to your room and play until dinner time. Okay?"

"Okay." Melinda slid off the enamel stool. At the door, she stopped to ask, "Are you going to be mad at Sarah, now?"

Taken aback by the question, Bea debated telling her the truth and decided on a compromise answer. "I'm going to have a talk with her."

"Are you going to make her go away?"

"She might have to leave, yes."

Melinda's face twisted angrily, and with her small fists held beside her cheeks, she cried, "Sarah *told* me not to *tell* you! She *said* if I did you'd send her *away!* I don't *want* you to send her *away!* I *love* Sarah!"

"Go upstairs now, Melinda," Bea said quietly but firmly. "We'll discuss this later, when your father comes home."

Melinda started screaming. Horrified, Bea got herself out of the tub as quickly as she was able, wrapped herself in a towel, and moved to embrace Melinda, anxious to calm her down. *"Don't you touch me!"* Melinda shrilled. *"I want my Sarah!"*

Her cries brought both Lucy and Sarah running. Melinda threw herself against Sarah's thighs, shrieking incoherently, while Lucy asked, "What's going on?"

Bea didn't answer for a moment, her attention fixed on Sarah who was attempting to disengage herself from Melinda's fierce hold. Sarah looked as if she were trying to free herself from an octopus. Her expression, Bea thought, revealed anything but fondness for Melinda. She actually looked as if she hated the child. Her eyes still on Sarah, Bea said, "Lucy, would you please take Melinda upstairs?"

"Sure." Lucy turned and attempted to separate Melinda from Sarah. "Come on now, Mel," she coaxed.

"Go with Lucy," Sarah told the child. "Go along. Do as Mummy and Aunt Lucy say."

With enormous reluctance, Melinda allowed Lucy to lead her away.

Once Melinda was out of earshot, Bea's eyes returned to the tall, thin nanny. "What the *hell* have you been telling Melinda?" Bea raged. "How *dare* you tell her that her father and I aren't *real parents* to her, and that Lucy isn't her aunt! Are you out of your mind? How could you *say* things like that to a small child?"

Sarah remained surprisingly cool. "One could hardly say this household was typical, or normal. I was simply clarifying certain matters for Melinda. Someone should."

Bea stared at her in amazement. "She doesn't *need* matters clarified. And if she does, she has a mother and father who'll do that for her. And what *you* call 'clarifying' comes down to trying to turn a child against her parents. You've got half an hour to pack your things and get out of here. We'll send whatever we owe you, along with a very detailed letter, to the agency. It'll be a sunny day in hell before you get a chance with another child!"

"You needn't carry on in such hysterical fashion," Sarah said with infuriating self-control. "I'll be more than happy to leave. It's been an unpleasant position here from start to finish. I've always believed Americans to be crude, and you've simply confirmed that. And I shouldn't threaten me, if I were you. I'm not some illiterate tart off the street. I've a public-school education, *and* I merely accepted this position in order to satisfy my curiosity. It was scarcely worth the effort. You're frightfully common."

Bea's control snapped. "God help us!" she said in soft, deadly tones. "You're one of those demented creatures who thinks she's above the rest of us. Let me tell you something, Miss Public School Girl. You're not above *anyone*. You've got a brain as full of holes as Swiss cheese. And," she continued, zeroing in, "there isn't a man alive who'd ever want anything to do with you. So I'd give up that particular dream, if I were you. And as for using all of us to satisfy your warped curiosity, I hope it's been a real show because if you don't get your skinny ass out of here right now, I'm going to give you something to remember for the rest of your life."

Sarah huffed, drawing in lungfuls of air as she backed away from the frightening light in Bea's eyes. "You wouldn't dare touch me!" she said, not at all sure of that.

"Don't bet on it!" Bea took several steps toward the girl, her demeanor menacing. "Have you any idea," Bea said very softly, "how *ugly* you are? It's positively tragic," she said, her lips curving into a smile. "You'll spend your whole life alone. It's really very sad. I could harm you terribly," she whispered, "in unimaginable ways. You're not as clever as you think, Sarah. You picked the wrong family. Look!" Holding the towel around her with one hand, she raised her other to point to Sarah's face. "Festering sores are starting to appear all over your face. And in a few minutes, you're going to start to bleed. The blood will come out of your ears and your eyes and your nose. It'll run down your legs. See! It's already started."

Sarah emitted a thin scream and fled from the bathroom.

Letting out her breath, and clutching the towel around her, Bea went to the foot of the stairs and bellowed, "LUCY! BRING MELINDA DOWN HERE!" then stormed into the bedroom to get dressed.

"I *knew* you'd send her away!" Melinda accused tearfully as Lucy brought her over the threshold. "I knew you would!"

"Sit down and be quiet! I'll talk to you in a moment." Bea puffed furiously on her cigarette, then set it in the ashtray while she finished pulling on her clothes.

"Lucy, please make sure that girl doesn't help herself to anything that doesn't belong to her on her way out. I'll explain everything after she's gone."

"I *hate* you!" Melinda repeated over and over as she sat with her arms tightly folded in front of her, glaring at Bea. "I hate you hate you hate you!"

"Now you listen to me!" Bea said, going over to her. "Sarah told you things that just aren't true. You did the absolutely right thing to tell me, in spite of the fact that Sarah made you promise you wouldn't. Children don't keep secrets from their parents, Mel. Parents are the people you can talk to about anything, absolutely anything; because your parents are the people who're always going to love you best, no matter what."

"*Sarah* loves me!" Melinda insisted defiantly.

"Sarah's a goddamned mental case!" Bea snapped, then gentling her tone, added, "She can't help herself. She sees things one way, and your father and Lucy and I see them another way." Crouching painfully in front of the girl, putting her hands on Melinda's knees, Bea said, "You have to understand, Mel, that your father and I do work that lots of people see. And it's a funny thing about movies, but very often the people who go to see them start thinking they actually know the people on the screen. Or they feel as if they love them. But sometimes, with people like Sarah, they want to prove to themselves that they're just as *good* as they are. None of it has to do with the real, actual people that I am, that your father is, that other actors are. It's the parts we play in pictures. I've done it for a very long time now, so there are many, many people who know what I look like. And that's why sometimes when you and I go out together, strangers talk to us or ask me to sign autographs. It's their way of showing they like the work I do, the parts I play in the pictures. And it's also very very important to my work, Mel, because if those people didn't like me, then I wouldn't be able to work anymore. And that would make me sad because I like what I do. Do you understand?"

"A little," Melinda conceded. "But I still don't see why Sarah has to go away."

"She has to go because she's been trying to teach you things about your daddy and me that have nothing to do with the way we really are. You know we love you, don't you?"

"I guess so."

"You *know* we do," Bea told her. "Come on, now. Admit it. You know your daddy and Lucy and I love you better than anything."

"I know," Melinda admitted, still keeping her eyes averted and her arms tight across her chest.

"Mel, I want you to listen very carefully to what I'm saying. Okay?"

"Okay." Melinda sighed.

"You've got famous parents, sweetheart. That means that wherever you go, maybe for the rest of your whole life, people are going to ask you questions about me and your father. And there'll be other people, like Sarah, who'll try to convince you of bad things about us because they're jealous, or they don't know what to make of us. You have to know that your father and I will always do our best to make you happy. Sometimes we may do things that won't make very much sense to you, and when that happens, you've got to come and ask us to explain, no matter what it is. You're a very bright little girl, and you'll see things you *think* you understand, but you won't really, and if you don't ask you'll only get confused. And if you don't feel comfortable asking us about something, you can always talk to Aunt Lucy. Will you promise me you'll try to do that?"

"If you and Daddy are famous, does that mean I am too?"

"Sort of, in a way. But you're very lucky because people don't know what you look like."

"Why is that lucky?"

"Because you'll have a chance to lead a normal life, if that's what you want, without people bothering you."

"D'you like being famous?" Melinda asked, finally relaxing her arms and letting her hands drop to her lap.

Bea thought for a moment about how to respond. "Yes," she said, "I do."

"Is Daddy as famous as you are?"

"In his own way, yes he is."

"But people don't come up to him when we go out for a walk the way they do when you take me."

"That's because your father works *behind* the camera, and not in front of it the way I do. He's the one who gets all the people together and actually makes the picture. The work he does is very important, and far more difficult than mine."

"How can you be famous if people don't know what you look like?"

"There are different kinds of fame, Mel. Writers and painters, directors like your father, all kinds of people are famous without having famous *faces*. Maybe, when you're a little older, it'll be clearer to you."

Relenting, Melinda draped her arms around her mother's shoulders. "I don't think it'll ever make sense to me. I'm hungry. When're we going to eat?"

"Not until Daddy gets back. But we could go down to the kitchen and see if Mrs. Pepper can fix you a little snack to tide you over."

"Okay. Carry me!"

"Mel, you know I can't. Let me up now, sweetheart." She tried to remove Melinda's arms from around her neck, but the child simply tightened her hold. For just a moment, Bea was overwhelmed by rage. She wanted to tear away Melinda's arms and heave her against the wall. She couldn't bear having those small, but powerful, limbs locked around her neck.

"*Why* can't you?" Melinda asked.

"I've told you over and over," Bea said, working to be patient. "I'm not strong enough to carry a great big girl like you. Now, let go, Melinda."

Melinda continued to hold on, so that Bea had flash visions of breaking both her daughter's arms in order to free herself from the suffocating embrace. She closed her eyes and breathed deeply, willing herself to remain calm. "Melinda," she whispered, "let go now. I thought you said you were hungry."

Melinda studied her mother's face, taken by the way her mother was working not be angry. She wondered what would happen if she just held on and on. She knew it would make Mummy very angry, and she'd have liked to know what Mummy would do when she got very angry.

Behind Bea's closed eyes, a torrent of blood seemed to rage against her reason. She was powerless. Dickie knelt on her arms, and terror shot through her system, screams of fury died in her lungs. Bea opened her eyes, her heartbeat heavy against her ribs as she looked at her daughter, trying to imagine what Melinda could be thinking. As usually occurred when she looked at Melinda, she became so captivated by her child's beauty that she temporarily forgot what had preceded this viewing. There was a certain light to Melinda's eyes that was new and mildly alarming. She looked as if she were prepared to take Bea right to the end of her limits. "Let go now, Melinda," she said sharply, "before you make me angry!"

On this command, Melinda let her arms go limp so that they slid and fell away to her sides. The air was released from Bea's lungs, and she lurched to her feet, in pain from her protracted crouching.

November 21, 1951

Darling Bobby,

I'm thrilled you'll be here for Christmas. It's the best possible news I could've had just now. I feel as if if I don't see you soon, I'll be forced to do something desperate. All I've thought about for months now is making love to you. I'm starting to feel as if everyone who looks at me can read what I'm thinking. So hurry up and get here.

Of course you'll stay with us. There's plenty of room. But if you insist on staying in a hotel, let me know the exact dates and we'll make reservations for you.

We've now had a total of three nannies for Mel. I don't know if we've been unlucky or if Mel tends to act up when we're not around. She still talks about Sarah, and no amount of explaining will convince her Sarah wasn't the most wonderful girl who ever lived. Fortunately, now that she's started school, Mel's made some friends, and she's not throwing quite as many tantrums.

The school's very good, and there are several American kids there. Currently, Mel's best friend is the daughter of a couple from New York. They seem nice enough, and their girl Nancy gets along very well with Mel.

Yes, I read about the Wage Earners Committee picketing theaters, but I hadn't heard about the Catholic War Veterans picketing poor Judy Holliday in D.C. From the sound of it, you're not having much fun. We'll do our best to make sure you have a wonderful time while you're here. We've got a big Christmas dinner planned (I mean the amount of food, not the number of guests). Lucy's still in the thick of it with Brian and admitted the other night that he asked her to marry him. She turned him down, but he's being very persistent. Anyway, you'll get to meet him because he'll be here for Christmas dinner, too.

I'm so lonely for you. And Hank's pining away for Hero, who'll be coming over too. (Maybe the two of you could travel together?) Please don't decide you want to stay in a hotel. Every time I go past one of the guest rooms I think about having you here, about being able to come to you at night so we could sleep together. I start getting shaky just thinking about it. God! I hope you're keeping your promise to destroy these letters.

November 22, 1951

Here I am, back again. We had another scene with Mel, and the latest nanny quit on the spot. So I had to phone the agency again. They're sending several women over for me to interview this afternoon.

Mel's becoming more and more difficult, and it makes me feel horribly guilty, as if there's something I should be doing that I'm not. Lately, she's taken to getting up in the middle of the night and climbing into bed with me. And since she's become friends with Nancy (the NY couple's girl) she's started comparing our two households and asking why Hank and I sometimes sleep in the same bed and sometimes in different rooms. Hank was so good, explaining to her. He's amazingly patient, which only makes me feel even more guilty. But then she doesn't behave with him the way she does with me.

Anyway, enough domestic complaints. Write me back right away and let me know when you'll be arriving, and whether or not you'll stay here with us or at a hotel.

For now, all my love,
Bea

381

Thirty-Five

"**W**HY d'you always do that?" Melinda wanted to know. She was sitting cross-legged in the doorway of the dining room, watching her mother and Lucy making themselves all red in the face. "How come every day?"

"It's exercise," Bea gasped.

"But *why* do you do it?"

"Because it's good for you," Bea answered, resting for a moment.

"But if it's good for you, how come everybody doesn't do it? Nancy's mummy and daddy don't do it. *My* daddy doesn't do it."

Bea lay flat on her back, catching her breath. "I've told you, Mel. I used to be a dancer, and so did Aunt Lucy. It's very important to a dancer to keep her body in shape."

"But you don't dance anymore, either one of you."

"Mel, let's give the questions a rest now. Okay?" Lucy smiled over at her. "It's pretty hard to do this and answer your questions at the same time."

"Well, I still don't know *why!*" Melinda glared at Lucy.

"It's good to exercise, that's all," Lucy told her.

"*I* think it's silly!" Melinda declared.

Bea rolled over onto her side and leaned on her elbow to look at her daughter. She knew it was absurd, but Melinda's comment irked her. Every so often, Melinda would say things in a certain way, or she'd take hold of a stubborn attitude, that triggered in Bea a blend of anger and impotence that had combustive potential. On these occasions, she studied Melinda, trying to decide just what it was about her daughter that made her so angry. Along with the anger came even more guilt, because these were moments when she felt such a strong dislike of Melinda that it had to be a reflection on her worthiness, or lack of it, as a mother. Surely she wasn't supposed to feel this way about her own child. Yet because she felt as she did, she tried extra hard to compensate by being as tolerant as she possibly could, attempting to offer truthful replies to Melinda's limitless supply of questions and refusing to be blackmailed by her bursts of angry, bad behavior. "There are loads of things for you to do, Mel," she said now. "You don't have to stay and watch us. I'm sure it must look very silly to you." She gave Melinda a smile she hoped would convey both her understanding of a child's impatience with odd adult actions and a good-natured acceptance of Melinda's right to her own views.

"I'm going to go play house," Melinda announced, and skipped off.

Still winded, Bea stretched out again on her back. "Sometimes," she confided to Lucy, "I feel like the worst mother in the world, as if I'm doing everything wrong. Other times, I feel no one could possibly do a better job. I don't know why, but I thought this would be easier, more fun that it is."

"Who ever told you it was going to be easy?" Lucy asked.

"Oh, you know what I mean," Bea said impatiently. "I never thought she'd be so . . . I don't know."

"Did you think you were going to have a quiet little kid who'd sit in the corner, reading? I mean, for God's sake, Bea. *You're* hardly ordinary. Did you actually think you'd have an ordinary child?"

Bea thought about that, then, with a laugh, sat up hugging her knees. Somewhat sheepishly, she smiled at Lucy. "I think I did. That's pretty ridiculous, isn't it?"

"Just a little," Lucy agreed.

"I wonder sometimes what she makes of it all. You know? Leaving California to come here, living in somebody else's house, seeing Hank and I get mobbed by fans. I can't imagine how it must seem to her. D'you remember that trip to New York when you and Mel came along?"

"I remember."

"We stayed at the Pierre, and we took Mel to see *High Button Shoes* and went backstage to say hello to Nanette, and Phil Silvers. And we saw *Annie Get Your Gun* and went back to say hello to Ethel. We took Mel to just about every goddamned thing going. And I'd look at her at some point during every show, and she looked bored silly. But when I'd ask her after if she'd liked the shows, she'd make a fuss and say yes. Everywhere we went, I had to sign autographs and I kept looking at Mel to see how she was reacting. At first she seemed confused. But after a while, she looked angry. A couple of times I actually saw her pushing at people's legs, as if she wanted everyone to go away. It was awful. I had the feeling she thought people were trying to take me away from her, and I felt so deeply, terribly sorry for her, because she couldn't understand any of it.

"She doesn't do it anymore. Now, she just seems—resigned, in a way; as if she knows it'll be over soon and then everything'll be back to normal. Except I have no idea what's normal for Mel."

"Kids have to adapt to whatever their parents do. What if you were a teacher, and she had to be a student at the school where you taught? She'd have to get used to that and to the razzing she'd take from the other kids because of her mother."

"That's hardly the same thing."

"It's not so different," Lucy argued. "And anyway, the point is: You are who you are, and any kid you had would have to live with that. It's not as if she's growing up deprived. She's got the best of everything, and you're a damned good mother. Hank's a wonderful father. She's one lucky kid. I can't see why you agonize over it the way you do."

Bea rested her chin on her knees. "I want her to be happy, Luce."

"She's sure not suffering. What're you so worried about?"

"I don't know. Maybe I'm just anticipating. We're going to have a houseful of people with Hero and Bobby here. And Becky might change her mind and come after all."

"So?"

"I don't know. Maybe people in the movies shouldn't have kids. Maybe it's not fair to them."

"Jesus! Spare me, would you? You're driving yourself nuts because Mel's an energetic kid who likes to ask a lot of questions and periodically throws temper tantrums. Kids do things like that, Bea. It's got nothing to do with you and Hank being in the movies."

"I'm not so sure of that, Luce. I'm really not."

"And what if you quit, and the two of you settled down somewhere and started being parents full time? D'you suppose that'd turn Mel into an ordinary kid?"

"Maybe I'm being silly, but I have to worry. She *is* my child, after all."

"Being her mother doesn't mean you quit enjoying yourself, that you give up your whole life for her. Long after you're dead and gone, kiddo, Melinda will still be around, living her own life and thinking her own thoughts."

"That's charming. Thank you so much for helping me put everything in perspective."

Lucy swatted her lightly on the arm. "You worry too damned much about her. Whatever she'll be, she'll be; and no amount of worrying on your part is going to change that. Are you ready to quit for the day?"

Bea nodded, preoccupied.

Lucy got up and stood gazing down at her, waiting for her to snap out of her sudden, trance-like state. Hands on her hips, she waited, for a few seconds caught by the realization of how much time had passed since she'd first seen the kid Bea had been go flying across the front lawn and away down the street. "*You* were no ordinary kid," she said with a fond smile.

Bea lifted her head and smiled. "I still dream of dancing. All the steps, the routines, they're still there. God, but it makes me sad sometimes to think about it. It's like remembering someone who died."

"I know, sweetheart." Lucy held out her hand to help Bea to her feet. "C'mon. You'll seize up if you don't get into the tub."

"D'you have the feeling things are going too fast now?" Bea asked as they climbed the stairs. "I do. A few months, and I'll be thirty-five. Then I'll be forty, then fifty."

Lucy laughed. "I refuse to get into this. You seem to forget I've got a few years on you, and I like to think I'm going to live forever."

The liveried driver carried the bags, and Bobby followed him out of the terminal toward the black Rolls-Royce waiting at the curb. The car's windows were dark-tinted, so it was impossible to see inside. Bobby stood, breathing in the cold, damp air, then the driver came to open the rear door. Bea looked up, and Bobby laughed, taken completely by surprise.

Quickly, she put out her cigarette, smiling as he got in beside her and the driver closed the door.

"I thought you'd be waiting at the house," he said, unable to take his eyes off her.

"I couldn't. If I had to wait, I wanted to be here."

"You look wonderful," he told her, oblivious to everything but the delight of seeing her.

"So do you." She could hardly breathe as he slid closer to her. "God," she whispered. "I almost think I could do it right now, in the back of the damned limo."

"Don't give me any ideas," he warned, clasping her to his chest. He held onto her hard, then she tilted her head back and looked at him in a way that made him suddenly overheated.

"Kiss me," she whispered, "then we'll behave ourselves."

He let go to open his coat and, reaching into his trousers pocket, brought out his handkerchief, then carefully wiped off her lipstick. He looked again at her mouth as he returned the hankie to his pocket, then drew her forward and kissed her.

She sat back, holding her hand to her breast, her eyes a little glazed and her mouth wet. As he watched, her eyes filled and overran. Then she wrapped her arms around him, whispering, "Thank God you're here. I thought I'd die, missing you."

At the last minute, Becky decided to come after all and sent a cable saying she'd be arriving on the twenty-third. A limo was hired to pick her up at the airport and bring her to the house. Melinda threw such a violent tantrum at being asked to give her room up to Becky that both Bobby and Hero volunteered at once to go to hotels. No amount of quiet reasoning would persuade Melinda to sleep in Lucy's room for a week. Hank tried to talk to her. So did Lucy, and the latest nanny, and the housekeeper, and, of course, Bea. Melinda threw herself down in the foyer and screamed, drumming her heels and fists on the floor until, with strength derived from embarrassment and anger, Bea lifted her to her feet and shook her until her cries abruptly ceased.

"How *dare* you behave this way in front of our guests!" Bea whispered, offended and frightened. "What's *wrong* with you? When *I* was a little girl I didn't even *have* a room of my own. Here you have an entire *suite*, and you're so selfish you won't give it up for a week! Go to your room and stay there! I don't want to *see* you until dinner." Bea thrust her away, saying, "Go on! Right now!"

"It's *my* room!" Melinda's tone matched her mother's. "*Mine!* I *won't* sleep with Aunt Lucy! I don't *have* to!" With that, she turned and pounded off up the stairs. The door to her room slammed so hard that the crystals in the hallway chandelier crashed together in a jangle of noise that made Bea wince, and several paintings tipped off-center. Trembling, Bea straightened and turned to face the others who appeared to be as shocked as she.

"I'm sorry," she apologized.

"She's overtired," Hank said.

"I'll move to a hotel," Bobby and Hero said together, then turned to look at each other.

"Maybe it'd be best," Hank said, his eyes on Bea.

"This is unbelievable!" She tried to smile, but couldn't quite bring it off. "I need a drink."

Hank went at once to get her one. Hero followed after him.

Lucy said, "I'll just go see how Edna's doing in the kitchen."

Bobby remained in the foyer with Bea. "I'll clear out and check into a hotel. I don't mind."

"*I do!*" she whispered fiercely. "I *need* you."

"Come on, Bea," he coaxed, reaching for her hand. "It *is* her room, after all. And she shouldn't have to move if she doesn't want to."

Her grip on his hand was so strong it was almost painful. "She frightens me when she gets that way, Bobby. It's impossible to reason with her."

"She's a little kid. She'll grow out of it."

"God! I hope so."

He directed her into the living room where Hank was waiting with her drink. She let go of Bobby's hand, took the glass from Hank, and downed half its contents in one go. "Jesus!" she gasped as the scotch seared its way down her throat.

"I didn't think you were going to chug-a-lug it," Hank laughed.

"I didn't know I was either."

"Look," Bobby told everyone. "It's settled. I'll get a hotel room and Becky can move right in here. I'll go make a couple of quick calls." He went off, and Hero said, "I really don't mind going to a hotel."

"*Please!*" Bea begged him. "Bobby will go. There's no need for you to do a thing. Not a thing. It means everything to me and Hank to have you here. You *can't* leave."

"I really don't mind . . ." Hero began, but Hank stopped him, seeing that Bea was ready to break if anything more on the subject was said.

"Have your drink and relax," Hank told him. "We'll be right back." Taking her arm, he steered Bea out of the room and up the stairs to their bedroom. "Go with Bobby and make sure he gets settled in," he told her, closing the door. "Take a few hours, have a drink or two, relax. You're making too much of this."

"How can you *say* that? You saw her, Hank. My God! It was one of the worst moments of my life. How can you say I'm making too much of it?"

"Because I happen to think it's true. The more she sees she's getting a rise out of you, the more she likes to act up. If you could ignore her when she gets that way, she'd stop doing it soon enough."

"How could I possibly ignore her screaming and practically foaming at the mouth? I wanted to *kill* her! I feel as if I still do."

"Bea," he chided, "everyone understands. Go with Bobby, see that he gets squared away, then the two of you will come back here for dinner. Lucy and I will be here to handle Mel."

She leaned against him, exhausted suddenly, as if she hadn't slept for weeks. He put his arms around her saying, "You're taking it much too seriously. Nobody's going to judge *you* by Mel's behavior."

"Of course they are," she disagreed. "I'm her mother. I'm responsible for her. What else can people think but that it's my fault she behaves the way she does?"

"Kids act up. Period. It's not a personal reflection on either one of us. I'll admit she's a handful, but not any more than any other kid."

"You actually think that?"

"Yes, I do."

"I want to believe you're right."

"Then, believe me." He held her at arm's length. "Go with Bobby. Go for a walk, the two of you. Have a drink in a pub somewhere. Do some last-minute shopping. Go make love. Just get a little distance from all this. Don't let one incident spoil the holidays, Bea. Another few weeks and we'll be leaving for Paris. You'll be up to your neck in the new picture, and you'll be phoning home every night to talk to Mel."

"D'you think things would be different if I were home with her all the time?"

"No, I do not. You've got a career. You've always had one. Mel's used to it."

"I can't help thinking she might feel ... more secure, something, if I were with her on a full-time basis."

"If *I* said that, you'd laugh and tell me I was being ridiculous."

She stared at him.

"Wouldn't you?" he persisted.

"Yes, I would," she answered. "You're absolutely right, I would. I feel like getting drunk. I so wanted us all to be together here."

He shrugged. "You'll only make yourself sick."

"I'll stop before I get to that point, but I definitely need several more good, stiff drinks."

He gave her a hug, then released her. "I'll hold the fort until you get back. It doesn't change anything, not really. You'll get to spend time with everyone."

"Henry," she began, as someone knocked at the door.

"What?" he asked, going to open it.

"Nothing."

"I'm set at the Ritz," Bobby told them. "I'm going to throw my stuff back in the bags. I've ordered a car."

"Oh, good," Bea said distractedly. "I'll be right there, to go with you."

"Okay." Bobby backed up and went off along the hall.

Hank closed the door after him, asking, "What were you about to say?"

"I don't remember."

"No, tell me."

She sat down tiredly on the side of the bed and leaned back on her hands. "Hank, maybe we should buy a house, find something permanent, if we're going to be here indefinitely. It might be better for Mel."

"But we've got this place for another fourteen months."

"But it's not ours. Maybe she'd be happier if she knew we were really staying."

"But *we* don't know that," he said reasonably. "And I'm not so sure permanency is the issue here, Bea."

"Then what is? Every time she throws one of those tantrums I feel like the worst kind of failure, that I'm completely hopeless as a parent. It's terrible, Hank; the worst feeling imaginable."

"It'll pass. Think about this for a minute, dear heart. We're talking about a child who's not yet six years old."

She sighed, and gave up, pushing herself off the bed. "I envy your confidence." She went to the dressing table to pick up her hairbrush. "If I'd known being a mother would be so..."

"You'd have done it anyway. I'm going back downstairs. Take some time off and forget about it."

She paused in brushing her hair to look at him in the mirror. "How do you manage to stay so sane?" she asked, giving him a smile.

"I've had eighteen years more practice." He blew her a kiss, and closed the door quietly behind him.

She stood to one side, her hands thrust deep into the pockets of her coat, watching with interest as Bobby filled out the information on the guest card, printing "ROBERT ELLIS BRADLEY," followed by his California address. The clerk glanced at the card, then over at her, then busied himself finding the room key before summoning the bellboy. Bobby linked his arm through hers, saying, "You look terrific. Have I told you that?"

"Since yesterday, about thirty times."

"Well, I mean it. You do. I like the mink. New?"

"We got it in New York before we sailed."

"You do realize the guy on the desk recognized both of us?"

"I do realize that," she said, as they stepped into the elevator. "He'll be discreet, however. The British are very discreet. That's one of the reasons I love it here."

Still in her coat, she sat down in an armchair in the sitting room while Bobby took care of the bellboy and the baggage in the bedroom. The door closed, and Bobby reappeared saying, "I've got some booze and ice on order."

"Good."

He leaned against the doorframe, studying her. "You're not your usual country-girl casual self," he observed. "I don't think I've ever seen you quite so—grown up."

"For every year Mel's been alive, I've aged five. And why are we talking about my clothes?"

"It's as good a topic as any," he said, removing his camel-hair topcoat and draping it over the back of the nearest chair. "I've been the loneliest man on earth," he told her, crossing the room to perch on the edge of the chair next to hers. "I guess I'm making up for lost time or something, taking mental notes, like how you look in a black mink coat and how well it suits you, and how your legs look in nylons. You still have the best legs of any woman I know."

"Isn't it a pity they're non-functional," she said, looking down at them.

"You planning to keep your coat on indefinitely?"

"Only until the bellboy comes back with the liquor. It would hardly do to have him come back and find the two of us stark naked on the carpet."

"But I thought you told me they were all so discreet."

"They're discreet," she laughed, "but they're not deaf, dumb, and blind."

"Round one to the skinny brunette," he grinned, as he got up to answer the knock at the door.

Having tipped the bellboy and placed the "Do Not Disturb" sign on the door, he came back to find she'd already poured drinks. She gave him his, clinked glasses, then took a large swallow of barely diluted scotch.

"Now," she announced, "I'll take off my coat."

She put down her drink to do it, then retrieved her glass and stood looking at him, a half-smile on her lips.

"You keep changing," he said, reaching out to touch her hair which, as always, fell precisely to her shoulders. It seemed to caress his hand as his fingers threaded into it.

"How have I changed?" she asked, leaning her head into his hand.

"Well, for one thing, I've never seen you drink the way you have since I got here."

"It's called dulling the edges. What else?"

"Dulling the edges of what?"

"Welll," she drawled, "it has been somewhat of a strain, these past

390

twenty-four hours. Or haven't you felt it?" She didn't move, yet somehow she was drawing closer to him. "It's been a *very* long time."

"We've had longer times than this."

"We were younger then." She took another swallow, set down the glass, and looked at him expectantly.

"Jesus!" he exclaimed, his eyes locked to hers. "There's no one else on earth who can do this to me." He put aside his untouched drink and reached for her, aligning his body to hers. He breathed in her perfume, playfully bit her earlobe, and whispered, "When I'm away from you, I sometimes get the feeling that maybe you're not real, that I dreamed you up just to drive myself crazy."

"I get scared nowadays, thinking how short life is. Do you think about that, Bobby? The past is gone, and the future's happening too fast. I keep wondering what it's all about, and I don't think I really know. *Everything's* changing, and if you don't change with it, you'll disappear. Nobody will know who you are or give a damn. And I want to be remembered. Is it terrible of me, to want to be remembered?"

"I'm the wrong guy to ask. I want the same thing."

"Do you? Why do we care? Why does it matter?"

"If I knew that, maybe it wouldn't matter, and neither one of us would care."

"I don't think we're vain, stupid people. I honestly don't. But I can't help thinking it must be vain and stupid to want to keep on being recognized. And yet, sometimes, I think if those crowds of fans really knew me, they wouldn't be interested; they'd be bored because I'm nothing special off the screen. I used to be," she said sadly. "When we danced together, God, I *was* special. You still are, Bobby. As long as you can dance, you'll keep on being special. I envy you that."

"Why, for chrissake?"

"Because I'm just another actress trying for decent parts, like all the other actresses. I lost the one thing that made me special."

"That's bullshit, Bea. You're not 'just another actress.' You're Beatrice Crane. You could go practically anywhere in the world, and people would know your name. There's nobody who can do what you do. Nobody! I can't believe you really mean any of this."

"I do, though. Another ten years and I'll be fighting for my life, if I stay in pictures. I'm going to have to hang on by my fingernails just to get work."

"Then walk away from it!" he called her bluff. "Quit! Get out while you're ahead!"

"I can't." She shook her head unhappily. "I have to see it through. I don't *have* anything else."

"Bea, that's just more bullshit. It's your choice. It's always been your choice, just as it's been mine, and it always will be. If you're scared, then quit. But don't make out that you have no alternatives, because you do. This isn't like you," he said, a little angrily. "You don't run scared. Nothing really scares you, not when it comes to your work."

She broke away from him to pick up her glass and drank the last of the scotch. Then she stepped out of her shoes and began undoing her suit jacket as she walked past him into the bedroom. He remained where he was until she turned and extended her hand to him. He went toward her, feeling uncertain, wounded by the images she'd drawn of her future. He let her get as far as removing the suit, then stopped her. "I want to do the rest," he murmured, his hands slipping around over the backs of her thighs. "Don't be afraid," he told her, lifting the silk straps of her slip off her shoulders, "not of anything. Don't you know I'll always look out for you?"

She stopped his hands, her expression serious. "I know that, Bobby. But I've still got to live my life. And it's turning out to be a lot harder than I thought it'd be. I *do* get scared. I can't help it."

"I *told* you: I'm going to be here for you. Now, shut up and let me do this!" He threw off his clothes, then adeptly stripped her of hers.

"Shut me up, why don't you?" she suggested, and when he looked puzzled, she opened her mouth over his, her hand gliding down his belly.

His body, his hands and mouth were like poultices pulling the poison out of her system. She could open herself, and he could close out the world by filling her so fully that there was no room for anything else. And as long as they could do this for each other, she needn't ever capitulate to her daily-growing tally of concerns. She could close her eyes and forget everything.

Thirty-Six

"**B**RIAN wants to get married," Lucy said. She and Bea were sitting together at the dining table, finishing a late dinner. Hank was on location in Spain. Melinda had been put to bed over an hour earlier. They could hear Edna loading the dishwasher in the kitchen.

"Are you going to do it?" Bea asked, lighting a cigarette.

"I can't say I haven't given it a lot of thought."

"I'll bet you have. You've been seeing each other for almost three years now."

"I keep coming up with the idea that if we get married, we'll ruin whatever we've got. Brian's too straight-laced to handle 'living in sin' as he calls it. So I've been given an ultimatum. Either we get married or we break it off."

Bea looked appraisingly at Lucy through the smoke from her cigarette. Suddenly, they were all much older than they'd been the last time she'd noticed. Lucy was almost forty-nine. She didn't look it. She was still very trim; there was very little gray in her hair. Nevertheless, she was close to fifty years old. "Why does it have to be one or the other? Why can't you keep on the way you are?"

"Reasons," Lucy said tiredly. "All of them his. You know what I'm like. I'd love things to stay the way they are. Maybe it's because he's younger. I don't know. I don't like being forced into a corner. On the other hand, I'm not crazy about the idea of giving him up. At my age," she smiled, "it's not easy finding men."

"What crap!" Bea laughed. "You should look behind you sometime when you walk into a restaurant. All those men ogling you, with saliva running down their chins. D'you want a drink? I'm going to have one."

"Sure. Why not? Saliva," she scoffed.

Bea went to the bar. Gin and tonic went in one glass, neat scotch in the other. Sliding back into her seat, she picked up her cigarette, then swallowed some scotch as she watched Lucy poke at the ice cubes in her drink.

"You're very sexy," Bea said in a voice that left no room for argument. "I swear you get more sexy every goddamned year. Anyway, tell me all the pros and cons, and we'll decide."

Lucy looked over and laughed. "Sexy or not, we both know I'm lousy marriage material. There's no point in going over the pros and cons. The minute we get married, I'll start wondering what you and Hank and Mel are doing; I'll worry that your appointments aren't getting made, or that you're not being reminded about them. I'll keep myself up nights worrying about your bank deposits, and this and that, and the next thing anyone knows, I'll be knocking at the door, asking to have my room back. I wish I knew why men always have to force the issue, why they can't leave well enough alone. I was hoping it'd just go on forever. I mean, I could see the point if either one of us was still young enough to be thinking about having kids. But I'm not. He claims not to want any. We've both been married before, and his wasn't any better than mine was. Sometimes, you know, I really am jealous of Becky."

"*Becky?* Why?"

"Because she's stuck to her guns all the way. She didn't want to get married, and she's never backed down. I really admire her for that."

"I've always admired her *talent*," Bea said. "How funny that you'd admire her for staying single."

"It ain't easy, you know, sweetheart."

"It's not all that hard, my darling. In any number of ways, it's far easier to stay single. You never have to worry about anyone but yourself. You don't have to compromise on any level. Your time's your own; your life's your own. You can do what you damned well please, and you don't have to answer to anyone."

"You left out the part about your bed's your own, and you get to sleep in it alone. Anyway, you've got all those things, and you're married."

"You could hardly call it a typical marriage." Bea crushed out her cigarette. "I'm scarcely qualified to say. I've been involved with precisely two men in my whole life. For any length of time, that is."

"For any length of time," Lucy repeated, beginning to smile. "Have you been keeping secrets?"

"Lucy, for God's sake! You know what it's like on a shoot, especially on location. Everybody's in everybody else's pocket. There you all

394

are, cut off from your families, away from home. You're on the set all day with some man, doing a kiss for fifteen takes. Then that night, you're sitting in bed by yourself in some motel room out in the sticks, and so's the man you spent the day kissing. It happens." She shrugged and drank some more of her scotch.

"You really surprise me," Lucy admitted. "Are we talking about a lot of times, a few, or just once?"

"A few, three or four. Maybe five."

"Why, little Beatrice, I'm shocked. Who were they?"

Bea laughed. "You'd love a list of names, and all the details, wouldn't you?"

"Damned right, I would. Are you kidding? I never dreamed you got up to such high jinks."

"It was a very long war."

"*That* far back?" Lucy said, disappointed. "I thought you were going to tell me *recent* news."

"Sorry." Bea busied herself lighting another cigarette. "Nothing recent. Just Bobby, as usual. And Hank, occasionally."

"And that's enough to keep you satisfied?"

"Let's just say it suffices." She was about to say more when her eye was caught by something at the very edge of her vision. Slipping silently out of her chair, she went to the doorway to look up the stairs just as Melinda disappeared out of sight down the landing. She stood for a moment, then went back to the dining room where she grabbed her glass and drained its contents.

"What?" Lucy asked.

"Melinda," Bea whispered. "Christ! She was sitting on the stairs, listening." She sat down abruptly, rattled. "I wonder how long she was sitting there," she said, meeting Lucy's eyes. "I need another drink."

"I'll get it." Lucy took Bea's glass to refill it. "So what if she did hear?" she asked, returning. "So what? Kids love to listen in on grown-ups' conversations. They think they're going to hear something about themselves. I used to do it all the time, and I never did hear one thing worth repeating."

"You didn't happen to overhear them talking about how many men your mother had slept with."

"No, that's true."

"I keep reminding myself of how I was at her age, of how I felt and the things I thought about. She's nothing like I was. When I think of how many nannies we went through before she got old enough to stop needing one. And the dozen of tantrums she's thrown since we came to England."

"She's a lot better now than she was."

"I'll admit that. She is. No question. But she does things that completely mystify me."

"Like what?"

"Like the other afternoon, when you and I came back from Harrod's, I went up, and there was Mel going through my desk. She said she was looking for a pen, but she wasn't. She'd been going through that file Hank and I keep for important papers. I wouldn't have minded if she'd told the truth and said she'd been curious so she'd had a look. It's that she lied without even considering telling the truth."

"You're making too much of it."

"No," Bea disagreed. "I don't think I'm making enough of it. I look at her sometimes, Luce, and she's so beautiful that seeing her makes my bones ache. I'll go into her room at night and watch her sleep. I kiss her, I fix her blankets, and I feel capable of murder at the thought that anyone might ever wish to harm her. Then it's another day and she's defying me, and *I'm* the one who'd like to harm her. I have visions of beating her silly, of throwing her against a wall."

"You couldn't lift her, let alone throw her against a wall."

Bea laughed, reached for her glass, changed her mind, looked at the burnt-out cigarette in the ashtray, and lit a fresh one. "Tell me all mothers go through this."

"All mothers go through this."

"God!" She gazed at the glass in front of her. "I've developed quite a fondness for this brown stuff lately. I can see now why people become alcoholics. It's very tempting. Throw down a couple of ounces of scotch and the world and everyone in it can go straight to hell. Are you going to marry Brian?"

"Nope! But it doesn't matter."

"It *does*," Bea begged to differ. "He loves you. You love him. If you say no, it'll be over, and what'll you have?"

"The same things I had before."

"Only less."

"Only less," Lucy agreed. "I'd miss sleeping with him. I would miss that. And we don't bicker constantly, the way Ike and I used to."

"Brian's a grown-up."

"He certainly is. Except for his talent for ultimatums. That puts him back in the playpen with all the other little boys. Men! Wouldn't life be perfect if we didn't need them!"

"Do you think she heard?" Bea looked toward the doorway.

"And what if she did? What did we say that was so terrible?"

"I wish Hank was here." Morose now, she picked up her drink and stared at it. "I hate it when he's off somewhere and I'm not working. Do you realize it's getting on for a year since I did anything?"

"You've turned down one script after another."

"They were dogmeat, garbage. I'm not that hard-up, not yet anyway. You ought to marry him, Luce. He's an awfully nice man, and he thinks the world of you."

Lucy put her hand on Bea's arm and smiled, saying, "You know what I like about you? First of all, you're the world's cheapest drunk. A couple of scotches, and you're gone. And second of all, you're too goddamned generous—with everything: your time, your money, your emotions. Hold some back for yourself, kiddo. There might come a day when you'll need it."

"I thought it was now. This feels like a crisis point. Are you telling me I've got the timing wrong?"

"Yup. I'll keep Brian dangling for a while longer. Might as well get all the mileage I can out of this."

"You sound as if you're talking about storing up nuts for the winter."

Lucy gave her arm a squeeze, then let go to pick up her own drink. "I like this big old barn," she said, looking around the wood-paneled dining room. "I like Hampstead. And I'm used to you people. It's too late in the day for making major changes. Anyway, it was nice to be asked, nice to feel wanted."

"I'm going to go check on Mel. I'll be right back." Moving somewhat unsteadily, Bea went up the stairs and along to Melinda's room. The door was ajar in order that the landing light could spill in, serving as Melinda's night-light. Bea sat down on the side of the bed, murmuring, "I know you're not asleep. Are you all right, darling?"

"I'm all right. I couldn't get to sleep because the two of you were talking so loudly."

"We weren't talking loudly at all." Bea bent to give her a kiss.

Melinda said, "Ugh," and turned her face away.

Stung, Bea straightened, asking, "Why did you do that?"

"You smell of whiskey," Melinda said disgustedly, "and of cigarettes. It's horrible."

"I wanted to give you a kiss."

"I *hate* it when you smell of drinks and smoking." Melinda kept her face averted.

"Have a good sleep," Bea said quietly, then got up and left. She walked slowly along the hall and back down the stairs to the dining room where she sat down, folded her arms on the table, dropped her head, and began to sob.

"What's the matter?" Jolted, Lucy at once sought to comfort her. "What's wrong?"

Bea couldn't speak. She wept for several minutes, then sat up, gulped the last of her drink and lit a cigarette. "You're right," she said thickly. "I am a cheap drunk. A few shillings worth of scotch and my daughter has me cast as an alcoholic. I reek of cigarette smoke and booze. Why is it she can say and do things I wouldn't put up with from another living soul? Why is that, d'you know?"

"She'll never be allowed to get away with it with anyone else. Mothers get hit with the stuff kids can't pull on other people. Whatever she said or did, she didn't mean it."

"Probably not. But it hurts. One drink, and she's got me set to join A.A."

"You are a bit on the tiddly side."

"I know that."

"Well, if you know that, then you also know that kids go to extremes. Everything's an absolute when you're eight years old."

"That's true," Bea said, considering it.

"Of course, it is. You need some coffee. I'll go tell Edna. Stay put, okay?"

"Where would I go?"

While Lucy was gone, Bea looked at the items on the table: her drink, the ashtray, a pack of Players, and the gold Dunhill lighter that had been a gift from Bobby the previous Christmas when he'd made what he'd started calling his "annual pilgrimage" to spend the holidays with them. Holding the lighter in her hand, she was suddenly awash with loneliness and would willingly have given anything to see Bobby, or Hank, just then.

Lucy came back, followed by Edna carrying a tray with the coffee and two cups. Lucy poured while Edna cleared the table.

"Drink this!" Lucy pushed a cup in front of Bea. "Then we'll go for a walk. Edna will hold the fort for an hour while we're gone."

"Edna," Bea asked the housekeeper soddenly, "will you do that?"

"Of course," Edna winked at Lucy, then carried the tray of dinner dishes out to the kitchen.

"I saw that!" Bea narrowed her eyes at Lucy. "What are the two of you up to?"

"Don't be paranoid," Lucy said. "Nobody's up to anything."

"I'm *not* paranoid," Bea said indignantly. "And even paranoids have enemies, you know."

Lucy clapped her hands together and laughed loudly. "That's a good one! C'mon, kiddo. Drink up. Then we'll have a nice leisurely walk and get back in time for Hank's call."

"He's so good, isn't he?"

"Yes, he is. Drink up."

"You're not going to marry poor Brian?" Bea asked after her first sip.

"Nope. I'm not going to marry Brian. And what's so poor about him?"

"You know what I mean. Everyone knows he's rich as Croesus."

"Close, but not quite."

"Well, if you've definitely made up your mind, I'm very glad for me. I'm sorry for Brian, but glad for me. I don't know what I'd do without you. I love you, you know, Lucy."

"I know you do, and I love you, too. Why else would I still be here after all these years?"

"I sometimes wonder about that. I wonder if I haven't stolen your life." Bea drank some more coffee, then studied Lucy over the top of the cup. "Why *do* you stay?"

"I signed on, remember?"

Bea gave her a slow smile. "So as far as you're concerned, I'm still thirteen?"

"Only sometimes. Like now, for instance. Finish that, and let's go."

Bea downed the coffee. "Okay, Mom. Let's hit the road and sober up the kid."

It had stopped raining, but the air was weighted with the promise of more to come. They walked down to Finchley Road, their arms linked, moving along in companionable silence until Bea said, "I'm homesick. Not," she qualified, "for Los Angeles especially, but for cars with left-hand drive, and Mexican food, and great big supermarkets, and fresh vegetables of every kind. What about you?"

"Me, too, a little."

"Bobby wrote to say he's going to be in New York for a while. He said Becky's there for good now. She's finally taken American citizenship."

Lucy looked over at the fish-and-chip shop on the opposite side of the road where a girl in a white smock stood with her arms crossed on the counter, talking to a young man in jeans and a black leather jacket. "Why don't you go over for a couple of weeks?"

"I hate to leave Mel."

"Hank'll be back soon. And I'm here. So's good old Edna Pepper."

"I really would like to."

"Then go. There's no reason why you shouldn't. You don't need anyone's permission."

"No, but I seem to need my own." She paused, and Lucy waited. They kept walking, their footsteps muffled by the last of the autumn leaves clinging wetly to the pavement. The streetlights gave off a thick orange-yellow glow. Up ahead, outside a tobacconist's shop, a young couple fed coins into a cigarette machine. The sound of the coins falling into the slot was clearly audible.

"I love it here," Bea said at last, "but I don't feel as if I really belong. Mel's got a genuine English accent." She smiled at that. "I keep thinking of Becky talking about being permanently displaced, belonging nowhere. It's how I feel right now. I get nostalgic about Hollywood and the way things used to be. Then I have to bring myself back, remembering how it was when we left. We'll probably never be able to go back."

"There are other places."

"Everything feels wrong, Luce. Soon it'll be a year since I did any work, and I can see it stretching out to two years, and then five, and before I know it, I'll be someone who *used to be* Beatrice Crane. Hank can work anywhere. I can't. And I miss all our old friends, and the premieres, the parties."

"You must be joking! You *hated* all that when you were there."

"All right, I did. But I liked knowing I had the option of going. I'm starting to feel invisible, as if this is the beginning of the end."

"The end of what?" Lucy challenged. "You get half a dozen scripts a week. You still get bags of fan mail. People recognize you and ask for autographs. So what's ending?"

"Something. I don't know what. I look back and see all the years like a row of books on a shelf. I can go back, pull down one of the books, and see that that was the year I made four pictures, one right after another. Twenty-eight takes to get one sequence right, and our feet were bleeding by the end of it. I'll bet there aren't more than a handful of people who even remember those pictures. We're dinosaurs. Well, Bobby's not, but that Beatrice Crane sure is. Christ! There are female impersonators who do me as part of their acts. They do the Crane walk, as if I'd ever have *chosen* to walk the way I do. And they mimic the way I talk, the way I smoke. They're better at me than I am, for chrissake!" She gave a brief laugh. "I don't want to end up doing impersonations of myself. God! That would be scary. I'm going to go to New York for a few weeks, to try to get in touch with things that're familiar." She stopped walking and searched her pockets for her cigarettes. After managing to get one lit, she took a hard drag and said, "I miss being mobbed, Luce. I need confirmation that people still know who I am. It shouldn't matter, and I hate myself because it does. It's petty and selfish, but it damned well matters. I want to keep on working. I want people to know who I am and what

400

I can do. I want all that, and I cringe inside saying it out loud, but I can't help feeling what I did was important. I want it to keep on being important. And that says something about me that's not very nice."

"Oh, yeah? What might that be?"

"It's 'movie star' stuff. It's Crawford and Shearer and Bennett stuff. I always swore I'd never let myself get sucked into all that crap."

"Could we keep walking?" Lucy said. "It's too cold just standing here." She started along the pavement and after a moment Bea hurried to catch up with her. "You know what I think?"

"What?"

"I think when you don't have enough to keep you busy, you start navel-inspecting. You *are* a movie star, for chrissake! You did it; you earned it. Why the hell should you think you've got to apologize for it? Get out of here, go to New York and see everybody! A few weeks of the mob scene ought to satisfy you that you're anything but forgotten. A few weeks and you'll be itching to get back here where people leave you alone for the most part and you can do pleasant things like going for a walk in the evening after dinner. And you know what else I think?"

"What?"

"I think this is the way it's going to be from now until forever. You'll be happy for a while staying home, and then you'll start getting nervous about being out of circulation for too long. As long as I've known you you've been proving things to yourself. You're not about to stop now, and I don't see one reason why you should. I sure wouldn't apologize for wanting to be sure I'd made the kind of impact on people that you have. And since we're having this little heart-to-heart, and at the risk of being crude, you need to go to New York and get laid. All this breast-beating and self-reproach and exaggerated fear is just so much hot air. Go sleep with Bobby, and get it out of your system. We'll all still be here when you get back."

"Jesus!" Bea exclaimed, nonplussed. "You certainly cut right to the heart of the matter, don't you?"

"If I left it up to you, you'd spend years trying to undo all the knots you manage to tie yourself into. I know the score, Bea. What I can never quite figure out is why you'll waltz all around an issue, but you'd rather die than come right out and admit you need to be with Bobby, need to do all the things that make you both feel good. Why the hell d'you think I'm still seeing Brian? Because I'm no spring chicken, but he can't keep his hands off me. It's the real confirmation, the real validation; it's what keeps the you inside happy. The work is something else, and you don't need to fret about that, because it's

401

always going to be there for you. You've gone way past the point where it's even legitimate for you to be worrying about it. So do everyone a favor. Let me make the arrangements, and then get yourself out of here, go to New York and wrap your little self around your fella."

Thirty-Seven

MELINDA'S existence was a perpetual source of joy to Hank. From the moment he first saw her, through the glass enclosing the nursery at the hospital, he'd been astounded and elated by the miracle he and Bea had managed to create. There was never a day when he didn't pause to think about Melinda, marveling at the fact of her reality. And because Bea had given him this extraordinary gift, his love for her had expanded proportionately. With the conception, and then the birth, of his child, he'd come to view women in general in a new light. They were, without question in his mind, the stronger, better, segment of humanity. That his private life was crowded with females seemed an added bonus. He could watch Bea, and Lucy, and Melinda, even the housekeeper, Edna, and be fascinated by their mannerisms and movements, by their grace and efficiency and humor, by their very femaleness. He felt comfortable and content in his home, gently buffeted by the ebb and flow of the female forces around him.

When Bea went off to New York, he saw this as a fine opportunity to spend time alone with his daughter. There were temporarily no extraneous demands on his time, and he could have breakfast every morning with Melinda, then deliver her to her school; he could be there, waiting, at the end of the school day; he could enjoy the evenings in her company.

She was a wonderful-looking child, with her mother's large, deepset eyes, pale complexion, and dark hair, and her father's short, straight nose. But she was her own self in every way, with pronounced attitudes and appetites, and a questioning, stubborn nature. She had, even at eight-and-a-half, ingrained notions of wardrobe and decorum. She favored dark colors, and when Hank asked her why she so often appeared in a chocolate brown, or navy, or deep gray dress or pinafore, she answered, "I don't like fussy colors. Pinks and yellows and pale blues are for *little* children." When he smiled at this, she turned to him very seriously, and said, "I'm not a small child anymore, Daddy."

"Of course, you're not," he agreed, as always charmed by her English accent. Somehow, Melinda's impeccable party manners and precise diction were altogether incongruous in a household populated by North Americans—with the exception of Mrs. Pepper. It was likely Bea felt the same way when hearing Melinda speak. Yet, they didn't talk that much about their child. Oh, they'd discussed her tantrums, and they'd deliberated over the wisdom of Melinda's being educated in a foreign country. But for the most part, when they spoke of her, it was in generalities and only infrequently of specifics.

The first few days of Bea's absence passed uneventfully. Lucy was busy getting caught up answering fan mail, seeing to the household bills, and going out most evenings with Brian who, despite her turndown of his proposal, continued to telephone daily to ask her out.

Edna took advantage of the opportunity to do a thorough housecleaning in preparation for Christmas.

While Melinda was at school, Hank read scripts, made calls, had a few business lunches—with some people from the Rank Organization, with friends who were passing through on their way to Switzerland. Then he collected Melinda from school. She went directly to her room to change clothes, before returning downstairs to do her homework on the living-room floor while Hank read, glancing over every now and then to study her as she chewed on a pencil before printing something in one of her notebooks.

Watching her, memories of her entire lifetime thus far—like slides tossed haphazardly into a viewer—came into focus: he and Bea with the baby on the beach; the living room of the house in Beverly Hills and their breath-held viewing of Melinda's first, precarious steps; Bea, radiant, gazing at the newborn Melinda and then at him; that dreadful Hollywood birthday party Bea had taken Melinda to when she was about two—the rear of the property transformed into a scaled-down amusement park, complete with pony-rides and games of chance where the prizes were wildly expensive baubles the tots carried off home with them. Several dozen children, all formally dressed; the little girls in starched, itchy organdy dresses with their hair elaborately

403

curled; the boys in spiffy Eton suits, their hair pomaded. No spontaneous laughter, no pleasure; it had been a social occasion primarily for the benefit of the parents, not the children. He'd seen it all when he'd come early, at Bea's request, to take them home. "They treat their children like props," Bea had stormed. "I couldn't *stand* it."

Life here was infinitely saner, on many levels, than their life in California. The weather, however, was horrendous. It was the major disadvantage to living in England, aside from the great distance between them and the circle of friends they'd once had.

Near the end of the first week, Melinda asked over dinner what Hank initially thought was an altogether amusing question.

"Are you very old to be my father?" she wanted to know.

"Does it seem as if I am?" he asked with a smile.

"I don't know. How old are fathers supposed to be?"

"I think they can be any age, really, Mel. Why?"

"I was only wondering because Nancy's mother is thirty, and her father is thirty-four. And Nancy says that you and Mummy are quite old to have a child my age."

"Nancy said that, did she?" His smile held. He was curious to see where this was leading. "And what did you say to Nancy?"

"Well." Melinda took her time, dragging her fork back and forth through the mashed potatoes, making a grid design. "I told her Mummy's going to be thirty-eight, and that's not all that old."

"No, it isn't."

"But you're ever so much older than Mummy."

"Eighteen years."

"That's quite a good deal older."

"A fair amount," he agreed.

"Are you really my father?" she asked, her eyes very round.

"Of course I'm really your father!" he told her, thrown.

"If you are, why is it that sometimes the two of you sleep in the same bed together, and sometimes you sleep in different rooms? Nancy's mother and father always sleep together in the same room."

It was on the tip of his tongue to tell her just what he thought of Nancy, and Nancy's opinions, and Nancy's parents. Instead, he took a steadying breath, and said, "I've told you quite a few times before, Mel. Not all married people share a room or a bed. Sometimes, it's because the husband snores or the wife is a restless sleeper, and it disturbs one or the other of them. There are all kinds of reasons why people sleep apart. You can understand that, can't you?"

"Uh-huh." She went back to work on the mashed potatoes with her fork.

"You really should eat, before your food gets cold."

"I'm not very hungry." She put down her fork, asking, "So it's because you snore and Mummy's a restless sleeper?"

"No. I said *sometimes* that's why."

"But if you only sleep in the same bed together sometimes, then how could you make me?"

He laughed, in automatic response to what he thought was the outrageousness of her little-girl's reasoning. "Back when we were trying very hard to 'make you,' as you put it, your mother and I slept in the same bed most of the time. Okay?"

"I see. I do *know,*" she said a shade belligerently, "how babies get made. Mummy told me, and so did Aunt Lucy. And we had a class about it at school, as well."

"That's very good."

"We had a film, actually," Melinda went on. "It had to do with butterflies and flowers, but it was really about people. It was frightfully boring."

"I'm sorry to hear that," he said. Not only was the conversation beginning to put him on edge, but for all her childish appearance, Melinda didn't, right then, seem in the least childlike.

"Is it because you're a restless sleeper and Mummy snores?"

He laughed again, relieved. "No. Your mother's a very quiet sleeper, and neither one of us snores."

"Uncle Hero snores," she said, and Hank tensed. "Is that why you only sleep in his bed sometimes when he comes to stay?"

"Melinda, where did you get the idea I sleep in Uncle Hero's bed?"

"I saw you," she said simply. "I saw you go in, and you didn't come out again, because I wanted to get into bed with you and Mummy, and Mummy was all by herself, sleeping."

"When was this?" he asked, striving to keep his tone casual.

"Last Christmas."

"I think you're a little confused, Mel," he said, feeling faintly queasy. "You may have seen me go into the guest room to have a talk with Uncle Hero, but he certainly wasn't asleep, and I certainly didn't stay!"

"I *saw* you, Daddy," she insisted. "And I *heard* him!" She looked hard at her father. Inside herself, a different Melinda from the one asking all the questions felt very badly at upsetting Daddy and wanted this to stop. But the other Melinda, the one who hated being told tales all the time, who hated being treated as if she didn't know what she knew, simply wouldn't let up. It felt awful, having the two parts of herself so at odds, but there didn't seem to be anything she could

405

do—either to leave the matter alone, or to stop feeling so badly at making Daddy unhappy.

She couldn't remember when this had first started, this one Melinda feeling all sorts of things inside, while another Melinda who was dreadfully angry said and did other things outside. She only knew that it had been going on for quite some time, and the result was that part of the time she felt confused and sad, and another part of the time she felt angry and very clear-headed. She thought sometimes about the inside Mel and the outside Mel, wondering which of them she really was, or whether a person could actually be made up of two different selves. Overall, the inside Mel annoyed her, because she was such a soppy little girl, forever anxious about Mummy and Daddy. The outside Mel was clever—everyone said so—and hadn't much time for feelings; she was more interested in the truth. And in this household, the truth seemed to depend on who you talked to.

"You must have dreamed that, Mel," her father said at last, "because it simply didn't happen." Feeling edgy, he reviewed Hero's visit of the previous year, trying to recall an occasion such as the one Melinda had described. He couldn't think of one. "If you're really not hungry, don't bother eating that. But I don't want you complaining an hour from now that you're hungry. Okay? It's not fair to go asking Edna to fix snacks for you once she's cleaned the kitchen and settled in her room for the night."

The inside Mel was simply wretched at what the outside Mel had done. She did wish she had two voices to go with the two different parts of her, but it was almost always the outside Mel who seemed to snatch at the words. "I won't be hungry," she said, carefully aligning her knife and fork in the center of the plate of barely touched food. Her eyes lowered, she wondered what her father would do if she asked him why, that very same night last Christmas, Mummy had been kissing Uncle Bobby in the hallway. They hadn't thought anyone could see them. But from where Melinda had been sitting on the floor, she'd been able to see their reflection in the hall mirror. She was about to mention it, but the inside Mel said, "May I be excused now?" and so she didn't get to ask, or to see her father's reaction.

"Sure. You go ahead, honey."

She went skipping off, and he looked down at his plate, his appetite gone. His instinct was to telephone Bea in New York and tell her to come home at once. He wasn't equipped to deal with Melinda and what he guessed would be a continuing interrogation. He also had no idea how to decipher the expression she'd worn throughout their exchange. She'd looked, he thought, like a pros-

406

ecuting attorney, presenting a very solid case against the defendant to an attentive jury.

Nothing was going right. Bea had arrived at the hotel to discover a message asking her to call Bobby at once in Los Angeles.

"I'm stuck here," he told her. "They want to reshoot the last couple of scenes. But I'll be there by Friday at the latest. I'm sorry, Bea. This is one of those last-minute things nobody ever expects. You're going to wait for me, I hope."

"I'll consider it," she answered, terribly disappointed. Then, with a laugh, she said, "I've come all this way to see you. Where else would I be? Just, please, make it Friday. You'll let me know if you can get away any sooner, won't you?"

"You know I will." There was a static-filled pause before he said, "I love you, Bea. Seeing you's all I've been thinking about. You know I wouldn't hang you up this way if it wasn't for a damned good reason."

"I know. It's just such a let-down."

"It is for me, too. I'll be there Friday."

"I'll be here," she told him, and hung up, trying not to slide into depression.

Informed by London that she was in town, the New York office had a number of scripts for her to read, as well as a number of highly lucrative offers for pictures in the preproduction stages. The scripts were delivered by messenger, and she dipped into them immediately, reassured that she hadn't been forgotten.

She refused several dinner invitations and ate room-service meals in her suite while she read the scripts, rejecting them one after another. By the time she got to the last of the submissions, the depression had taken hold. She sat with a glass of scotch and a cigarette, looking at the shadowy corners of the room, tired, lonely, and afraid. She felt even worse than she had in London and thought she probably shouldn't have made this trip.

"Are you sure?" Mark Rosenberg asked her when she called to give him her opinion of the various projects. "I thought a couple of them were right up your alley. Maybe you should have another look, reconsider."

Her anger flared instantly. "Look, Mark, if I know nothing else, I know what I can, and cannot, play. I'd be ludicrously miscast in every last one of those scripts. And you and I both know the only reason I'm being offered them is for my name value alone. *Please*," she said heatedly, "don't waste my time. And *don't* question my judgment. If you've forgotten what I do, go out some night and catch a double-bill somewhere. Then *you* take another look, and see if it's worth anyone's time sending them to me."

"But, Bea, they're all good parts. Are you sure...?"

"Goddamnit, Mark! Stop trying to tell me my business!" She slammed down the receiver, lit a cigarette, and paced back and forth, fuming. She hated her life, hated Mark, and the suite, and herself for bothering to come over here at all. She should've stayed home. None of what she'd anticipated was materializing. Bobby was delayed. The scripts were all wrong. She'd looked forward to seeing Becky, but Becky was at some damned conference and wouldn't be back until Friday. "Christ!" she muttered, pacing until her hips protested and she had to sit down.

Nine o'clock Friday morning, Bobby phoned again.

"You're going to hate me," he began apologetically, "but we're running behind schedule. It rained all day yesterday, so we couldn't do one damned set-up. I won't make it now before Sunday. I'm sorry, Bea. I really am."

"Oh, Christ! I've been cooling my heels here for five stinking days! And now you won't be here until *Sunday?*" She wanted to scream.

"Sunday evening, you have my word."

"All right," she sighed heavily, "but this is starting to get on my nerves."

"It can't be helped, Bea. You know how it is."

"I know, I know."

"Sunday night," he promised. "I've got the ticket right here in my hand."

Resigned, she said, "I'll be here." She hung up and stared at the telephone. The anger had gone, leaving only the depression. Anger required more energy than she had just then.

Half an hour later, Hank called.

"I thought I'd better let you know what's been going on," he said.

"Is anything wrong?"

"It's about Melinda. You're not going to like this, Bea."

"Henry! Please just tell me! I'm not exactly having the time of my life here. Bobby's delayed again, until Sunday night now. Mark sent me a truckload of scripts, none of which were right, then argued that maybe I don't really know what I'm doing. What's Mel done?"

He related to her the highlights of his conversation earlier in the week with Melinda, then went on to say, "This morning, driving to school, it was your turn. What did I think of the fact that she'd seen you and Bobby kissing in the hallway last Christmas? Bea, I don't know how to handle this. It's as if she's been studying the two of us through a microscope. I keep reminding myself she's only eight, but it's starting to feel like I'm living with the Gestapo. I'm getting self-conscious about everything I say or do around her. What should I be doing?"

"Right this moment," she snapped, "I wish I'd never *had* that child. And, God above, don't let anybody try to tell me *this* is typical! I don't know what you should be doing, Hank. Obviously, it's impossible to explain the fine points of our lives to her. The only thing you *can* do is keep on insisting she's misunderstood."

"I'm no good at lying, Bea."

"Then put an embargo on those topics, Henry. They're off-limits, not subjects for dinner conversation. Lay down the law. She's out of line, so tell her so! If we let her root around this way in our lives, there'll be no stopping her."

"You're right," he said, sounding stronger. "You are right. I'm sorry to drop this on you, dear heart."

"Don't be sorry, Hank," she softened. "I'm the other half of the team, remember. *I'm* sorry she's acting up. Talk to Lucy. She seems to know how to put Mel in her place. We'll talk again tomorrow, and you can let me know how you're doing."

"I probably shouldn't have unloaded this on you, but I was feeling a little out of my depth."

"I know the feeling."

"Are you all right, Bea? You sound down in the dumps."

"*I* probably shouldn't have taken this trip. Every last damned thing's going haywire. We'll talk tomorrow."

They exchanged good-byes, then Bea automatically fell to pacing. She was due at Becky's place in an hour. Becky would be a tonic; Becky would cheer her up. They'd have a good, long talk, go out for lunch somewhere.

The telephone rang again. She glared at it, wishing Lucy were there to answer. With a face, she picked up. The hotel operator said Mark was on the line. Not in the mood for anything more, Bea said, "Tell him I'll get back to him."

Becky's apartment on East Seventy-third Street was just as Bea had imagined it would be, with exposed-brick walls, books everywhere, and lush green plants. Twin loveseats faced each other in front of the fireplace, separated by a low, square coffee table.

"It's lovely," Bea said, after they'd embraced and she'd had a moment to look around. She felt better already, just being there. "Where do you work?" she asked, admiring the way the sun reflected through a panel of stained glass in the window.

"Come on. I'll show you." Becky took her by the hand and led her into the larger of the two bedrooms where she opened a pair of doors to reveal a fully equipped work area built into what had previously been a spacious closet.

Bea looked at the typewriter, the mugs of pencils and boxes of paper, and envied Becky for having a career that was so clearly definable and so readily contained.

"You're very lucky," she told her back in the living room, where they sat opposite each other on the loveseat, with freshly made coffee on the low table.

"Why?" Becky smiled to cover how odd she found it to have Bea there. It was one of those times when her awareness of who Bea was threatened to overcome her familiarity with the woman.

"Because you've got all that wonderful paraphernalia, for one thing, and because you can take whatever you need and work anywhere."

"But so can you, and you don't even need a typewriter." Becky laughed, watching as Bea lit a cigarette, then crossed her legs before taking another look around. "All your equipment's right there in you."

"It really is a lovely apartment, Becky."

She meant it, and Becky was once again confounded by this seeming dichotomy in Bea: that she could live as she did, surrounded by the most luxurious and expensive appointments, and yet be impressed by an apartment that would easily have fit into the living room of her Hampstead house. Becky didn't think she'd ever get used to having Bea notice and admire a pair of her shoes, or a jacket. One reason for this was that Bea's ability to appreciate the qualities or possessions of others in no way vitiated her personal expectations. She anticipated as her due a certain deference, primarily from service people, for which, of course, she was fully prepared to pay. She anticipated it as well from strangers and from the crews with which she worked. She was never condescending or patronizing; she simply expected a special brand of treatment, and she got it.

Naturally, staying in hotel suites and being driven around in limousines, and having production company and agency flunkies dancing attendance on her was all part of being Beatrice Crane, the movie star; but the truly amazing thing about Bea was that she never played out the role. She didn't have to. Everyone else did it for her. Off screen, at home, she wasn't a star. Away from home, she was a legend with a following.

The mention of her name was enough to send hotel managements into a tizzy. Calling a hotel and asking for Bea guaranteed a change of voice and attitude in the operator. If you knew enough to call that hotel and ask for Bea, then you, too, were someone of importance. Because not everyone's calls were accepted. The switchboard guarded access to Bea. It was the honored duty of the operators to keep members of the public away from her.

Bea had a privileged knowledge that was given to very few people: she knew intimately how it felt to live privately in the public eye. It required a most particular skill, and Bea excelled at it. She gave only as much as was needed, and not one iota more. Giving more would have rendered her too knowable and less worthy of respect; more would have reduced her impact and her image. When provoked, she could take a very hard line. She refused to waste either her time or her energy on people or situations that were inferior. The woman was extraordinarily potent, universally celebrated. And here she was, sitting in Becky's living room. It was incredible.

"You know something?" Becky said. "I still get a big charge out of knowing what hotel you're at, at being able to phone up and get put through to your room."

"That's ridiculous," Bea said lightly, dismissingly. "You're very important in your own right."

"But you're an honest-to-god movie star, Bea. It's very damned impressive."

Smoke curled from Bea's nostrils as she looked over at Becky who, shoeless and clad in an old University of Toronto sweatshirt and faded jeans, sat with her feet propped on the coffee table. There was a hole in the toe of one of her socks. Her long, red-brown hair was scraped back into a pony tail; her face was completely free of make-up. She was beautiful, fresh-looking. The sight of her had always given Bea pleasure. "It's only impressive," Bea said, "to people who don't know me. They have no idea who I really am."

"Sure they do," Becky said eagerly. "You're there, in every frame. It's all just an extension of you."

"Becky, that's *acting*. Don't tell me you've never been accused of being one of the characters in some book or script you've written."

"People don't go berserk over writers the way they do over movie stars."

Bea shrugged and took another puff on her cigarette. She was growing uncomfortable and wished Becky would change the subject. She'd managed to elevate herself out of the depression of the past week and didn't want to fall back into it.

"Seriously," Becky went on. "It's a positive phenomenon. And one of these days I'm determined to write about it. Oh, not about you personally. But something along the lines of how it feels to be on the inside of the transparent box, looking out; how it feels to have everybody looking in; about the way people look to you to help them realize their fantasies."

Bea laughed. "Transparent box?"

"It's the way I sometimes see you—sort of like a bubble trapped in amber. Would you ever consider writing your autobiography?"

"Giving interviews is as far as I'm willing to go."

"Come on, Bea! You've been giving variations on the same interview theme for as long as I've known you."

"I amend them to keep current. But it's no one's business what I do in my private life." She thought of Melinda, and of what Hank had told her. Picturing herself making love with Bobby, she was suddenly in the grip of anxiety at the idea that anyone, let alone her daughter, could have seen them. "It's hard enough even *having* a private life," she said, wishing fervently that Becky would find something else to talk about. "Whatever curiosity people have about me will have to wait until after I'm dead to be satisfied." She gazed at her old friend, willing her to understand and to leave these hazardous areas for a safer one. Please, she thought, don't make me talk about any of this. Not now, not today. I can't do this.

Becky found herself disarmed as always by the heat of intelligence and speculation emanating from Bea's eyes. She'd seen people literally wither beneath the weight of one of Bea's visual inspections; she'd also been witness to some amazingly candid and spontaneous demonstrations of admiration. Five minutes in Bea's company and either people were displaying the very best of themselves in order to prove worthy of being in her presence or they were made speechless by the realization that they had nothing of value to say to her. Naturally, there were some who simply failed to see they were on probation and so went blithely forward only to have Bea quietly turn away from them. She seemed to have an infallible bullshit-detector, and it worked in every area but one. And that area was Melinda.

As far as Becky was concerned, Melinda was on her way to becoming a first-class little horror. But Bea never appeared to see it. She expended enormous energy on the girl, for which the rewards were negligible at best. No matter how hard she'd tried, Becky couldn't like Melinda. "Don't tell me," she said coaxingly, "you still don't trust me, after all these years."

"But I *do* trust you," Bea contradicted her. "And that makes you dangerous." She was feeling increasingly disturbed. The blood seemed to be bubbling through her system, fizzing like soda water. Why wouldn't Becky stop? Why wouldn't she find some other, safer, subject?

"Don't you think if I was going to do you in in print I'd have done it a long time ago?"

Bea chose not to respond and busied herself lighting another cigarette.

"It's very interesting, you know." Becky sat up and leaned forward, folding her arms across her knees. It intrigued and bemused her to see Bea lean slightly back in guarded response to the move. "I'm forever bowled over by what you dare to let people see and know about you in your pictures. But you know what? I honestly think it's safer for you to put your soul on view in a movie than it is to allow yourself to be approached in real life. In the flesh, you're too vulnerable to sustain any prolonged exposure. So, it isn't *you* who handles the crowds of fans and all the hoopla. Beatrice Crane does it for you, doesn't she? And you're there inside, somewhere, under a couple of thousands' worth of suit—that's an honest-to-god Chanel, isn't it?—and a few tastefully subtle pieces of jewelry that would run twenty-five or thirty thousand at Cartier's."

A tremor in her hands, Bea put out her just-lit cigarette. "What am I supposed to say to all this?" she asked, her voice growing thicker. "Most of the people out there"—she waved at the windows—"have more real freedom than I do. Becky..."

"But that's part of what I'm talking about," Becky jumped in. "The other part has to do with the way you try to live, the way you work at being a mother. Then there's Hank, and Bobby..."

"*Of course*, I work at being a mother," Bea exclaimed. "Children don't raise themselves, you know."

"I know, but *look* at Melinda..."

"What *about* her?" Everything was going out of control. Bea wanted to weep; she wanted to throw herself across the coffee table at Becky and physically shut her up.

"It's just that I can't help wondering if your being what and who you are isn't responsible for Mel's being what *she* is."

"And *what* is she, in *your* view?"

Becky saw suddenly that she'd backed herself into a corner. She hadn't meant to get into a discussion of the things she felt were wrong with Melinda. Yet weren't friends supposed to be able to tell each other the truth, to talk about anything and everything? "Bea, you've admitted yourself—I don't know how many times—what a difficult kid she is. There's something about her. I'm not even sure how to articulate it. I guess what I'm saying is it's pretty strange, speaking of trust, when you feel as if you can't trust an eight-year-old kid. But that's how I feel around her. There's an awful lot going on in her head, but it's hard to figure out what any of it is. Every time I see the two of you together, I'm convinced she's happiest when she's running you around in circles. I'll never forget the show she put on that first Christmas I came over, when she screamed and kicked you because she wanted to open her presents Christmas eve and you'd planned to wait until morning. I watched you and Hank, and the two of you looked as if you couldn't imagine where she'd come from, or why she was behaving the way she did. And the whole time it was going on, the only explanation that made any sense to me was that it was because you and Hank were who you were. I'll remember it as long as I live," Becky said fervently. "It was nightmarish."

"I don't think you know what the hell you're talking about," Bea said shakily. She felt betrayed and ashamed. Her eyes filled.

"I think I do."

"Then elaborate, by all means. Since you have such a clear picture of my entire existence, do recite chapter and verse."

"I can't do that, Bea. That's not what I'm getting at. I mean, I don't have it all cut out like words from newspapers and magazines to make up some kind of ransom note." She hesitated, tangled up not only in her words but also in Bea's visible distress. "I have a *sense* of you, Bea," she diligently forged ahead. "Some of it's based on what I've seen between you and Melinda. And I'm concerned because I can't help thinking that maybe Melinda's part of the price you pay to be Beatrice Crane."

Bea couldn't speak for a moment. She was working too hard to stop the sudden flood of tears from her eyes and the mass of conflicting emotions that prompted them. She shook her head, both hands fastened to the handbag in her lap. Melinda, Melinda, Melinda. A scream was working its way into her throat.

"Oh, damn!" Becky said. "I . . ."

"*Shut up!*" Bea cried, finding her voice. "I'm not the fraud you make me out to be. Who and what I am doesn't get put on or taken off with my *goddamned* clothes, and it also doesn't have one damned thing to do with Melinda. Why did you have to do this? Why?" She was on her feet now, desperate to get away. "I don't *have* answers for every last thing, the way you do. I do what has to be done. You're not different, or better, than I am. Except that I have the wits to know when to leave some things alone. I'm sick to goddamned death of everyone giving me their interpretations of who I am, what parts I should or shouldn't play, what kind of child I have, and whether or not I'm raising her properly. Why do you think you have the right to *do* this to me?" She had the front door open, and stood a moment on the threshold. Eyes wide, Becky got up from the sofa. "How would *you* know what it means to be a mother?" Bea demanded. "How would

414

you know about the pressures on me or the crap I have to take from people? I'm her *mother,* you idiot! Why would you think for one minute I'd be willing to sit here and dissect my child with you? Maybe one of these days you'll start *living* life instead of sitting around endlessly *talking* about it. And maybe then you'll give the rest of us a break."

"Wait a minute!" Becky called to Bea's stiff, retreating back. "I wasn't trying to ..."

"Have a child of your own, and then we'll talk!" Bea glared at her from the top of the stairs, furiously wiping the tears from her face. *"Why did you do this to me?"* With that, she stormed down the stairs and out of the building.

Becky ran back inside and got to the window in time to see Bea slide into the rear of the black stretch limousine.

"Shit!" Becky pounded her fists on the window sill.

She went to the sofa and sat with her arms wrapped around herself, going back over the conversation. She'd never seen Bea in such a state, and she couldn't believe it had anything to do with what she'd said. "God damn it!" She grabbed the telephone even though she knew Bea couldn't possibly have arrived back at the hotel yet.

"Please have her call me!" she told the hotel operator. "It's urgent."

She hung up, knowing Bea wouldn't return her call. Their friendship was over. But why had Bea jumped so hard on what she'd thought was being said? She should never have talked about Melinda, she told herself.

As she'd predicted, Bea didn't call back. When Becky tried the Pierre again, the operator said, "I'm sorry. Miss Crane's not accepting any calls."

It couldn't end this way. It was too irrational. She hurried to change clothes, then took a cab to the hotel. She went directly up to the suite, but she knew as she approached the door that Bea wasn't going to be there.

She left a note at the front desk and then, in the grip of a melancholy more acute than anything she'd ever experienced, she went out to flag down another cab. For the first time, she wished there were someone waiting at home for her. She dreaded facing the empty apartment.

Safely hidden from view behind the dark-tinted windows of the limousine, Bea fought to hold herself together. She felt like a basket full of writhing snakes. Smoking a cigarette, she stared unseeing out the window, trying to think what to do. Becky was bound to phone or come to the hotel, hoping to clear the air. And Bea didn't care if she never again set eyes on the woman as long as she lived. She felt ill with disappointment and anger, wounded by the things Becky had said—about her clothes, about her duality, about Melinda. It wasn't bad enough she was inundated with rotten scripts, pestered by argumentative agents, spied upon by her own child, and left dangling alone in New York, she had to go to visit a friend and be subjected to a speculative running narrative on the why's and wherefore's of her life.

"I want you to wait," she told the driver. "I have several calls to make, then I'll be going to the airport."

In her suite, she put a call through to Bobby and, luckily, managed to reach him at the studio.

"Hey!" he said happily. "I'd love you to come here. Just leave a message with my houseboy saying what flight you'll be in on, and I'll be there to meet you."

"No, don't meet me. Arrange for a car, please, and I'll go directly to the house."

"Are you all right?"

"No! And I can't talk now."

"Okay. I'll see you later."

She had the desk book her a ticket on the next available flight and told the hotel manager to leave the suite as it was, that she'd be back in a few days. "Have the switchboard say I'm not taking calls."

She put down the phone, threw a few things into a small suitcase, then waited for the desk to call back with her flight information. She smoked one cigarette after another, frenzied with the need to escape. When at last the telephone rang, she noted the information, then tore out of the room and down to the waiting limo.

It wasn't until a good two hours after take-off and her consumption of several scotches that she was able to unbend to any degree. And even then, she couldn't stop thinking about Becky's remarks, and about the idea that now that she was free of the studio and its massive interference in her life, her own daughter had undertaken to play the role of silent, suspicious observer. She refused to allow anyone, Melinda included, to invade the interior of her life. She'd be *damned* if she'd let that happen. Her anger cooled, then escalated, then cooled again, throughout the flight. She was, however, sufficiently back in possession of herself to sign an autograph for the stewardess, and even to smile, as they touched down in Los Angeles.

Thirty-Eight

BOBBY'S Hawaiian houseboy offered to get her a drink or something to eat. She thanked him but declined. "I'm really very tired, Frankie. I think I'll just lie down until Bobby gets back." She carried her suitcase along to Bobby's bedroom where the overhead fan revolved silently and the curtains were drawn against the afternoon sun.

The door closed, she took off the Chanel suit. Letting it drop to the floor, she circled it suspiciously, as if these pieces of fabric were, in fact, a menacing, predatory creature. She kicked at the suit with her foot, knowing she'd never again be able to wear it. And to make certain of that, she snatched it up and pushed it into the wastebasket beside the dresser. One sleeve dangled over the rim and, with a furious swipe, she shoved it inside.

Why was everything going wrong? She'd gone along to see Becky hoping to be distracted from a week of unpleasant and distressing incidents. Now she felt as if she'd been living in some kind of dream world before this ill-fated trip, and only the hateful confrontation with Becky had been real. Had she been deluding herself for years? Was she not the person she believed herself to be? She couldn't make sense of the things that had happened, but the hurt was real enough. It throbbed in the center of her chest as she examined the items on the dresser top: the silver-backed brushes she'd given Bobby years and years ago; a framed, candid shot of her Bobby had taken eight or ten years earlier on the terrace at the rear of the house; another photo, this one of her, Hero, Hank, and Melinda, that Bobby had taken the first Christmas he'd spent with them in London. Bobby took good pictures. He had a feeling for light and composition. It didn't surprise her. He was stylish and tasteful in everything—his dancing, his clothes, his hobbies, even his blondes.

417

Fatigue swept over her. Stepping out of her shoes, she walked to the bed and lay down. For a few minutes she watched the rhythmic rotation of the ceiling fan, lulled by the faint whirring of its blades.

At some point she was aware of the telephone ringing and, awakening with a start, reached out to lift the receiver before remembering where she was. Frankie would answer, she told herself and, turning, plunged back into sleep.

Bobby sat on the side of the bed for quite some time, watching her sleep. Her hair was almost black against the white bedding, and it partially obscured her face. He'd come rushing home from the studio, half afraid she wouldn't be here. He'd opened the bedroom door to see that she was asleep, and then the telephone had rung and he'd made a dash for the extension in the living room.

After the call, he'd tiptoed in to sit close enough to her to breathe in her perfume as he admired the rounded curve of her shoulder and the supplicating look of her outflung, exposed palm. He studied her fingernails, clean and carefully shaped, coated with a clear polish. He looked at her wedding rings and felt, as he always did, somewhat inadequate with the proof of her commitment to Hank reflecting the dim light of the room. Still, he was reassured by the sight of the heavy gold-link bracelet he'd given her, worn on the wrist of the same hand that was weighted with Hank's rings.

He got a hollow feeling in his stomach just looking at her knees and at the deep incurving line from her hip to her waist. Her skin was so white, so translucent that he could see the deep blue veins swimming just beneath the surface. He touched the lace edging of her slip, allowing it to rest against the tips of his fingers, thinking foolishly what a lucky garment it was, getting to lay next to her skin all day. He smiled at himself and pulled back his hand, determined not to give in to his need to touch her, not while she was sleeping. He could wait, content to watch the slight rise and fall of her chest as she breathed.

His scalp itched under the damned hairpiece, and he rubbed the spot with two fingers, looking forward to being able to take the stupid thing off and let the air get at his head. For no reason, he thought of that piece of film—God only knew where it was, or if it still existed— that had been shot by some news team at the Canteen one evening shortly after he'd come out of the navy, showing him breaking into an impromptu routine for the GIs who were passing through, on their way home. He'd completely forgotten he wasn't wearing the toupee, and after about sixteen bars, he'd called it quits, realizing he didn't have the thing on. He'd made a hasty exit because the studio hadn't wanted any documented footage that showed him as he really was: bald on top, and no kid anymore.

Bea sighed deeply in her sleep, shifting so that the hair fell away from her face, and he couldn't wait any longer. He drew his hand down the outside length of her arm until her hand was enclosed in his and waited for her to awaken. When her eyes opened, he held her hand to his mouth for a moment, then said, "You'd better tell me about it. Becky called a while ago, looking for you. She's beside herself. I told her I'd give you the message. And what are your clothes doing in the trash?"

She wet her lips. "What time is it?"

He kept hold of her hand while he turned his wrist to look at his watch. "Almost eight. I hated to wake you."

"Have you been home long?"

"Not long. Maybe an hour. So, what's the story?"

"I should call Hank, let him know where I am. If he tries to reach me in New York, he'll be worried when he can't get through. What's the time difference, eight hours? It's four in the morning there. Don't let me forget to phone home, okay? Midnight should be about right."

"What happened with you and Becky?"

"I really can't talk about it. We had a falling-out. It's over. That's all."

"You're not going to call her?"

"I need to take a bath. I'm very stiff from the plane ride."

"I'll start the water going," he volunteered, and went through to the bathroom. When he came back, she was sitting on the side of the bed, head down, the nape of her neck temptingly exposed. He let his lips graze the downy skin there, then sat beside her. "You and Becky are kaput, and you're not going to tell me why, or what happened?"

"She said quite a number of things that upset me. If I repeat what she said, I'll get upset all over again." She turned to look at him through her lashes. "Do you see any possible benefit to be derived from my getting upset again?"

"I guess not. Frankie's making dinner. I assume you haven't eaten."

"No, I haven't." She lowered her head once more.

"Okay. Go have your bath. I'll grab a shower, wash the goddamned adhesive off my scalp, then we'll eat."

She caught hold of his hand as he got up. "Have your shower, then come talk to me. I'm not ready to eat yet, and I need to soak for a while." She sat up straighter, making a face. "I'm sorry, but I really do need some time in the tub. Will you come keep me company?"

"I wouldn't miss it for the world." He gave her a quick kiss, said, "I'll be in in a few minutes," and went off to the guest bathroom.

Fifteen minutes later, he was back, trying to absorb the impact of seeing her naked in his tub. She'd pinned up her hair and was sitting with her arms resting on the sides of the tub, looking dazed by the heat.

"Are you all right?" he asked, causing her to jump. "Sorry. Didn't mean to give you a jolt."

"I'm fine, just bone-weary." She gave him a drowsy smile. "Look at the two of us: you with your naked head showing and me with everything showing. We're quite the attractive couple."

"That's your opinion. I, personally, find us extremely attractive." He lowered the lid on the toilet and sat down. "It's all I can do to restrain myself from dragging you out of there and having you on the bathmat."

She laughed and slid a little lower into the steaming water. "You'll have to have me on your bed. It's been a very long time since I was able to do it on the floor."

"Proof positive we're getting old," he said, stretching his legs and crossing his ankles. "Time was when we wouldn't have waited for anything. Now, we sit around talking, taking baths before we get to it. A few more years and we won't bother doing it at all, we'll just reminisce about it. I might as well tell you," he said without a change of tone, "that Becky's extremely upset and begs you to call her so the two of you can clear the air."

She shook her head and said, "No."

"That's it? Flat-out no? You're not even going to give her a chance? It must've been one hell of a conversation the two of you had."

"Bobby, it's taken me *hours* even to *begin* to calm down. I don't want to hear you plead her case. The matter is *closed*."

"Well, Jesus! I hope you never decide to get this mad at me."

"Let's drop it, please."

He shrugged and said, "Okay. But I have to tell you I think you're making a very big mistake."

"Since you *weren't* there and *don't know* what was said, *I'll* be the judge of whether or not it's a mistake. And if it is, I'll live with it. *All right?* If you don't drop it, I'll start screaming."

"Fine. Soooo, how are Hank and Mel? What's up with Luce?"

"I can't discuss them, either."

"I see. Okay. How's the work situation?"

"Hank's had an offer to do a picture they want to shoot in North Africa. I have a few offers on hold in England. I'm dying to get back to work. It's been a hell of a long time between drinks."

"I guess it has."

"The best offer is for the worst script, naturally. And the one script I'd really like to do, they're offering peanuts and points. Plus, it's a French co-production deal, which means I'd have to learn the entire script phonetically with a coach. I would get to do the English dubbing, so at least there wouldn't be some dreadful voice coming out of my mouth, with the lip-synch all wrong."

"You going to do it?"

"I haven't decided yet. Jerry had the New York office send over a bunch more scripts. Abysmal. I'm not old enough for mother parts and not young enough for most of the good leads. Practically no one sees me in character roles, even though that's what I've been playing all along. I'm not willing to do nude, semi-nude, or partially nude features for the European market, so that eliminates a lot of properties right there. Most of the rest of the scripts have wonderful parts for men and one-dimensional parts for women. They're just not writing for women now. So, I have to be very careful about what I decide to do. On top of that, Hank and I seldom get to work together anymore, and I'm a nervous wreck when I go into a European shoot with people I don't know who half the time don't even speak English. They have to have interpreters on the set to translate for the actors and crew. Every goddamned thing's changed."

"Yes, it has," he agreed.

"D'you think about the old days and miss the way it was?" she asked him.

"Sometimes."

"Bobby, I'm afraid. We had a system, and I understood it. Sure, they ran our lives, and told us what to do and when to do it, and slapped us on the wrist when we were naughty, but they *built* us. They kept us working nonstop, they made our names. Now the system's gone, and I feel like an orphan, floating in space. Nothing's familiar, but I go ahead anyway, pretending everything's the way I expect it to be. *Nothing's* the way I expect it to be. Ludie died, and then they started those revolting hearings, and now there's television, and most of the people we knew have either taken to the hills or lost their stature in my eyes because they denounced their friends and did it with smiles on their faces, puffed out to there with righteous indignation. My daughter has just about come right out and accused her father, to his face, of being homosexual. Not only that, but she's started dropping bombs about certain things she's seen you and I doing together. If that isn't bad enough, Mark Rosenberg has the temerity to tell me I don't know a good script when I read one. And then we have Becky . . . I'm coming to pieces, Bobby."

"Sounds like you've been having a pretty rotten time."

"The worst of it is I'm trying to keep up, but I don't know with what. What we had here was supposed to last forever. I wasn't going to be living thousands of miles away, shopping around as an independent. I was going to have my golden moments and then vanish, somehow, in the final dissolve. It's as if I'm trying to hold on to a handful of mercury, but little drops of it keep spilling over. I've never felt so scared."

"I don't see that your footing's all that shaky, Bea."

"I didn't *pick* it, you know! I didn't reach into the hat and select fear as my primary emotion for the decade."

"I dislike it intensely when you snap at me that way. Don't bite my head off just because you've had a shitty week and a blow-up with Becky! This is me! Remember me?"

"I remember you," she said quietly, chastened. "I could sing you a few bars, if you like."

"Never mind. Are you planning to sleep in there?"

"I'm ready to get out. Please don't stay and watch. I'm at my graceless best climbing in and out of bathtubs."

"I know the drill." He went into the bedroom where he listened, smiling, as with muttered epithets, she levered herself out of the tub. "One of these days," he called out, "I'm going to sneak over and watch."

"Don't you dare!" she called back. "And anyway, you'd be disappointed. I'm nowhere near as bad as I was."

"Still exercising?"

"Every day." She came through the door wrapped in a towel. "It's all ridiculous, isn't it? *I'm* ridiculous." She sat beside him and began removing the pins from her hair, dropping them on the bedside table.

"I'd never call you ridiculous."

"What, then?"

He laced his fingers behind his head, leaned back against the headboard and looked up at the ceiling. "I'd call you—energetically neurotic. What did Mel see us doing, anyway?"

"I should hit you for that."

"Why? You'd dispute it?"

"No. But you could've lied and said something flattering."

"Oh, shit on that!" He undid the towel and slid his hand over her breast, coming forward to kiss her shoulder. "What'd the kid see?"

"So far as I know, nothing more incriminating than the two of us kissing in the hallway last Christmas."

"And with her Dad?"

"Nothing at all, evidently."

"Well, good."

"Tell me that the fact that I'm falling to pieces mentally and physically doesn't bother you."

"It doesn't bother me," he parroted obediently. "You're *not* falling to pieces. Now please shut up!" He pulled the towel out from under her and dropped it on the floor. "Don't you know I wouldn't care if you came in on crutches? I'd still think you were beautiful."

She sighed and stretched out beside him, his body cool against hers. His mouth opened on her breast, and she held his head to her, feeling the reaction start in her knees, in her belly, along the length of her spine. "Doctor Bob," she whispered, "my personal attendant."

He lifted his head. "You're way behind on your office visits, sister."

She laughed and kissed him, murmuring, "I need a complete check-up."

She twisted away out of his grasp. Damp strands of her hair trailed across his belly. The air rushed from his lungs. "Jesus!" he whispered from between his teeth, temporarily immobilized and unable to touch her. He closed his eyes at the pleasure, then opened them to see her sitting on her heels, watching her hands as they caressed him. Then her head dropped again suddenly, and his whole body lurched in response. It was so goddamned personal, so alarmingly wanton the way they made love, that sometimes he had the irrational idea that even *he* shouldn't see it.

She kept on until he had to stop her. He had to taste and touch her, to hold her to his mouth as if she were a cup that would never be empty, a vessel that would always slake his thirst. He could read her body as well as he could his own. He knew how to interpret the tremors of her belly and upper thighs; he might have been blind, her flesh Braille. When he lowered himself over top of her and looked into her eyes they were unfocused, glistening. Her hands played over his ribs as her hips rotated slowly, steadily against his, her knees rising either side of him. She lifted. All he had to do was glide back, then move gradually forward, watching her eyes dilate, her eyelids flicker, her mouth open as she arched upward. Glutted with emotion, he felt suddenly like weeping at the privilege of knowing and seeing her this way. "God, I love you," he told her, feeling her contract around him.

"You know I love you," her husky voice responded. "You're my *life*, Bobby. I couldn't live without you."

He retreated almost completely, then surged forward again. Her eyes grew very round, her arms tightened around him. He couldn't look away and felt pure anguish as tears collected and spilled from her eyes. He paused, uncertain, suddenly guilty at the thought that he'd minimized her fears, her experiences.

"No," she implored him. "Don't think about it. Please, don't. Not now."

He watched as she talked, first to Hank, then to Melinda. She sat on the bed with her knees drawn up to her chest, holding the receiver with both hands, as she listened to her husband and then her child. She smiled—it appeared to Bobby as a reflex action—at the sound of Melinda's voice and spoke quietly, admonishing the girl to be good to her father. She talked in fond, serious tones again to Hank, and then the call was ended. She put down the receiver and let her head rest on her knees.

Bobby waited, smoking a cigarette, feeling very separate from her now. He could, for hours at a time, forget her other obligations. Yet, inevitably, the reality of her life away from him intruded, severing their tenuous ties. He had no option but to wait for her to make good again their connection. And even though he'd long ago accepted the terms, nevertheless they seemed unfair at moments like this when, such a short while before, she'd been so unrestrictedly his that nothing could ever find a space between them in which to insinuate itself.

"I never," she said finally, "want to go through another week like this one as long as I live. Every time I talk to Melinda, I get the feeling she has no idea who I am. She addresses me as if I'm someone who came to visit once who she scarcely remembers. I say, 'I love you, Mel,' and, very politely, she says, 'Thank you,' as if I'd just complimented her on what she was wearing."

"You know how kids are," he said, his fingers walking up her vertebrae. "They get peculiar sometimes with love stuff."

"I know, but I still feel cut off when it happens."

"I feel cut off when I think that every so often you make love with Hank."

She lifted her head to look at him. "You've made love with *dozens* of women."

"True. That is true. And you've had a couple of affairs I know about, and probably some more I don't."

"I didn't know you knew."

"I knew."

"Does any of it have anything to do with you and me?" she asked.

"I don't know. Does it?"

She put her head back down on her knees. "You know it doesn't.

Christ almighty! It's odious to think you can't do a thing here without everybody knowing about it."

"It's a small town, a company town."

"So we can read about ourselves in tomorrow morning's paper and hear Hopper talk about us on the radio. I'm glad we'll be going back to New York on Sunday night. At least we can get lost there, if that's what we want."

"I'm buying a place," he told her.

"In New York?" Her head came up.

"An apartment on Park near Seventy-second."

"Bobby, that's wonderful."

"It's an investment."

She noted the lack of interest in his tone and placed her hand flat on his chest. "What's the matter?"

He covered her hand with his own. "The same old thing," he answered. "It's hard on me, you know, having to sit here and listen to you talk on the telephone, to see how your face changes when you talk to them. I start feeling jealous, wishing *I* was the husband and Mel was my kid. I have to share you, and sometimes it's a little rough."

"You don't *share* me," she said softly. "When will you ever see that what I have with you isn't something I could ever have with anyone else? I *need* you. I rely on you. You're the one I come running to when things go wrong. I'm *desolate* about Becky. Maybe it wouldn't seem like much to anyone else, and maybe it shouldn't seem as much as it does to me, but every last one of us has different needs that different people fill for us. And Becky was the one who was always so much her own person that I counted on her as a kind of sounding board. Bobby, she sat there and talked about my child, my clothes, and my jewelry; she put price-tags on all of it and made me feel superficial, *artificial*, like plastic flowers in a Steuben vase. You *know* how important my friends are to me, how much store I place in them."

"She's going to keep calling," he said. "How're you going to handle it?"

"I don't know. I shouldn't have started discussing it. I don't even want to think about it." She unfolded herself and eased over against his side. "Please don't ever think or feel you're only getting little bits and pieces of me, Bobby. Hank and Mel are one side of my life, and you're the other. I know it's hard on you. It's hard on me, too. I despise my life right now. And the only aspect of it that's good and right and feels safe, is you."

"Let's get some sleep," he said, pulling the sheet up over them. "We're both worn out."

"Wake me, and I'll have breakfast with you before you go."

"That's a deal. I love watching you do your exercises. It's very erotic."

"You're demented. There's nothing erotic about watching a middle-aged woman grunting and sweating."

"That's what you think, sister." He laughed and pulled her over closer.

Becky called at nine the next morning. Bea told Frankie to say she'd gone to the studio with Bobby.

At ten-thirty, Becky called again. Frankie looked over inquiringly to where Bea was sitting reading one of the books she'd tossed into her bag before leaving the Pierre. She shook her head, and Frankie said she hadn't come back yet.

Becky called at noon, at two p.m., at four, and again at five. At last, Bea stomped across the room, took the receiver from Frankie's hand, and said into it, "I can't and won't talk to you, so don't say a word. Just listen! Whether I'm right or wrong in how I interpreted what you said doesn't matter. You said cruel, hurtful things to make whatever point it was you were trying to make. You sat there and examined me like I was a lettuce you were considering buying in the supermarket. Maybe someday, later on, we'll be able to get together again, and all this will be behind us. But not now, not yet. Sooner or later you're going to have to learn how to read the signals other people give you, Becky, or you're going to wind up all by yourself, because no one will be willing to suffer through your endless goddamned excursions into their brains. I don't want to hear your explanations. I don't *care* about your explanations. I don't want to do anything but put the whole situation out of my mind. So, *please*, stop calling me!" She put down the receiver, then went to the bar to pour herself a drink. Her hands were shaking so badly she couldn't hold the glass. Leaving the drink on the bar, she went into the bedroom and stood by the window, staring out at the impossibly turquoise water in the swimming pool, until her hands were steady again. Rolling her shoulders to ease the tension, she returned to the living room for her drink and the book.

By the time Bobby got home, she'd managed to calm down and was seated outside on the terrace, staring at the sky, the book abandoned on the table nearby and a cigarette between her fingers. He came out and squatted in front of her, resting his chin on her knee, looking up at her. "You look very pretty. I like you in my clothes."

"I didn't think you'd mind. I packed in a hurry and didn't bring anything casual."

"I don't mind. If you want to, we can go out for dinner. I could shower and be ready in half an hour. Or we can stay in and have Frankie fix us something."

Her hand came to rest on his cheek and she looked at him with open affection, so that he felt truly loved and secure. "What d'you think? In or out?" he asked her.

"I think in. D'you mind?"

"Not one bit. I'll go tell Frankie."

She took another puff on her cigarette, put it out, and sat very still, her eyes again on the sky. There'd be no more long, newsy, type-written letters; no more unplanned visits; no more hours-long conversations; no more working together on a script; no more sudden bursts of laughter; no more friendship. Now she'd concentrate very hard on putting it out of her mind. She'd enjoy the warm breeze and the fragrance of the flowering bushes rimming the terrace. She'd enjoy Bobby's face, the freckles splashed across the bridge of his nose; she'd enjoy the sound of his voice and the reaffirming proximity of his body in the night. She would breathe slowly and deeply, and she would not prolong her grieving.

But, oh, she thought, it felt too empty. And how could she help but break into tears at the loss? Never to see Becky's lovely face again; never to hear her ramble on about some idea as she wound a strand of her autumn hair around and around her finger. Why had she talked about Melinda? Anything else but Melinda. She was locked into a spiral, spinning, everything going out of control. Circles, and at their center, Melinda.

Returning, Bobby halted for a moment in the doorway. Then he went once more to drop down in front of her, closing her into his arms.

"It'll be all right," he told her.

"It won't be," she sobbed. "How *can* it be?"

"You'll see. Things'll work out."

She pushed him away and got up to go stand by the side of the pool. He followed and stood beside her. She wanted to tell him how afraid she was that Melinda had taken complete control of her life. But not only couldn't she say it, she wondered how she could even think it was true.

"There isn't one of us," he said softly, "who hasn't felt the way you do right now. Not one of us, Bea."

She turned to look at him, ready to challenge his words. But his expression stopped her. She wiped her eyes on her shirt sleeve and nodded. His arm slipped across her shoulders, and she leaned closer to him. Bobby wouldn't let her drown.

Thirty-Nine

MELINDA was almost eleven the year her previously vague, rather muddled feelings knitted themselves into a definite antipathy toward her mother. This coincided almost to the day with her first period, and she experienced a profound sense of disgust at the treacherous turn her body had taken against her. The fact that her mother claimed to be proud of her and displayed a solicitous concern aroused in Melinda both a deepening of her disgust with herself and a raw lump of contempt in her throat for her mother.

While Bea went about gathering up sanitary napkins and the rest of the things she told Melinda she'd be needing, she watched her mother, all but laughing at the transparency of Bea's performance. It was just another acting role, so far as Melinda could see, and she'd have been far happier if Bea had simply left her alone instead of making such a fuss. But no. That couldn't be, because Melinda was, after all, the daughter of Beatrice Crane, and so the whole dismal event had to take on the dimensions of an awards ceremony. Mercifully, her father was off somewhere on the coast of the Mediterranean, working on a picture, so he wasn't there to see Bea get red in the face and positively giddy over the whole business.

If that wasn't bad enough, Bea had to announce it, not only to Aunt Lucy, but even to Edna, the bloody housekeeper. Melinda could have died but smiled instead as Aunt Lucy clucked and hovered over her and Edna said, "They're startin' younger all the time," before going off to empty the clothes dryer.

"I wish you wouldn't keep on about it," Melinda told her mother at last. "You're embarrassing me."

"I'm sorry," Bea apologized, back at once to looking concerned. "You should have said something. I had no idea you felt that way."

"It's hardly something everyone's interested in hearing, and I hate having people staring at me, knowing."

"But Mel," her mother draped an arm around her shoulders, "it's a perfectly natural thing. It also means you're not a little girl anymore. It *is* an occasion. It's the start of your life as a woman."

"Oh, *don't!*" Melinda shrugged off her mother's arm. "I'm nowhere near old enough to be 'starting my life as a woman.' I do so hate it when you say things like that."

Her mother looked so bewildered and hurt by this that the inside Mel immediately felt guilty for having spoken. She couldn't have said, though, which bothered her more: her mother's constantly being "on" or the hurt look she got whenever someone said or did something that didn't sit right with her. Melinda had to admit that the hurt look had the edge, because every time she saw it, the inside Mel got a crushed feeling in her chest and a metallic taste in her mouth, as if she'd been sucking on a penny. So, seeing this look now, she was compelled to say, "I'd rather keep it private. And I'd rather you didn't go on and on about it. That's all."

"Of course," her mother said, her features smoothing as she reached out to run her hand over Melinda's hair. "It's hard getting used to it at the beginning. Do you feel all right? Would you like to go up and have a nap before dinner?"

"I'm perfectly fine." Melinda dredged up a smile, perpetually exhausted by all the things she had to do solely for her mother's benefit. "I've got some schoolwork to finish."

Her mother then wanted to hug her, and Melinda suffered through it until she was finally free to go up to her room. She didn't actually have any schoolwork left to do, since, in fact, she'd completed it as soon as she'd come home from school on Friday afternoon. She sat down and deliberated ringing up Nancy, then remembered Nancy had said she and her parents were going to the country for the weekend. Nancy was terribly lucky. Her parents were so nice, so pleasingly ordinary and predictable. They weren't forever discussing this actor, or that actress, or locations, or budgets, or shooting schedules. Nancy's mother wasn't always either about to go off somewhere for six, or eight, or twelve, weeks, or about to return from somewhere. Life was very orderly at Nancy's house. There were never exotic people popping out unexpectedly of a morning from the guest rooms; there were never lengthy, loud parties with people arriving dressed in outrageous, overpriced clothes, people who drank too much and stayed until all hours of the morning. Nancy wasn't lumbered with someone like Aunt Lucy who so doted on Bea that she all but licked her shoes and sat up on her hind legs for attention. The only one who seemed even remotely normal was her father, and he, too, was forever about to leave, or on the verge of returning. He, at least, didn't make a great to-do of everything and listened quietly when Melinda had something to say. But she'd felt for ages that there was something odd about him, too, that she could never quite figure out. Some of it had to do with her mother and Uncle Bobby, and the fact that her father wasn't outwardly bothered by the amount of time her mother spent with Uncle Bobby. Melinda was bothered, though, and had been becoming more and more bothered since the previous summer when she'd gone to New York with her mother and Lucy, and her mother had disappeared for entire days and, occasionally, entire nights. It was during that trip that Melinda had really begun to see the way her mother and Uncle Bobby looked at each other and how they managed to find excuses for touching one another. They were forever kissing hello and good-bye, and Melinda could never shake the recollection of seeing them kissing one Christmas in the hallway of the London house. It happened again in New York.

They'd been staying at the Plaza in a huge suite with three bedrooms, and Melinda had awakened in the middle of the night to go to the bathroom. Hearing low voices, she'd peered into the living room to see her mother and Bobby standing very close together, by the door, whispering. Her mother's dress was unzipped, and Bobby had been standing behind her with his hand inside the dress. But they weren't moving; they were simply talking. Curious, Melinda watched them, wondering what they were talking about. But then they stopped talking, turned, and stood looking at each other for ages. Then her mother shook her head, as if she were saying no to something, and Uncle Bobby sort of shrugged. They'd looked at each other some more, and then they'd collided, as if invisible people had shoved them, and they kissed very hard before her mother made it end and opened the door. Uncle Bobby had put his hand on her mother's face, then he went out; and her mother closed the door and stood there for ages with her dress half falling off.

Melinda had run back to her room before her mother could see her. She'd climbed into bed and lay there for ages listening to the traffic— New York was frightfully noisy, not like home—thinking about what she'd seen. It gave her a peculiar, twisting feeling inside, thinking about it, a feeling that made her weak somehow. It had been hours before she'd been able to get back to sleep, and when she did, she dreamed about her mother and Bobby. After that, she couldn't stop thinking about the incident, and for some reason it made the inside Mel deeply sad—for her father, and for her mother, too, because there was something so very odd about *all* of them, and it seemed a secret they all shared.

The outside Mel didn't want to feel sad about her mother. The sadness merely got in the way of the outside Mel's anger with her. The sadness would have had Melinda believing that her mother wasn't truly forever acting in the things she said and did, and Melinda didn't want to believe that because it would've meant she was wrong about her mother, that her mother really was as sweet as she pretended to be. And if the outside Mel was wrong, then it meant something not very nice about Melinda, and that couldn't possibly be right. She knew very well what she saw and heard with her own eyes and ears.

What addled her more than anything else was that her parents not only slept together sometimes in the same bed, but they actually *did* it. She'd heard the sounds one night, and it had taken her a few moments to figure it out, and when she had, she'd felt positively ill, picturing the two of them and what they were doing to each other. She'd stood outside their closed bedroom door, hearing the faint telltale sounds, and she'd wanted both to run away with her hands over her ears and also to weep because nothing made sense to her, nothing at all. And as if in confirmation that she hadn't imagined anything, Melinda came to recognize a certain look her mother wore after she'd been 'doing it.' She'd come down to breakfast or out of her bedroom at some hotel, and she'd look softened, as if someone had taken a very stiff brush to her and rubbed her until she shone. She'd move languidly, and her eyes would be large and distant and very light so that you could almost see clear through them. Melinda had to wonder if this wasn't another portrayal, intended to convey things to Melinda that were simply beyond her comprehension. And yet, her mother, at these times, was unutterably beautiful, with her long dark hair hanging about her face and her skin glowing.

There were times when Melinda would sit with her mother and she'd forget herself and feel really very happy, while her mother mussed her hair and hugged her and smiled into her face. At those times, she'd feel as if there was a great rock lodged in her chest that made it hard for her to breathe, and she'd study closely her mother's face trying to decide if Mummy was actually real now, and this wasn't a trick of some sort. She'd look at her mother's eyes, and they were so big and such a rare slate color that they seemed to become bigger and bigger until Melinda became afraid she might actually tumble into Mummy's eyes and disappear.

There were other times when it was just the three of them, Mummy and Daddy and her in the middle, holding both their hands as they walked across Hampstead Heath or out to dinner on their own. The inside Mel felt wonderfully special then because Mummy and Daddy were famous, and that made her unique, too, because she was there with them. And when people came asking Mummy to sign autographs they always smiled over at Melinda, and Melinda knew they envied her and wished they could be her and get to live with Mummy and Daddy. But the outside Mel also got angry when people came, interrupting her time with her mother and father. It was supposed to be only the three of them, and it wasn't fair that strangers should come smiling over to their table, breaking in, telling Mummy how much they loved her, and asking if she wouldn't mind signing this piece of paper, please. Mummy never minded, never got annoyed. She smiled, said of course, and wrote her name on the pieces of paper, and then the people went away, and Mummy got on with her dinner or her drink or whatever they'd been saying to one another before the interruption. And that was something else Melinda found extraordinary: that her mother could pick up precisely where they'd left off, if they'd been talking. It was as if she'd memorized what had been said, and she was proving over and over how clever she was at being able to remember.

There were also times when her mother took her completely by surprise by seeming to know to the letter what Melinda was thinking. She'd say, "Don't let it bother you, sweetheart. They're only trying to be nice. They don't mean to interfere. My face is familiar, and they're not sure why. Then they realize they know who I am, and they want to tell me how much they liked a picture I did and to ask for my autograph. They mean well." Or, she'd say, "I know how hard it is being young, Mel, and trying to figure out what everything means, especially the things adults like to do and talk about. I honestly do know," she'd repeat, and then she'd smile. For a few seconds Melinda would feel elated, having her mother smile at her that way. But if they were out somewhere and her mother gave her one of those smiles, Melinda always had to look around to see if anyone was watching, because she couldn't help wondering if Mummy was smiling that way because she knew other people could see her, and she wanted everyone to think what a splendid mother she was to smile that way at her daughter.

Sometimes she'd get dizzy trying to decide what was real and what wasn't. She'd gone a few times with Aunt Lucy to see Mummy when she was working on a picture in London. She'd sat quietly watching Mummy act in front of the cameras and had been surprised and distraught to see that Mummy could cry right when she was supposed to, and do it several times again if the director wanted her to. Or she could say the same lines five, or six, or seven times if they asked her to. And, Melinda reasoned, if she could cry, or laugh, or make the words she said sound so real, and it was nothing more than pretending, then perhaps it was more pretending when she laughed, or cried, or said certain things to Melinda.

Aunt Lucy said, "That's acting, Mel. It's what your mother does. And she's very, very good at it."

If she is so very, very good at it, Melinda thought, then how am I supposed to be able to tell when Mummy is acting and when she isn't?

Her mother took her one afternoon to see a revival of *The Wizard of Oz*, and Melinda was mortified to realize that when Dorothy began singing in the farmyard, her mother started to cry right there in the cinema. It was dreadful, and Melinda had no idea what to do or why her mother was crying, so she sat without moving and kept her eyes on the screen, watching but not paying any attention to the film. She was listening to her mother crying and crying and finally clicking open her handbag to get a handkerchief. When they were on their way home and Melinda, quite angry, asked to know why she'd carried on that way, her mother had looked at her and, with a sad little smile, said, "She was such a lovely kid, Mel, so talented, with such heart." She'd looked off somewhere, saying, "It all went sour. Everything changes, everything."

Melinda hadn't the foggiest what she was talking about, but she couldn't forget that afternoon, and the way her mother had wept so broken-heartedly over some girl in a film. She really couldn't see what there was to cry about, and she began wondering if there were important things about her mother she was meant to know that nobody had ever told her. Because her mother was in no way remotely similar to other mothers Melinda had encountered; because her mother could weep over films or in front of a camera; because her mother could do things behind closed doors and then allow herself to be seen in the aftermath. So, more and more, it felt to Melinda that people weren't telling her the things she needed to know.

Probably the single worst example of that occurred the year Melinda was twelve. She arrived home from school one afternoon and knew the instant she came through the front door that something was going on. Her parents and Lucy were in the lounge—she disliked their American way of calling it the "living room"—sitting on the edges of the furniture wearing somber faces and talking in hushed tones. When she stopped in the doorway, all three of them went quiet and looked over at her. She became frightened when she saw her father. His face was gray, and his eyes were very red. She was about to ask what was wrong when her mother got up and came over to put her arms around Melinda, saying, "We've had some very sad news. Uncle Hero died."

It didn't mean a thing to Melinda. But obviously it meant a very great deal to her father because between the time she'd seen him at breakfast before she'd left for school and now, he looked years and years older. Since she knew it was the appropriate thing to do, Melinda said, "I'm very sorry. That's too bad."

"Your father's leaving tonight to go to California for the funeral," her mother told her, her arms still around Melinda.

"How long will you be gone?" Melinda asked him, not knowing what she ought to be saying. She'd delivered her only good line.

Her father didn't seem able to speak. His shoulders rose and fell, as her mother said, "We're not sure. Perhaps a week or two." Her mother finally let go of her, and Melinda took several steps toward her father, then stopped. For the first time, she could see that her father was old. He had wrinkles around his eyes and mouth, and the skin under his chin was loose and soft-looking. He wore the same clothes as always, with a bow tie at the neck of his white shirt, and one of the cashmere sweater vests Mummy was forever buying him. But he was old, and seeing this sent fear chilling through her system. She was suddenly so upset that she threw herself into his arms and burst into tears.

Everyone interpreted this as a display of her grief at Uncle Hero's death, and they collected around to pat her shoulder and stroke her head and she couldn't tell them her upset hadn't anything to do with Uncle Hero. She'd hardly known the man, even though he'd spent every Christmas with them the whole seven years they'd lived in England, and he'd always given her fabulous gifts. She'd certainly recognized him, with his silver hair and blue eyes and springy walk. She just hadn't any idea what sort of person he'd been. No, it was her father she was crying over, because she now understood that he wasn't always going to be there, that he'd die and she'd never be able to see him again, and she hadn't realized until this very moment that she loved her father more than anyone else in the whole world. And he was the only one who truly loved her. So what would she do if he died, and she was left with just Mummy and Aunt Lucy? She couldn't bear to think about it; it was too terrible.

She cried so wretchedly that her mother seemed very impressed and even shocked. And later on, after her mother and Aunt Lucy had returned from seeing her father off at the airport, Melinda overheard the two of them talking in the lounge, and her mother saying, "I had no idea Mel was so fond of Hero. I've never seen her so upset."

And Lucy said, "I think she was upset because Hank was. I don't think it had anything to do with Hero."

Melinda was taken aback by this observation. She'd never guessed Aunt Lucy was quite so clever or perceptive. She decided she'd pay closer attention in future to Aunt Lucy. Obviously there was more to her than Melinda had believed.

Later that same evening, as she was headed along the hallway, thinking of fixing herself a snack, she heard her mother talking on the telephone and slowed her steps in order to catch her mother's end of the conversation. It only took her a second or two to figure out that her mother was talking to Uncle Bobby in California, and she stopped outside the door in time to hear her mother saying, "Look after him, will you? He's in a terrible state, Bobby. You know how close he and Hero were. No, I just can't get away. We're starting principal photography the day after tomorrow in Cornwall. Darling, I can't. Aside from everything else, we need the money right now. Everything's hit us at once, and I couldn't possibly ask Hank at a time like this. Please, just look after him for me. No, I know that. No, I do. You know I do. You'll call me, won't you. I love you, too. And I'll see you as soon as we wrap this one, I promise. I'll take the time and meet you in New York. Yes, I promise. Yes, all right. You know I'm grateful. Bye-bye."

Melinda could never have explained why she did what she did. It was something that seemed to happen by itself. She didn't know she was going to do it; she didn't think about it. She simply found herself in the doorway, screaming at the top of her lungs at her mother, who was so startled she literally jumped, and then stood holding her hand to her heart, open-mouthed, as the words shot out of Mel's mouth.

"WHY ARE YOU ASKING HIM TO LOOK AFTER DADDY? DADDY DOESN'T NEED HIM! THE TWO OF YOU ARE ALWAYS SNEAKING AROUND WHEN YOU THINK DADDY DOESN'T KNOW, BUT HE DOES KNOW, HE'S NOT STUPID. AND NEITHER AM I, AND YOU KNOW WHAT I THINK, I THINK DADDY'S NOT REALLY MY FATHER AT ALL. I THINK HE IS, BOBBY IS! I KNOW THE THINGS THE TWO OF YOU DO. YOU THINK YOU'RE SO CLEVER THE TWO OF YOU BUT I KNOW WHAT YOU DO AND I HATE YOU FOR IT ALWAYS PRETENDING, ALWAYS SMIL-ING AND ACTING SO NICE WHEN OTHER PEOPLE ARE AROUND TO SEE, BUT I KNOW WHAT YOU'RE REALLY LIKE. I KNOW!"

Her mother stood there, and her hands slowly came up to cover her ears. She gaped as Melinda screamed and screamed at her. And finally, she got this look on her face that made the inside Mel want to die, but it was too late. She couldn't stop herself until her mother somehow, almost like magic, wasn't over there beside the telephone anymore but right in front of Melinda, and her arm was swinging way back and then she hit Melinda very hard, right across the mouth. Then Melinda was quiet, and the two of them were standing, glaring at each other, breathing so hard it was all Melinda could hear, their breathing, and a kind of rushing noise inside her head. She had no notion of how long the two of them stood there before her mother began speaking in a low, deadly voice that made the hair on Melinda's arms stand on end. "How *dare* you spy on me! I thought you'd stopped all that years ago, and now I find you standing outside doorways, listening to private conversations." Her eyes huge, her mouth hard, she said, "You stupid, *stupid* girl! It revolts me, the things you do. You *know* nothing, *less* than nothing! I can't *tell* you how it sickens me to think I could have a child who'd spy on her own parents, who'd say the filthy things you've just said! Henry Donovan is your father! *You know he is!* How could you *say* a thing like that? My God!"

Aunt Lucy, having heard, came running up the stairs, and Melinda could feel her eyes on her, but Melinda didn't care. She didn't care about anything.

"I know *all about you,*" Melinda spat. "You don't fool me. Oh, you're very good at fooling other people. The great Beatrice Crane. I've *seen* the two of you and the things you do. I'm not stupid. *You're* the one who's stupid, always pretending, when I know that's what you're doing. I know what I see with my own eyes." As the words hurtled out of her mouth, the inside Mel saw something happening to her mother, and she was mesmerized and terrified at the same time, powerless to stop any of this. It was meant to happen, and there was nothing she could do about it. She was firing words at her mother and way, way back in her brain, the inside Mel was pleading, Stop it! Stop it! You're hurting her! Look at the way you're hurting her! But she couldn't stop. It was as if years and years of words had been stored up inside her, and now they were rushing out with their own force, and they'd keep on coming until either she died or her mother did.

Aunt Lucy was saying something, but neither Melinda nor her mother was listening. Their eyes were fused together, and Melinda was recording every single thing that was happening, and still she couldn't stop. Not until her mother's hands clamped onto her shoulders, and she began shaking Melinda, shaking and shaking her until Melinda's teeth were rattling together and the outside Mel was glad her mother was so angry and hurt. Maybe she'd punish Melinda in some terrible fashion, and then Melinda would never again have to think awful things or say them; she'd be able to be the inside Mel who really did love Mummy more than anything else, and Daddy, too; she'd be the inside Mel who thought sometimes what a lucky,

lucky girl she was, because her mother was a famous film actress and all the rest of it; the inside Mel knew the truth. She knew that Mummy was real and cared very much and never pretended, about anything. The inside Mel felt very bad because the suspicious Mel had said such frightful things and had hurt Mummy horribly. But something was going wrong, and the inside Mel seemed to be sliding away, as if she was sinking in something thick and dark. It happened because Mummy very suddenly let go of Melinda and stood staring at her. Melinda could see she was shaking, her face very white, breathing even harder now. And Melinda thought if Mummy would only hold her now everything would be all right. The inside Mel would get rid of the angry Mel, the unhappy, horrible Mel who couldn't believe any of the things the other Mel did believe. The two Mels stood there, waiting for Mummy to choose, to pick one Mel or the other, either by taking hold and embracing her or by pushing her away because the bad Mel had gone too far, had hurt Mummy too deeply.

"Get out of my sight!" her mother said. "If I have to look at you for one second more, I swear to God I'll kill you!"

The good Mel inside made one last effort. She leaned forward inside, pressing against the walls of the other Mel, and said, "Mummy?" but it was too late. Her mother was already turning away. She turned her back and stood holding her hands out in front of her, looking at them as they trembled in the air. "Go to your room!" her mother whispered, her voice cracking.

Melinda hesitated for a moment, then turned and flew down the hall to her room, slamming the door as hard as she could. She stood with her back to the door, her fists clenched at her sides, concentrating on clearing the rushing noise from her head so she could hear what Aunt Lucy and her mother were saying to each other. She could hear her mother sobbing, and Aunt Lucy making shushing noises, and Melinda thought, "Good. Serves you bloody right!" She tried to hold onto that thought, but the sound of her mother's weeping was like knives cutting into every part of Melinda's body, and it was her turn to cover her ears with her hands. But she couldn't block out the sound. It was the worst thing Melinda had ever heard. It sounded as if her mother was actually dying. And standing there in her room in the dark, with her hands over her ears, Melinda felt the worst fear of her life and guilt that was so enormous that her body just couldn't contain it. She heaved again and again, and then was so weak she had to lay down on the floor, unable to get up.

Ages later, she was vaguely aware of the door to her room opening and the light going on. She curled tighter into herself on the floor, keeping her eyes closed, as she felt the reaction of whoever had opened the door. And then footsteps hurried down the hall, and the door to her mother's bedroom opened. There was a muffled, alarmed-sounding exchange, and then two sets of footsteps running.

She could smell her mother's perfume, and then felt her mother's hand pushing the hair away from her face. "Oh, God, Mel," her mother was whispering, "why is this happening to us? What's gone wrong with us?"

Melinda had so little strength that the inside Mel was actually able to get to the surface to hold Mummy around the waist and say, "I'm sorry, Mummy. I didn't mean it. Honestly, I didn't. Don't hate me, please don't hate me."

"I *love* you!" her mother cried, starting that awful sobbing again. "Lucy, help me!" her mother begged. "Help me with her."

Somehow, the next thing Melinda knew she was in her nightgown, in bed, her head on Mummy's lap, and her mother was saying, "God, I don't know what to do. What am I supposed to do about you, Mel?"

Melinda wanted to answer, but her mouth wouldn't open and her eyelids were so heavy she couldn't lift them. Her mother's perfume was in her nose, and her mouth, in her throat; she was choking to death on her mother's perfume.

Forty

A FTER Hero's death and Hank's trip to California for the funeral, everything was different. Bea felt that they'd reached a plateau in their lives, and she was deeply, privately, afraid that there would be a slow, steady decline now; matters in every area would continue to deteriorate until she was left with only handfuls of ashes.

The scene with Melinda haunted her; she had recurring nightmares where, with subtle variations, the horror played itself out repeatedly. For some bizarre reason she couldn't begin to fathom, her love for her daughter was the weapon Melinda had elected to use against her. No matter what she said or did, regardless of the truces that punctuated the weeks and months of their lives—periods of time when they seemed to draw close and to communicate most effectively— Bea was permanently on her guard, prepared at any moment to have Melinda seize hold of Bea's love for her and thrust it under Bea's nose like something rotting and rancid. Melinda had seemingly limitless contempt for Bea's emotions, and she displayed her contempt in ways so insidious that only those people at the very core of their lives were able to discern it. So, added to the existing complications in her life, was the awful reality that she was at her daughter's mercy. Melinda could withhold herself and knowingly make Bea suffer, and nothing Bea could display for her was enough to inspire Melinda to capitulate.

Hank, for the most part, simply didn't see it. To him, Melinda's very existence was commensurate with happiness. Because he'd never thought he'd have a child, the fact that he did have one blinded him to Melinda's faults. He saw only what she chose to show him, and what she chose to show him was the very best of herself. It was her father to whom she turned for approval; it was in him that she took public pride. Bea didn't have the heart to disabuse him, to try to get him to see that the daughter he loved was something of an illusion, created by his indulgence of Melinda and his refusal to judge her.

If Melinda happened to be present to hear someone praise her mother, and her mother was also present, Melinda's features took on a sagacious expression of boredom. And on one occasion that ever afterward Bea refused to believe had been staged intentionally for her benefit, she overheard Melinda talking in her room to her friend Nancy, saying, "It's positively sick-making how they go on and on about her. She's so important; she's so famous. She's so this, so that. *They* don't have to live with her. *They* don't have to put up with the things she does. She's a 'legend.' I sometimes think if I hear it one more time I'll go mad. And bloody Lucy forever telling me, 'Be nice to your mother, Melinda. Try to be nice, Melinda.' I don't hear anyone telling *her* to be nice to me. She's such a bloody *fake!*"

Bea had stood almost paralyzed, the words and the venomous tone with which they'd been delivered eating into her bones, her joints. She got away, to the bedroom and sat telling herself Melinda was a teenager, and teenagers were notorious for being overly critical and judgmental of their parents. It would pass, she told herself. Melinda would grow beyond this stage, and then the two of them would be close again. But what if it didn't pass? What if Melinda decided to feel the way she did about her for the rest of her life? No, no. She'd grow out of it. It was nothing more than a phase. She was nearly fourteen. Girls Melinda's age constantly took potshots at their parents, picking away at what they saw as flaws and failings. Parents were a constant source of chagrin and embarrassment to teenagers. Everyone knew that.

But it was so hard to reconcile the infant she'd held in her arms, the dependent, lovely infant, to the sturdy, very mature-looking young woman who gazed at her with such barely concealed dislike. The only people who seemed able to see through Melinda were Lucy and Bobby. And both of them, Bea knew full well, had time and again beseeched Melinda to relent and return some measure of her mother's love for her. And both of them had succeeded, in a lapidary fashion, only in adding further polish to Melinda's weaponry. She chose to interpret what Lucy and Bobby had to say to her as being further evidence of the ways in which everyone was attempting to manipulate her and not as proof of any kind that she was behaving so badly that people could actually see it.

Bea had tried everything she could think of to penetrate through to Melinda's central feelings. She'd taken her on shopping trips, and then to lunch. She'd gone with her on theater outings, to the movies, to museums and art galleries, and to antiques shops when Melinda had expressed an interest—promptly dropped thereafter—in old jewelry. She'd lavished gifts on Melinda, along with exquisite clothes, books, record albums; anything she thought Melinda might like. She'd planned holidays for the two of them when Hank was unavailable and had taken Melinda all through Europe and on regular visits to New York and California. She'd done everything conceivable, and the most she ever accomplished was another truce, during which time Melinda was pleasant and chatty, and seemed happy enough. But the moment Bea attempted, by words or actions, to move closer, Melinda shut down, retreating into stubborn silence. Bea refused to give up. There had to be a key somewhere, and she couldn't stop searching for it. Nor could she admit to anyone but Lucy and Bobby that she recognized the possibility that it was already too late. Even these admissions were veiled behind expressions of misgiving; she couldn't bring herself to make a flat-out declaration, to say, "I've lost her," because she wanted to believe there'd come a day when she'd be able to say, "I've got her back." It was bad luck to say certain things aloud; the very act of saying them might cause them to be true. And one never knew when superstition might prove stronger than one's own hope. So she went forward with determined optimism, willing to write off slurs and thinly disguised insults she'd never have tolerated from anyone else. Melinda was, after all, her child. It was a life sentence. She was going to be Melinda's mother until the day she died.

Two weeks before Melinda's sixteenth birthday, Hank awakened to discover himself too enervated to get out of bed. Rather than disturb Bea—it had been a night when he'd sought to have the warmth of her body against his—he lay back and waited for her to wake up. He felt very strange. He wasn't in any pain, and as long as he lay without moving, everything seemed normal. But the moment he again attempted to sit up, he became nauseatingly dizzy, and his heart pounded with such antic rhythm that he could hear the reverberations in his ears. He lowered himself back to the pillows and turned his head to look at Bea, who as ever, slept soundlessly, and in utter stillness.

The sight of her eased him, and he thought again of how fortunate he was to have had her in his life all these years. He found her as lovely and as lovable as he had the first time he'd seen her on the stage in New York. Her features in repose still seemed young to him, but then, he reasoned, his eighteen years' seniority was bound to influence his responses to everyone younger than he. Where once upon a time someone of forty had seemed old, forty-year-olds now looked to him fairly young. But Bea. It hardly seemed possible they'd been married for twenty-four years. Not when he could close his eyes and recall events that were so thoroughly detailed and clear they might have occurred only a few days before. He smiled to think of all the people who'd predicted the marriage wouldn't last a year at the outside, and here they were, still together, almost a quarter of a century later. They'd remained true to each other in all the important ways; they'd never dishonored the promises they'd made. And he had done what he'd set out to do: He'd made her into a star of the first magnitude. He'd taken her career and he'd shaped it into something that would outlive both of them. Directors didn't get remembered much, to speak of. But the world would remember Bea. He'd done everything in his power to see to that. And while he knew she sometimes had serious doubts about the career they'd engineered for her, and about her ability as well as her desire to keep it going, he was convinced it had been the right course. She had the talent, and the heart, and the courage, and the love of work, that were the components of staying power. She'd go down in the books as one of the great actresses of American film, and he'd played a primary role in that. His reward had been the privilege of spending his days and

441

nights with her, of watching her change, and grow, and become a woman he admired more than almost anyone else. She had a healthy sense of values, and she'd never allowed herself to be deluded into believing she was better than she was, or that she was no longer required to work hard at it. First and foremost, she was an actress. Incidentally, she'd evolved into a star. Being an actress had always interested and concerned her far more than anything quite so illusory as stardom.

And she'd given him the chance to know himself. With her exceptional generosity, she'd allowed him to satisfy questions that might have gone all his life long without answers; she'd taken him into her life, into her body, and she'd never judged him. She'd also given him a child. They had merged, and from the bittersweet pleasure of their thoughtful joining had come a child. Melinda had enhanced their lives. It really was quite miraculous.

There was an odd numbness in his fingers; his arm ached, and he thought he must have slept on it in that peculiar way that sometimes happened so when you woke up it seemed as if someone else was in the bed with you because there was no sensation whatever in that limb, and when you touched it with your free hand it didn't feel as if it belonged to you. But of course it did. The subcutaneous pricklings that took place as the bloodflow was restored always confirmed how foolish you'd been and how stupidly overimaginative, because whose arm could it possibly have been but your own.

He gently massaged his left arm, still looking as Bea, when all at once his heart began to swell inside his chest, growing larger and larger with each beat; each beat echoed inside his skull so that his ears hurt from the noise, and it was hard to concentrate on breathing with his racketing heart expanding so rapidly. He didn't want to disturb Bea and kept thinking this would stop in a moment or two and then he'd be able to catch his breath, but it wasn't stopping. His heart grew bigger and bigger; the pounding grew to a deafening roar. There was an instant of perfect silence, and he listened closely to it, awed. His heart ticked once more, twice, and then it detonated.

Bea opened her eyes and the first thing that registered was that Hank was awake. He was gazing up at the ceiling. She yawned and stretched, then sat up and looked again at him. A tremor started at a point very low in her body and moved rapidly upward so that when she put her hand out to touch him, it wavered so violently she was unable to control it. She brought the hand back and held it in her lap, but it refused to remain there and rose to cover her mouth. She remained with her hand over her mouth for minute after minute while her brain willed Hank to move, to blink, to do something, anything. But all the while she knew; it was a knowledge that had started in her cells and set her to quivering in the face of the utterly horrifying finality that shared the bed with her. She waited and waited, more minutes passing, but he was never going to move again, and it was up to her to close his eyes. She had the idea in her mind that he wouldn't be able to pay attention to where he was going if his eyes remained open. So, very carefully, she closed them for him, and whispered, "There." Now he'd be able to track his progress in that place he'd gone to without a word of warning, or a wave good-bye, or a knowing smile. Nothing. He'd simply left. Gone. That's all. Could this really be how it was? Would she, too, one day require someone to close her eyes so that she'd be able to see where she was going on that other side of life? She whispered, "Henry," knowing he couldn't hear. Whatever he was hearing now was beyond her capacity, beyond her range, beyond her conception. Nevertheless, she had to whisper, "Henry," once again and place her hand on his arm for confirmation that the blood no longer flowed in slender streams beneath the surface of his skin; there were no tiny pulses in the remote regions of his long body; there were no pulses, large or small; no blood flowing. Nothing.

All the times in her life she'd shed tears, for reasons valid or invalid, she'd wept with a knowledge of the comfort inherent in the act. But not this time. This time, her body wept of its own accord, with its own knowledge, and she couldn't connect herself to what her senses knew but her brain couldn't accept. Her tears exerted their own control; she was simply the channel through which they passed. They sprang from her eyes like tiny divers leaping from cliffs.

For a time, she and Melinda were reunited. Grief, undiluted and overrunning, bound them together. For hours, and days on end, the two of them clung to one another. Constantly touching, speechless with loss, they found a territory where they could stand side by side. Nothing else mattered; nothing was able to pierce the enclosing wall of their shared sorrow. They went step by step together through the process of committing Hank to his afterlife beneath the soil of an English cemetery. They made the arrangements, they selected appropriate clothes; they accommodated the people who flew over to attend the memorial service; they sat together, listening to the words his closest friends and associates used to laud his accomplishments both personal and professional; they stood, hand in hand, watching as flowers, one by one, were laid upon his coffin, and then, still joined, they backed away from the torn earth that would contain him for an unimaginable eternity. In the rear of the limousine, Melinda wept in her mother's arms, and Bea automatically applied her hands to the task of attempting to soothe a hurt that couldn't ever be eased by anything as simple or direct as mere touch. Lucy sat apart, a witness to the event, whose only real obligation was to tend to an endless unfolding of details. And since it was all she could do, she attended to the logistics of the death and to the problems and mysteries it created, in the process forcefully keeping people away from the fragile bonding of mother and daughter. She and Bobby were the temporary guardians of the dazed pair Hank had left behind, and they went about their duties with tacit complicity, hoping the bond would survive once the immediate shock had passed.

To Melinda, it made a kind of dreadful good sense that her mother should carry her grief down the corridor in the night and attempt to console herself with the other man who loved her. In this time out of time, all the old codes and rules were suspended; everyone understood and accepted everything. Like a ghost, Bea drifted out of her room and along the hallway to be taken in and embraced by Bobby into safe oblivion. Melinda could only watch her mother go, feeling the rightness of actions that were beyond her experience but not beyond her temporarily heightened sensitivity. She'd seen her mother scooped clean, gutted by her loss, and it was the only time in her life when she knew without question that it was not a performance she was seeing but the most alarming reality. Her mother was battered by grief, so debilitated by it, that were Melinda not to exercise the most extreme care, she stood to lose both parents. It was a responsibility she honored out of love for her father; she took hold of her mother because it was what her father would have wished her to do and not because of any spontaneous outpouring of newfound love for her mother. What she felt for her mother at this time was so complex, so tangled and twisted and unfathomable, that she lacked the energy to attempt to unravel and define it. Her skin, her pores, her nervous system dictated her actions, not her own will. Because for those few moments here and there when she focused her attention on her mother and everything became brilliantly, shatteringly clear, she found her mother's nakedness impossible to bear. It was safer, easier, to go forward by instinct. She obeyed. She protected her mother; she tolerated her blind need to be close; she even, in distant fashion, loved her during this time. It was the only occasion, she believed, when she was allowed to see her mother without benefit of camouflage. And what she saw, when she dared to look, was so potentially damaging to the barriers and beliefs Melinda had constructed for most of her life now, that she had to shut down her vision in order to be able to go on living herself. What she saw after the death of her father, and what she could never again acknowledge without suffering great personal damage, was that everything she'd believed to be true about her mother up until then had been intentionally distorted by Melinda herself out of a deep and abiding fear of being unable either to reciprocate her mother's enormous love for her, or to display for her mother any viable talent. Good grades were no match for Academy Award–winning artistry. And no matter what she might think of her mother on any other level, Beatrice Crane's talent was indisputable. It was an international given. She was so universally loved, and admired, and respected, that even the funeral of her husband would have been turned into a sideshow had the media been allowed to have their way. All unknowing, Melinda had been born to people of such impressive stature and ability that nothing she could ever do, beyond the pedestrian fact of her birth, would ever qualify her to stand on equal footing, either with her late father or with her still very-much-alive mother. It was an insight she was too young to accept or to live with, and so she had no alternative but to bide her time, do her duty, and wait for an appropriate opportunity to assert her right to her own life. She believed she had nothing else. There was only ever going to be one Beatrice Crane, and Melinda had no desire to spend her life as nothing more than a pale shadow of her famous mother. It was enough that she'd had people approach her for as long as she could remember, offering friendship, but in reality seeking an entrée to her mother. For too long, she'd had to watch the faces of the people who came into her life for signs of their secret priority: their true interest in her mother underlying their feigned interest in her. She was not some door people could open and go through to get to Beatrice Crane. She was Melinda Donovan, and a person in her own right, complete with feelings, and fears, and a great, hidden store of anger at having been used again and again as an access route to her mother. She was Melinda Donovan and worth more than secondary smiles simply because she happened to be in her mother's company. The death of her father meant the end of whatever naïveté she'd had left.

And yet, for a time, as she longed for her father and tried to comprehend the suddenness and monstrous totality of death, she floundered in the sea of her mother's love for her, adrift with need that only her mother could satisfy. So she held on; they touched; they were inseparable in their mutual bereavement and confusion. And during that time, she kept her inner eyes carefully closed, for fear of losing the sense she had of herself as Melinda Donovan. She might stand beside Beatrice Crane; she might have eyes like hers and a similar-sounding voice; she might bear in her body the genetic stamp only Beatrice Crane could have placed upon her, but she was Melinda Donovan; she would always be Melinda Donovan, and no amount of curiosity from strangers, no amount of media ink, no measure of her mother's need, or her own, would ever push her past the boundaries of her self-declared right to be Melinda Donovan.

Bea was so grateful at Melinda's compliance, at her demonstrations of emotion, that she simply opened herself wide and received Melinda into her in a rite as arcane and mystifying as the birth of Melinda had been. Beyond the immediate fog of her sorrow was a small, optimistic area where she saw Melinda's return as symbolic of the future they would have as a pair. Hank had died, but in dying, he'd given Melinda back to her. So the edges of her despair were lifted by her gratitude. It never occurred to her that this might be temporary, nothing more than another in the long series of truces that had exemplified their relationship for years. She believed positively that she and Melinda had managed to transcend their differences, that they'd at long last been reunited. Hank was gone, but Melinda had returned. There would be continuity.

She was therefore at a loss when, having decided to sell up the Hampstead house and returned to the United States, Melinda declared, "I want to stay on and finish school here."

"But it's all settled. The house is going to be sold, and we're going home."

"I haven't lived there since I was five years old," Melinda said quietly. "*This* is my home. All my friends are here, and I want to stay until I've finished school."

"You can't stay here alone."

"Nancy's parents said I could board with them. And once I've done my A- and O-levels, I'll find a place on my own while I go to university."

"But you're talking about *years*," Bea said, so stunned she had to sit down, at once lighting a cigarette. "I thought we'd go back, you'd go to school . . . Wasn't it *real*?" she asked in a near-whisper. "Did I imagine it all, Mel? We've been so close the past weeks. I thought . . ." She was all at once afraid to give voice to the thoughts she'd had, afraid that Melinda would take a verbal hammer to them and smash them into microscopic pieces.

Melinda sat down, too, but in the wing chair at the opposite side of the room and not, as Bea would have liked, next to her on the sofa.

"What I was thinking," Melinda began, "was that you'd go ahead, as you've planned, and find a place you like. And then I thought I'd come to you during the school holidays. It isn't as if we'll never see each other again."

"I see," Bea said, her voice gravelly with the effort she was making to battle down her disappointment.

"You've got loads of offers still, and you're bound to be away much of the time, the way you've always been. It won't make that much of a difference to you, if you're based there and not here. But it would make a tremendous difference to me. You *can* see that, can't you?"

"Well, I suppose I can, but..."

"It's always been my plan to read English, and I stand a very good chance of getting a place at Cambridge if I do well in my A- and O-levels."

Bea listened to Melinda's voice, arbitrarily thinking how good her accent was. No matter how hard she'd worked at it with diction and voice coaches, Bea herself had never mastered the English vowels. God! she thought suddenly, catching herself. She was being incredibly stupid. Melinda spoke the way she did because she'd spent two-thirds of her life in this country, and her having an American passport did not make her an American. "You're awfully young," she managed to say, knowing what Melinda's response would be even as she uttered the words.

"We both know I'm perfectly able to cope," Melinda said confidently. "I think I'll actually manage far better on my own."

Bea looked at her daughter's eyes. They were the same shape as her own, but they were an opaque brown color, so dark they sometimes appeared black. At certain moments, she could see glimpses of herself in Melinda, but for the most part, Melinda was Hank's daughter. She had his nose and his chin. But she had none of his sweetness, no hint of his compassion or his bursting enthusiasm for life. "You'll manage on your own," Bea said, "without me around to deflect any possible glory you might achieve."

"Don't make it sound as if we're in competition, Mother," Melinda said, her composure showing hairline cracks.

"That's what it's been, though, Mel, hasn't it?" Bea sounded surprised, even to herself. "I must be getting a little fuzzy with age. I never, until this moment, realized that that's what it is. It's been a competition, and you could never win. Poor Mel. I'm sorry. I honestly didn't see it."

"I'm *not* 'poor Mel,'" Melinda's voice acquired a strident edge. "I don't want to go back with you, and you're not going to force me into it."

"No," Bea said unexpectedly. "I wouldn't force you. No one's ever been able to make you do anything you didn't want to. I don't plan to start now."

"You've got your career, *and* your *love life*. You'll hardly notice I'm not there."

Bea crushed out her cigarette in the ashtray, then got slowly to her feet. "Let me tell you something," she said softly, but emphatically. "You do *not* know all the things you think you do. You never have, and you never will. You may be clever, but you're not nearly as clever as you think you are. On your longest day, Melinda, you'll never know the things *I* know. And you can spend the rest of your life trying, but you'll never be one hundred percent your own person. Part of you will always be mine, but you don't see that, do you? You haven't yet realized that every last one of us is a part of all the other people in our lives. No matter what you do, you'll never be able to · kill off the part of you that belongs to me, because no matter how hard you try to fight it, no matter how cruel you are to me, no matter what hurtful and damaging things you think of to say to me, I'm always going to love you. That's just the way it is. There's not even a question of choice involved. You can't have back a day, a minute, not a second, of that time when I loved the infant that you were, when I bathed you, and fed you, and worried about you when you were sick. You can't have even one of my memories of you, Mel. They're mine. *You're* mine. I don't know what I did, or why you're so set against me. I've tried to be the best mother I could possibly be. I thought we'd reached an understanding these past several weeks, but I was wrong. I'm very embarrassed to see just how wrong I was. But you've been wonderful since your father died, and I'll always be grateful to you for that. If you have your heart set on staying here, then that's the way it'll be. I've only ever wanted what was best for you. And if you change your mind, at any time, you can always come home. I'm very upset, and I know how you dislike it when I cry in front of you, so I'm going to go upstairs now. I'm sorry. Somehow, somewhere along the line, I let you down. If I knew how or when, I'd do everything in my power to correct it. But even that wouldn't be enough, would it?" She stood for a few seconds longer, then walked away.

Melinda sat and watched her mother's legs climb the stairs. Abstractedly, she noticed, not for the first time, that her mother had beautiful legs. Automatically, she looked down at her own, then yanked her skirt down hard to conceal them.

Forty-One

THE house was sold. The furniture was loaded into containers for temporary storage. Arrangements were made for payment to Nancy's parents for boarding Melinda. Lucy and Bea exchanged awkward good-byes with Melinda who then stood in the doorway of Nancy's parents' flat, watching as her mother and Lucy climbed into the rear of a limousine and headed off to the airport.

Bea had the feeling she was flying, not to the specific destination printed on their tickets, but rather into nameless space. In only a matter of months, she'd lost her husband and, to all intents and purposes, her daughter, and had given up her home. Now she was flying to New York where she and Lucy would stay, using the Pierre as their headquarters, while they searched for another house. She had vague ideas of what she was seeking and knew she'd recognize the place when she saw it. What she wanted was distance from neighbors, large sunny rooms, well-established shade trees, and country roads she might walk along without fear of encountering anyone but, perhaps, disinterested fellow travelers. What she wanted was a refuge, a sanctuary.

From time to time during the flight she turned to look at Lucy, finding it odd to realize that Lucy was fifty-seven years old. She wore her age well; her features had softened and blurred a little, but she looked a good eight or ten years younger. Nevertheless, she was fifty-seven. They'd been together for thirty-three years, and during all that time Lucy had been actively managing the minutiae of Bea's life— paying bills; answering fan mail; fielding telephone calls; playing bodyguard, mother, sister, confidante, friend, and adviser. She'd allowed herself to be uprooted without complaint, and now she'd left Brian behind. Perhaps it was too much to ask of anyone; perhaps she was wrong to anticipate that Lucy would merely fall into line with her plans.

"Would you rather have stayed, Luce? Are you upset about leaving Brian?"

Lucy closed the book she'd been reading, removed her glasses, and turned to look at Bea. "Do you really think," she asked, half-smiling, "I'd be sitting here with you if I'd wanted to stay in England with Brian?"

"I don't know," Bea answered. "I'm not sure anymore about anything."

"Well, let me hasten to assure you that I may be your friend, but I've never done a thing, not where you were concerned, that I didn't want to do. So don't even give it a second thought." She smiled and gave Bea's hand a pat.

Bea thought how much of a difference that smile made to Lucy's features. She was young again when she smiled, luring Bea into recollections of the afternoons they'd spent together in the living room of the house on Palmerston Boulevard, working up routines to the accompaniment of scratchy Gramophone records. It was a purely logical progression that her thoughts should shift to an image of Becky and Franny waving from across the street, curiosity propelling them forward to stand on the sidewalk watching Bea tap-dance with bottle-tops fastened to her shoes with rubber bands.

"What?" Lucy asked, tilting her head to one side.

"I was just thinking about Becky."

"Are you going to get in touch with her while we're in New York?"

Bea shook her head.

"Can't you forget that ancient history and make it up? Whatever the two of you fought about, surely it can't still matter." She watched Bea's eyes shift and focus somewhere distant. She could almost see the thoughts making their passage through Bea's mind as her jaw firmed and she blinked, bringing her eyes back to Lucy's.

"No. Not yet, anyway."

"For heaven's sake, why not?"

"Why not?" Bea repeated. "Why not. Because, unless you invited me to discuss it with you, I'd never dare speculate on your soul, on the essentials of who and what you are. It would be an unthinkable intrusion, an unforgivable presumption. It would mean that I believed myself to be so above criticism, not to mention reproach, that I could, with impunity, rummage around in your guts, then come up with my hands full of whatever I'd managed to find and wave it under your nose. There are things, even about the people we love the best, that don't sit well. It's a fact of life. Yet, because I have a career that

450

makes me recognizable, there are people who think they have the right to do that to me. And whether or not she recognized it, that is *precisely* what Becky did to me. She went on a fishing expedition inside of me, and then wanted me to approve of her catch."

"But she didn't mean..."

"Please, Lucy. Next you'll tell me that Dickie didn't mean to do any of the things he did, either. He was just trying to express himself, at my expense."

"Surely you don't equate what Becky did with what happened with that madman?"

"On a different level, yes I do. Picking up again with Becky would mean that I've either accepted what she said as the truth or that I've chosen to disregard it. I haven't done either. What journalists care to take from an interview I give them is one thing. What my friends decide to take out of my head, or my guts, or thin air, is something else. Aside from that, it made me furious that she constantly had to put me through all sorts of analytical processes in her own mind. She never could accept me at face value. Maybe it's my Achilles heel, but I am what I am, Lucy. What's the point of probing away at me, picking at the seams to see if maybe underneath there's something more real, or different, or truer than what's on the surface? You know I've never tried to present myself as anything other than what I am. I've never felt so *stripped* as I did that day. I felt as if I was on the table with my legs in the stirrups, and all of a sudden the doctor invited people in off the street to come have a look."

"Jesus! What a picture!"

"I'm glad you've got it. All I want to think about now is finding us a place to live. It's my first and only priority. That, and seeing Bobby, of course."

"Risking life and limb, dare I ask if you ever intend to work again?"

Bea shrugged. "I can't seem to handle more than one thing at a time right now. Of course, if something comes along...Somehow I've got to get used to the idea that Mel's going to be over there, and I'm going to be over here, and that it may be that way for good."

"She'll be home for three months in the summer."

"I thought we'd have longer, Lucy. I thought we'd have the time to work it all through. It never occurred to me we wouldn't have that chance. I was convinced she wanted it as much as I did." She turned and gazed out the window at the empty sky. "I was the only one thinking along those lines."

Lucy wisely decided to let the matter drop. She could see grief settling like a fine mist over Bea's features and knew nothing she could say or do would make a difference.

Bobby was wrapping up an hour-long television special in Los Angeles and would be flying in to New York in less than a week.

"Don't go ahead and buy anything without me there to see it," he told her. "Don't even make an offer. Will you promise me that?"

"Don't you think I'm capable of making my own decisions?" she asked testily.

"Of course I do. But I know about real estate, and there are things to ask that wouldn't occur to you. Besides, I have every intention of spending time with you, wherever you wind up, and I'd like to think I have something to say about where I'll be spending that time."

"You'd like to think that, would you?"

"Jesus! You're getting mean in your old age, sister."

"I'm not *that* old."

"No. But you're definitely mean." He laughed, then went on to say, "I've got a couple of things I want to talk to you about, a few ideas."

"You've had 'ideas' since you were sixteen years old. Why would I expect anything else? Let me know what flight you'll be on and I'll meet you."

"Do me a favor, don't. I'm going to be tired, and you can't go anywhere without attracting a crowd. I'll grab a taxi and meet you at my place. I'll let you know what time."

"Traveling incognito?" she asked.

"Hairless," he answered. "Gotta go. See you Saturday night."

Lucy lined up real estate agents in New Jersey and Connecticut, and the search began. After one day in New Jersey, Bea eliminated the entire state. "We'll concentrate on Connecticut. I don't care for it here at all."

They spent weeks looking at houses in Southport, Ridgefield, Westport, and Weston; they went through Norwalk, New Canaan, Darien, and Stamford. They walked through Dutch Colonials, ranches, split-levels, tri-levels, and converted barns. Nothing was right, and Bea was becoming more and more depressed as they returned to Manhattan after each day's drive to Connecticut.

"If we had some better idea of what you're looking for, we might have a chance of finding it," Bobby complained one evening, having persuaded her to come to his apartment for the night. "This is a pretty idiotic way to go about buying a place to live."

452

"Then *don't come!*" Bea shot back at him. "You *volunteered*. No one *asked* you."

"I had no idea when I volunteered that it was going to become a secondary occupation. Do you have any *notion* of what you really want? Or are we after the Holy Grail?"

"*Of course* I know what I *want*. And when I *see* it, I'll *buy* it!"

"Shit! You're nuts!" he told her, then started laughing. "You've had every goddamned real estate agent in the entire state of Connecticut pissing in their pants at the possibility they'll be able to go home that night and tell everybody they just sold a house to Beatrice Crane. Have you noticed their faces when you've said no? They look like little kids who've been told there's no Santa Claus."

"That's hardly my problem."

"Look, Bea," he tried to reason with her. "You can't keep this up indefinitely. For one thing, you're wearing poor Lucy out. She looks ready to drop on her feet. And for another, you're blowing a fortune on hotel bills and limos. Let's give it one more shot and see if you can't compromise and agree to something that fills *most* of the bill. Okay? You know you want to be settled before Mel gets out of school for the summer."

She turned her back on him and went to stand by the window, looking down at the traffic on Park Avenue. She'd lost weight after Hank's death, and she hadn't regained it. If anything, she seemed to be losing more. She looked fragile, and her rigid posture only accentuated the impression she gave of frailty.

"Are you pissed off with me now?" he asked, keeping his distance.

"No," she said almost inaudibly.

"What, then?"

Her shoulders lifted slightly, then fell. He got up and walked over. "What's the matter, Bea?" he asked, sitting on the window ledge and looking up at her.

"I've been impossible the past few weeks. I know it."

"Oh," he said, striving for lightness, "I wouldn't go that far."

"I miss him, Bobby. He set the standards and I lived up to them. Now I'm supposed to set my own, and I can't seem to care. So I'm covering everything up with anger."

"Come here." He directed her down on his knee, holding her secure against his chest. "It's your right to be sad, Bea. Nobody's going to think any the less of you for giving in to how you feel. I'd be pretty suspicious if you could just carry on, without turning a hair."

"But people don't want to *know* about grieving widows," she argued.

453

"I'm people. Lucy's people. *We* want to know. Who gives a shit about anybody else?"

"I don't know." She dropped her head onto his shoulder.

"Go ahead and be sad, Bea. It's really all right. I'm pretty sad myself, and so is Lucy. And don't worry about finding a place. Everything'll get taken care of."

She remained unmoving, while he rocked her tenderly, crooning comforting words that gradually became a soft melody he hummed to lull her into something that felt, for the first time in a long, long while, like peace.

A week later they found the house on Round Hill Road in Greenwich. It was a beautiful old house, with rooms of gracious proportions. The agent who showed it to them was an older woman who'd been in real estate since the war and knew the history of the house very well. While Bobby and Bea wandered through the upstairs rooms, the agent confided to Lucy details of the previous inhabitants.

"The couple who're selling now," she explained, "bought the house seven or eight years back. He's being transferred to Atlanta. Before that, there was a young couple had the place maybe three, four years at most. She was an interesting one, now, the wife. English, the daughter of—what was he?—an ambassador, something like that. She did all the restoration work. Just a beautiful girl she was, but so tragic. Tried to kill herself, I don't know how many times."

"She *died* here?" Lucy asked in a horrified whisper, fearful Bea might overhear.

"Oh, heavens, no," the agent laughed. "No, no. She was just a very unhappy girl. But she did love this house."

"I see," Lucy said. "Do me a favor, and don't mention any of this to Miss Crane. It could cost you the sale."

"Oh, dear me! I certainly won't say a word then. She does seem very taken with it, and we'd be thrilled to have her here."

"Don't say anything about that, either," Lucy cautioned her. "Just let the house speak for itself."

Upstairs in the master suite, Bea said, "This is the one I want."

Bobby closed the closet doors and said, "Okay. Please let me negotiate for you. I know you're capable of handling it yourself, but let me do this for you."

"All right," she acquiesced. "Go ahead."

They returned downstairs and Bobby approached the agent to say, "We're prepared to make an offer. Shall we go back to your office and work out the details?"

Delighted, the agent said, "Certainly, Mr. Bradley."

Bea sat and smoked a cigarette while Bobby enumerated for the agent the various contingencies upon which the offer would rest. "We'll want a termite inspection and a general building inspection of the whole house. I assume you have a list of people locally."

"Oh, yes, we do."

"It'll be a cash offer, so there'll be no mortgage contingency. And since the house is already vacant, if there are no structural problems, we'll want a thirty-day closing. I'm a little concerned about the wiring, and the roof needs to be redone. I don't like the look of the foundation near the furnace, and I'll want to know how old the oil tank is."

The woman wrote quickly, getting everything down. "If you like," she said, "I can try to call now with your offer. Or, if you'd prefer, I can get back to you later."

"Call now," Bea said, glad she'd allowed Bobby to handle this. She was most impressed by his knowledge and by the way he was dealing with the agent.

"You'll have to write a check for ten percent of your offer, Bea," he told her.

They both looked at the agent who was busy putting in a long-distance call to the owner. She raised her head, and, with a wide smile, said, "If you wouldn't mind, dear. Make it out to this office, in trust. All by the book, you know." She sat back, listening to the ringing on the other end.

"Let's go stretch our legs," Bobby suggested to Bea. "It's better not to sit here and listen. Want to come, Luce?"

"I'll stay and finish my coffee. You two go ahead."

Bea put out her cigarette and let Bobby lead her out of the office. "Don't be nervous," he told her.

"But it's such a low offer. What if they turn it down?"

"You're going to get the place, Bea. There's not a thing to worry about."

"I never dreamed you knew so much," she said, slipping her arm through his.

"There are all kinds of things I know about. It's a nice town," he said approvingly as they walked along West Putnam Avenue. "And the house is a beauty. You've got plenty of room for a pool, if you want to put one in. Even a tennis court."

"I don't play tennis."

"Just a thought."

"You'd want a pool, wouldn't you?" she asked him.

"I am kind of used to having one. It'd be nice to be able to take a dip now and then when I come to visit. Be good for you, too. Half

455

an hour doing lengths in the pool would do you more good than an hour of exercises."

"What're you angling at?" she wanted to know. "You've got something on your mind, I can tell."

"It's just an idea I've been working on."

"What idea?"

"There's no rush. Let's get the house business settled first. There'll be plenty of time later to talk about my idea. One thing at a time, okay?"

"When d'you have to go back out West?"

"Ah, well," he said. "That's another thing we have to talk about."

"You're starting to get on my nerves. Will you *please* give me just *one straight answer?*"

"Let's turn around and head back now." He made an about-face, towing her along. "Okay," he said. "Straight answers. Number one, don't get yourself all worked up because I'm not going to ask you to marry me. Hah!" he laughed, pointing a finger at her. "That's exactly what you thought I was going to do, isn't it? Come on, admit it!"

She blushed. "Well, I . . ."

"Never mind. I know how your mind works, and you're wrong. I'm in no mood for a turn-down, so I'm not going to ask you. Number two, I am, as of next Monday when the story hits the trades, officially semi-retired."

"Bobby . . ."

"Number three," he sailed on, "I've sold the house. I offered Frankie the chance to come East with me but he figured the winters would kill him, so he's taken his settlement and gone home to Oahu. I've liquidated some of my real estate holdings, and I'm hanging on to the rest until the market goes up a little higher. I haven't decided yet what my cut-off date's going to be, but I want to wait a while longer on that score. I've got an agency screening people for me in the city, and they're going to be sending the first batch of applicants over tomorrow. I'll never be able to find another Frankie, so I think a married couple will be best. You know. For the cooking and cleaning and running the apartment. I hate having a service that sends people in to wipe off the tops of everything, so it'll be a relief to have the place really clean. Your mouth is open. Do you know that?"

"You're not going back? You're not going to work anymore? What'll you *do?* And what about the blondes, the divorcées? Who'll console all those women? Bobby," her voice dropped, "you're doing it for me, aren't you?"

"Nope. I'm doing it for me, and only incidentally for you. And I said *semi*-retired. I didn't say deceased. I told you: I've got an idea or two I'm working on. But I'm not ready to talk about any of that yet."

"You sold your house? What about your furniture, everything in the house?"

"Sold the whole thing, lock, stock, and barrel. I've got a few pieces, and a couple of trunks with the stuff I wanted to keep. The rest of it's gone. I always planned to come back someday. I'm a Brooklyn boy, don't forget."

"You did it for me, didn't you?" She stopped walking and waited for an answer. He took several more steps, then backed up.

"Yeah," he admitted, "I did. I don't care what the terms are, Bea, but I'm not going to blow it a second time. I want to be near enough to come on the run if you need me. And the way I see it, it's an hour tops from here to my place. It's a tolerable distance. If you feel like coming into town, you've got someplace to stay. And if you feel like company, I can be here fast. Listen," he said, taking hold of her arm. "The game's different now. We're not in the studio's pocket anymore. We don't have to keep looking over our shoulders, worrying about who might be watching. We can do pretty much what we want, and it's not going to be in anyone's column in the morning. Nobody's going to care but the two of us. And if you weren't hoping for something like this, why did you come back? Why didn't you stay in London? You don't even have to answer because *I* know, even if you don't, that it *is* why you came back. Okay, so I know and you know. And what's wrong with wanting to be closer to the people you care about? Huh? Is there something wrong with that?"

"No. There's not a thing wrong with that. God, Bobby! You grew up and got smart on me. In fact, you're way ahead of me."

"We're about in stride, I'd say. And we'd better get back there so you can hear your offer's been accepted."

They started walking again, and after a minute or so, he said, "I think the whole place needs painting, inside and out. What d'you think?"

"I think we'll get this house business taken care of. Then we'll drop Lucy off at the hotel so she can make her call to Brian. And then I'll come back to your place and let you undress me and take me to bed."

"Jesus!"

"And I think perhaps after we've finished, I'll be ready to tell you how I feel about everything you just said. How does that sound?"

"Perfect. And as soon as my blood pressure drops back to normal, I'll escort you into that goddamned real estate office. Jesus Christ, Bea!"

"Would you risk giving me a kiss right here on the street?"

He kissed her, and she hugged him for a long moment, then whispered, "Thank you," and they went inside to close the deal.

Forty-Two

BEA went flat-out at decorating the house. Although she knew it was unrealistic, she had the idea matters between her and Melinda would be improved once Melinda arrived and saw the house and the rooms Bea had arranged for her. Melinda's furniture from the London house occupied the large bedroom situated between Lucy's at the front of the house, and her mother's at the rear. Bea had painters and paperers in to do up the adjoining sitting room like an English country-cottage lounge, with sprigged wallpaper and pale rose-painted trim. Centered in front of the fireplace were a pair of comfortable armchairs, and discreetly positioned in one corner was an entertainment unit complete with a twenty-one-inch television set, a hi-fi/radio console, and shelves for Melinda's books and records. The rest of the house got attention only after these rooms were completed to Bea's satisfaction. Then, in the month and a half before Melinda was due to come home, Bea got busy organizing the living room and kitchen while Lucy interviewed housekeeping applicants.

Lucy opted for a very pleasant English couple in their mid-thirties whose previous employer gave them such a glowing recommendation that there was no question of holding further interviews. Until the apartment over the garages could be made ready, they moved into one of the guest rooms. Gertie saw to the house, and Albert tended the grounds and played chauffeur when the occasion required it. He adored the new Mercedes Bea had bought, and when he wasn't busy mowing the lawn or running errands at Gertie's or Lucy's behest, he could be found in the garage, lovingly polishing the car's chrome or adjusting the timing so that all eight cylinders fired to silent perfection. He was, from the beginning, positively crestfallen when Bea would climb behind the wheel and drive off alone.

Lucy settled into the spacious bedroom at the front of the house and spent her free time arranging and rearranging her bits and pieces, until everything was the way she wanted it. Periodically, in the evenings, she'd look up from the book she'd been reading, or away from the checks she'd been writing, or from the call to Brian she'd just completed, and wonder about the young English girl who'd tried to take her life in this house. The story haunted her, and she found herself thinking about it at the oddest times. At those moments, she could almost hear the echo of voices on the landing or floating up the curving staircase from the foyer. She told herself that she was substituting interest in an unknown girl for the physical absence of Brian from her life. She hadn't thought she'd miss him to the extent she did. She also thought frequently of Ike. It wasn't that she was unhappy with the present circumstances of her life, she just felt at times that there was rather too much distance between herself and the two men who'd played such pivotal roles in her life. But for now, it was more important that she be with Bea, who seemed utterly driven. The only thing to which Bea paid any attention was the house. Everything else was sliding. Lucy had the inescapable feeling that Bea had pinned her hopes on something that could never materialize. Regardless of Melinda's reactions to the house and her rooms in it, she'd never capitulate in the way Bea hoped she would. Lucy wished Bea could somehow see that. And yet Lucy knew she'd have to discover this for herself; no one else could ever make her accept that Melinda was never going to be a loving, demonstrative child.

Once the major work on the house was completed, Bea found herself agitated and unable to establish any sort of routine. The only constant in her life was the hour she spent each morning working out in her bedroom. Every other hour of the day represented a hateful challenge. Gertie planned the menus; she ordered the groceries, the liquor, even Bea's cigarettes. And Albert drove into town to pick everything up. Bea wandered along the upstairs hallway two, or three, or four times each day to stand at the door to Melinda's suite, anticipating Melinda's reaction when she saw their new home. She was counting weeks and days and at the same time telling herself she was riding for a fall.

"Why don't you take a break and go spend a few days in town with Bobby?" Lucy finally suggested. "You're roaming around here vibrating like a tuning fork. By the time Mel does get here, you'll be a mental case."

"I've been thinking about getting some estimates for a pool," Bea said, flinging herself into the Queen Anne chair in front of the window in Lucy's room and immediately lighting a cigarette. "Bobby's right. There's plenty of room out there. And a pool would be good when the weather's really hot. Then there's the question of air conditioning. I imagine these upstairs rooms will be stifling. We should find out about a central-air system. Don't you think? I mean, we'll suffocate up here in the summer. Can you put in central air with an oil furnace? I wonder if you can."

Lucy turned from the desk and rested her arms along the top of her chair as she looked over at Bea. "Would you like me to phone around and have some people come give us estimates for a pool? And while I'm at it, would you like me to call some plumbing and heating people and find out about air-conditioning the house? Would you like me to do that, Bea?"

Bea jumped up and went over to the bedside table, looking for an ashtray. There wasn't one there, so she walked back, flicked her cigarette ash into the fireplace, then sat down and looked inquiringly over at Lucy. "What did you say?"

"I said, I'll take care of the estimates for the pool and for central air. Anything else? How about a barbeque pit? Or some garden furniture? No, maybe we should wait until the pool's in before we get garden furniture. We could always convert the breakfast room into a small gym. Or maybe we could go whole hog and have not only a pool, but cabanas out there, for changing in. And we could have showers. That way everybody could wash off outside so they don't track all kinds of muck into the house."

"What're you talking about?" Bea stared at her and then, before Lucy could answer, she jumped up again to toss her cigarette stub into the fireplace grate.

"Will you *please* go pack a bag and get Albert to drive you into the city? Get out of here for a few days! I'll find out about pools and air conditioning and whatever else you can think of. Go take a break before you drive us all crazy. You should see yourself. It's a picture. She's down, then she's up, then she's down, then she's up. You've got yourself wound up so tight you're making everybody nervous. Bobby's been begging you for weeks either to let him come out or to have you go there. Call him and tell him you're coming."

"Maybe you're right. I'll do that. I'll go call him right now." She flew out of the room, and Lucy listened as she picked up the extension in her room and dialed Bobby's number. Once Bea started talking, Lucy turned back to the desk and got on with the deposit she was preparing for Bea's account. She was just totaling the checks when Bea came back to announce, "I'm going into town to spend a few days with Bobby. You'll be all right on your own here, won't you?"

"Bea," Lucy said patiently, "are you really losing your marbles or is this some nutty game? If you'll think back a few minutes, you'll remember that I was the one who suggested you take yourself into town. And I'll hardly be on my own, will I, with Gertie and Al not fifty feet away? Go get laid, and come back rational, please. Let me know when you're ready to go, and I'll come down with a white handkerchief and wave you off."

"You *bitch!*" Bea's features grew mottled with instant rage.

"Now, now," Lucy said coolly, putting down her pen and pushing away from the desk. "You know perfectly well I'm not a bitch at all."

"Talking to me as if I was some sort of mental defective!" Bea ranted, livid.

Lucy walked the half-dozen steps from the desk to where Bea was standing and, without hesitation, closed her arms around Bea and held her so tightly that Bea was immobilized. "The last few weeks you've been like a flea on a griddle," Lucy said in that same cool tone, using every bit of her strength to hold Bea. "Don't waste my time and your energy getting mad. You're not alone, and we all still love you. Now give me a hug, then go pack your things and get out of here." Initially, Bea was rigid. She held out for a few moments as Lucy's sensible words penetrated—or was it simply the contact?— then she softened, and gave herself up to the embrace. "Take it easy," Lucy told her. "Whipping yourself into a frenzy isn't going to bring Hank back, or make Mel like this place any better or worse than she will. Whether or not she likes the house won't change her. I know it sounds like a hard line, but don't invest too much more in her, Bea. You may find you can't afford it."

"She's my *child*. You don't know what that's like."

"You don't think so? What've I been doing all these years, if not playing mother to you? There are more ways than one to give a life, Bea. Sometimes, I think we're all just displaced mothers and daughters, looking for the right mother, the right daughter, because the one we got wasn't the one we should've had. So we go out in the world and find people who fit our needs. Go on, now," she said kindly. "Get yourself ready."

Bea backed away, shaky inside with the feeling that what Lucy had just said was the truth. And she didn't want to believe it, because if she accepted that as the truth, either she wasn't the right mother or Melinda wasn't the right daughter, or . . . No! That couldn't be. The fact that Melinda had taken form inside her body, had grown there through months of enforced bed rest, and had, at last, been delivered from a neat incision that bisected Bea's belly had to make a difference.

She'd tried for years to have that child; she'd suffered to have her, and she'd succeeded. All of that had to be significant. Otherwise, what was the point? Why had she gone through the pain, and the sickness, and the years of waiting? No. The problems she and Melinda experienced were rooted in Melinda's youth. And Melinda would grow beyond resentment and her need to compete. She'd mature and eventually see the extent of the effort her mother had made all along on her behalf; she'd see, and understand, and they'd find ground to meet on; they'd come close again, as close as they'd been during the first months of Melinda's life when, even separated by miles, Bea had been able to sense the infant's need to be held, or changed, or simply loved. She'd leaked milk, knowing her baby was hungry.

Melinda was her child. She didn't want to find herself out searching the world for some other girl who'd more appropriately play out that role. She wanted the one child she did have, the true child, the real one, the one she'd made out of parts of herself and parts of Hank. Surely the fact of her having physically created Melinda had to be important, not only to her, but to Melinda, as well.

She undressed before the mirrored wall of Bobby's bathroom, then stared at herself, thinking, My God! I'm a ruin. Scars, and flesh that no longer had the elasticity or texture of youth, a belly that at certain angles resembled nothing so much as an abandoned balloon, bones poking against every surface of her body, stick-doll arms, ankles like thin twigs. She couldn't stand the sight of herself. Dead-white, transparent skin. Miles of dark and lighter blue veins riding just beneath the surface. Small knots of muscle in her thighs and calves from all the years of stretching and sweating, straining against the everpresent pain of ancient injuries. There was gray in her hair, and wrinkles around her eyes. A veritable ruin.

"You look as if you just discovered you're standing barefoot in dogshit," Bobby said from the doorway behind her. "What's wrong?"

"How can you *ask* me that? Can't you *see*?"

"See what?"

"*Me!*"

"I see you. What about you?" he asked, coming to stand beside her, studying her reflection in the mirror.

She couldn't believe he didn't see it. "Don't be polite! I know what I can see with my own eyes."

"Polite?" He looked puzzled. "About what?"

"Bobby!" She was beginning to quiver with frustration at his refusal to be honest. "I'm *old*. My *body's* old. *Jesus Christ!*"

He debated jollying her out of it, decided that would be a major mistake, and said, "Your body's not old. It's actually not bad, all things considered, for a forty-six-year-old. Your muscle tone's good. Your breasts don't sag. There's not an excess inch of fat on you anywhere. As far as I'm concerned, it's a very attractive body. I even like your scars. You've taken good care of yourself, and I'd say you have a good forty more years' usage left. It's definitely *my* favorite body. I've always enjoyed it. In fact, I've been out there waiting, looking forward to enjoying it again. It's been a while, almost a month and a half, as a matter of fact, since you started trying to turn that house into a minor-league version of San Simeon."

She snatched up a bath towel and held it in front of her. "Don't lie to me," she said hoarsely. "I know how I look."

"You know what?" he said. "You're wrong. You have *no idea* how you look. And you want to know why?"

"Why?"

"It'll take a couple of minutes, so why don't we go sit down while we talk." Sliding his hand under her elbow, he moved her out of the bathroom and over to the bed. One hand placed firmly on her shoulder brought her down. Her knees bent, and she sat. He sat beside her, took hold of her hand in both of his, and said, "There are a couple of reasons. One of them has to do with something called stasis. In your case, I think it's caused by two forces of equal strength. One force is your own personal portion of intestinal fortitude, otherwise known as guts. The other is a combination of Mel, and the mental and emotional energy you've been putting into trying to make it all come right with you and her. The way I see it, you're caught in the middle, and all that energy is fighting against itself, so things are starting to go stagnant. And since stagnation's not your favorite sport, you're turning it into self-hatred."

"*I don't understand a single word you're saying!*"

He continued toying with her hand, rubbing her knuckles with his thumbs, running his fingertips over the edges of her nails. "Neither do I, really," he admitted with a smile. "But I told you a while ago I had some ideas, and we're going to talk about one of them now. You and I are going to work up one or two of our old routines."

"Are you crazy...?"

"No," he cut her off. "We'll do maybe one from *Big City,* and one from *Early Birds.* The simpler numbers that are primarily ballroom, with no tap steps. I've got prints of all the pictures, so we can run them and decide what we want to tackle first."

"Bobby, I can't..."

"Sure you can. And you're going to. And here's why: I've been talking to a very sharp young fella who's come up with the bright idea of a Crane-Bradley Film Festival. The timing, of course, is up to us, but the basic idea is to show, say, three pictures on each of two days. The first evening, at a gala, they'll have an M.C. introduce a half-hour reel of clips that ends with the intro to whatever number we've decided we're going to do. The orchestra picks up from the film cue, and you and I are there, going into the dance. Since it'll be a subscription deal, the audience'll have seen all three of the pictures that day, and after they've finished applauding their hearts out at seeing the two of us do our stuff, we'll come downstage and do questions and answers for an hour. Howard wants to kick off the festival in New York, and there's no reason why, if it goes here, it wouldn't go in all the major cities, maybe even on an international level. You and I would, naturally, wear the costumes we wore in the picture."

"Those gowns would be in tatters now, for God's sake."

"Copies," he said tolerantly. "You'll wear copies of the originals."

A tingle of excitement started up inside her, but she was still far from convinced. "No one's interested in those old pictures, Bobby."

"According to this fella, there's all kinds of interest. People have been lining up to see them at the rerun houses." He stopped chafing her hand and held it motionless between his own. "You can't sit out in the country indefinitely, Bea, making Mel the whole focus of your life. You haven't even been reading the scripts the agency's been sending you. Why not give this a try? It'll be like old times, working together again."

"It's all right for you. I mean, you've never stopped. But do you *realize* how long it's been since I danced?"

"But wouldn't you like to? I mean, why else've you been working out, exercising every day, all this time? You're in damned good shape. You're not walking like a half-drunk sailor anymore, with your hips caroming off the furniture. Will you at least think about it?"

"Why bring Melinda into it?" she wanted to know.

He dropped her hand, jumped up and, leaning with his face only inches from hers, said, "I'm sick and tired of her and the effect she's having on you. She's all you think about. Christ! Even goddamned housewives in the goddamned suburbs occasionally think of something else besides their goddamned children! It's about time you stopped hiding the real problem behind this bullshit about your poor, aging body, and the rest of it. You're only her mother, you know. You're not her *life*. And let me tell you something else! *People have rotten kids.* It happens. What makes you think you're exempt? Maybe she's one of those rotten kids. It's possible, very possible. And not

464

one goddamned thing you can do is going to make her any more or less rotten. What it *will* do, if you keep on the way you're going, is wreck your life. I'm fed up to the *teeth* with Melinda. D'you honestly think *she's* giving herself an ulcer worrying about *you?* I sincerely doubt it."

"What the hell are you so damned angry about?" she demanded, matching his tone.

"Because it's time you paid some attention to *me.*"

"Oh, wait a minute! I want to be sure I've got this right. Everything would be just fine if I was doing all the things you accuse me of doing, but for you, not her. Is that it?"

"Right! Exactly!"

"That's ridiculous!"

"No, it's perfectly reasonable. Because, for better or worse, at least the two of us are adults. If I piss you off, you can fight back, or walk away, or tell me to blow it out my ass. And vice versa. But what you're doing with Mel is completely one-sided. Are you going to sit there and tell me you honestly, truly, believe she spends even one-tenth of her time or energy worrying about pleasing you? *Do you?* No bullshit. The truth."

"No," she answered truthfully. Then, more quietly, "No."

"Right! At least with me and you there's someone putting equal energy into whatever the fuck you and I have. At least with *me* you know where you stand." Satisfied that he was getting through to her, he sat down again. "Nobody's saying you've got to give Mel up. Just back away a little. You can't force people to change, Bea. And chances are, the way you've been acting the past five or six months, you'll only drive her farther away. Maybe it's cruel of me to say it, but I think the harder she sees you trying, the more she's going to dance you around. Shit!" he said, seeing her eyes had acquired a glaze. "Look, Bea. I'm the first to admit I'm no expert on kids. And there is a kind of mystery when it comes to mothers and their children. I hate it when you cry." He put his arm around her shoulders. "And I hate it even more when I'm the one who makes you cry. But what I'm saying is the truth, and you damned well know it."

She used the edge of the towel to blot her eyes, then held the towel bunched in both hands, saying, "Sometimes, when I'm face to face with her, I can see everything so clearly. Oh, not everything. But the dimensions of that moment, and its dynamics. You know?" She looked at him with hope-filled eyes. "At those times, I'm capable of saying the most objective, intelligent things, to let her know I'm aware of how she operates. But when we're apart, I lose it, and I start thinking maybe I was wrong, or maybe I didn't really make myself clear. I get caught up in worrying about it, and I lay awake at night making lists of the things I want to say to her; I get trapped in it, and I can't stop. I don't want to *do* anything, or have to *deal* with anything, or make any *decisions,* or even *consider* anything unless it has to do with making everything come right with Mel. It's as if, if I keep digging, I'll come up with the solution I've kept on missing so far."

"You've got to stop, Bea. You really do."

"It's so hard. You don't *know* how hard it is."

"I have some idea, I can tell you, after watching you go high as a kite one minute, down the next, because Mel wrote, or you haven't heard from her in weeks. Or you sent her something and she didn't like it, or she didn't bother to thank you, or she wrote telling you to stop sending her things. It's been endless," he said tiredly. "The smallest things getting blown into full-scale melodramas."

"I'd make a fool of myself, Bobby, embarrass both of us," she said, abruptly switching subjects.

"D'you really think I'd let you set foot on a stage if I didn't think you could do it? That's what we're going to find out. That's the point of getting to work: to see if you can still cut it. I may love you, but there's no way I'm going to make a complete ass of myself in front of a live audience just to keep your spirits high, sister."

"I do like the idea."

"One word about the kid while we're working, and I'll throw you out the nearest window."

"I can't promise that."

"Promise you'll try."

"I will try. I know you're right. And Lucy's been saying the same thing. It's just that some things die hard."

"All I ask is that you try. That's all. So, are you hungry?"

"Unlike you, arguments don't give me an appetite. They make me feel sick." She leaned against him, finally letting go of the towel. "I've never seen you get so mad. That was scary."

"Scared myself. I've never known two people argue as much as us. We'll probably kill each other one of these times. All that crap about your body. Christ! I love your skinny body, always have. You make me look bad when you start with that stuff, like I've got no taste, and I'd sleep with any old bag of bones that happened by."

She smiled up at him. "Only if she was blonde and newly divorced."

Forty-Three

BEA would have liked to be at the airport to meet her, but Melinda wrote suggesting that since so many things could go wrong—delayed departure, tie-ups in customs, and so forth—the best idea would be to send a car. It was one thing, she wrote, to keep a paid driver waiting; it was quite another to have her mother hanging about the airport, perhaps for hours. So Lucy made arrangements to have a limousine at the terminal, and Bea kept returning upstairs to look at Melinda's rooms, to be sure everything was perfect. Fresh-cut flowers, a supply of the latest magazines, even a box of imported biscuits on the bedside table, in case Melinda got hungry in the night. There were books and an assortment of record albums on display in the entertainment unit. A special dinner had been planned, with Melinda's favorite foods. Every conceivable type of snack food had been laid in, along with cases of half a dozen kinds of soft drinks. There was an entire range of Twinings teas, as well as three different varieties of ground coffee. Theater tickets had been booked for all the top shows so that Melinda would have something to look forward to for weeks to come. Bea anticipated taking her into the city for shopping expeditions and excursions to the museums and art galleries. She and Bobby had agreed to put their rehearsal plans on hold until after Melinda's visit, and since he'd been planning to go to California in August anyway to take care of some business, it seemed that everything would work out splendidly.

The flight was scheduled to get in at five-thirty, and the driver had been instructed to take up his post at the arrivals gate at precisely five-fifteen. At Bea's urging, Lucy called the company to confirm that the driver had been given all the information and would be there on time.

"Everything's under control," Lucy told her. "Why don't you put your feet up and relax for a while? Even if things go like clockwork,

467

she won't get here before seven, more likely closer to seven-thirty or eight."

"You checked that the flight left on time?"

"It's on schedule. Go on," Lucy said. "Take your bath and relax. You've got plenty of time."

"D'you honestly think she'll like her rooms?"

"If she doesn't, she's crazy. Go on! You've been on the run all day. You'll be worn out by the time she gets here."

"All right. But you'll let me know if anything happens?"

"You know I will."

"Should we have Gertie put a carafe of ice-water in her room?"

"I'll take care of it."

"You think I'm behaving like a fool, I know. I'm just so anxious for her to get here, to like what we've done."

"She will. You've thought of everything, even Ovaltine, for chris- sake." Lucy laughed and gave Bea's hair a tug. "Since when does she drink Ovaltine?"

"You never know. Okay." Bea backed toward the stairs. "I'm going."

By seven, the two of them were seated in the pair of wing chairs by the windows in the living room, glancing every so often out at the driveway. Bea was sipping a light scotch and water. A cigarette between her fingers, she was trying to read the previous Sunday's *New York Times Book Review.* Every week, she made a list of books culled either from the reviews or the ads. Lucy then phoned the list in to the manager of the largest bookstore in town. What was on hand was picked up by Albert; anything else was ordered and Lucy was notified when it arrived. The bookstore sent a monthly bill that, in appreciation of Bea's trade, reflected a fifteen-percent discount. It was a handy arrangement that provided the entire household with reading matter. The flow had stopped in the past few weeks, since Bea had become so progressively nerved up about Melinda's visit that she found it hard to concentrate.

"You've already got so many books upstairs," Lucy said, "your bed's starting to look like a walled fortress."

"Help yourself to anything you want," Bea said, distracted.

"My point is maybe you should slow down with your orders for a while, until you get caught up."

"But then I might miss something I really want to read."

"You could always wait until they come out in softcover."

Bea shook her head and glanced out the window. "She should be here any minute."

"Uh-huh." Lucy went on turning the pages of the magazine in her lap.

Part Three / 1947–1976

By seven-fifteen, Bea had abandoned her book list and was standing at the window, wondering aloud if they should put on the exterior lights.

"It won't be dark for at least another two hours," Lucy said as Bea turned from the windows and dropped back into her chair. Her legs crossed, one foot swung back and forth metronomically.

"Maybe the plane was late."

"Would you like me to call?"

"Would you?" Bea looked grateful for the offer.

Lucy got up. She returned five minutes later to say, "It was on time."

"Maybe the traffic's heavy."

"That's possible."

"I think I'll freshen this." Bea jumped up and went to the bar to add more scotch to her glass. She lifted the lid on the ice bucket, looked inside, then replaced the lid. She was about to take a swallow of the undiluted scotch, reconsidered, grabbed a couple of ice cubes and dropped them into the glass.

At seven–forty-five, Lucy went to telephone the limousine service.

"I was about to call you people," the dispatcher said. "My driver phoned in ten minutes ago to say your party didn't come off the plane. Or if she did, she walked right by him. He swears he was right there, where she couldn't miss him, with her name on the card. He says he checked, and everybody on that flight's cleared customs."

"I see."

"I sent him on another call. We'll just bill you for the waiting time. I'm really sorry."

"You're sure he's reliable?"

"Lady, believe me, he's one of our best drivers. And, seriously, we don't like foul-ups like this. It's no good for business. He covered all the angles. It's possible your party just didn't see him."

"Okay. Thank you."

Lucy went back to the living room, trying to imagine where Melinda could be.

"What did they say?" Bea asked anxiously.

"The driver waited for more than two hours. I can only think Mel didn't see him."

"Didn't *see* him? You mean she wasn't..."

"He waited until every last passenger cleared customs."

"Where *is* she?" Bea asked frantically, looking once more out at the driveway. "She *was* on the plane, wasn't she?"

"I'll call the airlines and see if they've got any way to check that."

While Lucy went off to the telephone again, Bea opened the front door and walked the length of the driveway to look in both directions along Round Hill Road. After a minute or two, she told herself this was stupid. She didn't even know what she was looking for. Lucy was waiting in the doorway to say, "She was on the flight. I'm out of ideas."

"We could have her paged."

"It's getting on for eight," Lucy said as Bea stepped into the foyer. "The flight landed two and a half hours ago. It's unlikely she'd still be hanging around the airport."

"What should we do?"

"I don't know. I honestly don't. I guess we'll have to wait to hear from her."

"Oh, God! What if someone's..." She stopped herself from pursuing any of the dreadful ideas that occurred to her.

"Come on," Lucy said. "We'll finish our drinks. And if we haven't heard from her by nine, we'll consider our alternatives. She's not a little kid, Bea. She's traveled a hell of a lot more than most adults. She knows her way around airports and around Manhattan. You're bound to hear from her any time now."

During the next half hour, Lucy witnessed a change in Bea. Her thoughts and feelings played over her features in a way they hadn't since Bea was a child, in that era before she'd perfected her acting skills and learned to use them to mask her true emotions when in the company of strangers. This situation, the terrible uncertainty of waiting, forced Bea into the confrontation with herself regarding Melinda that neither Lucy nor Bobby had been able to bring about.

She reviewed the small cache of never-discussed fears she'd had from the first moments of Melinda's birth, when she'd imagined the many aspects of harm that could come to the newborn. She'd progressed into the injuries toddlers had been known to sustain; from there, she'd suffered periodic nightmares and daytime sweats at the prospects of Melinda's being kidnapped, or raped, or beaten, or murdered. There hadn't been any time in Melinda's life when Bea didn't, at some moment, turn inward to consider, with horror predicated on her own experiences, the dangers that surrounded her child. She'd always believed the majority of her fears to be the common property of all mothers, but with an exception: she was famous, and those with incomprehensible grudges, or those with a yearning for blood-spattered money, had been known to prey upon the children of the well-known. So Melinda was doubly imperiled. And Bea was always, on one level, prepared to receive word of disaster. In the main, her fears had been a tolerable burden, something she was more than

470

willing to shoulder as her responsibility for having given the child life in the first place.

But now as the air outside grew cooler and heavier, and night turned the windows into mirrors reflecting the details of the room and its occupants, Bea began to grow angry. And the anger, like a second child she'd just given birth to, raced through an accelerated growth spurt to arrive fully formed beside the fund of her fears. She sat in the neutral, middle, territory, with her anger on one side, and her fear on the other, making a number of long-delayed decisions.

It had been fifteen months since Hank's death. She hadn't worked, hadn't even considered it in that time, initially because of her shock and grief, and then because of her absorption with finding the house and preparing it for Melinda. For fifteen months she'd been more than a little crazy, and she could see very clearly now just how crazy some of her actions had been. She'd had rational moments when Lucy or Bobby had hauled her back to earth to issue warnings, but they'd only been isolated moments. Suddenly, she'd come past the craziness and was able to see things accurately.

She hadn't worked because Hank was no longer there to bolster or criticize her decisions; because Hank had been her sounding board right from the beginning and, without him, she'd been unwilling to trust her own judgment as she always had in the past. But his legacy was far more than just the financial estate he'd left to secure her and Melinda's futures. He'd left her the knowledge he'd acquired throughout his lifetime, and had shared actively with her, of everything that went into the making of a good motion picture. He'd taught her to recognize the components that rendered a script not only workable, but inspired; he'd taught her how to play down for the camera, how to think and feel and react for the camera; he'd taught her how to splice film, scraping off the emulsion, applying the cement, then clamping the next piece onto it, before holding the join between the hot metal plates. He'd taught her that you could make film do anything you wanted it to; that it could lie or tell the truth; it could make people laugh or cry, or inspire or confuse them. He'd taught her how to work with it so that the end-product said the things she wanted said. There was a great deal she knew, and if she didn't put her knowledge to use, then she'd be dishonoring not only the man, but all he'd worked so hard both to teach her and to achieve. She couldn't waste any more time ignoring scripts, ignoring offers, ignoring her fundamental need to work. She also couldn't continue to indulge the crazed, desperate part of her that had, for all these months, pinned itself to Melinda in the hope of some sort of satisfaction. As long as

471

Melinda could read this hope in Bea's letters and telephone calls, in her conversations and behavior, Melinda had a power no one should be allowed to wield over anyone else.

Lucy got up to go turn on the outside lights. When she came back, Bea stood up, saying, "I'm going to go up and change. I'm a little overdressed for the occasion." At the bottom of the stairs, she stopped and called out. "Lucy?"

Lucy immediately hurried to the door. "What?" she asked nervously.

"It's late. Why don't you tell Gertie to go ahead and start dinner? There's no sense in the two of us starving to death."

This was further evidence of the alteration taking place. Lucy smiled, said, "Good idea. I'll tell her, then come up, and get changed myself."

As she went through to the kitchen, Lucy marveled over the way Bea was handling this. It was as if she'd decided this was a routine misadventure to be experienced as the parent of a teenager, and so she'd treat it as such. They'd been at the breakpoint, but Bea had refused to be broken. Lucy was feeling better than she had in months as she sailed into the kitchen and told Gertie to put the steaks under the broiler.

"We won't wait for Melinda," she told the housekeeper.

"Right you are, dear," Gertie said, apparently unflappable. "Will you be wantin' Al to uncork the wine?"

"Why not?" Lucy said. "Give us a shout when dinner's ready."

"Won't be long. All the veg're done, dear; I've been keepin' 'em warm."

On the way to her room, she paused, hearing Bea talking on the telephone to Bobby. Good, Lucy thought. In spite of everyone's concern for Melinda, life had started up again. Lucy could feel it in the air which was no longer leaden with the weight of impossible expectations but electric with the regeneration of Bea's special energy.

Over dinner, which Bea ate with rare speed and appetite, Lucy ventured to say, "What d'you think?"

"I think this is a stunt," Bea replied with conviction. "It's a goddamned stunt, and I'm furious. She's in for quite a surprise when she gets here."

"A stunt? You think that's what it is?"

Chewing furiously, Bea put down her knife and fork to drink half her glass of burgundy. Then, knife and fork in hand once more, sawing away at her steak, she said, "I know it! Mel's making a statement, and it's about to blow up in her face."

Lucy was impressed. "Yeah? What're you going to do?"

"I'll know that when I see her."

Welcome back, Lucy thought, gazing across the table at Bea who seemed to be shedding years with each mouthful of food. She'd taken off the Worth dress, unpinned her hair from the sophisticated, loose top-knot she'd started wearing in public in the past few years and, in the gentle light of the chandelier centered over the table, could have passed for a teenager in an old shirt of Hank's, and a pair of jeans, with her hair center-parted and tucked behind her ears so as not to interfere with her eating.

At the end of the meal, Bea said, "Let's watch television," and led the way into the room that Bea had made into a den, with a large-screen TV set built into an oak wall unit that also contained a hi-fi system with components Bobby had picked out. Bea flipped the channel selector, found "Gunsmoke," and curled up on one end of the soft leather sofa, beckoning Lucy to join her.

This, too, was so unusual an occurrence that Lucy's time was divided between watching James Arness and watching Bea, as, in a way so reminiscent of Hank that Lucy could only smile, she commented on the show and its origins.

"William Conrad played Dillon, you know, on the radio. When CBS wanted to put on an adult western back in '55, they were after a John Wayne type, and it was Duke who suggested Arness. He's very good, isn't he? In fact, I like the show. She has a nice edge, Amanda Blake. Don't you think?"

"I thought you didn't like television, that you never watched it."

"I watch," Bea said, her eyes on Milburn Stone. "When I can't sleep, I watch. And if I'm up early, I watch the 'Today' show. I like Hugh Downs."

"You're just full of surprises, aren't you?"

Bea shrugged, lighting a cigarette. "If you can't sleep and you can't read, you watch television. I really am going to kill her," she said, making her first reference to Melinda in almost two hours. It was also the first time ever when Bea sounded like an ordinary mother.

"You think she'll show up tonight?"

"Oh, she'll show up, all right," Bea said knowingly. "She doesn't have the balls to keep me waiting *that* long. These commercials are so terrible," she complained. "My favorite is the one they show at two or three in the morning, for that little wonder tool that dices and slices and cuts potatoes into julienne strips and does amazing things to an ordinary tomato."

Lucy laughed happily. "The Ronco Vegematic."

"You've seen it, too! Isn't he amazing, that poor man? The words come flying out of his mouth, and he's hacking away, making cole slaw and French fries. *God!*" she exclaimed appreciatively. "He's the Academy Award–winning announcer of all time."

They watched the eleven o'clock news, then Bea got up and turned off the set. "You go to bed if you want to, Luce. You don't have to stay up to keep me company."

"I'm not tired."

"How about some coffee, then?"

"Fine."

They went to the kitchen, and Lucy sat down at the table while Bea ground beans, then filled the percolator. "Doesn't this remind you," Lucy said, "of those days when we were first in New York, and we used to sit around with Bobby, drinking coffee until three or four in the morning, planning our futures?"

"It does," Bea agreed, setting the percolator on the counter and plugging it into the wall outlet. "We had such good times, didn't we? Remember the landlady?"

"Mrs. Jolly."

"That's right. She was so dear. I suppose she must've died years ago. It's incredible," Bea said. "Sometimes I think back, and it's as if it all happened to somebody else—me and Bobby on the cover of *Life,* and then my *Time* cover. All those magazines we were on, and we were so high. I remember walking by a newsstand about fifty times when that issue of *Life* came out, trying not to give myself away by bursting out laughing with excitement. God! We were *so* young."

"Maybe it's time to bring all that stuff up from the basement," Lucy suggested.

"I guess we could put out the awards and hang the pictures in the den. Might as well, huh?"

"Damned right. You earned them, might as well show them off."

The doorbell rang, and Bea froze for a moment. Then she pushed up her shirt sleeves and started toward the door. Lucy went along after her.

Bea cracked open the door and stood with her hand on the knob. There was Melinda, looking a little giddy. And, behind her, carrying the luggage, was a long-haired, scruffy young man, also smiling. Bea opened the door a little wider.

"Sorry I'm so late," Melinda said blithely. "Oh, this is Skip. Skip was my seat-mate on the plane. Skip, I'd like you to meet my mother."

He dropped Melinda's suitcases and wiped his hand down the side of his jeans before offering it to Bea. "Good to meet you, Mrs. Donovan." He gave Bea's hand a shake that nearly dislocated her elbow, then bent to pick up the suitcases. "Just tell me where you want these."

"Just a moment," Bea said quietly, causing both the young man and Melinda to stop what they'd been doing. "Why didn't you take the limousine?" she asked Melinda.

"Oh! Well, Skip offered to give me a ride, and I thought..."

"It didn't occur to you to tell the driver or to call and let *me* know there'd been a change in your plans?"

"Well, Skip had to pick up the rental car, and that took a bit of doing. And then, we'd neither of us eaten much of the meal on the plane. You know how dreadful the food is. So we stopped to have dinner. It took ages to get out of the city. The traffic was just..."

"You went into Manhattan for dinner?" Bea asked.

"Yes, but..."

"And the restaurant didn't have a telephone?"

"Uh-oh!" Skip said under his breath, backing up a step.

"Of course it did, but we had to wait ages at the bar, and then they didn't want to give us a table because Skip didn't have the right clothes, so I had to tip the maître d' and then they loaned Skip a jacket and tie, and..."

"I've made a reservation for you at the Motor Inn on the Post Road in town. Perhaps Skip"—Bea looked over at him—"would be good enough to take you there."

"Oh, sure," he said, frowning with confusion.

"Good," Bea said. "I'll talk to you in the morning, Melinda. Call me when you're ready, and I'll send Albert with the car. Thank you for looking after her, Skip. Goodnight, Mel." In one smooth gesture, Bea glided backward, swung the door closed, and turned the lock. She stood facing Lucy, her eyes glittering, as they listened to Melinda and the young man muttering. Then the car doors slammed, the engine turned over, and, spitting gravel, the car reversed and drove off.

"I will not," Bea said firmly, "put up with any more crap from her I wouldn't take from anyone else. Let's go have our coffee." Pushing away from the door, she put her arm through Lucy's, and they walked back to the kitchen.

"I *can't believe* you did that!" Lucy said, when they sat together at the kitchen table with their coffee. "I mean, I saw and heard it all, but I can't believe it."

"Either she plays by *my* rules in *my* home, or she'll have to play somewhere else. I refuse to let her get away with any more nonsense. Jesus Christ, Luce! I have to draw the line somewhere, don't I?"

"Sure do. As far as I'm concerned, you did the right thing."

"I think so. Of course, I'll be up half the night worrying that some-body's broken into her room and attacked her. But I'll be *damned* if being her mother means I get victimized on a regular basis. She set the whole thing up, right from the beginning, when she wrote asking me not to meet her. She had no intention of coming here in the limo. If she hadn't met that, that *Beatnik,* she'd have found someone or something else. Imagine doing all that just to get her own back at me! It'll be quite some time before she tries anything like that again."

"I'm sure she'll be a reformed Melinda when she gets here in the morning," Lucy agreed.

"Bobby's coming at noon. To lend moral support, in case I weaken." Bea smiled. "He's prepared, he says, to take a belt to her ass, if necessary."

"Did you *see* the *look* on her face? It was priceless, just priceless."

"I saw. Tonight, I finally understood that we're two completely separate people. I almost backed down. I almost did. But then I thought that, if I did, it would all go on and on until she drove me out of my mind for real. So I did it. And I feel very good about it, all things considered."

Forty-Four

L UCY had spent the morning and most of the afternoon closed away in her room, seeing to odds and ends. Her desktop at last cleared, she sat for a few minutes gazing out the window, almost able to feel the heat that held the trees and flowers immobilized. It had been an unusually hot summer and everyone was glad Bea had gone ahead with centrally air-conditioning the house. It was a pity they hadn't also gone forward with the pool, because it would've been wonderful, just then, to go out into that baking air and plunge into an expanse of cool water.

Part Three / 1947–1976

Lucy sat toying with her fountain pen, the silence of the house all at once too complete. Bea was in the city for the weekend, with Bobby. Gertie and Al had gone to visit some cousins in Scarsdale. Where was Mel? Lucy wondered, putting down her pen.

The doors to Melinda's suite were both closed. Lucy knocked, got no answer, opened the sitting-room door and peered inside, sucking in her breath in instant annoyance at the chaotic upset. Magazines and newspapers, record albums, candy wrappers, apple cores, dirty dishes, abandoned clothes draped over the furniture, an open window defeating the push of cold air from the floor vents. She went at once to close the window, then stood sniffing the air. The place smelled of stale cigarette smoke, leftover food, the soft-rotting odor of apple cores. Disgusted, she left, closing the door on the mess, and proceeded along the hallway, halting at the top of the stairs to study the door to Bea's room. It had been pushed to. Since Bea never shut her door unless she was inside, Lucy moved closer, her footsteps silenced by the thick carpeting. She eased the door open a few inches and peered inside to see Melinda sitting on her haunches, going through letters and papers from Bea's desk. So intent was she on her reading, Melinda was unaware she was being observed. She finished the letter she'd been reading, folded it back into its envelope, and reached—greedily, Lucy thought—for another.

Who was this girl? Lucy wondered. What drove her to do the things she did, say the things she said? Everyone tolerated her frequently arrogant behavior and her patently false displays of interest and affection, only because she was Bea's child. Had she been anyone else's daughter, not only would she not have dared be so disrespectful, so unconcerned with the feelings of others, and so mightily involved with her own, but she'd have had some manners knocked into her long before now. But she was Bea's daughter, and everyone knew how much Bea adored her, and so Melinda's sometime sullen silences, and her abrupt departures from the dinner table, and now, her daring to violate her mother's personal papers was dismissed as the, perhaps to-be-expected, eccentricities of a girl who, after all, had a heavier than normal load of attention to bear because she was Bea's daughter. They were forever making excuses for Melinda, forever refusing to rise to the provocations she offered. But not this time.

"What the hell d'you think you're doing?" Lucy snapped, shoving open the door.

Melinda jumped, turning wide, momentarily fearful, eyes on Lucy.

"I *asked* you a question!" Lucy declared, standing hands on her hips, glaring.

"I was just looking..." Melinda turned to survey the evidence spread on the carpet.

"For *what?*" Lucy wanted to know. "You were 'just looking' for what exactly?"

"Nothing actually. I uh..."

Lucy had to admit she was impressed by how quickly Melinda collected herself and sought to take the offensive.

"You haven't the right to question me!" Melinda asserted, getting to her feet, one of the letters still in her hand.

"You're amazing!" Lucy held out her hand for the letter. "Give me that!"

"Oh, take it!" Melinda said snidely, shoving it into Lucy's hand and attempting to stride past her out of the room.

"No, you don't!" Lucy grabbed hold of her arm. "I don't know what you were up to in here," she said, her eyes taking in the material spread on the floor, "but you ever again so much as step past the door of this room when your mother's not here, and I personally will give you a walloping you'll never forget."

Melinda shook off Lucy's hand, but instead of leaving, as Lucy had thought she would, she stood her ground. "Don't you *dare* touch me, you dotty old bitch! You think you're so bloody grand because you're my mother's old friend and no one can get to Beatrice Crane without going through you first. You're halfway round the twist, and anyone with eyes could see it. Forever ringing up that dreary little man in London, keeping the great romance alive. *You* wallop *me!*' That's too funny. You'd better watch yourself, *Aunt Lucy,* or the next thing you know you'll find yourself being carted off to the local nuthouse. All that codswallop about ghosts in this house, and that poor, dear soul who lived here. The only truly odd thing around here is you!"

Lucy hit the girl, as hard as she was able—an open-handed slap across Melinda's face, with all her weight behind it. The girl reeled back, her hand at once going to her cheek.

"You vicious viper!" Lucy said breathlessly. "The only reason *anyone* puts up with you is because of your mother. Don't push your luck, Melinda. You don't have that much of it left. From now until you leave to go back to London, you'll treat your mother with respect, or by God you'll be one very sorry girl. It's bad enough you sneak around, listening in on other people's conversations. But what d'you think she'd do if she knew you'd been in here, going through her desk? Think about that before you open your mouth to anyone around here. And that includes Gertie and Al. They're not slaves, you know. They're people, and I'll be damned if I'll put up with you ordering

478

them around. Now get down the hall and clean up that disgusting pigsty! And don't ever make the mistake of judging people by your standards, because most of us can't even *point* that low! Now, go on!"

In tears, Melinda fled down the hall and into her room. The door slammed.

Lucy bent to pick up the letters and documents, then returned them to Bea's desk. She had no intention of telling Bea about this, but she was gratified to have a weapon she might use, if necessary, to keep Melinda in line.

Bea was shocked and guilty at how relieved she felt after seeing Melinda safely through the departure gate and onto the aircraft. She sat in the back of the car as Al drove toward home, thinking her relief must be indicative of some failing on her part as a mother. But, God! It had been a long three months, during which time Melinda had been restrained and polite, but for the most part distant, as if in anticipation of further peculiar behavior from Bea, as on the night when she'd been refused entry to the house. She'd turned down Bea's offers of clothing, of shoes, of anything but a number of classic novels from Brentano's; she'd been noncommittal in her responses to the shows they'd seen; she'd been barely civil to Lucy and, initially, positively rude to Gertie and Al; she'd spent most of the summer holed up in her sitting room, reading and listening to records or the radio at a volume that finally drove Bea to burst in one afternoon, shouting, "IF YOU DON'T TURN THAT DOWN AND KEEP IT DOWN, I SWEAR I'LL RIP THE GODDAMNED THING RIGHT OUT OF THE WALL!" Melinda had taken hours writing lengthy letters to Nancy and to her other friends in London; she'd accompanied Bea into the city to spend the weekend at Bobby's apartment, only to refuse, at the last moment, to go along to the dinner and concert outing that had been planned. So Bea and Bobby had gone without her and, upon returning, Bobby had looked around his bedroom, noticing things slightly out of place, saying, "This doesn't look right." Somewhat confused, Bea had watched him lift the lid of the old trunk he kept at the foot of the bed. He'd stood staring down into the trunk and swore once, furiously. When she'd asked what was wrong, he just shook his head, closed up the trunk, and locked it. "Nothing. It's okay," he'd told her, but she guessed Melinda had had a look through his things and felt disgraced even to think Melinda would do such a thing.

Arriving home, she went upstairs to discover Lucy and Gertie standing in the doorway to Melinda's room, gazing in with expressions of utter disbelief.

"What is it?" she asked, and the two stepped aside to allow Bea to see. She covered her mouth with her hand, appalled at the condition in which Melinda had left the place. There were stains all over the carpet and on the upholstery of the armchairs; there was garbage everywhere, even dirty underwear tossed into a corner; the TV set and the hi-fi were both minus knobs, and the arm of the turntable was sitting at an angle that clearly indicated it was broken; the wall unit itself was scratched and ruined by overlapping rings from soft-drink bottles and hot coffee cups; the curtains in the bedroom were hanging askew and tinted irreparably with something that looked like nailpolish; the bedspread had several cigarette burns, as did the carpet immediately beside the bed. And the bathroom was a nightmare of filth, the wastebasket overflowing with soiled Kotex pads, grimy cotton balls, and Kleenex; the tub and shower stall were greasy with dirt and hair, as was the basin.

"She wouldn't 'low me in to clean," Gertie explained tearfully, "not for the last fortnight."

"It's all right, Gertie. I certainly don't blame you for this. Call a cleaning service and have them send some people over to take care of it. I wouldn't *dream* of asking you to do it."

"I'm that upset, I am, Miss Crane." Gertie dolefully surveyed the rooms.

"Don't be," Bea told her. "This is another statement from Mel to me. Luce, could you dig out the name of the people who installed the carpet and get them to come replace this?"

"Oh, sure," Lucy said hotly. "And I'll put them on standby for Christmas, so they'll have everything ready for the next time."

"I don't think there's going to be a next time," Bea said, herding the women ahead of her out of the room and closing the door with finality. "I think we'll meet on neutral territory from now on."

"I've been waiting lunch for you," Gertie said. "Got some of that cold potato soup you like, a lovely salad, and the leftover roast sliced up nice."

"We'll be down in a few minutes," Bea told her. "Just set the table in the breakfast room."

"Right you are, Miss C." Gertie raced away down the stairs, visibly grateful to be putting some distance between herself and the disaster Melinda had left behind.

"Don't try to tell me you're not mad," Lucy said as soon as Gertie was out of earshot.

"I feel more sick than mad. I've never seen anything so revolting. She's always been fanatic about keeping her things clean and tidy."

"Yes, but these were *your* things, not hers."

"I know." Bea stood with her hands on her face, looking shell-shocked. "You don't have to tell me, Luce. I know. It's so awful. I'm not sure I want to live here anymore."

"You *love* this house! Don't you let her spoil it for you! I love this place myself."

"She really hates me. She must, to do that."

"I don't know about that. As you say, it's a 'statement.'"

"I just feel sick."

"You'll feel better after you eat something."

She actually did feel physically ill, and lunch didn't help, nor did the nap she took afterward. When she awakened just before three, there was a pressure in her lower belly, and she went to soak in the tub for half an hour, convinced this was part of her ongoing reaction to Melinda's destruction of the rooms. She lay with her head resting against the rim of the tub, deciding she could never again risk inviting Melinda to stay in the house. She closed her eyes, letting the tears come, admitting defeat. She'd done her best, and it hadn't been good enough. It wouldn't ever be good enough, so there was no point to making any further special effort. In future, she'd allow Melinda to advise her as to when she wanted to visit. It would all be up to Melinda from now on.

The rehearsals exhausted her. After an hour, she had to sit down and rest. Bobby was patient and understanding, but did say, "You'd be in a lot better shape if you cut back on your smoking."

"Ah!" she said. "The zeal of the recently converted! I'd be able to breathe beautifully," she gasped, "but I'd be a raving lunatic. I'm addicted to the goddamned things, and you know it."

"I'd help you quit."

"How?"

"I don't know. I could think of something. Seriously, Bea. We work for an hour, then you collapse and have a cigarette. It's no good."

"I tried a while back to go one day without smoking. It wasn't pretty."

"We could go somewhere, break your habit by changing your routines. I did it that way."

"Maybe," she allowed. "I'll think about it." She pressed her hands into her abdomen, making a face.

"What's wrong?"

"I'm in such rotten condition. I ache."

"That's kind of a strange place to ache. How long's that been going on?"

"A while. Since before Mel left."

"Maybe you should get it checked out."

"I'm just out of condition, and I don't even have a G.P. here. I've been meaning to ask around."

"I'll ask around for you. How long's it been since you had a checkup anyway?"

"Bobby," she smiled at him, "stop making such a fuss. We've been at this for weeks, and it's hard work. I did warn you."

"You warned me, but you were in better shape a month ago than you are now."

"Let's drop it, okay?"

"Okay. But I'm going to start seriously nagging you about your smoking."

"Fine. Nag me about that. You never know, you might convince me. Having a sore throat every day of my life isn't exactly my favorite thing. Let's go back to work. I'm breathing again."

He gave her a hand up, then went to rewind the tape. While he was waiting for the machine to finish, he watched her limbering up in front of the portable bar he'd set against the far wall. Her movements were all inward, self-protective. "I like you with a ponytail," he told her, telling himself he was reading too much into things. "You look cute as hell."

She looked up at him in the mirror and laughed. "I like you without your rug," she countered. "Let's go on with this."

She missed a period, then got out of bed one morning and blood gushed down her legs. Dizzy, her belly cramping, she went into the bathroom to get cleaned up. She was so weak, she had to call Bobby to tell him she couldn't make it into the city. "I seem to be having a minor-league hemorrhage," she joked. "I'm sure I'll be fine by to-morrow."

"I'll hop on the train and come out. Al can pick me up. Let's make it the midday."

"There's no need..."

"Send Al to meet the train," he said sharply, then added, "You know I worry about you, so don't be stubborn. I'll see you in a couple of hours."

"You're working yourself up over nothing."

"That's my privilege," he said, and hung up.

Gertie brought in a tray, and Lucy came to have coffee with her. "You look lousy," Lucy said, pouring the coffee for them both.

"You're white as a sheet, and you've been losing weight again."

"It's just a bad period, probably the start of menopause or something. I'm old enough, God knows."

"Interesting new habit you've got lately of talking about yourself as if you're two weeks younger than Methuselah."

"Well, I *am* old enough. How old were you?"

"Older than you are now."

"How *much* older?"

"About four years."

"Pooh!" Bea drank some coffee, then put her cup down to light a cigarette. "I won't be sorry to have the whole business finished. That's probably what it is."

"Yeah, well since I've never seen your diploma, Doctor Crane, I've taken the liberty of making an appointment for you to see someone here in town."

"Have you been talking to Bobby?"

"Yup. We've hatched a plot against you. Please," Lucy said. "You haven't seen a doctor since your insurance medical for the last picture, and you know how long ago that was. You're going next week, and no arguing."

"Fine. No arguing. I'll go. He'll tell me it's perfectly normal for a woman my age, and then everyone will be happy."

"Right. Now eat something!"

"Bobby's coming. Will you ask Al to meet his train?"

"For how long?"

"I didn't ask. And what d'you mean 'for how long?'"

"Go back to bed when you finish that, and I'll come see how you're doing before Al leaves for the station. You really do look lousy."

"Thank you. I can't tell you how much I appreciate your encouragement."

Lucy got up, taking her coffee with her. "By the way," she said from the door. "There's a problem with the carpet. They can't match up the color. Something to do with the run. What d'you want to do?"

"I don't know. Get the next shade lighter, or the next one darker. Whatever."

"What about the bedspread? It's ruined."

"Call Porthault in the city and order all new linens with a matching spread. The sheets are ruined, too."

"I wasn't going to mention that."

"I went back for another look," Bea admitted. "It was a mistake. I'm beginning to think she really does hate me. I can't imagine why else anyone would do what she did. It was so pretty. Didn't you think?"

"It was gorgeous, and she's a mean-hearted little bitch."

Bea looked away, busying herself with her cigarette and the coffee.

The telephone call filled Melinda with cold fear. She couldn't ever have predicted the reaction she had to the sound of Lucy's voice saying, "Your mother's ill, Melinda. She's in the hospital for surgery." So many times she'd wished her mother dead or disadvantaged in some critical fashion so that Melinda might, finally, get an opportunity to have the upper hand, to show she was considerably more than just the daughter of a famous woman. But that had been something else, another part of her that wasn't connected in the same way the part of her was that at once said, "I'll come straightaway. I'll have the airlines ring through with the flight information so Albert can meet me."

Her mother was ill in hospital and required surgery, and all Melinda could think was, Oh, please, don't die! Please don't die! I'm sorry for that silly nonsense last summer, sorry for everything I've ever done. It was a litany that ran nonstop in her brain, played under her every action while she threw clothes into a bag, rang Nancy to explain, then pushed her passport into her handbag and flew down to the street to stop a taxi. All the way to Heathrow, she was silently urging the driver to hurry, while wishing she'd thought to ask Lucy for details. But she'd been so overwhelmed and so immediately fearful she hadn't wanted to waste a moment. She had to get to her mother, to see her mother, talk with her, *love* her, before it was too late.

There was a flight departing within the hour, with first-class seating available. Melinda wrote out a check for the fare, then suffered further while the woman behind the counter fussed about approval for such a large amount. *"Please!"* Melinda begged the woman. "My mother's ill, and we're wasting time. I simply *can't* miss this flight. Copy down my passport number. Ring my bank. They'll verify the check's good. But please, give me the ticket and let me go board the airplane before it's too late."

She made the flight with merely minutes to spare before they closed the doors and the plane began to taxi into position for takeoff. She fastened her seat belt, then turned to watch the ground glide away as the plane lifted into the sky. She'd forgotten to have the airline notify Lucy! There'd be no one to meet her. There might be long queues for taxis and limousines.

484

Part Three / 1947–1976

"Are you quite all right?" the stewardess asked.

"Would it be possible for the captain to radio ahead with my arrival information? My mother's ill, and there wasn't time to notify her staff what flight I'd be on. She lives in Connecticut, you see, and it's very important there be someone to meet me."

The stewardess began to say, "I'm afraid we couldn't..."

"Look!" Melinda said, overwrought. "My mother's Beatrice Crane. She's ill. That's *not* for public consumption, you understand. But it's imperative my family be informed I'm on this flight."

"Oh, I see." The woman underwent a change of attitude that at any other time would've maddened Melinda beyond measure. This time, she was simply appreciative. "I'll have a word with the captain. I'm sure we'll be able to arrange something." Her hand on Melinda's shoulder, she said, "Try to relax now. You've got six hours ahead of you, Miss Crane. I'll have a word, and let you know."

Under any other circumstances, being addressed as Miss Crane would've prompted Melinda to correct the offending person in no uncertain terms. Now, she could only offer the woman a weak smile and say, "Thank you so much. I'm most grateful."

The stewardess returned a short while later to say, "If you'll give us the telephone number, we'll arrange for New York to ring through and advise your family of our arrival time."

Melinda quickly printed Lucy's name and the Connecticut number, gave it to the young woman, then sat back feeling as if enormous weights were pressing against her lungs, preventing her from breathing properly. When the drinks trolley came by, she asked for a gin and tonic, and gulped it down, feeling the effect of the alcohol almost immediately. She had a second drink which she consumed more slowly and was able to breathe in and out again, without that frightful pressure on her chest. She could not, however, rid herself of the dread that her mother would die before Melinda had a chance to tell her that nothing really mattered except that she loved her. She was willing to discount everything, positively everything, if her mother would just be alive when she got there.

She imagined all the possible illnesses her mother might have; like a mole, worrying herself ever more deeply into the darkness of the possibilities. Surgery. The word conjured up images of her mother's body, already scarred to such an extent that Melinda hadn't been able to look at her without wincing for years, not since she'd given up going in daily for her afternoon tub-side visit while her mother sat wreathed in clouds of steam as she soaked in water so hot that Melinda could never understand how it could be beneficial. Thinking of her mother endlessly holding court in some bathroom or other aroused Melinda's anger. She pushed it down. This wasn't the time for anger or for old resentments.

She had the idea she'd rush to her mother's bedside, they'd clasp each other's hands, and make good their understanding of, and commitment to, each other. Only the two of them really knew how it was, how they felt. Her mother knew Melinda loved her. Hadn't she said it that day when Melinda had broken the news to her that she wouldn't be returning to America with her? And hadn't Melinda showed it during those weeks after her father had died, when they'd been so close? But, bloody hell! She'd ruined those lovely rooms her mother had gone to such trouble to do up for her. And she'd gone about it with such bloody-mindedness she'd even shocked herself with the depth and breadth of her anger with her mother for turning Melinda away from the door as she had, and in front of that revolting Skippy! No! All that was in back of them; she wouldn't think about any of it. She'd think only good thoughts, and her mother would still be alive when Mel got there.

"**H**ow is my mother?" were her first words to Albert as she thrust her bag into his hands and hurried with him out to the Mercedes.

"Afraid I can't rightly say, Miss," he answered. "Course we're all 'oping for the best."

He drove her directly to Greenwich Hospital where Lucy and Bobby were waiting.

"What's wrong with her? Is she all right? You must tell me!" Melinda burst out upon seeing them.

Lucy took her by the arm and steered her along the corridor to a small waiting area where she sat Melinda down, and said, "You've kept this quiet, I hope."

"Who the bloody hell would I have told?" Melinda raged, thinking guiltily of the stewardess and the captain. God only knew how many of the crew might have shared the secret.

"Calm down!" Lucy ordered. "You're not going to help anyone by getting hysterical."

"I'll be calm *after* you tell me what's wrong with her!"

"It could be very damaging to her career if word of this got out. You know how things get twisted around," Lucy said, trying to determine if Melinda's apparent concern could possibly be real. She was such a pretty girl, Lucy thought, irrelevantly, admiring her flawless skin and long, dark eyelashes.

"I *know* all that! For God's sake! Will you please get on with it?"

"They did a biopsy," Lucy explained, deciding Melinda's atypical and passionate concern was, indeed, real but unable to fathom it. "She has cancer of the cervix."

"Oh, no!" Melinda blanched and wedged her hand between her teeth to keep from crying out.

"Just a minute," Lucy went on. "It's not as bad as it sounds. She's having surgery in the morning, a hysterectomy. They've assured us she'll be perfectly all right."

"But *cancer* . . ."

"You're not listening!" Lucy exclaimed. "She'll be *perfectly all right*. It hasn't spread, so far as they can tell."

"You're sure? They're not just saying that? Doctors always lie. They think they're sparing you, so they don't tell you the truth."

How, Lucy wondered, did Melinda know something like that? "I'm positive," she answered.

"Can I see her? I want to see her!"

"Calm yourself down, have a cigarette, then I'll take you to see her. I don't want you going in there, upsetting her. D'you hear me?"

Melinda nodded, groping around in her bag for her cigarettes. How could she explain to Lucy that the old rules no longer applied, that everything was suspended now? She couldn't. And, in any case, it was her mother who'd understand. It didn't matter whether or not Lucy did, although, at that moment, Melinda would have liked everyone to know.

"I'm warning you," Lucy said in a low voice. "You say one word, do one thing to upset her, and I'll make sure you regret it for the rest of your life."

"You don't understand," Melinda said, holding a match to her cigarette with a trembling hand.

"You're right. I *don't* understand. I'm too old to buy a complete change of face from anyone I know as well as I know you. So I'm warning you: you behave."

"I can't wait!" Melinda crushed out the cigarette. "I want to see her now!"

"Okay! But don't forget what I've told you."

The pressure was back on her lungs at the sight of her mother looking so *little* in the hospital bed, with everything so very white all around. She felt abnormally large and unseemingly healthy, seeing her mother so pale, her arms so thin. Why hadn't she ever noticed how *tiny*, how delicate her mother was? Melinda could barely speak, and when she did, her voice was rusty, and didn't sound like her own. She said, "Hello," and her mother looked at her with those great, sunken eyes, and smiled as if seeing Melinda was nothing short of miraculous. She held out her bony hand, and Melinda took hold of it, stifling the momentary revulsion she felt at the sights, and sounds, and smells, bombarding her senses. She'd been told both by Lucy and by the nurse that she wasn't to stay for more than a minute or two, and she was glad of that limitation. Having traveled all this way expressly for the purpose of declaring her love, she was incapable of getting the words out. She just couldn't. Not when she'd seen the proprietary glint in the nurse's eyes and had been aware of the inquiring looks of the other nurses she'd passed on her rush to this room. It was the same bloody thing all over again. Even seriously ill, even down to skin and bloody bones, she was Beatrice Crane, and the hospital had been sanctified by her illustrious presence in it. Melinda wanted none of it to matter, but it did. She couldn't help it; it mattered. She'd have given anything to have an ordinary mother, just another woman who happened to be ill, instead of someone so important that every last person wanted to stake some sort of claim on her. Coming up against these people wore Melinda out; they seemed to resent as well as envy her, and she loathed having to cope with their emotions when the only one who had any real right to be here was she.

"It's wonderful of you to come," her mother said, "and so quickly. There's nothing to worry about."

"No, I know." Melinda nodded her heavy head, wishing she could look away from those eyes, that face. "I wanted you to know," she began, determined to get the words out, but unable, so she rapidly switched directions, and said, "I'm truly sorry about what I did to the rooms. It was dreadful of me, and I'm sorry."

"Never mind," her mother said, her eyes creating in Melinda a familiar drowning sensation. "I'm happy to see you."

The nurse appeared in the doorway and gave a subtle little cough. Melinda whirled around and made an angry face at the woman who, looking affronted, scurried away.

"Mummy," Melinda began, turning again to her mother, "I uhm ...I...I'll be back," she promised, and kissed her mother's cheek before escaping into the corridor where she whispered, "Bloody bloody hell!" under her breath as she went back to Lucy and Bobby. Nothing *ever* changed. There would always be people who'd come to stand between her and her mother. And because of her mother's damned career, those people had a right to be there. It wasn't bloody fair. But she'd make a good show of it, stay until her mother was out of danger, then go the hell back to London where no one stood between her and the people who'd proved themselves interested in her and not in her mother.

"Why does she look so horribly pale? And why is she so thin?" she asked Lucy.

"She hasn't been feeling well for quite some time, but she didn't want to mention it. Your mother's anything but fond of hospitals. Albert's waiting to take you to the house. Gertie's fixed you some dinner. If you want, he'll bring you back here later."

"What about you?" Melinda wanted to know.

"Bob and I will be here. We haven't been flying all day. Rest for a couple of hours and then, if you want to, you can come back."

No one believed she actually cared about her mother. She could see it in Lucy's face and in Bobby's. She could tell by the way Bobby kept his distance, as if he thought this was nothing more than an inept performance on her part. For a few moments, looking at their faces, she realized she was responsible for their mistrust; she'd worked years to create it. And the only way she could ever regain their faith would be by spending the rest of her life demonstrating her love for her mother. She couldn't do that, and she didn't feel she should have to prove herself to anyone except her mother. Yet this, too, mattered. These two people cherished her mother; they adored her for reasons that hadn't anything to do with her celebrity. It shamed her because she, of all people, should have been the one to cherish most, adore the most, love the best. And she never could. It wasn't some bloody contest.

She ate the meal, then went back to the hospital because she knew it was expected, and there were limitations on her defiance just now. Her mother was asleep, so Melinda only had to stay for a moment. She used the time to notice the gray in her mother's hair, and the lines encircling her throat, and, again, how diminutive she was. She studied her sleeping mother, fearful of a power this woman had that she never used.

She waited while Lucy and Bobby took turns tiptoeing into the room for brief visits, closing her eyes at hearing her mother murmuring tearfully to Bobby. She shivered and went to the waiting area to smoke a cigarette. At last, the three of them went out to the car, and Albert drove them back to the house.

Throughout the night, Melinda drank black coffee and chain-smoked, tempted to ring for a taxi and go back to the hospital. She had the arbitrary idea that the lateness of the hour and being there on her own with her mother would allow the sort of confessional conversation she'd had in mind. But she couldn't bring herself to do it. She imagined some night nurse, all fired up with protective indignation on her mother's behalf, trying to stop her from going to her mother's room. And how could she prove who she was? Every document she owned stated she was Melinda Donovan. It was really just good luck that the stewardess had believed her. Hopeless. It was all hopeless. She couldn't be Melinda Donovan *and* Beatrice Crane's daughter. The two were not synonymous; and she'd never wanted them to be.

They were told the next morning that the surgery had gone beautifully. There wasn't a thing to worry about. Bea was in the recovery room, and they'd be bringing her up shortly. Lucy wept with relief, and Bobby consoled her. Melinda sat apart, watching them and smoking a cigarette. If Lucy had been so convinced, why was she weeping now? More of the same. Everyone lied to her or tried to keep the truth from her. Melinda wanted to stand up and scream at them, for their attempts to keep her in ignorance of the reality of the situation. Yet, oddly enough, she couldn't shake the feeling that Lucy and Bobby had more right to be there than she, because they'd always been there, because they knew things about her mother no one else, not even Melinda, was supposed to know. And hadn't Melinda been doing her damnedest for a very long time *not* to be there, to disassociate herself from the entourage?

When it was allowed, she went in for a last, quick visit. Again, she struggled to bring the words out of her and into the air, but they wouldn't come, and, finally, she gave up. "I'm glad you're all right," was the best she could manage. "I must get back. I hope you understand."

"Thank you for coming," her mother whispered through cracked, dehydrated lips. "You know I love you, Mel. It means everything to me that you came."

All but blinded by sudden tears, Melinda kissed her good-bye, then fled from the room, past Lucy and Bobby, along the corridor, through the exit door and down the stairs, out to the circular drive at the front of the hospital where Albert was waiting with the car to take her to the airport.

She wept bitterly throughout the flight home, pounding her fists against each other, tearing at her fingernails with her teeth. She couldn't stop seeing her mother, pale, and vulnerable, and so awfully small, in that hospital bed. She despised herself for caring. For all the good it did her, she might as well have been another of the hundreds, thousands, of fans who'd queue up for hours in the rain to catch a glimpse of Beatrice Crane emerging from a limousine to enter a hotel, or a restaurant, or a theater. She felt just as anonymous, just as helpless in her inability to make contact with the woman. There was simply too much to get through. And Melinda loathed herself for loving her, for being so afraid of losing her.

490

Forty-Five

BOBBY chartered a small jet to fly himself and Bea and his live-in couple to the house he'd rented at the Mill Reef Club in Antigua. In the jet's cargo bay was a supply of frozen meats and poultry, tinned foods and juices, and a van had been hired to pick up these supplies and deliver them to the house. Since the owners were old friends of his, he'd made sure to get details on everything from the need to use sparingly the household water supply—which was collected in a pair of catchments on the hillside across the road from the house—to the peculiarities of the electrical system. Power outages were a regular feature, so there was a stock of kerosene lamps and candles. He'd ascertained that mail and telephone calls could be directed to the club and that the commissary stocked basic staples at whopping markups. He'd found out where in St. Philips Parish to buy fresh vegetables and the name of the people in St. Johns who kept chickens and sold eggs. He'd agreed to give the four regular household staff their salaries for staying at home during the time he and Bea would be using the house. His couple, Paul and Gerry, would run the place and see to it that no one got past the front gate who wasn't invited.

The house was simple, with the master suite elevated above the other two bedrooms. All the rooms had windows on two exposures in order to catch the breeze as it came off the water that lapped against the sand not fifty feet beyond the open-plan living/dining area. The staff quarters were situated out beyond the pantry and kitchen, at the opposite end of the house, and were locked up for the duration. Paul and Gerry took the front bedroom and bath that was closest to the water. The middle room remained available for Lucy and Brian, should they decide to join them at some point. Lucy was in London for an extended visit and would return, either to Connecticut or to the island, should she be needed.

491

Paul and Gerry divided the work equally, both of them doing the cleaning, and laundry, and cooking, but remained for the most part out of sight. The only evidence of their presence was the music from their transistor radio that rode gently on the breeze and in through the louvered windows.

The simplicity of the house itself was in direct contrast to the equipment the owners had in the way of a top-quality hi-fi system, long- and short-wave radios, games of every conceivable variety from backgammon to Chinese checkers. The everyday china was white Wedgwood; the special-occasion service was gold on black Egyptian-key Wedgwood. The white wrought-iron furniture in the living room had pillows covered in gaily printed, sturdy cotton fabric that matched the seats of the dining chairs. The table was also white wrought iron, with a slab of thick plate glass inset on top. The view from the dining area was of the daily encroaching sea-grapes and, beyond their rolling, rich green surface, the pale to deep turquoise of the water. A few hundred yards offshore was a reef that sheltered the wide scoop of the inlet, at whose apex the house sat, and kept the water temperature mild enough so that it never shocked sun-heated flesh but was still refreshing.

During their first few days, Bea slept for long stretches of time, while Bobby, Paul, and Gerry familiarized themselves with the eccentricities of the Calor gas stove, the plumbing, the fresh-water unheated showers, and the lime trees that grew just inside the bougainvillea-covered shoulder-high wall that shielded the house from the road. Paul and Gerry, pleased at being home again in the Leeward Islands—they were natives of Barbuda—made the acquaintance of the staff from neighboring houses and sat for long hours in the shade of the bay tree in the courtyard enclosed by the staff quarters, listening to their radio and talking in the low, rapid dialect that was incomprehensible music to Bobby. He'd hired the couple because of their affability and their competence in almost every area. Paul could take apart a TV set or a toaster that was malfunctioning and reassemble it in perfect working order. He could cook, he could drive anything with four wheels, he could repair a broken toilet or a badly hung door, he had no qualms about cleaning house or doing laundry, and he complained only when there was no work to be done. Geraldine could sew; her home-baked bread was better than the best cake, and her pumpkin soup inspired Bobby to raise their salary; she was stronger than most men and regularly lifted the furniture in the Park Avenue apartment in order to track down devious dust-balls. They were both in their late twenties, and childless; they loved music and often, spontaneously, got up to dance in the white-hot afternoon sunshine, while the laundry hung motionless from the lines, bleaching as it dried. If he chanced to be passing through the courtyard on his way to the storeroom for something, Bobby would stop to dance with them. Their laughter would hover, caught in the dome of heat that contained them, so that often, upon awakening, Bea would turn her head toward the sound and smile.

Bobby donned a mask and flippers and paddled about for hours— the sun turning his flesh a deep red-brown—studying the fish and plantlife on the reef, sometimes accompanied by inquisitive parrot fish or schools of tiny, darting angel fish. He collected samples of the different kinds of coral, and Gerry dipped them in ammonia and water before setting them around the perimeters of the courtyard to dry.

By the end of the first week, Bea felt strong enough to put on a thin, sleeveless cotton dress and a broad-brimmed straw hat and dark glasses and walked barefoot through the white sand, hand in hand with Bobby, all the way to the perimeter of the Club beach and back again. The Club members and other guests said hello in passing but otherwise left them alone. They encountered few people during these long, slow walks.

The top of Bobby's head was sunburned and freckled, his nose was peeling, and, when he smiled, his teeth were startlingly white in his darkly tanned face.

"You look wonderful," she told him, newly intrigued by his smile and by previously unseen aspects of him. He appeared to thrive in this environment. She sat for an hour or two in the afternoons watching him float about in the water, then listened as he described the extraordinary sights he'd discovered only a few feet beneath the surface.

"You look too white," he said critically. "You don't really intend to stay out of the water, do you? I told Lucy to make sure you had bathing suits."

"It's been ten weeks and I don't have much control of my stomach muscles yet."

"So that's why we're dressing and undressing in the bathroom these days. You don't want me to see you with a big, sagging gut."

"It's hardly that." She poked him in the ribs, then looked longingly at the water. "I would love to go in, though."

"Okay!" He veered sharply to the right and walked straight into the water, pulling her along with him. She laughed as he stopped to remove her hat and sunglasses, tossing them onto the sand before taking both her hands and leading her in until they were standing up to their necks in the clear, mild water. "Okay?" he asked.

"It's paradise." She put her arms around his neck, allowing herself to float against him. "Who are your old friends who live in this incredible place?"

"You won't believe it, but he's my insurance broker. He and his wife are in Europe indefinitely, so we can have the place for as long as we like."

"He didn't just *give* it to you?"

"Of course not. No more questions."

She let her feet find the bottom, but kept her arms around his neck. "Were you scared?" she asked him.

"Terrified. I thought you were going to die, and I didn't want to think about having a life without you in it. If you could've *seen* what you looked like. Jesus! Don't tell me you weren't scared."

"Oh, I was. But it was strange. You have all these experiences and you use them to measure other things. For example, I used to tell myself that nothing could hurt as much as it did when Dr. Shannon had to fix me up after that botched breast job. That was my yardstick for quite a long time. You know? And nothing had been as painful as that was, until this. This got to be so awful that I was beginning to think it really might be a relief to die. But I honestly wasn't afraid to die. I really wasn't, Bobby. I thought about it, and I decided I'd done pretty well everything I've ever wanted to do. I might miss out on a few things, but I had a lot to be proud of, too. Are you afraid to die?"

"Nah," he answered readily, tilting his head back and looking straight up into the sky. "It strikes me kind of funny that you don't pick that business with Dickie as your yardstick."

"That's because it didn't have anything to do with me. I mean that was something that was *done* to me."

"So was the breast job."

"But that's different."

"Maybe. Anyway, I'd kind of like to work it out so we'd both kick off around the same time."

"Oh? What did you have in mind, some sort of suicide pact?"

"Don't be a jerk." He lowered his head and brought his hands to rest on her waist. "I just want to be able to look after you. Your physical history's pretty rotten, you know."

"No, it isn't. I've always been healthy as a horse. I've never missed a day's shooting. I've never even had the 'flu, not once in my life. I'd love a cigarette right now, though. I'm never going to make it. I keep thinking my reward for all these weeks without smoking's going to be a cigarette."

"Your reward is that you're already breathing way better than you were. And you smell great. By the time we go back, your little lungs'll be pumping away good as new."

"My little lungs," she laughed.

"Well, how big could they be?" He looked at her breasts through the thin, soaked dress.

"D'you suppose anyone's watching us?" She craned around to look at the shoreline. There wasn't a soul on the beach.

"They're all in having their siestas." His hands moved upward over her ribs, and he drew her closer to kiss her.

When they separated, she said, "I was afraid I wasn't going to be able to feel anything anymore, but I just did."

"You did, huh?" He smiled, his eyebrows lifting.

"I'm starting to feel a little chilled, Bobby. I think we'd better go back now."

He picked up her hat and glasses and watched her put them on, then took her hand as they headed back toward the house. There was a huge, thatched umbrella-like structure on the beach in front of their house, with chairs arranged in a circle underneath. In the spines supporting the roof were wedged mismatched flippers, snorkeling gear, bottles of suntan oil, odd pairs of sunglasses, and a variety of hats. Bobby liked to come down here in the early morning with his coffee and a book and dig his toes into the morning-cool sand while he read and sipped at his coffee and, nearby, the boy who came daily raked the sand free of tendrils of sea-grass and occasional bits of coral and broken shell.

"I wouldn't mind living here," he said, as they rinsed the sand from their feet in the small water-filled well to one side of the open rear entryway to the house.

"It would be heavenly," she agreed, pulling the wet dress away from her skin.

"But only for a few months at a time. I have a hunch that after a while there'd be too much temptation to start hitting the juice at ten or eleven in the morning, so you'd be pissed by eight at night. There's not enough to do. You go ahead and use the shower. I'll just check with Gerry and Paul about dinner."

Leaving the bathroom door open, she stepped into the shower stall and stood beneath the water, noticing her arms were already dark from their strolls along the beach. And those walks in the sand had turned her feet smooth as silk. Perhaps it was time to surrender her vanity and put on a bathing suit. Her belly wasn't flat, but it wasn't immense, either, she decided, testing its laxity with her fingertips. The surgery hadn't left her with any additional scars. The doctor had simply excised the old incision by cutting along either side of it, removing that strip of skin, and then stitching the two sides together.

"I don't know why you've been hiding out all this time," he said, having made a silent entry into the bathroom. "You look fine, a little round in the tummy, but fine."

"It's going to be ages before I get back to where I was before the surgery."

"So? Is there some rush?"

"I was really looking forward to doing the festival thing."

"We'll do it later." He threw off his wet shirt and shorts and ducked around the curtain to join her. "Pass the soap, kiddo."

She handed it to him, moving aside to give him more room. His body was in such excellent condition she was momentarily daunted by the sight of it. She slipped out, reaching for a towel.

The afternoon was an especially hot one, and she went to the windows to open the louvers to the maximum before turning on the ceiling fan. All the bedrooms in the house had twin beds, which led her to believe the owners must either be getting on in years or not interested in sex. The first thing Bobby had done was to push the beds together, and he had encouraged Paul and Gerry to do the same, saying, "It's uncivilized and downright unfriendly," which had sent the couple into fits of laughter.

The sheets were cool. The fibers contained the scent of sunshine from their time over the line in the courtyard. The water went off in the bathroom, and Bobby appeared a minute or two later. His intent was so obvious, she felt suddenly boneless as he crossed the room and lowered himself down on her, bearing his weight on his elbows as he gazed at her for a moment before engaging her in a kiss that created for her a series of slow inner contractions.

She went tense with apprehension when he began to push slowly forward. But there was no pain, and her capacity to respond was still intact. They rested together, joined, and he silently questioned her.

"It's all right," she whispered. "I just don't have any flexibility in my legs."

"Then let me do all the work for a change. As long as it doesn't hurt, or anything. That's all I care about."

"God! It doesn't *hurt*."

It happened so quickly she was caught totally by surprise. Holding her legs locked together between his own, be began a measured thrusting that in moments had her curving into him in an engulfing need to satisfy the rhythm. She soared to the peak of pleasure, went rigid in his arms, and convulsed. The spasms continued as he accelerated, then shuddered violently before subsiding. She held him tightly,

496

until he raised himself to look at her, and then they laughed.

"You've been saving up for that one," he teased, always enchanted by the way she looked—purified, and a little startled—in the aftermath. "Christ! That was fantastic!"

"I love you." She smiled up at him, her hands caressing his neck and shoulders. She sighed deeply, her eyelids suddenly heavy. "I'm falling asleep, but I don't want you to move."

"If I don't, you'll suffocate." He withdrew slowly, then arranged her with her back to his chest. "Nap time," he said softly, but she was already asleep.

They stayed for five months, then the charter jet came to take them home.

A month later, Lucy got a call from California and, at the end of it, told Bea, "Ike died. I've got to go out for the funeral."

"Oh, Luce. I'm so sorry. Would you like me to come with you?"

"No, I'll go on my own. It'll just be for a couple of days."

"Are you all right? Is there anything I can do?"

"No." Lucy sat down abruptly and covered her eyes with her hand. "Damn!" she swore. "I kept meaning to go see him, but I put it off. I always thought we'd get together one last time. I really did love him, you know."

"I know that, Luce."

"I'm getting too old to put things off." She wiped her eyes on her sleeve. "It's a big mistake. You put things off, and then the people all of a sudden aren't there anymore. It's only been a month since I was with Brian, but now I feel as if I want to go back."

"Why not do that? You could go directly from Los Angeles."

"I hate to leave you in the lurch."

"Don't even think about it!" Bea told her. "If I have problems, I can always call a temporary agency and get someone in to answer the phone and type a few letters. Go ahead and make your plans. Take as long as you like. Maybe I'll stay with Bobby in the city for a while."

"It's such a mistake," Lucy said again, shaking her head, "putting things off until later. We're getting short on laters. I guess I'd better go up and make some calls."

Lucy phoned from London after six weeks to say, "Bea, I hate to do this to you, but I'm going to marry Brian."

"You're not doing *anything* to *me!*" Bea exclaimed. "Don't be silly!

I'm thrilled to death for you. When's it going to be? You *are* going to let Bobby and I come over to be with you, I hope."

"It's short notice, I know. But I really do think it's the right thing. You don't think I'm out of my mind, do you, marrying a man who's so much younger?"

"He's only eight years younger. And I don't think you're out of your mind at all. When is it?"

"We thought we'd do it quick and dirty at the registry office, the end of next week. Is that too short notice for you?"

"I'm sure it isn't. I'll call Bobby right away, and we'll come. I'm so happy for you, Luce. D'you want me to ship your things over?"

"Don't you do it! Get Gertie and Al to take care of it. And there's no rush about it, either. Brian's been running all over London buying me things. I'm having one hell of a good time."

"We'll be there. Don't you dare do anything without us!"

"We won't. Let me know when to expect you, okay?"

"You deserve this, Lucy. I couldn't be more thrilled. I'll be in touch as soon as I've talked to Bobby. This'll give me a chance to visit Mel, too. It's marvelous, just marvelous! Give my love to Brian, and I'll talk to you very soon."

The only dark spot in the whole affair was the fact that Melinda was off on a trip to Switzerland with some friends from Cambridge and so was unable to attend the wedding or the small reception afterward. Bea did wonder about the timing of the trip, occurring as it did almost simultaneously with her and Bobby's much-publicized arrival at Heathrow when they happened to be photographed emerging from the plane. The presence of the photographer created a burst of public recognition that attracted so many people the airport security staff had to be summoned to escort them safely to the waiting Rolls. Somehow, word got from the airport to the Ritz, and by the time they arrived at the hotel there was a huge crowd waiting to greet them. The public response was tremendously encouraging and, upon their return home, Bea began reading the submitted scripts in earnest, anxious to be working again.

In the meantime, she resumed her daily exercises while Bobby went to California for two months to do another television special. She worked out; she read scripts; and she tried to fill the hours of each day. It was an effort. For the first time in her life, she was alone, and when she stopped to think about it—roaming through the house, pausing to look into Lucy's denuded room and Melinda's suite—it unnerved her. She found herself thinking about Becky and felt chagrined and embarrassed to think that something as absurd as a bad week, culminating in a disagreement, had caused her to push Becky out of her life. She thought of calling her up but was stopped every time by the knowledge that, not only had far too much time gone by, but she was also too ashamed to do it.

Somehow, she got through the days. A local woman who'd come to her through a personnel agency in town spent two afternoons a week taking dictation, packaging rejected scripts to carry to the post office, and answering the trickle of fan mail.

There were brief visits from old California friends who drove up to spend an afternoon or a few days. But it simply wasn't the same as having people actually living in the house with her. She did speak regularly to Lucy on the telephone and received occasional letters from Melinda; other friends called just to stay in touch, and there were offers that came through the New York office, but none she cared to accept. Not one of the scripts she read had a part in it she felt well-suited for, although some of them were so good it was heartbreaking to have to say no.

While Bobby was away, she found herself unable to sleep and stayed up late into the night. She'd go into Lucy's room, or Melinda's suite, and sit staring into the darkness, remembering Hank, thinking back over the years, recalling moments that made her smile and, at the same time, heightened her loneliness. Wonderful, elegant Hero danced in her reveries. And she thought fondly of Ike and the way he'd fussed over his camera and lenses.

While the house gave off occasional creaks as it continued its long settling process into the earth, she sat, resisting the craving for a cigarette, selecting memories to review. Inside, she felt the stirrings of fear, but she refused to allow it room for growth. It was one thing to acknowledge loneliness, something else altogether to surrender to it. This was temporary, she told herself; and she'd get through it. But, God, she thought, it was hard. And the idea of spending the rest of her life coping with the emptiness *was* alarming.

As a litany to fend off the darker thoughts, she recited voicelessly the names and fine qualities of those who were no longer a part of her life. It was a way in which to keep them all alive and to help her to get through the nights.

Bobby was worn out after his time in California, and spent his first week back in New York lazing about the apartment. "I'm lousy company right now," he apologized. "I've got one more of these specials to do, and then that's it. I'm getting too old for all the bullshit out there. It'd be fine if I could go, get the show done, then turn around and come home. But there's always got to be wheeling and dealing; there're people you've got to see or they'll never talk to you again. One more, and that's the end of it. I've had enough."

At least with Bobby home, she didn't mind quite so much being alone in the house; and he came out for the weekends once the weather turned warm.

"In case you were wondering," he told her, "Howard's still interested in the festival idea."

"We could start working out again," she said tentatively.

"We could do that. All you've got to do is say the word."

"I just wish a script would come in that had a part I could do. I've never gone this long without working."

"Something'll turn up," he said confidently. "D'you know there are quite a number of handsome silver threads overtaking the old brunette?"

"I know. It's about time, wouldn't you say?"

"No, I wouldn't say. Jesus! Are you going to start that age crap again."

"I wouldn't dream of it."

"Good. Don't!"

"Mel's avoiding me, staying away intentionally. It's been over a year since I saw her."

"Maybe it'll get to be two years, or five. There's nothing you can do about it, if that's the way she wants it. She's grown up, Bea. She's got her own place, her own money, her own life. She'll come around in time," he added, seeing how the prospect of not seeing Melinda distressed her.

"I don't know what to do," she admitted.

"There's nothing you *can* do. She's made her choices; she's doing what she wants."

"I miss her, Bobby. It's as if she thinks I've commited crimes against her. But what did I ever *do?* That's what I don't understand."

"I can't help you there. I don't understand it, either."

She was standing outside, surveying the garden, later that summer when Gertie came to the back door saying, "There's a Mr. Greenswag on the tellyphone from Los Angeles."

Breaking into a smile, Bea hurried inside.

"Jerry, are you still actually alive? You must be a thousand years old by now. And why haven't I heard from you for so long? How *are* you?"

He chuckled. "I'm hanging on by my teeth, but I'm alive. How're you, sweetheart? What're you up to in Wasp country?"

"I was just out looking at the garden, trying to decide for the hundredth time whether or not to put in a pool. How's Brenda, and the children?"

"Brenda's fine. And the children have children, if you don't mind. Listen to me, Bea. You're not kidding when you say I'm a thousand years old. I'm getting ready to retire. I got one last deal here to put together, and then Brenda and I, we're off on one of those around-the-world cruises. God forbid either one of us should be seasick! We'll be sick for three solid months. Anyway, this deal. There's something I want you to do for me. You listening?"

"I'm listening."

"I've got a wonderful package. A terrific thing. Everything's set, but one thing. And I want you to do something for me. I want you to say you'll do this, without asking one question."

"But what is it?"

"Okay. Here's what it is. It's a 'Hallmark Hall of Fame,' a two-hour production. You and Bobby starring in a piece you'll win Emmys for. *And,* for old time's sake, I got Elizabeth Hansen signed to play the daughter."

"It sounds perfect! When do I see the script?"

"Here's the deal: You say yes right now, before you read the script. The New York office is sending it up to you. It should be there any minute. But you say yes, right now, let me go retire in peace with a happy mind."

"Bobby's already agreed?"

"He's all set. Everything's set. Say yes, and let me finish with this already."

"What's the catch?" she asked suspiciously. "There has to be a catch here somewhere."

"Say yes!"

"I don't like this. But yes, all right. God! You wouldn't sell me down the river, would you, Jerry? You haven't gone strange in your old age, have you?"

"You'll have the script any time. You'll read it. You'll call me back, thanking me. I gotta call the production people, confirm you're set. You'll be happy, I promise you."

Fifteen minutes later, the script was delivered by messenger. She tore open the envelope and stared at the title page, not sure how to feel. Carrying the script with her, she went back to the telephone.

"You son of a bitch!" she shouted at him. *"You tricked me!"*

He laughed happily. "You know you would've said no without

501

reading it. You go read now. Never mind your personal feelings. The woman's written you another award-winning part. Go with God, sweetheart! It's a *mitzvah.*"

Stiff with reservations, and feeling somewhat betrayed, she sat down to read *Good-bye, Emily Skye*, by Rebecca Armstrong.

Forty-Six

I T was Bobby's first dramatic role, and Bea's first project since Hank's death almost three years earlier. On the flight to Los Angeles, they joked grimly over which of them was more reluctant.

"At least you've done television before," she argued.

"I've never done *anything* where I didn't have to dance."

"Why are we *doing* this? I want a cigarette."

"Have a drink instead. In fact, let's get smashed. That'll solve all our problems."

"My God!" she said, after a time. "I was just trying to think how old Elizabeth must be by now. She has to be at least thirty. This is going to be very, very strange. I'd kill for a cigarette."

"Good thing they don't sell them on planes. Have another drink."

She started to laugh. "We'll come staggering off, they'll take one look at the pair of us and send us home again."

"In that case, I'll definitely have another drink."

"There's no chance Becky's going to show up, is there?"

"Nope. I checked, like you asked me to. Why're you such a hard case where she's concerned, anyway?"

"I'd just prefer not to see her."

"I see her every so often, you know," he said casually.

"Don't tell me she's one of your girls!"

"Go on! You know you're the only dark-haired type I've ever socialized with. No, she's stayed in touch. She always asks after you."

"You knew all about this script, this whole business, didn't you?"

"The hell I did! I knew about it the same day you did, when Jerry phoned and said he couldn't retire until he put this deal together. Did you know she'd been married?"

"No. Really?"

"According to her, it lasted about twenty minutes one day. But she's got a very nice kid, girl, must be twelve, thirteen now."

"Is she still living in New York?"

"Same place in the East Seventies. She bought the apartment next door, knocked out the walls, and made the place bigger. It's pretty much the way it was, with bare floors, and a couple of sofas, wall-to-wall books. The only difference is she's got herself a nice IBM type-writer these days. And the daughter."

"How often is 'every so often'?"

"Oh, two, three times a year. I told you, she's stayed in touch. I think the only reason she has is so she can keep tabs on you through me. She thinks the world of you, Bea."

"No comment."

"You're both nuts. Why the hell don't the two of you make it up and forget about all that crap?"

"Bobby, I can't."

"If you want my opinion, that's bullshit. Of course you could, if you wanted to."

"Why would I want the opinion of a bald, middle-aged, semi-retired dancer who's willing to risk his reputation on a straight acting job?"

"Probably for the same reason I'd bother trying to convince a middle-aged, long-time-unemployed, sometime Award-winning actress whose favorite sport is turning down my offers of marriage. And *why* can't you make it up with her?"

"It's been too long; I'm too embarrassed; I wouldn't know where or how to begin. Now, let's drop it. More drinks."

"Yeah." He signaled to the stewardess.

Good-bye, Emily Skye had a simple, uncomplicated plot. The power of the script lay entirely in the characterizations and the dialogue, and in the issue of a woman's fight for the right to die in her own home, with her family around her. The major portion of the action revolved around the various battles Emily engaged in, initially with her husband and daughter, and then with doctors, friends, and family. It was wonderfully well written, without false sentiment and with a surprisingly upbeat ending.

The director, the cameramen, the crew, all seemed too young, until Bea took the time to realize she hadn't been as old as these men when

503

she'd started in films. And Hank had been in his early twenties when he'd begun with von Stroheim in San Francisco. She relaxed, so did Bobby, and they got on with it.

Elizabeth was also doing her first work in more than ten years and, after the second day's shooting, brought her five-year-old daughter to the hotel to meet Bea. Lindy was so like her mother at that age that Bea had a little trouble with the odd tricks her mind seemed to want to play on her.

"She's exactly like you were," she told Elizabeth.

"Do you remember this?" Elizabeth asked, revealing at her neck a gold chain with a small heart on it. "I've still got Leonard, too. Or rather, Lindy does. You were so good to me," she said, suddenly choked up as she gave Bea a hug.

"You were a lovely little girl."

"No," Elizabeth said. "Nobody else would stand up to my mother. But you did, and it made such a big difference to me. I'll never forget that day you and Mr. Donovan came to the house to get me and take me back to the wrap party. You *fought* for me. Seeing you do that made me feel that maybe I was worth fighting for, so I started standing up for myself. She'd have ground me into dust, if it weren't for you. I thought you'd like to know just how important you were to me then. And I wanted you to know how much you've always meant to me, so Lindy and I, we brought you something. Didn't we, Lin?"

The girl came to stand by Bea, holding out a large, flat, gift-wrapped package, then leaned against the arm of the sofa at Bea's side to watch her unwrap it. It was a framed, signed, and numbered print of a Hurrell portrait of Bea and Elizabeth that had been taken for *Jeannie*.

"I hope you like it," Elizabeth said. "I have one in the living room at home. I feel good every time I look at it."

"Like it?" Bea said, overwhelmed. "I *love* it. I'm speechless. Thank you."

Bea gazed at the photograph, for a few moments struck by the thought that Elizabeth was offering her everything Melinda had always refused to give. Recalling Lucy's comment, Bea looked at Elizabeth, wondering if this was the good daughter, the true daughter. The idea of it made her throat hurt.

Lindy bent forward to look closely at Bea, so closely that Bea could see the child's pupils dilate, as she asked, in hushed tones, "Are you gonna cry?"

"I might." Bea put an arm around the girl. "Do you know you look just like your mother?"

"I know that," Lindy answered seriously. "I thought this was me."

She twisted around to point at the photograph. "That's you," she said, smiling suddenly and pointing the same finger at Bea's nose.

Bea set aside the photograph, her arm still around Lindy, and said, "Could I give you a hug?"

In answer, the child wound her arms around Bea's neck and hugged her so hard her narrow body vibrated.

"My God!" Bea laughed. "You give hugs that last for days!"

"You're nice," Lindy decided, rubbing her nose against Bea's.

"You are, too. And I'm going to put that picture in a very special place when I get home."

"Lin and I better be going," Elizabeth said, and Bea got up to walk with them to the door. "I'm a nervous wreck doing this show. It's been a long time. I couldn't believe it when Mr. Greenswag called. I mean, I don't even have an agent anymore. I've been a housewife the last ten years. I hope I don't let you all down."

"I'm sure you'll do beautifully," Bea assured her.

"You haven't changed one bit." Elizabeth smiled, then gave Bea a shy kiss on the cheek. "I can't tell you how excited I was about seeing you again. If there's ever anything I can do for *you*, just let me know."

"You may have to hold my hand to get me through this," Bea laughed.

"We'll all hold each other's hands."

"I'm sorry Bobby wasn't here to meet Lin, but perhaps you'll bring her to the set."

"Maybe. If I don't overdose on Valium trying to stay calm. C'mon, Lin, say good-bye."

"'Bye." Lindy held up her arms, and Bea bent to embrace her.

"Come and see me again. Okay?"

"Okay," Lindy said.

Bobby walked into the suite, saw the portrait, and said, "If you don't let me have that to hang in my bedroom, I'm going back to New York on the next plane. I mean it. Where did you *get* this?" He picked up the photograph and held it at arm's length. "This is mine. I don't *care* where you got it. Christ!" He looked over his shoulder at her. "It's Elizabeth, right?"

"Uh-huh. You really want it?"

"Too late. I've got it. You want to run lines? I can't remember a single word. I'm gonna blow this, I know it. Christ! Look at you. What a face. Right on the bedroom wall this goes, so I can lie in bed and look at it. Will you run the lines with me?"

"Of course. It's a good omen, the nerves. I think everything's going to be fine."

Instead of attending the Emmy Awards ceremony, Bea went to visit Lucy and Brian. She spent a pleasant two days of shopping, and dining, and walking with Melinda.

Bobby flew out to the coast with Becky and was present when *Goodbye, Emily Skye* won six Emmys. Bobby won for best actor and ran onstage to accept the award in a state of total disbelief. Then Becky won for her script and said, "I've been very fortunate in having a friend who, over the years, has inspired my best writing." She held out her Emmy saying, "This one's for you, Bea," and the audience cheered, anticipating more to come. Sandy Greenberg thanked Bea, too, in accepting his directing award. And then Bobby had to go back to receive Bea's award for best actress. For a moment, he could only stare at this prize, then he looked up and said, "She's always been my favorite dancing partner," and the audience went berserk, applauding, whistling, stamping their feet, and cheering.

The production itself won an Emmy, as did Elizabeth for her supporting role. Everyone, unanimously, expressed gratitude to Bea.

When later at Bobby's apartment, he ran a tape of the show for her, she began to cry at seeing Bobby win his award, and when she saw him go up to accept hers, she held her breath, as if this were the actual moment. On the screen, he bent his head for a moment, then looked directly into the camera and said, "She's always been my favorite dancing partner," and she burst into tears again, amazed by the reaction of the audience.

"It's true," he said, passing her his handkerchief. "You always have been."

She sniffed, drying her eyes. "The offers are coming in from all sides, since the show aired."

"You're on your own on that score, sister. It'll be a good long time, if ever, before I'm willing to go through anything like that again. I don't know how the hell you do it. You know that? I mean, Christ! I watched you every day, and half the scenes I was right there with you, but I was just me, delivering the lines the best way I knew how. You *were* Emily. It was like playing it out with someone who only *looked* familiar. And most of the time, whatever reactions I gave were the goods because that was how you made me feel."

"That's acting, Bobby."

"Uh-huh. Oh, yeah, maybe *I* was acting. But you, *you* were living and dying Emily, and it scared the shit out of me. It was just like the way it was when I sat with you in that doctor's office in Greenwich, and he told you about the cancer. It was the same damned thing all over again. I won that thing"—he pointed to the Emmy on the cabinet across the room—"because I'm a song-and-dance man who managed to deliver his lines without disgracing himself. You won because you climb inside other people's skins and walk around *being* them. So, you're going to pick out the parts you want to play, and I'll tag along to make sure you stay out of trouble. Just don't plan anything that comes up at the same time as that last goddamned special I've got to do and, that way, we can go on location, or whatever, together, and I can sit around and watch you do your stuff. Sound reasonable?"

"I should probably marry you."

"Yeah, but you won't. So forget it. I like gossip. I'm used to it. And besides, nobody gives a shit anymore who's living with whom. The only part of it I'm never going to understand is how you could sit here and listen to Becky say what she did and still not give one inch in her direction."

"Bobby, I can't. I've left it too long, and now I wouldn't know how." She looked away. "She *gave* it to me, just wrote her heart out and gave it to me. I'm too ashamed to face her now." She turned back to him. "She was so special to me. And both of us screwed it up. I don't know how to change any of it. Have you seen her with her daughter? What's her name? What are they like together?"

"They're great. She's a swell kid."

"But what's her name?"

He stared at her for a long moment. "You know her name."

"I do?"

"Oh, sure. You've signed it maybe a couple of hundred thousand times."

"She called her daughter *Beatrice?*"

"Yup. Beatrice Fitzgerald. Everybody calls her Bones."

"Bones," she repeated. "Becky named her daughter after me." She got up, poured herself a glass of neat scotch and tossed it down, then stood holding the empty glass. "They get on well? They're close?"

"Uh-huh."

"I'm glad," she said feelingly. "Bones. Is she skinny?"

"Skinny and taaalll! What is she, fourteen? Six feet easily."

Bea laughed softly. "Does she look like Becky?"

"Spitting image."

Bea shook her head, smiling. "Six feet tall and she looks like Becky."

"You're a shmuck. You both are. She says all the same imbecilic things you do. You needed her; she let you down; now there's too much water under the bridge. Shmucks, the two of you."

She shrugged, put the glass down and came back to the sofa. "Maybe we'll grow out of it."

She did a picture in England that summer. Melinda managed one free afternoon, then left for an extended cruise with friends through the Greek Islands. Bea and Bobby spent two weeks in London with Lucy and Brian and persuaded them to come to Connecticut for Christmas. Melinda sent a telegram at the last moment saying she'd be unable to join them. She had mononucleosis and was confined to bed.

In February of '66, Bea accompanied Bobby to Los Angeles while he fulfilled the last of his contractual obligations and did the final special. Then, after a few weeks' rest, they flew to New York where Bea filmed on location in the city and swore, when it was done, she'd never repeat the experience.

They spent the summer going over the old dance numbers and working, in between times, with an editor to put together a thirty-five-minute selection of clips from their six musicals, with both of them writing, and then reading, the voice-over narrative. It was planned that the festival would be in June of the following year.

Since they couldn't decide which of the gowns they preferred, they went ahead and had two of them copied. Bobby came along to the fittings to make sure she had no opportunity to change her mind. She was far more fearful of doing one seven-minute dance number, he thought, than he'd been about doing a two-hour TV movie.

"I'm forty-nine years old, for God's sake!" she exclaimed. "I've got plenty of reason to be nervous. Don't think for one minute that every single person in that audience—and especially the women—won't be watching and waiting for me to be an aging caricature of myself!"

"They'll all be sitting there, those women, wishing they looked half as good as you do."

"Oh, right! The journalists will start in on my beauty *secrets* and hint around, trying to find out how many times I've had my god-damned face lifted."

"How many times *have* you had it lifted?"

"Bastard!"

"Calm down. Okay?"

"*You* be calm. All you've got to do is put on your stupid top hat and tails, and they'll be falling over in the aisles. I've got to worry about my goddamned crepey arms."

He laughed until his eyes ran and his sides ached. When he finally managed to stop laughing, they made love. And while she was sleeping, he watched her; watched her eyes shift, dreaming, beneath their lids; he watched the slow rise and fall of her chest, and the way one

508

strand of hair slanted across her cheek; he watched so closely he could see a faint pulse throbbing in her throat and another in her breast. He felt completely happy.

The festival tickets sold out an hour after the box office opened. Tickets for the opening-night gala, a black-tie affair, were also grabbed up, at a hundred dollars each. The first five rows of orchestra seats had been held aside for people Bobby and Bea might care to invite and for special guests such as the mayor, and the governor, the state senators, and sundry other personalities and dignitaries.

Lucy and Brian promised to be there. But as the date for the festival drew closer, there was no word from Melinda. Hearing from Bea that Melinda hadn't responded one way or the other, Lucy decided to take up the matter personally. She telephoned and told Melinda, "I want to see you. I'm coming right over. Don't you dare go out!"

Melinda hesitantly let Lucy into her Knightsbridge flat, having guessed the reason for this visit.

"I've decided not to go after all," she told Lucy at once.

"Could we sit down here?" Lucy asked, making herself comfortable in one of the starkly modern, yet yielding and capacious, chairs.

Melinda followed suit and lit a cigarette.

"Nice place," Lucy said, looking around. "No garbage on the floor, no cigarette burns on the rug, no nailpolish on the curtains. Very nice."

"Oh, *please*," Melinda said impatiently. "I've long-since apologized to Mother for all that. I see no need to apologize to you, as well."

"What're you doing with yourself these days, Melinda?"

Melinda took a long look at the woman seated opposite, impressed, in spite of herself, by Lucy's handsome appearance. With her silver-gray hair, and a white gabardine suit, black and white spectator pumps, Lucy looked chic, well turned-out, and well loved. She simply shone with good health and happiness. "This and that," Melinda answered. "There are several positions I'm considering."

"Oh, really? Well, good. Interesting positions, I hope."

"They are, actually. I've had an offer from the British Museum and another from the Tate."

"Doing what?" Lucy asked skeptically.

"Historical backgrounds, researching documentation, that sort of thing."

"Oh! Well, if it's what interests you, good."

"It interests me. Why have you come?"

It was Lucy's turn to take in Melinda, wondering why someone so truly lovely-looking worked so hard to play it down. Her long hair was pulled back behind her ears and held in place by something that looked like half an old wallet, pierced by a chopstick. She was clad in a shapeless blue pullover and a long, voluminous skirt, neither of which allowed any indication of the form of the body underneath. "If you never do anything else for your mother as long as you live, Melinda," Lucy said, "you've *got* to be there for the opening of the festival."

"*Why* have I *got* to be there?"

"What is it with you?" Lucy asked, genuinely puzzled. "Why are you so set against her? She's your *mother*. She loves you. No one could love you more. But all you do is back away every time she tries to get close to you."

"Spare me that." Melinda laughed unpleasantly. "Everything the woman's ever done has been a performance of one variety or another. And she's so bloody good at it, she's got the lot of you bamboozled."

"Elaborate on that for me, would you? I think I'm missing something."

"It's all a great show. She doesn't care about me. I admit I think she's truly fond of you, and undoubtedly she feels something for Bobby. But where I'm concerned, it's all just performing."

"I don't know *how* you can *think* that. I honestly don't."

Melinda relaxed fractionally, seeing that this was true. "No, I don't suppose you do," she said, carefully putting out her cigarette. "But then, I'm uniquely qualified to judge, aren't I?"

"How?"

"Because you couldn't be there one hundred percent of the time to witness her behavior, could you? And you couldn't know how we were with one another when we were on our own, could you?"

"I was there to see a hell of a lot of it, and I truthfully don't know what you're talking about. I've never seen *anyone* work harder at being a good mother than Bea. Just what sins has she committed against you, Melinda, that you find so unforgivable?"

"Well, for one," Melinda said, adrenaline suddenly gushing into her system, "there's the matter of my father."

"Your father?"

"My *real* father."

"Your real father. Your real father was Henry."

"Don't be absurd!" she said scathingly. "Of course he wasn't. Henry Donovan was a homosexual. And for another thing, she's been sleeping with Bobby for God knows how long."

Was the girl crazy? Lucy wondered. "Melinda, Henry Donovan was your father. What on earth ever gave you the idea Bobby was?"

510

"I happen to know it's the truth. We do share a common birthday," she reminded Lucy.

"You happen to be wrong. I know for a positive fact Henry was your father. I mean, God above, you look just like the man."

"What did you do, sleep in the same bed with them?"

Lucy had the feeling she was trying to go down an up escalator and making no progress whatever. "Bobby was away in the navy when you were conceived. How do you explain that?"

"They simply changed the dates."

Lucy laughed. "By two whole months? I can assure you you were *not* premature. You weighed almost eight pounds, for heaven's sake. You tell me how a seven-month baby gets to be that big."

"I know what I know."

"This is nuts! I can't sit here and argue this with you. Listen to me! If I have to get down on my knees and beg you, I will. You've got to do this for your mother. If you're not there for that first night, you'll break her heart. Do you *really* want to hurt her that much?"

Melinda lit another cigarette, taking her time to study Lucy's pleading features. Do I want to hurt her? she asked herself, and suddenly, like a distant echo from somewhere very deep inside her, another voice reasoned, It's nothing, one night out of your life to make your mother happy. It wasn't such a lot to ask. Her mother would pay for it, had already offered everything from first-class air fare to a suite at the Plaza, or the Pierre, or anywhere else Melinda might care to stay. She'd even promised a designer gown complete with the trimmings. All Melinda had to do was agree.

"Would you care for something to drink?" she asked Lucy. "Tea, perhaps, or coffee. I know how fond you are of coffee."

"You actually need time to think about it, don't you?" Lucy said, convinced she'd never be able to make sense of this girl. "All right, coffee."

"It'll just take a few minutes." Melinda got up and went to the kitchen where, while she plugged in the kettle, then poured ground coffee into the Melitta filter and set out cups and saucers, she tried to understand her sudden, renewed longing for a connection her common sense told her was impossible. She was no longer able to judge what in her mother was real. There were times when, like some trick of light, she thought she could see truth emanating like a glow from her mother. At other times, she was dazzled, and her eyes stung from the brilliance. Her instincts told her to disbelieve her eyes, because there were all sorts of magicians, not merely the types who produced rabbits from hats and miles of silk scarves from innocent pockets. There were sorcerers—and her mother was one of the best—

511

capable of transforming their very selves, so that the beholder lost all notion of what was real and not real and could only wonder about the validity of the identity being presented. Always, underlying every thought, was the idea that this time the presentation would be the real one, the ultimate, true one. And it was this idea that lured her into repeated confrontations with her mother, only to discover, yet again, she'd been the victim of illusion. Nevertheless, she hadn't reached the stage in her own life where she could resist the lure. And so she pulled the plug on the kettle and went back to the lounge to say, "All right. I'll go. I've changed my mind about the coffee, and I'd be most grateful if you'd leave now."

Lucy didn't say a word. She simply got up and went toward the door, stopping when Melinda said, "Just one thing."

"What's that?"

"Don't ever again do this to me! My decisions are my own. I've said I'll do this, but I'm not entirely happy with it. I very much dislike being coerced. However, I'll write and tell her I'll be attending."

"Good," Lucy said. "Thank you," she said, and then hurried away, chilled in spite of the day's warmth.

Forty-Seven

THE preparations were more complex and time-consuming than anyone had anticipated. It was originally thought a live orchestra would be used, but after much discussion with Howard Kramer, who had originated the idea of the festival and was producing it, it was decided that not only could a live orchestra not reproduce the proper 'thirties' sound, but it wasn't a practical consideration either in terms of the expense involved or for traveling purposes. So they recorded the original dance track, as well as lead-ins and lead-outs, electronically enhancing the sound and cleaning out the background noises. The results were even better than they'd hoped for.

They hired a lighting man, a rear-screen projectionist, a sound man, a stage manager, an assistant stage manager, and two men to crew backstage. And then they all met to plot out the light and sound cues. Since the theater was only available to them between midnight and eleven a.m., they had to do the initial walk-throughs late at night. It was a slow, tedious procedure of blocking, then waiting while the lights were adjusted, then set and marked. The physical blocking alone took two entire nights. Then came the audio cues, and the proper placement and levels of the microphones downstage for the question-and-answer segment. After that, they had to integrate both sound and light, and then do a technical run-through from start to finish to be sure all the cues were right. Finally, there were the "unknown" contingencies.

"There's bound to be flowers," Howard said. "The two of you can't stand there for an hour or more with armloads of flowers, trying to field questions. We've got to figure some way to get the flowers offstage without having one of those awful, stop-dead moments while the audience sits and watches the two of you fumble around, trying to think what the hell to do."

To satisfy the entire roster of "unknowns," it was agreed that the techies would wear dark suits, white shirts, and ties, so that when they had to come on stage, for any reason, it would not only appear prearranged but would look good.

"We want this classy," Howard said over and over. "It's got to flow. We don't want any embarrassing hitches. I want every last cue to come in right when it should. And you guys," he told the crew, "better make sure everything that has to fly, flies, and everything that has to move has the best casters and rolls without so much as a squeak. I want the downstage floor mikes turned on right on cue and off at the cue. Get those gels on the spots; make sure you know the light board backwards, upside down, and sideways. And, the most important thing: You keep your eyes on Mr. Bradley for the final cue. You see it, you hit the lights, the sound, you get ready to bring down the screen and close those curtains. You got any problems, any questions, I want to know now! I don't want to hear about it at the half-hour. Okay? Okay!"

Gertie, Ellen, the newest secretary, and the hairdresser would be backstage to help Bea. Paul and Gerry would be with Bobby. The stage doorman had a list of names of people who'd be allowed backstage after the gala. No one else would get in.

They did a final run-through. Everyone was happy. Bobby and Bea went back to his apartment. Bea went at once to telephone the Pierre to make sure Melinda and Lucy and Brian had arrived.

Lucy said, "We're all here. Brian says to tell you he thinks the champagne's a nice touch, and why are you wasting your time on us?"

"It's not a waste of time. What a thing to say!"

"Are you nervous?"

"Paralytic. How's Mel?"

"Quiet. She's been quiet since we met up at Heathrow. Friendly enough, but quiet. She spent the whole flight reading."

"Are the rooms all right, Luce?"

"Everything's perfect. Go rest up now, and don't give us a thought."

"You've got your tickets?"

"We've got the tickets. We'll be there, and we'll see you backstage after. Break a leg, sweetheart."

Melinda said, "Everything's lovely, thank you. Are you well?"

"I'm a little shaky, but fine."

"Good. I'll look forward to seeing you. I expect you're tired, if you've just come from rehearsing, so I won't keep you. Good luck. And to Uncle Bobby."

"Thank you. Sleep well, darling."

"You, too. Goodnight."

"She sounds so . . . warm," she told Bobby as she filled the tub and poured in Epsom salts. "Maybe everything's going to work out, after all."

"Maybe." He was examining his face in the mirror at very close range. He raised his eyes and gave her a smile. "I think I'll join you. This has been as bad as one of those damned specials."

"I love the way you're forever bitching about them, and they've won you a closetful of Emmys."

"Yeah, well. Everybody's got to have something to complain about. D'you think you'll sleep?"

"God, I hope so. What if they ask questions we don't want to answer?"

"Then you'll say, 'I don't want to answer that. Next.'"

"You don't think anyone'll notice that my shoes aren't right, do you?" she wondered.

"So what if they do?"

"It's just that we've copied everything else, even my hair."

"Let's agree to something, okay? Let's not say one more word about tomorrow night until tomorrow. Okay?"

"Okay. But I keep remembering last-minute things."

"Howard's covered everything. and what he hasn't thought of, Ellen certainly has. She's so efficient, it's unnerving. And talk about devoted! The woman's a walking compendium of facts about you. I

514

think she's seen every movie you ever made at least three times. Doesn't she kind of get to you?"

"I don't have to tell her what to do," she said, stepping into the tub. "It's heaven, after the last three. She *anticipates*. Do you know what a pleasure it is, to have someone around who doesn't hem and haw on the telephone, who takes a problem and solves it without having to be told how? And she's old enough not to get rattled. The only reason she gets under your skin is because she's not good-looking enough to suit you. You like them young, blonde, newly divorced, and with the dew still damp on their earlobes. I thought you were coming in."

"I am. I'm just waiting until it gets below boiling. Christ! From the chest down, you're a lobster."

"God! I'd love some lobster right now. Wouldn't you? Cold, with fresh mayonnaise."

"I think the closest we could come is some canned crab. I think there's some. We'll go raid the kitchen when we finish in here."

"A cigarette," she said longingly. "A package of English Dunhills."

"Quick transition, from one to an entire package."

"Do you know, I was talking to someone—who was it? I can't remember—anyway, this person was telling me it's been known to take as long as *twenty years* before the urge goes away altogether."

"Only another sixteen to go, sister." He tested the water, then withdrew his hand.

"Sometimes I actually dream I'm smoking a cigarette, and I feel so guilty. I wake up sweating, for God's sake."

"It's tough, I know."

"If you wait till the water's cold, it's not going to do you any good."

"I hate pain."

She laughed. "Get in and stop being such a sissy."

Gritting his teeth, he climbed in at the opposite end of the tub and inched his way down into the water. "What I could do," he groaned, finally seated with his legs either side of hers, "is open a couple of tins of crab, get the mayonnaise, mix it up, then spread the whole mess all over you, and eat it off."

"That takes care of you, but I'm the one who wanted the lobster."

"Okay. I'll spread it all over me, and you can eat it off."

"That is sick and twisted, you know that?"

"I like it. We'll get out there tomorrow night, and the whole time we're spinning away, I'll be thinking about how I licked crab salad out of your navel."

"I thought we agreed not to talk about tomorrow night."

"Bobby's a bad, bad boy."

"Sick and twisted, and a dirty player, too. If that's the way it's going to be, there's a little number I could do with some peanut butter. You could think about what that might be while we're out there, dancing."

"*I'm* sick and twisted? Christ! What *would* you do?" he asked with a leer.

"One hint: It takes a *very* long time. God! This place isn't bugged, is it?"

"Can't you just see the headlines in the *Enquirer:* 'Award-Winning Actress Gives Cardiac Arrest to Aging Playboy Dancer ... See page two, under "Peanut Butter." ' "

"All this talk of food is quite stimulating."

"Peanut butter," he said thoughtfully. "How much longer d'you plan to sit in here?"

"Fifteen minutes?"

"Give me some more hints."

Lucy was elated to discover Becky in the seat next to hers. They threw their arms around each other, then separated to make the introductions.

"My husband, Brian Fairleigh. And this is Mel. I don't know if the two of you remember each other."

Brian shook Becky's hand warmly, saying, "I've long been an admirer of yours. It's a great pleasure."

Melinda was diffident, but polite, and offered her hand, taken aback when Becky kissed her, then said, "It's been such a long time. You look just like Hank. It's incredible. I want you all to meet my daughter, Bones."

Lucy couldn't help comparing Bones and Melinda. Melinda seemed older than twenty-one, stiff and cool, her exceptional good looks spoiled by her apparent inability to smile. Bones was very tall, a young fifteen, with Becky's auburn hair, wide-set brown eyes, and freckles. She was immediate and open, and so enthusiastic it was impossible not to like her. And the link between mother and daughter was visibly loving and good-natured.

"I guess I'd better explain that Bobby sent us tickets," Becky told Lucy once they were all seated.

"Don't tell me you and Bea haven't made it up yet!"

"I'm afraid not," Becky admitted.

"Well," Lucy said firmly, "there's no time like right now."

Becky shook her head. "It wouldn't work," she said softly. "Eventually, it will. Neither one of us has managed to figure out yet how to take the first step. But I know we'll get it sorted out one of these days."

"Boy! I'm so excited," Bones said, looking at the stage. "I had to go to the bathroom about sixty times before we left."

"Bones is a big fan of both of them," Becky told Lucy and Brian, smiling.

"I wanted to go into dance," Bones stretched forward to see them all, "but I got way too tall. So now I'm concentrating on acting."

"She's very good," Becky said in an undertone to Lucy. "She's so good, it's scary."

"Have you done anything yet?" Lucy asked the girl.

"Mostly I've done modeling. But I had four lines in one picture and six in another. I'm trying to get my union card. I've already got an agent and everything. Mom won't let me work outside New York. Not until I'm eighteen. I have to finish school first. I'm up for a small part in another picture, though. I've already read once, and I've got a call-back, so I'm keeping my fingers crossed."

Lucy turned to look at Brian who was studying Bones with considerable interest as he reached into his inside pocket for one of his cards. Beyond him, Melinda was staring fixedly at the stage, her hands knotted together in her lap.

"I don't suppose," Brian asked Bones, "you do an English accent?"

"Oh, sure. I can do four or five different ones. My best is Cockney."

"Perhaps you'd ring me tomorrow. We're at the Pierre." He gave her his card. Bones read it and emitted a high-pitched little squeal. "There's a film we're about to do that might just have something for you in it."

"Oh, Mom!" She gave her mother the card. "Will it be okay?"

Becky looked at the card, then at Brian, and said, "It'll be okay."

Melinda thought she just might be sick at her stomach. Another bloody actress, making deals right in front of God and the assembled masses. And Lucy proud as punch because she was married to a big film producer. *Why* had she agreed to be here? It was dreadful. At least a thousand people, all dressed to the nines; everyone craning about looking for famous faces, as if it was of any importance whether or not one saw someone famous. She hated having to dress up, hated having people here and there glance at her, then whisper, no doubt commenting on the fact that she looked not at all like her mother. People on all sides speculating about every one of them—Rebecca Armstrong and her daughter; Lucy and her frightfully important husband; herself, of course.

She glanced at her watch. Five more minutes before it was to start.

She'd have to sit through what would likely be a dismal show, then go backstage to her mother's dressing room after, where crowds of people would be pushing forward to gush and lie and rave about how fabulous it all was. The lights flickered, and the last people rushed to their seats, the volume of conversation far too high. Out of the corner of her eye, she saw Brian take hold of Lucy's hand and, as he did, the diamonds on her finger fractured the light. Bloody interfering old cow, forcing her into this! She had no idea why she did it, but she turned to look at Lucy, beyond Brian, and found Lucy's eyes on her. One had to admit she looked bloody good for her age, very trim and terribly smart in a black velvet evening suit, a black crêpe de chine shirt under the jacket open just far enough to show a fair bit of cleavage and a whopping diamond pendant nestled between those opulent breasts. Lucy smiled at her, and Melinda smiled back, for a moment, feeling a remembered affection for the woman, recollecting suddenly an afternoon years and years ago when Lucy had walked with her along the beach, carrying Melinda's sand bucket and spade and singing some silly song. For one terrible moment, Melinda wanted it all back again, wanted to be a toddler once more, with a talent for believing.

The lights dimmed, and her insides went tight. Music came up softly, gaining in volume as the curtains rolled apart, revealing an enormous screen. The film started. Her mother's voice emerged from the speakers, and then Bobby's. The two of them sounded as if they were sitting together on a sofa somewhere, reminiscing, as on the screen, an incredibly young Beatrice Crane sang a chorus that led into an astonishingly complicated and energetic dance with Bobby. Her tension eased slightly. Nothing new here, except the voice-over, and it was really quite pleasant. Somehow there was no connection between that girl on the screen and her mother.

Lucy clutched Brian's hand, glad she'd thought to go out at the last minute and buy some waterproof mascara. She was already on the verge of tears. By the time the two of them came onstage, she knew she'd just dissolve.

Bones took her eyes from the screen for a moment to look at her mother. Her mom looked so sweet, Bones thought, all kind of dewy and nostalgic. She reached for her mother's hand and gave her a big smile when their eyes met. Then they both looked back at the screen.

Up in the booth, Howard smoked furiously, watching through what was normally the projectionist's window. So far, so good. Better than good. Great. The audience was enjoying the hell out of the clips and the narrative. Laughs here and there, the kind that had this great fondness for what was being shown. Great. They were getting to the end. "Without You" was up on the screen now, the clip of Bobby singing the full number, before the dance. God god god! Nobody fuck up the cues! Cue the sound, fly the screen. His hands were soaking wet. Good, great! Screen all the way up, and people already applauding as the two of them hold one beat, two, and then into the dance. He groaned, wiped his hands, lit a fresh cigarette.

The screen disappeared upward as the old music was replaced by a version somehow stronger and truer than it had been a minute before during the clip. It cascaded out of the speakers, and there they were, Bobby and Bea; and the whole original set had been reconstructed. Everything was exactly the same as the film. The audience broke into spontaneous applause at the sight, and for a moment, no one was entirely sure this was real, or possible, so still were the two onstage and so exactly like their younger selves.

And then they began to dance. People sighed with pleasure.

Melinda gripped the arms of her seat, sitting up straighter. This wasn't what she'd expected. She didn't know what she'd thought she'd see, but it wasn't this; it wasn't this slim couple who stood posed for one unforgettable moment—her mother in the gown from the film, white with short puffy sleeves, scooped at the neckline, the bodice embroidered and adorned with tiny beads, the fabric molded to her torso then flaring to the ankles. And then they danced, and everything Melinda had believed until then to be tricks played by lights and cameras was a fiction she'd created somewhere, for unknown reasons.

They turned, they separated, came together, turned and turned; they traveled over the stage as if they were halves of the same body. Their smiles, their pleasure in each other and in the dance was undeniably real. Oh God! she thought. That's my mother. *My mother.* She felt as if she might actually die, seeing this, noticing the way the skirt lifted as they turned, revealing those delicate ankles and long, flawless legs; noticing the supple arch of her mother's spine, the turn of her chin, the length of her neck, the flex of her fingers reaching through space to connect with Bobby's waiting hand. Something felt as if it might be breaking inside Melinda, her hands gripping harder and harder on the arms of the seat.

Lucy gave up trying to hold in her emotions and let the tears run unchecked, her heart suddenly enlarged at the sight of the two of them. All these years, and look at her, she'd done it, she was dancing. There she was, *dancing.*

Becky cried, too, and felt a piercing regret that a few badly timed remarks had had to separate them for so many years. I miss you, Bea, she thought. But I'm so happy for you. You're amazing, the two of you. It's just like that night of the talent contest, when they wanted to give your prize to that sappy blonde singer. You were astonishing, rocketing around that stage, the spangles catching the light; you sparkled, you glittered. And here you are, shining. I'm so proud of you.

Bones sat open-mouthed, blown away; all this time and she'd never even known Beatrice Crane could dance, hadn't ever seen *one* of those movies. Everybody in the entire world had seen Bobby dance, but the two of them together were the most incredibly beautiful, sexy, sensational, stupendous thing she'd seen in her whole entire life. And that *dress!* That dress was the all-time best. The whole thing was too incredibly fantastic. And Uncle Bobby in that ultra-sensational set of tails, his shirt front just so white and totally perfect. The dancing killed her totally dead, totally. She could hardly breathe.

Howard was glued to the projectionist's window, checking out the audience in the first half-dozen rows, visible in the spillover from the stage. Half the people were crying. He could see men handing their wives their hankies, hands blotting eyes all over the goddamned place. "I was *right!*" he crowed, his breath fogging the glass. "I was one-hundred-percent goddamned right!" They were winding down onstage; they finished dead on the beat, and the whole place was thunder as everybody jumped up out of their seats and started shouting and clapping. "Jesus Christ!" Howard whispered through his teeth. He'd never seen anything like it.

It felt so right; it *was* right. Bea could feel it in every step. This was the way it had always been, each of them knowing what the other was going to do every time, how to melt together into the turns, the separations effortlessly synchronized because they could read each other's breathing; each other's eyes, and hands; the parts of them where they touched; the music in their eyes, in their lungs, in the air they shared. She even knew he'd be thinking, Right on the money, when they pushed it up into double time, silently laughing with the pleasure; then the retard and his body was joined to hers, and he held her, leaning way, way into it to bridge the transition back into four-four, and the lift-turns all the way around the stage, four bars dancing apart, and then the final steps to the locked pose. The music out, and then, to her astonishment, he kissed her on the mouth, whispered, "Peanut butter," and they split apart to take the call, skipping downstage, hands held, as the curtains glided closed behind them, and they stopped on the apron, flabbergasted by the noise. People ran down the aisles with flowers and were intercepted by the dark-suited techies who materialized to accept them, handing them up to Bobby and Bea who were laughing aloud now, clutching armloads of flowers as they took bow after bow, and still the audience continued shouting and applauding. There were no more flowers from the aisles and, as instructed, the techies went stage-left and stage-right and came on to carry the bouquets offstage. Keeping hold of Bea's hand, Bobby signaled for silence and, reluctantly, the audience seated itself.

"We'd like to thank you," Bobby began.

Someone from the audience shouted, *"We'd* like to thank *you!"* and set off another wild round of applause.

Again Bobby signaled for silence, and someone shouted, "How do you feel?"

"We're very happy," Bea said.

And then, naturally and easily, the questions and answers began.

Melinda was distraught, wrung out. She listened to her mother's familiar throaty voice answering questions with what seemed admirable candor—if you didn't know her. After a few minutes, Melinda stopped listening altogether. The disparity between what she'd seen and what she was now hearing was more than she could tolerate. She simply tuned out and studied the pair less than twenty feet away, finding both of them beyond her ability to comprehend. For an hour, to the joy of the audience, her mother and Bobby fielded questions, gave answers, and then, suddenly—that magic, again—the curtains opened, the music came up, and they danced back into the set, the curtains closed, and they were gone.

In the crush of people heading backstage, Melinda had no difficulty slipping away. She had to walk several blocks to get a taxi. Back at the hotel, she wrote a note on a piece of the Pierre's stationery, then changed her clothes, checked out, and took a taxi to the airport. For fifty dollars, the doorman had guaranteed her that her note would be hand-delivered to her mother before she had a chance to leave the theater.

There simply wasn't time to stop and read the note, and so it was after four in the morning, when she and Bobby finally got back to the apartment, that Bea remembered, and fished in her evening bag for it.

Dear Mother,

Tonight was a triumph for you, and I hope many more follow. Forgive me for not staying to congratulate you, but I expect there were a great many people eager to talk to you, and I've never been especially keen on large gatherings. You truly are remarkable, and I wish with all my heart I could know who you really are. Too much of what passes between us rarely seems to me to be actual. And I doubt anyone could love you in the way you wish I would. We each care in whatever way we're able for the people in our lives. Thank you for allowing me to be there. It was an unforgettable experience. I'll be in touch soon.

Mel

PS: I paid the air ticket and the hotel bill.

Bea exhaled slowly and gave Bobby the letter. "Do you understand this?" she asked him.

"It's a whole load of push-me pull-me."

"What?" She frowned at him.

"Just more of the same old crap. What d'you want me to do with this?" He held up the letter.

"Oh, I don't care. Throw it away. Let's go to bed."

Forty-Eight

IN the course of the next two years, festivals were held in Boston, Chicago, Houston, Seattle, San Francisco, and Los Angeles. When Howard called to ask if they'd be willing to go to Toronto, Bea said yes without hesitation.

"I'd love to go back and see the city."

"Well, good, because the interest is tremendous. They claim you as 'Toronto's own,' you know, and we can get the Royal Alexandra Theatre for the opening-night gala."

"Go ahead," she told him. She had a sudden interest in seeing the places where she'd lived, the streetcars, the corner downtown where she'd held a tin can and sang and danced for pennies.

Almost inevitably, her thoughts turned to Becky, and she studied that long-empty space in her life that Becky had occupied, yearning to see Becky again. It had all gone horribly wrong, and she was compounding the wrongness by allowing more and more time to go by without making some effort to put things right. And yet when she went to the telephone, she couldn't make herself dial the number. She would call, she promised herself, just as soon as she got past the shamed reluctance that prevented her from taking the first step.

"I've never been to Canada," Bobby said cheerfully. "It ought to be fun."

Before the plans were anywhere near firmed up, Howard called again to say, "How do London and Paris sound? And if they sound good, does a side trip to the Cannes Film Festival make it sound even better? Mark called to say they'd had a feeler, wanting to know if you two'd be interested in judging. We could tie it all together so you do Toronto, have a few days off, fly to London, a couple of weeks to organize crew and so forth, then to Paris, a couple more weeks, then on to Cannes."

"Let us get back to you on it," Bobby told him, then sat down to discuss it with Bea. "We could wind up spending the rest of our lives on the road with this show," he said. "It's fun and all the rest of it, but you're turning down work, and I think maybe that's a mistake."

"What about you? You've got something in mind, haven't you?"

"Not really. Well, okay. There's a script I kind of like, with a part I think I could do. They want to start principal photography the end of June."

"Where's it shooting? What kind of part? Will you let me see the script?"

"Sure I will. I wasn't keeping it a secret or anything. It just came in a couple of weeks ago, and I've been mulling it over. The whole thing's going to be done in San Francisco."

"Dancing?"

"Not really. You'll have to read it."

"But you want to do it."

"Yeah, I guess I do. It didn't hit me all that hard when I read it, but it's stayed with me, so it must have something. I wouldn't mind your opinion."

"Well, give me the script and I'll tell you what I think."

"We have to decide about London and Paris," he reminded her.

"Let's make that the end of it. We'll put it to bed in Paris, do the Cannes thing, and then come home. It's a chance for a few weeks in London."

"And you think maybe Mel would be there for a change, and the two of you would get together. And this time it'll be perfect."

"I know it's hard for you to understand," she said hotly, "but she's my child. It's not a part-time job, you know, Bobby. Whether any one of us likes it or not, it's what I'm going to be for the rest of my life. I can't change it, and I can't stop myself from hoping, every single time, that somehow it'll turn around and be the way it is with other mothers and daughters. I *love* her. I can't help it. I'm always going to love her. I admit I don't know what makes her tick. I admit she's cold, and distant, and goes out of her way to avoid me, but she's *mine*. She's the only child I'm ever going to have, and I have a moral obligation, as well as a whole lot of others, to try in whatever way necessary to *be* her mother. I know she's odd. But *she* thinks *I'm* the odd one. I know she's not as warm and outgoing as Becky's girl, and I'd give anything to know what would bring her around. I've *got* to *try*. Please respect that. *Please!*"

"Okay, okay," he backed down. "Don't take my head off!"

"I'm sorry. But it's painful for me to hear you talk about her the way you do. Most of the time I write it off because she's unpleasant and arrogant and she hasn't been especially nice to you. But for chrissake, Bobby! I'm her *mother*. Sometimes I think you forget that. I can't *ever* forget it, and every time you make a crack about her it hurts me. You're supposed to love me. Stop cracking wise about Mel, because every time you do, there's something inside me that hates you for being sensitive to every damned thing about me but the fact of my being a mother."

"Have you ever stopped to consider that there's something inside *me* that hates *her* every time she pulls another stunt and fucks you over? *I* hate seeing what that kid does to you. I *do* love you, and I understand far better than you think how much of you is involved in being a mother to that lifeless, hard-hearted, selfish bitch of a kid. I'm sorry if my cracks upset you. I'll try to stop. But don't expect me to like her, Bea. I couldn't like anyone who treated you the way she does. And you've said yourself a hundred times you wouldn't put up with crap like that from anyone else."

"All right. We've each had our say. We both know where we stand where Mel's concerned, so let's put it on ice. Do we do London and Paris and Cannes?"

"Yeah."

"Fine."

They sat in silence, each stung by what the other had said. Bobby recovered first, saying, "I'm sorry. I'll try to stop making cracks about her."

"I'm sorry, too. D'you want something to drink? Are you hungry? I think I want some coffee. While I'm getting Gertie to put the pot on, why don't you call the apartment and get Paul or Gerry to send the script up by messenger. I'd like to read it."

Toronto wasn't the city she'd known as a child. Her memories had been of a somber place, with dark buildings, brick houses; a cautious city that lacked edge. There'd been no sense of excitement, no special energy; the people had been conservative, quiet, reserved. The city she came back to in 1969 had a skyline, highrise office buildings, and vitality.

She had the chauffeur drive them along Dundas Street to the neighborhood where she'd lived all those years before. "It's still a hardware store!" She pointed it out, laughing. Palmerston Bouleverd was exactly as she remembered, and she had the driver stop for a moment. "That's where Lucy lived," she told Bobby.

"Pretty nice house."

Bea gazed at the house, seeing herself standing on the front porch, dancing along to the class taking place inside. She saw herself returning, with a fistful of coins, to knock at the door and beg Lucy to teach her. Ah, Lucy, she thought, look what we did with our lives.

"If you don't mind my making a suggestion," the driver said. "I was thinking you might like to see Yorkville."

"Give us the whole tour," Bobby said. "We've got time."

"D'you know what pisses me off?" Bobby asked after dinner as he leafed through a directory of what was on in town.

"What?"

"Downstairs here, in the Imperial Room, they've got Ray Charles appearing. I'd love to go down and catch him do a set."

"So why not?"

"Come on! You know why not. We wouldn't get two feet inside the door and there'd be a commotion. Every so often, I think it'd be great to be able to go places without having to worry about being spotted."

"Nobody's bothered us so far," she said.

"We haven't been sitting in a night club, stationary, for a couple of hours."

"You could phone down, ask if they have an out-of-the-way table."

"You want to?"

She shrugged. "You can take off the rug. I'll cream off my make-up, put on something casual."

"Jesus!" he said excitedly. "Let's do it. I love that man. Just to hear him sing 'Ruby' it'd be worth it."

"You phone. I'll change."

The maître d' was very discreet, led them to a table off to one side, whispered, "The waiter will be right along to take your order. Enjoy yourselves," and backed away. The show had started about ten minutes earlier.

"I hope he hasn't done 'Ruby' yet," Bobby said in an undertone, as the applause ended and Charles began the intro for 'Ruby.' Bobby sighed contentedly, took hold of her hand, and paid rapt attention, his feet noiselessly keeping time.

They managed to slip out just before the end of the second encore. While Bea soaked, Bobby danced around the bathroom singing "Hit the Road, Jack," and she said the "no more, no more, no more, no more" part.

"Looking good, sounding good." He executed a neat double-twist turn, finishing up seated on the rim of the tub. "I figure we've spent a total of close to four thousand hours in bathrooms, here and there."

"World's longest bath. I wonder what kind of reception we're going to get."

It was one of their most successful evenings. The audience asked informed, intelligent questions and were every bit as hearty and enthusiastic in their ovation as the New York crowd had been. About a hundred people had discovered the location of their limousine on Pearl Street behind the theater and began applauding when Bea and Bobby appeared. They signed dozens of autographs, accepted more gifts and flowers, and after half an hour, succeeded in getting into the car and heading for the airport.

"Weren't they wonderful?" Bea said. "And I love that theater, although the dressing rooms left a little something to be desired."

"On to London. Isn't it clever how Howard managed not to give us the extra time here, after all that bunk about days to rest up."

"We have a whole week in London."

"That's what you think. I'll bet my life he's got plans for our free week. Knowing Howard, he's lined up the crew and everything else; the everything else being a raft of interviews and all kinds of personal appearances."

"Mel's promised to keep a day free."

He bit back the remark that sprang to his mind, saying instead,

"That'll give me a chance to go to Turnbull & Asser for some shirts and see about a few new suits."

"I swear to God you're more interested in clothes than any woman I've ever known. You always have been. I remember you spending every last cent on clothes way back when in New York."

"I like good clothes. What's wrong with that?"

"Nothing. Just an observation. I find it harder every year to have any interest at all in what I wear."

"Hah! Lack of interest is what you call the Chanel outfits, and the Dior, and the Givenchy, and the rest of those size-six numbers? You've got plenty of interest, sister."

"I really don't."

"Yeah. Well, we'll talk about this again after Paris."

"You can't expect me to be in Paris and *not* shop!"

"I rest my case. Two more of these 'evenings' and then I'll never answer another question as long as I live. I'd make book that these people study up for weeks in advance."

"I couldn't believe it when the man tonight asked about *Moonlight*. For one awful moment, I thought he knew something. Then I realized the accident was in all the papers, and the picture had to have been mentioned somewhere along the line. But it really threw me. I couldn't think what to say. I was so glad you took that one. I went numb."

"You were just fine." He patted her hand.

"I was afraid, Bobby. So silly, but for that one moment, I actually was. Here it is all these years later, and just the thought of that night makes me afraid."

"Don't you worry, kid. Big Bob's here to look after you."

"Big Bob?" she guffawed.

"Little Bob?"

"No, I adore it. Big Bob. It's heaven."

Melinda came along to the Ritz to have breakfast with them. Bobby did his best to be friendly, to keep the conversation moving, but Melinda scarcely glanced at him. He excused himself and went off to Savile Row. Bea poured more coffee while Melinda lit a cigarette, and Bea casually observed, "You smoke quite a lot, Mel. Don't you feel awful when you wake up in the morning?"

"I feel simply splendid when I wake up in the morning," she replied tartly.

"Well, good. As long as you do."

"What's this in aid of?" Melinda wanted to know. "Are you giving me subtle hints now about my cigarette-smoking?"

"Not at all. I simply noticed you're smoking a lot."

"And naturally now that you no longer smoke yourself, you take note of those of us who do."

"No. As a matter of fact, I like having smokers around. I enjoy the smell of tobacco. I still want one, every so often. I thought we could go up Bond Street," Bea changed the topic. "Or we could start at Oxford Street and walk down. There's a shop in the Burlington Arcade that has lovely cashmere sweaters, and I thought I might get one or two for Bobby."

"Clever exit he managed, I thought. Very subtle."

"What're you talking about?"

"All that chat about leaving the two of us on our own. He's always disliked me. I'd have respected him a good deal more if he'd simply left, without going through that farcical routine."

"He's been planning for weeks to see his tailor today. Have you any idea how paranoid you sound?"

"Now, I'm paranoid. I smoke too much, and I'm paranoid."

Bea could feel her ears getting hot but was determined not to be pulled into an argument. Why, instead of growing more mellow with age, did Melinda seem to become narrower, and tighter, and more argumentative? "It's a lovely morning," she said, "and I've had enough coffee. I'll get my bag, and we can go." She moved to get up.

"Why is it you've always got everything planned to the last detail? Every time you come over here, you've got time allotted and plans made for where we'll go and what we'll do. Why is nothing ever spontaneous?"

Bea sat back down. "Have you got something in mind?" she asked. "I'm perfectly willing to change my plans, such as they are. What would you prefer, Mel? What would please you?"

"Now you're being sarcastic."

"I'm being nothing of the sort. Tell me what you'd like to do and we'll do it."

"I don't *have* my life planned down to the last minute the way you do. I don't *know* what I want to do."

"Have you any objection to going for a walk along Bond Street?"

"Not in particular. What I do object to is the proprietorial stance you take toward me. It's been this way from the start. You've got everything planned, from where we'll go to how I'm expected to behave with you. I'm sick of it. And I'm fed up with your bloody paramour leaving rooms the minute I enter them. I'm fed up with being expected to drop everything because you're arriving and you want to walk on bloody Bond Street and go to the Burlington Arcade to buy cashmere bloody sweaters for that patronizing, fatuous fool you're so besotted with."

With every word Melinda spoke, the blood pounded louder in Bea's eardrums. Her vision seemed to become clouded by a film of red that descended over her eyes. Her heart rate quickened, her hands clenched, and when Melinda finished her tirade, Bea let go. "You've got some hell of a *nerve*, talking about Bobby that way! On your longest day, you'll never have a *fraction* of his kindness, or generosity, or sensitivity. You came here this morning determined to be unpleasant. It didn't matter what I did, did it? Because you were going to have your say. It could've been anything. Right? I could've talked about going to the zoo, or mentioned the weather, anything. You came for a fight. Well, okay, miss! You're going to get one!" Bea jumped up so quickly her chair toppled backward. "I'll tell *you* what I'*m* fed up with! I'm sick of being judged for every goddamned thing I say, do, or think. I'm sick of having you set yourself up as the virtuous child who can do no wrong. You're a vicious, cold, self-centered bitch, and you've been this way for so long I've almost managed to get used to it. I don't *like* you! I haven't liked you since you were about six years old. I don't know where you got it from, certainly not from your father, and not from me, but you're selfish, sneaky, and arrogant. *My God!* I've never *known* anyone more arrogant! What did you think, Melinda? Did you think I'd just go on taking this shit from you indefinitely? Did you think I was so stupid you could keep piling it on and I'd be too dumb to notice? I notice! *And you go too goddamned far when you dare to talk that way about Bobby!*" She was so enraged, it was either hit Melinda or hit something else, so she threw out her arm and swept everything off the table. Pleased to see the gesture alarmed Melinda, she pushed over the table too. "Here's more ammunition! You can go back and tell Nancy and whoever else you hang around with these days that your crazy mother wrecked a hotel room. You can go back and do whatever the hell you want because I don't give a shit anymore *what* you do! It appalls to think I could've given birth to someone who'd turn out like you. And if you don't get out of my sight right now you're in danger of being hit by me. Maybe I should've hit you years ago, when it might've done some good. It's obviously too late now. *Get the hell out!* GO ON! GET OUT OF MY SIGHT!"

Looking truly frightened, Melinda backed up several steps, saying, "This won't win you any awards."

"GET OUT!"

Melinda turned and ran awkwardly to the door.

"DON'T COME ANYWHERE NEAR ME EVER AGAIN! THE SIGHT OF YOU

MAKES ME SICK!" Bea picked up an ashtray from the table and threw it against the door just as it closed. She stood, panting, hearing the echo of her shouts inside her head. Finally, she turned to look at the mess and stared at that for a time, before going to the telephone to call housekeeping.

"I'm afraid we've had an accident up here. Please have someone come to clean it up."

Her next call was to room service to ask them to send up a bottle and a package of cigarettes.

When Bobby arrived back, hours head of schedule, he found her sitting on the sofa, smoking a cigarette and holding a glass of neat scotch balanced on her knee.

"What're you doing back so soon?" she asked.

"What're you doing here at all? And why are you smoking?"

"Smoking and drinking." She held up the glass for him to see.

"You're sloshed, and you've had"—he counted the butts in the ashtray—"eight cigarettes. What happened?"

"I'm sloshed from the cigarettes. I've only had two drinks. This is my second."

"Where's Melinda?" He looked around.

"Melinda," she said carefully, "is gone. I threw Melinda out. We will not be seeing her again for quite some time. If ever. Probably never."

He dropped down beside her on the sofa, took the glass from her hand, drank half the remaining scotch, then gave it back to her. "I ordered my shirts and was about to go the tailor, but I had a hunch, so I decided to come back. Please don't smoke any more. It really makes me feel bad to see you smoking again." He held out the ashtray. "Please?"

Making a face, she stubbed out the cigarette and made no comment when he pocketed the package. "Okay," he said. "Are you going to tell me what happened?"

She shook her head, finished the drink, and put the glass down on the coffee table.

He watched her closely, imagining any number of things Melinda might have done. This must've been something big for Bea to throw her out. She removed her hand at last from the glass and flung herself against him, the control she'd been exercising for the past two hours gone. Trembling, she held on hard to him as she repeated what had gone on. In a breathless, reedy whisper, she got it all out, then clung to him, saying, "Hold me, hold me. This is terrible. I can't stand to feel this way. Bobby, I don't want to be here. We've got to leave.

Please talk to Howard, tell him I'm ill, anything, but I've got to get out of here now, right away. Please, will you?"

"You want to cancel out on the festival?"

"I've got to get out of here. I couldn't face people, those questions."

"Okay, Bea. Okay. I'll take care of it." If she had shed tears, he wouldn't have been as concerned as he was. But she didn't. She was dry-eyed. It was the tremors that frightened him. She shook so fiercely, held on to him with such desperation, that he was afraid to let go of her. So he kept his arms around her, and said, "Don't worry. I'll take care of everything. Don't worry." All the while he was filled with near-murderous anger at what Melinda had done. He thought if he ever did see her again, he just might kill her.

Forty-Nine

THEY flew directly back to New York, where Albert was waiting to drive them to Greenwich. Exhausted and silent, Bea went upstairs to undress, allowing her clothes to fall to the floor. She got into bed, pulled the blankets around her, and lay wide awake with her eyes closed, trying to get warm. She could hear Bobby downstairs talking to Gertie and Al, then his muffled footsteps on the stairs and along the hallway. He turned on the lights and automatically began to pick up her clothes.

"I'll run a bath for you," he told her after hanging up the clothes. "Gert's making coffee. How d'you feel?"

"Old, cold, and tired."

"Back in a minute." He went to start the tub filling then came back to sit beside her. "You okay?"

"I'm okay, glad to be home. You don't really mind about canceling out, do you?"

"Nope. I was getting tired of the whole thing anyway."

"I'll come to San Francisco with you for your picture."

"You will, huh?" He smiled.

"And then you can come to Boston with me to do mine."

"You sure you want to sit around all day, cooling your heels, while I do it? You know how goddamned boring it is, waiting for set-ups."

"We'll play gin rummy," she said. "It'll be fine."

"What's the picture in Boston? You've been holding out on me."

"The script's in the drawer there. You can read it, if you like. I figure you can play an old con man, I can play an old hooker. What the fuck!"

"Beatrice Crane! I can't believe my ears!"

"Want me to repeat it?"

"You trying to kill me?"

"The tub's going to overflow." She pushed back the bedclothes and went into the bathroom.

He found the script and carried it into the bathroom, pulling off his tie as he looked at the title page. "*Nightlife?* You really are going to play a hooker?"

"Ex," she said. "It's a terrific part. Oh, God! I need this." She slid down until her chin was resting in the water. "I never want to go through another twenty-four hours like this again. Want a plot break-down?"

"Sure. But I don't want to steam the suit. Give me five minutes." When he came back, he sat down on the floor with his back to the wall, and said, "Okay. Give it to me."

"Here it is: Boston ex-call girl, hasn't been in the business for years, got wise, got lucky, saved her money. She's got this long-term thing with this cop who's craggy and shaggy and wise. Lots of nice, biting dialogue. They're a couple of old-time toughies. She's got this homey, middle-range restaurant. Nice, but not Lutèce. Anyway, she closes up one night and goes out the back door to her car, and blow me down if there isn't a dead body parked in it. Face shot off. She gets kind of rattled—you know how it is when you open your car and there's a body in it, a little upsetting—so she goes back inside to call her chum. He comes along with a bunch of the boys and a meat wagon, and they cart this stiff off to the morgue. The stiff turns out to be a big hot-shot doctor, and the mystery is: what's he doing dead, with no face, in her car? There are all kinds of nifty twists and turns while they try to track down the murderer. We get some more dead people, and one way or another they make the connection that all these guys are former clients of hers, and some psycho's knocking them off. Maybe she's next. We've got some swell backflashes as each of the bodies turns up and she makes the mental connection. I get to sleaze around in some lurid lingerie, and the cop saves my ass from this psychopathic former hooker chum of mine who wants revenge because when I went straight I gave her my john book and one of the johns turned out to be her father. And he was the doctor parked in my car back in reel one. End of story."

"This I've got to see. Lurid lingerie?"

"Well, obviously they're not going to have me running around in a bra and panties with my Wonder Bread flesh hanging out, not to mention a fair amount of scar tissue. It's a great part, actually. She's never been married, she's got this rotten past, and a decent present. And the two of them together, her and the cop, are great." She sat up a little. "I'm starting to feel better. Thank God for work."

"I can't wait to get to Boston. Little Bea as a reformed hooker."

"The thing is, she's not the heart-of-gold type or the type with the 'dark secret' in her past. She's just tough, and straight, and what she is: a restaurant owner who used to screw men for a living."

"You really think you can do that?"

"Yes, I do. And I will."

From the bedroom, Gertie called, "Coffee's in 'ere, Miss C."

"Thanks, Gert." Bobby pushed up from the floor, walked over to the tub, and bent down to give Bea a kiss. "Perhaps we could do a little research when you're feeling up to it."

"I was hoping you'd offer. I shouldn't have smoked those cigarettes. My throat's sore. They tasted wonderful, though. I'm okay now," she said softly. "Thank you for bringing me home."

He dropped down on his heels, folding his arms on the rim of the tub. "You scared me, Bea. I've never seen you like that."

She looked away. "I've never *felt* like that. Remember what I told you about the pain that time? How the previous worst pain was the yardstick? I never thought anything could hurt the way today did." She looked back at him. "I don't want to think about it or talk about it. Will you bring me some coffee?"

"Yup. Any idea what you'd like to do for the six weeks we've got to kill?"

"Let's get estimates and put the goddamned pool in. We discuss it every year and never do it. Let's finally do it."

"But we'll be gone the whole summer."

"So we'll use it next summer. But at last it'll be there, and we can stop talking about it."

"Okay, whatever you say."

"Let's just stay here until it's time to go California. Okay?"

"Okay."

533

Nightlife earned her another Academy Award. Since she was on location at the time of the Awards ceremony, and since she didn't believe for a moment that she'd have the remotest chance of winning, she watched the show on television in her motel room in Tacoma, with Bobby beside her. Both of them were stunned speechless when she was announced the winner, and the film's producer went up to accept on her behalf. It was seven months before she succeeded in getting the statuette away from the producer who was reluctant to part with the added prestige he felt it lent to his office. In the end, she had to go to New York, barge into his office in the middle of a meeting, snatch it off his desk, and walk out with it, leaving in her wake half a dozen slack-jawed businessmen, and one producer she'd crossed off her list.

After the stint in Tacoma, she and Bobby took a year off. They met up with Lucy and Brian in Zurich and traveled with them down to Italy where they chartered a yacht and cruised the Mediterranean for six weeks before disembarking in Athens. Lucy and Brian returned to London. Bea said, "Let's go home," and they made a connection from Athens to Paris and another from Paris to New York.

"I think that's it for me," Bea said, and resumed reading scripts.

There was no shortage of offers, and Bea would only accept one if the timetable suited Bobby. She turned down a number of scripts in order to be in the studio with him when he recorded a double album of all the songs from their six films. It was a sentimental project, and the album sold surprisingly well, especially when he agreed to autograph copies in a Manhattan record store. People lined up for blocks to buy the record and have a chance to say hello.

With time, Bobby came to notice that when Bea referred to Melinda, which she did infrequently, she talked about Melinda as she'd been as a small child and not as the woman she'd become. It seemed as if, in this way, she could still have the child, but without the painful associations. And since Bobby had been very fond of the little girl Melinda had been once upon a time, he found he could accept and respond to Bea's recollections with honest pleasure.

Life had settled. They were together either at the Park Avenue apartment or at the house in Greenwich. They took days apart but rarely an entire week; they spoke every day on the telephone when not together, and made all their plans jointly. They socialized with old friends wherever they happened to be and exchanged visits with Lucy and Brian regularly, and always at Christmas. It seemed as if they would simply continue to move forward at the same pace—

which was alternately overly busy with preparations for some picture one or the other of them was about to do or pleasantly uneventful with long afternoons out by the pool in summer, and evenings reading, or playing Scrabble, or just talking in front of the fire in the winter.

It was during one of those three-day separations, when Bea was getting caught up on correspondence with Ellen and reading scripts in-between time, that Bobby had a call from Becky.

"We have to go see Bea," she said straight off. "I've ordered a car, and I'll be over inside the hour to pick you up. I'll explain everything on the way up there."

"What's happened?"

"It's about Melinda."

"What *about* her? Don't do this, Becky! I can't stand mysteries and drama."

"She's written a book. It's about Bea. I'm on my way. That's my buzzer. I'll be at your place in fifteen minutes."

By the time they arrived in Greenwich, Bobby felt ill. "I don't know how to tell her. This'll *kill* her."

"I'll wait out here. I know I'm probably the last person she'd want to see."

"Don't be too sure of that." He threw open the limo door and burst into the house, startling Gertie who had the vacuum cleaner going and leaped back with a cry at the sight of him. "Where's Bea?" he asked her.

"Miss C.'s upstairs with Ellen, doin' dictation."

"Thanks."

He took the stairs three at a time, raced down the hall and slid to a stop in the doorway, saying, "Ellen, please go have some coffee or something. I have to talk to Bea."

Ellen put down her steno pad and pencil and, staring at Bobby as if he were deranged, left the room, closing the door behind her.

"What's going on?" Bea asked.

He just stood there, not sure how to do this.

"Bobby! Has something happened?"

"Yeah, something's happened. I think we'd better sit down. Jesus! You'd better. I don't know if I can. Sit down, okay?"

"Who died?" she asked fearfully.

"Nobody. Nobody died. I'm sorry. I didn't mean to scare you. Bea, listen. There's a book. It's about you."

"Oh, for God's sake." She laughed. "There's half a dozen of them: films of Beatrice Crane, a biography in pictures, on and on."

"This isn't a photo book. It's a *book*."

"God! I *knew* she'd do it someday. It's Becky, isn't it? She's finally done it."

"Jesus Christ, *no!* It isn't Becky. It's *Mel*. Becky's the one who told me about it. She's downstairs in the car. She found out about it a few days ago."

"Mel's written a book about me?"

"Bea, I'm sorry. Let me get Becky in here. She can tell you about it."

"Mel? Why would she write a book about me? This doesn't make sense. Yes, maybe you should get Becky. I might as well have all my shocks at once."

"Listen to me." He went over and took hold of her by the shoulders. "You've both been total shmucks for years, and yet the two of you are better friends than any other two people I can name. It's time to stop all that now. I'm going down to get her, and you'll talk."

"I'll come down. I can't talk in here."

"Okay. Whatever." He let go of her, raced down the stairs and out to the car. "Come on!" he told Becky. "You've got to tell her this. I'm making a hash of it. I'm no good at stuff like this. *Come on!*"

Bea stood near the fireplace trying to guess at what she was about to hear. She was so overcome by dread, and by snippets of information about her life all jamming together like little blocks in her brain, that she could only observe for the moment the things going on—Bobby opening the front door, Becky hesitantly stepping inside and glancing around—and perform by rote with politeness hastily applied to the surface of her apprehensiveness like a piece of Scotch tape intended to hold together the lips of a gaping wound.

"Please come in, Becky," she said, oddly aware of the workings of her throat, tongue, and mouth to produce these sounds. "Would you like some coffee, or a drink?"

Becky shook her head, coming to a stop at the opposite end of the room, some thirty feet away. It was there, as always, the extraordinary energy emanating from the small figure in the gray dress and low-heeled black shoes.

"Sit down, Becky," Bobby said. "I'm going to get a glass of milk. My stomach's upset. D'you want anything?" he asked Bea, who shook her head, unconsciously duplicating Becky's gesture.

"Please sit down," Bea repeated Bobby's invitation.

"This isn't how I thought it might be," Becky said, choosing to sit in one of the wing chairs by the window. "When I projected images of our reunion, this wasn't one of them."

"No, I know," Bea agreed, openly studying her old friend and the way the late-afternoon sun set fire to a portion of Becky's hair and

536

softened the effects of age on the half of her face that was turned to the light. Becky wore her familiar uniform of faded jeans and Shetland pullover atop a button-down-collared shirt.

Bobby returned with his glass of milk and stood, trying to figure out the geometry the women had attained in the way they'd chosen to place themselves. Bea remained by the fireplace, her stance reminding him of her posture in the immediate aftermath of the accident when she'd had to lean slightly backward for balance, her hips thrusting forward. "Are we just going to stand around?" he asked, on very uncertain ground. "Could we at least sit down?"

Bea withdrew her gaze from Becky and turned it now on him. All her actions and reactions seemed fractionally delayed, as if something was impeding the flow of information to her brain. She looked at him, then went to sit on the sofa, keeping distance between herself and Becky. To offset this, he took the other wing chair by the windows, as Becky opened her handbag and took out several folded sheets of paper.

"I heard about it five or six weeks ago, through a friend of mine. The book's scheduled for February '76."

"That's five months from now," Bea said unnecessarily.

Becky nodded. "As soon as I heard, I started asking around. My editor at the house that reprints my stuff in paperback put me on to a sub-rights woman who'd been offered the reprint. Luckily, I know Liza; we've had lots of contact over the years. And she was about to go over to Crompton's to read the galleys in house. Crompton's," she explained, "isn't letting the galleys out of the office. They're being kept in the safe there, and the people who're interested in the reprint have to go read the galleys on the premises. So, she promised she'd report back to me as soon as she'd been there, and I made these notes"—she lifted the pages to show Bea—"when she called. It's very bad, Bea," she apologized. "Liza turned down the book. So far as she knows, nobody's offered on it yet, but word is there's going to be an auction. Crompton's is going out very big. A hundred thousand first printing, a big ad budget, and they're setting up an author tour."

"You mean Mel's going to publicize this book?" Bobby asked.

"Uh-huh. National television, print, the whole thing. I think you should know what she's going to be saying," she addressed herself to Bea. "I have to tell you, she hasn't left anything out."

"Excuse me." Bea got up and walked in her old hipshot fashion out of the room, returning a few minutes later with a package of Al's cigarettes, some matches, and an ashtray. "Don't say *one word* to me!" she warned Bobby, tearing off the cellophane and then lighting a cigarette. "Okay," she said to Becky. "Tell me."

"Bea, she's written about things . . . I've been hoping maybe a lot of it isn't true, and you could get your lawyer to try to halt publication. I did ask Liza if that was possible, and it's Liza's opinion that Crompton's legal staff has been very careful to make sure no one living's been slandered. I don't know. Anyway." She cleared her throat, and referred to her notes. "She starts with your being illegitimate, the daughter of a woman just a notch above a prostitute. She tells how you went off to New York with Lucy, and hints around about Lucy's morals, but stays just this side of coming right out and smearing her. She covers how you lied about your age. She has all kinds of stuff about you and Bobby, and an abortion. There's this big, long thing, complete with newspaper clippings, about the accident and Dickie DeVore, how he beat and raped you and accidentally got killed trying to kill you, and how the studio police and Ludie Meyers covered the whole thing up." She stopped to look at Bea who'd gone white. Lowering her eyes, she went back to her notes. "There's tons about Hank and his being homosexual and his long-term affair with Hero; speculation about why the two of you got married. There are quotes from all kinds of people—I can only think she interviewed them under false pretenses—including Molly and Mrs. Pepper in London. Then there's the second abortion, and studio memos from Ludie's files about the deals you and Hank made to do *Jeannie*. It goes on and on. The part that's incredible, according to Liza, is how she lays out evidence intimating Bobby's her father, and not Hank."

Bobby jumped up, livid. *"What?* Jesus Christ! You can't be serious! Surely to God, my lawyer can do something about that!"

"Maybe," Becky said quietly. "You'll have to discuss it with him, *if* he can find some way to get hold of the galleys. There's more," she said miserably, looking from Bobby to Bea. "Do you want to hear the rest of it?"

"Go on," Bea said, her voice flat and deep.

"It's one long diatribe against you. She sets out to show you 'as you really are' which is: insincere, ruthless, determined everybody, and especially her, will perform to your specifications. You're always 'on,' and everything in your life is an act, from your holding court in the bathtub, to your faked candor at the festivals. You and Bobby, according to the book, have been sneaking around screwing each other everywhere and anywhere since you were kids. You had all kinds of plastic surgery for reasons of vanity, and you'd do anything short of murder to maintain your stature and your image for the public. Liza says Mel has set herself up as an archetype, the child who suffers all her life because of her mother's death grip on stardom. Liza also says Mel has made herself a goddess of household virtues and goes to incredible lengths to prove how significant that is, in view of *your* inability to cook, or clean, or even iron a hankie. Liza said she was appalled that Crompton's would even consider publishing the book, but that clearly they were doing it for the money, and so was Mel. She got sixty-five thousand for the hardcover rights." Becky paused, wet her lips, then said, "That's everything I've got. I'm sorry. I can't *tell* you how sorry I am. Perhaps your lawyers can get an injunction, stop publication. I don't know."

Bea was on her second cigarette. Her small, tense, figure seemed ghostlike, with the sun holding the smoke in the air all around her. Bobby was tempted to have a cigarette himself, or a drink, or something. He felt like screaming and, he reasoned, if he felt that way, God only knew what Bea was feeling. Both he and Becky sat, waiting for her to react, but Bea continued to pay attenton only to her cigarette, drawing the smoke deep into her lungs and holding it there for a very long time before it began to coil lazily from her nostrils. At last, after perhaps five minutes, when the cigarette was burned down, she said, "I'd like to talk alone with Becky. We'll go for a walk. I'll get my coat. Please stay, Bobby."

Becky got up, pulled on her sheepskin jacket, and followed Bea to the foyer, where she grabbed her mink coat, shrugged it on, then opened the front door and waited for Becky to precede her.

"We won't be long," Bea told Bobby, then went out.

They walked without speaking past the waiting limousine and down the long driveway toward Round Hill Road. "We'd better cross and walk against the oncoming traffic," Bea said, and they went to the far side of the road. Her hands shoved deep into her pockets, her eyes on the road, Bea at last began to talk. "You took quite a chance, coming here," she said.

"I know. But I was willing to have you kill the messenger. I believe it's your right to know. I tried everything I could think of to get a copy of it for you, but it's impossible. If it means anything, I don't think people're going to believe any of it. Oh, maybe the background stuff, but not that you're the way she depicts you. It's just so unbelievable that she'd do this. It's too cruel."

"I don't want to believe it, but I do. What I can't understand is how she found out those things, and why she'd want to use them against me. It's all true, Becky. All those things did happen, just not, probably, the way she says they did. We haven't seen each other in six years now. She sends polite, impersonal Christmas cards every year, and the occasional postcard. How is your daughter?" she asked out of the blue. "I thought she was so lovely that night when she came backstage with Lucy."

"She's great. She's got a good supporting role in the picture she's doing now. I feel awkward talking to you about Bones," she admitted. "I feel guilty discussing her with you because the two of us are close."

"Don't feel that way. I'm glad for you. I hoped for years and years Mel and I might come to have some of that. I'm sure you're a wonderful mother."

"So were you!" Becky cried angrily. "I know what I saw with my own eyes. You worked just as hard at being that monster's mother as you did at everything else you've ever done. This is so fucking unfair! I've never felt so frustrated in my life, because there's nothing I can do to help you, or to stop this, or to make it better. Nobody can really do that for you. I tried to imagine how I'd feel, if it were me, and it hurt so much just trying to imagine it . . . I had to stop. What will you do?"

"I don't know. I'm going to have to think about it very carefully. I feel . . . I feel *murdered*." She lifted her head, looking straight down the road before them. "She's taking my private life, she's taking me, and eviscerating me in print. I feel naked. I don't want to believe this is actually happening, but I do. I believe it. But I don't understand *why*. Mel doesn't need the money. Her father left her half of everything; she got the balance when she was twenty-five. She probably has a lot more now than I do. She doesn't have a house to maintain, or the expenses . . . I'm looking for all the wrong reasons. None of this has to do with money. It has to do with Mel, and her anger. And I don't know why she's angry, or what it's really about."

She stopped and looked up and down the road, then crossed to the far side, turning back in the direction they'd come.

"I think it has to do with talent," Becky said, "and the fact that everyone in the family had it, everyone all around you had it, except for Mel. And nothing she did could measure up, not against you."

"We're not supposed to be people? We're not supposed to have private lives and give birth to children? Is that it? We're supposed to be stars and nothing else? Jesus Christ, Becky! All my life, I've refused to buy that package. You know that! You know I've never subscribed to *any* of it, beyond what had to be done."

"Of course I know. And so do an awful lot of other people. There's going to be one hell of a fuss when that book comes out."

"But it won't matter. Don't you see? People will buy it because it's about me. What's she calling it, anyway?"

"Private Lies."

"Christ! Catchy," Bea said caustically.

When they got back to the house, they stopped a few feet away from the limo, and Bea turned to look at Becky. "I've missed you

540

more than you'll ever know. Over the years, I've had so many conversations with you in my head, thinking of the things we'd say to each other, how we'd laugh at what a complete idiot I was that day, to get so upset and storm out the way I did. I've loved you since we were kids, Becky. You were my only friend, the only one who didn't laugh when I made up those crazy stories and danced on the front walk. I was wrong. In the end, I felt so goddamned ashamed I didn't know how to set it right. Please come back into my life. I need you."

They embraced and held on, then Bea pulled slowly away.

"I have to be with Bobby now. You understand?"

"Of course."

"But you'll come back?"

"I've missed you, too. We were both wrong. I'll keep trying. Maybe somehow I can get you a set of the galleys." Becky opened the rear door of the limo. "Please, don't let this defeat you. *Please* don't let that happen. You're too valuable, and too important to too many people." When Bea didn't answer, Becky said, "I'll call you tomorrow. I love you, Bea."

"Me, too." Bea stood with her hands still in her pockets and watched the car reverse and drive off.

Bobby heard the door open and got up to go to the foyer, watching while Bea hung up her coat. She closed the closet door, then turned and walked into his arms. "It's like another death in the family," she said thickly. "Only this time, it's mine. It's obscene, but all I want is to make love to you, the way I did after Hank died. It's all I can think of, to have you hold me and tell me lies, tell me everything'll be all right."

"Come on." He took her hand. "Let's go upstairs. Maybe it's obscene, but I feel exactly the same way. I want to have you next to me."

She started to cry and kept on until it was over. She wept and clung to him as if his body might save her from quicksand. In the end, the pain seemed to travel out through her limbs, through her skin, and seep into him, and he cried with her, while he tried to convince both of them it would be all right.

Fifty

SHE couldn't get away from the book. It was everywhere, in some form or another. A big ad in the *New York Times Book Review*, cover stories in national magazines, reviews she refused to read, dozens of telephone calls from reporters and journalists asking for comment, for interviews. It was no longer safe for Bea to pick up the telephone, so Ellen took to screening every call. Lucy telephoned from London, to tell her about the afternoon she'd found Melinda going through Bea's private papers, and apologized guiltily and at great length, claiming a major portion of responsibility for the disclosures in the book. Bea absolved her, as she did Bobby, when he admitted his thinking on the connection between Melinda's last-minute refusal to join them for dinner one evening some years earlier and the disturbed contents of his trunk.

"I've kept all the letters you've ever written me," he confessed. "I know you asked me not to, but I had to keep them."

"It's all right, Bobby. I kept yours, too. Obviously, she read everything she could get her hands on. We all trusted her. I certainly never dreamed she was capable of something like this. The other night, I got every paper out of my desk, thinking I should put them somewhere safe. Then I realized there'd be no point. It's all been made public."

"What're you going to do?" he asked, not for the first time.

"Ellen was in the shower this morning, and Gertie had gone into town with Al to do the marketing, and the goddamned phone kept ringing and ringing, and finally I couldn't stand listening to it anymore, so I answered. And naturally, it was a stringer for the AP. Had I read my daughter's book, and would I care to comment on it. I said, 'What daughter? What book? If Henry Donovan wasn't her father, how could *I* possibly be her mother?' He said, 'That's great! Great!

542

Anything more?' and I said something unprintable and hung up with such a crash his head must still be aching."

"Jesus!" Bobby whistled appreciatively.

"I hung up and tried to get back to my exercises, and while I was working out, I started getting very, very angry, just the way I did that morning at the Ritz when I started heaving the furniture around. Bobby, I was so goddamned mad! I've been going around here for months feeling so *guilty*; going backward and forward, looking for the things I did wrong, searching for reasons why this is happening. It's all I've done, even in my sleep, for God's sake! Looking at every last little thing, digging around trying to come up with answers. And suddenly, I thought, why the hell am I feeling so guilty? I've never done anything but love Mel and try to get through to her. I did my best, so why do I feel like a criminal? Yes, I made lots of mistakes with her, and maybe I was too indulgent, and maybe I couldn't see her in any kind of accurate light, but whatever I did, it was with the best intentions in the world. I did my best, Bobby. I really did."

"Of course, you did," he agreed. "I was there. I should know."

"So, I got angry, good and goddamned angry. Why should I feel guilty, or ashamed, because she has—at least according to you—told the entire world that I did a number of things when I was young that she doesn't approve of? I'm not ashamed of any of it. I'm really not. Some of it wasn't my fault, and a lot of it was my choice. But I'll be *damned* if I'm going to spend the rest of my life hiding out here like some kind of criminal because of Mel."

"Damn right!" he agreed again.

"So when Ellen came in to say somebody from CBS was on the phone, and would I be willing to do an interview for 'Sixty Minutes,' I said, okay. Why the hell not? I might as well answer the goddamned questions once and for all, and maybe we can get on with our lives."

"You're going to give them an interview?"

"At least it's a responsible show, not like some of the others that've called. And they have an enormous audience. I might as well go public with the biggest possible exposure." She paused, then asked him, "Do you think I'm wrong not to read the book?"

"*No!* Listen to me, and listen good! I've known you most of my life, and there were moments when I was reading that thing when I wasn't so sure I knew *any* of the people she wrote about, let alone you. No, you *don't* want to *read* it!"

"I've been so paralyzed; unable to think, unable to *do* anything. I kept feeling I wanted to be somewhere else, somewhere far away from this whole horrible mess, but I just couldn't move, and I couldn't think of anywhere to go. People have been hounding me day and

543

night. The phone still won't quit, and I'd like to know how in the hell, suddenly, everybody's got my number."

"Come stay in the city with me."

"They'd only call there. You and I are now common knowledge. It's bad enough they won't let up on me. I'm not about to inflict this three-ring circus on you."

"Hey! I'm a part of this, you know. Let *me* worry about whether or not I want to have it inflicted on me."

She gave him a kiss and said, "Bless you. I know you feel that way, but I'd prefer you to retain whatever privacy you've got left. And by the way, if you'd like to see the afternoon papers, you'll find the stringer managed to make an item out of my fifteen-second outburst. He put it on the wire, and it's probably in every paper in the country."

"Should I look at it, or will it just piss me off?"

"Oh, look at it, by all means. I did. I actually laughed for the first time in months. It felt wonderful. Go on, have a look. It's in the entertainment section." She watched him read the brief piece, then said, "Short, but to the point, wouldn't you say?"

"Says it all. 'What book? What daughter?' D'you really mean that, Bea?"

"I mean it. She may be trying to kill me off in print, but as far as I'm concerned, I'm always going to love her but I never want to see her again. About the CBS thing, they want it fast so they can get it to air right away."

"When?" he asked.

"Day after tomorrow. Will you be here, please?"

"If you want me to, sure."

"I've asked Becky to come stay, too. Bones might come with her. And Lucy said if I'd let her know as soon as I find out the air date, they'll fly over and we'll make a bash out of seeing the edited interview."

"Sounds good."

"It's going to be a tough one, Bobby. They're going to ask some very tough questions."

"They always do."

"My only defense is to tell the truth. People know when they're hearing the truth. They do, don't you think?"

The evening before the interview, Ellen took a call, then covered the mouthpiece to say, "Elizabeth Hansen?"

"I'll take that. I'll pick it up in the bedroom."

Bea said hello, and Elizabeth said, "Bea, I don't know how to tell you how I feel about what's happened. I haven't slept for nights, thinking about you. I've been afraid to call because . . . How are you?"

"I'm alive."

"There's something I want to say to you, and maybe it's not what you want to hear. I don't know. But I just have to say it anyway. I'm forty-two years old, and probably the last thing in the world you want or need is somebody calling up, getting all emotional; but I've loved you all my life, Bea. You've always been the one for me; you stood up for me; and every good thing that's happened in my life has been because of you. And because I love you, Lindy does, too. So what I'm trying to say is, maybe you didn't actually have me, but I've always felt like I was yours. And Lindy wanted me to tell you she'd love to be your honorary grandchild. Please, could we come to see you?"

Bea couldn't answer for a moment. Then she said, "Elizabeth, I've always loved you, too. Yes, come. I have to go now, but yes, come see me." Bea put down the receiver, then stood concentrating on her breathing.

Bea was nervous while the crew set the lights, and wires turned the living room into an obstacle course. The pair of wing chairs by the windows where they'd sit for the taping, the room itself, had taken on the look of a set. The sound man fussed with his equipment, checking and rechecking his tapes, his batteries. She stood for a few minutes looking into the room and finally decided she had to have some fortification. Bobby and Becky were in the kitchen with Gertie and Al. They had already given interviews—Bobby's had taken place outside; he'd tramped through the snowed-over garden while a hand-held camera had followed; Becky had spoken her piece in the kitchen, at the table, with a cup of coffee in front of her.

Gertie was busy setting cups and saucers on a tray while Al prepared a large pot of coffee. Promising to buy Al a carton of cigarettes when this was over, Bea took a pack from his supply in the cabinet above the stove, then had to defend herself to Bobby.

"I can't do it without smoking. Let me just get through this, and then I'll go back on the nicotine wagon."

"Are you sure about this?" he asked, drawing her into the den to talk privately.

"I am, yes. Is my make-up all right, or do I need a touch-up?"

"It's fine. Talk to me for a minute. It's not too late to call it off, you know. You don't have to bare your soul to the public."

She looked a little surprised. "I'm not going to bare my soul, Bobby.

545

I'm just going to answer some questions and show everybody that I'm not afraid, that I have nothing to hide. That's all. If I don't like the questions, I won't answer them. Don't look that way!" She put her hand on his face. "Nothing's going to happen that I can't handle. I'm a big, grown-up lady. I've had interviews before."

"You're a small, grown-up lady. And you've refused for years to give TV interviews."

"This is different. My honor and integrity are on the line. I'm not going to argue my case against the book. I couldn't, anyway, since I've no intention of reading it. I'm going to answer the questions once and for good and try to defuse the situation. I want to feel free to go out again, Bobby. If I don't do this, it'll seem as if I really do have things to hide. And I don't believe I do. Those things we thought so shocking thirty years ago are things nobody cares about now. So why not just get it all said?"

He linked his hands together around her waist, and looked at her, taking his time to study her face. "Christ, but we've been through it all, haven't we?"

"I can't think of a thing we've missed." She gave him a smile. "You know something?"

"What?"

"You learned how to fight, Bobby. It happened so gradually, I guess, that it's taken me a very long time to see it. You've turned into an honest-to-god world heavyweight champion."

"Couldn't stay in the ring with you unless I learned," he said off-handedly.

"We were too young. I wanted too much."

"No, you didn't," he disagreed.

"I did. But I'm not sorry. Are you?"

"Nope. I wouldn't've missed any of it."

"Me, neither. I do love you."

"I know," he said. "But how much?"

"Oh, lots and lots."

"Okay. I've got plans."

"What plans?"

"Tell you later." He kissed her cautiously, so as not to spoil her make-up, then released her. "Go get this done, and then we'll talk. Knock 'em dead, sister!"

Melinda was in Los Angeles, resting up for a few days before returning to London. All in all, she was very pleased with the way things had gone. She'd heard only two days earlier that the paperback rights to the book had been sold for three hundred and seventy thousand dollars. Since her share of those rights was sixty percent of everything over one hundred thousand, she'd be receiving two hundred and twelve thousand, less the hardcover advance. A net of a hundred and forty-seven thousand dollars. And that didn't include the book-club advance, or actual royalties on copies sold. It was a very nice sum, and it proved to her that the book was indeed important, that people wanted to read what she had to say.

Of course her mother was outraged. That was to be expected. The world was finally being given a picture of her as she really was, and she could hardly be grateful to Melinda for that, although, really, she should have been. She'd given her mother an opportunity to tell the truth, for once in her life, but of course she'd never risk it. And it was also possible there wasn't a *real* Beatrice Crane. Or, if there had been, once in time, she'd long-since been mislaid somewhere.

Melinda lit a cigarette and switched on the television set, interested in seeing the interview. She was most curious to know what her mother would say. It would undoubtedly be a complete whitewash job, another superlative performance. The familiar ticking clock came on the screen, and Melinda raised the volume as brief clips of all the segments were shown and introduced. Her mother's segment would be first. Good. That meant she wouldn't have to sit through the entire program. She disliked American television, especially the endless commercial interruptions. She couldn't wait to get home and talk to Nancy, hear what she thought of the book.

The segment started with a close-up of the cover of *Private Lies*, while the host told a bit about the book and the furor it had created everywhere. Then there was a clip from *Jeannie* showing her mother with that little girl, one of those moments in Hollywood films meant to be tender. It was all Melinda could do not to laugh. The clip ended, and suddenly there was her mother sitting in the living room of the Greenwich house, and the camera was in very close on her, getting her reaction to the opening remarks being made.

"There are a number of fairly damning statements made about you in the book, but I'm curious, Bea, about the specifics. In particular, the claim your daughter makes that you were, in fact, the illegitimate child of a woman of, shall we say, loose standards."

"That's absolutely true, although I wouldn't say she was loose. She simply wasn't too bright. She wasn't a bad woman, or a bad mother, for that fact. Her biggest failing, to my mind, was her greed. She was a very greedy woman."

"And you supported her for years, did you not?"

"I sent her money regularly, yes. She raised me. It seemed a fair return. Men support their families. Why should it seem unreasonable or odd for me to send my mother money?"

"No, I agree. But she allowed you to leave home with your dancing teacher when you were fourteen years old. Does that seem reasonable now, looking back?"

"Oh, eminently. I wanted to go. She wasn't particularly interested in having me stay. And it was during the Depression, don't forget. Times were hard. If there was the possibility that I could make some money and help them—her and my grandmother—then why not?"

"You had two abortions?"

"That's right."

"Why?"

"Why?" Bea paused to light a cigarette and, seeing this, Melinda did laugh aloud at her mother's smoking again; although the way her mother was responding to the questions—taking her time to think before answering—didn't seem much like a performance. She looked well enough, certainly younger than she was. But the *feeling* was odd, and Melinda found herself leaning closer to the screen so as not to miss her mother's answer. "I had the first one because I was told to by the studio. My career was just beginning. It wasn't an opportune time for me to be having a child. Especially since I also wasn't married. The second one . . . that's more complicated. Let's just say it had to be done, so I did it."

"But you were married by then to Henry Donovan."

"By then, yes."

"Let's back up a little and talk about Dickie DeVore. Did all that actually happen? Did he really take you up into the Hollywood Hills, beat and rape you, and then attempt to kill you?"

"I knew you were going to ask about that, and I've given a lot of thought to how I wanted to answer it. Yes, it all happened. But I read about that sort of thing happening to women every day in the papers. Why is it important because it happened to me, but not as important when it happened to them? It happened. I don't think we need to go into the details."

"But it ruined your dancing career. And according to an interview you gave—Wait a minute, I've got it right here—here it is. In this interview from *Hollywood Quarterly* in January of 1946, you said, and I quote, 'I still wake up in the morning thinking I'll jump out of bed, put on my rehearsal clothes, and get to work. Every morning, it's a jolt to realize I'll never have it back.' End quote."

"But I did get it back," she said with a smile. "It took me almost thirty years, but I did. And isn't that the important thing now?"

"Okay. What about Bobby Bradley?"

"What about him?"

"Isn't it true that the two of you have been involved since long before your marriage to Henry Donovan?"

"Yes."

"And all the way through your marriage to Henry Donovan, right up to this very minute?"

"Yes."

"You were married to one man, but involved at the same time— in fact, before, during, and after—with another?"

"Could you tell me where it's written that we're allowed to care for only one person at a time?"

"No, but..."

"There are men *and* women who've had lovers on the side for years on end. Hearst, for one, with Marion. Everyone accepted it."

"So you're saying everyone accepted you and Bobby?"

"Everyone who mattered."

"Yet your daughter contends, and makes a good argument for the fact, that it is he, and not Henry Donovan, who is her father."

Bea laughed and turned to put out her cigarette, at once lighting another. Melinda was perspiring, seated now on the floor only inches away from the screen. None of this was what she'd expected. "All anyone has to do is take one look at Melinda, and there's no question who her father was. She's the image of Hank."

"She must have got the idea somewhere."

"She got the idea because Bobby's return from the navy coincided fairly closely with my becoming pregnant. But I was two months' pregnant by the time he came back."

"So Henry Donovan was, in fact, her father."

"Of course he was. It's ridiculous to suggest it could've been anyone else." She played for a moment with her gold Dunhill lighter, then put it down on the table beside the ashtray.

"You really see nothing wrong in being involved with two men at the same time?"

"I loved them both. If that makes me immoral, then so be it. I'll have to live with the stigma. But I've been very lucky to have two men of their stature in my life."

"What about the cosmetic surgery?"

"My God!" She laughed again. "More studio orders. As long as I was dancing, no one was going to pay very much attention to my face, or so they reasoned. But once I was no longer able to dance, then everyone was going to be looking more closely, and my face was all wrong, so it had to be fixed. They wanted everything: my jaw redefined, my wisdom teeth pulled to make my cheekbones more prominent, my hairline altered, my nose remodeled. And that was just my face. In the end, all that was done was my nose. And my breasts, but that went sour, and whatever they'd put in had to be taken out again."

"That's it? And it wasn't your decision, but the studio's?"

"Have you ever had surgery of any kind? Would you volunteer for it if you didn't need it? I agonized over it, but in the end, I had to give in. I hadn't worked in over a year after the accident—after Dickie— and there was a chance for me to work *if* I agreed to the surgery. So I agreed."

There was a cut from the interview to a clip from *Fancy Dress*, followed by a close-up scene from *Strange Paradise*, with a voice-over commentary on the "before" and "after" Beatrice. Melinda lit another cigarette, very confused. They cut now to the garden of the Greenwich house, with Bobby, in a smart topcoat, walking through the snow.

"So it's true about your affair?"

"Does it matter?" Bobby answered. "Isn't the point here why Bea's being put on trial, why her life is being turned inside out for public consumption?"

"But where's the morality? Didn't you ever think it was wrong, your involvement with a woman who was married to someone else?"

"Let me tell you something. Henry Donovan was one of the finest men who ever lived. Not only was he a hell of a director, he was the most knowledgeable man I've ever known when it came to making movies. There wasn't any aspect of it he didn't know inside out. On top of that, he was gentle, and sweet, and completely principled. Yeah, there was a conflict. There sure was. I loved *both* of them. The problem was we both couldn't be married to her, and we knew it. So we made the best arrangements we could. But I'd never have knowingly hurt Hank, and neither would Bea. She adored him. I don't know where morality comes into this."

"And you're not Melinda's father?"

"That's just absurd. You tell me how I could do that from a ship in the middle of the Pacific."

"Is it true you're starting an action against her?"

"No. I figure she has to live with herself. That should be punishment enough for what she's done."

Melinda's heart was thumping with anger as there was another cut, this time to Becky, sitting at a kitchen table, holding a cup of coffee with both hands. The voice-over bridged the cut. "We visited with Rebecca Armstrong who wrote a number of starring vehicles for Bea and who's known her longer than anyone else. You know Bea, probably better, certainly for a longer time than any other person. *Is* she always 'on'? *Is* everything a performance? And did she, quote, 'hold court,' end quote, in the bathtub wherever she happened to be?"

"That's three questions," Becky said. "First, the only time Bea is ever 'on' is when she's working. She's too accessible, if anything. That's something that's hard for most people to understand. The assumption is if you've accomplished as much as Bea has, you've had to fight all along the line, so therefore you must be hard as nails. Well, yes, she's fought all along the line. But she's a soft woman. It's very easy to hurt Bea, because she doesn't have the defenses most of us do. But it's also part, or maybe all, of what makes her such an exceptional actress. And as for that crap about holding court, that makes me furious. Bea's lucky to be alive. She was horribly injured that night. And for years and years after, just standing for an hour caused her terrible pain. Yes, she soaked in hot tubs. To help ease the pain. Her back was broken, so were both her hips, and her left leg was broken in *five* places. On top of that she was beaten almost to death and raped. She was *in pain,* and it stayed with her for years. She still can't stand for any length of time. And one more thing, too. In all these years, I've never *once* heard her complain. Not once. I hope that answers that goddamned question once and for all. I'm sick and tired of hearing someone courageous and caring being depicted as a monster. Bea's just *human.*"

Cut back to the Greenwich house, close-up on Bea.

"Rebecca Armstrong is a staunch friend, and she refused to discuss your relationship with your daughter, as did Bobby Bradley, as did most of your other friends. Would you like to comment?"

"Next question," Bea said.

"Okay. The matter of Henry Donovan's relationship with the choreographer Hero."

"They're dead. Is there really any point to dishonoring them?"

"Would it be a dishonor?"

"Possibly. I'd prefer to have them both remembered for what they achieved and not sit here and pick apart their personal preferences, especially when they're not here to defend themselves. Let's stick to me. Okay? I'm still here."

"To defend yourself?"

"Whatever from? No, to answer your questions. You've got pages of them on that clipboard."

"Fair enough. *Nightlife.* In the August '64 issue of *Show,* you said, quote, 'I was never willing to do semi-nude, partially nude, or nude scenes,' end quote. There was a fair amount of you on display in *Nightlife.* Why the change of attitude?"

Bea laughed hugely. "I displayed my legs and, as I recall, my shoulders. I wore undergarments that were far more concealing than the bathing suits most women wear sunbathing. I wouldn't *dare* display my body. People would run screaming from the theaters." She laughed some more, tremendously amused. "Unless," she added, "it was a horror movie."

"But you have very strong feelings about nudity in films."

"I don't think they're quite so strong as they were, but yes, I do have some feelings on the matter. The issue came up of using a body double in *Nightlife* in order to do several more explicit scenes. First of all, I think that's grossly dishonest. And second, most nudity today's gratuitous. We accomplished precisely the same effect in the early films without robbing the audience of the right to *imagine* what took place after the dissolve. We leave an audience very little these days. I think our films were more romantic. But then we were living in a much more romantic era."

"You don't think the 'seventies are romantic?"

"Not generally. Do you?"

"No, not particularly. What about the four years you added to your age?"

"God! That's right. I'm sixty-three in a lot of reference books. I was too young to work when we arrived in New York, so I simply made myself four years older. If people want to believe I'm sixty-three, I have no objection."

"The word is you're a very tough customer on the set."

"Is that the word?" Bea considered that for a moment. Melinda studied her mother's every move and gesture, feeling some vital part of herself dissolving in the course of this interview. Her teeth ached slightly, and there was a faint ringing in her ears as she lit another cigarette. Everything was going wrong. Not a single answer seemed planned or rehearsed. "It's my work. I don't fool around when I'm working, and I'm not interested in people who do. If tough is being serious about one's work, then I suppose I'm tough. When I'm waiting for a set-up, I don't want to sit around gossiping. I want to concentrate on where we are in the script. It's difficult nowadays when almost everything's shot out of sequence to keep a feel for where you are and what you're supposed to be doing. I suppose I'm tough. There are worse things. Aren't you tough about your work? I didn't notice you horsing around while the crew were setting up the lights and testing the sound levels. As I recall, you were there in the corner going over your notes."

"Point made and taken. You've made only one public comment about the book. You said, and again I quote, 'What daughter? What book?' End quote. What's your reaction, really?"

"What book?" Bea said, her eyebrows lifting.

"Okay. Answer me this: How do you feel knowing millions of people out there are reading *Private Lies?*"

"There are only a few areas over which I have any control. One is the work I choose to do, and the other is how I live my life. It's not up to me to select other people's reading matter. What they read or don't read is certainly not in my control. How a person responds to what he or she reads is up to that individual. I've always believed the average level of intelligence to be considerably higher than television networks would have us believe. People aren't stupid. They're capable of making their own value judgments."

"But people *are* curious about the private lives of celebrities. How do you feel having them read such shocking facts about you?"

Bea sighed, and Melinda knew, finally, that it wasn't going to matter that she'd written the book, not only because her mother wasn't going to acknowledge it specifically, but because none of it was true. Oh, the skeleton, the information, all that was true. But the stance she'd taken, the things she'd believed to be the truth, were wrong. She felt ill. It hadn't ever been performances that her mother had given, it had been a caring Melinda had been utterly unable to reciprocate because her mother's love, like her talent, and her generosity, and her concern, were all too large to be supportable. It had been *Melinda's* performance, *her* show, *her* interpretation, *her* judgment that had been out of whack. Not that woman sitting there, so relaxed, so calm, admitting to things no one should ever have had to admit to with millions of people watching. And yet she was turning these admissions into an act of courage that would, undoubtedly, inspire other women. Melinda had been wrong. Totally, hideously wrong. A lifetime of wrong. *What daughter? What book?* This had to be a trick, more distorting magic. It wasn't possible she'd been mistaken on so epic a scale. People would ridicule her, accuse her of profiteering on her mother's reputation after all she'd done to achieve her independence. She kept her eyes on the screen, more and more frightened and confused. Could she have voluntarily thrown away everything she'd wanted all along because she'd failed to recognize it? Was this reality, or did the book represent it? It was this. God! she thought, starting to curl in on herself on the floor. She'd been wrong, wrong.

"How do I feel?" Bea repeated the question, then gave a little shrug. "I know the truth. I sleep well at night. I'm not ashamed of the things that happened. I could hardly be held responsible for my mother or for Dickie DeVore. I am responsible for going along with what Ludie Meyers and the studio wanted me to do. I had a choice there, but I did what I believed was right. That's all anyone *can* do. I've believed

for a long time now that being an adult means assuming full responsibility for one's actions. I assume responsibility for my own actions."

Melinda was panic-stricken, dreading the end of the interview. It
might be her last chance ever to view her mother in conversation
with anyone, because she'd believed she'd never want to go back,
but she'd never considered the probability that she wouldn't be *allowed*
back. She'd finally managed to kill it. The welcome was gone forever.
What daughter?

"Last question. If it was possible to go back in time and change
things, do things differently in your career, or in your personal life,
is there anything you'd change?"

The camera moved in even tighter so that her eyes, smoke-colored,
dominated the screen. Her fingers rested for a a moment near the
corner of her mouth as she took her time, giving careful thought to
the question. Then her head tilted slightly to one side, her eyes on
an angle now, her face a fascinating study in light and shadow. "I
would not," she said at last, with positive conviction, "change one
single thing. Not one moment, not one experience, not any of it."
And then, her fingers steepled beneath her chin, she smiled radiantly.

MARRIAGE DISCLOSED: Two-time Academy Award–winning actress Beatrice Crane, 59, widow of noted director Henry Donovan, and celebrated actor-dancer Robert Ellis (Bobby) Bradley, 61; she for the second time, he for the first, in Antigua in the West Indies, April 15.

TRANSITION/*Newsweek*/July 22, 1976

Selected Bibliography

Affron, Charles. *Star Acting.* New York: E. P. Dutton, 1977.
Anger, Kenneth. *Hollywood Babylon.* New York: Dell, 1975.
Astor, Mary. *Mary Astor: A Life on Film.* New York: Delacorte, 1971.
Atkinson, Brooks. *Broadway.* Rev. ed. New York: Macmillan, 1974.
Balio, Tino, ed. *The American Film Industry.* Madison: University of Wisconsin Press, 1976.
Beaton, Cecil. *Cecil Beaton's Scrapbook.* New York: Charles Scribner's Sons, 1937.
Buckley, V. C. *Good Times.* London: Thames and Hudson, 1979.
Capra, Frank. *The Name Above the Title.* New York: Macmillan, 1971.
Castleman, Harry, and **Walter J. Podrazik.** *Watching TV.* New York: McGraw-Hill, 1982.
Crist, Judith. *Take 22: Moviemakers on Moviemaking.* New York: Viking, 1984.
Croce, Arlene. *The Fred Astaire and Ginger Rogers Book.* New York: Vintage Books, 1972.
Davis, Bette. *The Lonely Life.* New York: Putnam's, 1962.
Dmytryk, Edward. *On Screen Direction.* New York: Focal Press, 1984.
Dody, Sandford. *Giving Up the Ghost.* New York: M. Evans & Co., 1980.
Dooley, Roger. *From Scarface to Scarlett.* New York: Harcourt Brace Jovanovich, 1984.
Drutman, Irving. *Good Company.* Boston: Little, Brown, 1976.
Dyer, Richard. *Stars.* London: BFI Publishing, 1979.
Ebert, Roger. *A Kiss Is Still a Kiss.* Kansas City: Andrews, McMeel and Parker, 1984.
Fireman, Judy, ed. *TV Book.* New York: Workman, 1977.
Fordin, Hugh. *The Movies' Greatest Musicals.* New York: Frederick Ungar, 1975.
Green, Stanley. *Broadway Musicals of the 30s.* New York: Da Capo Press, 1971.
Higham, Charles, and **Joel Greenberg.** *Hollywood in the Forties.* London: Tantivy Press, 1968.
Kanin, Garson. *Hollywood.* New York: Limelight Editions, 1984.
Katz, Ephraim. *The Film Encyclopedia.* New York: Perigee Books, 1979.
Koszarski, Richard, ed. *Great American Film Directors.* New York: Dover, 1984.
Lawton, Richard. *A World of Movies.* New York: Bonanza Books, 1974.
Levin, Martin, ed. *Hollywood and the Great Fan Magazines.* New York: Arbor House, 1970.
Leyda, Jay, ed. *Film Makers Speak.* New York: Da Capo Press, 1977.
Lloyd, Ann, and **David Robinson,** eds. *Movies of the Forties.* New York: Orbis, 1982.
———, eds. *Movies of the Thirties.* New York: Orbis, 1983.
Mast, Gerald, ed. *The Movies in Our Midst.* Chicago: University of Chicago Press, 1982.
Michael, Paul. *The Academy Awards: A Pictorial History.* New York: Bonanza Books, 1964.

————, ed. *Great American Movie Book.* Englewood Cliffs, N.J.: Prentice-Hall, 1980.

Mordden, Ethan. *The Hollywood Musical.* New York: St. Martin's, 1981.

————. *Movie Star.* New York: St. Martin's, 1983.

Morell, Joe, and **Edward Z. Epstein.** *Gable & Lombard & Powell & Harlow.* New York: Dell, 1975.

Newquist, Roy. *Conversations with Joan Crawford.* Secaucus, N.J.: Citadel Press, 1980.

Niven, David. *The Moon's a Balloon.* New York: Putnam's, 1972.

Parish, James Robert. *The RKO Gals.* New Rochelle, N.Y.: Arlington House, 1974.

Parish, James Robert, and **Donald L. Bowers.** *The MGM Stock Company.* New Rochelle, N.Y.: Arlington House, 1974.

Parrish, Robert. *Growing Up in Hollywood.* New York: Harcourt Brace Jovanovich, 1976.

Peary, Danny, ed. *Close-Ups.* New York: Workman, 1978.

Pike, Bob, and **Dave Martin.** *The Genius of Busby Berkeley.* Reseda, Calif.: cfs Books, 1973.

Quirk, Lawrence J. *The Great Romantic Films.* Secaucus, N.J.: Citadel press, 1974.

Ragan, David. *Movie Stars of the 30s.* Englewood Cliffs, N.J.: Prentice-Hall, 1985.

Scherman, David E., *et al.* *Life Goes to the Movies.* Alexandria, Va.: Time-Life Books, 1975.

Schulberg, Budd. *Moving Pictures.* New York: Stein and Day, 1981.

Sennett, Ted, ed. *The Movie Buff's Book.* New York: Bonanza Books, 1975.

Silver, Alain, and **Elizabeth Ward,** eds. *Film Noir.* Woodstock, N.Y.: Overlook Press, 1979.

Stallings, Penny, with **Howard Mandelbaum.** *Flesh and Fantasy.* New York: St. Martin's, 1978.

Steinberg, Cobbett S. *Film Facts.* New York: Facts on File, 1980.

Stine, Whitney, and **George Hurrell.** *50 Years of Photographing Hollywood: The Hurrell Style.* New York: Greenwich House, 1983.

Swindell, Larry. *The Reluctant Charles Boyer.* New York: Doubleday, 1983.

Thomas, Tony. *That's Dancing.* New York: Abrams, 1984.

Torrence, Bruce. *Hollywood: The First Hundred Years.* New York: New York Zoetrope, 1982.

Wallis, Hal, and **Charles Higham.** *Starmaker: The Autobiography of Hal Wallis.* New York: Macmillan, 1980.

Walsh, Andrew S. *Woman's Film and Female Experience.* New York: Praeger, 1984.

Warren, Doug, with **James Cagney.** *James Cagney.* New York: St. Martin's, 1983.

Weis, Elisabeth, ed. *The Movie Star.* New York: Viking, 1981.

Wilkerson, Tichi, and **Marcia Borie.** *The Hollywood Reporter: The Golden Years.* New York: Coward-McCann, 1984.

CHARLOTTE VALE ALLEN was born in Toronto, Canada, and her love of movies dates from her earliest childhood. After three years in England, she emigrated to the United States in 1966, and has lived in Connecticut for the last fifteen years. She began writing full-time in 1976, and since then has published twenty-three books. Along with her interest in film, she is a mystery buff, as well as an avid photographer.

Allen, Charlotte Vale, 1941-

Time/steps.

(Fiction)

PL 31996

Oberlin Public Library